LAST MESSAGE TO BERLIN

LAST MESSAGE TO BERLIN

"PHILIPPE VAN RJNDT'S new novel blends history with espionage to produce a first-class thriller."

The Hamilton Spectator

"A World War II espionage thriller of breathtaking scope . . . an extraordinary tale of treachery and vengeance, romance and heroism . . . Moving with lightning speed from London to Berlin, Geneva and Washington, this is a page-turning hypnotizing blockbuster of high treason and high adventure."

Cameron Publications

"LAST MESSAGE TO BERLIN IS A CORKER . . . The book is exhaustively researched, exquisitely detailed and wonderfully convoluted — yet all very clear. It's got movie written all over it."

Calgary Herald

LAST MESSAGE TO BERLIN

"The story is exciting and the surprise ending leaves the reader wondering just how much is fact and how much fiction."

Toronto Sun

"A remarkable blend of truth and fiction... one of the most exciting and complex spy tales to come along in some time... The story is packed with surprises."

Kitchener Waterloo Record

"VAN RJNDT CHECKS IN WITH ANOTHER COMPULSIVELY ABSORBING SPY THRILLER... THIS BOOK DELIVERS NONSTOP EXCITEMENT."

Publishers Weekly

LAST MESSAGE TO BERLIN

"Van Rjndt doesn't overlook a twist of the plot or a trick of his trade."

The Ottawa Citizen

"This book amazes me by its intricacy and detail!"

Hugh MacLennan

"A THRILLER OF TOP RANK."

London Free Press

LAST MESSAGE TO BERLIN

PHILIPPE VAN RJNDT

A Division of General Publishing Co. Ltd.
Toronto, Canada

Stoddart Publishing edition
published in 1984

General Paperbacks edition
published in May 1985

Cover design: Brant Cowie/Artplus

ISBN 0-7736-7097-1

Printed and bound in Canada

ALSO BY PHILIPPE VAN RJNDT

Samaritan
The Trial of Adolph Hitler
Blueprint
The Tetramachus Collection

For Allan, the best of friends.

"For nothing is hid that shall not be made manifest, nor anything secret that shall not be known and come to light."
The Apostle Luke

PROLOGUE
1940

The evening of May 15, 1940, had, without warning, turned cold. A bitter wind coursed low over the flagstones set in the garden of Ten Downing Street. It whispered through the diamond pattern trellises, rattling them against the walled enclosure, then rose suddenly to stir the barren branches of the centenarian oak.

Beneath the tree, seated at a wrought-iron table that would have been more in place at a French *bistro*, the Prime Minister of Great Britain and Northern Ireland, Winston Churchill, reached for the bottle of cognac. He was alone, sitting in the almost total darkness, a thick-bodied figure wrapped in great-coat and red scarf, illuminated by two pale-yellow carriage lamps burning over the French doors that opened up onto the garden. His fingers trembled as he snatched the bottle, gripping it hard by the neck. He held it in his lap, staring down at the embossed gold foil depiction of Napoleon on a charger.

"Cold," Churchill whispered. "I am so very cold!"

He wrenched out the cork with such force that it flew from his fingers, bouncing soundlessly into the gloom. The bottle tinkled nervously against the rim of the snifter.

Churchill cursed, the epithet expelled from his lips on a cloud of vapor. It was not the cold that had seized him. He would not deceive himself for that comfort. Inside his padded jacket, he felt his shirt clinging to his skin, soaked through at the chest and shoulders. It wasn't the cold nor the drink that was shredding his nerves.

This is how utterly barren a man who has degraded himself must feel, he thought silently. A man who has sold his birthright with a few dozen words, spoken softly so that his friends and countrymen might not hear him.

Churchill pressed the balloon glass hard against his lips. The fiery drink made him shudder, but just as quickly as its warmth flared within him, it died, swallowed whole by icy bitterness.

"I cannot endure it!" Churchill whispered. "I have betrayed them all, my friends, my people, my country. I suffer for my treachery but suffering brings me no relief, much less forgiveness . . . If they knew what I have done in their name they would vilify me, cart me through the streets towards mob justice . . . And there would be nothing I could say in my defense!"

As the glass was raised once more two fat tears spilled from his eyes, rolling swiftly, streaking the gray jowls. Winston Churchill had no way of knowing whether these had come because of the wind or because he had at last accepted that no one could ever comfort him on his lonely journey to hell.

I
PROMETHEUS

1

The events germane to inflicting such a nightmare upon the Prime Minister had begun early on the same date, May 15, 1940. However, their seed had been cast on fertile ground a week earlier.

On May 8, at 11:10 in the evening, Neville Chamberlain had at last resigned as Prime Minister. Nevertheless his conservatives retained their eighty-one-seat majority in the House of Commons, prompting Churchill to mutter his scandalous phrase: "It is as hard getting rid of him as getting a leech off a corpse."

In spite of such forthrightness, which only buttressed the poor opinion of himself held by King George VI, and the misgivings of the Labour Party as a whole, Churchill became Prime Minister two days later. He immediately instituted a Parliamentary bloodletting that would last six full days.

But even as Churchill cut a swath through Chamberlain's political appointments—the appeasers, isolationists and party hacks—he could not fail to see that the pace of events in Europe had made the power he had coveted for so long almost redundant: Two days after Churchill's triumphant entry into Downing Street, German Panzer divisions, victoriously bloodied in Belgium and Holland, pierced the French frontier at Sedan and Dinant.

Sequestering himself in the Admiralty cipher rooms, the new Prime Minister drafted one cable after another, had these routed through the neutral facilities in Lisbon, Portugal, and waited for a reply from the recipient in Berlin. The silence in the German capital remained unbroken until May 14.

Upon receiving the Lisbon cipher Churchill was consumed by cold fury. The man across the Channel had been toying with him, using silence to buy time. Yet there was nothing more the Prime Minister could have done. It had been agreed from the outset that his opposite number would have final control over both the time and place of the meetings. Any attempt to change the ground rules would result in immediate suspension of the rendezvous.

As he reread the Berlin text Churchill laughed bitterly at the irony. . . . Or had his opposite already known that Churchill would, of necessity, be in France the following day, May 15, 1940?

He was the last one to leave the Whitworth bomber that had flown the official party from London to Le Bourget aerodrome outside Paris, staying behind to hear out Charles Lindbergh's broadcast on behalf of American isolationism.

"The wars of Europe are not wars in which our civilization is defending itself against some Asiatic intruder. There is no Genghis Khan or Xerxes marching against our western nations."

"Cretin!" Churchill muttered and heaved himself to his feet.

He considered Lindbergh a dangerous fool, a pioneer hero who had overextended himself, straying into areas he knew nothing of, gullible yet persuasive, with an adoring public that kept the ego inflated.

If only you were here now, Mr. Lindbergh, to look upon these pathetic faces! Churchill thought savagely, emerging at the top of the ramp, clutching his bowler against the stiff breeze.

All of Le Bourget aerodrome was a mass of activity, save the areas cordoned off for Churchill's plane and the hangar reserved for his meeting with Paul Reynaud, the Premier of France. On the eastern runways what units of the French Air Force remained were preparing for takeoff, their destination the river Meuse. Standing orders read that they were to provide support for a counterattack to be launched by the Fifth Army under General Lefebre. The truth of the matter was that the aging fighters would cover the retreat of these same soldiers—so long as the Luftwaffe stayed out of these skies.

Internal commercial air traffic was being routed out through a single northern strip, as quickly as controllers could direct a plane to an open field. From where he stood, Churchill saw hundreds of people straining against the crosswire barriers between themselves and the aircraft, barriers reinforced shoulder to shoulder by armed French paratroops. The wind snatched up their cries and shouts, the urgent pleas and shameless bribes. Fistfuls of money were shaken in the hope of attracting official attention. Reservations and tickets had become meaningless, as had destinations. London was as good as Lisbon, Manchester better than Jersey. Along the side of one hangar, piled high against the curved sheet metal wall, were thousands of crates, packages, suitcases, trunks and tightly bound bundles. Freight offered no incentive to those *fonctionnaires* determining who would board. Churchill was certain that even cargo holds now carried human traffic.

Yet for all this a polished French honor guard had been turned out to pay homage to pomp and circumstance. As he walked past the glittering gold and red jackets, Churchill caught the scent of rifle oil, boot polish and faint cologne.

Parade soldiers! he thought contemptuously. You still believe you will never have to sully those pretty white gloves, that the Maginot magic will somehow save you. Fools!

Churchill turned up his collar against the damp chill that hung in the aerodrome. Detective Inspector Thompson, his personal bodyguard, and the six members of the elite Advance Strike Force who constituted his security force on this trip fell in on either side of the Prime Minister, following the lead of a French colonel. At the far end of the enclosure was a jerry-rigged desk, a sheet of plywood mounted on two sawhorses. Through the open door that led into a back lot Churchill saw rows of ashcans, flames licking at the tops of the rusted metal.

"My dear Winston!"

Paul Reynaud, a short slim man with plastered down black hair and pencil mustache, offered his hand. His skin was pasty and the consumptive cheeks were covered in stubble. Bewilderment brought on by a loss too profound to grasp emanated from his eyes.

"Paul," Churchill said softly, permitting himself to be embraced in the French manner.

"Thank you for coming so quickly, my friend," Reynaud whispered.

Churchill drew back, embarrassed for the other man. Reynaud's telephone call to Ten Downing had come through at seven o'clock this morning. Haltingly, the French Premier informed Churchill that the fall of France was imminent and begged him to come to Paris as quickly as possible. They were the last coherent words Reynaud had been able to utter. Whatever else he had wanted to say to Churchill had been swept away on a torrent of tears.

Over Reynaud's shoulder Churchill watched as men lined up before each of the ashcans, their arms laden with files and documents. Behind them, through the open doors, he saw a half dozen trucks being unloaded. He asked the question for form, even though he had been monitoring the German attack since its inception . . . nine hours before Reynaud called him.

"What is happening, Paul?"

"The same scene is being repeated all over—in Paris, Lyons, Nice, Bordeaux," Reynaud said, as though he hadn't heard the question. "We are burning everything, my friend, that could possibly be of use to the *Boche*. Everything and then some, just to be sure, you understand?"

The Frenchman laughed, an ugly hysteria curdling his voice.

"In Quai d'Orsay we are using wheelbarrows. There is a giant bonfire in the Minister's sacrosanct rose garden."

Churchill placed a hand on Reynaud's shoulder, guiding him away from their entourage and the noxious odor of fuel and charred paper that the wind had carried their way. He faced Reynaud and spoke very softly, conscious that the aerodrome's metal hemisphere roof was an excellent sound conductor.

"Paul, I have been receiving hourly reports—from my people *and* yours—on your situation since the Germans crossed the Meuse. There is nothing I am not privy to. Yet you were most insistent on meeting personally. What else has happened, Paul, that you could not tell me about over the telephone?"

Reynaud's gaze dropped with the butt of his cigarette, which he then ground under the sole of his shoe.

"The Meuse line has disintegrated," Reynaud said woodenly. "Our air force is being systematically destroyed. Stukas and Messerschmitts are targeting airfields, support facilities, planes on the ground. Those aircraft we did launch were unequal to the German machines. I understand pilots continue to fly only because they prefer to die in the air rather than on the ground. For them honor is still something worth salvaging."

Reynaud jammed another cigarette into the corner of his mouth. "Our ground forces have been utterly routed. To add to complications, commanders have to deal with thousands of Belgian infantrymen and civilian refugees. The situation on the roads is chaotic, making an orderly retreat and reestablishment of line positions next to impossible."

The voice finally cracked.

"As for the Maginot Line, it is worse than useless. German aircraft flew over it, their tanks and armies circumvented it. When I look at it now I see a relic, a piece of architecture that belongs in the Middle Ages. The Line has been revealed for what it is—a myth. But there is still your British Expeditionary Force . . ."

Paul Reynaud couldn't bring himself to say the rest. These were not his troops, not under his command, yet he badly wanted to commit them to the fighting, commit them utterly and completely in a savage desire to see others suffer as his own people were suffering. It was a vile, atavistic emotion but he could not help himself. It was the reason he had begged Churchill to come to Paris.

"I'm sorry, Paul, I can't give them to you," Churchill said. "Not under these circumstances. I have to save what I can. Not only my people but yours as well. I must get them to Dunkirk, then back to England."

Reynaud's eyes glittered, more because of the tears of shame than an anger to which he knew he had no right. Churchill had known all along what he would ask of him. And he had had his answer ready.

"Some of my generals . . ." Reynaud whispered, humiliated. "Almost *all* my generals expect the British not only to stay and maintain positions but to have their forces augmented. They have visions of endless rows of tanks, limitless fighters and bombers. They expect field artillery, the new infantry rifles, ammunition . . ."

Suddenly Reynaud fell silent, horrified by the bitterness in his voice, a rancor that indicated exactly where he placed the blame for the French debacle. Now Churchill understood that it hadn't been for himself but on behalf of his generals that Reynaud had pleaded he come to France. Of course the French military would have demanded that Reynaud drag the British into their failure!

"What of de Gaulle?" Churchill demanded coldly, trying to turn away his anger.

"He has said nothing. I take his silence to mean he has a more realistic assessment of our situation."

"It grieves me to say this, Paul, but I feel you should come to London," Churchill said. "You can form a government-in-exile, temporary to be sure—"

Reynaud held up an open palm. "I thank you for the offer, my friend. I am deeply moved by the spirit behind it. But the next time we meet—if we meet—I will be an ordinary citizen."

He blurted out the rest. "There is no question but that I must resign."

And Churchill knew this as well. By his refusal he had made Reynaud's position untenable. The posturing, strutting French military had handed him its broken sword and with it the ignominy for what the military itself was responsible for. The generals then compounded the outrage by demanding that Reynaud guarantee them British troops with which to fight their battles. If Reynaud failed to procure them—as he knew he would—it would mean the end of his career.

"No, I suppose there is no question," Churchill said softly. "But should you reconsider my offer, you have only to contact the commander of the BEF. If you wait until after the withdrawal there will be different means available."

Reynaud's head bobbed like that of a jack-in-the-box. "I wish I had better hospitality to offer you," he said, obviously unaware of the non sequitur. "Perhaps you have time for dinner?"

"I'm sorry, no," Churchill replied. "Under the circumstances it is imperative I see Weatherspoon in Enghien before returning to London this evening."

He opened the hunter. "Arrangements have been made and I'm already overdue."

"I will see to it you have an escort," Reynaud declared.

"No need, my friend. My staff is perfectly adequate."

It was unthinkable that Reynaud should learn the true reason for this journey to France, that Churchill would have been here this day even if Reynaud had not summoned him. . . .

Churchill walked to the car, a Rolls-Royce belonging to the British Ambassador, Reynaud at his side, hands behind his back and head bowed. He had all the appearance of a mourner walking toward the grave.

More trucks had pulled up. The French soldiers were rolling up more barrels, filling the bottoms with kerosene-soaked charcoal.

They are in a hurry now, Churchill thought. They waited

until I came and confirmed what all suspected but were loath to believe: We can no longer help them.

Paul Reynaud himself opened the door.

"*A tout à l'heure*," Reynaud whispered.

"In better times . . . Goodbye, Paul."

As the car surged forward Churchill looked back and caught a final glimpse of Reynaud, hands stuffed deep in his pockets, eyes fixed, unblinking, on the retreating vehicle.

"Perhaps I will be able to salvage something even for you," Churchill whispered. "God knows, this is the last chance any of us has."

The members of the Board of Governors for the Enghien casino were prescient men. No sooner had the first German soldier stepped onto French soil than the Board ordered the casino closed. All gaming tables were dismantled and stored in the cavernous basement. Everything else, from museum-quality paintings to the house chips, was inventoried and similarly locked away. Under the supervision of the executive chef, the restaurant's perishable delicacies were wrapped and buried in frozen-meat lockers. Only the wine cellar, with its complement of twenty-one thousand bottles, was moved in its entirety to an undisclosed location.

The Board had calculated its losses for drawing the shutters. These were not insignificant, but far less than the damage that would ensue if the public, driven to panic, stormed the casino for its food stores if nothing else.

The German was quietly amused by such businesslike logic. He had been to Enghien in better times, so now, standing in what had once been the magnificent central lounge, he had a melancholy sense of déjà vu. Only the floor-to-ceiling windows, opening onto a cut-stone balcony, remained. The damask curtains had disappeared, as had the black and oxblood leather chairs. The inlaid ivory convenience tables were gone, the Persian and Chinese carpets rolled up, the paneled walls revealed patches where priceless works had once hung. The ceiling, a collage of cupids, dancing nymphs and satyrs set within a woodland expanse, seemed almost shabby without its grand Venetian chandeliers.

The bar, nine meters of solid mahogany with leather padding and brass rail, had been wrenched from its floor moorings and somehow taken out, probably through the windows via a hoist.

The German sighed and drew on a cigarette, standing full face to the windows. The Egyptian Sobranie was half consumed when he saw the Rolls-Royce turn into the gravel path.

Churchill's driver guided the limousine around a circular, crushed stone drive. The two outriders had remained at the front gates, some sixty yards away, close to another vehicle which flew the Swedish flag from a pennant mounted on the left fender.

Churchill didn't bother to wait for his man to come around but opened the door himself. If he said anything to the driver, the German did not catch the lip movement. Taking the steps of the main entrance, Churchill disappeared from his line of vision. Below, a door opened then slammed shut as the wind caught it, followed by the whine of the elevator's electric motor.

The heavy glass doors with frosted designs swung forward. Churchill entered, walked twenty feet into the room and abruptly halted, gazing around at the emptiness.

"Herr Jaunich, it is a pleasure to see you again," Churchill said, the irony verging on sarcasm.

Gerd Jaunich, the man to whom Hitler had entrusted these secret negotiations with the British Prime Minister, inclined his head, seeming to take no notice of Churchill's tone. He was an individual of medium height, with the carriage and physique of a horseman: a slim torso that sat on developed muscular legs and supported wide shoulders, powerful arms. Churchill knew him to be fifty-five years old, but the clear blue eyes, taut cheekbones and jawline, and iron-gray hair cut *en brosse* worked to reduce this figure by a decade.

As far as British SIS had been able to learn, Jaunich had no contacts with any other member of the British government, official or otherwise. The reason why he had approached Churchill through Lisbon while Churchill had still been First Lord of the Admiralty was still a source of mystery for the Prime Minister. As well as respect. As soon as Churchill had ascertained Jaunich's credentials, he realized that this man, who stood closer to Hitler than any other, could have chosen a dozen other men—holding far greater power at the time—with whom to open a secret dialogue. But Jaunich had selected him. Years later, when he remembered that moment, Churchill could only conclude that the German had been something more than an astute observer of British political reality. It was as though Gerd Jaunich had lifted the veil over the future and glimpsed the sequence of events which would catapult Churchill's fate.

"I trust you had an uneventful journey, Prime Minister?" Jaunich asked politely.

"Thank you, yes. And yourself?"

"Quite comfortable." The German looked around. "I'm sorry I can't say the same for our surroundings, however . . ."

"Why the invasion?" Churchill cut him off, his voice soft, honed by anger. "Why step into France when there was still an opportunity for negotiations?"

Jaunich inclined his head, giving the impression he was surprised by the directness of the question.

"Negotiations, Prime Minister? I should think the Führer extended more than ample time for you to come to the table. The two of us met in thirty-eight, then a year later. The discussions were, shall we say, inconclusive."

"It is somewhat difficult to believe in the good faith of the other party when, while he is talking, his armies are marching into Austria and Czechoslovakia."

The subdued outrage in Churchill's tone lent his voice a blustery quality. Jaunich was not taken in.

"One must always have a contingency plan, Prime Minister," he said dryly.

Churchill scowled, tapping his walking stick impatiently on the dusty floorboards.

"You haven't answered me: Why has Hitler invaded France and the Low Countries?"

"The Führer is of the opinion you are procrastinating," Jaunich told him. He delivered the sentence in the manner of a succinct message. "He believes you have not, at *any* time, been negotiating in good faith. You have been taking advantage of his patience and goodwill to *buy* time—time for your armed forces to strengthen themselves, to establish a European beachhead such as now exists near Dunkirk."

"Preposterous!" Churchill flung at him. "You must remember that until now it wasn't within my power to speak for Great Britain openly, much less formulate policy."

He mustn't know how close he is to the truth. I need still more time. My country cannot fight now, undermanned, underarmed . . .

"No, of course not, Prime Minister," Jaunich said solicitously. "And forgive my rudeness: I haven't offered you my congratulations on your new appointment." He paused. "But do understand: this is the final opportunity for me to receive your proposal—if in fact you have one. I suggest you do not squander it."

"There is time for a settlement," Churchill said woodenly.

He was anxious to steer the conversation from references to the past. The words he had to say now, even though they were laden with deceit, would nonetheless be dragged out of his throat, whether by fear or cunning or even some fragment of honesty—he couldn't say. If he were able to speak quickly, get them out in a rush, even he himself might be taken in by them.

"What is it you have to offer the Führer that he cannot take for himself?" Jaunich shrugged.

Churchill said it. "Peace." He stepped closer to the German. "It is painfully obvious that whatever the Führer may *like* to think, whatever illusions his sychophants foster, the *German people* are not ready for a war. They have had two decades of economic misery. In the last seven years they have been cheated further because Hitler chose to construct a military machine rather than the basis for an economic recovery. Outside the armed forces you have seventy million citizens who eat meat and butter twice a week, if that. These same millions bathe only on weekends when there is hot water—the same water that is later used to boil cabbage or potatoes for the onion sauce."

Churchill shook his head. "Goebbels may brag all he wants about the average German feeling towards the war as the man with a recurring toothache—the sooner it is out the better. He *wants* war, is ready to impose it. I am offering an alternative."

Jaunich asked skeptically, "A concrete proposal, Prime Minister?"

"In the West, German armed forces would withdraw from France and the Low Countries," Churchill stated. "The opening negotiations would encompass Alsace-Lorraine and the Danish protectorate of Schleswig-Holstein."

"And in the East?"

"Certain arrangements would have to be concluded in respect to Czechoslovakia. On the face of it I would think a plebiscite in the Sudetenland would be in order. If the population wishes to annex itself to Germany, then a separate government would be formed."

"Austria?"

"I feel that issue has been settled."

"Poland?"

"I suggest that it would be wiser, in the long term, to leave Poland as an independent buffer—after German claims on Danzig have been settled."

"You are beginning to echo your predecessor, Prime Minister," Jaunich observed, a trace of condescension in his tone. "Was it not Chamberlain who said—and forgive the paraphrase: a weakening or dismemberment of Germany would destroy the natural barrier against Bolshevism?"

"The wording is close enough, the context entirely different," Churchill bridled.

"But what is not different, Prime Minister," the German retaliated, "is the fact that England needs the peace as badly as you seem to think Germany does. Is it not true, for example, that your own Ministry of Information estimates four million of your citizens would settle for peace at *any* price? Have you not already evacuated three million Londoners, half of them children with their mothers? Are your own people not rationed to four ounces of bacon, butter and twelve of sugar each week? Lastly, Prime Minister, is your expenditure on this war not crippling you financially—*to the sum of four and a half million pounds each and every day?*"

"I will not deny that," Churchill answered quietly. "We too are paying a price. But I suggest to you, Herr Jaunich, that in spite of the impressive beginning to Germany's ventures, she does not have the wherewithal—physical, human; nay, nor the moral—to continue a prolonged indecisive conflict."

He stared at the German. "On the other hand, *we have!*"

The German threw up his hands. "*Ach, die Amerikaner . . .*"

"No, sir, *not* the Americans!" Churchill thundered. "I do not deny their contribution. But matériel is valueless unless used by men of bravery and conviction. *That* is what I suggest your Führer consider. Yes, we can fight. Our two nations can send wave after wave of human fodder at one another. Yet with every soldier who falls, our backs will stiffen. His blood shall be poured into our resolve not only to win, but to avenge. In the end it is people, not chancellors or prime ministers or generals, who decide the outcome. Yours are already tired.

You cannot coerce a people to fight, much less expect victory from them!"

The momentum was his, for he had seen the German flinch, his eyes lose their composure. He was listening, Churchill knew, and listening hard.

"Your General Staff is no different from my own," Churchill said quietly. "They have been bred for battle. But your soldiers, as mine, would much prefer to remain at the jobs, in their homes, to build lives for their families rather than destroy those of others. I ask you to convey the following message to your Chancellor: There can still be peace—for us, for all Europe. There is still that precious room in which to turn around. I can extend, and now guarantee, certain agreements. I can persuade other leaders to follow where I lead. But I can do this only if your Chancellor joins me, not in words, but by example. Otherwise . . ."

Churchill exhaled a deep breath. There, he had said it all, as best, as convincingly, as he could. With the grace of God he had bought himself and Britain invaluable months. during which, beneath the ramblings of useless negotiations, he would arm his island and strike once and for all at Berlin. Yes, he had bought something . . . *But how much*?

Jaunich regarded Churchill steadily, with no uncertain evaluation but without fear or even concern. It was as though he had already settled on the tone and texture of his report to Hitler. In fact, what Churchill didn't know was that Gerd Jaunich would, within hours of Churchill's return to London, be the recipient of a message which would confirm or deny the truth of what Churchill had so eloquently uttered.

"I will convey both the text and the tone of your proposal to the Führer," the German said without inflection. "I shall communicate with you in the usual manner, as soon as possible."

Jaunich extended his hand and Churchill took it, returning the grip.

"And now, Prime Minister, I believe it is your turn to leave first."

The first streetlights flickered and glowed to life as the Prime Minister's car turned off Whitehall into the cul-de-sac of Downing Street.

Winston Churchill erupted from the car and walked swiftly to the front door. He tossed his coat at Playter, his manservant, and stomped through the dining room into the kitchen. He flung open the door of what appeared to be a pantry and disappeared, much as the rabbit had into the bolthole of Alice's Wonderland. Detective Inspector Thompson followed, locking the door behind him.

The stairwell was steep, the individual stone steps covered by strips of carpeting to prevent one from slipping. The plastered walls gave way to raw timber beams. Above, high-intensity bulbs swung lightly in the recirculated air.

At the bottom landing two Royal Marines snapped to port arms as Churchill brushed between them, slipping through an open steel-sheathed door into the central corridor of the warren. He was in the Hole.

Three years previous, the Transport Authority of Greater London had announced that it was considering extensions to its Westminster line and improvements along the existing thoroughfares. No one paid any great attention to the holes that were being bored into the earth for preliminary tunnels. There were even fewer questions, when, a year later, the project was quietly shelved, the streets repaired, new green put in the public squares and workmen given a generous cancellation settlement.

But the tunnels remained. They were not the giant avenues used by the Underground, but they were sufficiently high and wide to accommodate an army of one thousand people who would eventually work there. Bounded by Number Ten Downing Street in the north, Whitehall to the east and the Houses of Parliament to the south, was a warren of halls, chambers, kitchens, sleeping quarters, communications rooms and offices which totaled four meandering miles. This was the secret heart of Britain, buried one hundred twenty feet below the streets, linked to the major nerve centers by boltholes such as the one Churchill had used. It had been designed to withstand the heaviest bombardment, and was the invisible fortress of the last stand. In 1939 few had believed it would ever have to be used. By spring of the following year, after Churchill had activated the Hole, all secret meetings between the body politic, the military and selected members of the diplomatic corps took place in it. The offices of Whitehall and Parliament were still used, but now they were part of an elaborate smokescreen, empty jerry-rigged sets whose substance—the secret files on defensive and offensive plans, industry capacity and production direction—had all been removed into the Hole.

Clerks, messengers, warrant officers, members of Britain's War Security Council, saw Churchill rumbling down the hall, glimpsed at his set expression and maneuvered out of his way. Arms swept up in salutes but no words were exchanged. Almost invisible smiles creased the lips of those who were in earshot to hear the Old Man mutter: "Must get to the bloody bog!"

Churchill's private bathroom was perhaps the only object of humor in the Hole, whose lack of sanitary facilities was legendary. The Hole's architects had thought that Transit Authority workers might raise their brows at installing plumbing and toilets in barren chambers. Until a few months ago Churchill's quarters, as everyone else's, had been equipped with a large pot, emptied and cleaned twice a day. Then a strange contraption appeared courtesy of Major General Emery Carlton of the Army: an outhouse on wheels. Standing six and a half feet tall, five in length and width, this portable toilet was equipped with six little wheels fixed to the base crossbeams. The rattling that ensued whenever the "bog" was moved was so loud that even those who couldn't see it were aware of Churchill moving around. Drawn by two Marines, the bog followed him from his spartan quarters to his cubbyhole of an office to the large rectangular hold that served as the War Security Council chamber. Needless to say, the peculiarities of Churchill's digestive tract were discussed at great length.

No sooner than Churchill turned the corner toward his office did he hear the telltale cacophony of the bog being moved up the corridor. He fiddled with the key to the door, entered and waited with hands on the small of his back as the privy was wheeled inside, drawn up directly in front of his desk.

"Splendid," he told the two Marines, who, sweating profusely, saluted and stepped outside. Thompson leaned inside and drew the door shut. He positioned himself in the corridor, directly under the glowing amber light.

"At last!" Churchill growled and locked the bog door.

There was no bathroom inside. Instead, a rather old but comfortable leather club chair whose fold sank gently beneath his weight took up half the available space. On the left was a writing board which he positioned before his lap, the paper already clipped in place. Churchill withdrew a fountain pen from his breast pocket, then a cigar. He spat out the end into a gleaming brass spittoon, struck a match on the emery board fixed to the side of the armrest and drew on the cigar. When he was wreathed in smoke, the Prime Minister lifted the receiver from the telephone fixed to the righthand wall.

He did not have to say a word. At the American embassy on Grosvenor Square an operator instantly became aware of the glowing light on her switchboard. The *only* light on the board. Neither she nor her sister operators who shared the continual twenty-four-hour shifts could determine the origin of the call. It might be Downing Street, an office in the Houses of Parliament, Chequers, or a cruiser in Scapa Flow. It might be local, national, continental or overseas, rerouted via a half dozen different exchanges.

Churchill drew too deeply on the cigar, coughed, and expectorated the phlegm into the spittoon.

The nation could demand my head for what I am about to do. The military and the High Court would gladly and rightly give it to them. But, God help me, there is no choice!

He stared at the receiver in his hand, the grip hard, moist.

"Hello . . . hello, Winston?"

Churchill brought the receiver to his ear. Delicately he removed the cigar, placing it in the ashtray by the writing board.

"Yes, Franklin, I'm here."

The connection was, as always, mediocre. Distance, switching equipment, the scrambler, all played havoc with transmission. Nevertheless the good-fellow tone of President Franklin Delano Roosevelt was instantly recognizable.

"How was your trip to Paris, Winston?"

"I have nothing to add to what you and I discussed last night, Franklin. Reynaud can hold out for another couple of weeks, no more. He's begging for more troops, matériel . . ."

Roosevelt did not take the hint. Static crumbled in the background.

"I don't have anything more to give him, Franklin. My job now is to get my men out of Dunkirk."

"Hitler's bent on going for the whole shooting match, is he?"

"He wants it all. And I am obliged to snatch what I can from his grasp."

"*Can* you get your people back, Winston?"

"With some luck and a great deal of effort, yes, I believe so."

Churchill hesitated. "Franklin, the moment is at hand. Britain will become at once the last refuge and the future staging ground. In the next few weeks I shall require no less than fifty additional destroyers, all the troop ships you can spare, two thousand antiaircraft units—"

Churchill felt his anger carrying him away.

"Everything that is on the list you have. That and whatever else you can sell me. Time is the critical factor now.

"There is nothing to stop Heinz Guderian's tanks. The Luftwaffe is already moving its forward bases into Alsace-Lorraine. Within days the naval yards at Saint-Nazaire will fall and a week later U-boats will have found new pens. In short, Hitler can kill or capture three hundred and fifty thousand of my men at his convenience. Even if I could move posthaste, I could save only half, perhaps two-thirds, of that number."

There was a pause.

"I am not unfeeling towards you or your circumstances," Roosevelt said.

"I realize that, Franklin."

"But I'm working under constraints over here. You have to give me something to take to Congress."

This time it was Churchill who remained silent.

Let him say it, he thought viciously. Let him come out and demand it!

"Winston, given the circumstances, am I to understand you've reconsidered your position on Prometheus?"

The words came out in a rush, as though he had to say them before they were dissolved by their own cruelty.

"Yes, Franklin, I have. I suggest to you that Prometheus be put into effect at once."

2

"Good night, Joe."

"'Night, Miz Davis."

The young negro janitor pulled his mop back to allow the

woman to pass. As she stepped by, Beth Davis bestowed a cocky smile upon him. The janitor grinned back and leaned against the mop handle, watching her wait at the elevator.

The janitor knew a great deal about Beth Davis. She was thirty-four, engaged to an Army Air Corps lieutenant stationed at Forest Lake in upper New York, but was having an affair with a White House staffer. She had worked at this address, 141 South N Street in Washington for Section B (Cryptanalytic) of the Signal Intelligence Bureau, for the past two years. She had two commendation letters in her file and was a conscientious analyst who often, as tonight, worked late.

She was also, he thought, a very classy lady. Tall—at least five ten—with a magnificent proud body set off by thick auburn hair and riveting green eyes. Beth Davis knew exactly the effect she had on men. As the elevator doors opened she glanced back at the janitor. He caught the flash of a smile, the soft curve of her throat, the play of slim elegant fingers, a ring sparkling as she waved goodbye. For an instant he wondered if she had ever made love with a black man, what she would be like in bed. The thought evaporated. The janitor knew that like most white people Beth Davis considered negroes invisible. They existed only to serve, not to be taken into account. Which was precisely why he had drawn this assignment.

The janitor replaced the mop in the pail and watched as the elevator needle swung counterclockwise. When it reached "G" he withdrew a set of keys, opened the door to the office Beth Davis had just left and made a telephone call.

At approximately the same time as Beth Davis was making a left turn out of the government lot on N Street, taxi number 112, belonging to the Yellow Diamond Cab Company, was picking up a passenger at the corner of R Street and Madison Boulevard. The driver, a negro about the same age as the janitor, threw his arm across the top of the seat.

"Where to, sir?"

"The Spike."

The driver nodded and slipped the car in gear. But his eyes constantly flitted to the rearview mirror.

His passenger was a short but powerfully built man, with a gleaming bald pate, thick mustache, and two gold teeth glittering in the smile. His beige suit was cut along a Continental line, his complexion was dark, his accented English suggesting a Spaniard or South American. The driver knew that his passenger did not belong to either nationality.

It was still the cocktail hour and traffic was light. The driver stayed in the righthand lane behind a bus. At the next traffic light the passenger leaned forward and told the driver he was in a hurry. The cab pulled around the bus, swerved back into the right lane and ran a red light at the corner of Madison Boulevard and Pennsylvania Avenue. There was no way the driver could have avoided hitting the light-blue Ford sedan that was making a right on Pennsylvania.

The impact tossed the passenger into the corner of the cab, his head striking the edge of the window. The shriek of metal shredding metal shattered the murmur of traffic as the driver wrenched his steering wheel to the left. The two cars were running parallel to one another. The driver looked across at the woman behind the wheel and saw her gaze was on his passenger. A glance into the rearview told him the foreigner was staring back. Suddenly the blue Ford accelerated, swerved in front of the cab and roared down Pennsylvania.

"You see what she did!" the driver screamed as he slammed the cab against the curve. "She's gone! When the po-lice comes—"

"Drive on!" the passenger shouted.

"Mistah, I can't—"

"Drive, nigger bastard, and I will forget that you did not stop on the red light!"

For a moment the only sound in the car was the gasping breathing of two men, then the driver slammed the gearshift along the column and popped the clutch. The cab fishtailed from the sidewalk and into the center lane of Pennsylvania Avenue.

Less than a minute later the valet at the Spike opened a cab door for a European gentleman who was gently dabbing the crown of his shaven skull with a white handkerchief. The man brushed past the valet, cursing softly in a foreign tongue.

The valet leaned through the open window on the passenger's side.

"What the hell was wrong with him?"

The driver shrugged. "Some guys don't like to be taken for a ride."

The valet laughed and shook his head. He was heading up the steps and so never saw that instead of pulling into traffic, cab number 112 from the Yellow Diamond fleet circled around to the rear of the hotel.

"Nice of you to get here on time," the janitor said, flicking away his cigarette and sliding in beside the driver. "Did you hit it off?"

The driver grimaced. "The lady has no left fender and a banged-up door. A tail couldn't lose that car if it tried."

The Spike was never referred to as a hotel. That particular designation was not inscribed on its stationery, cutlery or service, on the uniforms of its staff, nor even on the matchbooks nestled in sparkling crystal ashtrays. It advertised neither in print nor in neon. Although its location was prominent—on the banks of the Potomac, precisely three minutes from the White House in a measured walk—most Washingtonians passed it by without a second look. This was due in part to its architecture, which was scarcely inspirational. The Spike was a mass of Victorian Gothic, granite blocks angling out into turrets and trestles, topped by slate shingles and oddly sculpted lightning conductors. All the windows were lead lined, further adding to its unappealing grayness. However, such was precisely the anonymity its founders intended.

Prior to the Depression, the Spike was known as the Railroad Club. Founded by Lawrence Pullman and William C. Van Horn, the membership was strictly limited to those men who built and owned railroads. In its heyday the club had over one hundred and fifty members from sixty countries around the world.

But in 1929 the age of baronetcy crumbled and personal fortunes melted away. Nonetheless a few of the members managed to save, if not themselves, then something of this preserve they loved. The doors of the Spike were closed between February 1930 and May of the following year. When they reopened, they did so to the public. The one hundred fifty member suites had been modernized, the kitchens revamped, the lobby renovated. The Spike, the non-hotel hotel, opened its doors on a brilliant spring morning to, among others, the Prince of Wales, Garbo and a physicist whose taxi driver had brought him to the wrong address: Albert Einstein.

With the outbreak of war in Europe, the hotel became the stalking ground for a new type of clientele: the high-ranking military from both sides of the Atlantic, personal assistants to ambassadors who quietly laid the informal groundwork for their masters' public utterances, foreign correspondents proclaiming fiction as fact, and civilians in a particularly sensitive line of work who adopted the Spike as their off-duty headquarters. Beth Davis, along with a number of others from the Signal Intelligence Bureau, was on a first-name basis with the staff of the Aviary Lounge.

The cryptanalyst allowed the manager to press his lips to her hand but declined to be seen to a table. She crossed the central area of the lounge, which was dominated by a spectacular ten-foot brass cylinder that was in fact an aviary. The birds inside were multichromatic parrots and cockatoos from Mexico and South America, mynahs and birds of paradise. The cylinder was encircled by a padded seat that a long-forgotten Spike member had brought up from a New Orleans bordello. To the right, beneath a soft-green, glass ceiling lighted from above, oxblood leather settees and club chairs were carefully arranged around a small dance floor, music provided by a string trio. This part of the lounge was full, with military uniforms predominating.

Across the room, on a second tier set eighteen inches higher, was the discreet service bar and a series of semicircular booths which shielded its occupants from the floor level. Beth Davis made directly for this area, slipping onto the banquette just as a waiter was arranging two very large, extra-dry martinis.

"Felipe, you poor dear! Shall I give your little head a kiss and make it all better?"

The scowling expression of the passenger in the ill-fated Yellow Diamond taxi vanished immediately.

"Ah, Beth! How lovely to see you! I am quite well, I assure you. A little bruise, nothing more."

"I'm so glad to hear that."

The green eyes were lowered, the words, spoken between a whisper and murmur, disappeared into the excellent martini.

"But you must tell me, Beth," Felipe Schecker carried on. "Why did you leave so quickly?"

The green eyes drifted up and seized his own.

"Because when I saw it was you in that taxi, I didn't know whether to laugh or throw up," Beth Davis said. "The last thing I wanted was the police to show up and have our names linked because of some idiot nigger."

The gold teeth reflected the lamplight as Schecker laughed

silently. He looked up at the glass ceiling, then out across at the part of the room he could see from his vantage point.

"A magnificent place, Beth," he announced. "I am grieved we were not able to meet here before. In fact I recall your telling me we should *never* meet here because you are known."

Schecker's smile faded. "An exception tonight?"

Beth Davis set her glass down.

"An exception that has to get to *Berlin* tonight," she said softly, the command unmistakable. "Believe me, it's important enough for me to have broken the rules."

"I hope so, Beth," Schecker answered levelly. Although he was loath to admit it, he was intimidated by this formidable woman, in spite of the fact that he was her control.

"The Portuguese Ambassador would be most distressed if his personal secretary was arrested on espionage charges," Schecker continued. "To say nothing of Berlin."

Schecker sipped his drink.

"Where is it?" he asked softly.

"I passed it to you while you were still licking your wound. It's in your lefthand pocket."

Schecker raised his glass, keeping both hands in view. He had no reason to doubt her. He maneuvered his body around to the other side of the banquette and stood up.

"You must excuse me for a moment, Beth." He winked. "Nature calls."

Beth Davis watched him approach one of the waiters and ask for directions to the men's room. She returned to her drink, found it warm and snapped her fingers at a waiter.

Schecker strode purposefully to the end of the landing and turned left, pushing open the designated door. The washroom was small and very cool, due in part, he supposed, to the green vein marble from which the sinks and floor had been carved. The five urinals on the left were unoccupied, but Schecker moved past them to the stalls. Of the three, the center one had an out-of-order sign posted on it. Schecker slipped into the last one, inadvertently stepping on the paint-spattered tarpaulin.

"Just don't tinkle on it, mac," a voice grunted at him.

Schecker heard the two things simultaneously: the opening of the washroom door as someone else came through, broken by the screech of a wrench loosening a rusted nut. He opened the envelope, read the transcript, then replaced it and dropped the envelope on the tarp. The tarpaulin was slowly pulled from his stall.

Schecker urinated, flushed the toilet and stepped out of the stall. He washed his hands carefully, taking note that the third stall was now occupied, picked up the towel and, when he was through, magnanimously handed the attendant a dime. Adjusting his tie, he left, satisfied that the drop had been achieved without incident.

Felipe Schecker had had reservations about meeting his agent in a place he did not frequent, much less have any control over. But neither could he refuse her: Beth Davis wasn't one to exaggerate the necessity for a meeting. The quality of the information she had brought must have ruled out the usual, and slower, transmission via dead-drop. And Schecker had told her he would come. The detail about having a backup man, the plumber working on the toilet, who would be the actual carrier, was his own precaution, mandatory under the circumstances but one Beth Davis did not have to know about.

"Very nice, Beth, very nice," he murmured, slipping into the booth. The gold smile flashed again. "Rest assured your payment is also in place."

Beth Davis laughed softly. Of that she had no doubt. Most of the men who worked with her coveted her body, but all stood a little in awe of this sexually electric woman who faithfully, once a week, went calling on her mother at an expensive Georgetown nursing home. Beth Davis was not their idea of the dutiful daughter, especially not in the minds of certain female co-workers who made it known that Mrs. Endersby Davis, widow of a wealthy Du Pont executive, was well worth the weekly visit. Beth Davis could scarcely support her lifestyle swathed in designer clothes, furs and jewelry, on the $6500 salary of a cryptanalyst without some patrimony.

Beth Davis was well aware of the cat talk and silently reveled in it. True, her mother had been well provided for, and she herself received a monthly check from the Morgan Bank. The details of her financial arrangements had been thoroughly checked by the FBI when she had applied to the Signal Intelligence Bureau. But her weekly visits were scarcely made out of filial devotion. Beth Davis loathed her mother, despising her wretched seesaw battle against alcoholism. Yet she suffered the once-a-week Wednesday visit because between twelve-thirty and one, while Beth was wasting her lunch hour listening to geriatric prattle, a package addressed to Mrs. Endersby Davis would arrive by special messenger. The nurses looked forward to this package as well. Invariably it contained expensive Swiss chocolates, and since Mrs. Endersby Davis's diet forbade sweets and her daughter didn't seem to care for them either, the chocolates were given to the staff. But not until the box had been opened.

Beth Davis would lift the cardboard cover and remove one sweet for show. While her mother mooned on about the gift, she would discreetly slide the cover into her handbag, always a large one on such occasions. That the cardboard was heavy didn't surprise her in the least. In fact she would have been able to tell by weight alone whether or not the gold imbedded between the cardboard covers was the correct amount.

Twelve coins, once a week, for almost one hundred weeks to date. In 1940, not so small a fortune. Today, when she had picked up the bounty, she wondered what her mother and the nurses would think of the anonymous sender, Felipe Schecker, if they were ever to meet him in the flesh.

Beth Davis ran a blood-red fingernail around the wide diameter of the cocktail glass.

"You know, Felipe, with things in Europe blossoming as they are, I can expect more and more work." She gave him a sweet smile but the eyes were hard. "You might consider asking Berlin to take that into account. After all, even the wages of sin have to rise sometime."

She paused. "I was thinking of diamonds, Felipe, say four to begin with, one perfect carat each. Berlin must be rolling in them what with all the Jews who are disappearing."

Schecker raised his eyebrows, stirring the martini with the swizzle stick.

Three years ago he had been servicing half a dozen German agents. In the last twenty months Beth Davis had been his sole "client." Berlin considered her contribution so important that the other agents had been parceled out among different controls. When Davis had caught him shaving her coins prior to receipt, the dead-drops had been empty for three weeks. After a furious Berlin learned of Schecker's cheating, the Portuguese had had to make up much more than he had stolen.

Yes, Berlin would undoubtedly acquiesce. It might even add further inducements because it knew, as Schecker did, that in Beth Davis it had a perfect agent: a human being who was completely amoral, with no understanding (or perhaps it was acceptance) of the concepts of right or wrong, good or evil. The concept of loyalty was as foreign to Beth Davis in her professional work as it was in her private life. She had become a cryptanalyst because her mind was able to read mathematical concepts and equations the way most people read words. She could be engaged to an officer in the U.S. Armed Services but carry on a liaison with at least one other man, seemingly unburdened by the weight of deception. She had meritorious letters in her SIB files but regularly supplied Schecker with copies of top secret traffic between the White House and the American embassy in London.

Beth Davis, Schecker reflected, under different circumstances would become either a saint or a psychopath. He hoped that whatever the factor that maintained her equilibrium, kept her functioning as a societal being, would not fail until he was done with her. Because when Beth Davis fell she would not do so alone.

Schecker covered her hand with his own, but she drew back, shaking her head, the eyes mocking him.

"I am sure Berlin will have no objections to certain, ah, bonuses," he said smoothly, showing no offense.

"After they read that I'm sure they won't either."

Beth Davis reached for her purse. "I wish I could say it was a pleasure, Felipe, but I really am sorry to have brought you here. It was bad form. Besides I really do like this place and right now it seems somehow dirty."

She smiled sweetly at him. "I'm going to the little girls' room. Be a dear and wait until I come back for my coat."

Felipe Schecker watched her disappear around the corner of the booth. He felt no anger at her insulting manner, only relief that she was gone. He was certain he had glimpsed at something terrible that churned within Beth Davis, the red-eye demon of psychosis which had winked at him.

Out of the corner of his eye Schecker saw one of the colored waiters approaching. Automatically his hand dipped into the inside breast pocket of his jacket for the billfold. Before he could withdraw it he was taken.

In one motion the janitor, now wearing a striped shirt, bow tie and red vest, slipped into the booth, slid along the smooth leather and drove three stiffened fingers into Schecker's midriff. The Portuguese diplomat gasped and fell forward. The waiter seized his right ear, jerking his head back, and with the other hand jammed a linen napkin into his mouth. Schecker's flailing arms almost knocked over the glasses on the table. The waiter hit him again, a fist hammering into the right temple. The blow stunned Schecker. He felt himself being dragged out of the booth. A pair of arms came under his shoulders. As he stumbled he managed to raise his head. The stockroom door behind the service bar was open. In front of wooden crates filled with soft drinks stood another man. The driver of cab number 112.

In spite of the pain Schecker began shaking his head furiously. The door was kicked closed behind him, his jacket ripped open, the sleeves jammed down around his arms, immobilizing him. Somewhere in his consciousness he heard one of his gold cuff links hit the floor. But he failed to see the glitter of the needle. There was a smell of alcohol, the prick of steel, oblivion . . . The musical trio, which had been playing a somewhat raucous version of the samba, switched to a soft mood piece.

Beth Davis went into the ladies' washroom but she never entered a stall. It wasn't because these were occupied. The lavatory was empty. Nor had she forgotten her purse at the table and had to return for it. Beth Davis couldn't quantify what it was that made her abruptly turn around and open the door and walk slowly, softly, down the carpeted hallway that connected the washrooms with the lounge. Yet she followed her instinct without hesitation or second thought.

Beth Davis stepped around the corner into the lounge, feeling the heat of the pink spotlights above her. She moved along the wall until she came to the dance floor and looked across to the raised section where she had been sitting with Felipe Schecker. In that split second she saw the face of the janitor who worked in the N Street building, with whom she had tauntingly flirted on her way out tonight . . . to meet Schecker. There was no mistaking the face, and so it didn't matter that she never saw what it was the red-jacketed negro was pushing through the stockroom door at the end of the service bar.

Beth Davis closed her eyes. The image of herself as a little girl on a roller-coaster car plummeting down a run sprang into her mind. It was one of the very few memories she had of childhood, that and how, when the ride was over, everyone had laughed because her face had become so white from terror.

Her hand dipped into her purse, cold fingers caressing the cold barrel. Her grip tightened around the butt of the Walther. She felt warmth creeping along her cheeks.

Beth Davis began to make her way across the lounge toward the exit. The fall of her heels created a staccato rhythm she thought was too loud. But no one was watching her. Men would glance up as she passed by, but only to smile appreciatively. She entered the foyer without incident.

To the left of the central staircase which wends to the second-floor dining room was a door with a square, frosted pane. Beth Davis pushed it open, shivering as the cold air in the stairwell cut through her black linen jacket. Leaning against the cinderblock wall, she ripped off her shoes, then ran down the steps so quickly she scarcely felt the cold. Three flights down, she reached the garage.

The individual parking areas were large, designed to hold the mammoth limousines favored by the founding members of the Spike. Beth Davis paused briefly, glanced around and made for her car parked twenty feet away. The gun was in her hand, swinging gently. She did not put it away after getting into the Ford, but laid it on the seat beside her.

No one was waiting for her at the entrance to the garage. No one tried to cut her off when she turned out of the driveway onto Pennsylvania Avenue. The evening traffic was moderately heavy as official Washington began its social whirl, and although she constantly checked her mirrors she couldn't tell if anyone was following her.

Not that it mattered. This was the endgame that was being played out, and she was the embattled queen, her protective knight taken. Beth Davis refused to think about Felipe Schecker. The man she had toyed with so casually over the last two years, baited with words and her body, had suddenly gained the capacity to instill terror within her. Thinking of him was to invite madness. There would be enough time later, when she was safe, to try to understand what had gone wrong.

Once out of the mainstream traffic Beth Davis made good time to her cottage in Rockcliff Park. She drew the Ford into the driveway, left the lights on and engine running but automatically picked up the gun. The house was dark. There were no shouts, no lights snapped on when she opened the door.

Beth Davis pulled back the hall closet door, swept her arm across the array of hats and scarves on the shelf above the coatrack and opened a panel which resembled a fuse box. Except that in the crevice was a chamois bag. She gripped the strings and slid the bag off the shelf. It was terribly heavy in her hand but that very fact caused her to smile. She stepped over the strewn clothing, slammed the door behind her and returned to her car.

They hadn't been waiting for her in the garage. They hadn't picked her up en route. No one had been waiting at her home. As long as she could get to the Maryland shore she would be safe. After that the gold would take her anywhere she wanted to go. It was this tantalizing mirage of freedom that blinded her for a brief moment. Beth Davis was backing out of the drive-way, intent on turning left. She didn't see the Packard until it was almost too late.

The heavy sedan was in the street, its front half partially blocking the drive, cutting Beth Davis off from the direction in which she had intended to go. She hesitated only a fraction of a second, swearing at the driver because she at last realized she had been in the trap all along. Fury slammed her foot onto the gas pedal. The spinning tires screamed out a warning but the Packard did not move. Beth Davis spun the wheel to the left, her right rear fender scraping the other car, then accelerated down the street.

The Packard's headlights split the night, two rattler's eyes catching her in their glare. Seemingly without effort the car drew alongside her and with a casual cuff, slammed the Ford. Beth Davis turned the corner, the Ford rocking on its chassis. The chamois bag slid off the seat, hitting the floorboards.

The glare of the lights blinded her momentarily, then the Packard was on her left, cruising less than a foot away. Beth Davis grabbed the Walther with her left hand and thrust the barrel partially out the window. Before she could fire, the Packard rammed her again. The gun fell into her lap, the hammer digging painfully into her thigh. In the last instant Beth Davis swerved. The car's momentum brushed a lamp-post, carried it onto the sidewalk, razing the undercarriage.

The Packard moved over onto her right, trailing in the stream of sparks. Beth Davis felt the Ford shudder as the heavier car slammed into her sedan, and this time did not move away. She felt the car drifting to the left and spun the wheel in the same direction, skidding into an alley. The single headlight illuminated an onrushing brick wall. Beth Davis slammed the brakes with both feet, the metal curve of the horn ramming painfully into her breasts. When she looked up she saw that she had come to a stop only inches away from the wall. A dead end. The spring of the trap.

Beth Davis staggered out of the car, clutching the Walther. Only the Packard's parking lights were on, but beneath the yellow lamplight she could see the driver very clearly.

"It's over, Beth."

He was a tall man, well over six feet, whose height was emphasized by a large, heavy-boned frame. He stood with his legs slightly apart, hands stuffed into the pockets of his raincoat. For some bizarre reason she recognized the expensive cut of his jacket, the silk sheen to his shirt and tie. The face too was not what she would have expected. It was fleshed out, the nose long and almost Roman in its curve. Curly chestnut hair tufted around his collar. It was a warm, open face, that of a priest or farmer. Except for the eyes. The eyes gave him away—dark, almost black and opaque. Eyes she had never seen before, that bored into hers without a hint of mercy. This was not a Hoover man. He was worse, much worse.

"Put the gun down, Beth."

The voice was soft, extending an invitation rather than issuing an order. She raised the barrel level with her eyes, the stock gripped in both hands.

"Beth, you won't kill me," he said. "You're not cut from that kind of stuff. I think it would be better for all concerned if you were to surrender, don't you?"

Beth Davis didn't reply. Her mind was churning furiously, the thought of escape being pursued by the image of prison. She couldn't go to prison. She would never survive it. It would be impossible . . . To continue to exist she would have to kill. Kill and keep on killing until she made it to safety, somewhere . . . And this man, this stranger whom she had never seen in her life, yet who had run her to ground, would be the first.

"Beth, usually you don't carry your gun. But today, knowing you were to meet Schecker, you did. You removed it from the lefthand drawer of your night table. I know this because you're a very conscientious person who keeps her weapon clean. I found traces of machine oil in the wood.

"The gun was in your purse. At work you placed your purse

in the well of your desk, next to the wastepaper basket on the right. At ten thirty-five this morning you were called into Murray Feldstein's office. Feldstein is your supervisor in Section B. Ostensibly the meeting concerned the possibility of liaisoning you with Naval Intelligence. That was a lot of garbage. Those twenty minutes allowed me to remove your gun and remove certain parts. Without those parts, Beth, the Walther 7.62 you're holding will explode in your face."

"Who are you?" she screamed. "*Who*?"

He started to move toward her. "It's better for you to be alive, Beth. You can tell us a great deal we have to know. Perhaps you could even work for us."

He was no more than five feet away.

"Liar!" Beth Davis whispered, her throat hoarse. "Goddamn lying son of a bitch!"

Beth Davis pulled the trigger and died before her consciousness could register her disbelief.

At eleven o'clock on the evening of May 15, a black sedan with curtained windows stopped at the checkpoint before the western entrance to the White House. The Secret Service agent shuffled through the papers handed him by the driver, then shone a penlight across the features of the lone occupant on the rear seat. Satisfied, the agent waved the car in and returned to his post to telephone the Marine security desk. Neither the visitor's name nor the time of his arrival was written into the official White House log. The entrance into the Oval Office had been chosen so as to minimize the chance of any staff member inadvertently catching a glimpse of the visitor, even at this late hour. The precautions were eminently justified because this man, powerful in his own right, could never be officially connected to the President of the United States in any way.

At forty-eight, Allen Dulles cut a tall, somewhat corpulent figure with a leonine head of full, silver-gray hair, bushy eyebrows and a buccaneer's mustache. Born to privilege and authority, he was, in 1940, a partner in the family firm of Sullivan and Cromwell, controlled by his elder brother, Foster. For the most part Allen eschewed the firm's domestic business, preferring to concentrate on the European clients. The majority of these were in Germany and Switzerland—several provincial governments, Reich industrial combines, U.S. branch corporations and a handful of wealthy individuals.

In 1936 Dulles led a junior partners' revolt which ultimately shut down Sullivan and Cromwell's offices in Germany. But Allen himself did not return to the United States immediately. Instead he expanded the firm's Swiss bureau to incorporate the German clients who stayed with him. Whether this was merely a fortunate coincidence or a carefully structured move, it nonetheless resulted in Dulles's having what he termed "a window on Berlin." In less than six months Allen Dulles knew more about what was going on in the German capital than any Allied secret service. His sources, some clients, others who used clients as a conduit, were men who held the highest offices in the Reich. This informal network would become the basis of Dulles's power, a power that would expand in the same geometric progression as the number of his sources. It was also the reason why Roosevelt had summoned Dulles to the presidential retreat at Hyde Park in the spring of that year.

Although the Dulles clan had always been staunch Republicans, Allen favored the President's foreign policies, especially the unequivocal White House support for Britain. He had long ago declared himself bipartisan but never considered that he might be called upon to serve. Yet when Roosevelt tabled his proposal the Wall Street lawyer was stunned: a new, strictly unofficial office was to be created, that of Security Advisor for European Affairs with Dulles at its head. Because of the furor that would erupt within the Democratic Party if the appointment were made public, all arrangements would be constructed under the umbrella of national security. Dulles was to continue working at Sullivan and Cromwell, although he would lighten his duties. Offices would be set up in New York and Washington, manned by specially screened staff. Access to the President would be immediate. The new bureau would have three directives: to coordinate and evaluate the information from Dulles's vast number of European sources; to expand these resources by whatever means Dulles saw fit; to create a small security group which would work independently of the FBI in dealing with internal subversion (where necessary) and whose members could be sent abroad to either ferret out or bring back vital information.

The office would be funded by a series of bogus defense contracts (Sullivan and Cromwell would do the paperwork).

Allen Dulles would report to the President by telephone or, in the event of an emergency, in person.

In the four years the office had been in existence Dulles had never had to resort to the latter. The call from Jonathan Baylor Cabot, only six hours ago, changed all that.

Dulles strode into the Oval Office, closing the door behind him.

"Mr. President," he said, tossing his coat on a loveseat. "Forgive my tardiness, but traffic from Union Station was horrendous."

"No apologies are necessary, Allen," the President replied. "Take a drink. Mr. Cabot just got here himself."

Cabot, who had been slumped in an easy chair, drew himself up and came over to the trolley bar.

"How bad is it, Jonathan?" Dulles asked softly, pouring for both men.

"Very."

The two men took their places before the President's desk. Cabot spoke unbidden.

"I have given the President the background on this case," he said to Dulles. "You, sir, are aware of the pertinent details. If I may I'll pick up the thread after the killing."

The soft tone, with its shade of New England twang, almost concealed the horror of what was to be told.

"We found nothing in Beth Davis's clothes, nothing on the body itself," Cabot said. "Nothing in the Georgetown apartment or in the nursing home. The gold on her person has been confiscated. The Rockcliff Park address, the house she and her fiancé had bought, is clean."

"What about Schecker?" Dulles queried, not taking his eyes off his man.

Cabot shrugged his broad shoulders. "He has diplomatic immunity so we'll let him go in a little while."

"There is protocol to be observed," Roosevelt objected. "Even if the man is an agent of a foreign power."

"Schecker has been cooperating with us, Mr. President."

Cabot did not think it necessary to inform Roosevelt of the use of sodium pentothal. By the time he was ready to hand him back to the Portuguese, Schecker would be ready for the trash heap. The control had held out far longer than Cabot had anticipated. When Cabot finally broke him he anticipated a mother lode of information. Instead Schecker had begun talking about something Cabot didn't even know existed. Which meant that one or both men in this room had been holding back on him. A violation of their contract with him.

"But it took me a long time to induce Schecker's cooperation," Cabot said, looking at Dulles. "He was very reluctant to tell me about Prometheus."

He caught the telltale warning flash from Dulles's eyes as they darted toward the President. But Roosevelt's did not even attempt to mask his reaction. The President sighed and inserted a cigarette into the famous holder. He wrapped both hands around a heavy lighter.

"Would you pour me a glass of sherry, Mr. Cabot?"

"Certainly, Mr. President."

"And while you're at it, could you explain to me exactly how you centered on Miss Davis as the informant as well as the implication this unmasking has for us?"

He wants to understand how much I already know, Cabot thought. What I've inadvertently blundered across . . .

"Mr. President," Cabot began softly, "for the past three months you have been using the telephone link with our London embassy more and more often. Within this time frame, my bureau within the Special Advisor's office came to suspect a tap or some other form of intercept on the communications channel. Mr. Dulles spoke to Friedmann, chief of the Signal Intelligence Bureau, secured his cooperation, and I infiltrated their offices."

Cabot handed the President his Amontillado.

"Thank you, Mr. Cabot," the President said between clenched teeth. "And how did you manage this without anyone being any the wiser?"

"Better than half of my agents are negroes, Mr. President. No one pays any attention to a janitor, cabdriver, elevator operator. They were my eyes and ears inside SIB."

"Devastatingly simple," Roosevelt murmured. "Continue."

"An agent of ours in Berlin was the final connection. He made it painfully clear that Berlin was receiving information within days, sometimes within hours, of its having been transmitted from London. When we learned the nature of this information we were able to ascertain the date it was sent, by whom, and which other details had been sent in the same transmission. Whoever was taking was taking only the most sensitive traffic, leaving the chaff."

Cabot returned to his chair and raised his own glass.

"For eight weeks I checked and rechecked the rosters of SIS, Army and Navy Signal Corps. I traced everyone even remotely connected with all these units, not only those personnel who have access to the White House London channel. Nothing. I backtracked, got out the lists for our people at Grosvenor Square. But the inquiries could only go so far. London's four thousand miles away.

"Then, two weeks ago, I took a different tack. Instead of going after personnel, I had copies made of that day's London messages to State. I matched the transcripts with ones made of the actual messages sent. Twice there was a discrepancy in content. Hidden in the traffic received here was a phrase, six innocuous words, meaningless to anyone except the person who was looking for them, to whom it was a signal to lift and subsequently deliver a specific piece of that traffic."

"And Miss Davis was the one dealing with this traffic," the President said quietly.

"Every piece," Cabot confirmed. "But I had to let her have that one final piece to be sure it was her. I also wanted to see where she took it, to whom."

"So you waited until today, when you *would* be sure?"

"That's right, Mr. President."

Cabot hesitated. "Except Schecker had a backup. My people lost sight of him for a couple of seconds when he went into the washroom. That's where he passed it on to a third party. A very careful man, Schecker. Even though he had no reason to suspect surveillance on Davis, he nonetheless arranged for a third party to walk out with the traffic."

Cabot looked away. "It's one transmission Berlin should not have received. It was my oversight, my responsibility."

"If a third man carried out the message, how did you come by the reference to Prometheus?" Roosevelt queried.

"Schecker read the message, Mr. President. It seems he has a photographic memory. Once we got into his skull he played it back for us word for word."

Cabot didn't miss the subtle exchange of looks between the President and Dulles. A decision was being made in that loaded silence . . . something based on what Schecker had managed to pass on. Prometheus. Cabot waited for the President's opening gambit but didn't get it.

"And what, Mr. Cabot, is the upshot of all this?" Roosevelt asked. "What conclusions are we to draw?"

"We have a spy—a deep-penetration agent—somewhere in the heart of Grosvenor Square," Cabot said.

Roosevelt, who had leaned forward in his wheelchair, abruptly sat back. Cabot's tone was cold and dead, as though the voice came from some distant part of hell. Roosevelt had known many men who wielded power and who were ruthless in their execution. But never one like Cabot. Never the finality, the awful inescapable certainty.

"A deep-penetration agent," Cabot repeated. "Someone so valuable to Berlin that he or she is under orders not to intercept traffic at source. Instead this person alerts a fellow agent at the Washington end—in this case, Beth Davis. Given that *all* traffic, military and civilian, between Ten Downing Street, Whitehall and D.C. is routed through our embassy, I would say we have one hell of a problem."

Roosevelt looked sharply at his Security Affairs Advisor. Dulles had informed him of Cabot's investigation, cautioned him against speaking openly on the trans-Atlantic line. Roosevelt still believed the reference to Prometheus was circumspect enough that the Germans could not divine its meaning. But the evidence of a traitor in the London embassy shook him to the core. London's integrity was crucial to Prometheus.

"And how long has the other side been reading our mail, Mr. Cabot?" he demanded.

"I wish I could tell you, Mr. President." Cabot shook his head. "Let's highball it and say a long, long time."

There was a pause as Roosevelt twisted another cigarette into the holder.

"There's more of a problem than you may appreciate, Mr. Cabot," he said finally. "London and the Grosvenor Square embassy are Joe Kennedy's turf."

The President's fingers drummed on the wooden wheel of the chair.

"Technically Kennedy is my representative in Washington. For a while it was quite a joke to have an Irishman as your top man to the Court of St. James."

Roosevelt snorted. "It also got him the hell away from domestic politics. But Kennedy has become very tight with the British isolationists. Churchill doesn't like or trust him and resents like hell having to deal with him. He warned me—and was probably right—that given time, Kennedy could become the center of formidable domestic opposition to involving the U.S. in another European war. You understand the potential ramifications, Mr. Cabot."

Cabot inclined his head but said nothing. Roosevelt was a master of saying one thing while meaning something totally different. Obviously Kennedy didn't have a clue that he was harboring a spy at Grosvenor Square. It was also possible that the Ambassador's own appeasement/isolationist tendencies had fostered a climate where an agent could work not only effectively but with greater access to information as well as greater security. To terminate this individual would mean handing Roosevelt Kennedy's head on a platter, neutralizing, if not destroying, the Ambassador politically.

"The agent must be rooted out," Allen Dulles said with finality. "Regardless of the effect upon the embassy or its personnel. Given time, we can reroute the President's communications to a direct Downing Street–White House line. The only real reason we haven't done so until now is because Kennedy would bitch and gripe about being left out of the scene. We can reduce the importance of military traffic flowing through Grosvenor Square, but that still leaves us with an incredible mass of communications coming out of Whitehall to deal with."

To Cabot the implication was clear.

"Do you want me to handle it or should I brief Pearce and let him run with it?"

"As chief of Grosvenor Square security, Pearce is too visible for the mission," Dulles said flatly. "Whoever is operating inside the embassy knows Pearce isn't on to him—or her. If Pearce were to start asking questions, the plant would either cease operating or run. Counterproductive in both cases. But over there no one knows you from a hill of beans. I'll speak with Redman at SIB, we'll concoct a file for you and you'll become just another technician from their basement."

"Are you thinking Pearce might be involved?" Cabot asked quietly.

"No, Jonathan, not at all," Dulles replied. He was aware of the friendship between the two men and wouldn't have placed Cabot anywhere near London if he felt there was any chance of Pearce being tainted.

"Brief Pearce, let him familiarize you with the terrain, use him where you can. But you control the overall operation. I will contact Churchill to tell him you're coming. Undoubtedly he'll want one of his own people working with you."

Dulles held up his hand to Cabot's objection.

"Your cooperation would be appreciated," Dulles said dryly, ending the matter.

"Yes, sir. And what about the Ambassador?"

"No!" Roosevelt said at once, emphatically. "Joe Kennedy is not to be made aware of your activities, not under *any* circumstances."

Cabot received the message clearly: Roosevelt wanted to know not only how deep the rot had gone but how high.

"I'll have to move very quickly," he said. "As soon as Schecker gets back to the Portuguese embassy Berlin will know we've taken Davis. Berlin will flash instructions to London for our person to sit very still. That will make the search that much more difficult."

"Unfortunately time is a factor in another way," Roosevelt said. "This spy must be unearthed within the next two weeks. No later."

Cabot stared hard at the President. "Sir, there's no way I can guarantee—"

"Mr. Cabot, you *will* guarantee me this!" Roosevelt shot back, eyes blazing. "Because there's more riding on this than just the integrity of our embassy. More than you would possibly imagine!"

3

At eight o'clock in the evening of May 15, light still clung to the sky over Berlin, but Adolf Hitler was oblivious to it. He was sitting with his back to the seven-meter windows that studded the length of the Chancellery banquet hall. The one-way glass between the frames was invisible behind drawn curtains, red velvet with gold thread and a white border. Three candelabras, laden with fat candles, burned along the length of the rosewood table, their light reinforced by the tepid glow from three magnificent chandeliers set into the twenty-meter dome.

Adolf Hitler raised the crystal goblet and wet his lips with mineral water. It had become warm, its effervescence dissolved. He replaced the cup and came around to the back of his chair, parting the curtain. In the glass his silhouette appeared to shiver, but perhaps this was only a trick of the light.

Where is he?

Abruptly Hitler pivoted on his heel and glared into the darkness, at a door he knew to be there yet could not see. Beyond waited his generals: Jodl, Rommel and Mannerheim had been in the Chancellery for the last eleven hours. Goebbels waited. Ribbentrop, Himmler. To the west hundreds of thousands of fighting men, in infantry, tanks, in the seats of bombers and fighters, in the confines of submarines, destroyers and battle cruisers—all waited. And behind them the people of Germany, who would follow his lead over the radio, in the newspapers . . .

And Hitler too waited, for the one man whom he trusted above all others, who was neither a general nor a statesman nor a courtier. The man who had saved his life in the trenches along the Somme twenty-three years ago. The most faithful and honest of men . . .

That day the shelling from British guns had been ferocious, bearing the intangible yet undeniable quality of victory. Time and time again the shells landed on pockets of German infantrymen huddled in trenches as though the gunners had had divine—or infernal—inspiration in choosing their coordinates. Corporal Adolf Hitler watched as one of the last salvos literally blew eight members of his company out of the trench, catapulting them through the air onto their own barbed wire. A dozen others were buried alive when the trench walls collapsed. As he was scrambling in retreat, Hitler heard the British bugles, and in their echoes the obscene, inhuman screaming of charging Tommies.

Perhaps it had been a shell that had knocked him unconscious, or he had twisted his foot in the mud, falling and jarring his head against a rock. When he opened his eyes Hitler saw the swirling dust that blotted out the sky. Through that murkiness a shadow loomed. He reached for his carbine but his back blazed with pain. The clawing, grasping fingers managed to clutch only at mud.

He lay there like a fish with a broken back, watching as the shadow shouldered its rifle and took aim. He did not realize he was screaming, or that the shadow was laughing.

It was the laughter that saved him. Had the British soldier shot immediately, Hitler would have died. Instead Tommy's forehead disintegrated under the velocity of the sniper bullet. The rifle slipped, the barrel falling. The shot discharged, missing Hitler by inches, splattering his face with mud.

A moment later Gerd Jaunich appeared. With one arm he hoisted Hitler over his shoulder. He backed away toward the German lines, his rifle held at his hip, the barrel pointed in the direction of the fallen British soldier . . .

By the end of the war Jaunich had risen to the rank of captain. Hitler did not chance to meet him again until five years later, after the abortive *putsch* in 1923. It was the ignominy at Munich that sealed the fates of the unemployed painter and the discarded war hero. While Hitler pursued the political course, plotting the demise of the Weimar Republic, Jaunich worked ceaselessly to recreate a German military machine. A decade later, in 1933, when Hitler shunted aside the aging Hindenburg and assumed the post of Chancellor, Jaunich handed him an armed force so well trained and equipped that the rest of Europe could not believe it had been constructed under the very nose of the Versailles Treaty.

Yet for all he had achieved Jaunich refused Hitler's wish to make him a general. He resigned his commission in 1935 and instead became an unofficial advisor to the Chancellor. Jaunich had no need of the pomp and circumstance that surrounded a Goering or Jodl, nor of the trappings Ribbentrop demanded. He had the one thing which all others lacked: the absolute trust of Adolf Hitler in Jaunich's judgments and opinions. It was on the basis of this trust that Hitler allowed, indeed encouraged, Jaunich to open a dialogue with Winston Churchill while the latter was still in the political wilderness. Somehow Jaunich had perceived that at a critical point in Germany's expansion, Churchill would be the man who would speak for England.

The doors to the banquet hall were thrust open. The shaft of light from the antechamber pierced the gloom, severing Hitler's last thoughts.

"*Mein Führer!*"

The light disappeared as the doors closed. Soft clicks, leather soles on parquet flooring, sounded as Gerd Jaunich approached. He walked up swiftly, with a soldier's military gait although he was dressed in a suit.

Beneath the light, Hitler's face appeared sallow and worn. Jaunich could smell the sweat across the shining forehead, feel Hitler's body trembling in anticipation.

"Churchill told me he desires peace."

Hitler began to nod his head, a smile coming over his lips. The eyes widened like those of a greedy dreamer.

"My friend!" he whispered, reaching out to touch Jaunich. "Those few precious words—"

"But he lied to me, Führer!"

The dream crumbled and Hitler screamed: "Lied?"

Jaunich did not flinch, nor did his voice lose its composure.

"Winston Churchill wanted me to believe, wanted *you* to believe, that peace was still possible. He went to great lengths to convince me of this. But in fact he was only playing for time. Time, Führer, to organize and execute the removal of the British Expeditionary Force, as well as much Allied manpower—French, Belgian, Dutch—as soon as possible, from Dunkirk."

"But what of his treaties with the French?" Hitler whispered. "All the time he spouts rhetoric about standing by his allies."

"The British Empire did not fight on behalf of those it considers its inferiors—the Czechs and Poles," Jaunich replied. "It is reluctant to commit English blood to French soil. The English will not fight until they themselves are directly threatened. I suggest, Führer, that coming from anyone else the offer of peace could have been judged genuine. But not from Churchill. Beneath his honeyed lies was an understanding, a fatalistic certainty that England will *have* to fight the Reich. Believe me when I say that Churchill is very capable of inducing the British to engage in conflict. He will—already has—painted you as the dragon to his Saint George. And in the end his people will fight . . ."

Hitler brought the flat of his palm hard upon the table.

"I do not understand this! My armies are poised to deny Churchill three hundred thousand men. He begs for a meeting and speaks of peace. Yet you say he is lying. Is he not aware that I can wipe out his Expeditionary Force within a week? Is he inviting me to proceed with their destruction?"

"Churchill would not willingly sacrifice such a large number of troops," Jaunich said. "Today he used subterfuge in order to secure as much time as possible for their retreat."

"But there is a trap!"

From the breast pocket of his jacket Jaunich drew out a single sheet of paper.

"This was handed to me the moment I landed in Berlin," Jaunich said. "It is a partial transcript of the conversation held between Churchill and the American President, Roosevelt, earlier today. He asks for enormous amounts of supplies to be shipped from the United States immediately. There can be only two uses for such material, Führer: either to reinforce the troops already present at Dunkirk or to store the weapons in England as part of the building of Fortress Britannia."

Hitler read the transcript very slowly. He had not failed to recognize the excitement beneath Jaunich's measured tone. There was something in this message that held the key. Hitler read the words one more time.

"What is Prometheus?"

"The reason why I urge you not to unleash your forces upon Dunkirk immediately."

"Churchill lied to you!" Hitler said in that pitiless tone which even Jaunich feared. "This message to Roosevelt proves as much. He is requesting arms and now is willing to pay for them with something the Americans made a condition: Prometheus. Yet you are suggesting that I stand back and allow Churchill to play me for a fool!"

"No, Führer," Jaunich said quietly. "In fact I am asking for quite the contrary. It is the British who will be *our* fools. Within forty-eight hours you will have proof that Prometheus is the cornerstone upon which to engineer a British defeat. The English generals, our own, *everyone*, is obsessed with Dunkirk. But Dunkirk, Führer, is only a battle. Prometheus could well be the war!"

The portents of evening come early in the valleys behind the Jura Range, that irregular mountainous terrain which forms the spinal column between France and Switzerland. By four o'clock in the afternoon, even though the sun remains high in the sky, the shadows have completely settled over the valley floor. The conifers, evergreens and beeches lose their individual colors in favor of a uniform blackness. The meandering trails, old scars cut into the forest by smugglers, disappear and the sparkle from the torrential springs is lost, leaving only the rush of water over stone.

Two kilometers from the town of Bonneville, in the French district of Haute-Savoie, a soldier in French uniform with an MAS38 submachine gun slung over one arm was standing on the sharply angled west side of the valley. One shoulder was pressed hard against a slender birch for support, the boots firmly planted in the dank, dark earth. He was holding a pair of binoculars to his eyes, but he heard the sound before seeing its source. The train was on time.

Major Erik Guderian was a tall man, six feet three, with long legs and reach. At thirty-eight, his physique, sculpted by mountain climbing, was that of a man a dozen years younger. The sportsman reflected in the athletic body was tempered by a sensitive face. The eyes were gray and kind, the mouth generous and often smiling. The brushed-back flaxen hair and the three sharp lateral creases along the forehead gave him an actor's countenance, or a poet's, as some women who had loved him remarked.

Erik Guderian shifted his weight slightly, causing the birch to crackle. He did not have to look at his watch to know that the train was on time. The locomotive with its coal carrier and four passenger cars had left the Gare de Lyon in Paris seventeen hours ago, staying exclusively on the *lignes nationales* which crisscrossed German-overrun territory. The engineer would have been given a set of special directions, combining the *lignes militaires* with other little-used, seemingly defunct feeder lines. Guderian knew all about these and hence that the journey would take one and a half times longer than necessary to reach Bonneville.

The other safety factor was the camouflage. The passenger carriages were a signal to German aircraft that the target was civilian. The French had gambled that if any Luftwaffe pilot did overfly the train, he would waste neither time nor ammunition on a strafing run. With the *Blitzkrieg* at its height, military targets had priority, not what appeared to be a trainload of refugees fleeing for the mountains.

Nor was there much chance of a pilot recognizing that the locomotive in the lead had never seen service with the Société

Nationale des Chemins de Fer, but was a model built for and used exclusively by the French Army.

As the train rounded the sharp bend and began to labor up the last grade before the valley, Guderian sheathed the binoculars and began skittering down the incline. The prize was almost in reach. Those on board—and Guderian had a fair estimate of their number—would be thinking that they had survived the gauntlet. In the midst of silent thanks they would relax their vigilance. Bonneville was only twenty minutes away. They had no way of knowing that the figure in the olive-green camouflage jacket, dropping diagonally across the valley slope, had ensured their safe journey. Major Erik Guderian could have exercised his authority and stopped that train anywhere along its route. But he hadn't.

The train had reached the narrowest part of the valley and was less than a hundred meters from the point at which Guderian cleared the trees and hit the brush which grew tenaciously from the dry soil above the narrow-gauge line. Guderian crouched low, running hard. As he pounded through the brush he counted off the men entrenched into the side of the hill. All three were in position. Although he couldn't see the others on the opposite side of the tracks, he knew they were there.

Guderian dropped prone beside a man so young he appeared to still be shedding his teens.

"Any luck?" he whispered.

The communications officer shook his head. "Quiet as the grave at the other end."

Guderian cursed, but his ears heard only the approaching train drawing closer by the second.

"Shall I signal the others, *Herr Major*?"

Guderian stared down at the tracks, listening to the high-pitched vibrations coming off the steel as though the rails were a gigantic tuning fork. A decision had to be made, based on the carelessness, inefficiency, stupidity or simply bad luck of those who were responsible for the back end of the plan. By all rights he should abort. It was his cardinal rule in any field situation that if the support facilities broke down, he would not countenance going at the target alone. The risk to his men was too great. If even one of them were captured alive, the efficacy and value of the entire unit would be destroyed. And he along with it.

"*Herr Major . . .*"

"No signal!" Guderian said under his breath. "Whatever is happening—or not happening—at Tholon may still be corrected. *We can't let go of what that train is carrying.* Just pray we don't end up in the position of the Russian dog who, having chased the cartwheel, doesn't know what to do with it once he has his teeth on the spokes."

The Army locomotive was panting fiercely, its stack spewing out billows of acrid black smoke mixed with twinkles of red ash. The gargantuan iron wheels passed within ten meters of Guderian, who was now lying prone on the forest floor, the barrel of the gun poking out from the underbrush. He let the first carriage go by, and the second, and the third. As the fourth came into view he adjusted the angle of the rifle with its discharger cup, lining it up with the shuttered windows that moved slowly past the sights. He counted off three, then squeezed the trigger.

Even though he had held the weapon hard against his shoulder, the thrust of the discharge drove the butt into Guderian's muscles. The sharp grunt of pain was lost in two subsequent sounds: the soft woosh! of a second—then a third—grenade being launched by the men beside him and the shrieking explosions that blended into a single holocaust as the high-explosive charges shattered the windows of the carriage and detonated on impact. The carriage bucked under the attack, lurching over to one side, only to be struck by two more rounds fired from the other side of the tracks.

The train was still moving, the last car blazing like the tail of a salamander crawling through flames.

"Get moving!" Guderian screamed, already half-rising out of the brush, the grenade launcher discarded, submachine gun cradled in his hands.

The order was superfluous. The men of Action Group were in step with him, sliding through the undergrowth, the barrels of the MAS38s spitting out controlled bursts of fire. From inside the burning carriage Guderian heard the screaming of men seconds from death. At one end of the carriage a door was smashed open and a figure resembling a human torch teetered out, arms flailing over his head in a parody of surrender. The French soldier took one step too many, missed the narrow platform and fell facefirst onto the gravel bed, clawing at the rock. Guderian didn't hesitate but shot the man cleanly through the head. There was no need for gratuitous suffering.

The train shuddered to a halt. Somewhere up ahead, over the crackle of flames consuming timber, Guderian heard shouting. Within seconds the second half of his team would have secured the locomotive.

As he threw himself under the carriage Guderian caught a glimpse of the men on his side running alongside the coach. On cue the pins from three grenades were pulled, the sticks thrown in a gentle arc into the inferno. Action Group flung themselves into the gully between the railbed and the incline, hugging the earth as the last explosions tore the belly out of the carriage. Bodies tumbled out onto the track, followed by seats shorn from their bolts, bits of clothing and scraps of wood. The screaming ceased as though it had been a single unified expression of agony.

Guderian scrambled between the ties, then flipped over onto his back. From a long deep flap pocket sewn onto his combat trousers he withdrew a railman's wrench and set to work on the coupling. After two vicious twists it gave way. Guderian unscrewed the bolt, pulled himself to his feet and removed the pin.

"Stand clear!" he shouted.

For an instant the blazing carriage seemed unwilling to move.

"Damn you!" Guderian whispered, bracing his feet against a tie and leaning all his weight against the car.

"Once more, *Herr Major*!"

Guderian glanced to his left and saw his second in command, the red-bearded ex-woodsman *Feldwebel* Karl Horst, setting his shoulder to the carriage. Both men counted off and threw every ounce of strength behind the push. The wheels moved a fraction, the angle of the incline did the rest: the burning carriage was rolling down the track, leaving half a dozen French dead in its wake. In seconds the carriage reached the curve, its momentum unchecked. It spilled across the track and plowed into the underbrush, the wheels shrieking as steel cut across steel. The back dug into the soft dirt while the front end, refusing to slow, catapulted across the track, spilling over onto its side, a grotesque parody of a coffin in which forty men would forever be interred.

"*Mein Gott!*" Horst murmured, fingers sweeping across his

chest in the Catholic ritual. Erik Guderian turned him away from the carnage. "Go up front and make certain the locomotive is secure," he said. "Get the engineer and stokers off. I'll walk through the other cars to make sure we're not interrupted."

"Request permission to accompany you, *Herr Major!*" Horst said softly. "The rest of Action Group can look after the locomotive."

Guderian hesitated, then said, "Permission granted . . . with thanks."

The giant smiled and in one motion jumped onto the ramp of the third carriage, one arm motioning the rest of the squad to move up front. Guderian followed, positioning himself on the other side of the door. He looked across at his *Feldwebel* and silently began to count down. He could not have denied Horst's request: although ten years younger than Guderian, Karl Horst had been Guderian's ubiquitous shadow since the Major had arrived at the Action Group training center an eternity ago. During each of the six operations the Group had undertaken, he had remained close to his superior officer, never overstepping the bounds of command, always adhering to strict military protocol, but nevertheless remaining no more than arm's length away during an assault.

The slow shudder of the locomotive starting up again passed through the train, throwing off the aim of the two men. But the MAS38 bullets splintered the lock on the door, which then fell back as Horst kicked out with his boot. Both men drew back, anticipating fire, but none was forthcoming. Guderian had judged correctly: this passenger carriage, along with the two ahead of it, had been cannibalized. The seats, overhead racks and toilet had been ripped out. In their place rested wooden crates, two meters long, one across, half that in depth. They were stacked in four rows, five high, with only a narrow aisle between them. No one could have hidden here even if he wanted to.

"Check the other carriages," Guderian told Horst. "The babysitter must be hiding in one of them . . . Tell Willi to generate as much speed as he can. We're falling behind schedule."

"*Zu Befehl, Herr Major!*"

Guderian looked back down the track and saw the engineer and two stokers standing on the track. Rage had replaced incredulity and fear. Guderian reached down and propped the door up against its splintered frame. He drew out his heavy knife and levering it under the slats of the nearest crate, wrenched the heavy-gauge nails from the wood. The top came free and he brushed away the wood shavings, drawing out a brick that weighed exactly twelve kilos. Even in the half-light of the carriage it glittered as though molten. Guderian tossed it in the air, catching it so that it landed on its other side. In the center was the stamp of the Banque de France, in the lefthand corner, the numerals indicating purity: .999 *or fin*. In the other corner was the serial number that told Guderian all he had to know: Action Group had successfully intercepted and pirated a third of the French national gold reserves which, in the best of all possible worlds, would have by this time passed through Bonneville en route to its ultimate destination: Geneva, only forty kilometers to the northwest. Action Group, known among its members—and to only two other individuals—by the sobriquet of *Die Piraten*—the Pirates—had triumphed one more time.

"*Bitte, Herr Major!*"

Shuffling ahead of Karl Horst, made all the more diminuitive by the *Feldwebel*'s stature, was the babysitter, a controller from the Banque de France, who was carrying the inevitable paperwork demanded by his Swiss counterparts.

"Where did you find him?"

"They left him a private compartment in the forward carriage." Horst laughed. "All the comforts of home."

Guderian was not surprised. This short, corpulent *fonctionnaire* with yellowing dentures, walrus mustache and porcine eyes would have had nothing to do with the soldiers sequestered in the last car, who had died protecting him and his cargo. Even now his sweaty fear betrayed his selfishness: He lived only for the yellow metal.

"What is your name?" Guderian asked him.

"Robert Foucault," the banker stammered, lips flapping.

Guderian stretched out his arm and crooked his fingers, indicating the *vache*—a worn black briefcase—Foucault was clutching to his chest.

"*S'il vous plaît.*"

The banker must have felt Horst's hot breath on him, for he surrendered the *vache* without a murmur.

Guderian spread the contents across one of the crates: a tally sheet listing the serial numbers of the bars, a letter from the director general of the Banque de France to his counterpart at the Banque Nationale Suisse, transfer papers for the frontier and the all-important Swiss customs documents, pre-stamped.

Guderian stuffed the paperwork into the *vache*.

Someone must be looking out for us, he thought.

Under the terms of the original plan it wouldn't have mattered at all if Foucault had been killed along with his escort and the documentation destroyed. Action Group was to have intercepted the train, neutralized the armed French escort and commandeered the freight across the southern shore of Lake Geneva to Tholon, where a Reich lake freighter, manned by naval commandos, was standing by. Nothing in the plans called for Action Group to cross any frontiers. Although Guderian and his men carried forged French Army papers, they had no documentation pertaining to the pirated shipment. None had been necessary . . . until now, when the German radio at Tholon remained obstinately silent . . . until Robert Foucault, the controller of the Banque de France had been captured alive, the *vache* intact.

"Is a managing director to meet you at the frontier or at the Gare Centrale in Geneva?"

The question startled the French banker, who had been scrutinizing this German who spoke his mother tongue so flawlessly. His face was familiar, yet Foucault could not place it, as though he were looking at a familiar landscape but one veiled in fog. Guderian was aware of the banker's persistent interest in him. It was not the first time such a thing had occurred.

"I do not believe you have the legitimacy to ask such a question," Foucault answered pompously. "You are German bandits—"

"Agreed," Guderian cut him off quietly. "But I can request that you be thrown off this train. At the speed we're traveling I doubt if you would survive."

To drive home the point Karl Horst clamped both hands on Foucault's shoulders, fingers digging into the Frenchman's collarbone.

"We shall have the bullion with or without your cooperation," Guderian continued. "It is merely a question of how much you value your life. Three seconds should be enough to decide."

"At the frontier," Foucault blurted out immediately, squirming under the *Feldwebel*'s grip.

"How very cooperative of him," Guderian murmured.

But it made sense. The managing director, sent ahead to deal with the Swiss government, would have been biting his nails to the quick during the last eighteen hours, desperately wondering if his cargo would make it across the country. The discomfort of waiting at a customs depot would be far outweighed by the relief of seeing the train arrive at the frontier. Then the entry into Geneva would be triumphant.

"And at the Gare Centrale, trucks from the Banque Nationale Suisse are waiting, with the appropriate escort," Guderian said.

Foucault's agate eyes glittered. "Exactly so. That is where your madness will come to an end."

Guderian shrugged. "Possibly. Our madness, your life."

He turned to Karl Horst. "Take him back to the compartment and truss him up. Tell the men to get ready for the crossing."

"We are not stopping before the frontier, *Herr Major*?" Horst queried, uneasy.

It is time to decide. Do I take them to Tholon, into the unknown? If the freighter has been seized, then the Swiss will be waiting. We will walk into an ambush, or worse, a firefight . . . without support, without hope.

The alternative was marginally better. Audacious, with only a razor's edge of a margin of error. But it could work, *be made to work*.

"No, my friend." Guderian smiled. "As the Americans are wont to say, we are taking this straight to the bank!"

Guderian followed his *Feldwebel* and the banker out of the car, but stopped at the canvas that bridged the two carriages. He pushed down the window on the door and leaned out into the twilight, the rush of air catching his hair.

The train was traveling at full speed, entering Bonneville, which lay in darkness just ahead. Bonneville was deserted. He had ascertained that for himself during the reconnaissance mission. Guderian imagined the chaos that had overtaken it when word of the German invasion had been received. A few brave or patriotic, or simply foolish, souls had stayed behind. But the temptation of Switzerland, less than a stone's throw away, had been too much for most. As the train thundered past the Bonneville station Guderian saw no lights. The stationmaster's last act had been to leave the track to the frontier open—orders from Paris to let freight proceed unimpeded. Guderian could not help but smile at the irony.

When the train was less than two minutes from the Franco-Swiss border, Erik Guderian brought his men together in the narrow corridor opposite the single compartment, which had become the bank controller's cell. Only Willi Trapp, his transportation specialist, was absent, at the controls of the locomotive.

"We have a choice," Guderian told them without preamble. "The original plan called for taking a feeder line at the frontier and heading east toward Tholon. However, complications have set in."

He looked down toward the bespectacled Thomas Braun, Action Group's communications expert.

"I still haven't been able to raise the boat at Tholon, *Herr Major*," Braun said softly.

He ran a hand over the golden-red stubble that he was vainly cultivating into a beard.

"There is nothing wrong with our equipment. I can only guess that the transportation promised us hasn't arrived."

"So we don't know if it will be there when we finish busting our asses over half of *unoccupied* France with God knows what in pursuit," Karl Horst added helpfully.

"We can *assume* that the transport will be in place when we get there," Guderian said.

"Begging your pardon, *Herr Major*, but when have we assumed *anything* positive when someone began fucking up on the other end?"

Thomas Braun asked the question so politely that even the coarse language sounded innocent.

"Which is why I want you to consider an alternative," Guderian said.

Quickly he outlined the plan he had been putting together as soon as the train had cleared the assault area.

"It's stuck together with string, baling wire and prayer," Guderian warned them. "Foucault has told us little, but that's to be expected: a controller is not necessarily privy to the exact physical arrangements on the other end. However, with a little luck we may get the information we need from the managing director, who was sent ahead."

Guderian paused. "We can be certain of one thing: if we

make it past the Swiss border patrols then our chances improve. But if there's trouble at the frontier . . ."

The rest need not have been voiced. His men knew well enough the devastating results of a firefight between German soldiers in French uniforms and Swiss Army regulars.

"We should go with the string and baling wire, *Herr Major*," Horst rumbled, and laughed. "After all, we are *Die Piraten*. Our reputation is at stake!"

Guderian counted off the assenting nods and said: "That's it then. Horst, you tell Willi the change in plans. Thomas, you look after our friend in the compartment. I wouldn't want him talking out of turn."

The French outpost was nothing more than a two-room shack stuck at one end of a long barrier pole. As the train sighed to a halt, Guderian and Horst, who had been riding the platform, jumped down. The door to the shack opened and two rifle barrels poked out.

"Identify yourselves!"

"Lieutenant Beauchamp and Sergeant Lalond, Third Parachute Brigade, escorting a special consignment from Paris!"

The door opened a little more and two men stepped out. They were both elderly, one limping badly, a legacy from the First War. Their carbines were ancient, the navy blue uniforms shiny and tattered, betraying their age in the yellow glow of a paraffin lamp. The one with the limp held back, the carbine lowered a few degrees but still trained on the two soldiers. His partner shuffled forward.

"Papers," he rasped. The hand he held out was trembling badly, as much from fear as from the alcohol that wafted on his breath.

"We heard shooting," he stuttered, watching Guderian undo his flap pocket and begin pulling out papers.

"There was trouble—"

A few feet away there came a faint sigh. The old man with the lamp jerked his head around to see the rifle clatter from his partner's hands. Because of the gloom he could not make out the black handle of the throwing knife buried to the hilt in the man's chest.

Guderian took two steps and his forearm was around the old man's throat. He reached around and pried the lamp from the gnarled fingers. He couldn't afford the lamp breaking, a sudden fire. One hundred meters away, on the Swiss side, border patrols would be watching.

Guderian held the lamp away from his body, his forearm cutting off the old man's wheezing gasps. There was a dry crackle as bone snapped and the head rolled to one side. Guderian lowered the corpse to the ground, stepped over it and ran toward the train. Horst had already lifted the barrier; the locomotive was moving into no-man's land.

"I'm sure they will be very happy to see us, *Herr Major!*" Willi Trapp shouted over the engine rumble.

Guderian, hanging on to the bar welded in beside the platform, saw what he meant. Illuminated by the giant spotlight at the head of the locomotive was the Swiss checkpoint. Not a shack but two concrete bunkers built on either side of the tracks. Manned not by elderly veterans but by Swiss Army regulars, with armored scout cars for support.

The train rolled slowly through the frontier. Guderian timed his jump and was off before it shuddered to a halt. A command was shouted and Swiss soldiers trotted down the length of the platform, taking up positions alongside the carriages. Behind the last car the barbed-wire barrier was being swung back across the tracks.

"What in God's name happened to you? Where's Foucault?"

The imperious voice belonged to a tall, distinguished gentleman whose elongated nose was pinched red at the tip. In one gloved hand was a crumpled handkerchief. Beside him stood a Swiss Army lieutenant.

"Lieutenant Beauchamp, Third Parachute Brigade, reporting, *sir!*"

"Lacroix, managing director of the Banque de France," the civilian replied brusquely. "Now, what happened?"

Guderian looked over Lacroix's shoulder at the Swiss Lieutenant, who hadn't taken his eyes off him. He too was waiting for an answer, would match it up against this French officer whose dirt-streaked uniform and muddied face almost spoke for itself.

"We ran into an ambush," Guderian said haltingly, the fatigue over his words real enough. "A German commando unit attacked us just outside of Bonneville."

Guderian stared hard at the banker. "We lost forty men, the engineer and his stokers. But we still made it over the border."

"With one car less!" Lacroix cried.

"The one my men were riding in!" Guderian said savagely. Out of the corner of his eye he saw the Swiss Lieutenant's lips curl in disgust at what the banker had uttered.

"Don't concern yourself," Guderian finished bitterly, ripping open the *vache* he had appropriated from Foucault. "The consignment is safe—all of it!"

"And Foucault?"

"He bumped his head," Guderian replied derisively and nodded at the lead car. "He's probably come around by now."

Lacroix regarded Guderian with shining hatred.

"Your insolence will be remembered, Lieutenant," he said and walked off toward the carriage steps, bumping into Karl Horst.

Guderian reached into the *vache* and brought out the already stamped customs and transit papers, handing these to the Swiss officer.

"Technically it is against regulations, Lieutenant," the Swiss said, leafing through the documents, "but if I can be of any assistance to your men you have only to ask."

"I am grateful for your consideration," Guderian said. "But aside from a flesh wound, some cuts and scrapes, we're all right. I just want to get this scrap to Geneva and go back. My men deserve a proper burial."

The Lieutenant handed him the papers.

"Godspeed, then," he said softly. "And I am very sorry."

The two men shook hands and Guderian signaled Willi in the engineer's cab. The train was on the move again, heading for the small suburb of Veyrier, the last town before Geneva itself.

Guderian opened the compartment door to see Foucault and Lacroix sitting across from each other, one's eyes downcast with shame, the other's alive with fury. But neither man spoke because between them, on a small stool, sat Karl Horst, carefully shaving a piece of wood with his long commando knife.

"Like mice, *Herr Major*," he said, not turning around but speaking to Guderian's reflection in the window.

Guderian moved toward the back of the car, four men following. He scrutinized the ceiling and immediately saw what he was looking for.

"You have twenty minutes to pull the bolts," he told them.

"I don't want to be in those freight yards a second longer than necessary."

The passenger carriages had been effective camouflage for the gold shipment, but the ruse also telegraphed to Guderian exactly what to expect in Geneva. Passenger cars did not have the wide sliding doors of the freights. Yet they were carrying crates whose dimensions and weight would have made it impossible for them to have been moved through the narrow doors. That left a single option: the roofs of the three cars had been cut away from the body, then slit in half, widthwise. Before loading, these panels had been removed and a crane had swung the gold crates through the opening. When the job was finished the crane had lifted the roof panels back onto the carriage, where they were fixed to the body. The presence of industrial bolts was the final giveaway. The only way in which the bullion could be off-loaded was to repeat the process. Therefore Guderian knew precisely what would be waiting for the train when it pulled in.

The Gare Centrale is Geneva's oldest rail terminal. Located in the southeastern half of the city, it is bordered by the Route de Frontenex and the Route de Chine, two major arteries in the city proper. To the east of the gigantic, green-glass station are the freight yards, small in comparison to those of other European cities but equipped to handle almost any kind of cargo. As the train veered from siding to siding, skirting the station itself, Guderian could make out the giant cranes mounted on flatbeds. The corner of the yards into which the freight was being guided was lit up with klieg lights. The cool night air and intense heat mixed into a filmy vapor that settled over the triple-axle Peugeot trucks that waited on the platform.

Guderian slipped back into the compartment.

"I have been explaining to your man that there is no way in which you can get out of this," Lacroix said quickly. "If you surrender now—"

"Where is your car?" Guderian demanded.

The banker looked away. He almost didn't feel the blade as it whispered across his wrist. But the blood was real enough. Horst wiped the tempered steel on the banker's dark overcoat.

"The next time the tendons will be cut," Guderian said tonelessly, ignoring the banker's horror. "You were going to tell me about your car."

"It will be with the trucks," Lacroix stammered, staring at the welling blood.

"With a driver?"

"Yes . . . of course."

"Do the trucks belong to the Banque Nationale Suisse?"

"No, but they are leased from the same firm the bank uses."

"Security?"

Lacroix had fished out a handkerchief and clamped it over his wound.

"Police!" he snapped viciously.

There had been an outside chance that the Swiss would have provided a military escort. But Lacroix must have reasoned, sensibly enough, that if the gold got as far as Geneva, surely no one was going to pinch it here. These days gold moved *into* Geneva; it was seldom brought out.

"This gentleman will escort you out as soon as the train stops," Guderian said. "You will both walk along the platform, past the trucks and toward your car. You will be close together and you will be speaking constantly to each other. I assure you that if any alarm is attempted you will not live to hear it."

He paused. "You have seen what a knife can do—in the right hands."

"You're insane," Lacroix whispered.

Guderian turned to Horst. "I'll come by the car before the trucks roll. Send their driver to me."

Horst raised his eyebrows.

"He's no good to you," Guderian said, "so he might as well help with the unloading."

The men of Action Group scrambled onto the roofs of the carriages as Willi Trapp slowed the locomotive and released the steam pressure from the boiler. Guderian was on the platform, trotting by the cars, shouting at his men to work the bolts free. Halfway down the cinder walk he stopped and surveyed the conditions.

As Lacroix had said, the trucks were there, three of them lined up with their canvases piled on top of the cabs, the drivers clustered together in a loose ring, smoking. On the adjacent rails was the flatbed with mounted crane. From where he stood Guderian could make out the operator in his cab halfway up the crisscross girder tower. He followed the man's gaze toward two men who were approaching him, one in a police uniform, the other in blue workman's overalls.

"What's holding you up?" Guderian shouted. "The roof is ready to come off!"

The supervisor hesitated, glancing at the official, who nodded briefly. A moment later the crane engine roared to life over the deserted yard.

"The border patrol informed us you had some . . . unforeseen difficulties, Lieutenant," the policeman said.

The cigarette remained jammed in the corner of his mouth, but the cold shrewd eyes never left Guderian. The papers he offered identified him as an inspector of the Bureau des Monnaies, the Bank Squad of the Swiss civil police. Guderian reciprocated without waiting to be asked.

"What happened was a bloodbath," Guderian said flatly. "With the grace of God we managed to get through."

The policeman returned Guderian's forged documentation.

"The Chinese have a saying," he murmured. *"May you live in interesting times*. People mistake it for a blessing. In reality it is a curse. And the curse is upon us."

Abruptly the policeman turned on his heel and began walking along the platform. Guderian fell in beside him in time to see the two French bankers step onto the siding. An instant later they disappeared behind the bulk of Karl Horst.

"How many men in your escort, Inspector?" Guderian asked the Swiss.

"Myself and three others. This is Geneva, Lieutenant. Your final destination is only a few minutes away. Nothing can happen to you now."

But something *was* happening.

Two of the roof panels had already been removed. As the soldiers of Action Group clambered off the carriages, they were met by Swiss officers who were now checking their identification.

"My men will be driving the trucks," Guderian said.

"Oh?" But the policeman did not break stride, making purposefully for the black sedan at the head of the convoy. Karl Horst had the rear door open, waiting for the controller and managing director to get in.

"It is a small point," Guderian said. "But my men have been through a great deal. The honor of delivering the bullion to the vaults should be theirs."

There was a glint of amusement—contempt?—in the policeman's eyes.

"It is your property, Lieutenant," he said in a neutral tone. "You may deliver it any way you see fit. But you will be paying for the drivers whether you use them or not."

Why does he have his nose in the wind?

The policeman was within ten feet of the car. It was clear that he intended to speak with one or both of the bank officials. And there was nothing Guderian could do to stop him. The presence of Karl Horst might be enough to keep Foucault in line. But the managing director, Lacroix, would be tempted by stupidity. Guderian saw Karl Horst move closer to the Frenchman, one hand hidden, fingers grazing the handle of his knife.

It can all finish right here . . .

But it didn't, because the last man on the carriage roof, Willi Trapp, who was securing the crane ropes to the metal hooks imbedded in the roof, had been watching the scene below. He tied the final loops and waved his arms at the crane operator, then scampered down the ladder. The ropes grew taut and the roof lifted away, swinging gently under the momentum. Trapp followed its progress, lips moving soundlessly as though in prayer. At this point the Swiss policeman had almost reached the car.

The knots fixed to two of the hooks held, but Trapp had deliberately left the others slack. The lazy swing put enough strain on the woven jute for it to unravel. As the crane operator began to reel in his cable to lift the roof over the carriage, the rope gave way. The roof panel seemed suspended as the ropes snaked to the ground, then one end angled down. The operator watched helplessly as the roof drove into the cinder platform at a sixty-degree angle, the impact sending out a thunderclap as it buried itself in the shining grit.

The Swiss policeman reacted instantly to the cries that went up. Like any commander his first concern was for his men. Guderian caught Lacroix's stunned expression as the Swiss turned around. The French banker opened his mouth, desperate words forming, but Karl Horst stepped in front of him.

Guderian started after the policeman. "*What the hell happened?*" he roared.

"The ropes—" Willi Trapp started to explain.

"Carelessness!" Guderian cut him off and squatted by the roof, both hands gripping the edges.

"Give us some help, will you?" he shouted at the Swiss.

The policeman hesitated, then gestured at his men, who positioned themselves on either side of the panel. Guderian signaled the crane operator and with a sickening lurch the wedged roof was freed.

"Stand clear!" the operator shouted.

"I'm sorry about that," Guderian said. "My men are tired . . ."

"We are fortunate no one was injured," the Swiss replied.

The crane was swinging back over the gaping opening in the carriage, the ropes dropping on the exposed boxes.

"Tell your men to stand down, Lieutenant," the Swiss said. "My people can supervise the transfer to the trucks."

Guderian hesitated, searching for the catch.

"I have coffee in my car, if you like," the policeman finished.

Guderian smiled faintly. "Is there enough for a cup each for my men?"

"But of course."

Guderian shouted out to Action Group, which fell in behind him. As they trooped down the length of the platform Guderian saw that the black sedan was gone. But it seemed that the Swiss inspector was no longer interested in the French bankers nor where they had gone or why.

A few minutes before ten o'clock on the evening of May 15 the convoy carrying a third of the auric patrimony of France left the rail yards of the Gare Centrale. Guderian rode in the lead truck, following the police sedan. Willi Trapp was behind the wheel, the hired driver sandwiched between him and Guderian. The seating arrangements were repeated in the two other trucks. There was no way in which any of the hired help would be able to interfere.

Guderian followed the Swiss policeman's vehicle out onto the Route de Frontenex, turned left and picked up speed. The two-lane highway was all but deserted at this time of night. Even though the war had not spilled over the borders, a curfew was in effect. Guderian pressed on the accelerator, heel-to-toe, bringing the truck's bumper to within a few feet of the police car. He knew that Karl Horst was out there somewhere, waiting. But the distance between the rail yards and the Banque Nationale Suisse was only a few kilometers. He would have to use the first opportunity that came along to rid himself of his escort.

At that moment Feldwebel Horst was three kilometers down the road, at the junction of Promenade du Lac and Pont du Mont-Blanc. He was sitting in the front seat, gently drawing on one of Lacroix's excellent cigars. Neither banker had cared to join him since both were bound and gagged, squirming in the rear seat. Horst was mentally counting off the minutes to the convoy's arrival, which he knew had to be coming. Lacroix had been told how painful blinding could be when inflicted by the glowing ash of a cigar. Feldwebel Horst had no doubt the managing director had given him the correct routing.

At twelve minutes past ten he heard the trucks. A second later the police vehicle came into view, yellow foglights glowing, a red light winking on the left fender.

"Make yourselves comfortable, gentlemen," Horst said cheerfully, throwing the cigar away and depressing the clutch.

He eased the car, lights blacked out, closer to the intersection and raced the engine. Then he chose his moment.

The Swiss inspector was at the wheel, concentrating on the narrow ramp that led onto the Pont du Mont-Blanc. He never heard the sedan hurtling at him because of the rumble of the heavy trucks and saw it only when it was too late. Nonetheless he managed to cut the wheel to the left—a move he realized a heartbeat later was patently wrong. Horst's vehicle careened into the police car broadside, pushing it off the blacktop and onto the gravel shoulder, only a few feet from the embankment. The cars seemed locked, but the banker's sedan was the heavier of the two. Feldwebel Horst grunted and spun the wheel again, slamming the accelerator to the floor.

For a moment it seemed that the police car would ride the shoulder and get far enough ahead to cut across the sedan. But the embankment grade was too steep, the momentum of the car too quick. The rear wheels spun furiously, tearing at the gravel. But the rubber could not hold its footing. With a slow, almost graceful motion the vehicle tumbled over twice, plunging hood-first into the lake.

Karl Horst rammed up the handbrake, sending his car into a controlled spin. The chassis was still rocking when he flung open the door and ran toward the lead truck, leaping onto the running board.

"Nice of you to join us, Karl," Willi Trapp said politely.

"Now if you would step back for a moment so our passenger can get off . . ."

Horst jumped down, then pulled the hired driver out. The doors of the other trucks were opened, bodies tumbling out. Erik Guderian threw the truck into gear, shaking his head. Not exactly a textbook operation, but they had the gold. All that remained now was to hide themselves and their booty from a combined police-Army force that would number well over two thousand men.

The Reich diplomatic mission is located off the Route de Lausanne, fourteen kilometers from the city proper. The property, composed of two acres of wood and pasture, backed up against the foothills, with a winding dirt road running from the manor to a gatehouse at the foot of the property along the Route. This night, according to the drill, there was only one sentry on duty. As usual he was having a second cup of excellent Swiss coffee before settling down with a forbidden Walter Benjamin text on literary criticism. The time was 10:42 when the tranquil evening erupted.

Erik Guderian brought the lead truck to within inches of the gate. Karl Horst, riding the running board, jumped off and ran for the gatehouse. The sentry was half out of his chair when the door crashed open and a hirsute madman had him by the throat.

"The keys to the locks, if you would, sonny," Karl Horst said amiably.

The young soldier inadvertently glanced at the peg on the wall by the door. Horst leaned over and took the ring.

"Don't even think of moving," he said, picked up the sentry's rifle and disappeared.

Less than a minute later all three trucks were racing up the dirt road to the manor. Behind them the gates were once again drawn, the lock in place, a sentry on duty in the lit guardhouse. Except that he was not the one who was partial to Walter Benjamin.

Erik Guderian wheeled his vehicle behind the manor, next to the stables that now served as a garage for the diplomatic fleet. Lights had come on in the various windows and when he jumped out he saw faces pressed against the glass. A door opened, throwing a shaft of light at him, and a tall, portly man in evening clothes was marching toward him.

A reception, Guderian thought in disbelief. I've driven into an evening of Mozart!

"What is the meaning of this?" the official brayed, the epitome of Bavarian manners. "Who are you men? How did you get in?"

But before Guderian could retort he heard a familiar voice in the darkness.

"It's quite all right, Baron," Gerd Jaunich said. "I've been expecting these men. I'm afraid we shall have to finish our chess game another time."

Subsequent opinions were divided as to whose expression of outrage was greatest: that of the French government, the Swiss government, the Swiss banking group or the apoplexy of the Banque de France. The men of Action Group placed their money on the Swiss, their reasoning being the patrol units of the Swiss *gendarmerie* which were parked outside the property gates, ostensibly for protection.

Within an hour of Guderian's dramatic entrance, the Ambassador, Baron Ottenheimer, was summoned to the home of the President of the Swiss Assembly and invited to answer questions pertaining to the theft of French gold. Jaunich, in his capacity as Hitler's personal roving envoy, insisted on being present—something the Swiss knew better than to refuse. Both men professed ignorance of the alleged crime and saw no reason why the Swiss bank police should be permitted to search the diplomatic grounds of the Reich. After all, nothing untoward had occurred in the compound. The mere presence of armed Swiss patrols outside the wall was enough to result in a diplomatic incident . . .

"No doubt you've some idea as to how to get rid of the bullion," Gerd Jaunich said conversationally.

He and Erik Guderian were sitting at the kitchen table in the manor house, finishing a very early breakfast. Ottenheimer had been put to bed with the help of sedatives, while *Die Piraten* were nowhere to be seen.

"We'll get a kiln in through the diplomatic freight, melt the bars down, recast them and stamp them with the Reich seals," Guderian said. "Then you can ship them to Zurich and deposit them in our account."

"And the trucks?"

"Burned and buried."

Jaunich smiled over the lip of his cup. "Whatever possessed you?"

"We couldn't contact the evacuation team at Tholon," Guderian said, blinking rapidly to keep his eyes open. "We had to improvise."

He paused. "And how did *you* happen to be here? The arrangement was to meet in Berlin."

Jaunich pushed his cup away and handed Guderian a sheet of paper.

"This came through yesterday. Hitler has already seen it. He wants to know what *you* have to say."

Guderian hunched forward, unfolded the paper beneath the lamp and read the words slowly.

"Source Morningstar?" he whispered hoarsely.

Jaunich nodded silently, watching as the leader of *Die Piraten* reread the text of the conversation between Winston Churchill and Franklin Roosevelt. The intercepted Prometheus text.

"The British are going ahead with it!" Guderian said, incredulous. "God help us but they're going to do it . . . Exactly as I said they would."

"That is why I need you in Berlin as soon as possible," Jaunich said. "You are the only man who can convince Hitler of what is about to happen."

Guderian leaned across the table, eyes shining.

"Gerd," he whispered, "I can deliver him England without sacrificing the life of a single German soldier. Not one."

Which were exactly the words Gerd Jaunich had expected to hear.

4

The illuminated clock in the Georgetown University tower struck six, its pealing intruding on Jonathan Cabot's concentration. He turned out the desk lamp and sat back in an old leather chair, surrounded by the gray light and silence of dawn. Before him, the massive attorney's desk was strewn with papers, notes and carbon copies. On either side of the chair, lined up against the base of the study's floor-to-ceiling bookcases, were cartons of documents and transcripts the Signal Intelligence Bureau archivists had delivered six hours earlier. Jonathan Cabot had spent the small hours of the morning tracing back Beth Davis's treacherous path. He had gone over each transcript she had been responsible for in order to determine exactly how much she had passed along. It was a lot—a hell of a lot.

Bracing himself on the armrests, Cabot heaved himself out of the chair and walked through the silence of the townhouse where he lived alone. From the kitchen icebox he took out a quart of orange juice, brought that back to the study, removed a glass from the liquor cabinet and poured. The bite of the juice stung his lips and dispelled the noxious taste of cigarettes. He swiveled the chair and stared through the French windows into the small garden. He saw the first roses and tulips, and the new ivy . . . and out of the corner of his eye something else . . . a photographic portrait on the third shelf of the bookcase.

It was the picture of a girl whose name was Orit Steinfeldt. She was German, a Jewess, and he still loved her so very much. Cabot had never seen her dead. He had only been told, by a man who knew, that she had been killed, and so he only remembered her as being alive. Sometimes, when her image suddenly confronted him, he thought she still was.

In 1933 Professor Aaron Steinfeldt arrived at Princeton University, New Jersey, from the Polytechnisches Institut in Berlin, a recognized world authority in mathematics, particularly the field of binary numbers and complex infinities. He had worked with Einstein in the early twenties and tutored Oppenheimer only three years earlier. It was during his sabbatical at Princeton that he met Jonathan Baylor Cabot.

Many thought it strange that such an immediate and close kinship should form between the young scion of a prominent American family and a foreign scientist whose roots lay in the Jewish Pale of the Ukraine. Yet the bond was recognized by both men and even though Cabot was in his final year at Princeton he returned the following September to audit the first semester of Steinfeldt's lectures.

But there was a second, equally compelling reason for Cabot's return. During the hot, lazy days of a campus summer Cabot had met and undeniably fallen in love with Steinfeldt's twenty-four-year-old daughter, Orit. Orit, who spoke five languages, had studied at the Sorbonne and was now apprenticing at Sotheby's, hosted the professor's dinner parties—at which Cabot had become something of a fixture. A stunning woman, tall, with agate hair that swirled about her shoulders and crystal blue eyes ("my Crusaders' eyes" she called them), she too was drawn to this American who had quite suddenly and naturally stepped into her life. By the end of August it was clear to the campus community that the relationship was something quite different from the usual June-to-September romance.

Years later, when hindsight was the cause of so much pain and grief, Cabot bitterly regretted not marrying Orit before he returned to Washington that Christmas. It had been the mistake of youth, the illusion that one had time to do almost everything . . .

The Steinfeldts returned to Berlin in the spring of 1934. Cabot visited them that fall and again in February of the following year. At that time he had tried to convince the professor to return to the United States—for good.

"I am ninety percent German," Steinfeldt had laughed. "Of the remaining ten percent five is Jewish and five belongs to the rest of the world. I don't think Hitler will begrudge me that much."

But in 1936 Hitler did. Professor Aaron Steinfeldt, thirty-two colleagues and over a hundred past and present students were rounded up by the SS. Cabot, who was in China, did not receive word of this until his escape from Nanking in the summer of 1938.

When Cabot arrived in Berlin the woman waiting for him was not the same as the one in his mind's eye. After the arrest of her father, Orit Steinfeldt had been ostracized by a society she had thought she was a part of. Terrorized as much by intermittent Gestapo interrogations as by the petty cruelty of neighbors, she had withdrawn into herself. There had been no one to protect her, comfort her, no one she could reach out for. . . .

After the tears and kisses of their reunion had faded she told Cabot what had happened.

"It was a special SS project, something so secret that the

work couldn't be carried on in the university laboratories. Father and his entire staff were taken to Regensburg, where a special compound had been built . . ."

"Have you visited him there?" Cabot asked urgently. "Has he ever been allowed to come out?"

"In the beginning I could go up every second Saturday," Orit replied. "I brought food and fresh clothes for him. Then the visiting period was reduced to once a month. That was over a year ago."

Her voice fell. "Since then I have seen him only twice. He's become ill, lost weight and his diabetes has gone unattended. They're killing him, Jonathan, as surely as if they were to put a bullet into his heart. They're killing him!"

He gathered her up in his arms, stroking her hair.

"What is he doing there, Orit?" he whispered. "Who is heading up the project?"

She drew back, cradling his face in both hands, then slipped out of his grasp. Orit pulled back the drawer of her night table and handed Cabot a packet of letters.

"They permitted him to write me . . . until a few months ago," she murmured, giving him the packet bound by a red ribbon. "Naturally the SS read the letters through before allowing them to be sent out of the compound. But I suppose they didn't believe that at such an early point there would be any information Father would want to smuggle out."

She hesitated. "They were wrong. They missed the microdots he planted in the letters. ENIGMA, Jonathan, that is what you have here. All the details for the machine he built for them. This was my father's legacy for you . . ."

She broke off, choking on sobs that didn't cease even after Cabot had her in his arms.

"Now you understand why I can't marry you, my darling," Orit whispered through her tears. "I am all that Father has in the outside world. Even though I can't see or speak to him, he knows I am out there. I couldn't live with myself if I were to leave, abandon him . . ."

"There's another way," Cabot said fiercely. "You can marry me and then your father becomes the dependent of an American citizen. We'll have the leverage we need to force Himmler—"

She placed a finger on his lips.

"You must go to your embassy right away," Orit said.

"Deliver ENIGMA, Jonathan, while there is still time. The Gestapo has my apartment under constant surveillance. By now word of your arrival has reached Himmler. In time he will learn of your relationship with my father. They will come for you too."

"Orit, I can't leave until I know who runs that compound!" Cabot cried. "I need a name, someone I can touch!"

"For my father, Jonathan," she pleaded, ignoring his words. "Don't let what he's done be in vain!"

The ferocity of her words robbed him of any alternative. But he was still loath to leave.

"You must," she said, reading his thoughts. "When you return—"

"When I return we shall *all* leave," he declared grimly. "ENIGMA will buy Aaron's freedom. Dulles will see to that."

The last memory Jonathan Cabot had of Orit was her standing in the doorway of her flat, eyes shining with tears. Joyful tears, he had thought, because she believed he would return, not only for her but also for Aaron Steinfeldt. It was not to be. Cabot delivered the packet of letters to the American embassy within the hour. On his way back to Orit he was arrested.

The Gestapo managed to hold Cabot for seventeen hours. They would have had him longer had Cabot not been expected back at the embassy. When he didn't show, the Ambassador, a tenacious Midwesterner, went to Ribbentrop's office and refused to leave until Himmler himself had arrived and personally tracked down Cabot's whereabouts. It was also Himmler who, between apologies for such an unfortunate case of mistaken identity, casually shattered Cabot's desperate hopes.

"I regret to inform you that your, ah, friend, the Steinfeldt woman, killed herself," the Gestapo chief said casually. "Threw herself out the window in an attempt to escape arrest."

Cabot's muscled forearm snaked around Himmler's neck. In one step he was behind the *Reichsführer*, his other hand twisting Himmler's head to one side. Cabot never felt the blows raining down upon his back and the sides of his head. He never tasted the blood streaming across his face as Himmler's escort flailed their truncheons. It was as though the pain that fell upon him only intensified his grip. The last thing he saw was blood; the first, when he woke up in an embassy bed, was a woman who didn't resemble Orit at all. She was the embassy nurse . . .

Jonathan Cabot came over to the bookshelf and gently lifted the silver frame, gazing down at the photograph.

After the embassy spirited him out of Berlin, Cabot based himself in London, in the midst of the deluge of European refugees. He worked day and night for six months, a man possessed, questioning anyone who might have had even the slightest connection with Regensburg. Only his own fury kept him alive, pushing back his despair as each rumor, innuendo and clue crumbled under investigation.

When he accepted the fact that he could do no more in London, that his resources were woefully inadequate for his goal, Cabot returned to New York and the office of Allen Dulles. To find the man who had taken Steinfeldt prisoner, who was directly responsible for Orit's death, he accepted the directorship of Dulles's nonexistent intelligence apparatus. Cabot had at last understood that his search might last years. Only a machine such as Dulles had created could give him access to all diplomatic and internal transmissions originating in Berlin. Buried somewhere in that morass was a magic word or phrase which would link a name to Regensburg, or to Steinfeldt himself . . . which in turn would end with a girl whose body had been buried in Berlin's ancient Jewish cemetery. Almost another year passed before Cabot was certain he had unearthed the right one.

Cabot slipped a file from the shelf and flipped open the cover to the snapshot of Erik Guderian.

Erik Guderian . . . Cabot had met the man who had been responsible for Regensburg, once in Washington in 1933, twice in New York the following year. The man was one of the preeminent financiers of his day . . . which was why Cabot could not fathom the link between Guderian and his control over the ENIGMA project. Worse, Guderian seemed to have vanished off the face of the earth. Four thousand miles away, Cabot couldn't even find a hint of the tracks Guderian must have left behind him . . .

Jonathan Cabot stared at the snapshot of Erik Guderian for a long time, asking himself why, in the name of all that was holy, this man should have been the instrument that caused him so much suffering.

For Jonathan Cabot was not by nature a violent or vengeful man. From his father he had inherited the belief that the greatest thing a man could strive for was to be worthy of his civilization, to preserve the best of what came before and contribute to what was to come. Yet somewhere along the shining road of ideals he had erred and found himself passing through the underbelly.

The city of Nanking, on the Yangtze River, was the capital of China until 1937, when Chiang Kai-shek withdrew to Hankow. Jonathan Cabot, who had been teaching mathematics at the university, remained behind. In the three months between Chiang Kai-shek's retreat and the Japanese occupation in December, Cabot moved over three hundred people—pupils, associates, friends—to the safety of the U.S. mission and vessels lying in the river. During his last sortie twelve Japanese fighters attacked and sank the gunboat *Panay*. Cabot and the refugees who survived swam back, not realizing that they had witnessed the destruction of their last hope for escape.

During the next sixty days Jonathan Cabot saw the gates of hell open beneath him. Forty-two thousand men, women and children were systematically murdered by the Japanese. The favorite method of killing was by bayonet practice on live victims. But Cabot survived—in the sewers and on the waterfront, beneath the floorboards of bordellos or in the freezing root cellar of a farmer's hut. He survived and learned to fight and then to kill, until he lost track of the number of men he destroyed. Even after the Japanese government was secure and the bloodletting stopped, he continued the carnage, leaving Nanking only after he had secured something which would give him the greatest vengeance.

Six months after the sinking of the *Panay* Jonathan Cabot was back in the United States. Discreet queries among his father's friends elicited the name of Allen Dulles as the man who not only had the President's ear but who, speculation had it, was actively involved in the White House. On a rainy March afternoon Cabot walked into the Wall Street offices of Sullivan and Cromwell for his appointment. Dulles rose to greet him but Cabot did not take the proffered seat.

"I believe these may be of interest to the President," he said, placing three sealed cylindrical containers on Dulles's desk, and walked out.

When a flabbergasted Dulles had scrutinized the blueprints, annotated with Japanese characters, translated, he understood: Jonathan Cabot had brought him the newest Japanese "B" ciphers, Code Purple, with which the United States could read any diplomatic traffic sent from any Japanese source in the world . . . When Dulles had tried to contact Cabot for a follow-up briefing he learned that the survivor of Nanking had already left for Berlin.

That was why Orit Steinfeldt had meant so much to Cabot. During the abomination of Nanking it was her image that had kept him alive, kept him alive only to survive her own death. Now he wanted vengeance one more time. He would go to London and take out the traitor at Grosvenor Square. That neither Dulles nor the President chose to tell him anything about Prometheus was immaterial. Cabot suspected it had to do with the embassy in some way. He would find out soon enough. But after London he would disappear, for he had an appointment to keep with a man called Erik Guderian. Cabot, who had survived Nanking, knew that he would find the killer. That he might not survive Berlin was something that mattered not at all.

Jonathan Baylor Cabot was the only passenger on board the Pan American C-54 transport. Although the Douglas aircraft still flew the airline colors and was piloted by a company crew, it was one of three the Federal government had quietly leased from Pan American a year ago. The engines had been overhauled by Air Corps mechanics, increasing the plane's top speed from 239 to 250 miles per hour, reducing the trans-Atlantic crossing to eighteen hours. Extra fuel tanks now gave the plane a four-thousand-mile range. Half the bulkhead had been redesigned to carry cargo. What remained had been subdivided into individual sleeping compartments and a working area.

Jonathan Cabot was awakened by the copilot an hour before touchdown. He washed up, dressed and took a breakfast of juice, coffee and biscuits. As a salmon-pink dawn separated itself from the dark-blue hues of night, and the green of England became visible under the starboard wing, Cabot reached into one of his overnight packs and withdrew two weapons.

Both were of Japanese manufacture. The ten-shot, 9mm Hanyatti revolver which he had used in China slipped into a shoulder holster underneath his left arm.

The second gun was also manufactured by Hanyatti. Weighing just over ten pounds, the machine gun was modeled on the German Erma-designed MP38, sharing a common folding metal stock and short trim barrel. But the Hanyatti carried a twenty-four-bullet clip and its firing rate was almost twice that of the MP38, giving the weapon a tremendous close-in fighting capability. Finally, as with the revolver, the barrel had been rebored and the trigger mechanism redesigned to accept 9mm hollow point bullets.

Cabot had had two thousand rounds of ammunition altered to meet these particular specifications. The nose of each bullet had been removed, the metal core ground out and the cavity filled with a drop of mercury compound. Upon impact the mercury acted as a tiny detonating charge. The bullet had only to graze a man's arm to shatter it. The wounding of a thigh or shoulder could be fatal. If the bullet fragmentations did not catch a vital organ, they almost always severed a major artery. Shock and blood loss did the rest.

As the wheels of the Skymaster rebounded off the runway at Gatwick Airport, Cabot folded the Hanyatti stock and slipped the gun into the leather loops sewn into the lining of his coat. On a smaller man, the cylindrical bulge of the firing chamber would have been noticeable. But a glance at Cabot would only lead one to think the man could stand to lose ten or fifteen pounds.

Cabot pulled back the handkerchief-size curtain and looked out at the glistening tarmac, suddenly aware of the needle-point rain hammering across the aluminum skin of the aircraft. Beyond the blacktop was a patch of English green stretching toward the maple and elm glens that bordered the airport. Cabot caught a glimpse of something black and white moving past the trees. Perhaps a cow that had strayed from the rest of the herd . . .

"Mr. Cabot, your ground transportation is pulling up now."

The pilot was standing in the aisle, his eyes red rimmed from fatigue.

"I'll see that your bags are loaded onto the car, sir."

"Thank you." Cabot waited until the pilot had turned his back, then opened the coat and snapped in the clip. He stared down at the weapon, which had been designed solely for killing other men. Twenty miles away, in London proper, the clock started running for a man or woman or both.

Let me take you quietly, without harm, Cabot prayed. Let me find you quickly and excise you from that body you're feeding on.

But in his mind's eye he saw the twisted, hate-filled expression of Beth Davis as she pulled the trigger. The death aimed at him had instead propelled her into oblivion. And she had been only the Washington end. Important but not as crucial as her master/collaborator. Cabot reached down into his pack, pulled out two more clips and dropped these into his jacket pocket.

"Jonathan!"

Cabot didn't dare raise his eyes. With the rain slicing down, the metal steps of the ramp were slippery as moss. As soon as his feet touched blacktop two arms surrounded him in an iron bear hug.

"You've put on a few pounds, son. Living off the fat of the land in D.C., are you?"

Edward Pearce, chief of security for the U.S. mission to London, liaison with MI5 British counterintelligence, and on the board of the Anglo-American Security Committee, stood back, grinning.

"You still look good, you son of a bitch!"

Cabot gripped his hand in both of his.

"You too, Edward. It's good to see you again."

A Texan by birth, Edward Marlow Pearce had been in London since 1938. The climate hadn't faded his perpetual tan one degree. The sparkling blue eyes, squirrelly cheeks and perfect white teeth were as Cabot remembered them. Nor had Pearce made any accommodations about his dress. He still wore the familiar battered Stetson, sheepskin jacket, dungarees and handtooled boots which, bruised and scarred, nonetheless glowed of fresh polish.

Cabot reached out and removed Pearce's Stetson.

"You're still losing it, Edward."

Pearce snatched back the hat and jammed it on the golden curls that had once covered his entire head.

"Just the goddamn crown, Johnny. Christ, I just turned thirty-six!"

Cabot allowed Pearce to relieve him of his bag, then fell in step with the Texan's slightly bowlegged walk.

He knew. His friendship with Pearce went back twenty years, to the days when a tall lanky boy from Texas had arrived among the Establishment princelings at Choate. For all his family's oil money, Pearce had been considered a parvenu. Lonely and uncertain of himself, he had taken to using his fists to settle scores with those who thought him easy prey. Although Pearce held his own without help from anyone, he was grateful for the friendship shown him by the big, tall senior. Jonathan Cabot had evened the odds on a number of occasions, and Pearce, who had been taught on his daddy's knee how to recognize the character of a friend, knew he had found one in this soft-spoken Easterner who boxed with a wicked right hook.

Both Cabot and Pearce went on to Harvard, where they roomed together, shared classes, friends and girls. They and a circle that formed around them drank away weekends in New York, sailed the waters off Martha's Vineyard and passed long, hot days on the limitless Pearce ranches. Although their paths diverged after college, they kept in touch. Cabot was not surprised that Edward, the hell-bent of the two, had chosen the area of Federal law enforcement. Fifty years earlier he would have given Wyatt Earp a run for his money.

Age is showing in your legs too, Eddie, he thought.

Five years ago Edward Pearce had been a top-level FBI infiltrator, working the Mob rum-running operations near the Canadian border. An informer had singled him out. Pearce had managed to survive the assassination attempt, but two bullets were lodged forever in the backs of his knees.

Cabot stood by the open back door watching a young, fresh-faced man stowing the bags into the trunk. He touched Pearce's arm.

"Who's your driver?"

"Jamie? He's been with me for almost a year now." He bowed his head closer to Cabot. "His old man is Colonel Robertson of some uppity regiment—the Queen's Own or something. He never forgave his boy for being an asthmatic. Jamie flunked the physical and wound up in the civil service motor pool. He drove for us a few times when we were short, seemed to take a shine to Americans, so I had him posted to me full-time. The kid knows London like I do Dallas—or used to."

Pearce watched as Jamie Robertson flashed him a smile and brief salute, then slid behind the righthand-drive wheel. He motioned for Cabot to get in.

"Besides," he said, sliding shut the glass partition and drawing the gray, ruffled curtains, "I still can't understand how they manage to drive over here."

As the car moved off, Pearce twisted around toward Cabot.

"Listen, maybe I should have left the kid at home. Dulles sent a triple-X cable about your coming over—on a one-time pad, for Christ's sake. I didn't think we used the triple X for anything short of all-out war."

"As long as that partition is soundproof," Cabot said.

He refrained from an explanation. A one-time pad meant that not even the cipher-room decoders could unscramble the message—only the intended receiver, who had the appropriate key and book. Nor did Cabot mention that he had specifically asked Dulles to use the triple-X format.

Cabot rubbed the condensation away with his gloved hand. Beyond the rain-spattered windows, the countryside was shrouded in a light low fog.

He had been to London on four separate occasions, twice while still a student, twice when he stopped over on his way to the Continent . . . on his way to Orit. He loved the city as only a cosmopolitan could. It was a microcosm of the world, bursting with everything that centuries of Empire had bestowed upon it. He loved the grand houses of St. James's as much as he did the cobbled mews and alleys off Fleet Street, the mawkishness of the markets along the Thames and the glory of the Haymarket theaters. He could walk for hours at a time, passing from one architectural period into another, changing blocks to change whole centuries, and end up before the majesty of the Houses of Parliament.

But there was no joy in this arrival, no anticipation of revisiting old haunts or discovering new ones. A part of him was revolted by the thought of having anything to do with the city, as though suddenly it had become unclean.

When Cabot finally started to speak his voice was low, dispassionate, the way Pearce remembered it from times when Cabot was husbanding his energies, saving his strength for the unavoidable conflict rather than allowing the explosive details to unnerve him. There was also a sadness, but Pearce couldn't determine whether it was for himself or because of the dead, horrific events Cabot recounted.

"We have a high-level, deep-penetration agent in the embassy," Cabot concluded, "and we have to get at him or her in less than fourteen days."

"Unless you know who you're looking for, the time frame is impossible to handle," Pearce said flatly.

It never crossed his mind to deny or express outrage at what Cabot was telling him. There was no chance, *none*, that he was wrong. Pearce understood how difficult it must have been for Cabot to say what was necessary, speaking as he had to a friend who, as the words implied, had failed in his duty.

"I *don't* know who it is we want," Cabot said. "That's why I'm here. I went through the embassy roster but I can't get a feeling for the names and faces at three thousand miles. I need you on this, Edward. They're your people. You vetted most of them because there was a general rotation at the same time as you came over. Knowing you, you undoubtedly screened the ones who remained."

The car entered Leatherhead, the last suburb before Greater London: neat, trim row dwellings with claypot chimneys set in streets lined with rain-blackened trees.

"I've got to know one thing, Johnny," Pearce said. "Is Washington blaming me for the leak? No matter what, does Dulles want my head for this one?"

"Dulles wants the traitor. Your record is too good for Dulles to even consider a reprimand. You can't be on top of the entire staff twenty-four hours a day."

"But the number of those who have access to trans-Atlantic traffic is limited," Pearce murmured, looking at Cabot. "The bitch of the matter is, Johnny, that I ran a check on that section only two weeks ago. I came up empty."

"How many people are we talking about?"

"Churchill almost always makes his Washington calls from what he calls 'the bog,'" Pearce said, sitting back, chin on his chest. "It's a telephone booth cleverly disguised as a portable toilet. The call is picked up by a special switchboard at Grosvenor Square. I have three girls on it, eight-hour shifts each. Since the line isn't used that often, I've given the ladies some filing to do to keep them from going crazy."

"Can they listen in?"

"No. The board is set up so that as soon as the connection is made the operator is cut off."

"Then what?"

"The President's line is buried in the cable we set up for supersensitive communications. Besides the telephone link, the cable carries all cipher traffic, military and civilian, between Washington and London."

"Who handles the cipher traffic?" asked Cabot, his voice low but the urgency unmistakable.

"Four men on six shifts."

"Four . . ." Cabot murmured. "All right—I've been through transcripts of Roosevelt's and Churchill's conversations. They never—almost never—commit anything overt to the line. They speak in references to operations or circumstances, a kind of verbal shorthand. The details come later, over the cipher machines. What's the procedure when Churchill wants to send details via cipher?"

"Let's say they've been on an open line for four or five minutes, talking in that shorthand," Pearce said. "Now the details are needed. The trans-Atlantic line remains open but Churchill switches to a direct connection with one of our cipher people. He speaks to him exactly as though he were Roosevelt. The cipher clerk is typing Churchill's every word on the cipher unit, which simultaneously scrambles the text, then transmits it to the White House where its twin decodes it and gives Roosevelt a printed text of what was said. The process goes back and forth until the conversation is finished."

"You said the cipher clerk types in every word Churchill says," Cabot said slowly. "How easy would it be for him *to add* a few words; a short phrase?"

"Johnny, he could probably add an entire paragraph as long as the tone and context made sense with the rest of the message."

"But copies are made of the unscrambled conversations!"

"Sure. And they're sent to Downing Street every evening by armed courier as per standing orders. Do you think Churchill reads them back? Even if he does do you think he would remember, in the course of the kind of day he puts in, exactly, word for word, what it was he said to the President?"

Pearce shook his head. "I doubt it, Johnny. The cipher operator would have to be very careful, but if he wanted to tip someone off at the other end to pick up a message, and all it took was a couple of words, then sure, he could slip those in."

"But he'd need more than that, wouldn't he?" Cabot said, his voice deathly cold. "You said there are four cipher operators. Each works a six-hour shift. Each handles a lot more than just Presidential traffic. Assuming that the military and diplomatic stuff interests him a great deal, how could he get at the Crown Jewels? If he were not on duty at the time, how would he know that a Churchill-Roosevelt communication had been sent?"

"Oh, sweet Jesus!" Pearce whispered. "One of the board operators! She would have to be in on it. If she told him a message had been sent, he could get to the embassy copy of the text."

"That's right, Edward. Suddenly we have two to look for."

"But wait!" Pearce said, excited. "You got Davis. You know when she was at her machine. Couldn't we correlate the time she was receiving with the time when the message was sent? The duty logbook could tell us which cipher operator was on here at the same time as Davis on the other end."

"It doesn't work, Edward." Cabot shook his head. "Your operators have call numbers. Each week their shifts change. I have all four call numbers on the copies Davis was receiving."

"Son of a bitch!" Pearce muttered. "I'm sorry, Johnny, I wasn't thinking." He offered Cabot a cigarette, took one for himself and lit both.

"Three at the switchboard, four on the cipher units. Seven goddamn possibles."

"No one else?"

"No, Johnny," Pearce said quietly. "No one else."

He slumped into the corner, cigarette hanging between his lips, the smoke veiling his face. Cabot wanted to say something, reassure Pearce that for all the damage that had been done, the suspect list had at least been narrowed down. It was only a matter of time now. But he also knew that was poor comfort. Pearce was a professional.

"Edward," Cabot said quietly without turning around, "what do you know of a black Jaguar sedan, plate TRW-63?"

Pearce didn't bother to look over his shoulder but stooped down and lifted a piece of carpeting, then a panel cut into the floorboards.

"Nothing."

"It's been following us for the last three miles."

Pearce lifted out the Thompson submachine gun from a hollow beneath the carpeting and pulled down the glass partition.

"Jamie, the black Jag behind us—"

"Been there since the airport, sir. I thought it was one of yours."

"If it had been I would have told you!"

Pearce swung around to Cabot, who was holding the Hany-atti.

"I'm not sure we have a choice," he said tensely. "This heap will never outrun the Jag. All they have to do is follow us out of Leatherhead onto the last part of the highway to London. There won't be too much traffic right now. They can choose the moment, come alongside and either push us off the road or riddle us."

Pearce leaned across Cabot and pointed out the window.

"I've driven this route God knows how many times. For the next couple of miles all you'll see are deserted, half-bulldozed factories. If you want to check out their intentions, then let's do it here. It's the only place we can make a stand."

Cabot's eyes bored into Pearce, demanding answers.

"It may be nothing at all, Johnny," Pearce said softly. "But if it is, then it's not me they're after. Everyone knows who I am, what I do, where I can be found . . ."

"Then let's find out for sure!" Cabot said savagely.

Edward Pearce poked his head through the partition.

"Pick up speed and swing onto the second road, the one that leads toward that pile of rubble."

Jamie Robertson, both hands clamped high on the steering wheel, nodded. But he never had a chance to carry out Pearce's order.

The ambush team was waiting on the other side of the two-lane road, directly opposite the torn-up street the Austin Princess was approaching. The Princess's sudden acceleration surprised the driver of the Royal Mail army van, but he popped the clutch and shot across the road in time to smash into the sedan's left fender.

Jamie Robertson reacted exactly as he should have, swinging the Princess into the rutted lane. He had no way of knowing that he had just driven into a killing ground that within seconds would be covered by murderous crossfire.

The lone gunner hidden in the rubble by the road opened fire as the Princess lurched by. A stream of 9-millimeter bullets from the British-manufactured Lancaster submachine gun shot away the glass in the driver's window. Jamie Robertson kept his grip on the wheel even as the bullets stitched into his arm and shoulder. A second later two more buried themselves in his neck, their velocity flinging him away from the wheel. The car hit a wall on its left flank, plowing into the brick at a forty-five-degree angle.

The other two killers leaped from the truck parked on the side of the road, lifted their Bren guns and began to pour a steady fire into the still rocking chassis.

"*Move*!" Cabot screamed.

Pearce, who had been trying to wrench open the rear door, drew back and with both feet kicked it free. The two men tumbled out one after the other, glass splinters digging into their hands. They had a few seconds, no more, to return fire before the gas tank ignited. It would all depend on how determined the killers were, whether they expected their victims to be armed, if they were willing to risk a prolonged shoot at such quarters.

Cabot motioned at the front end of the car, which effectively cut them off from the single gunner. Pearce nodded, rose and was firing as the barrel of the Thompson cleared the hood. Even the ring of gunfire couldn't drown out the piercing scream.

Cabot dropped to one knee, poked the barrel around the side of the Princess and aimed for the half-glimpsed form behind the truck. The Hanyatti ripped through the clip and the gunners jumped back behind the army van. Pearce, who had already reloaded, started shredding the dirt around the retreating lone gunman, who was staggering toward the others.

Cabot drove in another clip and moved around the car. He hadn't forgotten the Jaguar, which had screeched to a halt a few yards behind the Princess, effectively cutting off any escape. A man dived out the passenger door, hitting the broken-up asphalt. The revolver in his hand was pointed at Cabot, who didn't hesitate. The mercury-tipped bullets disintegrated the door and caught the killer as he was getting ready to scramble. Cabot saw him fall, the gun clatter from his reach. He swung his weapon on the van, emptied the clip, then began running toward the Jaguar. He had one alive. If he could only get the driver . . .

She kicked open the door and thrust her arms out, the large Webley pistol held in a two-hand grip. The gun bucked, her golden hair flying. An instant before Cabot pressed the trigger he realized she was gunning for the mail van.

"Johnny, watch out!"

Pearce had vaulted the hood of the Princess and was running toward the van. The clatter of gunfire was replaced by engine roar as the mail truck bore down on Cabot. He flung himself to one side, the arm holding the gun swinging wildly. As he hit the ground Cabot felt the hiss of tires as the front wheels passed within inches of his face. He kept on rolling, the gun tucked into his chest, spinning away from the dual-axle wheels. The truck was out of range by the time he had his weapon up again.

"Johnny, are you all right?"

Pearce was beside him, holding him by the shoulders. Cabot nodded and stepped away.

"I know I got one," Pearce said, panting. "But they dragged him back into the van."

"Both of you bastards got one!" a woman's voice called out to them.

The girl was more beautiful than Cabot had imagined. She was kneeling down beside the fallen man, the honey-blond hair covering her face. All Cabot saw was long slim fingers working expertly to stop the bleeding from the facial wounds. Suddenly she rose and stepped toward him, the long legs moving swiftly, the turquoise eyes sparkling in anger. He saw her pale lower lip tremble as she was about to speak, but completely missed the hand snaking out and striking him, palm open, across the face.

"You stupid, stupid man," she half gasped, half shouted. "You could have killed him—both of us!"

The outraged expression stretched her peaches and cream skin across high cheekbones. Cabot trailed his fingertips across his cheek and stepped past her.

The man was in his late twenties, short, with a heavily developed physique of a weight lifter or wrestler. His face, roughly hewn, the nose broken at the bridge, glistened under a sheen of sweat. In spite of her ministrations blood was still pouring from his forehead and cheeks where glass and metal had sheared away the skin.

Cabot felt an iron grip on his elbow, muscles trembling in anger.

"*Who are you*?" the girl shouted at him.

Cabot looked over his shoulder at Pearce. The embassy security chief gently laid the body of Jamie Robertson across the front seat and closed the door.

"Who are they, Edward?"

"She's Mackenzie McConnell, our liaison with MI5," Pearce said. "He's her partner."

Cabot slipped the Hanyatti through the leather loops sewn into the lining of his coat and tightened the belt. The girl flinched when he touched her, but Cabot firmly steered her toward a pile of broken brick and mortar. Somewhere in the distance the telltale whine of a police siren sounded.

"My name is Jonathan Cabot," he said softly.

"I don't care—"

"Yes, you do!" He cut her off, never raising his voice. "Your partner is wounded. I can't tell you how I feel about that. But what he needs now is attention. *I* need to get to London without any questions from the police. That means I'll need your car. And you must use whatever authority you have to convince the police that it wouldn't be in anyone's interest for them to investigate what happened here."

"Who *are* you?" the girl asked him.

"When you get back to London, call Pearce, no one but him," Cabot continued, ignoring her persistence. "We'll want to know who the shooters were, how they knew I was coming."

Cabot hesitated. "I'm not going to ask you what *you* were doing following us. I'll take it on trust that we're on the same side. I'm asking you to show me the same: let us go now, find out what you can about why this happened and call Pearce. I'll be waiting."

Abruptly Cabot turned around, motioned to Pearce and got into the Jaguar. He half expected the girl to come after him, but looking through the windshield, he saw her standing exactly where he had left her.

Jonathan Cabot had no way of knowing that Mackenzie McConnell had intended to do exactly what he himself had asked of her. She also knew who he was and where to find him. Now, she realized, so did someone else. Someone who knew Cabot would arrive today.

How could it have happened? The man from Washington was to have been sterile!

5

In Berlin the evening of May 16, 1940, was clement, with a warm wind that carried a hint of lilac along the Unter den Linden. At half past seven there was still daylight in the sky, and the Lorelei's glass veranda panels were drawn back so that the restaurant's patrons might enjoy the scene along the promenade.

Erik Guderian poured out what remained in the bottle of Riesling. Across at the opposite table a husband and wife raised their glasses as one and looked at their children, a girl of six and a boy of four, who were attacking their strudel and ersatz cream with concentrated ferocity. Crystal resounded softly. Over the rim of his glass Guderian watched the girl, a miniature of her father, with the same brown curly hair and dark, almost gypsy eyes. Except one did not refer to them by that name. The boy was his mother's: blond, mischievous, with a spry sense of humor.

"To the children," Erik Guderian whispered. "May they be spared all we have known."

Erik Guderian had left Geneva less than twelve hours earlier, traveling as Gerd Jaunich's valet under the cloak of diplomatic immunity. The men of Action Group would follow in due course, a few at a time, at staggered intervals, through circuitous routes.

In spite of the bone-numbing exhaustion Guderian hadn't been able to sleep on the plane. Instead he and Jaunich reviewed every facet of a plan which until a few hours earlier had been purely hypothetical. But Prometheus had changed all that. Prometheus infused theory and hypotheses with flesh and blood.

Upon landing Guderian was driven to his apartment in Jaunich's car. He showered thoroughly, set the alarm and slid in between the cool sheets. He remembered nothing after that.

Precisely five hours later he was up and donning a fresh Army uniform. His body felt stiff, the muscles pinched, but his mind was clear, sharp, eager to get on with what had to be done. He was also very hungry and although the food at the

Lorelei was better than the usual fare in wartime Berlin, he thought of nothing except Prometheus throughout the meal. Prometheus, the God-sent panacea.

Static crackled through the speakers fixed onto the corner above the bar and a woman's voice announced:

"*Achtung!* This is the kitchen speaking. There is no more Wiener schnitzel!"

"More of Goebbels's 'prosperous times.'"

Guderian glanced up, surprised to see Gerd Jaunich drawing back a chair.

"I trust you managed to get some of that Wiener schnitzel," he said.

"I bribed the waiter for the last serving of calves liver," Guderian said. "Sinful. May I order you a glass of wine, Gerd?"

Guderian's tone was light but already his stomach had begun to churn. The arrangement had called for him to meet Jaunich at the Chancellery . . . an hour from now. And the older man was too quiet, almost pensive.

"There's news from America you should know about before you walk into Hitler's parlor," Jaunich said as though he had read Guderian's mind. "Two hours ago Lisbon reported that its control in Washington, Felipe Schecker, had been taken. The arrest occurred after his meeting with Morningstar."

"But we received the Prometheus text!" Guderian exclaimed. "How could Schecker have gotten it to us—"

"Somehow Schecker managed to pass it before he was taken," Jaunich interjected. "The Americans held him for twenty-four hours before diplomacy prevailed. We don't know how much Schecker told them but . . ."

"It's Davis," Guderian said, his voice low. "He told them about Davis."

"Beth Davis is dead, Erik," Jaunich said quietly. "She was shot during the attempt to arrest her."

Erik Guderian stared out at the chestnut trees bordering the broad avenue. He had never had occasion to see the file on Beth Davis. He did not know if she was young or old, beautiful or ugly, single, married or a widow. At that moment he was grateful for his ignorance.

"Is Hitler aware of this?" Guderian demanded.

Jaunich nodded. "It couldn't be helped. Ever since I spoke

to him about Prometheus he has insisted on daily reports on everything concerning the operation, no matter how remote."

"There is no reason not to go ahead," Guderian said softly, drumming his fingertips on the rim of the glass. "The Americans may have cut off the Washington end, the receiver, but the sender in London is secure."

"They will send a hunter to London, Erik," Jaunich said. "Hitler knows that, I do, and you must. We have no way of ascertaining how much Schecker told the Americans, but we must proceed on the assumption that they know we are aware of something called Prometheus. Given the restrictions on the Anglo-American operation, the hunter will enjoy a narrow range in which to find his quarry."

"Are you suggesting we should allow Prometheus to go ahead unchallenged?" Guderian asked incredulously.

"You know better than that," Jaunich rebuked him sharply. "I am only forewarning you. Yes, you predicted the British and Americans would do something like this. Now you must convince Hitler that *in spite* of the hunter you can bring him England. Everything, Erik, rests on what you say to him today!"

Jaunich withdrew his billfold and placed some notes beneath the saltcellar.

"There are files in the car, on men London and Washington have to choose from. We have time to drive a little. Look through them; perhaps something will jar your memory."

Guderian followed the older man toward the Mercedes sedan, slipped past the driver and huddled against the corner. He pulled a file from the stack on the writing tablet and opened it. But even as his eyes scanned the words and his mind flashed to align them with what he already knew, a part of Guderian remained withdrawn, savage and angry. Two years ago he had been given a mandate. The results he had brought about exceeded all expectations. Now he was on the verge of the greatest triumph of all, a feat which would make the piracy of the French gold seem like a schoolboy's prank. No one would stop him. No one *could* stop him any longer. He had come too far, suffered too much, to permit that to happen.

The leader of *Die Piraten* was not a Guderian by birth. He had been adopted by the Iron General, as Heinz Guderian was known, after his natural parents, Anna and Helmut Bittner, had been killed in an avalanche that had all but destroyed the ski resort of Kitzbühel.

At age twenty-two Erik Guderian had graduated from Oxford with Firsts in Economics and Political Science. He stayed on for another two years as a special student to John Maynard Keynes before accepting a graduate position at the Harvard School of Business. He was granted his degree three days before the stockmarket crash of 1929.

For the next seven years Guderian was employed first by Alfred Krupp, whom he served as an international consultant, then by Edward E. du Pont, who brought him back to America as vice president for international affairs. By the mid-thirties Guderian spoke American and British English, French, Italian, Spanish and Dutch in addition to his native German. A natural linguist, his ear retained the exact pitch of any given accent. Twice a year he produced economic treatises for scholarly publications on both sides of the Atlantic. By the middle of the decade, senior civil servants, bred for longevity, remembered him long after their political masters had been ground into dust. The directors of central banks as well as the owner/operators of large independent concerns such as Rothschild monitored his progress from a distance. They watched for signs of faltering or overreaching, of *hubris* or weakness of flesh. They found none. In the great exchange houses of Berlin, Paris, London, to New York, Erik Guderian's capital, both physical and moral, was without limit. He had become a man who never carried on his person any keys nor any currency.

In March 1936 Erik Guderian abruptly disappeared from the international stage. Although his departure was swift and silent, his absence created a void too large to be ignored. Rumors sprang up and quickly fed off each other. Erik Guderian had contracted cancer and was being treated at an Innsbruck sanitorium. He had instigated a massive swindle and was, any day now, expected to flee to Switzerland. He had a falling out with Hitler, who had personally imposed exile upon him. There was a woman involved, perhaps royal, and a child . . . The truth was, in comparison, mundane.

The stage-managing of Guderian's "disappearance" had been conceived by Gerd Jaunich during the final months of 1935, when Jaunich had turned his attention to what he believed was a completely overlooked but vitally important factor of any future conflict: finance. After voluminous research he created a blueprint for a totally new office, which he named the Reich Directorate for Economic Intelligence. This bureau would be wholly autonomous among all existing intelligence organs, including the military, Canaris's Abwehr and Himmler's SS. It would bear Hitler's personal imprimatur and have a mandate to use any and all resources of the other services. But the flow of information would go only one way: into the new Directorate, and even then through a blind. In no way could the existence of this new group ever come to light.

Gerd Jaunich presented the plan to Hitler on January 2, 1936, at a private meeting at Wolf's Lair. The Führer's endorsement was enthusiastic: Jaunich was to proceed immediately in his selection of the man who would control it. And it was here, in the area he least expected to be problematic, that Jaunich encountered his major obstacle.

In his search for that one particular individual, Jaunich pulled over a hundred files of men currently serving in the Finanzministerium. Each was eventually rejected. What he was seeking was not an accountant, administrator or banker. There was a legion of those. The individual he wanted had to have exceptional qualities . . . which in the end led him to Guderian.

Jaunich was a close friend of the Guderian family and knew that Heinz Guderian had been seeking a suitable post for his adopted son. He knew too that while the elder Guderian favored a Wehrmacht appointment, Erik was far too valuable to go into the officers' corps.

There was a further complication: Erik Guderian had never joined the Nazi Party. His earliest schooling had fashioned a cosmopolitan attitude, and although his loyalty to his native land was unquestioned, he had cultivated a detached attitude toward national politics. Gold, currencies, multinational corporations were all entities that transcended state borders. Moreover, Jaunich had learned that Guderian scrupulously avoided mentioning Adolf Hitler in any conversations, much less committing opinions to paper. The very lack of comment was, in itself, telling. By others it could be construed as a sign of treason.

Nevertheless Gerd Jaunich knew that sooner or later someone would claim him. He explained his proposal to the Iron

General and two days later Guderian arrived at Jaunich's border retreat.

Erik Guderian met every single operational requirement Jaunich stipulated. His knowledge of international financial systems was encyclopedic. He had had entry into the most guarded halls and offices of Continental finance, knew intimately the men who resided in those offices, their strengths and failings, their personal lives, the levers that could be used upon them. But most important of all, he was privy to the locations of the caches.

Every nation had special vaults buried somewhere on its territory. These were separate and apart from the central bank reserves, which at any given time held only a fraction of a country's bullion and foreign currency assets. The locations of such holds were state secrets of the highest order. Erik Guderian had ferreted out and memorized the sites in each European country.

Guderian's personal life presented no obstacles. His adopted family was a tight-knit clan. Three brothers held senior positions in the Wehrmacht, another was an engineer for Messerschmitt, and the fifth was to serve on board the battleship *Bismarck*. There was no question of any family member inquiring as to what Erik was doing for the war effort. Moreover, because he traveled so frequently, there hadn't been the time, and with it the opportunity, to marry, and his sexual exploits, while numerous, remained discreet.

Erik Guderian listened to Jaunich's exposition, interrupting only when a point required clarification or a reference was unclear. Otherwise his expression betrayed nothing. At times Jaunich noticed Guderian's elegantly manicured fingers toying with the miniature gold cross he wore around his neck, the only legacy he had kept of his natural parents. He did not speak until Jaunich was through.

"You realize, Gerd, that I am against the waging of war," Guderian said.

"There is no war," Jaunich objected. "Certain territorial questions—"

"Let us call it by its true name," Guderian interrupted quietly. "The momentum has been established. I doubt if Hitler could slow it down even if he had the desire, which he doesn't. I tell you right now that if Germany overreaches herself in this effort she will be destroyed. Utterly and for all time. I confess I do not understand the need for such 'territorial claims.' But I realize that unless I choose exile, humiliate and possibly endanger my family, I must serve." He paused. "After all, I too have to live with myself."

He paused, staring out at the falling snow. "Now let us accept certain facts. Germany is a nation rich in certain resources, incredibly poor in others. She relies heavily, possibly fatally, on basic imports—oil, rubber, aluminum, copper, to mention a few. There are two ways to overcome this problem. The first is to create a navy so powerful that it will not only usurp the British maritime presence but literally rule the Atlantic Ocean, particularly the African and South American sealanes. We do not have such a navy at the present time. Furthermore, the greater number of capital ships that do exist would be lost in battle with the British. This leaves us with the sole alternative: Germany must be rich enough to buy *and have delivered* whatever resources she needs until hostilities cease and normalization returns to international trade.

"That, Gerd, means she must have gold reserves. Far, far more than she possesses now.

"I understand exactly what it is you have planned," Guderian continued slowly. "The schema is brilliant. But the man who organizes and executes the program will become known as the greatest thief in history, a plunderer the likes of which the world hasn't seen since Tamerlane. I don't wish anyone to turn away from this fact to try to camouflage it with pretty names or impressive titles."

Guderian paused.

"That is also why I must insist on absolute secrecy. When I meet with Hitler I don't want any of his entourage nipping at my heels—no Himmler, Goebbels, no one from OKW. This operation is too important to become compromised by interdepartmental or interservice rivalries, which, as you well know, breed more security breaches than anything else."

"Given the mandate of the Directorate for Economic Intelligence, I can assure you of that," Jaunich said.

"There's also two other matters," Guderian carried on. "I have not joined the Nazi Party, but under the circumstances I should do so now—even though my loyalty to my country has never been questioned. Secondly, no one in my family, with the exception of Father, is to know what I have undertaken. I want you to promise me that."

"You have my word on both counts," Jaunich told him quietly. He was about to rise when Guderian restrained him.

"There are several more considerations," he said. "Please bear with me."

Uneasiness stirred in Jaunich.

"I want," Guderian went on, "an overt department, differently named but with the same function, set up at the Finanzministerium. Once the operations begin, word of the plunder—and that is exactly what it will be—will inevitably reach the appropriate circles in Britain and France. The subsequent inquiries through their intelligence services should meet with a *cul-de-sac* at this ghost office at the Finanzministerium."

"A sound precaution," Jaunich agreed.

"I also expect to lead the operational unit, its members screened by me personally."

"An active unit?" Jaunich smiled skeptically. "Erik, you're too old—"

"You are asking me to throw over three decades of life, to 'disappear,' as you put it," Guderian said coldly. "When you think about it there is no other way to proceed. But I am serving notice, Gerd: this plan may be your idea, but it will be done my way or not at all. And I do *not* intend to fight the war from behind a desk."

"What are you driving at?" Jaunich demanded.

"I will need reconstructive surgery."

"What is this surgery?" Jaunich whispered.

"There is a chance of my being recognized by former associates in the course of these operations," Guderian said. "Remember what I said about piracy. I cannot be recognized . . . because one day the war will be over . . ."

"This is insanity!"

"Listen to me!" Guderian said urgently. "I loathe the thought of mutilating myself. But under these circumstances it is necessary. For God's sake, think! My face may not be a household familiarity like that of some cinema star. But I can be recognized by hundreds of people in every European financial capital. That alone could jeopardize everything."

And Gerd Jaunich had no comeback, perhaps because he acknowledged, with whatever self-loathing, the irrefutability of Guderian's argument. Nor could he deny the awful premonition that events would somehow outstrip him, carrying the man who would be his instrument in a direction Jaunich could not follow, much less control.

The next two months Erik Guderian trained at a special base outside Regensburg in the Bavarian Forest. Drill instructors recruited from the Parachute Forces stationed at Mühldorf ran him sixteen hours a day, but at the end of the allotted time Guderian walked away with written commendations attesting to his skills in hand-to-hand combat, jumping and small arms.

From Regensburg he was moved to Starnberg, south of Munich. In the Starnbergersee, a lake cordoned off for military maneuvers, he learned infiltration by water. Already a strong swimmer, he spent endless nights practicing with aqualung equipment copied from French and American designs. By day, calm, quiet-spoken men tutored him in the fine points of demolition and small arms.

Erik Guderian returned to the Regensburg base on July 30, 1936. The reconstructive surgery was scheduled for the following afternoon.

Dr. Felix Rheingold, a short, bespectacled man of sixty, with a goatee and an immense waxed mustache, carefully probed Guderian's face, his short, stubby fingers touching every centimeter of flesh. He had Guderian go through an extensive examination, after which he pronounced him both mentally and physically fit to undergo the operation. Shortly after two o'clock Felix Rheingold broke the cartilage in Guderian's nose. A few seconds later the first incision was made.

In 1936 the techniques of reconstructive surgery were far from perfect. It was a field of medicine that had developed of necessity, out of the carnage of the Great War, when men returned home with limbs deformed by shells and faces seared away by gases. Three weeks after surgery, as he watched Rheingold slowly remove the bandages for the first time, Guderian realized just how far ahead of his time the Stuttgart physician stood. At first glance he was startled by the change in his facial structure. The nose, which had bent upward slightly at the bridge, had been straightened out, the nostrils taken in. The flesh beneath the cheeks had been tucked in, accentuating the bone structure. The area around the eyes had been elongated so that the eyes themselves appeared larger, the effect heightened by extending and thickening the brows. Across the forehead, three horizontal scars ran almost from hairline to hairline.

"Four weeks recovery period," Rheingold pronounced, examining his handiwork. "No water on the face for six more—sponge baths only."

Erik Guderian gazed into the hand mirror. The man staring back was himself . . . Yet it wasn't. He looked carefully at his hands, at his arms. The golden hair, the light freckles, the scar at the side of the right elbow where he had caught himself on a piton, they were the same. The way he thought, the memories that flashed through his mind, were all his . . . And yet something else had changed, had been lost besides the flesh. He didn't understand what that could be.

"Erik—"

Guderian held up his hand and Jaunich fell silent.

"Not Erik but Helmut Kleemann," he said, pronouncing each word slowly, savoring it as an oenophile would a rare wine. "My name is Helmut Kleemann."

That was the name they had agreed Guderian would be known by from this day on. The final vestige of the man he had been was gone.

In the first week of 1937 Erik Guderian was sent to a camp at Neustadt in the province of Württemberg. There he was introduced as Major Kleemann, of the OKW Special Detachment, to the six men who had been selected for his unit. For all intents and purposes these men no longer existed as members of either the Parachute Forces or the Wehrmacht. Any dossier pertaining to them had been excised from military records.

The youngest of the men was nineteen, a former chemistry student who could fashion lethal explosives from the contents of a household medicine cabinet. The oldest, Karl Horst, a sergeant from the elite ski-parachute Talon Regiment, was twenty-seven, with a hundred jumps to his credit. Among them the unit members were fluent in every European language including Portuguese and Russian. All but one of the men was unmarried; half had no families to speak of. Their mail, incoming and outgoing, was screened as a matter of course. They were permitted to write out one letter a month, which was dispatched to its address via Hannover, five hundred kilometers to the north.

From February to the middle of June, Guderian trained with his unit. What he did not know in the way of tactics, or was unfamiliar with in terms of weapons, he learned from his men, never hesitating to call upon their expertise.

By June, when the unit members were comfortable with each other to the point where actions and reactions could be anticipated, Guderian moved them all to a new compound several kilometers from Regensburg.

There, in a twenty-hectare compound that Allied intelligence supposed was an SS training camp, obviously so since it was patrolled by members of the SS Das Reich Division, Gerd Jaunich met them and, upon Hitler's instructions, revealed not only when Germany would fuse war but what the primary targets would be. Their primary targets.

Fifteen hectares at Regensburg had been cordoned off into one-hectare grids. In the center of each one was a copy of a particular building, built to exact original specifications. In most cases the structures were merely shells. What lay beneath their foundations, however, was accurate to the last detail. The street names on the sides of the buildings were the true addresses, written in Dutch, French or Czech. The SS personnel who served as "clerks" represented the accurate number of inside personnel.

After they had toured each facility, Guderian brought his men to their operational quarters.

"*Meine Herren*, you are to become the greatest group of thieves the world has ever seen." Guderian paused to glance over the incredulous expressions. "No, that is not quite true," he corrected himself. "That the world will *never* see.

"Each of the buildings you have seen represents a secret depository of the nation in question. These caches are separate and apart from the central reserve banks and major financial institutions. The locations and true purposes are among a country's most prized secrets. I am privy to these secrets, as now you are. I assure you that each location not only exists but will hold, upon the outbreak of war, *at least* the estimated number of gold, silver and platinum bars as well as paper currency.

"As soon as war is declared, the central banks will attempt to move their bullion reserves and negotiable securities out of our reach. To a very small degree they will be successful. The reason for this lies in the figures before you. It is physically impossible to transfer such bulk and weight within the time the banks will have. In fact, I predict that the banks and houses will employ a two-tier move: the central vaults will be emptied and their contents deposited in these secret holds. Only later will an attempt be made to spirit the holdings out of the country.

"Essentially this will make our task easier. The enemy will *expect* an assault on its financial nerve centers. He will not be disappointed, as feints will be arranged to accommodate the expectation. But he will not foresee a swift, direct attack on the secondary caches, which he believes are unknown to us.

"Our responsibility, gentlemen, is to enter with the first assault wave, work our way toward these caches, seize them and at the same time prevent the enemy from destroying the reserves.

"Our operations will have no code names. For our own purposes the Führer has decreed that this unit be called Action Group. It remains unlisted in any Wehrmacht records. Its uniform will have only one distinction: commando flashes designed by myself for identification purposes. The sole method of communication will be the new ENIGMA units, which were designed and constructed specifically for our use. They are almost ready for field testing, and from what I understand may be adopted for general field use. The chain of command is quite simple: you answer to me, I to Herr Jaunich, Herr Jaunich to the Führer. The only time anyone else will know of our existence will be at our point of penetration. Before we enter a specific location, the commander of forces in the field will be advised by OKW, Berlin, that a special commando group will operate in his area. Whatever assistance by way of men or matériel will be instantly forthcoming upon request from any member of this unit. We shall locate, penetrate and secure the caches, gentlemen. As soon as they are ours we will commandeer regular or SS troops to move the booty out. While this is being done, we remove ourselves and monitor the operation at a safe distance. This has nothing to do with our courage; rather we must never permit our identities to become known. Not if we are to take every one of the twenty caches on our lists.

"Finally, gentlemen, allow me to give you a rough estimate of exactly how much booty we intend to seize from our quarries: the projected conservative figure is the equivalent of twelve billion United States dollars."

Guderian paused, noting the disbelief on the faces of his men.

"But that is not the whole of it. A country without money

cannot fight, no matter how many alliances it belongs to. When we succeed in our mission we also make it very clear to the powers that be that further conflict is valueless. In this way, gentlemen, we save German lives. We are the radical scalpel which excises a vital organ, thus shutting down the entire corpus quickly and effectively. The funds we remove will of course help the Reich's war effort, but I hold that our contribution lies as much in sparing life.

"Now, *Meine Herren*, our first assignment . . . "

In March 1939 Adolf Hitler marched into Czechoslovakia, challenging France and Britain to honor their treaty with the Czechs. But while the Allies wrung their hands, Erik Guderian's unit swept in alongside the invading forces. On the second day they captured the bullion reserves that had been removed to Pilzen. Bypassing Prague, they made directly for Ostrava, near the Polish border, and took the second repository. The operation was concluded at Brno one week later with the capture, contents intact, of the third cache.

Adolf Hitler had spent some three million marks on the creation and training of what he had personally designated as the Action Group. After the Czechoslovakian campaign alone his gold reserves swelled by the equivalent of one hundred twenty million United States dollars.

The unit retired to its Regensburg headquarters, and for the rest of the year lay dormant, out of sight but not inactive. Erik Guderian supervised the erection of other structures on the compound. When these were completed, he and his men began to perfect their command of the Polish language.

In September of 1939 the marching orders for Poland were issued. While Stukas pulverized the cities from the air and General Guderian's tanks overran all resistance on the ground, Erik Guderian and his men were parachuted into the outskirts of Gdansk. Slipping into the city, they mined two freighters that were to ferry Polish gold to London. The ships sailed as far as Hel in the Gulf of Danzig. As they were clearing the shallows, explosions ripped open their engine rooms and drove them down into ninety feet of water. By then there was no Polish organization, civil or military, left to attempt a salvage. The ships lay in the water for three months before Guderian returned to supervise their raising.

After the Danzig operation the unit regrouped behind German lines at Lebork. It flew overnight to Cracow and there seized the Customs building, an innocuous structure whose hidden subbasement was the hub for a series of caverns, each one laden with precious metal. The success at Cracow eliminated the need to go to the capital. The serial numbers on the bars confiscated at the Customs House matched those on ingots that had once been held in Warsaw.

The pattern repeated itself in spring of 1940 in Belgium and the Netherlands, leading up to what *Die Piraten* believed to be the largest prize they could ever win: a third of the immense national reserves of France.

They didn't know, Guderian thought, closing the last of the dossiers, that long before the French action, I was already dreaming of the unattainable . . .

The briefing quarters Adolf Hitler preferred to use were hidden in the warren of the Chancellery basement. There were few concessions to comfort: the chairs were hard and straight-back; the concrete walls were covered with large maps of Europe, as was the oversized drafting table which Hitler favored, walking around it, tapping the map with a long pointer.

As the closing of the steel-sheathed door resounded behind him, Erik Guderian squinted to adjust his eyes to the glare of naked lightbulbs set in wire nests.

"*Mein Führer!*"

Hitler did not return the salute but continued to stare at the officer before him, weighing, assessing. He did not so much as glance at Gerd Jaunich, who stood off to the side.

"Major!" he barked suddenly. "I have been informed that you have an audacious plan to present to me. Tell me the premise upon which it is based."

Guderian folded his hands on the small of his back.

"The premise, *Mein Führer*," he said clearly, "is that England can be placed in a position where she *must* surrender and sue for peace. Putting her in that position need not cost the life of a single German soldier."

The room was deathly still. Guderian could feel Hitler's eyes, blazing with excitement, boring into his own.

"And how do you propose to maneuver the English into such a position?" Hitler demanded.

"*Mein Führer*, the foundation of Britain's ability to fight is her immense gold reserves and negotiable securities. So long as she is able to pay, the United States will continue to supply arms. But what if such reserves ceased to exist?"

Guderian let the question hang.

"Yesterday, *Mein Führer*, I received the transcript of the most recent conversation between Roosevelt and Churchill. It is clear from the wording that the British Prime Minister has been forced into doing something he had hoped very much to avoid. The code name for this action is Prometheus. I believe it refers to only one thing: *the transfer of England's entire fiscal wealth to America either by submarine or capital ships*."

"Your reasoning?"

"Based on a number of factors, Führer. One: We know that Churchill has been desperately buying time by meeting with your representative to discuss terms for a possible peace in Europe. It is clear now that such meetings were a feint.

"Two: But why does Churchill need time? Part of the answer lies with the British Expeditionary Force in Dunkirk. Churchill cannot reinforce them, so they must be withdrawn. That requires time. But this is not the entire answer.

"Three: To prolong the conflict, Churchill requires American arms. We know the Congress of the United States is reluctant to involve its country in another European war. Nevertheless this body has been pressured by Roosevelt to accept the following condition: As long as Britain pays cash for its arms, weapons will continue to be sold. It is therefore imperative for the British to maintain credit at the Federal Reserve Bank in New York City. We know that their account is very low. The time has come to replenish it.

"Four: Since the British must send tens if not hundreds of millions of pounds to the United States, I believe they will use this opportunity to send *everything* they have. There is sound reasoning for them to do so: Your armies stand unopposed in France. The French coast will be yours in a matter of weeks, and then the threat of invasion becomes imminent for the British. I cannot think of a greater disaster, from the British point of view, than *the Third Reich succeeding in such an invasion and thereby capturing Britain's entire fiscal resources*. This will not only force an immediate surrender—a country without financial resources surely cannot fight—but will also add untold millions to the wealth of Germany!

"I put to you, *Mein Führer*, that the British would sooner risk sending the gold to America than leave it in their vaults for us to confiscate. Even if they were not obliged to pay a penny for the American arms, they would still move the gold and securities."

Guderian paused. "And at that point, when the booty has been assembled and is en route, is the time to strike—and either steal or destroy the treasure. Whatever course we adopt, so long as we are successful, Britain will be bankrupt. She will surrender. She will be taken without spilling a drop of German blood."

"And you are convinced, Major, absolutely convinced, that Prometheus is the code name for such a transfer?"

From the inside pocket of his tunic, Guderian withdrew a page of newspaper, unfolded it and read aloud.

"The *Times* of London, May 3, 1940:

"'In a written reply to a Parliamentary question the Chancellor of the Exchequer disclosed that an Order in Council had been made to empower the Treasury to give instructions as to the custody and disposition of reserves and securities held in this country. In order that transactions outside the United Kingdom may continue to be realized in an orderly fashion, it is convenient for them to be held in North America . . .'"

Hitler leaned across the table at him, eyes shining.

"Are the British now telling us—telling anyone who cares to read!—exactly what they intend to do?" he demanded.

"Precisely, *Mein Führer*," Guderian said softly. "I hasten to add that this quote, of such immense importance, was buried on page eight in the 'City in Brief' column. No one recognized its significance. There was no outcry, no demands as to why tens of thousands of small investors were suddenly to have their securities moved—without explanation. In short, nothing."

"There can be no other explanation for the meaning of Prometheus?" Hitler asked.

In the few seconds it took Hitler to utter the question, Guderian realized that the slightest hesitation, a nuance of doubt in his voice would condemn his proposal.

"None, *Mein Führer*. The English will move their gold soon, very soon. They understand that once the Reich armies control the French ports, especially the naval base at Saint-Nazaire, our U-boats will be operating much more effectively. It would be madness to wait until then. I suggest to you that plans for the transfer are being drawn up at this very moment.

The actual shipment is three, maximum four weeks away from being realized."

Adolf Hitler stepped forward and stood very close to Guderian.

"*Herr Major*, is it not true that the agent who provided you with the transcript alluding to Prometheus has in fact been killed in Washington and her control arrested?"

"That is, unfortunately, the case," Guderian said tonelessly.

"Does not the catastrophe in the American capital endanger your primary source of Prometheus, the agent in the U.S. London embassy who worked in tandem with Washington?" Hitler pressed on.

"London's integrity remains intact, Führer. As soon as the catastrophe, as you put it, occurred, this agent was silenced. He or she or they will not move until further instructions are received from Berlin."

"But that is scarcely the issue, *Herr Major*," Hitler said softly, a cold note of triumph to his tone. "You must agree that the Americans at least surmise there is a London penetration. They will send in the hunters."

Guderian did not flinch. "All the more reason to move quickly. Permit me to be frank, *Mein Führer*. Our London agent has been invaluable. I would do everything in my power to preserve this person. But if I have to make a sacrifice to rob England of two hundred and fifty million pounds sterling, if by making abnormal, dangerous demands I can bring about British surrender and save German lives, then by God I will do just that!"

The cold fury and determination of Guderian's voice broke Hitler's attack. The Führer stepped away and for a moment stood with his back to Guderian.

"Major, obviously you have thought this matter out," he said, not turning around. "What is it you require to carry out your mission?"

"I have divided this operation into three stages," Guderian said, doing his best to keep the excitement from his voice.

"First, it is necessary for me to enter Great Britain and establish myself in London.

"It is true that my face was well known in the English capital from previous visits. However, since the reconstructive surgery my appearance has been altered to such a degree that not even former acquaintances have been able to recognize me.

This being the case, I shall be able to work quite freely in London."

"Do you propose to go alone?"

"I do, *Mein Führer*. One man, operating on his own, with an intimate knowledge of the British banking system and its moves, can penetrate the operation that is being set up. It would be pointless, and above all else dangerous to myself and my men, if I were to try to bring them with me."

"But you will require assistance," Hitler objected.

"Certainly, *Mein Führer*. And this brings me to the second stage: I will need the names of all British agents under SD and Abwehr control, a complete list of specialists whose services I can call upon, and shelter houses I can use in case of emergency. Although I believe British counterintelligence, MI5, has been unsuccessful in pinpointing our agents, I cannot take the chance that some have been secretly turned. I must have as many alternatives available as possible."

"What else, Major?"

"The third aspect of this operation requires that the Luftwaffe begin immediate bombardment of British positions at Dunkirk. Given time, the British may organize an orderly retreat. It is imperative they be denied the opportunity to do so.

"At the same time, I need access to all OKW intelligence files concerning British and Canadian units operating in the area of Boulogne and Calais. If I do not find the man I'm looking for, then raiding parties must go out, and under cover of Luftwaffe bombardment, capture enemy units."

"You ask that major military strategy be brought into line with a single clandestine operation?" Hitler demanded hoarsely. "Have you taken leave of your senses, Major?"

Guderian ignored the intimidation.

"*Mein Führer*, it is essential that the British retreat be burdened with as much confusion as possible. I do not feel such circumstances interfere with OKW planning . . . not unless the Chief of Staff is of the opinion to permit the British to sail away without attempting to crush what remains of their forces."

Hitler stared at Guderian, lips twitching in a smile.

"Any why are these raiding parties so vital, Major? What is the intention behind them?"

"To create a new man," Guderian said softly. "Somewhere in the POW holding camp or in a still active unit is one soldier, British or Canadian, who will not see his native land for a long, long time . . . if ever again."

6

"The doctors aren't sure how much of Ogilvy's face they'll be able to save."

Edward Pearce leaned back against the door to his office, his hands stuffed deep in his coat pockets. Cabot looked away from him and at the dossier in his lap.

Robert Ogilvy: twenty-six years old, working class background out of Manchester, scholarship student at the University of London, a fine athlete who hadn't missed by much in making the British wrestling team that had gone to the 1936 Berlin Olympics. A life that would never be the same again.

"Repercussions?" Cabot asked softly.

"You have Mackenzie McConnell to thank for the lack of those," Pearce said, tossing his coat over the back of a chair. "She sealed up the entire incident. As far as the Leatherhead constabulary is concerned, nothing happened out there this morning. MI5 investigators have brought back every scrap of evidence they could find."

Pearce's voice broke. "And I had to tell Colonel Blimp that his boy Jamie died today."

Cabot rose and threw his arms around his friend.

"I'm sorry, Edward. God knows how sorry I am!"

Pearce managed a weak smile. "I need some real coffee in me. Meanwhile here's the file you wanted on McConnell."

Cabot knew Pearce well enough to let him be. He pushed the remorse from his mind and started to read slowly, concentrating on every detail.

Mackenzie McConnell had celebrated her twenty-seventh birthday three days ago. The only child of Hortense and Edmund McConnell, the archeologist and explorer, she had been born in Alexandria, Egypt, where McConnell was heading up an expedition that had just returned from the southern fringes of the Nile. By the age of ten she had traveled throughout the Holy Land, as much at ease on a Bedouin camel as in the Rolls-Royce driven by the young adventurer who would later become known as Lawrence of Arabia.

When Edmund McConnell was sent to India and Ceylon,

Mackenzie took her schooling with private tutors along the way. It wasn't until 1931 that she came to England for the first time in her life and completed a First at Cambridge in less than three years. But her native land was too tame for her expansive and restless spirit, and upon graduation she rejoined her father in South Africa. For the next four years Mackenzie trekked by his side from the Horn of Africa to Malaya, Singapore, Thailand and finally into Hong Kong.

By the time Edmund McConnell realized he could no longer keep up this pace, his daughter knew his every secret. She was present at the quiet ceremony in London, where he received the medal he was not permitted to keep in his possession and listened as the director of the British Secret Service quietly thanked him for his selfless service to the Crown. Four days later Mackenzie McConnell signed the Official Secrets Act and was inducted into the same netherworld.

"The old man still works for them," Pearce commented, looking over Cabot's shoulder. "He's retired but serves as advisor to the code sections."

"An archeologist deals in symbols," Cabot remarked. "What better training?"

"Which also explains why the daughter was in on the Double-cross System. With what she's seen and heard she could turn the King himself if she put her mind to it."

"But what the hell were they doing tailing us?" Cabot asked softly.

"According to McConnell they always tag along when someone new arrives."

"If that's the case—"

"They're lying, Johnny," Pearce said softly. "I've picked up dozens of people and never had a shadow. You know what I think? That someone tipped off British counterintelligence. How many people knew you were coming over?"

"The President, Dulles, Churchill and you."

"Then it must have been Churchill," Pearce said flatly.

Cabot flicked his cigarette butt into the fireplace.

"You know what you're saying, Edward? That Churchill passed that bit of news to his own people . . . and one of them was a high-level Whitehall leak."

"How else can you explain it?" Pearce shouted suddenly. "For Christ's sake, I almost lost you out there, Johnny!"

"What about the shooters?" Cabot asked him.

"That's another reason MI5 suddenly has a hair up its ass. You've heard of the Double-cross System?"

"A little."

"MI5 has been incredibly successful in rooting out Nazi sleeper agents. They've turned most, shot the rest. Those who cooperate keep sending phony intelligence back to Berlin—and the Abwehr doesn't know it. Not only that, but these same agents are alerted by Berlin as to when and how new agents are to arrive. You can imagine the surprise when MI5 is there to greet them at the drop zone.

"Given all this, why were three heavily armed, well-organized shooters waiting for you to arrive? MI5 is going crazy, because it's very possible they've missed a key nest right here in London."

"What about you? Could the Germans or whoever have decided it's time you were gone?"

"If there is an operational cell in town it could take me out any time it wants. I'm public, Johnny. They don't have to make such a production when a bomb under my bed would work just as well."

Cabot rose and walked over to the fireplace.

"If MI5's been taken by the Nazis on one operational unit, is it possible Berlin has managed to plant someone right in its belly?" Cabot asked, speaking to the empty grate. "I don't like coincidences. Not the kind where we drive into an ambush and a tailing car just happens to pull in behind us with armed personnel inside."

"McConnell would never admit such a possibility, at least not to me," Pearce said. "But yes, given what happened, what you're suggesting is possible."

"Kennedy has a deep-penetration agent burrowed away somewhere in Grosvenor Square," Cabot said. "I'm supposed to get to him or her as quickly as I can—with the cooperation of British counterintelligence."

He looked up at Pearce. "How can I do that if they're rotten?"

"It's simple," Pearce said. "I'll be covering your back. Anywhere you move I'll be right behind you. I'm going to be your long gun, Johnny."

He glanced at his watch "You're going to be late for your meeting. In the meantime be thankful for the little things: You're still secure at the embassy. As far as anyone knows, you're just a poor cipher mechanic from Washington. If we're lucky Kennedy will never hear of Leatherhead, which means you'll have free rein in here. Use it, Johnny. Get the son of a bitch before he can turn on you!"

"Your armament, sir, if you would, please."

Detective Inspector Thompson greeted Cabot in the antechamber of Number Ten Downing Street. Cabot shrugged off his coat and handed it to him, holding it with two fingers tucked under the collar. Thompson saw the submachine gun and hung up the coat without comment. But he blocked the way when Cabot tried to step by him.

"The revolver as well, please, sir."

Winston Churchill's office was a study in maritime lore. Over the Adam fireplace hung an oil of Henry VIII's flagship, the *Mary Rose*. Across the way, in an immense glass-enclosed mahogany cabinet, was John Harrison's first maritime timekeeper, a model of an eighteenth-century merchant ship, the figurehead off the 1809 HMS *Ajax*, and the centerpiece: the mounted uniform of Lord Nelson, complete with the hole in the left shoulder made by the fatal French musketball.

"Accurate to the final detail, Mr. Cabot—even the hanging epaulet dislodged by the ball."

Cabot turned around at the booming voice, watching as Churchill, bedecked in a three-piece pin-stripe, strode up to him.

"My humblest apologies, sir, for the manner in which you were received this morning. And my thanks to Providence that you were spared."

He gripped Cabot by the elbow and guided him to a sitting area in the corner of the room.

"I believe you've met Miss McConnell."

She walked into the room and took Cabot's breath away. Her hair fell in billows over her shoulders, framing the smooth, sculptured face. The navy sweater, matching her eyes, clung to a generous bosom, while the long riding skirt emphasized a high slender waist and long legs. She did not avert her eyes from Cabot's gaze, but there was no warmth in them. They regarded Cabot with suspicion, resentment, impatience.

"Miss McConnell, about your partner . . ."

"He's as well as can be expected," she replied coldly. "It

could have been worse, but then again his injuries need never have been inflicted."

"A drink, Mr. Cabot?" Churchill interjected.

"Scotch, neat, please."

"And you, Miss McConnell?"

"The same, thank you, Prime Minister."

"Now, Mr. Cabot," Churchill grunted as he poured out the drinks, "I understand you have a message for me from your President Roosevelt."

"The text is for your ears only, sir," Cabot said pointedly.

Churchill settled back with his port and regarded Cabot over the rim of the glass.

"Mr. Cabot, I truly regret the circumstances under which you and Miss McConnell were introduced. It is obvious, sir, that there is bad blood between you. Mistakes were made, compounded, and as a result one man was killed and another almost shot to death by someone who was his ally.

"But I wish to make it clear to you, sir, as I am certain your President already has, that there *will be* British participation in this operation. I chose Miss McConnell from a dozen possible agents. You will find her not only capable and experienced but extremely intelligent and persuasive. In addition to being *your* associate she will be *my* liaison in the field."

"Mr. Prime Minister—"

"Pray, allow me to finish. I am sufficiently familiar with your assignment, Mr. Cabot, to conclude that your spy *is* an American and that he or she operates from your embassy, technically American soil. However, it is quite likely that this person continues to conduct his treasonous affairs *outside* Grosvenor Square. And that, sir, places him in *our* domain. Moreover, there is the possibility of accomplices who are likely to be British subjects. Thus, Mr. Cabot, both nations have jurisdiction, not to say anything of the fact that both President Roosevelt *and* myself are grievously inconvenienced by this person's activities."

Cabot sipped his Scotch and kept his eyes low.

"Prime Minister, I'm aware of the cooperative arrangement, but I have no authority to discuss intrinsic details with anyone except yourself—not until I receive instructions to the contrary from either the President or Mr. Dulles."

"Very well, Mr. Cabot. You have only to ask and I shall see to it you can avail yourself of my trans-Atlantic line."

Churchill sipped his port while Mackenzie McConnell arched an eyebrow at Cabot. A hard smile played on her lips. He knew she was waiting to see how he would handle himself.

"Mr. Prime Minister, your offer is generous but it is also ridiculous."

"Really?"

"Since security of communications is the matter I was sent here for, calling Washington would be a pointless—and dangerous—exercise."

Churchill nodded. "I see."

Mackenzie McConnell raised her glass at Cabot, acknowledging his capitulation.

"Therefore," Cabot continued, ignoring her, "the message from the President is as follows: he asks you, sir, to avoid using the current method of communication, that is, the line which is plugged into our embassy circuits and cipher machines. Instead, the President asks your Army Signal Corps— he was very specific here, sir, about it being an Army operation—design a new circuit system which would bypass our embassy completely.

"Since this changeover and my mission here are secret, no one on our embassy staff except for the security officer, Edward Pearce, has been given any details. This includes our Ambassador, Mr. Joseph Kennedy.

"You appreciate the delicacy of such a situation, Mr. Prime Minister. If Ambassador Kennedy were to become aware that he was being kept in the dark, a very awkward and unpleasant situation would develop." Cabot decided to twist his own knife a little. "For both President Roosevelt *and* yourself. So, in order to keep up appearances, normal military and diplomatic traffic will continue to be sent through Grosvenor Square. This will have the added effect of making the agent inside believe that everything is on the up and up. I don't want this person spooked. I don't want him to run until I'm ready."

"This all seems very straightforward, Mr. Cabot," Churchill rumbled. "I'll see to it our chaps construct something for me for the interim period."

"Excuse me, Mr. Cabot," Mackenzie McConnell said coolly. "But have you considered the possibility that the person you seek was somehow privy to your arrival—and arranged that little reception?"

"Miss McConnell," Cabot said coldly, "only four people

knew I was coming over—your Prime Minister, my President, Allen Dulles and Edward Pearce!"

Her eyes blazed at the implicit accusation.

"What are you suggesting, Mr. Cabot?"

Cabot turned to Churchill. "That given what happened I have to know whether my mission was compromised on *this* end! Did you, sir, ever discuss it with anyone other than the President?"

"I did, Mr. Cabot," Churchill answered calmly. "With Miss McConnell."

"I resent the inference!" Mackenzie McConnell cried. "How can you even suggest—"

Churchill held up his hand for silence.

"You see what is happening, Mr. Cabot," Churchill said, a sadness weighing on his voice. "Someone is driving a wedge between us. An attempt was made upon your life because of indiscretion. You cannot believe Washington was responsible; we assure you that the fault does not lie with London. Yet we are already at odds—before your mission has even begun.

"I suggest to you, sir, that we all take a step back to the point of good faith. Otherwise we might as well throw up our hands right now. And neither of us can afford to do that, Mr. Cabot. There is so much at stake!"

Almost the same words Roosevelt used, Cabot thought. Prometheus again!

Cabot filed away the thought, at the same time realizing that further antagonism would gain him nothing. If MI5 was dirty, then he needed Mackenzie McConnell where he could see her—and that meant making the first gesture.

"The Prime Minister is right," he said. "I'm going to need as much help as I can get. I'll be counting on you."

"That you may, Mr. Cabot," Mackenzie replied softly. "Rest assured I'll be with you every step of the way."

"I quite agree with you," Philby said languidly, uncrossing his long, thin legs. "It's quite ridiculous to have this Yank charging about London without a leash." He fixed his iron gaze on Mackenzie McConnell, sitting behind her desk at Queen Anne's Gate, home to the British Security Service, MI5. "But then again, unless I misread the situation, you *don't* have anything to show Churchill, who seems to have worked himself up into quite a tizzy over this encounter. Is it *possible* the old man could have let something slip?"

"As far as I am concerned, the attack on Cabot is directly related to the problem at Grosvenor Square," Mackenzie said, leaning across to accept his light. "There is no doubt that our American cousins have a badger in their woodpile and that he, in turn, has made a nice little nest for himself on the outside."

"So you're saying that when the Americans unearth their little problem, they shall, by the same stroke, solve ours," Philby drawled.

"Not in the least, Kim!" Mackenzie snapped at him. "I cannot wait for the Yanks to clean up their house. I will not have terror in my city, which is exactly what has already ensued with arrival of this . . . this cowboy!"

Philby blew a smoke ring. "What *I* find puzzling is how such a protection unit, assuming there is one and it is under the control of Grosvenor Square, has escaped detection by the Double-cross System."

"Nowhere is it written, Kim," Mackenzie said dryly, "that MI5 has touched each and every agent the Germans have sent over."

"Kindly do not mix apples and oranges, my dear," Philby corrected her. "MI5 has located and either turned or neutralized every *active* agent the Abwehr threw at us. But we cannot go after something we didn't know existed. We have no names, covers, to identify these people by. We have no addresses to check. Nor have we a history on such a group, which at least might offer a starting point. It is obvious that somewhere in London there are men who are *not* part of the regular Abwehr force. They could well have been spirited into the country very early on, in thirty-eight or thirty-nine, told to organize lodgings, equipment, armament, that sort of thing, and then to do absolutely nothing. Their identities would not be known to the agents we've netted. Not even their existence. Which would explain why we've never heard mention of a group like this from our tame sources."

"It's possible," Mackenzie admitted grudgingly. "And *if* that is the case what are we to do, since Cabot is obviously their target?"

"What do we know about Cabot?" Philby asked suddenly.

"Not very much that relates to the matter at hand," Mackenzie said. "His background is accessible enough. He's the son of Baylor Cabot, the banker and diplomat. Conventional education, after which he taught in China. We lost track of him after Nanking in thirty-seven, but picked him up in London the following year. That's when we learned he was very close to Aaron Steinfeldt, the mathematician. Steinfeldt had tutored him at Princeton—"

"Wasn't there a girl?" Philby interrupted her. "A Jewess?"

"Steinfeldt's daughter. By the time Cabot arrived in Germany Steinfeldt had disappeared. His daughter was taken just after Cabot called on her. He was arrested and . . . and she was killed."

"Who was Cabot reporting to?"

"As far as we know, no one," Mackenzie said, but quickly added, "However, I don't really believe he had come over only to see and possibly bring out Orit Steinfeldt. Cabot was, and is, very well connected. He could have been working either for the State Department or Dulles—even at that point."

Mackenzie was silent for a moment, then spoke thoughtfully.

"Cabot is compromised. We are, therefore, in the stronger position. For this reason alone I wouldn't share any of our information with him, no matter how much authority he comes with. Surveillance on our major suspect must be maintained without Cabot's being aware of it."

"Are you sure your position is all that secure?" Philby countered. "The attack at Leatherhead may have been directed against Cabot, but it was your partner who was wounded." He paused. "And it was Jamie Robertson, your man inside the embassy, who was killed."

Mackenzie McConnell's eyes flared, hurt and pain feeding her anger. Robertson had been her recruit. She had trained him, devised his cover and maneuvered him into the position from which Edward Pearce had innocently plucked him for the factotum job. Jamie had been her eyes and ears inside Grosvenor Square. A solid, methodical agent, it was he who had brought out the bits and pieces which had finally produced the composite sketch of a possible enemy inside the U.S. embassy.

"Jamie Robertson's death was tragic," Mackenzie said softly. "But we have an opportunity to make up for his loss, possibly get even closer to our suspect than he did. By virtue of being liaisoned to Cabot, I am in a unique position: not only will I have access to the man himself, but he will be obliged to share whatever he knows with me."

"Who knows what interesting highlights you may learn about American operations in general, my dear," Philby murmured.

"There is one further possibility," Mackenzie said slowly. "The Americans trust Cabot implicitly. That has been made patently clear by the Prime Minister himself. But given his rather unusual record and the fact that our cousins either can't or won't share any information about him with us, isn't it just possible that Jonathan Cabot is not who he appears to be?"

She paused. "What, for example, would happen if I were to ascertain that he is working *with* the traitor at Grosvenor Square?"

"In that case, Mackenzie," Philby said sadly, "when you have evidence of such collaboration, you should make every effort to take Cabot alive. But failing that, you'll have to kill him."

7

"The eyes of the Empire are upon Calais!"

With these words, Minister of War Anthony Eden finished his address to the House of Commons on the evening of May 22. His recital on the deteriorating situation faced by the British Expeditionary Force in France had been lengthy. Time and time again he reiterated the necessity of holding the port city, which was, after the fall of Boulogne, the last obstacle to a German assault upon Dunkirk itself.

The Parliamentary correspondent for the BBC summed up the impact of the Minister's words as follows:

"The Prime Minister," the correspondent said to his audience, "shuddered visibly at the final words of Mr. Eden's address. Indeed his complexion became ashen and he seemed to sink into his chair as though trying to hide from something quite horrible . . ."

Erik Guderian switched off the radio set.

A travesty, he thought to himself. Churchill could not order the Calais regiments to retreat even if he wanted them to. It is not a matter of holding Calais until reinforcements come up. There are none! No, his soldiers must stay where they are because there is no more room at Dunkirk! The beaches are swollen with troops. If the British public knew how chaotic the retreat really was, they would hang Churchill!

Abruptly Guderian rose and began to pace, feeling as much a prisoner of his circumstances and environment as Churchill must have of his. Not that the Congress Hall at the Chancellery was a confined area. But its three hundred square meters had been converted by Hitler into a war conference center and that meant the room was barren. Gone were the priceless Vermeers and Rubenses adorning its walls, the silk tapestries from Japan and thick carpets woven in Persia and Afghanistan. All furniture had been removed and replaced by bare essentials: a large mahogany desk for Hitler's personal use, an immense table assembled from three individual pieces, which dominated the center of the room and held large-scale maps of Western Europe, a dozen hardback chairs, and a smaller table from which to serve refreshments. It was also the room Erik Guderian had occupied for the last two days.

Guderian returned to his desk, once again switched on the gooseneck lamp. He ran his fingers over his face, marveling at how he had almost come to think of the stretched skin, with its smooth rubbery quality, as natural. Only now, when he was overtired, did he feel the slightest burning sensation underneath the skin, as though there were a layer of tiny coals imbedded in the flesh. Guderian readjusted the angle of the lamp, trying to push the pain away from his consciousness.

He had divided the operation against Prometheus into two parts, referring to them as *Before England* and *After England*. It had been easier to start with the latter.

Jaunich had been as good as his word: Not only had he provided a master list of all Abwehr agents operating in England, but also the names of men and women controlled by Himmler's Sicherheitsdienst, the Security Service of the SS. From the lists Guderian had chosen only the names of agents entrenched in London. He reviewed each piece of information the agents had sent in by courier, each transmission received. In the end he discarded every man and woman on the list and moved on to the sleepers . . . those dormant men and women who, in some cases, had lived and worked in London for decades, had become British citizens if they weren't so already, and waited, like some mythical figures, for the magic phrase which would raise them from their slumber.

Guderian scrutinized the smallest details. How had these people spent the money paid to them by Berlin? Had they succumbed to the temptation of throwing it around ostentatiously? Who had come into their lives—a wife or husband or lovers—to whom they might unveil their secret world? Where was the all but invisible clue that they had been turned and were now working for the British?

There wasn't. The sleepers were all secure, and from the names available to him Guderian chose three. Three men who would complement Darius, Jaunich's virtuoso agent, who operated from within the heart of Grosvenor Square. He chose them with utmost care, the criterion being their ability to furnish him with the tools he would need to tear Prometheus asunder. Although it might be possible for him to procure what was necessary by his own means, Guderian could not afford the inherent risk. Besides, these men were also his communications link with Berlin as well as the escape route in case he had to run. Unknown to one another, they would never be told of the overall operation, but only that part in which they had a role to play.

After he had outlined the battle plan in London to the last possible detail and was satisfied that he could work effectively within the circumscribed parameters, Guderian turned his attention to *Before England*, the task of infiltrating the sceptered isle. Unexpectedly, it was here he encountered a problem that seemed insoluble.

Guderian stared at the forty stacks of documents on the table before him. Two-thirds of these were prisoner of war records culled from the combined Records Offices of the OKW and General Gehlen's Military Intelligence (Abwehr) Group West. The remainder were the General Staff Intelligence Division estimates of exactly what units of the BEF and French forces were still fighting in the northwest sector of France.

In the last week, since his presentation before Hitler,

Guderian had read over three thousand pages of military and intelligence data in an effort to crack the riddle posed in *Before England*. He worked twenty hours a day, often collapsing at the table when sleep could no longer be denied. When going home proved too time costly, he had ordered a cot, a hot plate and small icebox brought in. The Chancellery staff responded to his commands instantly, all too aware that the man in the Congress Hall had been given absolute authority by Hitler himself before the Führer had departed for Berchtesgaden. But neither the orderlies who had brought the bedding and food nor the OKW dispatch riders who delivered the voluminous data on POWs ever saw Erik Guderian. The locks on the door responded to electronic signals. Whenever a consignment arrived, Guderian activated the locks from a gloomy recess in the Hall. Those who entered did so quickly, keeping their eyes front and center. They retreated just as quickly.

Three thousand pages . . . And nothing! The slamming of an open palm against wood resounded across the ceiling.

There was too much material, too many names, facts, dates, locations, figures, for a single mind to absorb in such a short time. As prepared as he had thought himself to be, Guderian was nonetheless staggered by the sheer weight of information that continued to flow in.

Yet, he thought to himself, why should I have been so unprepared for it all?

Germany was no longer a geographical entity. It was a voracious juggernaut that had swallowed Poland in seventeen days, Denmark in two, Norway in twenty-four, Holland in five and Belgium in seventeen. As each campaign was initiated, a separate army of clerks and archivists moved alongside the fighting troops. They meticulously recorded the names of the battalions, regiments, companies and squads that disintegrated before the Wehrmacht thrusts. Volumes six inches thick and more sprang up overnight, between their bindings the lists of thousands of names representing every Allied nationality. And beside these, the names of the individual soldier's commanding officer, his unit, and a brief but succinct description of its total strength, armament, position and purpose.

Three thousand pages read and scrutinized. All to no avail. Frustrated, Guderian had attacked these records a second time, plowing through the prisoners' list, scanning the new material as it was delivered each morning from the front lines via OKW, Berlin.

Nothing. Now all that remained were the still active troops belonging to the British Expeditionary Force, who, having been squeezed out of Louvain, had fallen back across the Belgian border.

It was no good. Hitler had given him until the twenty-fourth to present the first phase of his plan. Guderian knew that if he had nothing by then the Führer would let slip the generals' leashes. He thought it ironic that the fate of so many British lives, the possibility of at least some sort of evacuation of the BEF to England, rested upon the shoulders of an unknown face somewhere in German intelligence files.

Erik Guderian noticed that, without his being conscious of it, his gaze had come to rest upon the radio on the table.

"Calais . . . the eyes of the Empire are upon Calais . . ."

He shook his head, pitying the hollow defiance of Eden's words. Calais was a lost cause. Guderian pulled the file containing lists of the still active units in the town. He had gone over the names before and found nothing new. Perhaps because in his mind they were already dead men, or at best, beaten prisoners . . . Yet for a reason he could not define he opened the file.

The British commander at Calais was Brigadier Harold Nicholson, who had one thousand French and three thousand British troops to deploy in defense of the port. The British units consisted of a battalion of the Queen Victoria Rifles and Territorial Motorcycle Battalion. There was also a unit of the Royal Artillery, whose soldiers manned the searchlights and, on the outskirts of the city, a battalion of the Royal Tank Regiment, which, as the first line of defense, was being chewed up by the Wehrmacht Panzers.

A dim but steady alarm began to sound in Guderian's mind. Quickly he checked the dates on the intelligence reports and found the cause: the first mention of the Royal Artillery had come in overnight. A crosscheck served to determine that three of its soldiers had been captured and proved most cooperative under interrogation. Guderian understood why: the Royal Artillery unit had no secrets to hide—no new weapons, no prominent role in any counterattack, nothing that would cause a man to suffer under the inquisitors. There appeared, on the surface, so little to tell that the German interrogators had padded their report with the names, ages and fighting experience of the entire unit. The captured soldiers had thought that the more information they gave, the more lenient their treatment would be. What good would their comrades' names be to Berlin in any case? If Calais fell these men would either be dead or captured. The lucky bastard or two unaccounted for might have slipped through German lines, heading for Dunkirk.

Erik Guderian realized that the inactive unit was no good to him. The criteria for the man he was seeking required that he belong to a quasi-civilian unit, recruited at the last moment, one that was near the battlefield but separated from the main combat forces by the nature of its duty. Finally, the unit had to be small in numbers. This, above all else, was crucial.

Guderian pressed on, reading what the prisoners of the Royal Artillery had to say about their support facilities. Halfway down the list his gaze froze. Very slowly, Guderian sat back. For almost a full minute he stared at it as combinations and permutations tumbled in his mind. He knew that he would not act at once, that the first order would be to gather more intelligence on this particular unit. He pushed up the sleeve of his tunic and glanced at his watch: 5:45, almost dawn. There was no time left.

Guderian reached for the telephone which connected him with Hitler's personal switchboard. The operator came on instantly.

"Call the military field at Schlepel," he ordered. "I want a Dornier bomber, with crew and escort fighters ready for take-off within the hour."

"*Sofort!*" the operator replied smartly.

"*Einen Moment!*" Guderian told him. "I also want an open circuit to the Führer at Berchtesgaden—immediately!"

Sometime in the dawn hours of May 24, Corporal Henry Schiffer, manning one of the searchlights at Calais Citadel, turned twenty-one. Slumped against the tires of the mobile platform, the young soldier celebrated his reaching the age of reason with a canteen of tepid tea and a half bottle of excellent brandy he had secreted away from the prying eyes of his mates since finding it two days ago. But a far better gift than the cognac was the shift in the air battle, which had moved from the docks to the outskirts of the city.

The young Canadian pressed his back against the tires, raised the bottle to his lips and drank deeply. The explosions that continued to reverberate around him were, for an instant, dispelled. Schiffer closed his eyes, willing the thunder from the air and the quaking of the earth beneath him to dispel. He had heard enough of the hellish screams of dive bombers, the infernal whine as bombs slipped their racks and fell to earth, of the staccato drumming of machine guns as their bullets raked his position time and again. Yet somehow the lights pinpointing the Nazi air assault on the Citadel and the harbor had remained intact. Hour after hour, night after night, the wavering fingers of light searched out the Nazi armadas, silhouetting them against a black-gray sky, following their flights so that the antiaircraft guns on land and the floundering destroyer *Wessex* could find targets of opportunity.

But four days of uninterrupted battle was more than the soul could endure. Henry Schiffer was not a man bred and toughened to withstand the screaming agonies of men around him. He could not remain at his post hour after hour, guiding the twenty-thousand-candlepower light across the sky while every second staring at the death that rained down from endless aircraft in the skies. So, when the air battle abruptly shifted from the harbor to outlying areas of the port, the young corporal collapsed. His eyes were burning from too much exposure to the lights, his hands and fingers trembled as much from fatigue as fright, a deep ingrained terror he perceived he would never rid himself of. Sitting there in the cold mud of Calais, listening to the battle, Corporal Schiffer guzzled more brandy and wondered how soon the end would come.

A short war, Schiffer thought to himself. A bloody, useless, short war. Gripping the truck's chassis with one hand, he staggered to his feet. To the east, its reflection shimmering in the oily, bloodied waters of the Strait, dawn was streaking along the rim of the sky. He took a final swig of cognac, knelt and deposited the bottle in a groove in the earth behind the rim of the tire. Drinking on duty was a court-martial offense, but Henry Schiffer didn't give a damn anymore.

Henry Schiffer staggered to his feet and came around to the side of the truck. The scene was exactly as he had anticipated: strewn around the body of the truck were the supine figures of his unit, the five of twenty left alive. Three were fast asleep, only their rising chests singling them out from the dead. The other two had their backs propped up against the tires, knees drawn up, vacant eyes staring into infinity. Schiffer shuffled past them, feeling their utter resignation and fatigue as he passed by. He kicked aside shell castings and leaned on the waist-high parapet, unbuttoning his collar so that the morning wind could refresh him.

Beyond the stone wall was the harbor of Calais. As the sun pierced the gloom augmented by dust, diesel fumes and smoke, Henry Schiffer saw the horrible finality of his condition and that of the garrison of Calais.

There were hundreds of men on the sandy dunes of Calais. Motor launches, trawlers, tugs and fishing boats, and other shallow-draft vessels which had slipped into Calais harbor during the night were still taking on the wounded: the blind, the crippled, the maimed; the conscious groping into the salt waters with open wounds, the unconscious being carried on the backs of those who deposited their burdens and returned to the shores for more. In the harbor itself the skeletal wreckage of what once were cranes was being unveiled by the dawn. Schiffer turned his head slowly, following the trail of devastation: the ruptured docks, their concrete bays now rubble, the wooden pilings choking the deep-water harbor, the warehouses and sheds that had collapsed amid the shriek of metal, the older timber buildings which still smoldered even though they had been the first to vanish, swallowed by the fires erupting from overhead incendiaries; the railway jetties with their splintered tracks, ruptured ties and gravel beds scattered.

Calais would surrender once more, no matter how valiant its defenders, regardless of the bloody singlemindedness of its commander. Only a matter of time now—days or perhaps only hours. The weight of butchery would in the end collapse its defense and then . . . then there would be nothing left. No time for retreat, perhaps a bullet through the heart . . . or a prisoner-of-war camp.

Suddenly Henry Schiffer began to tremble, his entire body shuddering as spasm upon spasm of fear swept through him. A prisoner . . . he had never conceived of the possibility! And as images of his mother and father, his home and his room, the family store and a girl flashed across his mind, he began crying, shoulders hunched forward, his breath coming in gasps broken by sobs. Far away he heard someone calling to him, but he did not move until he felt the hand upon his shoulder.

Three days earlier, on May 21, General Kurt von Hoven, commanding the first of two armored divisions that had moved up to the outskirts of Calais, had sent his opposite number an offer to surrender. Brigadier Harold Nicholson had replied with machine gun fire.

During the next seventy-two hours von Hoven's temper, stung by the Englishman's bravado, boiled over into wrath. A brilliant tactician, he had promised himself Calais in a single day. When he failed to take the port in the allotted time, he swore at his men to redouble their efforts. By the end of the third day, with the British holding out, von Hoven was at his wits' end. He had decided that the British were no longer worthy of being spared. To that end he had drawn up his tanks in a spearhead formation, prepared to assault and utterly demolish whatever stood in his way. The ground assault was to be coordinated with a Luftwaffe bombing run. Von Hoven was convinced that by the end of May 24, not one building would remain erect in the city he had come to loathe with such utter fury.

And undoubtedly everything would have gone as von Hoven had planned had it not been for the arrival of a certain Major Kleemann from Berlin late in the evening of May 23.

The General had made his field headquarters in an abandoned farmhouse half a kilometer from the city proper. It was in the kitchen that the two men had first met and now, after four hours, had not stirred from.

Von Hoven looked across the scarred wooden table at the younger man. From the first time he had set eyes on him the General had been bothered by a sense of familiarity. He swore to himself that somewhere he had met this Kleemann, but under what circumstances, or when, he couldn't place. A clock on the counter chimed midnight.

"*Herr General*, I trust you have examined my suggestions for deployment of your troops and have found everything satisfactory?"

Erik Guderian, whose papers from OKW, Berlin, identified him as Major Helmut Kleemann, drew his arm in an arc over the half dozen maps spread out on an adjoining surface—the family dinner table that had been unceremoniously dragged into the kitchen.

General von Hoven did not answer at once. Since Kleemann

had arrived carrying with him the imprimatur of OKW itself, armed with authority to order, *to order*, von Hoven to do his bidding, the General had burned up communication channels to Berlin. Yet every reply to his increasingly frantic demands for elucidation was the same: Kleemann is acting on the authority of the Führer himself. Every request is to be met and expedited. No queries into either Kleemann or the nature of his operation are in order. All replies had been signed by Chief of Staff Jodl.

"Yes, Major, I have gone over your strategy," von Hoven said slowly, intertwining his long, thick fingers. "Just so there are absolutely no misunderstandings, allow me to reiterate what it is you propose."

Von Hoven's tone was rich with irony.

"*You* say that instead of proceeding with my scheduled attack, which would take the Panzers from their current position *south* of the city into a north arc, splitting the British forces in half, I should move my tanks to the *east* and attack the sections farthest from the harbor."

"That is correct, *Herr General.*"

"And you also say that this attack is to be coordinated with bomber squadrons whose orders would be changed from attacking the harbor and Citadel to leveling the northeastern sector of the port."

"And those orders to the Luftwaffe should be transmitted as soon as possible, *Herr General*," Guderian suggested, "just so there is no misunderstanding."

Von Hoven ignored the implied command.

"At the same time as my soldiers are engaging the British, you, with your five men, will enter the city, dressed in civilian clothes, to initiate an operation whose details you cannot reveal to me."

"Exactly, *Herr General*. I suggest to you, and your own intelligence will bear me out, that the British are expecting an attack from the south. As weakened as they are, they will nevertheless fight with tenacity to keep the port open. Mere hours mean that many more lives saved, men evacuated. But if you attack from the east, they will have to shift defenses. And what will they be able to shift, General? Not the heavy artillery they've set in the harbor and Citadel. That will be of no use to them. They'll have to try to stop tanks with mere bullets."

"This venue will be slower," von Hoven retorted. "In the

end I shall slog my way *through* the city and *still* have to confront that artillery."

"I will do what I can to help you in that respect, *Herr General*," Guderian said quietly, "but only if my own mission has succeeded."

Von Hoven rose to his full height of six feet seven inches and glared down at the unknown officer.

"It would be far better, Major, if we were to coordinate our efforts," he said coldly. "Then perhaps we could accomplish both objectives, not just your own."

Guderian glanced down at his watch.

"It is now half past midnight. Your attack, as we've agreed, is scheduled to begin in two hours. I respectfully recommend, *Herr General*, that you make the appropriate arrangements with the Luftwaffe."

At 0200 hours Erik Guderian received a radio communication from Air Marshal Goering, Luftwaffe headquarters, Berlin. The air assault on Calais would take place as scheduled, the bombers unloading their death-dealing cargo along the coordinates Guderian had asked for.

At 0215 Guderian had his last meeting, a brief one, with von Hoven, and again went over the exact route he and his men would take into the city.

Twenty minutes later Guderian was reunited with his squad, which had moved into an old gasoline station on the southern outskirts of Calais. He adjusted the level of the kerosene flame and glanced at the men ringed around him. All of them, including himself, were dressed in civilian clothing, the usual baggy workman's trousers, field jackets and boots. But the clothing, while of French origin and design, had been modified. Interior pockets had been sewn in to carry the necessary equipment, sleeves and trouser legs widened to accommodate weapons strapped to forearms and thighs, shoulders padded so that the backs of jackets fell away from the body, hiding more matériel taped along the spine.

Guderian examined each man carefully, making certain nothing was amiss, then addressed the last three on the end.

"Latest intelligence reports only three skylight batteries in operation," he said. "They are within a hundred yards of each other, strung out along the Citadel wall."

He paused.

"Gentlemen, as you're all aware, we shall have very little

time once we reach the target area. Fortunately, there should be no more than six men to each searchlight battery. In fact, given the casualty rate there will probably be fewer.

"The man we are looking for should not be an officer, but rather a recent recruit: young, approximately my height and weight. If we can find one with the same complexion and hair color, so much the better."

"*Herr Major,*" the young veteran, Karl Horst, spoke up. "Are we looking for *any* man who fits that description or someone who might have intelligence value?"

"*Any* man, *Feldwebel,*" Guderian said. "He may be taken unconscious if necessary, but under no circumstances is he to be hurt—or, God forbid, killed.

"Under optimum conditions it should take us no longer than thirty minutes to examine the men in each of the remaining batteries. A team, which I lead, will go in first. B team will follow within fifteen minutes, tracing our route exactly. If, for any reason, A team is detected and a firefight erupts, B team shall withdraw.

"When we get our man, it shall be A team's responsibility to get him back, *alive*, to our lines. Our ingress and egress corridor has been deemed a no-fire zone. I personally saw to it that unit commanders understood this order. It is therefore of paramount importance that we move back the way we came in. B team will cover our retreat."

"*Herr Major,*" Karl Horst spoke up again. "We have discussed this mission and we feel that strategically it would be wiser for you to remain behind. We have just as good an idea of the man we're looking for as you do. Given the reasons we have to bring this man back alive, there is no point in your accompanying us."

Guderian smiled faintly. He had heard similar arguments, presented much more forcefully, by Gerd Jaunich in Berlin.

"*Herr Feldwebel*, your point is taken." Guderian hesitated, then added, "And your concern is appreciated. But in comparison to our other little ventures, Rotterdam, for instance, this foray should be accomplished without much ado, don't you think?

"And now, gentlemen, I suggest we move out. Goering himself has promised that this time the Luftwaffe will not be late."

Everyone, including Guderian, laughed.

On May 24, the German air offensive against Calais erupted at 4:14 in the morning. The Luftwaffe was almost a quarter hour late, but its attack fell along the coordinates Guderian had specified. The British, who had been anticipating the assault but not its location, were thrown into disarray.

As British troops desperately shifted across the city to meet von Hoven's Panzers, Erik Guderian and A team were crouched along a hedgerow fifty meters beyond the main road that skirts Calais to the south. As soon as he saw the Very-lamp signal, Guderian was moving, running hard across the meadow, headed straight for the light.

One of the reasons Guderian held the mission risks to be acceptable was the presence and discipline of the fifth column in Calais. These men and women were not expected to relay radio intelligence, although a number managed to do so. Their prime duty was to act as guides and spotters for Wehrmacht artillery and tanks. That Calais held out as long as it did was testimony to its defenders' ferocity rather than German strategy or lack of intelligence.

A few minutes before five o'clock, a half hour before dawn, A team had successfully penetrated the tattered British line. Staying off the main thoroughfares, alive now with the grinding of trucks and shouting of men as the British struggled to move across the city, Guderian led his unit through the back alleys, the lanes and courtyards, each of them had memorized. Failure to have done so would have spelled an end to their mission. There were few if any street signs left standing; those on the sides of buildings—what buildings were standing—had been ripped away.

Across the city the earth quaked under the whistling bombs. Staying well in the shadows, using the wreckage of houses for cover, A team made its way across the shattered port toward the Citadel. When they were within sight of the searchlight batteries, Guderian thrust his hand into a trouser pocket whose lining had been cut away. He withdrew it, his fingers clamped around the hard rubber handle of a twelve-inch commando stiletto. They were in the killing ground.

Guderian moved out first. Slipping out of the shadows, he made for the parapet in a crouching run. Slowly he straightened up and began to walk along the edge of the Citadel, affecting the staggering gait of a drunk, one arm clamped on Karl Horst's shoulder.

"Hey, Frenchie, save any of that wine for us fighting lads?"

Guderian braced himself on the parapet and twisted his body around. Ten or twelve meters away, he saw the indistinct shape of huddled men.

"Comment?" he rasped.

"Booze, Frenchie! *Vin!*" one of the soldiers snarled.

"Ne comprends pas," Guderian mumbled and lurched over, carefully looking at each of the men.

"Fucking frog arsehole!"

Guderian didn't answer. He was listening for the telltale scraping of boot leather on gravel, someone following. But after the oaths died away he heard nothing.

The *Feldwebel* left his side, went over to the soldiers and threw one a small, half-full bottle of cognac. Guderian watched as his sergeant squatted with the men, accepted a cigarette, then heaved himself to his feet and came back.

"Not even a resemblance," Horst muttered under his breath.

By the time the sun had swum over the horizon, A team had passed through two other batteries. It was an exhaustive, time-consuming search, broken by scrambles for cover whenever the Luftwaffe pilots overflew their bombing patterns and released their loads near the harbor. Guderian knew that the charade could not last much longer. Sooner or later they would be challenged.

Guderian was approaching the final searchlight battery when he noticed a soldier leaning heavily on the stone wall. Guderian caught sight of the man's face, smelled the drink on his breath, but reacted too late. Karl Horst was already by the man's side, helping him lean over the wall. Guderian heard the sickening sound of retching, and saw his *Feldwebel*'s brief nod. Then the soldier turned around and Guderian knew the hunt had ended. Quietly he slipped away, making for the last battery.

Tea. That was the first smell that caught his nostrils as Guderian approached the battery. The next was that of cold rank sweat, the dirt and debris men had lived with and in for days on end. They were a pitiful lot, the three soldiers huddled together in a shallow bomb crater, their coats wrapped tightly around them, hands thrust out over the steam that rose from a tin bucket suspended over glowing coals.

"'Ay, English!" Guderian called out softly, his voice hoarse.

One of the three turned around to see a Frenchman weaving his way toward the crater, his hand patting his jacket pocket.

"Lord love a duck—a Frenchie with some booze!"

The soldier closest to Guderian scrambled out of the ditch. He was young, no more than twenty, with blond hair and skin that was so crusted with dirt that the eyes appeared white, like a death's-head.

"What have you got for us then, Frenchie?"

Guderian took one more step, so close now he was repelled by the soldier's rancid breath, and slid the stiletto in hard. The babyfaced Englishman stared in terror at Guderian. His hand shot out and dropped on the German's shoulders. His mouth opened, the lips trembling. But he died as Guderian knew he would, with only a sigh.

"Get on with it, then. Where's the bloody drink?"

The two remaining soldiers were looking at them over their shoulders. Guderian gripped the dead man by his waist and began dragging him to the hole. The knife was already in his right hand.

"Christ, Charlie, one dram and you've had the biscuit—"

The soldier's laughter died as Guderian dumped the body on top of him. In the same instant he jumped into the crater, his forward motion carrying him over the steaming bucket and onto the third soldier. In one motion Guderian slit his throat. Then, without pause, he jumped onto the last soldier. As the knife went in, Guderian heard a rib snap. The soldier groaned and began to thrash his arms, hitting Guderian on the side of the head. The knife was withdrawn and thrust again, held deep in the chest cavity.

Guderian did not move. He remained like that, leaning hard against the soldier, his head held up, ears straining for the sound of someone approaching. His ears were deafened by the thunder of exploding bombs, the return fire of antiaircraft guns. But around him, as in the eye of a hurricane, nothing moved. In the midst of so much destruction, this silent killing had gone unnoticed. Guderian pushed himself off the body, wiped the knife on the dead soldier's coat and climbed out of the crater, running back to the wall, where Karl Horst was still standing beside the soldier.

"Corporal!" Guderian said briskly, using his best British accent.

Slowly the cadaverous, fear-torn face turned toward him, the reddened eyes glistening with tears.

"It's time to go, Corporal," Guderian said. "You're wanted at HQ."

For a moment Schiffer didn't reply. His mouth was working but no words emerged. "No," he whispered at last. "My mates . . . I have to stay with my mates." He looked at Guderian, pleading.

"I understand," Guderian said gently. He reached out as though to comfort the man, but instead his thumb and fore-finger circled the side of Schiffer's neck and the carotid artery was pinched hard.

At 0556, units A and B were back behind German lines, their prisoner still unconscious.

8

"What I wish to know, Mr. Pearce, is what exactly provoked that bloody incident involving you and Mr. Cabot and, more to the point, *why wasn't I told about it?*"

Joseph Kennedy was seated behind his desk, a slim, erect figure with freckled scalp, round clear plastic frame glasses, a tight mouth that spat out his words. He was wearing his habit-ual gray suit, cut for him by Lankin of Savile Row, with a red-and-black-striped tie and white linen handkerchief in the breast pocket.

Beneath his patina of earnestness Edward Pearce was watch-ing carefully to see if the falsehood would hold. A scant half hour before they had been summoned by the Ambassador, Mackenzie McConnell had telephoned Pearce, tipping him off that somehow Kennedy had gotten wind of the shooting at Leatherhead. A brief three-way conversation that included Cabot resulted in the subsequent fabrication.

"Mr. Ambassador," Pearce began in his best Western drawl, "I was asked by British security to sit on what happened out in Leatherhead. You're aware, sir, of just how embarrassing this is for the Brits, Americans being shot at on their home turf. They wanted time to find out who was responsible so that they could give you something concrete by way of explanation."

"May I remind you that your first responsibility is to this office and this embassy," Kennedy said icily. "I have not yet lodged a formal complaint with the Home Office, because this matter just came to my attention. I also wanted to speak with you first. But rest assured I will not permit this issue to be treated lightly!"

"I assure you, Mr. Ambassador, the British are just as concerned as we are—" Pearce started to say.

"Precisely my point," Kennedy retorted. "And if by the end of the working day I don't receive satisfaction from their efforts I'll light a fire under them myself!"

Kennedy paused.

"But perhaps *you* can enlighten me further, Mr. Pearce."

"Mr. Ambassador, I have nothing more to add to my report," Pearce said. "Until the British get hold of the gunners we won't know why I was targeted—"

"You or Mr. Cabot?" snapped Kennedy.

"With all due respect to Mr. Cabot's skills, Mr. Ambassador, there is no conceivable reason why he, a cipher technician, should have been the target of *any* violence. Besides, no one knew he'd be arriving when he did—"

"Precisely, Mr. Pearce!" Kennedy interjected. "Not even *I* was informed."

Pearce reached into his vest pocket and drew out a carbon copy green sheet.

"A memo I forwarded to your office four days ago informing you that State was sending a man over to restructure our cipher machines."

Kennedy took the carbon copy, barely glanced at it before tossing it aside.

He walked from behind his desk, past the two men, running his fingertips along the glass-enclosed bookcase that housed his library of Irish literature, mythology and poetry.

"And you, Mr. Cabot?" he asked suddenly. "Have *you* any idea why your arrival provoked such a spectacle?"

"Mr. Ambassador," Pearce protested, "Cabot's arrival had nothing—"

"I'm addressing Mr. Cabot!" the Ambassador cut him off.

"Sir, my arrival was kept secret by Washington and on this end by Mr. Pearce," Cabot said. "There is no way anyone, excluding those parties concerned, could have known otherwise. Therefore it is simply not feasible to think the attack was directed against me."

"Perhaps," Kennedy said thoughtfully. "Mr. Cabot, have you been involved with our embassy before?"

"No, Mr. Ambassador."

"Have you been to London?"

"Only briefly, a couple of years ago."

"I see." Kennedy came around and planted himself a few feet from Cabot so that he wouldn't have to incline his head to look up at him.

"You're from Boston, aren't you?" Kennedy said softly.

"Yes, sir."

"Baylor Cabot's boy?"

Kennedy's lips curled as he spoke. The contempt was naked, born of generations of resentment by families such as the Kennedys, whose clan was founded on the Boston docks and in the saloons, while the Cabots had already established their pedigree.

"Baylor Cabot was my father, Mr. Ambassador."

"And his son is serving in the United States State Department as a telephone repairman?" Kennedy snorted. "Do you really expect me to believe that, sir?"

"I am a mathematician by training, Mr. Ambassador," Cabot replied.

Kennedy shook his head. "I want to see your file, son."

"I'm sure State will forward it as quickly as possible," Pearce offered.

"That they will, Mr. Pearce, that they will."

Kennedy narrowed his brows, the light from the chandelier making his glasses opaque, his eyes disappearing.

"I have read your orders, Mr. Cabot, at least those which accompanied you. I shall be frank with you and say openly that I do not believe your responsibilities here are as limited as they or you make them out to be. Therefore, sir, I shall be watching your progress very keenly. Keep that in mind as you proceed.

"As for you, Mr. Pearce, when you're speaking to your

opposite numbers in London, don't forget to mention that I will have satisfaction!

"That is all for now, gentlemen. Good day!"

Joseph Kennedy waited until he was sure Cabot and Pearce had passed through the waiting room, then depressed a button on the intercom.

"Miss Dunn, call Frye and have him come up immediately."

While he waited for his head cryptographer to appear, Kennedy reread the memo concerning Cabot's arrival. The Ambassador had a prodigious memory for trivia—or for details—depending on whom one asked. The words he was reading were completely unfamiliar. He would swear he had never read the original of Pearce's memo. On impulse Kennedy jabbed the intercom button again.

"Miss Dunn, get me a memo original, dated May 18, from Pearce."

"Yes, Mr. Ambassador. And Mr. Frye is here. Shall I send him in?"

"Please, Miss Dunn."

Physically Leonard Frye was not, in the Ambassador's opinion, a handsome or appealing man. He was of medium height but appeared shorter because he was substantially overweight. His skin always had a pale, unhealthy hue to it, as though for some reason Frye avoided sunlight where possible. He used excessive amounts of brilliantine on his hair, plastering it down across his scalp; and his teeth were crooked, stained, like the short stubby fingers, by too much nicotine. The thick-lens glasses magnified the watery eyes, and a slightly rumpled suit gave off the distinct odor of stale food. As if his appearance were not enough against him, Leonard Frye also had a speech impediment which caused him to stutter when he was nervous.

"Sit down, Leonard," Kennedy said.

"Th–thank you, sir."

Leonard Frye eased his bulk into a chair before Kennedy's desk and smiled at his boss. Whatever Frye's shortcomings may have been, there was no question about his personal loyalty to the Ambassador or his brilliance as a cryptographer. Frye was a genius not only at deciphering codes but at constructing new ones which were virtually unbreakable.

"Frye, does the name Jonathan Cabot mean anything to you?" asked Kennedy.

The cryptographer considered the question for a moment

even though he already had the answer. Frye's memory was encyclopedic and he was certain he had never come across that name.

"N–no, sir," he said firmly.

"You're sure?"

"I am, sir."

"Do you recall Edward Pearce receiving a priority cable concerning such a man?"

Frye shook his head slowly. "No, Mr. Ambassador. I can tell you with absolute certainty that I never decoded any transmissions for Mr. Pearce in which a Jonathan Cabot was mentioned."

The cryptographer paused. "That's not to say, Mr. Ambassador, that Mr. Pearce couldn't have received communications concerning this man. You're aware that as chief of embassy security Pearce has his own machine and link with State."

Kennedy tapped the tip of a silver letter opener against the leather blotter.

"Yes, I know," he said quietly. "Tell me, do you know of any reason why State would send a technician over to overhaul our cipher machines?"

Frye's heavy black eyebrows furrowed.

"No, sir. Our communications are secure and all the equipment is functioning properly."

Frye hesitated. "Excuse me, s–sir, but *has* State sent someone over for an overhaul?"

Kennedy smiled and turned to the intercom.

"Miss Dunn, that memo from Pearce . . ."

The voice that answered him was clearly flustered.

"I'm sorry, sir, it's not in my files. I've checked back two weeks in case I misfiled it or the date was incorrect. But it's simply not here."

"That's fine, Miss Dunn. Forget about it for now. Thank you."

"You see, Frye, State tells me only what they wish to tell me," Kennedy said, the bitterness light and smooth upon the words. Frye recognized the danger signals. He lowered his eyes, not wanting to be a part of Kennedy's embarrassment.

The letter opener dropped with a rattle.

"But we're putting an end to that, Frye," Kennedy said sharply. "Slowly but surely we're putting an end to it!"

"Yes, sir!" Frye said enthusiastically. Better than most the cryptographer was aware of the constraints Kennedy worked under. Frye dealt frequently with his opposites at Whitehall. Although the British decoders were under strict orders not to discuss their work with the Americans, most tried to be decent about Frye—which meant including him at parties and pub gatherings where liquor loosened tongues. After such encounters Frye reported faithfully to Kennedy.

"Frye, you have good contacts in State."

"Yes, sir, I trained most of State's cryptographic p–personnel," Frye said modestly.

"I want to have information on Cabot," Kennedy said tightly. "Over and above what is in his file—if I ever get his file. If he does have genuine connections with State cryptography I want to know about them. If not, then I *must* know who the hell he is, who sent him and why!"

"I understand, sir."

"I want nothing on paper about this," Kennedy warned him. "We do this on our own initiative, in our own way. However, if for some reason State queries us or our communications to the White House—"

"That won't happen, sir," Frye promised him. "I c–can assure you of that."

"But if it does," Kennedy finished, "I will take full responsibility."

"Sir—" Frye pleaded. He couldn't bear to have his Ambassador expose himself like this.

"No, Frye. I can tolerate so much. But if Cabot is not who he says he is, then I'm afraid the President has gone one step too far . . ."

"Y–yes–sir," Frye stammered.

He understood only too well the acrimony between his Ambassador and Roosevelt. Kennedy cut an independent, sometimes infuriating, always controversial, figure. He visited Lord and Lady Astor at Cliveden, whose "Cliveden Set," composed of influential writers, politicians and bankers, conspired none too silently to keep Britain out of another European conflict. Three weeks after the Munich appeasement, at the annual Trafalgar Day dinner at London's Navy League, Kennedy preached the common ground between democracies and dictatorships, stating that they had to live together in a single world whether they liked it or not. Comments like these, coupled with Kennedy's undisguised pro-isolationist sentiments, infuriated British public officials and caused resentment throughout the country. As a result Frye had discovered that more and more Washington-London traffic was routed around Kennedy, who was quick to take offense. But by the time Churchill took office it was a fact of embassy political life not to ask the Ambassador certain questions pertaining to the unannounced Anglo-American alliance. More often than not Kennedy had no inkling of what was going on between Roosevelt and the State Department, and Whitehall.

"I will do my very best, sir," Frye whispered.

"I am counting on that," Kennedy told him heavily. "Very much so."

"Kennedy's scared," Cabot said after they were back in Pearce's office. "For some reason I've rattled him. And it's not the Boston connection. He knows better than to believe that I'm a technician, but he doesn't have anything concrete to disprove that. You can bet he'll be smoking the channels between here and Washington to try and find out exactly what it is I am doing here."

"He won't get much," Pearce said.

"He won't get anything—and that will make him even more vicious. But there's something else. Kennedy *suspects* I'm an investigator. The shooting ground would confirm as much to someone who was already worried about skeletons. But *what* is he worried about, Edward?"

"If he suspects what you're here for, then that means he also suspects a leak," Pearce said, his voice harsh. "If that's the case, and we come up with someone who's a favorite of his, I'm going to hang Joe Fucking Kennedy out to dry! Because he hasn't said a word to me about anything!"

"I take it then that Kennedy has his own little Mafia here?" asked Cabot.

"He loves his favorites," Pearce acknowledged. "Anyone who's not a Roosevelt man is gold to him. If the election were called tomorrow, and only Grosvenor Square counted, Kennedy would win by sixty, seventy percent. To work here is to know what side the butter is on."

"Do you think Kennedy will talk about his suspicions?" asked Cabot.

"One way or another, if he thinks you're gunning for someone here—himself for instance—word will get out."

"Time," Cabot murmured. "The son of a bitch and that shooting are going to cost me time."

"I wish I could do more, Johnny." He paused and looked across at Cabot. "I don't like the idea of you walking around out there like an arcade duck."

Cabot drained his cup and rose. "I'll be all right as long as I know you're covering my back."

Outside, the city was veiled in a fine mist that drifted across the streets. It clung to the steeples of churches or wove itself around trees, then was shepherded across the sky only to ensnare itself on a smokestack or one of the great towers that guard the bridges across the Thames.

Cabot paused under the embassy portico, drew up the collar of his trenchcoat and looked out onto Grosvenor Square. The park was empty, its gravel paths quickly filling with puddles as the fine incessant rain streamed from invisible clouds. The green of the grass contrasted sharply with the wet black trees and the wrought-iron spiked fence that ran along the perimeter. Not even the caretakers would be out today. There would be no one to clean up after. Thousands of London children who, even on a day like this, would have passed through here, had been evacuated into the country along with their mothers.

Suddenly Cabot moved, descending the wide stone steps two at a time, his eyes flitting from left to right, scanning the sidewalks on either side of the embassy, watching for a telltale movement in a doorway down the street or the emergence of a car. Nothing. He hunched his shoulders into the wind and moved down Grosvenor. Five minutes elapsed before he spotted a cab.

The driver was an elderly man with wispy hair flying out from under his cap and knobby arthritic fingers. He cupped the steering wheel in his palms.

"Where to, guv?"

"Harmsworth Hospital on Brooke Drive," Cabot said, slamming the door.

"Yank, ain't ye?"

"Yank," Cabot agreed. He leaned forward and dropped a five-pound note on the seat beside the driver. "And in a hurry."

The driver slammed down the meter flag.

"Your kind always is," he said with a satisfaction of a man expressing a self-evident truth.

The room was functionally soulless. A threadbare carpet was tacked onto the floor. There was a scarred old dresser in one corner and a rickety night table with a lamp beside the hospital-issue bed. The flowers Mackenzie McConnell had brought were in a thin vase on the windowsill.

Robert Ogilvy's eyes had been closed when she had come in. And just as well, because Mackenzie recoiled at the sight of what she saw. In that instant she permitted the full horror of her reaction to spill across her features. Robert Ogilvy opened his eyes, saw her revulsion and Mackenzie knew he had tricked her.

"Doesn't look all *that* bad, does it now?" Ogilvy asked, his voice cracked.

Mackenzie came forward and sat on the edge of the bed, unable to keep from staring at him. Just above the forehead the thick black hair had been shaved so that the surgeons could get at the scalp wounds. A deep black furrow, running from the corner of the right eye to the edge of the lips completely disfigured half the face. The lower lip had been split open and was swollen to twice its normal size. Another fragment of metal had gouged away the flesh over the left cheek. Mercifully, part of that damage was hidden by a bandage. But the full effect could not be diminished: Robert Ogilvy, once a handsome man, was mutilated for life.

"You can't bear to touch me, is that it?" Ogilvy asked, reaching for her hand. He found the fingers lifeless to his touch.

"I'm afraid to hurt you, Robert," Mackenzie said, the turquoise eyes made enormous by welling tears.

"They say there will be scar tissue," Ogilvy said conversationally, as though he were rendering a clinical evaluation. "But as soon as that heals they can begin reconstructive surgery."

His hand trailed up her arm, but couldn't reach past the elbow. Mackenzie did not move closer.

"I'm glad you came," he whispered. "You don't know how much I've thought about you."

His voice broke. "I was afraid you wouldn't be here."

"I will always be here when you need me," Mackenzie said, and bit her lip.

Ogilvy did not miss the hesitation. Deep in his heart he knew there was no hope, but lying in that bed, with the memory of what his face looked like in the mirror, he could not abandon the illusion.

"Do you want to know about the investigation—" she started to say.

"No!" he said sharply. "Not now. There have been too many investigations, too much damn work already. That's what came between us!"

Ogilvy fell silent and Mackenzie knew exactly what was going through his mind. The same memories had streamed through her mind when she had heard him cry out, saw him lying in the dirt, his face a bloodied canvas.

Their attraction had been instantaneous, their lives fused together as soon as Ogilvy had walked into the offices at Queen Anne's Gate. They became lovers the first night, each feeding on the other in a desperate attempt to fill appetites long unsated. For a long time, or so it seemed because of their voracity, their bodies spoke for them and they did not believe consummation possible.

But those were the days before the war, when work was a routine and hours could be stolen. After September 1939, Mackenzie's work became more and more pressing. Conferences, travel, meetings that would go on for days, all conspired toward separation. When she did return home it was to a man who could be told nothing of where she had been or what she had done. Unlike Mackenzie, who was an executive officer at MI5, Robert Ogilvy was only a field agent. The beginning of the end came when both realized that one would have to execute the orders of the other. The imbalance had at last been struck.

Still they tried to preserve the frailty, civilly at first, then desperately, two people seeing but refusing to accept the erosion that had set in. And every day, as Mackenzie withdrew into her secret world, a little more of the passion died to be replaced by recriminations, insults and mindless anger. When passion was extinguished even respect began to crumble.

"You'll be back soon, Robert," Mackenzie said softly.

God, her heart went out to this man! But not for the reasons he still believed in . . . because of the past. She felt for him as she would for any person she worked with who had been injured in the line of duty. Mackenzie almost lost her resolve then. Line of duty . . . cold words, yet that was all she had left for him.

". . . you?"

"I'm sorry, Robert, I wasn't listening."

"Back with you?" he repeated. "Together?"

"No, Robert," she said quietly in a firm voice that would not deceive him. "We can't have it like that, not ever again. We have to work together—"

"Damn the work!" Ogilvy said harshly, the venom in his words almost choking him. "We can do it differently, I swear—"

"Don't start, Robert, please!" she begged him. "Not now . . . not ever. Can't you understand?"

"It's my face, isn't it," Ogilvy said wonderingly. "It's what's bloody happened to me, isn't it?"

His fingers tightened on her elbow. Instinctively Mackenzie bent his wrist back and jumped off the bed.

"You told me you would never hurt me, Robert," she said, her voice dead. "Is this how you keep your word?"

"But you won't understand!" Ogilvy cried.

"No, Robert, I do. You want me to pity you, and come back to you for that alone. But I think you're better than that. I could never pity you. Only you could do that to yourself."

She left so quickly that Ogilvy almost thought she had never been there. Except for the lingering scent.

"Mr. Cabot?"

A young, bespectacled physician whose fresh face and shock of red hair made him appear no more than twenty crossed the checkerboard floor of the reception area.

"I'm Cabot."

"Doctor Griswald. Terribly pleased to meet you."

The physician's grip was exceptionally strong. Even beneath the shapeless smock Cabot could see the bulge of the forearms and shoulders. Dr. Griswald was a cutter.

"I'm looking for a Robert Ogilvy."

"Ah, yes, Mr. Ogilvy. Not my patient, but then again Doctor Fine isn't on duty at the moment. You're not a relative by any chance, are you?"

"I was with Ogilvy when he was injured."

"Oh, I see, yes," Griswald murmured. "Nasty cuts, but fortunately nothing major. Come along, I'll take you to him."

They took the birdcage elevator to the fourth floor of the house and Griswald guided him down a carpeted, paneled corridor. The hospital was a mixture of old genteel and hastily put together new rooms.

"The decorating leaves *much* to be desired," Griswald laughed. "But really the facilities are first-rate."

"I'm sure they are."

"Mr. Ogilvy's in this room," said Griswald, indicating an unstained oak door that still had the smell of the sawmill to it. "He hasn't been sleeping all that well, so please don't tire him."

Cabot pushed open the door and stepped inside.

"Well, aren't you a brave one!"

The voice was cracked through with dry hatred. Robert Ogilvy was lying on his bed, propped up by pillows. It was all Cabot could do to keep his eyes on the agent's face and not flinch.

"I'm Cabot—"

"I know who the bloody hell you are! Come to have a look at your handiwork, have you?"

Cabot approached the bed. "I came to say I'm sorry for what happened, to see if you were all right . . . if there was anything I could get you."

"No thanks, Yank," Ogilvy rasped, each word causing him obvious pain. "Go peddle your fags and nylons to someone else."

The wounded man pushed himself up by the elbows, the coal-black eyes riveted on Cabot.

"You might say I got off lucky," Ogilvy spat out. "If one of the bullets from your fucking gun had even nicked me, I'd have bled to death."

Slowly the wounded agent moved a trembling hand across his face, speaking as he did so.

"Is that what you're using these days, Yank, mercury tips? Enjoy disfigurement, do you?"

"I didn't know—"

"That's right, Yank, you didn't! And you were too stupid to wait, weren't you? Started shooting even before you knew who the enemy was."

Ogilvy's fingers hovered over his facial wounds and his voice dropped to a whisper.

"When I become active again, Yank, you'd better not go anywhere near me. Because the minute I see you I'm going to remember that big gun of yours. And I'll kill you, you smug bastard, so help me, I'll shoot you fucking dead!"

"Robert, that's enough!"

Neither man had heard Mackenzie McConnell enter. Neither knew that on her way out she had chanced to glimpse Cabot rounding the corner and guessed exactly where he was going . . . and what would happen once he got there. She had run back to Ogilvy's room to prevent just that. Mackenzie gripped Cabot by the arm.

"Leave him alone now," she said, the command unmistakable.

Cabot took a long last look at Robert Ogilvy, his eyes absorbing every feature of the agent's face, memorizing the hatred and loathing. He thrust open the door and walked to the end of the corridor into a small sitting area beneath a stained-glass bay window.

"I must apologize for Robert, Mr. Cabot," Mackenzie said, taking a seat on the padded sill. "Before joining us he worked undercover in Germany. Three years without a scratch. Now this . . ."

Her voice trailed off and she looked away. The light refracted off the glass behind her, bathing her face in a golden-green glow, cascading off her hair. She was wearing a long tweed skirt, set off by tall, oxblood boots. When she turned back to Cabot he saw a cameo pinned to her lime-colored blouse just below the throat.

"I wanted to tell him I was sorry for what happened," Cabot said. "See if he was going to be all right . . ." He paused. "Does Ogilvy have a problem with Americans?"

Mackenzie McConnell drew out a cigarette from a tin and struck the match. He saw her fingers trembling.

"Not really," she said softly, the smoke flaring her nostrils. "It's something altogether different."

Her fingertips brushed Cabot's hand.

"But it's still no excuse for his behavior. I am sorry."

"So am I," Cabot said quietly. He was suddenly overwhelmed by her presence, all too conscious of her scent, the frank appraisal in her eyes. Deep within him, beyond the pain and the loss, something stirred and reached out toward her. Perhaps because he recognized pain in another, in her.

"I think we ought to go," he said at last.

Her car was a white Jaguar, the supercharged SS100, which

she drove like a champion. Between the roar of the engine and wind shrieking through the cracks in the canvas, conversation was impossible. She got them across the river and across to the southern side of St. James's Park in what Cabot figured had to be record time.

"Where did you learn to drive like that?" Cabot grunted, extricating himself from the sports car seat.

"At Le Mans for Aston Martin."

Queen Anne's Gate ran off of Birdcage Walk, at the eastern boundary of the Wellington Barracks. It was one of a warren of quiet, seemingly residential streets whose town houses were all bloated red brick, white window shutters and shining black doors with ornate brass knockers. Number 12, home of the British Security Service, trade name MI5, was no different.

"Before you say it's such a little operation, let me say that we own the entire block. None of the other front doors will open."

"Rule number one," Cabot murmured, cupping her elbow as they walked. "Never put your foot in your mouth."

Mackenzie McConnell smiled. He wasn't, she decided, an unattractive man. She liked the way his brown curls framed his face, open and honest when his features were relaxed, as they were now. His hands were large, the fingers long and very powerful, yet the nails were carefully manicured, a sign of the attention he gave to detail. His height and the way he carried his weight were instinctively reassuring. The confidence he projected was quiet but unmistakable. But beneath the obvious breeding, the education and refinement, Mackenzie McConnell concluded that Jonathan Baylor Cabot had never truly mastered the violence within him. She had seen other men in the circumstances of an ambush. None of these even came close to Cabot's instantaneous response at Leatherhead. None had had the ferocity with which he used his weapon, the murderous singlemindedness that had made his gun an extension of himself.

The young man who opened the door might have been the doorman to an exclusive club—warm smile, empty hands. But out of the corner of his eye Cabot caught the real security: another agent standing in what once had been a coat closet, arms thrust straight out, a Webley magnum gripped in both hands, pointed at temple level. Mackenzie McConnell pretended not to notice anything. She swept straight through the postage stamp size reception area, pecked a kiss on the cheek of the elderly switchboard operator, and made for the staircase. Across the way in another room a typewriter was being battered with singleminded ferocity, while down the hall a kettle whistled. Over everything hung the inoffensive odor of lemon tea.

"Let me take your coat," Mackenzie McConnell said once they were in her office.

"Are these your father's works?" Cabot asked her, indicating the calfbound row of books on the shelf.

"Yes," she answered, smiling. "From his meandering days in Arabia and North Africa."

"With Harry St. John Philby."

"That's right." She paused. "Philby's son, Kim, works for our opposite number as liaison. But then I imagine you knew that."

Cabot came over to her desk. "I did."

There was nothing, he thought to himself, in the office to give an indication as to what kind of person occupied it. Nothing except her father's books.

"I travel very lightly," Mackenzie McConnell said, reading his thoughts.

"Sometimes that's the best way."

"Before we get started, Mr. Cabot, is there anything you would like to know about me?"

He offered her a cigarette but she declined. "I prefer my own, thanks."

Cabot leaned forward and lit hers. "Just one thing: do you think you could call me Jonathan?"

She laughed, a deep rich throaty laugh that warmed him.

"Yes, I could. And you can use my first name too, as long as you don't follow the tendencies of your countrymen and reduce it to 'Mac.'"

"Fair enough."

"Now, then—where shall we begin? I take it you've ingeniously explained away Leatherhead to your Ambassador after he managed to learn about it."

Cabot gave her an abbreviated version of his and Pearce's meeting with Kennedy.

"All of which means that you and I will have to move very quickly. No time for niceties."

"How do you mean?"

From his inside jacket pocket Cabot produced a single sheet of paper with seven names typed on it.

"The three operators who handled the Churchill–Grosvenor Square switchboard and four cryptographers who work at the embassy. Two of the operators are British, two cryptographers have married British girls since coming over for the posting."

"And you propose to concentrate on these first?" Mackenzie McConnell asked, a hard edge to her voice.

"No, I suggest we split up. You handle the British. You know what to look for. You can go where they go without being obvious, ask questions I could never get answers to."

"Then you'll take the Yankee side, as it were," Mackenzie McConnell said. "Even though there's more of them."

"That doesn't matter," Cabot told her. "By the time we finish with the first few the rest will know what to expect."

"What do you mean?"

"Exactly this," Cabot said, leaning forward to grind out his cigarette.

It took him a full hour to explain the plan he had formed, another hour to answer Mackenzie McConnell's objections and agree with some suggestions.

"You're a very hard man, Jonathan Cabot," she said when they were through. "You appreciate what this is going to do to the innocent parties?"

"I wish I had a fairer alternative," Cabot said softly.

9

Erik Guderian poured out two glasses of brandy and pushed one toward his prisoner. Schiffer's fingers trembled as he reached for the glass, and even though he had both hands on it he spilled half the liquor on his mud-caked field jacket. Guderian raised his own glass and quickly downed the fiery drink.

The interrogation took place in the barn next to General von Hoven's field headquarters. It lasted six and a half hours and had been conducted by Guderian alone. The transcript of questions and answers had been written out in his longhand, an old door mounted on sawhorses serving as the desk. No one else had been permitted near the prisoner. While Guderian had sequestered himself with Schiffer, *Die Piraten* quietly regrouped, changed from civilian clothing into field uniforms, gathered their armament and waited for the interrogation to end. They had been advised at the start of the mission that their duties would end only after Schiffer had been safely delivered to the Action Group camp in southern Germany.

"Are you hungry?" Guderian asked Schiffer. "There's some cold meat and cheese if you like."

Henry Schiffer shook his head with what appeared to Guderian to be a great deal of effort. The Canadian corporal pushed his glass toward the bottle and Guderian obliged.

Henry Schiffer had been born in the small Canadian town of Kitchener in the province of Ontario. Before the Great War Kitchener had been known as New Berlin, testimony to the thousands of German and Austrian immigrants who had settled there at the turn of the century. Schiffer's father had immigrated to Canada after the German defeat of 1918. In a few short years, despite the silent contempt of local English residents, he had established a thriving butcher's trade which quickly expanded into a small meat packing plant.

The elder Schiffer married a Canadian girl ten years his junior, and when the son was born, deferred to her preference of a name. Henry Albert Schiffer was his true name, but at home his father invariably called him Hans.

The success of the family business was such that Henry Schiffer completed not only undergraduate studies in Toronto but was funded for further studies at the University of London, where he started the first stage of his master of engineering degree. Then, on February 2, 1940, for a reason which now escaped him, he had enlisted in the British Army.

As a Canadian Henry Schiffer had not been required to register. Although Canada, following the rest of the Empire, had declared war on Germany in autumn of 1939, Schiffer could have either returned to his native country for induction or waited until the overseas Army had arrived in Britain. But he didn't. Whether it was the bent-for-hell fever of young men around him, the embarrassment (which he readily acknowledged) of being an ablebodied man not in service, or some notion of patriotism, he couldn't say. Still, one morning Henry Schiffer presented himself at an Army recruiting center and subsequently disappeared within the khaki bureaucracy. After five weeks of basic, the Army in its infinite wisdom sent him not into the Engineers Corps, where Schiffer might have provided a valuable contribution, but into the Royal Artillery. Without any training in the use of deployment of antiaircraft weapons or their attendant searchlights, Henry Schiffer arrived on the docks of Calais scarcely a week before the Germans launched their offensive against the French port.

Guderian knew that better than half the battle for control of Schiffer's mind had been fought for him even before he had reached the Canadian soldier. Schiffer's senses had been pounded by battle for the last fourteen days. He had lived in the midst of blood and screams, had watched his comrades fall into muddy graves, had had to breathe the air of retreat . . . defeat. When Guderian had sat him down, Schiffer refused to speak, not out of duty or truculence but simply because he couldn't put into words a single coherent thought. So instead of questioning Schiffer for military information, Guderian had taken a personal tack, carefully leading him back through his time in London, then onto the liner that had brought him over from Canada, to Halifax, where the ship had sailed from, and before, to the train ride that had taken sixteen hours from Toronto to the Nova Scotia port.

With infinite patience, supplemented by hot coffee and fresh crusty bread, which Schiffer could keep down, Guderian spun the boy's life back like a movie reel in reverse. The more Schiffer talked, the more details he provided of his own accord, which led to even more delicate, tentative questions. Several times he stopped and regarded Guderian suspiciously, as though he had caught him at something.

"I'm not saying anything about my mates!" he said loudly. "I won't be giving you any information like that . . ."

And Guderian assured him that he wasn't going to ask Schiffer to compromise himself.

"What do you want then?" the corporal had demanded. "I keep telling you about me but . . . but that's all you'll get. Why do you want to know?"

Guderian told him there were other men, hard men, who

asked for the military details, intimating that he could protect the boy from them. All he wanted to know was what kind of troops had been holding Calais, where they came from, what they had left behind . . .

The explanation was so veiled that of his own accord Schiffer went back to his personal history. Guderian was certain Schiffer never suspected that in fact he was telling Guderian exactly what the German had to know. Young, cold, swept with fatigue and alone without any possible help, Henry Schiffer talked for hours on end, in that dead monotone of the war-torn, his voice breaking with emotion only when he stumbled across memories that still had the power to make him feel. And as he spoke he felt the occasional flashes of pride and self-respect that here he was, a prisoner, getting the better of his German victor. For his part Guderian kept on writing, steering the narrative monologue with subtle questions here and there, the way a master sailor uses the delicate touch of his ropes. So it was that both men knew, at the same instant, when there was nothing more to say. Only then did Guderian give him the brandy which in a matter of minutes would bring the exhaustion crashing upon Schiffer's head.

"What will you do with me now?" the Canadian asked thickly.

"You'll be transferred to a camp in Germany," Guderian told him.

Schiffer stared into his glass. "Bloody short war, wasn't it?"

"Sometimes those are the best kind."

"Tell that to my mates!" Schiffer shouted at once. "They'll get back. You'll see! Gort'll never leave them behind. They'll get back."

Guderian said nothing. All surviving soldiers in Schiffer's battery had had to be killed. Guderian couldn't have taken the chance of even one getting out of Calais alive and back to England. There could be no one left in London who could identify Schiffer. When the bodies were found, if they were found, the British Army, in the course of panic and retreat, would—should they bother to examine the bodies closely—presume that the men had been murdered by fifth columnists. If a head count were made and Schiffer were unaccounted for, then he would become just another one of the thousands Missing in Action. No great search would be mounted for a lone corporal.

There were enough "ifs" to hide behind. Erik Guderian felt secure.

"It's time," he said gently, getting to his feet.

Guderian came around and helped Schiffer to his feet. At the door, flanked by two of Guderian's officers, the corporal turned back to his captor. Tears were streaming unashamedly across his cheeks, streaking the dirt that could not be washed away.

"They won't hurt me, will they?" he sobbed.

Guderian gripped Schiffer's face in both hands.

"No one will hurt you. I promise you that!"

Guderian watched as his men escorted Schiffer to the truck and clambered aboard.

Do it now! he thought fiercely. Do it now and get it over with!

Guderian gestured to Karl Horst, who trotted across the muddy road.

"Zu Befehl, Herr Major!"

"There is something I must ask of you," Guderian said, turning the *Feldwebel* away from the direction of the truck. He dared not take the chance of someone reading his lips or seeing Horst's reaction.

But Guderian needn't have worried. Karl Horst's features remained expressionless as the Major explained what had to be done. Only the eyes betrayed an infinite sadness because there was no place for Horst where Guderian had to go.

"We'll meet in Berlin, *Herr Major*," Horst said softly.

"In Berlin," Guderian echoed, handing him the briefcase with the transcripts. *"Auf Wiedersehen, mein Freund."*

The *Feldwebel* saluted, then quickly ran back to the truck. Guderian stepped aside to avoid being splattered with mud churning beneath the rear wheels. Slowly he returned to the farmhouse.

"Herr Major!" the Lieutenant said smartly, moving around from his field transmission unit. "A message from Berlin came in over an hour ago. It was marked urgent but your men prevented me from delivering it."

"Those were my orders, *Herr Leutnant*. I'll look at it now, please."

Guderian swung a chair around and draped his arms across its back, holding the flimsy yellow sheet before him.

The text was surprisingly long. Darius, the London agent,

was reporting the arrival of an American, the hunter from Washington who had tracked down and murdered Berlin's agent, Beth Davis. Now this man was looking for Davis's opposite number at the U.S. embassy. By the length of the text Guderian realized Darius had stayed on the air too long, flirting with the counterintelligence homing trucks that bore down on unauthorized transmissions. Yet the agent in place had obviously felt that the security risk was more than justified: the hunter was dangerous to the entire embassy operation. Even though Darius believed himself to be secure, there was no telling where the investigation would lead. And the hunter was in a hurry.

Jonathan Baylor Cabot. Guderian remembered the name from Jaunich's files. He was Dulles's very best.

"I was instructed to give this to you after you had read the transmission, *Herr Major*," the Lieutenant said. He passed Guderian a leather pouch, the locks sealed, the red wax stamped with Hitler's personal insignia. "It was delivered from Berlin by special courier."

"I have a message to transmit to Chancellery," Guderian said quietly, and gave him the code numbers which would activate the ENIGMA machine in Gerd Jaunich's bureau.

The Lieutenant, his back ramrod stiff, positioned himself before his unit and punched in the identification codes. He glanced at Guderian, indicating he was ready to transmit.

MESSAGE AND APPENDIX RECEIVED AND UNDERSTOOD.
AM PROCEEDING AGAINST THE HOLDER OF FIRE.
PRISONER EN ROUTE.

"Is that all, sir?" the Lieutenant queried.

"That's all," Guderian replied, his voice breaking.

He had been going too long on too little. He wished to God he could remove himself instantly from this Godforsaken mudhole and be standing in the same room as Jaunich. He wanted to say words that would inevitably be bastardized by distance and the wretched anonymity of code. He wanted so badly to feel the grip of that last handshake.

"Incoming, *Herr Major*," the Lieutenant called out as the ENIGMA began its clatter.

GODSPEED.

"No further transmission," Guderian said, turning away.

He closed his eyes and summoned forth the features from the photograph in the file, a file he had first leafed through in Jaunich's car. He brought the chair around to the table, uncorked the brandy and began to read the detailed report Gerd Jaunich had appended on Jonathan Baylor Cabot.

At two o'clock on the morning of May 25 Erik Guderian finished the reading. He opened the door to the potbelly stove and fed the sheets in one by one. Then he made the mistake of returning to the table and sitting down. His head dropped on his arms and he was asleep in seconds. But it wasn't the sleep he deserved, because behind every veiled dream that crossed his subconscious stood the figure of the man who had unwittingly placed himself between Guderian and the destruction of Prometheus.

10

During the last week of May, the London Metropolitan Police investigated two forced entries at the homes of staff accredited to the United States embassy.

On May 23, Maureen Ryan, a U.S. citizen and one of the three operators on the Churchill–Grosvenor Square switchboard, finished her twelve-to-eight P.M. shift a few minutes later than usual. Her replacement, Dianna Sparks, had been waylaid again by her boyfriend, an officer of the Polish Army-in-exile. Maureen brushed aside Dianna's apologies, bundled up her things and made it out to Park Lane in time to catch the Number 7 bus, which would take her to Norfolk Place, off Sussex Gardens. When she stepped off the rattletrap vehicle she didn't notice the tall man standing across the street from her address. Even if she had, she wouldn't have recognized the face since she didn't know what Jonathan Cabot looked like.

Maureen Ryan took forty-five minutes to freshen up, change and be out on the street again. Cabot watched as she went across the street to the pub fifty yards up from where he was standing and emerged a minute later with a cabdriver in tow. After the cab drove off, Cabot entered the Boar's Head and parked himself at the end of the bar by the telephone. He had scarcely touched his half pint of Whitbread when the phone rang and the barmaid called out his name. The conversation with the MI5 legman was brief: Maureen Ryan had arrived at her scheduled destination, the Palace Gardens Club in Soho, and was dancing up a storm with her RAF beau. The music in the background was Big Band sound. Cabot hung up, drained his beer and left the pub. Twelve minutes later, after making certain no one had followed him out, Cabot had jimmied the lock on the tradesmen's entrance at Number 14 Norfolk Place and was moving up the staircase. Maureen Ryan's two small rooms were on the second floor, next to the end of the corridor's communal bathroom. Cabot forced the lock and was inside within seconds. The curtains were across the windows; the lights on.

Maureen Ryan was not the neatest of people, a trait which made Cabot's job all the easier. He tossed the unmade bed first, then quickly moved to the single dresser, clothes closet and dirty-laundry hamper. Moving to the next room, Cabot pushed the sofa and chair into one corner, lifted the fraying carpet and carefully examined the floorboards. He went over the walls, concentrating on the wood panels. He examined the furniture, then went into the alcove that passed for a kitchen. The hot plate was taken apart, the kettle and pans removed from the drawers, the cutlery and crockery cupboards emptied. Just as he had done in the bedroom, Cabot tested the floors and walls. Nothing.

Without pause he went back to the bedroom and carefully went through Maureen Ryan's personal effects—the letters from home she kept in the bottom vanity drawer, pictures of her beloved and mementos of their affair, a diary he pried out from underneath the center drawer which detailed the polarities of despair and hope this girl lived between. The officer was already married.

Thirty-five minutes had elapsed since Cabot had entered the apartment. He began to move the furniture back into place—but not quite into place. The bed was returned to its approximate disheveled state; from a partially open bureau drawer he let one stocking trail. In the kitchen he returned everything to its not quite proper place, then took stock of his handiwork. There was one more thing to do, in case Miss Ryan arrived, as he suspected she would, drunk.

Cabot went into the living room and removed a potted spider plant from its place in the mantelpiece. He loosened some dirt with his fingers and dropped some on the carpet. With his knuckles he broke the pot in three quick jabs, setting down the wreckage on the carpet. Even in an inebriated state Maureen Ryan would wonder when that could have happened.

And that's what Cabot wanted her to think about. Even before he had broken into the flat, Cabot was all but certain she wasn't the target. Maureen Ryan's life was too much of an open book and Cabot knew it by heart. But when she came back she would know someone had been in her home. She would call the police. At the very least she would talk about it at work, which was exactly what Cabot wanted. Whoever had buried himself away at Grosvenor Square would hear Maureen's story. Whoever had known Cabot would be coming to London, knew that he was coming to investigate, who had set up the killing ground in Leatherhead—he or she would know Cabot was on the move. And that was where Cabot wanted him or her: worried, off-guard, being faced with Cabot offensive, not defensive. He wanted the son of a bitch to start sweating . . .

A few minutes after eleven o'clock Jonathan Cabot was walking into a pub off the New Fresh Wharf, between Billingsgate Market and London Bridge. In the blackout it had taken him a half hour to find a cab, and even then the driver, who had been ferrying military men on the strength of their passes, thought twice before accepting the princely bribe of ten pounds.

"Wouldn't do this if ye wasn't a Yank," he said at last. "But if I'm stopped you bail us out, lad."

Like most pubs in the city's market centers, the Pelican had a special license which permitted the owner to open at eleven at night and close at five, after the day's catch was brought in, cleaned and hauled away. When Cabot pushed his way in past the double doors he realized he was already late: the fishermen were three deep at the bar, passing drinks back shoulder over shoulder. Over the cigarette smoke, made thick by the heat from the blazing fireplace, hung the rotting stench of fish, diesel oil and bodies that had been exposed to the sea nets and everything that was dredged up with the catch. He looked around for Mackenzie McConnell, suspecting that either this was the wrong place or else she had fled.

"Jonathan, over here!"

Mackenzie McConnell was seated next to the fire, her long legs stretched out toward the flames, toes wriggling in heavy socks. Her coat was carefully draped behind her in the manner of a royal cloak. The fishermen gathered at her table, their caps doffed, were toasting her in undisguised admiration.

"Gentlemen," Mackenzie McConnell smiled upon them as Cabot struggled through the press, "I'm afraid you'll all have to excuse me."

The fishermen offered one last toast. A couple of them slapped Cabot on the shoulder and gave knowing winks.

"Do sit down, Mr. Cabot," Mackenzie McConnell said grandly. "I've taken the liberty of ordering you a whiskey."

She reached out and poured Cabot a glassful from the earthen pitcher.

"Do you come here often?" Cabot asked. "Or is this your fiefdom."

"Very good, Jonathan." Mackenzie McConnell laughed softly. "Draw yourself a little closer. After all, we're expected to be lovers . . . Oh, you're blushing!"

"It's the whiskey," Cabot said thickly. "How can they drink this stuff?"

"Special brand, Jonathan." And through the smiles came a hard question. "Any luck?"

"Nothing. Maureen Ryan's as clean as we suspected. Any late developments with her bank account?"

"She has four pounds ten to her credit," Mackenzie McConnell said. "But that's because she sends most of her salary to Philadelphia. The money orders are made out to Meagan Ryan, her mother. Pearce confirmed that she's an invalid, getting by on some kind of pension as well as what the children contribute."

"Dianna Sparks," Cabot said quietly.

"Miss Sparks is a horse of a different color," Mackenzie McConnell said, tapping down a cigarette. She leaned forward and cupped his hand while drawing off the flame of his lighter.

"Thank you. Dianna lives in St. John's Wood, Scott Ellis Gardens. The house, along with not an inconsiderable yearly allowance, was left to her by her grandmother. Sir Stafford

Sparks is a City financier; Lady Cornelia still believes that George the Third is on the throne and fighting the Colonies. There are two brothers—or were: Dennis, the elder, was shot down three weeks ago. The Air–Sea Rescue people didn't reach him in time. Timothy is at Dunkirk with Gort. The family has a high tradition of service, ergo Dianna's insistence on helping in the 'effort,' as this little affair is known in her circle."

"But why the embassy?" Cabot queried. "With her connections she could have gotten a job closer to kith and kin."

"My dear Jonathan, it was precisely those connections which got her the job in the first place. Daddy is banker to the entire Churchill clan. Up until recently they were, as you would put it, drinking buddies."

The whiskey burned Cabot's throat, choking his words.

"A possible."

"Not unless I missed something awfully big," Mackenzie McConnell replied. "You'll recall Dianna's on the board right now. I got in as soon as she left and spent a leisurely hour checking the house. Nothing—except that our lady has a decided interest in French lingerie . . . which undoubtedly helped her get into her predicament."

"Which is?"

"Dianna Sparks is pregnant," Mackenzie said softly. "From what I found in her room—besides his clothing—the father is one Miroslav Zaruzelski, an officer in the Polish Free Corps, Artillery. And before you ask, yes, the man exists. We could go after him, since he's stationed in London, but I don't see any point in it."

"What are you getting at?"

"That Dianna Sparks will, of necessity, leave her job in two, possibly three weeks' time. Pregnant women are not allowed to handle security work, and by then she will be very evidently with child. Between the man she loves, the child she's carrying and the family she'll have to contend with, I would say our Miss Sparks hasn't time to act as the deep-penetration agent.

"I also checked her passport records. She's a homebody. Never been off the island."

Mackenzie McConnell paused. "I really would eliminate her from the running, Jonathan."

Cabot, who had been concentrating on Mackenzie's report,

now let his mind drift, the boisterousness of the pub filling his ears.

"All right," he said at last. "Let's leave her. I take it you left a calling card."

Mackenzie's eyes clouded over and she turned away. In the light he could see the down beneath her lower lip.

"It was a shitty, shitty thing to do," she said savagely. "But if that doesn't push her over the edge, nothing will . . . I left the letter from her doctor out where she could see it. It had been hidden away . . . with her silk undies of all things."

"Mackenzie . . ."

"Smile, Jonathan. My faithful legions are watching us."

"I'm sorry—"

"It had to be done," she stopped him and quickly continued on. "What about yourself? Are you through for the night?"

Cabot shook his head. "Cliff Hastings is on the cryptography unit for the next six hours, starting midnight. I want to get to him as well."

Mackenzie reached out and touched his arm.

"I'd like to come with you, cover the flanks as it were."

The flames cast her hair into a molten gold stream, her skin, a tender pink. Cabot saw, heard, felt nothing but her. Without his being aware of it his hand reached out and cupped her cheek.

"Come, then," he said softly.

And she was so good that he never saw the shadow of guilt flit across those turquoise eyes as it sped the way of her ulterior motive.

The appearance of Leonard Frye's office hadn't changed in the three years he had been stationed in London. Located on the ground floor of the embassy, its French doors opened up onto a flagstone terrace which was part of the back gardens. However, these doors didn't "open" in the literal sense. As soon as Frye had taken possession of the office, he required that Pearce not only seal the doors but prime them with the most sophisticated electronic alarms available.

The interior was pristine, a reflection of Frye's obsession with neatness. Instead of bookcases, olive drab filing cabinets took up one wall. Opposite them was Frye's battery of telephones which connected him to the cipher room in the basement where his juniors worked, to sister departments at British

Intelligence, a half-dozen internal and external lines and one directly into the Ambassador's office. There was no art work on the walls save a small photograph of the President tucked away in one corner and a picture ten times as large of Ambassador Kennedy which hung in the place of honor behind a desk which was almost always spotless. Leonard Frye did very little paperwork at the desk. As head of cryptography he had had a personal cipher unit built into it. Information from which others were excluded, information which was to be found only in the maze of letters, numbers and symbols, was the only kind Frye valued. What was available to anyone held no interest for him.

On the afternoon of May 25 Frye took his lunch at his desk. There was nothing unusual in this since he seldom went to the commissary for anything more than coffee. As he listened to the rains slice down on the flagstones, Frye finished his liver paste sandwich, daintily wiped his mouth with a linen napkin and watched as the hands of the clock reached one. He swiveled his chair toward the cipher machine, and as though on cue the unit erupted to life. Frye leaned forward, watching as the typewriter moved across the newsprint-quality paper, pushing out steady inches of sentences whose words were totally garbled. At the same time the deciphering unit was translating the scrambled text into clear. Frye had insisted on the dual machines so that in the event that the clear text was in some way ambiguous or its meaning in doubt, he could manually decode the passages, one of several checks to determine whether there was an error and if that error was human or technological.

For the next hour the machine clattered away at five- to ten-minute intervals, falling silent long enough for Frye to tear off the copy and examine it before starting up again. The texts carried a uniform, if differently worded message: little or no information is available on one Jonathan Baylor Cabot as regards his connection to the State Department.

Frye set out the clear copies side by side across his desk. The evening before, he had sent out coded messages to men in Washington who owed him. In his six years as cryptographer at State, Frye had pocketed many favors. He had chosen his pupils carefully, selecting on the basis of what he saw as their characters rather than qualifications. As head of a wholly new department, Frye's word was final. If he made errors in judgment there was plenty of time in which to remove those whose loyalty to him was questionable. As a result of his careful selection Frye's pupils went on to assume control of cryptographic departments at Treasury, the Passport Office, the Post Office, Defense and a half dozen other departments in Washington. Before he left for England in 1937, Frye visited each of his pupils for a personal farewell. It was a gesture that was now repaying itself many times over: Frye had heard from each one of his pupils before the day was out.

Jonathan Baylor Cabot . . .

His passport had been issued in 1932, renewed in 1937. No visas had ever been applied for, no diplomatic documentation had ever been issued . . . at least not under that name. The Post Office had one mailing address for him in Georgetown. Treasury didn't even have him listed. State confirmed only that Cabot was a technician who had been sent to London. No further details were in the file.

Which in itself told Frye something: the Ambassador was right. Cabot was not who he said he was. If State had in fact sent him over as a cipher technician, then even if Frye hadn't been informed due to an honest oversight, State would have had a far more exhaustive record for him. So who had sent Cabot over? With what instructions? And did his mission really pertain to ciphers or was it, as the Ambassador suspected, targeted elsewhere?

Abruptly Leonard Frye bolted out of his chair and walked quickly into the washroom, where he washed his face and hands. Whenever he was anxious or tense Frye's skin oozed perspiration. Doctors had told him it was a glandular problem and Frye despised it. But the washing had become a sort of ritual which not only calmed him but also allowed him to see the problem in what he believed was the correct perspective. By the time he returned to his desk, Frye had decided not to follow his initial impulse, which was to present the clear texts to the Ambassador at once and at the same time provide his analysis of the situation. It would be much better, he thought, to try one more avenue. If that one turned up nothing, then the Ambassador could truly lay Cabot out on the carpet. And Frye, who detested meddling in his preserve, would help him.

The cryptographer gathered up the pages of the scrambled text and carefully folded them away into the inside breast pocket of his jacket. He placed the clear copies into a small safe beside the radiators. This done, Frye checked his watch and went to the closet for his overcoat. If he hurried he could arrive at his destination before the party in question left.

At the age of thirty-three Patricia Burns had found a new lease on life. On that birthday, two years ago, her bedridden mother had at last passed away, and although Tricia had wept genuine tears there was a part of her which soared as the last notes of the church service died away. Tricia Burns was free—free to sell the row house for which her father had killed himself at the mill in order to pay off, free of her loutish brothers who had tried to fight the last will, which gave her everything, free of a mother who had made her a virtual prisoner for the last four years with a disease that would neither recede nor do away with her in merciful dispatch. Tricia left the grimy industrial suburb of Leeds two days after the funeral. She severed all connections when the solicitors sent her a check for the sale of the house and never thought twice of the life spent there. A few months later she had her flat in London's Southwark district, had applied for and gotten a job as a Whitehall operator and was living more happily than she had ever remembered.

Tricia Burns was a pretty girl, tending toward being overweight especially around the hips, but with a lovely round face whose flawless skin was set off by long chestnut hair. Through the Whitehall mills she had met young men who at first appeared genuinely interested in her except that they never stayed the night and after a week rarely called again. There were also those who, from office gossip, had learned of Tricia's substantial savings book account, which drew enough interest to permit her a generous monthly stipend. But while she had had little formal education and at times allowed loneliness to cloud her judgment, Tricia was nobody's fool. She had been used the better part of her life. False flattery was as easy to spot as her mother's guilt-intended whining. Tricia carefully weeded out the gold-diggers and was for the most part content to go without Friday night or weekend dates. She had unbounded optimism and firmly believed that one day she would meet her true man. On October 17, 1938, when she was selected as one of three operators to work at a certain switchboard at the United States embassy, that moment arrived.

Tricia Burns carefully adjusted the scarf at her throat and

took one final look at herself in the bathroom mirror. The soft eye shadow was perfect, although she wished she had had time to pluck out the few offensive brows that made her eyes a little too large. The lipstick was a bold red she would never have worn to work, but her lover had often told her how much he liked it. That could come off later . . . along with a few other things. The *crème caramel* blouse seemed even lighter against her dark-brown hair and complemented the soft tartan skirt clipped with a large gold pin. Tricia dearly wished the other girls could see her now. At the office she dressed simply, almost to the point of drabness. It was just another way of not drawing attention to herself or creating jealousy or envy among the other working girls.

Tricia turned out the light and hurried into the living room, whose bay window overlooked the traffic in Southwark Street. Since the telephone had rung a half hour earlier and she heard his voice, listened to him say that he was coming over right away, she had asked herself over and over again what it was that was bringing him here. Tricia blushed at the first answer that came to mind. Yet she had told him that she had agreed to change shifts with Maureen Ryan and would be going on duty at three. He knew this yet he was still coming! She shivered in anticipation.

Tricia Burns sat sideways on the sofa, one arm draped across the back, staring out through the rain-slicked window. The top part of the glass was fogged over, but the sidewalk was visible as were the people who hurried along it, umbrellas held low. That was all Tricia needed to see.

"What's she waiting around for?" Mackenzie McConnell asked under her breath, checking the time. Beside her the temporary replacement for her injured partner, Robert Ogilvy, provided a confirmation.

"Two thirty-seven," the agent murmured. "There's still time, mind you . . ."

"She's usually on her way by now," Mackenzie McConnell told him. "The word is she arrives at least thirty minutes before her shift, sometimes to get something to eat, sometimes just because she is so conscientious."

"Maybe she's waiting for someone," the agent said thoughtfully and straightened up in the driver's seat.

He was, Mackenzie recognized, one of the younger breed, all dash and derring-do. Sitting in a cold, garage-issue Jaguar with rationed petrol that would be next to treasonous to burn just to keep warm was not his idea of counterintelligence.

But something was wrong, or perhaps only different. Mackenzie McConnell had gone over the operator's file carefully. By now she probably knew more about Tricia Burns than did the girl herself. Miss Burns was not supposed to have a boyfriend at this time. In fact, according to the office rumor mill, a check of the neighbors, and the accounting of her whereabouts for the past month, Tricia Burns hadn't been seen or linked with a man for the past month.

So what are you doing sitting by that window pining like some Jane Austen heroine?

Mackenzie McConnell's attention was so fixed on the second-story window that she almost didn't hear her partner.

"Hello, and what do we have here?"

She caught sight of him as soon as she lowered her eyes. Even with the overcoat collar thrust up and umbrella held low, the identification was positive. The man turned off the sidewalk and walked up the few steps to the front door of the terrace flat. At the same time as he pressed the doorbell, Mackenzie McConnell's eyes flitted to the window. Tricia Burns was no longer at the window. She looked back to the door just in time to see it draw to a close.

"Right—I have to make a call," Mackenzie McConnell said, digging in her purse for the change. "There's a call box up the street. If either or both come out get my attention."

"But how?"

"Sit on the bloody horn!"

In the middle of the afternoon this section of Southwark with its farmers' market stalls was packed with women meandering from one kiosk to the next. Mackenzie moved fast, angling her body sideways to cut through the crowds. Behind her a woman started to shout and Mackenzie looked over her shoulder to see that the woman's coat was drenched. She was paying no heed to the puddles that collected in the shallow concaves of the sidewalk.

The phone booth at the corner of Hopton Street was occupied. Mackenzie swore savagely, then wrenched the door open. A startled housewife, curlers under her kerchief, stared at her like some demented hen. Mackenzie thrust a phony CID card under the hen's nose, reached around and depressed the call button.

"Police business, madame, I'm dreadfully sorry. Thank you so very much."

Before the woman could turn around she was out on the street and Mackenzie inside with one foot against the door. While she fumbled with the change she looked back down the street. The car was nowhere to be seen. There was no way the agent could signal her. The din of Southwark would absorb even the most insistent car horn.

The tuppence dropped and the line was ringing. Ninety seconds had passed. Then Cabot was on the line and she was speaking rapidly. He listened without comment until she was finished, asked two questions and hung up. The door to the phone booth flew open and Mackenzie was back in the street. Even before she reached the car, engine running now, she caught sight of the agent's face between the flashing wipers. He was shaking his head.

Right, Miss Burns, Mackenzie McConnell thought as she slid into her seat. Before I had some misgivings about this job on your flat. But not anymore. In fact I'm awfully curious to see what you have to show me.

Twelve minutes after he had hung up with Mackenzie McConnell, Cabot was in Pearce's office at the embassy.

"I need equipment to tap the Downing Street lines," he said without preamble. "As well as the one open line the operators have for nonsecurity calls."

Pearce, who had been going over the daily digest sent over from MI5, was stunned.

"Johnny," he started to say, "those lines are sacred. No one—"

"Damn it, Edward, I need that equipment!"

Pearce regarded him for a moment, then sighed.

"We have our asses out this far . . ." he muttered. He came over to a filing cabinet, stooped carefully to avoid putting sudden pressure on his legs and unlocked the bottom drawer.

"You know the Brits monitor the Downing Street lines from their end," Pearce warned him, pulling out a wooden container the size of a shoebox. "If they're sharp—and they are—all hell will break loose, very quietly of course, as soon as they pick up the tap." Pearce hesitated. "They'll go to Churchill first but someone may jump the gun and try to get through to Kennedy."

"Wouldn't they come straight to you?" Cabot demanded.

"Sure, but—"

"Then there's no problem." Cabot smiled thinly. "Because you'll be babysitting the tap for a while."

"Oh, Christ, Johnny, what the hell's this all about?"

"Who is on the Downing Street switchboard right now?"

"Tricia Burns. Why?"

Cabot gestured at the telephone. "I don't think so. Call up and see for yourself."

Confirmation of what Cabot inferred took less than a minute.

"That's not like Tricia." Pearce shook his head. "If anything it's she who covers for the others."

"Did you know that she and Leonard Frye are at her apartment right now?"

"Frye! Johnny, you've got to be kidding!" Pearce cried. "Jesus, he's married to a shrew and Tricia's on her way to becoming a spinster! In fact she probably crossed that line a long time ago."

"Why don't you call up Frye right now?" Cabot suggested.

"You mean these two . . ."

"McConnell had Burns's place under surveillance," Cabot explained. "She was waiting until Burns left so she could toss the place. But it appeared that Tricia Burns was waiting for someone. And who should come walking down the street—"

"But Frye," Pearce finished for him. "Look, Johnny, those two may have something going on the side. Unlikely as it is, there's no law against cheating on one's wife. That they've kept such a low profile is understandable. And maybe, just maybe, I should have known about it—"

"I'm not saying you had to know," Cabot interrupted him. "And you're probably right—their meeting in the middle of the day means nothing to anyone but themselves. Maybe. But I can't afford the luxury of writing it off. Tricia Burns is going to be late for work—not like her. Especially when she's covering for someone. And Frye. Why would he suddenly bolt the office and go home—simply for a nooner? Doesn't sound right."

"Then what does?"

"That's why I want the tap," Cabot said quietly. "I'm assuming those two are up to something more than just an extramarital fling. I think Frye is telling her to do something. I think that when she is back at the embassy she will do it. I'm betting that it's going to be over the phone because Tricia Burns can't move off that switchboard until eight o'clock!"

Pearce tucked the box under his arm and opened the door. "If you're wrong, Jonathan?"

"Then I go on to the others who are left," Cabot said coldly.

Being at the end of the hall, Pearce's office was next to the stairwell that led to the basement. The two men slipped past the storerooms, the huge mail room and the warren of cubicles occupied by Frye's cryptologists.

The room housing the telephone switching apparatus was no larger than a closet, with no ventilation save for a grille that covered an exit of a heating duct. The wiring panels covered two complete walls, leaving just enough room for a single technician to move around in. Pearce locked the door behind them and from the box removed a long, slender screwdriver. Within seconds the metal face was off, the wiring exposed. Pearce ran his fingertips over the array of red, blue, green and white plastic, lips moving silently. Using the screwdriver, he made nicks on four wires, then asked Cabot to start handing him the necessary equipment.

"In case you're wondering," Pearce muttered, fingers moving swiftly to cut away the plastic, trim the leads and hook up the alligator clips, "I helped install this gizmo when the lines were hooked up."

Ten minutes later the last wires had been connected to a field telephone. Pearce lifted the receiver and listened to the telltale hum of an open line.

"I've hooked us up to both the Downing Street lines and the outside channel," he said.

"I'll take first watch, until Frye leaves for the day," Cabot told him.

"Fine by me," Pearce answered. "You want me to bring you something to drink?"

"No, thanks, but there is one thing you can do: does Frye have a safe in his office?"

"Sure."

"Do you know the combination?"

Pearce shook his head.

"I need the combination, Edward," Cabot said. "Even if you have to go to the manufacturer to get it."

"Which is why you so generously offered to take the first shift," Pearce said dryly.

Cabot glanced at his watch. "I do need it," he said, then sat down on the cold concrete floor and brought the receiver to his ear.

11

Tricia Burns was thirty minutes late for her shift. When
she entered the switchboard room, Dianna Sparks, snapping
back the pages of a fashion magazine, threw her a withering
look. Before Tricia could say a word the other woman gathered
up her purse and stormed by her.

Quietly Tricia closed the door and locked it. She came over
to the counter before the switchboard and emptied the overflowing ashtray. Carefully she wiped the counter, then glanced
at the day sheet. Dianna Sparks hadn't bothered to write in the
time she left, so Tricia filled in the appropriate columns, making a note of her tardy arrival. All the while she kept one eye
on the white bulb in the center of the board. Not that she had
to. As soon as Downing Street called, both the light and a
sharp bell would be activated. When she had settled in, Tricia
adjusted her headset, sweeping the curls behind her ears, and
started to reach for the jack which would connect her to the
outside line.

Her fingers refused to insert the plug.

Don't you dare lose heart now! she thought fiercely. You're
not some criminal. He hasn't asked you to do anything wrong!

But the reservations that had surfaced when Leonard Frye
explained why he had had to see her were still gnawing at her.
As soon as she saw him at the door she knew something was
wrong. After their embrace he held her and still had one arm
around her shoulder as he led her over to the couch. Terrified,
Tricia waited for the marital ax to fall. Leonard was quick to
assure her it was nothing like that. There was no question of his
ever leaving her, not now, not ever. But a problem had arisen
at the embassy, a difficult matter, delicate. He needed her help.

Her heart was so full of love for him that Tricia almost missed what Leonard went on to say. But the words he used, "an unknown man," "an investigator" who was "involved in a shooting in Leatherhead," "trouble for the Ambassador," were cold, ominous. As was what Leonard wanted her to do.

In spite of her misgivings Tricia did not protest. She answered Leonard's questions carefully and accurately. She repeated the instructions he gave her without hesitation. Only when he took her face in his hands and gently kissed her did Tricia's resolve, ironically enough, weaken. She wanted to tell him she was afraid, uncertain that she was doing the right thing, uncertain he was acting as he should. A part of her demanded that she tell him she wanted no part of this filthy, secret business, that it shouldn't touch them and what they had.

But she said nothing of the kind.

For God's sake, girl, you can't let him down now! With that thought Tricia Burns jammed the plug into the switchboard and the outside line hummed. Her gaze dropped to her watch. There was at most an hour and a half to do what Leonard had asked of her. Tricia began to dial the first number.

She had always been popular among the girls at Whitehall. Plain, dowdy Tricia didn't threaten their femininity. No one's boyfriend would even dream of making a pass at her. She was also a good listener. Office gossip or secret revelations about romance all made their way to her ears. The girls trusted her because she was sympathetic—and safe. Tricia Burns had a reputation of never divulging what was said to her. She offered advice when asked but never carried a story any further.

The number at the Defence Ministry was ringing. She would have to be careful in what she said. Leonard had warned her not to appear too anxious or inquisitive. Play on the mystery, he had advised her. On the shooting, which everyone had heard about by now. See if you can unearth that one link . . . just one.

A woman's voice answered. Tricia took a deep breath and said, "Hello, Corrine? Yes, it's Tricia . . ."

At 5:35 Edward Pearce unlocked the door to the switching chamber. He saw Jonathan Cabot sitting on the floor, his jacket spread out beneath him on the gray concrete floor, a notepad resting against drawn-up knees. Beside him were half a dozen legal-sized sheets of paper covered in Cabot's small, precise handwriting.

Cabot was holding the receiver between his ear and shoulder and writing very quickly. Pearce locked the door and stood back, waiting until Cabot replaced the field telephone. "Read it and weep," Cabot said, gesturing at the pages. His voice was hard, the words clipped by bitterness. He got up slowly, massaging the muscles in his thighs and calves.

"Our little wallflower has been burning up the wires all over town," Cabot said. "The outgoing calls have been almost non-stop—to MI5, Defence, the Home Office. You name it—she's called there."

"Who?" Pearce demanded.

"All her old friends who work the switchboards, run the receptionists' desks, take notes for people like you and me." Cabot shook his head. "There's a regular gossip network throughout official London. You wouldn't believe the amount of information that I've picked up just listening to this girl-talk."

Pearce glanced at the pages. "Yes, I would."

"The most interesting part is that Tricia Burns had only one purpose in mind with all these calls," Cabot said. "And that was to get a line on me."

"Oh, Christ," Pearce groaned. "You were right, Jonathan . . . Goddamn it, you were right!"

"Every person she talked to was asked, in a roundabout way, about me," Cabot continued. "On the face of it the questions sounded innocent enough. Except that they were variations on the same theme: Who is Cabot and what is he doing here?"

"I'm almost afraid to ask." Pearce laughed nervously. "Did anyone answer?"

"The rumor mill hasn't gotten to me yet."

"Do we have enough with which to pick Burns up?"

"Yes. And once MI5 gets hold of these names, it's going to be a bloody day for most of the people Burns spoke with."

"Then let's take her—now!" Pearce said coldly. "Get her off that damn board—"

"What about the safe in Frye's office?" Cabot broke in.

"I stopped by and had a good look at it," Pearce said. "It's a Chubb antique. A crowbar will pop it."

The ringing telephone interrupted Cabot's reply.

"Busy little bitch, isn't she?" Pearce murmured.

"You take it," Cabot said. "Has Frye left for the day?"

"Checked out twenty minutes ago."

"I'll be back as soon as I've had a look," Cabot said. "We'll get Mackenzie, put a surveillance team on Frye whether or not I find anything, then take Burns."

Cabot looked over his shoulder at the field phone. "You'd better answer that."

At twenty minutes past six, Tricia Burns heard a faint knocking on the door of the communications chamber, followed by the scraping of a key being inserted into the lock. She put aside the volume of Galsworthy's *Man of Property* and checked the board in front of her. She had stopped her calls at six when official Whitehall closed for the day. The notes she had made had been carefully tucked away in her purse.

As the door opened she called out, "Come in, Charlie . . ."

Except that it wasn't Charlie, the elderly attendant with the tea trolley, who entered.

"Howdy, Tricia."

"Mr. Pearce!" she exclaimed, rising. "My goodness . . . I didn't expect you."

"Well, Charlie's a bit late with the coffee tonight," Pearce said, smiling. "By the way, there's someone outside to visit you."

Tricia Burns didn't know what to make of Pearce's suggestive, if not altogether lewd, grin. She felt herself blush but knew it wasn't embarrassment. She was paralyzed by fear.

"I . . . I'm not expecting anyone, Mr. Pearce," she managed to say. "Are you sure?"

"Yes, ma'am, I am. You'd better not keep them waiting."

The word "them" slipped by her altogether and curiosity propelled her forward. As soon as she crossed the threshold the door slammed behind her. Tricia Burns whirled around, her knuckles flying against her mouth in a feeble attempt to stifle her scream. When she drew her hand away she tasted the blood.

"Miss Burns . . ."

The woman standing before her was tall, extremely striking in the black trenchcoat that set off her golden hair. But the eyes, turquoise like the cold gem, belonged to an inquisitor.

"Who are you?" Tricia whispered.

An elegant hand extended a leatherbound wallet, open at the center.

"Security Service, Miss Burns. We'd like you to come with us, if you would."

Tricia backed away until she could feel her shoulder blades against the communications door.

"No," she said faintly. "Why should I? I haven't done anything—"

A man emerged from the darkened recess of the corridor. He was tall, and from what Tricia could see, heavily built. His coat was open and it hung away from his body, shapeless.

"My name is Cabot," the man said quietly. "We would like to ask you why you've been making inquiries about me."

At that instant Tricia Burns went numb. This man was the enemy! He was the one Leonard was suspicious of . . . the Ambassador wanted to know about . . . Yet she didn't protest or struggle when the woman took her by one elbow and the American, Cabot, by the other. They hurried her along the corridor, the trio of footsteps resounding off concrete as they passed the mailroom, the vault and the cipher chambers. At the top of the stairs the woman moved slightly ahead and pushed open the door that led onto the driveway. It was raining hard, the water spattering off metal, obscuring the twin yellow beams, but not the engine noise, of a powerful car. Tricia Burns saw this as the last chance for herself, for Leonard . . . everyone. She wrenched her arm away from the woman's grasp and came at Cabot with a roundhouse. Suddenly pain blinded her. She threw back her head and screamed, not believing what had happened. Cabot couldn't have been that quick, but he was, sidestepping her flying arm and in one motion stepping behind her, allowing her own momentum to carry her around. Tricia felt five fingers clamp onto her arm like a bulldog's jaw, then the arm propelled upward until she staggered forward, shoulder on fire as though the bones had been cleanly and mercilessly snapped.

Standing on her tiptoes, Tricia Burns was propelled into the evening rain. Someone pushed her head down and she was shoved into the car, falling to the floor, her hip jarring against the transmission shaft. Doors slammed as she was dragged onto the seat. When she looked up she saw Cabot sitting in the front seat beside the driver.

"He's not worth it," Cabot said coldly and turned away. The

car's acceleration drove Tricia into the soft leather seat, and then without warning she began to cry.

The ride to Queen Anne's Gate took all of seventeen minutes, testimony to the driver's skill at negotiating blacked-out London traffic. The car had barely skidded to a halt when the rear doors were thrown open and Tricia Burns pulled out, none too gently. Mackenzie McConnell left her with two of the internal security people who had been waiting beneath the cover of massive umbrellas and hurried around to Cabot's side.

"You're sure you don't want me to come with you?" she asked.

"I need you here, for her." Cabot glanced in the direction of the shivering operator. "Get what you can as fast as you can. If something develops I'll call for a backup."

"I'll have a squad waiting," Mackenzie promised. She reached out and touched Cabot's cheek with her palm.

"Be careful, Jonathan."

Cabot gripped her fingers. Then, as though he could not help himself, he kissed her hard on the lips, tasting the scent of her flesh, seeking its softness, warmth, comfort. Just as abruptly he pulled away, got back in the car and rolled up the window. The driver took this as a go signal.

Leonard and Beatrice Frye lived in Addison Gardens, a pleasant tree-lined street of three-story Victorian houses across from Holland Road. The black Jaguar stopped across from Number 17 and Cabot got out. He waited until the car had turned the corner before leaving the street. The driver would take up position in the alley that bordered Frye's back garden.

Cabot ran up the steps and pushed the door open to find himself in the antechamber. Quickly Cabot checked the nameplates and found the number of Frye's apartment. Ground floor, second on the left.

"Who is it?"

The woman's voice was high-pitched, underlined with annoyance. Even though the door muffled the tone, Cabot recognized it for what it was: tough, south Boston working class. Three years of London hadn't touched the way Beatrice Frye spoke."

"Embassy messenger," Cabot said.

He listened as the chain was slipped off the latch and the lock turned. The door drew back just enough to reveal a puffy, overly madeup face, scarlet on the lips, generous blotches of rouge on the cheeks. The hair, mousy brown, had been badly bleached and frizzed and the nails scraping against the door were chipped.

"What do you want?" Beatrice Frye demanded.

Cabot showed her his embassy security identification.

"Is your husband here, Mrs. Frye?"

The sharp glinting eyes, which couldn't camouflage a lifetime of resentment and struggle, lost their arrogance. In its place Cabot saw fear.

"He ain't home," Beatrice Frye snapped.

"Can you tell me where he is?" Cabot asked patiently.

"You should know that better than I," she retorted and was about to close the door.

Beatrice Frye screamed as the door flew back at her. In one motion Cabot was in the central hall, moving into the living room. There was someone on the sofa. Not Frye but a young Army corporal, not more than twenty. He was fumbling with his zipper while looking at Cabot fearfully.

"Yer not her old man!" he snarled suddenly. The soldier rose and started to move in Cabot's direction.

"Who the hell you think you are, mate, bustin' into a lady's home like this?"

Cabot's arm shot out, grabbing the soldier by the shirt.

"You have ten seconds to get out of here," Cabot said tonelessly. "After that I take you in."

He released the soldier, who staggered back, then scrambled to grab his jacket. Behind him Cabot heard Beatrice Frye laughing and then the door slammed.

"Well, well, what a show!" she applauded, entering the front part of the double parlor. "Why did you have to go and upset that poor boy like that?"

But Cabot didn't hear her. He was listening hard for other sounds—the creaking of floorboards above him, the scraping of a shoe on the staircase, the creak of a door being closed. He was listening for Frye trying to make his escape.

"I told you, lover, he isn't here," Beatrice Frye said, smiling at him. "Lennie and I don't have much left, but that darling boy wouldn't have been here if hubbie had been home."

As she approached him Cabot noticed for the first time that she was a short woman, perhaps five-three or four. Her floral print housecoat was loosely tied, the breasts pressed together by a black brassiere, the cleavage revealing soft, freckled skin.

Beatrice laughed throatily at his gaze.

"I know what you're thinking, lover. I *was* something else at sixteen. But I'm even better now!"

One hand was on his sleeve, moving up, the fingers curling around the lapels of the wet coat. Her other hand was pressed against the buckle of his belt.

"And I thought you spoiled my evening. . . " Beatrice smiled.

Cabot pushed her hands away.

"I'm sorry if I have," he said.

Before anger made her ugly there was another expression that crossed Beatrice Frye's face: pain, deep, shocking pain which allowed Cabot that sudden glimpse into the core of her life. Emptiness, that's all there was. A life as dusty and ordinary as the haphazard arrangement of scratched furniture in the parlor, where dirt lay on the windowsills and dust balls curled along the dull floorboards between the walls and threadbare carpet. A life of cracked dreams, like the ceramic ashtray overflowing with butts, or the glasses, stained, which held the remainder of the soldier's drink.

"Where is he?" Cabot asked gently.

"The hell with you!" Beatrice Frye spat back. "Who do you think you are . . . coming in here?"

"Does he always go out on Wednesday nights?"

Beatrice Frye shuddered and seemed to grow smaller before his eyes. She shuffled over to the hard, green-gray couch, sat down and fumbled with her cigarettes.

"What's he done?" she asked, the voice hollow, resigned.

"Perhaps nothing," Cabot said. "But I have to talk to him."

"You got to tell me one thing," she said, staring at him through a veil of cigarette smoke. "You've got to tell me if it has anything to do with her."

"Her?"

"You know damn well who I'm talking about!" Beatrice Frye screamed. "I'm not stupid! You think I don't know about that tramp he's been keeping on the side?"

The rage expended itself and crumbled.

"Tell me if it's because of her," Beatrice sobbed. "Just tell me that it wasn't his fault . . . whatever it is."

"She's involved," Cabot said. "I'm sorry . . ."

"But I'm not!" Beatrice Frye retorted viciously.

As she wiped away the tears, the rouge and mascara streaked her cheeks, turning her into a grotesque parody of the seductress.

"You think it was always like this?" she demanded. "You think I always ran after young stuff? It wasn't like that at all . . . I don't know when Lennie stopped caring for me . . . stopped being a man to his wife. Oh Christ, how bad is it for him?" she implored Cabot. "You must tell me!"

"Mrs. Frye, I can't tell you anything more because I don't know. I have to speak with your husband—"

"All right, all right!" Beatrice Frye waved her hand. "You're like the worst cop back home. You don't give a shit for anything but what you need. But you have to tell me one thing: Is she going to suffer too? If she hurt Lennie then I want her to hurt too!"

Cabot looked down at the hate-filled, almost maniacal eyes that wanted someone—anyone—else to share the pain.

"We took the woman in question into custody an hour ago," he said.

For the next forty minutes, as she drank her lover's now warm whiskey and smoked cigarette after cigarette, Beatrice Frye told Cabot more than he had ever expected to hear.

The mansion occupied the better part of the block bounded by Wellington Place and Cavendish Avenue. Across the street was the Lord's Cricket Ground and at the foot of Wellington Road, the St. John's Burial Ground.

Jonathan Cabot was sitting in the front seat of the Jaguar at the edge of the cricket grounds. On the right the grandstands threw up stark monolithic shadows across Wellington Place. The wind, light since the rain had abated, played the naked branches of trees like a xylophone. Cabot's eyes were fixed on the palatial Georgian mansion whose white stone shimmered in the light of the moon.

Mackenzie McConnell lit two cigarettes and passed one to Cabot. She had arrived fifteen minutes ago to find him already there.

"That's about all, then," she said quietly. "Tricia Burns kept neat little notes on her calls around Whitehall. Those were enough of a lever to pry loose the rest of the information."

"To get a line on me Kennedy used Frye, Frye used her,"

Cabot said tonelessly. "And she ended up plugging into the Whitehall gossip mill."

He paused. "Goddamn her to hell! Who knows how far my name has gone now!"

"We have a list of the women she spoke to," Mackenzie said quietly. "They're being tracked down now. We can contain the damage, Jonathan. After we use our influence none of them will want to even remember hearing of you."

Cabot did not reply. Instead he said: "Tell me about Blackthorne."

"Of all the names Beatrice Frye had to come up with why that one?" Mackenzie said rhetorically and shook her head. "Sir Francis Blackthorne is twenty-eight years old and as blue-blooded a bastard as you would ever want to meet. In addition he's also one of the wealthiest. In addition to being heir to land holdings in Devon, he also owns a good deal of the coal mines in Wales, textile mills in the Midlands and part of the P&O shipping line.

"That house was built by a great-grandfather at the turn of the nineteenth century. Apparently all manner of royalty for the last hundred years has stayed there at one time or another. Politically young Francis is somewhere to the right of Attila the Hun."

"Is he on the Grey List?" asked Cabot.

Mackenzie glanced at him in frank surprise. The Grey List was so secret that even its existence was never alluded to. It was a compendium of names kept by MI5 of notable persons who, because of their right-wing politics, were under constant surveillance by home security. For the most part these people knew that since the official declaration of war their mail was being tampered with, their friends, servants, employees questioned at random intervals, their private lives subjected to minute scrutiny. They knew but could not prove anything.

"We've kept a *very* close eye on Blackthorne," Mackenzie McConnell confirmed. "The family has strong connections in Germany. Before Blackthorne *père* passed away he worked out major industrial agreements with Hindenburg, then Hitler. There has been intermarriage as well. Blackthorne's sister is the wife of Manfred Krupp."

"And this little get-together tonight—how long has *that* been going on?" asked Cabot.

"For almost a year. We've tried to get information as to what goes on, but the servants are given the night off and some of Mosley's thugs are brought in to make sure no one except those invited is admitted."

Mackenzie McConnell hesitated. "There's one other thing, Jonathan. Churchill knows that Blackthorne's address is a vipers' nest. He'd give his right arm to get someone in there because, with the new security laws and proper evidence, we could charge Blackthorne with sedition at the very least. But because the guest list includes former Cabinet secretaries, directors of the major banks and corporations, Churchill's standing orders are unequivocal: we can move only when we're certain Blackthorne or anyone else will have no comeback. If there were any grounds for a false arrest, the scandal and its repercussions on the government would be enormous."

"They're going to be enormous anyway," Cabot said, his voice hard. "But this time Blackthorne will have to take up his complaint with Roosevelt. He has the head cryptographer of the embassy in there. That makes Frye a security risk . . . and *that* gives him to me."

Mackenzie McConnell leaned forward, flicked a switch and the Jaguar's parking lights glowed briefly. A few seconds later the second car pulled up. Mackenzie rolled down her window, issued instructions to the driver and three other agents.

"There are three entrances to the house—front, rear, and through the gardens that border Wellington Place," she said, looking after the Humber's pinprick lights as the car moved silently across the square. "We have people around the back already. That team"—she nodded in the direction of the Humber—"will cover the gardens."

She laid a hand on Cabot's arm. "Why not wait until Frye leaves here tonight? We can pick him up on the way home."

"Because maybe he won't be going home," Cabot said. "He might have tried to contact Tricia Burns after we picked her up. If so, and he got no answer, he's figured out we're closing in. Right now Blackthorne's house is the best haven he has. He'll stay there until he decides on the next move."

There was a distinct snap as Mackenzie flicked off the safety on her gun.

"Let's take him," she said tonelessly.

They left the car on the corner of the square and walked the rest of the distance. The property was bordered by a shoulder-high stone wall with black wrought-iron spikes imbedded along the top. The gate latch was open and creaked as Mackenzie McConnell pushed it forward. She waited until Cabot was in position on either side of the wide, black-enamel door. She took a deep breath and pushed the buzzer.

The man who opened the door was a disfigured parody of a human being. He wasn't tall but his girth was almost the same size as his height. The face was pockmarked and fleshy, dominated by a squashed broken nose. The left eye was almost completely closed while the right burned a perfect red. Beneath a gleaming bald pate the skin hung in thick, rubbery folds across the forehead. He was dressed wholly in black and the muscles of the torso and arms lay contoured against his woolen sweater.

"Yes, miss, please?"

He spoke in a raspy whisper as though his larynx had been shattered.

"I wish to speak with Lord Blackthorne, please."

"His lordship is not at home."

The troglodyte started to close the door on her when Mackenzie McConnell said:

"I'm afraid that won't do. This is a security matter."

The giant's one eye blinked rapidly as he looked down at Mackenzie's identification. To do so he had to open the door to admit his bulk and that proved to be the mistake.

In his eye Mackenzie McConnell saw the decision to slam the door. Her left leg kicked out, the steel-capped toe of the boot catching the giant under the knee. For a precise instant, when he had both hands off the door, Mackenzie threw her weight against it, slamming it open, and flew past him. Then suddenly her midriff connected with what she thought was an oak beam. Looking around she saw that the manservant had thrown one arm out to stop her. With his incredible strength, that was all he needed. Mackenzie saw the door closing behind her, pressing what must have been Cabot's arm into the frame. As she felt herself being dragged back, Mackenzie managed to pivot and bring down one hand across the giant's face. Blood erupted from the right eye as her gold ring studded with tiny points of sapphire ripped into the flesh. Swinging her elbow back, she smashed his jaw, the momentum sending him crashing against the radiator. A third blow, the back of the hand behind the ear, finally toppled him.

Mackenzie McConnell wrenched open the door and Cabot stepped over the body.

"Are you all right?" he demanded.

"Y—yes," she stammered. "But we have to hurry. They must have heard all the commotion."

As if to underline her words a voice called out from the vestibule behind the frosted glass door.

"Leo, who is it? What do they want?"

Footsteps came closer, the thick glass knob began to turn. Cabot didn't wait. He threw himself against the door and pinned the second guard against the wall behind it.

"Very quietly, friend," he whispered, jamming the gun barrel against the guard's throat.

Cabot motioned for Mackenzie to get inside, then turned the guard around, clamping both his hands around the back of his neck.

"Where is Blackthorne?"

"Billiard room," the man gasped. "Straight down the hall on the left."

Cabot increased the pressure around the man's neck and the guard crumbled.

He was running now, Mackenzie McConnell only steps behind him. He heard faint music somewhere up ahead, a string quartet, then the murmur of voices, the peal of crystal against crystal. Cabot reached the double doors and pressed his back against them.

"On my go," he murmured, scarcely moving his lips. Mackenzie McConnell nodded and drew her own weapon.

Cabot stepped back and sent a spinning side kick at the latches. The shriek of splintering wood cut the air and the doors burst open. Cabot saw four men immediately, but the room was so large he continued to move quickly, disregarding the astonishment and terror in the faces, seeking others who might have been out of his sight. There were three more, standing in a group by the massive, cut-stone fireplace. Cabot glanced at each face, then his eyes began to probe the nooks and crannies of the room. He didn't see Frye.

"Just what the devil is going on here?"

The speaker was by far the youngest man in the group, but a young man already grown old. Although he was tall, a lifetime of excess had fattened him, the flesh around his neck spilling over the wing-tip collar. His face was florid, the nose already tracked with broken veins. Beneath sparse, straw-colored hair, plastered against the forehead, were rheumy, gray-flecked eyes that stared out in hatred.

"I asked you who you are and what do you want?" the man repeated. Cabot caught a faint lisp to his words.

"Lord Blackthorne, my name is Mackenzie McConnell, I am from the Security Service. We are here to ask a Mr. Leonard Frye to accompany us to our offices."

Cabot listened but didn't look back at Mackenzie. His eyes roved around the room, watching the expressions of those before him while Mackenzie spoke. From two men he received the involuntary signal he had hoped for.

"Miss Mackenzie," Blackthorne said, venomously adding: "If that is indeed your name, in the first instance I shall require some identification. Secondly, even if you are who you say and work for the Security Service, that will not spare you the rather dire consequences of your intrusion here tonight. Rest assured—"

"Where is he?" Cabot cut him off. "Where's Frye?"

"I haven't the slightest idea as to what you're talking about," Blackthorne said disdainfully. "I would suggest to you, sir, that you put away that weapon before my manservant appears."

"You may have to wait a long time for Leo to come around," Cabot said. The use of his servant's first name unnerved Blackthorne.

"You have broken into my house," he whispered. "Threatened my guests and myself, assaulted my people . . . I think this has gone quite far enough."

"I shouldn't do that, my lord," Mackenzie McConnell said coldly, pointing her gun at Blackthorne's hand, which was reaching for the telephone.

Blackthorne smiled maliciously. "No, of course not."

The gun bucked in her hand and Blackthorne screamed as pieces of metal and plastic ripped across his fingers. The telephone, what was left of it, rolled across the ancient Persian rug, smoldering.

Cabot grabbed the man nearest him by the lapels of his black-tie.

"Where is Frye?" he whispered.

The man was shaking uncontrollably, lips quivering.

"*Where?*"

"In there!" the man whispered hoarsely. "He went into the bathroom—"

But Cabot heard him now—Frye moving somewhere in the next room, footsteps echoing off floorboards, the slamming of a door.

"Keep them all here!" he shouted and made for the door that stood between two floor-to-ceiling bookcases.

Cabot found himself in a narrow corridor. To the right was a small bathroom, the lights still on. He moved swiftly past the pantry and kitchens; then, cursing, reversed direction. At the end of the hallway was a door slightly ajar. Cabot pushed it open and with his fingertips felt for the switch. The lights illuminated a narrow passageway that descended at a thirty-degree angle. The air was cool, the rough stone dry, giving off a musty odor.

Frye had bolted into the wine cellar. Cautiously, with the machine gun held low and over the railing, Cabot made his way down.

By any standards the cellar was immense, with six-foot racks running the length. The racks divided the cellar into a perfect grid, with just enough space for one man to pass between them. There was nowhere to hide in the aisles, which meant that Frye had gone to ground somewhere else. Cabot checked each row carefully, making sure there wasn't a hollow space where a man could crouch. When he reached the last column he saw a small curved door, like those in a monastery. He pushed at it tentatively at first, feeling it give a few millimeters but no more. There was no lock, no knob on the face. Cabot stepped back, took aim at the hinges and pressed the trigger. Sparks and splinters of wood flew back at him. The door sagged but did not fall. Cabot reached around the hinges and, gripping the wood, slowly pried it back. A utility room, smelling of old paint and varnish, the walls stenciled with pegboard from which an array of household tools hung. Cabot knelt down and pulled up the sheet of wood that had fallen against the door, blocking his entry. He took one last look around but not even his fury could conjure up Frye.

Upon hearing Mackenzie McConnell's shot the outside security teams split in two. Heavily armed men raced for the house while their partners remained at their posts, weapons drawn, tense, alert. After Cabot emerged from the wine cellar a thorough search of the grounds was conducted but to no avail. The security teams assured Cabot no one could have gotten by them.

Blackthorne and his seven guests were in the billiard room in the company of four security agents. The two manservants had been handcuffed and placed in the pantry. When he came in from the night Cabot motioned Mackenzie over, well out of earshot of everyone else.

"Anything?" he demanded.

"Frye has been here," she told him. "I found his coat. He had his name sewn into it."

She watched Cabot examine the garment.

"Which means we have all the justification we need for being here tonight," Mackenzie McConnell finished. "Considering what's happened and who is present I would say that's just as well. The roster reads like a political and City who's who."

Cabot glanced over her shoulder.

"Threats?"

"Oh, plenty of those." Mackenzie smiled. "Except they don't mean a damn thing right now."

"I want twenty minutes with Blackthorne—alone," Cabot said.

"Jonathan, when I said that we have justification for being here and doing what we did, I meant it," Mackenzie said, holding him back. "But Frye *isn't* here now. If you want that lot taken down to Queen Anne's Gate, fine. We can talk to them there. In the meantime I'd like to get Scotland Yard in on this as fast as possible, get a full description out, start covering the airports and docks. In fact I'd like to have the entire Metropolitan Police Force out there!" She paused. "But I can't leave you and Blackthorne alone for twenty minutes, not with what that implies."

"Mackenzie," Cabot said urgently, "I can't beat the truth out of Blackthorne in twenty minutes. But maybe I can get him to trade some information in return for being left alone."

"I'm not sure I follow you, Jonathan," she said cautiously.

"As far as I understand, your War Measures Act is designed to *neutralize* people like Blackthorne. It's out in the open, a formal declaration of rules: they can sit and plot all they want in their billiard rooms, but until they actually offer concrete aid and comfort to the enemy you won't move on them. The Act is the sword hanging over their heads. Besides, Churchill himself knows that if a head count were taken tomorrow a lot of Blackthornes would surface and show the Nazis just how divided this country really is."

Mackenzie McConnell bit gently on her lower lip. "Point conceded . . . I'm ashamed to say."

"So right now Blackthorne is afraid he's overstepped that invisible line," Cabot continued on quickly. "If we lose the momentum, let him and the others collect their wits, we'll get nothing out of them at Queen Anne's Gate. But now, *right now*, maybe I can get him to talk to me about Frye. That's all we want. I don't know how Frye ties in with this bunch, but he can't be very tight. These people use men like him. But Frye could never be one of them. I'm gambling that under the circumstances, to save their own hides, they'll spit him back at us."

Mackenzie McConnell looked up at Cabot, her eyes probing his own, trying to determine if there was something he was hiding from her.

"All right," she said. "Twenty minutes, no more. But in the meantime the alert goes out. Agreed?"

"Agreed."

Mackenzie McConnell turned and walked back to where Blackthorne and the others were seated.

"My lord, you will please accompany this gentleman into the next room."

Blackthorne clamped his hands behind his head and grinned at her.

"Not bloody likely!"

Mackenzie McConnell turned to one of her agents. "Mr. Tytell, would you be good enough to ring for more cars. Also telephone the press and the Home Secretary. Inform both that the Security Service has just succeeded in breaking a major espionage ring—"

She got no further before Blackthorne was on his feet, shouting.

"You can't say that!" he exploded.

"My lord, given your actions this evening I can say any damn thing I please about you! Now I shall ask you again: do you wish for a chance to resolve this matter privately or do I parade you and these other distinguished gentlemen through the city, the press and all posterity as traitors? The choice, gentlemen, is yours."

The others were speaking now, whispering frantically with Blackthorne.

"All right!" the young nobleman snarled. "Where is it to be?"

A minute later Cabot and Blackthorne were in the kitchens, seated at a simple wooden table next to a tiled wall. On his way in, Blackthorne had seized a bottle of Armagnac. He was about to take a snifter as well when Cabot stopped him.

"If you want the brandy, fine, but no glass."

Blackthorne drew out the cork, casually lifted the bottle to his lips and drank deeply. He placed the bottle before Cabot, who pushed it aside.

"I'm going to make this very easy for you," Cabot said. "I don't particularly care what kind of politics you or your friends in there are playing. I want Frye for my own reasons. You can give him to me. Do that and we all leave as quietly as we came."

Blackthorne brushed aside a cowlick and sat back, arms folded across his chest.

"Who are you?" he asked softly.

"Cabot, Jonathan Cabot."

Blackthorne nodded heavily. "Poor old Frye was very worried about you, you know. He tried every which way to find out about you . . . couldn't. Upset him dreadfully."

"Where is he?"

"Said you weren't on the best of terms with old Joe Kennedy . . . That right?"

"Where is he?" Cabot repeated quietly. "Believe me, Blackthorne, he's not worth it to you."

"Oh, I *do* believe you," the nobleman said, reaching for the bottle. "Oh, by all means smoke if you must . . . Disgusting, unhygienic habit."

Cabot waited until Blackthorne had drunk.

"I really can't tell you where little Leonard has run off to," Blackthorne muttered. "Bloody stupid of him to have bolted like that."

"Stupid of you to have had him here," Cabot countered. "That's something I don't understand. What was Frye to you?"

"He was *nothing* to us!" Blackthorne hissed. "Frye was a

sycophantic little turd who was prepared to bow and scrape so low it was revolting."

"But still you took him into your circle. His wife tells me he's been coming here regularly for the last six months."

"That stupid sow!" Blackthorne barked. "How could she know anything?"

"Because she thought Frye was having an affair. She followed him here a number of times, waited to see if he would leave with another woman."

Blackthorne laughed. "From what I understand she was looking in the wrong place."

"You people were using Frye," Cabot said slowly. "He was head cryptographer at the embassy. If you deigned to let him enter this charmed circle of yours, he would have been suitably grateful . . . grateful enough to share whatever tidbits he thought might interest you."

Blackthorne slammed an open palm on the table.

"You can't make such accusations!" he shouted.

"Yes, I can. The way I see it, you *recruited* Frye on someone else's orders. I'm beginning to think that this little club of yours is just a little more active than MI5 had suspected. Perhaps it's time to open you all up."

"I tell you that no one, least of all myself, ever considered recruiting Frye!" Blackthorne shouted, his skin breaking out in florid blotches. "Yes, he was an amusing chatterbox and he did volunteer gossip. *But we never asked him for anything!*"

"Then why was he so scared tonight?" Cabot demanded. "Why was he asking questions about me and why did he turn to you when he couldn't come up with the answers?"

"I don't know." Blackthorne shrugged. "I curse the day I set eyes on the little bastard."

"Which was where?"

"Oh, at some embassy reception or something of that sort. I can't remember."

"Then you'd better remember this," Cabot said savagely. "There was a shooting in Leatherhead I think you know about. Some gunners tried to get me and the embassy security officer . . . I think Frye helped set up the killing ground. I also think you knew about and abetted—"

Blackthorne's hand shot out, gripping Cabot's wrist.

"I had nothing to do with that. I swear it! Frye never mentioned anything about shooting!"

"Then exactly what did Frye talk to you about?" Cabot kept
on relentlessly. "Frye passed you information, information *you*
used to set up the massacre."

"I didn't! For God's sakes I didn't!" Blackthorne cried out.

"But Frye was your source, your informant, inside the embassy, wasn't he?"

"*Yes*!" Blackthorne roared. "Frye had all sorts of gossip to
tell. Most of it was harmless, I swear. Occasionally there
would be something interesting which would be repeated . . ."

"To whom?"

"I don't know! I meet a great many people. I can't tell you
what every one of them really does."

"To whom did you pass on Frye's information?" Cabot hammered at him. "Think!"

"A fellow at the Spanish embassy," Blackthorne whispered.
"He's their American observer as it were—you know, collects
all the gossip, scandal, what have you."

"But he took a particular interest in Frye?"

Blackthorne withdrew a handkerchief and blew his nose
loudly.

"He made a point to tell me that he found my anecdotes
about Frye most amusing," the nobleman admitted.

"I can see where he would have," Cabot said softly. He
looked at the beaten, pathetic figure opposite him.

"Congratulations, Blackthorne. A couple of minutes ago
you were just another rank, pain-in-the-ass amateur. Now
you've made the big leagues."

"What do you mean?" Blackthorne rasped.

"I'm going to hand you over to that fine lady in there, and
I'm sure you and she will have a nice long talk about dates,
names and places. Then, later on, when you meet your Spaniard, you'll have much more to tell him—except that it will be
information *we* want passed along to Berlin. From this moment
on, Blackthorne, you're going to be under the microscope and
you thank the stars that you're here and not up against a brick
wall with twelve troopers taking a bead on your heart."

"You can't force me to do that," Blackthorne whispered.

"Not a matter of forcing you," Cabot corrected him. "You're
a volunteer, remember? Frye passed you information—con-
fidential or otherwise, it makes no difference. He turns out to

be at least a security risk, at worst a traitor. And you're his conduit."

"But you promised me that if I told you about Frye . . ." Blackthorne's voice trailed off.

"And you were a much more stupid man than I expected," Cabot finished.

12

As he sat in the rattling sub-way car, rocking back and forth with the motion of the train, Leonard Frye gave silent thanks to an unknown Blackthorne servant who had been dere-lict in his duty.

The basement would have become his coffin had he not found the coal bin, thrown himself onto the bricks and clawed his way toward the chute. Even then it could all have been for nought, if a servant had, as he was supposed to, pulled the chute away from the mouth cut into the foundation. Driven by an insane fury, Leonard Frye had split open his nails in the struggle to gain a foothold on the chute. As he dragged himself forward, splinters pierced his soft hands, the wood driving deep beneath the nerves to the blood.

Nonetheless he kicked and clawed his way to the top and wrenched open the small, square door, crawling into the pud-dle that had collected at the base of a roof drainpipe. He heard shouting all around him but paid no heed to it. The perimeter would have shrunk and with luck he was now on the outside of it. Leonard Frye had the presence of mind to shut the trapdoor behind him, then plunged into the hedgerow that bordered the servants' entrance. Within seconds he was over the wall and stumbling across the playing field.

In the odd moments the car lights flickered to life Leonard Frye saw exactly the toll his crawl up the chute had taken. His best suit, bought on credit in Savile Row, was filthy and tattered, the fine wool shredded at the elbows and knees. His hands were dirty, the fingernails clogged with coal dust. In the reflection of the window he saw streaks of blood across his cheeks. Mercifully there were few riders at this hour and those who came on avoided the miserable man who huddled in one corner.

Shortly after midnight Leonard Frye emerged from the Kensington High Street station. He walked in the direction of Argyll Road, moving quickly because of the bitter wind rather than fear, and came to a telephone booth. Trembling, he dialed, heard a voice on the other end and hung up.

Turning right on Argyll Road, Frye walked no more than a dozen yards before turning again onto Phillimore Walk. His fingers fumbled with the coins and keys in his pocket until he found the slim skeleton key he needed. Within minutes he was climbing the stairs of the boardinghouse where he kept a bed-sitting room. Here he was known as John Foster. The landlady, who seldom saw him, believed him to be a minor employee of an American corporation. She was pleased to have him there because Frye paid his rent promptly at the first of the month. When he couldn't come in person, a post office money order arrived instead. The landlady had no complaints.

Now it's finished, Frye thought as he locked the door behind him. Carefully he made his way over to the couch and turned on the single lamp. Frye slumped down on the old hard springs and looked around himself. In the pale yellow light the room appeared dingier than he had remembered. Brown watermarks blotched the ancient flowery wallpaper. Dust hung in the air, the motes dancing and finally settling in yet another layer on the shade. The furniture, old and heavy, with its varnish peeling, was pathetic.

Leonard Frye shivered in the still, cold dampness. He took out whatever change he had in his pockets and fed the coppers into the gas meter. By the time he returned to the couch the ancient radiators were creaking as the coils warmed. He thought of warming a can of soup on the hot plate but couldn't bring himself to move. Finally Leonard Frye couldn't hold back any longer. His shoulders hunched forward and his fingers covered his face as the tears burst forth. Sobbing uncontrollably, he lost hold of his thoughts blazing across his consciousness. His lonely boyhood, the struggles at school, the first meeting with the woman who was to become his wife, the marriage which had been doomed from the outset, every pain, insult and injustice was remembered. But when the memories came to Tricia Burns they slowed and the agony redoubled. He had at last found another human being who truly loved him, respected him and pledged her devotion. After so much pain he had honestly believed he had arrived at a point in life where he dared to be happy. To preserve this state he called upon and was astonished to find resources he never believed he possessed. Leonard Frye discovered he could ignore the whining of his wife, that he could work out a foolproof plan by which certain information that passed through his hands reached interested parties who paid handsomely for his efforts. These faceless men never asked him why he could be a traitor so easily, but Frye would have told them the truth as he believed it: he was owed—owed this one chance for a happiness he had never before tasted.

To preserve this love he began to spy, building his cache of gold so that one day he could walk out his front door, finish the day at the embassy, then walk to the pier where Tricia would be waiting. They would board the boat together and from that moment on turn their backs on everything that had happened in their lives. Nothing would matter after that. Nothing.

Leonard Frye wiped his palms on his trousers, his breath coming in shuddering gasps. Now they had him. How they had discovered his meeting with Blackthorne he would probably never know. Perhaps he had been under surveillance, perhaps others in the group had mentioned his name to someone . . . Maybe it had been Beatrice . . . But the whys and wherefores were not important. He had gone after Cabot only to find Cabot waiting for him. And the man who had no past, who had arrived like a shadow, also had the woman Frye loved. Tricia should have been at the number he had called. He had made certain she understood how important that was. But someone else had answered, in a deathly cool, detached voice . . .

"My fault!" he whispered through his teeth. "All my fault!"

But she wouldn't suffer, Frye promised silently. In a matter of days, a week at most, she would be with him. They would be together, as they had planned.

Leonard Frye moved across the floor on his hands and knees. When he reached the defunct fireplace his fingers pried loose the old stone that served as a grate. Beneath it he saw the key to their freedom: the complete embassy code texts, copied and smuggled out of the embassy a page at a time.

Frye brought out the waterproof oilskin pouch and looked at it hungrily. He had time—not much but some because no one, not even Tricia, knew about this miserable room which, according to his plan, he had rented as a refuge of last resort. Time . . . enough in which to contact Darius, a man he had never seen, knew only as a voice over the telephone. Darius . . . who worked for the Germans, the relay between Berlin and Frye, the courier of instructions, the courier who delivered what Frye took from the embassy, who in turn was Berlin's paymaster . . . He would contact Darius, using the emergency procedure. He would tell him to get Tricia Burns to safety. Somehow, any way—it didn't matter. As soon as Darius did this Frye would follow. And he would bring the codes with him.

But if Darius were to fail him, or desert him, then Frye would contact Cabot. A meeting would be arranged, an exchange offered: Tricia for the codes. A guarantee of safe conduct . . . somehow it would be worked out.

Leonard Frye replaced the pouch and positioned the stone in the grate, making sure it was flush with the floorboards. He staggered over to the couch and using what was left of his strength swung it lengthwise so that the front faced the radiators. No sooner had he stretched his legs out than a long, forlorn sigh escaped his lips and he was asleep.

Ambassador Joseph Kennedy was a man of regular habits and strict routine. At one o'clock on the morning of May 26 he had been asleep almost two hours. He did not take kindly to the insistent buzz of the telephone on the night table. Annoyance became anger when his valet informed him who had caused his sleep to be so rudely interrupted. As he struggled into his robe and searched for his slippers the Ambassador was already composing the scathing demands and questions he would hurl at Cabot and Pearce. As he stomped downstairs to his office he was almost delighting in the confrontation. Not once did he consider he had anything to be afraid of.

The two men were already seated before his desk. Cabot had helped himself to a brandy and was staring into the snifter on his lap. Kennedy swept around his desk, settled in his chair and glared at Pearce.

"This had better be very, *very* good," he said, emphasizing each word.

"No, Mr. Ambassador, it's very bad," Pearce replied quietly. "And it might be worse than we expect."

After Cabot had returned to the embassy and briefed Pearce on what had happened with Blackthorne, the two men agreed that Pearce, as chief of embassy security, should present Kennedy with the details. It took Pearce twenty minutes to do so, during which time Kennedy didn't utter a single word. He didn't have to. His expressions spoke volumes, running the gamut from shock and outrage to a fearful realization of the implications of Frye's actions.

Although the chief of security stopped short of accusing Kennedy of making it possible for Frye to gain access to information which otherwise he never would have seen, the implication was there that the Ambassador, by his rank favoritism, had provided Frye with opportunity.

"It's been two hours since Frye began to run," Pearce concluded. "We don't think he'll go very far tonight. He wasn't expecting to be caught. But even money says he has a safe house somewhere and a contingency plan to get out of the country. That's where the British can really help us out. They're already involved because Tricia Burns is a British national. They have the manpower to cover all exits out of the country, get Frye's description to every cop, taxi driver, railway porter, bartender in London. In short, Mr. Ambassador, they can shut London down for us."

Kennedy swung his chair around, sitting in profile before the two men.

"Has Frye taken anything with him?" he asked finally. "Papers, documents . . ."

"Nothing appears to be missing from his office, sir. But tonight's meeting wasn't a regular drop—"

"You don't even know for sure he *was* meeting someone regularly!" Kennedy flared.

"We know he passed information to Blackthorne," Cabot said, breaking his silence. "If we're lucky that's *all* he was doing. But I don't think so. Frye may have run off at the mouth at a pro-Fascist meeting but that doesn't mean he was careless or shortsighted. He would have had a bolthole—and a route worked out between it and Blackthorne's place. He's not wandering the streets in the blackout waiting for us to find him."

Kennedy began toying with a silver letter opener, twisting it between his fingers.

"The embassy will be in turmoil tomorrow," he said in a hollow tone. "Can you imagine the effect this will have on our people, their morale? The staff will be asking questions . . . the press will make everyone's life hell . . ."

"Not necessarily, Mr. Ambassador," Pearce broke in. "The British can slap a D notice on the newspapers and radios. A letter from the Home Secretary to the national editors will put a lid on the affair for as long as we need to have one. As for our people, I'll get the crypto boys in here right away. If Frye has taken anything they'll be the ones to find out what it is."

"I don't like it," Kennedy muttered. "I don't like it at all."

"Mr. Ambassador," Cabot said, "I believe this is the time to tell you exactly why I was sent to London."

Kennedy swiveled around, his anger riveted on Cabot.

"Yes, sir," he said softly. "I do believe you owe me the courtesy of an explanation."

In a few minutes Cabot explained the events in Washington, the unmasking of Beth Davis, the trail that led back to Grosvenor Square, the Presidential directive which had brought him to London.

"I think Leonard Frye was Beth Davis's source," Cabot concluded. "He kept a very low profile but tainted the crypto communications when there was an intercept to be made at the other end."

"If that's the case why would Frye have been communicating with Nazi sympathizers here in London?" Kennedy objected. "Surely if he was so valuable to them, kept in deep cover as you say, they would have instructed him to do nothing of the sort."

"We'll have to ask Frye about that when we catch up with him," Cabot replied. "But we know of Frye's relationship with Tricia Burns. We know his wife knew. It's fair to say Frye was approaching the point where this would have to be resolved. He may have gone into business for himself, started feeding Berlin more information directly out of London in return for greater payments."

For a moment Kennedy said nothing. Slumped back in his chair, he seemed older now, vulnerable, a man who had suddenly had the ground open up beneath his feet. Kennedy, Cabot understood, had just been gelded. Whatever political threat he represented to Roosevelt had just evaporated. Whether or not any blame for what Frye had done could be placed at his feet, the result was the same: he was head of the embassy. The scandal would be inextricably linked to his name as long as he remained in political life.

"There's one more detail," Pearce spoke up. He glanced at Cabot and held up his hand, warning him not to interrupt.

"As chief of security it was my responsibility to ensure the integrity of this embassy. I failed to do so. Until Mr. Cabot arrived I had no idea what was going on here . . . in one of the most sensitive posts."

Pearce hesitated, then spat it all out. "Mr. Ambassador, at this moment I am tendering my resignation. I will of course stay on until this matter is resolved. But as soon as Frye is caught I would ask that I be reassigned to other duties."

Kennedy nodded and a faint smile crossed his lips.

"Thanks to Mr. Cabot here," he said, not without malice, "both of us may be looking for a new job, Edward. Why don't you sleep on it and I'll do the same. Now if you'll excuse me I'll telephone Churchill myself and tell him to expect you shortly."

Jonathan Cabot descended into the communications chamber and from there sent a carefully composed message to Allen Dulles via the White House. On the ground floor Edward Pearce was quickly but methodically going through Frye's office, searching for anything that might give him a clue as to where the cryptographer had gone to ground.

"Nothing," he said when Cabot appeared. "But I've pulled some five-by-eight glossies of him from Personnel. Get these over to the British and they can run off as many as they need."

Cabot pocketed the photographs. "You're sure you can manage here?"

"Get going." Pearce waved at him. "You're keeping Churchill waiting."

"Edward, about resigning—"

"Not now, Johnny, please." Pearce's voice faltered. "We'll talk later, OK?"

Shortly before three o'clock Jonathan Cabot arrived at Number Ten Downing Street to see the Prime Minister's residence ablaze with lights and the driveway jammed with official vehicles. In addition to Mackenzie McConnell and Churchill, the chief of Scotland Yard's Criminal Investigation Division and the head of the London Metropolitan Police Force were also present.

"It seems to me that we're doing all we can," Churchill said gruffly. He was wearing a paisley houserobe that seemed quite out of character.

"We have Tricia Burns's residence under surveillance," Mackenzie McConnell confirmed. "As well as that of Mrs. Frye. Additional squads have been placed around the 'neutral' embassies of Spain, Portugal and others. If Frye tries to go anywhere it will be to one of these."

Churchill turned to Inspector General Malmouth of the Yard.

"Prime Minister," Malmouth said smartly, "I can put two hundred men into the streets within the hour. I would suggest that they concentrate on the Irish community here, particularly those places and figures we know are associated with the IRA. If this man Frye is planning to leave Britain, I would think a quick trip across the Irish Sea would be his ticket."

"Do so," Churchill said simply. "And you, Chief Inspector?"

The head of the London police cleared his throat and held up the photo glossies.

"In most precincts, Prime Minister, the relief shift comes on at six o'clock, about three hours from now. I would think there is enough time to make the necessary number of duplicates from these photographs and disseminate them to every station in Greater London.

"In addition to providing each constable with a picture, I would call up a double shift of personnel to cover such key areas as train stations, bus depots and hotels."

"Chief Inspector," Cabot broke in, "I would suggest you tell your patrolmen to carefully check the tenants of small boardinghouses. If Frye has gone to ground he would have chosen a small, innocuous place. Nothing fancy."

"Good point," the official murmured.

"Mr. Cabot," Churchill said, "I take it the two women involved have been thoroughly interrogated."

"Yes, Mr. Prime Minister. Tricia Burns has already confessed that she was telling Frye exactly when the London–White House line was active. When she wasn't on duty she made a point of calling in and chatting with one of the two other operators. In the course of the conversation it was easy enough to ask if a call had come through. Burns then immediately contacted Frye, who would pull the cipher texts. Given the irregularity of Frye's intercepts, the other cipher operators didn't see anything suspicious—just routine, random checks on their work, which Frye was always running."

"But didn't the damn woman realize what she was doing?" Churchill demanded.

"I think she did," Cabot said. "But she buried the truth so far below her love for Frye that it might never have existed."

He paused. "We're continuing the questioning of both her and Frye's wife. It's possible Frye may have let something slip that neither woman paid any attention to at the time but which could prove significant."

"If they can remember it," Churchill said sourly. "Very well, gentlemen. I suggest you get on with your respective tasks. Miss McConnell, Mr. Cabot, pray stay behind. I should like a few words with you."

After the others had filed out, Churchill rose and shuffled over to the liquor trolley.

"Scarcely the cocktail hour," he muttered. "But under the circumstances . . ."

Without bothering to ask if they would join him, Churchill poured out three snifters of cognac.

"I simply wanted to congratulate the both of you," he said quietly, raising his glass. "You achieved what you set out to do. Of course I am sorry that you were right . . ."

Churchill drained his brandy in a single swallow.

"I may assume, Mr. Cabot, that Ambassador Kennedy is fully cognizant of the matter."

"He was briefed earlier on, sir," Cabot said.

"He knows, of course, that when Frye is taken there will be a public trial," Churchill said. "There is no way around that, I'm afraid. We will request that under the circumstances diplomatic immunity be waived."

"I'm sure the Ambassador is familiar with the law, Mr. Prime Minister."

Churchill was silent for a moment, his great head nodding, the cigar bobbing like a seesaw.

"A damnable state of affairs!" he barked out suddenly. "No matter the individual profit, so much has been compromised."

"And more could have been, sir."

Churchill looked up at him. "You are a generous man, sir. Much more so than I. I applaud you for that."

The Prime Minister hesitated, as though he felt the need to say something more. But Cabot understood that Churchill could never apologize, for he was glad Kennedy had been gelded. And better still, by one of his own.

"Good night, Prime Minister," Cabot said.

They did not speak in the car and Cabot said nothing when Mackenzie drove them in the opposite direction from the embassy, into Pont Street Mews in Knightsbridge.

"Is this where you live?" Cabot asked, indicating the regal, fourteen-floor hexagon that was Harrods.

"Not quite," she smiled, stepping out of the sports car, and ran up the steps. Cabot followed, unbidden but understanding that he was meant to do so.

"Very nice," he murmured, looking around him.

The front room was very large, dominated by a fireplace with a gilt-edge mirror above the mantelpiece. Old Persian rugs hid most of the stained oak flooring, while the furniture was of the Art Deco period, comfortable but slightly bizarre in design. The walls were adorned with Cubists and Impressionists, all of them, by Cabot's estimate, genuine.

"Make yourself comfortable," Mackenzie called out from the kitchen. "I'll just be a minute."

Cabot swung off his coat. "Who lives upstairs?"

"No one now. The house belonged to Mum and Dad when he was working in London. They moved to the country a few years ago, stored a lot of books and things upstairs, and left the rest for me."

"Nice."

Cabot unbuckled the loops from around the submachine gun and carefully placed the weapon on a loveseat. He removed the revolver, then unclipped the belt holster and sheathed the weapon. He carried both weapons into the living room and, leaving them within reach, placed them at the end of the couch and covered them with his coat.

The house was too silent. Swiftly Cabot rose and walked soundlessly through the small dining room. The light was on in the kitchen. He discerned a shadow.

She was in the breakfast nook, on a large chaise longue that in summer would have been out in the garden beyond the tall window. Her head was bowed, her face covered with both hands, and she did not stir as he entered.

Cabot came over to her and gently took her shoulders, making her stand. Her hands dropped away, her expression that of a human being reaching for another. And then Cabot knew why she had been in Ogilvy's room at Harmsworth Hospital, that she had been with the injured man before he had arrived . . . That she and Ogilvy had been lovers and now she had nothing more to give him.

Without a word Cabot kissed her, first on the lips, then along the cheek, and finally in the soft well of her throat. He felt her lips tug at his earlobe, her arms snake around him and her mouth slide across to feed upon his . . .

Forgive me! Mackenzie cried out silently. Oh, please, if you ever find out, forgive me!

Because the man who raged within her heart was the same she had never trusted, always watched, had been prepared to kill. How sadly Philby had stated the awful truth. Yet it was no longer truth. Not when he was with her like this. There could be no deception, not anymore, not this way . . .

He had removed her blouse so swiftly she scarcely realized it. As his hands came around her back to free her breasts, Mackenzie undid his shirt, letting it fall to the floor. He came around her, one hand cupping her breast, fingertips stroking her nipples alive. She felt his hand on her buttocks, the soft rustle of silk along nylon.

When she was naked save for her garter and stockings, she faced him and looking into his eyes stripped him, devouring what she saw with her eyes. But as she reached for him, he moved her to the chaise longue and in one motion spread her legs and buried his tongue within her, feeling a shudder work its way through her thighs.

Mackenzie was lost in sensations she never knew existed. She arched her back and brought her legs around his back, holding him captive, thrusting her hips in a furious rhythm, urging him on, crying out his name when she spilled herself onto him . . . Then she jerked his head up, probed his mouth, tasting herself. Her fingers curled around his cock and she bent over him, her lips squeezing him, her golden hair flying as her head rocked to fulfill him.

"Come over me!" she heard him cry and swung her legs over him, feeling his hands press her buttocks down until his fingers parted her lips and his tongue was rife. She squealed in agony, pumping him faster with her lips until she felt his cock engorge and burst into her mouth. An instant later she ground herself against him with a last furious cry of release and heard him call out her name . . .

Again the house became silent.

Jonathan Cabot's eyes snapped open. For an instant he was disoriented, because nothing seemed right—not the lilac scent that was drifting in the air, the soft breathing beside him, the warmth of another body stretched out beside his own. Slowly Cabot rolled over, pushing the covers back. As he did, he remembered.

Mackenzie McConnell was lying on her stomach, one arm thrust under the pillow, the other tucked up against her breasts, a closed fist under her jaw. One leg was perfectly straight, the other bent high at the knee, a dancer in flight. Cabot reached across and brushed away the golden hair draped across her face, slipping the strands through his fingers very slowly. He covered one cheek with his palm, then let that hand slide down across her shoulders. She stirred and rolled onto her side, her lips and eyes opening at the same instant. But his lips were on hers already and his hand around her taut waist, moving across the gentle curve of the belly, fingers passing through the golden down.

His fingers came to rest between her thighs and she felt him caress the warmth and moistness. Her legs parted. Gently she pushed his head onto her breasts, feeling his lips on her nipples. Then both his hands came under her buttocks, lifting her so gently yet so easily and she called out his name, clutching the curls of his hair . . . An hour passed.

"We have to get up," Cabot said.

"Was she your wife, Jonathan?"

"Who?"

"The woman who taught you to love this way."

Cabot shifted so that he could look into those wondrous eyes and have them know he was telling the truth.

"If Orit had lived she would have become my wife," he said. "She believed in the sanity of man, that although history was filled with aberrations, decency and beauty would prevail. She was never able to see herself as a victim upon which such provenance had to be built. So she returned to Germany with her father, who once tutored me." He stopped abruptly, feeling an old pain in his chest. "I was going to bring them out . . . I came too late."

Mackenzie's fingers tightened on his shoulder.

"Is she still in Germany?"

"Yes, she is still in Germany," Cabot whispered. "In an unmarked grave, or a mass grave . . . or some ashes strewn in the field."

Abruptly Cabot sat up and got out of bed. Mackenzie saw the muscles quiver and tense in the arms, the great shoulders hunch forward, veins bulge out in the neck.

"Jonathan . . . Jonathan, I'm sorry."

He shook his head violently from side to side as though shaking off her comfort. If it were possible for a soul to bleed, that was what Mackenzie was witnessing now.

She was about to come to him when the telephone rang. It was Pearce from the embassy.

"No, I'm sorry, Edward, he just left," she lied quickly. "Yes, he was on his way to Grosvenor Square. Could you tell me what this is . . . yes . . ."

Mackenzie McConnell listened to what Pearce said, then cut the conversation short.

"Look, Edward, let me get over to the embassy and we can talk about it there. All right? Good. I'll see you shortly."

"What is it?" Cabot asked. He came to her and held her tightly and she knew the madness had passed, that she could cleanse him of it.

"Pearce just got a call from Frye. He wants a meeting with you tonight, alone . . . Pearce says he wants to make some sort of deal for Tricia Burns . . ."

"No, he doesn't," Cabot murmured. "That's not it at all. All Frye wants to do is to have another shot at me. He knows he'll never see Tricia Burns again for as long as he lives. He's gone beyond her now . . ."

13

On the twenty-third of May 1940, the commander of Army Group A, General Rundstedt, ordered his tank forces to halt their advance. In spite of this command the Second Panzer Division, operating under secret orders from OKW, Berlin, continued its assault on Boulogne and brought about the subsequent battle for Calais.

The following day an enraged Rundstedt received confirmation of the OKW orders from Hitler himself. All motorized regiments except those engaged in the struggle to take Calais here to halt. For the bulk of the German forces the pause was to last four days, until May 27.

Across the Channel London was watching the collapse of the Belgian Army with utter dismay. Although uncertain as to why the Germans had chosen this moment to retard their advance, Churchill understood that every hour the German armor was idle was an hour to get more troops off the Dunkirk beaches. On May 26 Churchill appointed General Dill as Chief of the British General Staff, replacing General Ironside, who became Commander in Chief of Home Forces. The same day saw the appointment of Admiral Ramsay, commander of the Royal Navy forces at Dover, as chief of what was to become the most ambitious evacuation in the history of warfare. Between themselves, Churchill, Dill and Ramsay examined and put into place the final details for Operation Dynamo. The evacuation of Dunkirk was born.

After he had seen his men off with the English corporal, Henry Schiffer, Erik Guderian returned to the farmhouse and slept for a while. The communications officer brought a decoded radio dispatch from Chancellery to his breakfast table. Guderian read it through and instructed the officer to send a receipt of confirmation to Berlin.

So the English side of the operation was under way. The best agent in Great Britain, probably anywhere for that matter, had been contacted and apprised of Guderian's arrival.

At half past six a quartermaster sergeant delivered what had been Henry Schiffer's uniform. Although Guderian had ordered the outfit not to be cleaned, a certain amount of tailoring had been required. Schiffer was not a big man but fortunately the British had issued him clothing that was oversized. The cuffs, which Schiffer had clumsily sewed up, and the waist, which he had tried to take in, had been let out. Although the trousers were still baggy they were comfortable and didn't drag at the bootheels. Similarly the tunic was left too large but the sleeves had been lengthened to the measure of Guderian's arms.

The quartermaster sergeant also brought with him a Bren Mark I light machine gun. Derived from the Czech ZB30, a 7.92mm weapon designed at Brno, this version had been manufactured by Enfield, thus the acronym BREN. With a drum rear sight and angled grip beneath the butt, the Mark I was fed by a top-mounted magazine holding twenty-eight rounds. It was also fitted with bipods for easy use in the prone position. While it was doubtful that Corporal Henry Schiffer would ever have been issued such a weapon, Guderian had no qualms about carrying it. The British and French were abandoning matériel as they retreated, this because as of May 10 they had had only some one hundred and sixty rounds to the gun, the "weapons issue" a man could comfortably carry. Those who still carried weapons would take only the best, leaving revolvers and rifles behind. The Bren was one of the finest LMGs ever produced. It would be only natural for a retreating soldier to carry and use it as far as he could.

By seven o'clock Erik Guderian had completed his checklist.

Every piece of clothing, including the gray, helplessly baggy underwear, had once belonged to Schiffer. The flashes on the tunic, identifying him as a soldier in the Royal Artillery, had been resewn. A personal letter from Schiffer's father and a picture of a pretty, dark-haired girl went into the right breast pocket. The wallet, with its odd assortment of papers, a few pounds in currency and, inexplicably, some French postage stamps, went into the left one. That left the military ID card.

When Guderian and his unit had flown into France there had been one more person on board: an Abwehr master forger who had brought with him a trunk of any and all tools he might require. While Schiffer was undergoing interrogation, his official identification was being meticulously altered to match

Guderian's physical characteristics. After six hours of uninterrupted labor the forger had managed to change the vital specifications, replace Schiffer's photograph with one of Guderian and duplicate the watermarks and double red bands that slashed across the entire card at a forty-five-degree angle.

Guderian spent a full ten minutes scrutinizing the effort and was satisfied that the identification was good enough to pass scrutiny at Dover. But somewhere in the cavernous holds of Whitehall, buried in the service and registration records, was a duplicate of this card in its original state as well as Henry Schiffer's military file. Such a permanent, conflicting record could not be allowed to exist.

"Major Kleemann!"

Guderian had been so engrossed in examining the identification that he failed to hear General von Hoven enter.

"*Herr General!*"

Guderian saluted him, causing von Hoven to smile.

"This is the first time in the whole of this campaign that I have been saluted by a British soldier," von Hoven said. He came forward and scrutinized Guderian from head to toe.

"Well, Major, you are to be congratulated," he said at last. "I'm sure any one of my men would arrest you as a Tommy."

"That is precisely what I intend to avoid, *Herr General*," Guderian replied.

"I have spoken to Luftwaffe command in Cologne," von Hoven said. "Within the hour eight squadrons of Stukas accompanying three flights of bombers will be over the road that leads from Calais to Dunkirk. As per your . . . recommendations"—von Hoven's words dripped sarcasm—"the flight will concentrate on the back end of the British retreat, that is to say to columns of soldiers closest to Calais. The objective is twofold: to keep our own troops at bay, discouraging immediate pursuit, and to hurry the British along in as disorganized a fashion as possible.

"The attack on the rear of the column will last exactly twenty minutes. Under its cover you will be driven as close as possible to the English lines. If Luftwaffe's timing and that of your arrival coincide, the bombers and fighters should be moving along the column in the direction of Dunkirk itself, leaving the road alone."

If . . . Guderian thought. *If* the Luftwaffe breaks its attack at precisely the right moment. *If* there isn't some trigger-happy, would-be hero who decides to take one last strafing run at the column. *If* the British run like sheep, away from the barking German shepherd, and there are no stragglers who decide to take on a sole German vehicle if only to get something back for their suffering . . . Too many *ifs*.

But Guderian didn't voice any of his doubts.

"I am confident that everything will proceed on schedule, as we expect, *Herr General*," he said.

Von Hoven smiled sadly. "You are a brave man, Major, whoever you are. You are going behind the enemy line dressed in a British uniform. If, God forbid, you are captured they will shoot you where you stand."

Von Hoven held out his hand. "Good luck, Major, and good hunting—for whatever it is!"

The scout car waiting outside the farmhouse was a Horch Sol Kfz 223. A four-wheel-drive vehicle, the Horch was powered by a V-8 engine, carried a complement of three behind thirty millimeters of armor and weighed in at five tons. Its armament consisted of only one MG34 machine gun, this because the Horch was used exclusively as a radio-equipped reconnaissance vehicle for armored battalions.

Von Hoven spoke briefly to the driver and gunner, pointing at Guderian, who stood a few feet away.

"They assure me they know what to do," von Hoven said. "Again, Major, good luck!"

Handing the Bren to the gunner, Guderian climbed on board, fitting himself into the tight seat a foot below the gunner's platform. From this position only his head was exposed and he could still see exactly what was going on around him. The driver reached up and handed him a map, their route marked in red. Guderian glanced at it, then tapped twice on the metal hood.

To make better time the driver took the circuitous route around the edge of the city. Guderian approved without comment. From what he saw of the Citadel and the sectors he had passed through to bring Schiffer back, he knew the roads of Calais would be clogged with rubble, abandoned wrecks and stunned refugees. There was also the possibility of snipers who might take a long-range shot at a moving German head. Unnecessary chances.

On the northern side of the city, beyond the pall of smoke that still hung over the harbor, the war stopped. On either side of the road were German troop carriers and trucks parked off to one side. Fires were going in the field kitchens and soldiers were foraging food from nearby farmhouses. Others were stretched out alongside their vehicles, sleeping like the tired dead they were, oblivious as much to the clatter around them as to the cold dampness of the earth which crept through the tarpaulins.

The scout car continued on, clearing the last of the German lines. The gunner tapped Guderian on the shoulder and pointed to the skies. From the east, flying at three to four thousand feet, came the Heinkel bombers, their droning engines effectively cutting off all other sounds. Squinting into the cold morning sun, Guderian saw the overflight of Stukas above and behind the bombers. The Stukas would wait until the Heinkels had lumbered over their targets and laid their carpet of death along the road and the beach. As the bombers moved on, the Stukas would go after the big secondary targets: trucks, armored vehicles, the odd tank, the mounted antiaircraft artillery.

Once their bomb racks were empty and the weight loss restored maneuverability, the Stukas would return for their strafing runs, the third level of attack.

As the bombers passed directly overhead Guderian slid into the seat beside the driver and motioned him to slow the vehicle. They could not risk getting too close to the end of the tattered convoy, no matter how accurate the Luftwaffe was.

The aerial assault lasted twenty-two minutes. The scout car had slowed to a crawl, moving off the road and into the meadows. Even through the armored chassis Guderian had felt the earth quiver as the three-hundred-pound explosives pounded the earth. He thanked God that he was still far enough away not to see the carnage and concentrated his attention on the planes' progress. The Heinkels had done their job and moved on. Now the Stukas roamed the skies, climbing high, then suddenly shifting and dropping in almost perpendicular flight, the air screaming off their wings, that shriek broken only by high-pitched whistles as the bombs fell away.

The scout car continued on, climbing a small knoll from where Guderian could see the road three kilometers away. Fire, nothing but fire, covered the landscape.

"The fools!" Guderian screamed.

The Luftwaffe was using incendiaries! Goering had gone mad. The British were beaten ragged. Conventional bombs would have been enough to push them along to Dunkirk. But this . . . this was indiscriminate slaughter!

"Follow this meadow for as long as you can," Guderian shouted to the driver.

The Stukas made only two strafing runs. Guderian figured that either they were satisfied with the bombing sorties or else they were blinded by the evil black smoke that hung over the road and so chose to save their ammunition for visible targets. The scout car continued to lurch over the grassy, uneven terrain, forded a rushing stream and climbed around another hill, gears grinding. If it hadn't been for the shell-shock of the bombing run the five British soldiers huddled in the woods fifty yards away would have heard its approach.

The driver heard the gunner's shouts at the same time as he saw the troops and immediately killed the engine.

"Jump!" Guderian hissed at the gunner, who obeyed instantly.

Always watching the British soldiers, Guderian helped the driver out, then followed.

"Listen to me," he whispered to him. "You're going to have to get back to our lines on foot."

The gunner protested. "We could run them down!"

"No! I can use them. Now go on! I'll give you as much cover as I can."

The gunner and driver exchanged looks, then both started off in a crouching run, following the wide tire swathes the scout car had cut into the grass. Guderian slipped down the edge of the knoll fifteen meters from the car, counted off thirty seconds, then opened fire.

The first six bullets shattered the scout car machine gun, leaving it dangling, the barrel pointed at the earth. The next rounds stitched a weaving pattern across the armor plate and passenger door, shattering the driver's glass visor.

Guderian heard the British shouting and yelled back in English, then immediately pressed the trigger and shot off the rest of the clip. He thrust his hand down and wrenched free the only grenade he was carrying. Clamping the pin between his teeth, he jerked the grenade away from his mouth and struck the cap, which set off the four-second delay fuse. An instant later the 2.5 ounces of Baratol high explosives ripped its casing apart, gouging out what must have been a good chunk of the knoll.

Guderian staggered to his knees, clutching the Bren against

his side. He was conscious of feet pounding in his direction, the sporadic rifle fire, then silence.

"Think you got 'em, lad?"

Ten feet away lay a beefy, hard-breathing man whose shoulder stripes identified him as a sergeant.

"I . . . I think so, sir," Guderian stammered.

He watched as the sergeant's eyes flicked restlessly across the terrain around the scout car.

"Nothing's moving. The way that gun's hanging you either got the bastard or else they both ran for it."

The sergeant moved crabwise across the wet grass. He was a grizzled man, probably the same age as Guderian but forty pounds heavier, with red, swollen eyes that betrayed his fatigue and a tic that sporadically tugged at the left eyelid.

"Mighty fancy, old son," the sergeant said hoarsely, nodding at the Bren. "Let's see if you're as good with it as you should be."

The sergeant rolled over and passed instructions to his men, then swung back to Guderian.

"You go round to the right, I'll take the left," he said, pulling up the Number 4 Mark I Enfield.

"Yes, sir!"

"Right then . . . Mark . . . Move!"

Instead of the crouching run adopted by the sergeant, Guderian rose almost to his full height. Ignoring the sergeant's curses, he ran up the hill, slipping just enough to give a hint of clumsiness. Gripping the scout car's fender, he hauled himself up and looked toward the line in the meadow beyond. His men were gone. Guderian grinned and staggered around the side of the car. The improvised maneuver had worked—thus far. The driver and gunner were safe. It would be a long hike to the German lines but they would make it. Meanwhile he had safely reached the British lines and would, if matters turned out as he expected, get to Dunkirk sooner than expected.

"Well, you got a piece of someone, lad."

The sergeant had wiped some fluid off the gunner's mount and held it up to his nose.

"Blood."

The gunner must have caught an arm or leg jumping down, Guderian thought. It was an unexpected convincing touch.

"But I missed them," Guderian said. "Missed them both."

He started to walk toward the sergeant when he realized the Enfield barrel was pointed at his chest.

"But I didn't miss that you speak a very strange English," the sergeant said. "Maybe you can tell me why's that?"

"I'm Canadian," Guderian said, mixing what he hoped would be the right measures of fear and anger.

"Says you, boyo. Why don't you put down the Bren and show me some writing, eh!"

As Guderian carefully placed the weapon on the ground, he saw two other infantrymen coming up behind the sergeant, weapons leveled. Guderian fumbled in his pocket for the Army card and passed it to the sergeant.

"Schiffer . . . That's a Hun name, son," the sergeant said softly.

"I'm a Canadian!" Guderian cried. "My parents are Canadian. For God's sake—"

"Where did you come from?" the sergeant cut him off.

"Calais, sir. The Royal Artillery unit at the Citadel. I was on the searchlights."

"Collins!" the sergeant shouted over his shoulder. "You were at the Citadel, weren't you?"

"Yes, sir, I was," Collins said in a soft Lancashire drawl. "That I was."

"Perhaps you'll hear Corporal Schiffer out then. See what he has to say of the Citadel."

"Pleased to, sir."

"And at the first wrong answer, Corporal, you have permission to shoot him between the eyes." The sergeant turned back to Guderian. "We're all ears, old son."

Guderian began to talk, quickly, but keeping everything he had seen in Calais in the forefront of his mind, leaving nothing out. He described what he had seen from the point of view of the British, repeating the small details which only an infantryman on the site would have experienced and remembered or had had told to him.

Guderian addressed himself only to the sergeant, but occasionally watched the soldier, Collins, out of the corner of his eye. The gun barrel was being lowered, very slowly, but nevertheless lowered.

"Well, Collins?"

"He had to have been there, sir, no question," the young corporal said.

"And you say you got out fourteen, fifteen hours ago, before the garrison surrendered?" the sergeant asked.

"Yes, sir—there was a route open along the docks—if you wanted to take the chance."

"And you were the only one so brave?"

"I was the only one left alive, *sir*!" Guderian snapped back.

"Sergeant—" Collins started to say.

"You're pretty old to be a corporal, aren't you, Henry?" the sergeant suggested.

"I'm a teacher, sir," Guderian said dully. "Came over to London to study at the University. When the Canadian Army got held up in Halifax I decided to enlist with the British, to fight now . . . with my friends."

Without bothering to ask for permission Guderian sat down heavily on the running board of the scout car. He leaned forward and covered his face with his hands. The moment, he realized, was now. Either the sergeant believed him or else he would have to kill him and the corporal before finishing off the others. Given position, relative strength and combat readiness, Guderian reckoned he had a better than even chance.

"Get up, Henry," the sergeant said gruffly, hauling him up by the shoulder. He grinned at Guderian. "The name's Mackelhose, Frank. That's Jimmy Collins, one of the best machine gunners you'd want to have beside you. Behind him is our company dago, Charlie Fontana. So you see, old son, you're not the only suspicious one."

Guderian laughed along with the crude humor.

"What about the others, sir?" he asked. "I thought I saw five of you."

"You did, but the other lads are wounded. Renny'll be all right, just a broken collarbone. But Lennon is in a bad way. Took two bullets in the thigh. Lost a lot of blood."

"I take it you're headed for Dunkirk, Sergeant."

"Just as soon as Jerry runs out of fuel and heads on home," Mackelhose confirmed.

"Sir," Collins spoke up. "What about this car, then?" You think we might commandeer it, like? Renny gets tired pretty fast and if we have to carry Lennon to the first field hospital we come across . . ."

"Good point, Collins," Mackelhose said, stepping behind

the wheel. He depressed the accelerator a few times, then pressed the starter button. The Horch roared to life.

"Sergeant, sir, there's extra petrol on the back, too!" the dark-haired Fontana shouted.

"Boys, it could be that meeting Henry here was the first piece of good luck to come our way in a long while." Mackelhose grinned. "Well come on, pile in. We'll pick up the lads and ride to Dunkirk in style!"

At first Guderian didn't understand Mackelhose's comment. A half hour later, when the scout car was back on the road and two miles closer to Dunkirk, the meaning became excruciatingly obvious.

Mackelhose, Guderian and Jimmy Collins crammed themselves into the space around the machine gun post. The gun itself, useless, was ripped from its moorings and discarded. Fontana, who Guderian learned was a bus mechanic, was chosen the new driver. The seriously wounded soldier, Lennon, was in the seat beside him, his shattered leg stretched out as far as possible. Renny, with his injured shoulder, was crammed into the narrow space behind the driver's seat used to store ammunition.

As soon as they were under way Mackelhose directed Fontana to head across the road and at the first junction turn off for the beach. Guderian thought the going would be much slower, the pain of traveling over sand and dunes greater on the wounded. He was right on both counts. But it was a better route than the road.

At times the beach narrowed to a point where it was no more than a dozen yards between ocean and road. From this vantage point Guderian witnessed a sight so forboding that at first he was loath to believe it. As far as his eye could see there was an unbroken column of men. They could not have said to be marching. Shuffling, staggering but not marching, their dead eyes ringed with dirt and soot. They had, Guderian learned, been marching for over twenty-four hours, tortuously wending their way in from such obscure places as Armentières, Roulers, Furnes, Saint-Omer and Poperinghe. Almost all carried a rifle, but the ammunition canisters had been thrown away long ago. In their midst, horses pulled wagons laden with the injured, the stench of blood-clotted dressings and the groans of men in agony punctuated by the clop of the horses. This phantom army marched into the smoke, emerged only when the wind shifted, then once again plunged into the blackness. They walked over broken glass, downed telephone lines and around bomb craters. They looked neither at the trucks and cars in the ditch nor at the makeshift first-aid tents which sprang up every few kilometers in a clearing or abandoned farmhouse. Passing one of the latter, Guderian saw that the huge Red Cross tarpaulin covering the roof of a barn was stitched with machine gun fire . . .

Whether on Mackelhose's orders or on his own initiative, Fontana kept the scout car moving as quickly as he could, driving carefully when he had to, accelerating when he saw a long, open stretch of beach. They moved on, without pause, for three hours. Twenty kilometers outside of Dunkirk they stopped to refuel from the reserve tanks and watched as the German planes returned over the horizon, roared overhead and began the second attack of the day on Dunkirk proper.

They are aiming for the ships and the mole, Guderian thought lifelessly. Not the troops on the shore or on the roads . . . getting ships *and* men in the same passes . . .

They drove on, in silence because there were no words left that had any meaning in the presence of defeat. The grinding of the Horch engine, which before grated on one's nerves, was now just another monotonous sound their consciousness had absorbed.

"How much further?" Guderian shouted in Mackelhose's ear.

"Another four hours, maybe less if the road stays as it is now," the sergeant yelled back. "But the closer we get, the more bodies we'll meet up with. Our only hope is that Jerry concentrates on the docks and ships and leaves the road alone . . ."

Mackelhose must have seen Guderian's shocked expression because he leaned closer and gripped Guderian around the shoulders.

"Listen, boy," he said, speaking directly into Guderian's ear. "Don't think bad of me. You and I and every bloke around us has been through the same thing. We all want to let the other fellow take it on the chin. And that's exactly what he's saying to himself. Understand? We just want to live a little longer. Pretty soon it'll be our turn on that godforsaken beach. You'll see, son . . ."

Mackelhose's voice faded away and abruptly he moved

away. Guderian stared at him, astonished not only at the words, which were somehow so eloquent, but also by the tears which at last were flowing from the big sergeant's eyes.

Mackelhose was wrong about the four hours' traveling time to Dunkirk. The scout car didn't approach the outskirts of the docks until late afternoon, nine hours after starting out only fifty kilometers away.

Guderian hadn't had occasion to pass through Dunkirk for over four years. What he saw now could no longer be called a city or town. The bombing had literally leveled the entire area from the docks right up to the main residential section four kilometers inland. All public services—buses and trolleys, fire fighting, police—had disappeared. When the electric plant had been destroyed so had the telephone and telegraph lines. Sewers had burst, causing widespread flooding and contamination of the water supply. The city also teemed with animals. Dogs and cats which had been abandoned and were starving had made their way into the streets to challenge people for what food remained.

Fontana brought the scout car to a halt on a dune which offered a spectacularly grim view of the future: thousands upon thousands of men were standing in a meandering coil a kilometer long, their muddied greatcoats giving them the uniform color of a hideous, mythic serpent.

"A division!" Guderian whispered. "Good Lord, there's twenty thousand men—more!—out there. . . ."

"Aye, and that's what they're all waiting for," Mackelhose said, pointing out to sea.

Guderian could not believe what he was looking upon. The last intelligence reports he had read stated that Goering intended to sink most of the Royal Navy singlehanded. The Air Marshal believed that Britain would not abandon its quarter of a million men under arms, would risk almost anything in order to bring them back. Goering had boasted how he would annihilate the destroyers, corvettes, offshore patrol boats—even the light cruisers—should they come, as he knew they must, to Dunkirk.

But there was no Royal Navy to speak of.

Staring out from the shoreline, Guderian saw one lonely destroyer, moored well beyond the mole, whose pilings were no more than matchsticks. Troops were being ferried across to it on launches. . . . And some of these, laden with wounded, continued beyond the big ship to the open waters. Closer in were the small craft—fishing vessels, trawlers, tugs, sailing yachts, power boats, ferries—running the risk of being run aground as they maneuvered to greet the troops wading out into the surf. As soon as a load was taken on, the boats turned around and headed for the open waters. Those soldiers left standing, with waves breaking against their chests, moved to the next available craft, throwing the weapons in first, then helping the wounded, and finally, if there was room, climbing on board themselves.

The beach itself was littered with splintered boards, bits of clothing and discarded equipment. A few feet from where Guderian was standing an entire mast, with part of a sail still tied to it, was rolling in the foamy, brown surf. . . .

"Right, lads!" Mackelhose was shouting. "Let's get Lennon and Renny over to the aid shelter. They'll tag 'em and get them ready for the next load. Come on, then!"

Guderian turned to help Renny out of the scout car and to gently lay him down on the canvas stretcher. He picked up one end, Collins the other, and they headed for the Red Cross tent.

"Remember, lads," Mackelhose shouted behind them, "once we get under way I want patience and discipline. Patience and discipline! We'll take our place in the lines and wait until, God willing, our turn will come."

Guderian squatted down, releasing his grip on the stretcher handles. He turned away and looked down at the beach. Patience and discipline, he thought grimly. If the Stukas come back there will be none of that either.

And they did, almost as though he had had the power to summon them forth.

The planes had been using the setting sun as a screen, coming in low over the water instead of flying over the city. Gone were the high-pitched shrieks which the British had used as a warning. The Stukas seemed to almost drift in over the horizon. By the time their motors could be heard, cannon rounds and bullets were kicking up sand.

Guderian saw his chance. He knew that sometime during the evacuation he had to separate himself from Mackelhose and the others. He didn't want to arrive in England—if he was to arrive at all—with someone who had spent any time with him at Dunkirk. The Stukas gave him the opportunity.

Guderian began running, the cramped muscles pumping as

he drove himself across the thick, heavy sand. Behind him the screams and shouting erupted. Guderian waited until the last possible instant, then dived headfirst into the sand. The German dive-bomber cleared the beach by no more than ten meters, the air roll spinning Guderian over twice. He scrambled to his feet and was running again, moving down the beach just above the tide line, unbuckling and discarding equipment he no longer needed. Fifty meters farther Guderian veered into the water, wading out quickly. Looking over his shoulder, he saw exactly what he expected: the serpentine line of troops had disintegrated. As soon as the Stukas had attacked, the soldiers had thrown themselves on the sand, taking whatever cover they could. The patience and discipline which Mackelhose had so proudly spoken of had become a death knell.

Guderian plunged into icy waters and, gasping, began to swim toward the CMB vessel he had spotted a moment earlier.

The Coastal Motor Boats which the British were using in 1940 weren't very different from the CMBs that attacked the Russian fleet at Kronstadt in 1919. Powered by Italian Isotta-Fraschini diesel engines, the seventy-foot, short, hard-chine hulls limited their payload. Originally used as submarine chasers and offshore patrol vessels, virtually the entire squadron of CMBs in the Dover Fleet was pressed into service during Operation Dynamo.

Although Guderian was certain the CMBs would be overloaded, carrying at least triple their usual complement of four men on the return leg across the Channel, they were still the fastest craft on the seas. If he could get to this one he would have a better than even chance of reaching the fabled White Cliffs.

Guderian swam without pause, using the power of his arms and shoulders to keep him moving. The sodden clothing hung on him like medieval armor, and his legs flailed helplessly against the weight of the heavy, waterlogged boots that felt like two concrete blocks. He ignored the frigid waters that heaved his body about in the shallow currents, the waves which descended out of nowhere, forcing him to hold his breath and kick as hard as he could to break their crests. The screams around him were the worst. Every time he heaved himself out of the water he heard men floundering, dying, around him. In the instant of panic those who didn't even know how to swim, who hadn't dropped their equipment, who stumbled into the water with broken arms, twisted ankles or head injuries, sought refuge in the water. Once in, the tantalizing specter of boats, seemingly so close, was too much to resist.

Meter by meter Guderian swam by such men, keeping himself well out of reach of their flailing arms, clutching fingers which, if they got hold of him, would take them both down forever.

"For Christ's sake help me!" he screamed over the rattle of gunfire.

No one appeared over the side of the CMB. Guderian swung away from the bow and began swimming to the stern, realizing that he had to keep moving, otherwise his own weight would drag him under. He started hitting the side of the vessel with his fist, his voice hoarse now, throat raw with seawater.

"Help me. . . ."

Now he was close to the engines, surrounded by rainbow-colored water—floating diesel from the exhaust ports. He swallowed a mouthful and went under, his head spinning from the noxious fumes. Surfacing, he drove his legs so hard that for an instant he was out of the water to midchest.

Sweet Christ, if I fall back now! He had made the cardinal error: his upward momentum would, in a fraction of a second, reverse itself and he would plunge feetfirst deep into the sea. In his condition, with the weight he was carrying, even two meters below the surface could be a fatal distance.

The water was up to his neck when suddenly an agonizing pain shot through both arm sockets. Guderian's head fell forward into the waves, his mouth opening involuntarily as he screamed. The pressure increased, but now he was aware of a strong grip on his forearms . . . and his wrist.

"Come on, you silly bugger. . . ."

His chest hit the gunwale as he was dragged over the side. A hand came around him and gripped his belt. With a final grunt, Erik Guderian was landed, heaved onto the hard, slippery deck like a dogfish. His head rolled against the reserve tanks, and although he tried to raise himself on his elbow, it was no good. He had no strength left.

"Keep his head out of the water there, mate!"

A short, elfin figure, dressed in a tattered pea jacket, life jacket, woolen sailor's cap and heavy gloves, gestured at the fallen soldier whose nose was only millimeters from the sloshing water on the deck. The man grabbed Guderian by the scruff of the neck and hauled him up, propping him up against another soldier.

"Take some of this, then. Keep the chills off!"

Guderian's trembling hands gripped the flask hard. As he swallowed the bitter tea, his throat and stomach were set on fire.

The elf cackled madly, swinging with the heavy machine gun mounted on the stern.

"Oh, me bucko, a little surprise!"

"Thank you," Guderian answered weakly, forcing the words between clattering teeth.

Gripping the railing with both hands, Guderian staggered to his knees, planting them a yard apart so that the boat's violent rocking motion wouldn't throw him. He saw the destroyer lying some four hundred meters astern. All around the CMB were dozens of craft, each one filled and overfilled, struggling against the Channel swells. In the CMB itself were over twenty soldiers, propped up against the gunwales, their legs stretched out in front of them. On the forward deck were two officers and the helmsman, who was steering in and out between the slower craft ahead.

"Tried to get us onto the mole, the skipper did," the elf said, salt spray covering his rimless spectacles. "Couldn't do it though. Too far gone, that wharf. Twenty men on top and the pilings would have collapsed—from under them and on top of us!"

He threw back his head and laughed again.

"Name's Fred Doust. Used to be turret gunner on the old *King Charles*. Who're you be?"

"Schiffer . . . Henry Schiffer."

Doust cocked his head at a peculiar angle and appeared to study Guderian.

"Eh. . . . Canadian. Am I right? You're a Canadian!" he said excitedly.

"From Kitchener!" Guderian shouted.

"Have a brother who lives in Toronto. A mechanic. Probably see him over here before this be all over." The laughter erupted again, then suddenly the boat swerved, rolling Doust to one side.

"Hang on to your skivvies, lad!" Doust yelled. "Y'ere lucky

to be with us. We'll get you home in time for dinner. Not like these poor sods—"

Twenty meters away a small power cruiser that until this day probably hadn't been beyond the Thames estuary erupted into a fireball. The bullets and cannon fire kept on coming through the explosion, piercing the flames and smoke, striking the water a scant few meters from the CMB's hull.

"Git down!" Doust screamed.

He swiveled the heavy gun around and began firing over the blazing speedboat. Guderian scrambled over the legs of the prostrate men and fell heavily against the ammunition canister. Scooping up an armful of the bullet belt, he lifted the belt so that there would be an even feed into the gun. Doust glanced down at him, roared with laughter and kept on firing. Suddenly a gust of wind shifted the black smoke billowing from the sinking boat, and the target was sighted.

The *Schnellboot* . . . or as the British knew it, the S18 motor gunboat.

Guderian stared across the waves at the oncoming monster. Twenty-five meters of round-bilge hull powered by a 20-cylinder V-form engine from Daimler-Benz, armed with two single 21-inch torpedo tubes, two 20mm cannon and a single 9mm machine gun . . . And a seasoned crew who knew its vessel could outrun, outshoot anything that moved in these waters, including an overloaded destroyer and an aging CMB.

The S18 had spotted the British CMB. Even from a distance of a hundred meters Guderian could see that the torpedoes had been expended, probably on the destroyer or some large rescue vessel. Lighter now, the S18 became a lone wolf in the sheep herd, selecting helpless victims at random. The CMB, overloaded and underarmed, qualified.

The CMB skipper turned his vessel to port, giving Doust a clear range of fire. The German 20mm got him first. One moment the old gunner was behind his weapon, the next he was dancing in midair as the copper-sheathed bullets tore his body apart, flinging him into the sea.

Guderian didn't hesitate. Slipping on the bloodstained gunner's mount, he clutched at the machine gun handles and pulled himself up. The S18 was less than fifty meters away now, plowing through the waves directly for the CMB. The German gunners must not have seen him behind the gun because they were concentrating their firepower on the bow of the

British boat. Forty meters now. . . . The CMB was zigzagging wildly, trying to stay out of a fire pattern. But the S18, sensing an easy kill, continued to close the distance. Guderian jerked his head to one side to see the skipper screaming words he couldn't hear. Twenty meters. . . .

Guderian leveled the gun at the bow of the S18 and squeezed the trigger. He had one advantage over Doust: he knew exactly where the S18 gas tanks were.

The bullets ripped through the hull, hot lead streaming into warm gasoline. The last act of the German gunners was to turn their weapons on the CMB gunner. Thirty rounds stitched the side of the British vessel before the S18 hull kicked up in the explosion, pointing the vessel bow-first into the water. The momentum of its own engines drove the S18 beneath the waves.

Guderian kept firing into the water until his ammunition was exhausted. Even then he couldn't pry his fingers off the machine gun handles. But something very hot was burning his shoulder and Guderian felt himself falling away from the gun. The last thing he saw was his one hand still on the gun handles, the barrel almost vertical, pointed at the sky where, instead of death, he saw the stars . . .

14

At eight o'clock, May 29, the second call from Leonard Frye rang in Pearce's office. The conversation was one-sided, Frye issuing detailed instructions which Pearce wrote down while Cabot and Mackenzie McConnell listened on the extensions. The call lasted less than forty seconds.

"Do you have a map of Kensington Gardens–Hyde Park?" Cabot asked as soon as Frye hung up.

"Right here."

Pearce spread a large-scale map of the area across his desk.

Cabot located Victoria Gate, then drew his finger across to The Long Water, The Fountains and beneath them, the statue of Peter Pan.

"Smart son of a bitch, isn't he?" Cabot murmured. "He has water on one side so we can't encircle him, Budge's Walk on the other for a fast out, and a patch of forest in between in which to become lost. Once he gets into the trees he could head in any direction."

"I can have thirty armed men into Kensington Gardens, with dogs, in less than two hours," Mackenzie McConnell offered.

"Frye anticipated that," Cabot replied. "Which was why he gave me forty minutes to get to Peter Pan."

"I'll bet he walked the distance from the embassy to the statue, timing it down to the second," Pearce said.

"He did," Mackenzie concurred. "And that was his first mistake. I can *drive* Jonathan as far as The Ring."

She turned to Cabot. "But you're not entertaining the idea of meeting him alone, are you?"

Cabot shrugged. "I have no choice."

"Jonathan, there's no way on God's green earth I'm going to let you walk into something like that," Pearce vowed. "Who's to say Frye hasn't already deployed his shooters in a killing ground? He could take you out any time after you step out on The Ring."

"I don't think Frye wants me dead, not yet," Cabot said. "I still have Tricia Burns."

"Unless he's already written her off," Mackenzie pointed out.

"Do you really think that's likely?" Cabot asked her.

"Do *you* want to stake your life on the fact I could be right?"

Cabot leaned forward on his arms, staring intently at the map.

"He probably made the call from a place on Bayswater," he said. "Which means he's at the statue by now. If he sees anyone but me coming he'll go to ground . . ."

"You're *not* going in there alone," Mackenzie said stubbornly.

"What if we were to do it this way," Pearce suggested. "I leave now, *right now*, take up a position across The Long Water. After Mackenzie drops you off on The Ring, she continues out by Alexandra Gate, turns right onto Kensington Road and parks right here."

Pearce's forefinger stabbed at the paper. "By the Prince Consort Memorial. That puts her at the end of Lancaster Walk, which goes straight up to the Speke's Monument, about a hundred and fifty yards through the trees from Peter Pan."

"A crossfire," Mackenzie McConnell murmured.

"Only if necessary," Pearce cautioned. "If memory serves, the walks are lit until nine o'clock, so even though we'll be at a lousy distance we shouldn't have any problem seeing either you or Frye."

"Weaponry?" Cabot asked.

"I'll take the machine gun," Pearce said. "Mackenzie's score with the sniper rifle puts mine to shame."

Cabot turned to Mackenzie. "All right with you?"

"As long as you keep your gun," she said quietly. "I won't have you going in there unarmed."

Cabot reached out and touched her cheek. "Done."

It took Pearce and Mackenzie McConnell less than three minutes to change into night gear: black trousers, heavy black sweaters topped off by woolen caps, warm, ankle-high boots with thick crepe soles. They parted at the rear of the embassy.

"Take it slow on the drive," Pearce told Mackenzie. "I'll leave my car on Bayswater and enter through the Victoria Gate."

"Watch out for yourself," Cabot said. "Remember, I'm going to try to take Frye alive. If he runs, shoot to wound."

A few minutes later Mackenzie guided her car out onto Park Lane. Traffic was light, buses and trucks mostly, and she easily guided the car through Grosvenor Gate and toward The Ring. As they approached Victoria Gate, Cabot kept glancing at the sidewalks on the righthand side.

"No one," he murmured. "Not a living soul."

"It's too cold," Mackenzie said. "What's the point of strolling if all you'll get are the chills for your trouble?"

As she turned into Buck Hill Walk she drew the car to one side.

"Are you all right, Jonathan?" she asked, slipping a gloved hand over his.

"Fine," Cabot nodded. "I'm just hoping that Frye makes it easy for me, that's all."

"We still have Tricia Burns," Mackenzie reminded him. "If she means anything at all to him he won't do anything foolish."

Her lips brushed Cabot's. "Good luck, my darling."

He was gone before she had a chance to say anything more.

Standing in the shadow of the trees, Cabot watched the sports car move off. He lit a cigarette and with its glowing tip as a tiny signal began walking along the crushed gravel path toward The Fountains. At the edge of The Long Water, a rectangular body which curved slightly as it descended to The Ring, he turned left, keeping to the side of the walk, in the pools of light cast by the dim yellow lamps. He arrived at the Peter Pan Statue and stopped, listening. Night birds, some brave crickets, the slight crackle of branches being moved by a gentle wind. Overhead the moon slid from behind the clouds, bathing the night with its glow, diminishing the sparkle of the stars.

Cabot walked around the statue once, came back to his original position, which faced the Kensington Gardens woods, and brought out another cigarette. He had smoked half of it before he heard the telltale scraping of shoe leather against gravel.

"I'm over here, Cabot."

Cabot knew where Frye was before the cryptographer had even stepped off the grass. But he let his gaze pass over that position. Better to let Frye believe he had the advantage of surprise.

"Step back from the statue, closer to the light."

Cabot was watching Frye come toward him. Frye's coat, a tan mackintosh, was faded, with dirty water-rings along one side. In spite of the cold evening Frye had neither gloves nor a hat. His face was an almost translucent white, only the cheeks and tip of his nose pinched with red. But the hand which held the long-barrel Colt revolver was rock-steady.

"Take your hands out of your pockets," Frye ordered.

Slowly Cabot withdrew them from the coat pockets, turning his palms up so that Frye could see there was nothing concealed in them.

The cryptographer moved in closer, glancing around nervously.

"I came alone," Cabot said. "That's what you wanted, wasn't it?"

Frye stared into his face, his dark eyes taking in every detail of Cabot's face, like a man who has finally come face to face with someone who, until now, he has only had described to him in minute detail.

"I want to make a trade," Frye said.

Even from where he stood Cabot could smell the rank odor of sweat on the man, could almost reach out and touch the fear that enveloped him.

"Why don't you come in with me, Frye," Cabot countered. "So far all you've made are a few mistakes. There may have been extenuating circumstances—"

"Shut up!" Frye hissed. "I said I wanted to make a trade!"

Cabot was silent.

"You have Tricia, don't you?" He waited for confirmation. " *Don't you?*"

"We have her," Cabot told him.

"I want her . . . safe passage out with her," Frye whispered.

"And where would you like to go?" Cabot asked casually.

"Lisbon!"

For a moment Cabot said nothing, then asked: "Why should we give you anything? You're a goddamn traitor."

Frye reacted as though struck across the face. His features contorted in rage, the lips moving soundlessly.

"Lisbon!" he spat out finally. "And Tricia."

"What do you have to deal with?"

"The embassy codes."

Cabot shook his head. "I've already ordered a new set from Washington. They're ones you've never even heard of. You'll have to do better than that."

"You're forgetting I worked on every major code for the last ten years," Frye whispered. "If I go to the Germans I can help them break *any* code you use. You'll have to keep on changing them every month because you won't know when I've taken them apart . . ."

"If you think the Germans will let you stay in Lisbon, you're a fool," Cabot lashed out at him. "They'll package you up and get you to Berlin on the first flight."

"Let me worry about Berlin."

"It's no good, Frye," Cabot said. "You'll have to give me a lot more before I let you and Burns walk out of London." Cabot paused. "The name of your contacts, for instance."

Frye laughed. "That would be tantamount to cutting my own throat. No, you'll have to get the others by yourself."

"That's where you're wrong," Cabot said quietly. "Your picture is all over London. Every cop on the beat is showing it around—to bartenders, landladies, taxi drivers, even school kids. I have fifty men out of Scotland Yard CID leaning on their snitches. The Security Service has an open warrant out on you, Frye. You know what that means? They will shoot first—shoot to kill—rather than let you slip away.

"This is your one and only chance. But either we come to terms right here and now or else you can count on seeing me again within the next forty-eight hours. You'll be lucky to have that much time before you're cornered or killed. Think about it, Frye."

The gun barrel dropped fractionally and for a second Frye took his eyes off Cabot. Depending on where she had positioned herself, how much she could actually see, Cabot thought that Mackenzie McConnell could risk firing. It could be the best chance she would have.

Cabot heard the cough of a silenced shot almost at the same time as the bullet slammed into his chest, knocking him to the ground. The next shot took out Frye, catching him in the throat just above the breastbone. A few seconds later the killers emerged from the darkness, three of them, dressed in black, moving swiftly across the grass and onto the gravel walks. Two carried high-powered rifles with long, perforated snouts at the end of the barrel. The third was the cover man, handling a submachine gun.

Cabot, lying on his stomach, one arm stretched out before him, the other thrust deep into his coat pocket, fingers gripping the Hanyatti butt, opened one eye. The killers moved through a pool of light. A few more steps and they would reach the bodies, prepared for the coup de grace.

Now! Cabot screamed silently. *Now!*

Twenty yards away Edward Pearce rose from behind the stone wall of The Long Water, a deadly apparition. Holding the Thompson at his hip, he pressed the trigger a second after Mackenzie McConnell's shot blew the machine gunner's head apart. The night exploded as the Thompson poured out its rounds, the .45-caliber bullets slicing through bone and cartilage, tearing at and shredding the two riflemen. It was all over in less than ten seconds.

Cabot staggered to his feet, his chest aching as though someone had hit him with a sledgehammer. He tried to breathe, but the bulletproof vest which had absorbed the bullet now seemed to have contracted around his lungs like a vise. Cabot managed to get over to Frye and dropped to his knees.

The cryptographer was dying, the severed arteries pumping out his life's blood onto the crushed stone. There was almost nothing left of his throat, and when Frye tried to speak nothing but a strangled gurgling sound emerged.

"Who did this to you?" Cabot whispered hoarsely. "Who set you up like this?"

Slowly Frye rolled his head to one side, his mouth open, gulping down air that never reached his lungs. The eyes were wide open, terrified, as though he were beholding some monstrous vision hanging over him out of the night sky.

"Who!" Cabot shouted.

He heard branches being snapped as Mackenzie ran through the woods, the heavier pounding of Pearce's footsteps only yards away. Cabot leaned forward, his ear almost against Frye's lips.

"*Who!*"

Before either Mackenzie McConnell or Pearce reached them, Frye was dead. Cabot rose and stepped away, unbuttoning his coat. He walked from one body to another, pulling off the woolen masks to expose the killers' faces. He didn't recognize any of them, but they were undoubtedly the team from the Leatherhead killing ground. Cabot guessed that they might be Irish Nationalists in German pay. But even if Scotland Yard CID or the Security Service could identify them, the trail would stop there. Triggermen were thrice removed from those who issued them their marching orders.

Cabot let his coat drop to the ground and unbuckled the armored vest he had worn. Mackenzie flew toward him, crushing herself against him, fingers running across his chest to convince herself he was whole.

"The son of a bitch was good," Cabot murmured, holding her. "But he should have gone for a head shot. Someone won't forgive him for a mistake like that . . ."

When Edward Pearce put down his cup the china rattled in the saucer. He swore softly at the spilled coffee and wondered which of the three disasters was most responsible for shredding his nerves: the fact that Frye had *not* been killed instantly; that Cabot had survived the bullet meant for him; or the implications of the message that had been waiting for him when he returned home.

Edward Pearce, age thirty-six, a native of Dallas, former

FBI agent, currently head of security for Grosvenor Square, and Berlin's most senior agent in Great Britain, sat back in his chair, staring at the stitching on his hand-tooled boots.

Buried deeper in the embassy infrastructure than Frye, he was Germany's ultimate weapon against England: a man who had his finger on the pulse of all American embassy activity, whose security clearance was unchallenged, who was known to Frye as Darius—a voice over the telephone issuing swift but detailed messages as to what Frye was to pass on.

Edward Pearce had not recruited Frye. That had been done by an agent operating out of the Spanish embassy. When there was no question of Frye's commitment, control had been passed to Pearce, who then set up the Grosvenor Square–State Department communications axis . . . Leonard Frye at one end, Beth Davis at the other.

This channel performed flawlessly. Frye had been so well primed by his Spanish contact that he recognized exactly the kind of material to lift from the stream of traffic that crossed his desk. In the first twenty-four months, Pearce had called Frye only a half dozen times, when Berlin wanted supplemental information. Otherwise he was satisfied with the cryptographer's judgment.

"Goddamn him!" Pearce whispered savagely.

Even with Beth Davis's arrest and killing, Frye might still have had a chance—had Cabot not been the investigator. As soon as Pearce received the transmission from Dulles telling him Cabot was en route, Frye was condemned. With someone like Cabot, tough, tenacious, with instincts that frightened even Pearce, the cryptographer had no chance. It had only been a matter of time, a process of elimination.

I could have saved him, Pearce thought. I could have tipped him off and he could have run . . .

But Pearce hadn't known how loose his hold on Frye had become. That Frye was having an affair with Tricia Burns. That he was hobnobbing with the Blackthorne crowd. That he had a bolthole Pearce knew nothing about. Worst of all, that Frye had gone into business for himself, was selling extra information to Blackthorne for more money. He hadn't known any of this until Cabot had unraveled it all. After that, when Frye had called him begging for help to get him and Burns out of the country, Pearce had smiled as he ground out the last of the cryptographer's desperate hopes. Afterwards Pearce had gladly issued Frye's execution order.

Leonard Frye should have died quickly last night. And Cabot before him. But Cabot, with the cunning of a serpent, had been wearing a bulletproof vest, something he had never thought to mention . . . And Pearce's shooter had gone for the heart instead of the head. It was a mistake which had allowed Cabot to reach Frye before Pearce did.

But what could Frye have told him? He knew me only as Darius—a muffled voice, not a face!

So Frye was not the issue. Nor Cabot, because Cabot would believe the hunt was finished. No, the essential problem was Berlin.

Upon returning to his apartment across the street from the embassy, Pearce had found a circular in his pile of mail. It seemed ordinary enough—advertising for a grocer . . . except that certain selections were much more than a bargain offered to save a few pence.

The first three letters of the advertising copy, corresponding to their numerical opposites in the alphabet, provided him with the page, line and words of Stendhal's *Red and Black* that was the key to the text. Pearce memorized these, then began decoding the message. He could not believe the result.

Was Berlin mad? Had it completely lost its sense of priorities?

When Pearce had made his pact with Berlin, he was assured that he would have no contact with any other agents operating in Great Britain. His work was too important for him to be risked as a control for agents outside the embassy who might have been turned by the Security Service. Pearce was inviolate.

But now Berlin demanded that he place himself in a position where he *could* be compromised. A man was due to arrive in England . . . a Berlin agent whose mission was sanctioned by the Führer himself. Pearce would be contacted by this agent. He was to help him in any way possible. He was to regard this man as Berlin incarnate, his orders were those of Hitler himself . . .

"Insanity!"

The ground-down heels of Pearce's boots slammed to the floor.

Not quite so fast, he thought to himself. Maybe Berlin had forgotten just how much it owes me! The Germans were stupid that way: they issued an order and thought everyone would jump. But not this boy. Yes, Pearce would meet this man when the time came. He would learn what he wanted. And then, if he could help him without compromising himself he might just do so. Otherwise, he would arrange for a small accident. Edward Pearce was very good at such things.

At daybreak Leonard Frye's room was found. A constable on the beat had shown the cryptographer's picture to the landlady, who immediately identified him. Cabot and Mackenzie McConnell arrived with a Security Service unit which included a forensic expert. They found the code books hidden underneath the hearth and gold cached in the panel behind the wall. But as meticulous as the search was, it yielded no clues as to who Frye had been in contact with, nothing to indicate where the still-anonymous gunmen had come from.

"Your job is done," Mackenzie said to him, surveying the squalid little room. "A D notice has effectively stifled the newspapers. As far as the public is concerned, the shooting of an American cryptographer was an Irish affair. In time the rumors at the embassy will die away. Pearce seems to have the situation well in hand there . . ."

Her voice trailed off and she looked up at him.

"You'll be going home soon, won't you?"

Cabot placed his arm around her shoulders and drew her close.

"It's not over yet," he said softly, and immediately put a finger to her lips. "No, don't ask anything now. Tomorrow, or the day after, I'll tell you everything . . ."

Cabot could promise her this because he knew Allen Dulles's plane was scheduled to touch down at Gatwick at eleven o'clock in the morning. Cabot was the only man in the whole of England who knew he was coming . . . because he was the one who had demanded Dulles's presence.

The Holborn Bars in High Holborn Street is London's longest pub. Twenty-five-foot beams, easily a foot square, rise toward an inverted V-shaped ceiling. High on the right are racks of casks, on the left a minstrel's gallery complete with an array of seventeenth-century instruments. Because of its proximity to Lincolns Inn, Holborn Bars enjoys a brisk trade from bewigged barristers and magistrates who congregate in gaggles of four or five to rake through cases over sherry. It was also a place Jonathan Cabot had never set foot in. Neither the proprietor nor patrons recognized him, and that being the case dismissed both him and his companion from their minds.

"You did very well, Jonathan," Allen Dulles said quietly. "The President sends his personal congratulations."

Cabot pushed a glass of Sam Smith's Old Brewery Bitter across the small table.

"The job isn't finished yet," he said tonelessly.

Dulles had gathered as much. There was a restlessness, an anger, still churning in the big man. But Dulles didn't let on.

"I was under the impression that Frye was the only one we were *directly* concerned about—that is to say, within the embassy. The rest is British territory," Dulles reminded him.

"*Frye isn't the only one.*"

Carefully Dulles rolled the cigar ash into the tray.

"I think you had better elucidate, Jonathan."

The gray eyes never betrayed the fear that stabbed through Dulles.

"There's one other person at the embassy. Someone deeper than Frye. Infinitely more valuable to the Germans. This agent will do, and has already done, anything to protect himself. He, not Frye, set up the ambush that almost killed Pearce and myself. He was the one who sent the assassination team into Hyde Park. He knew exactly where Frye would be, at what hour, how he would arrive and what he would want."

Cabot's voice became low, the tone brutal. "This man has been working Frye like a puppet. He, not some Second Secretary at the Spanish embassy, was the true control. And he belongs to us!"

"The setup of Frye is your proof?" Dulles queried. "That was why you hauled me over here?"

"That and the fact that I learned the British were keeping tabs on one of the three names I came up with."

"How did the British get involved?" Dulles demanded. "What goes on inside Grosvenor Square is our business, not theirs!"

"The Brits have been on to this man for the last nine months," Cabot told him. "From what I've seen they have all the circumstantial evidence they need. If the son of a bitch was theirs he'd be dangling from a noose at Wormwood Scrubs by now. But he's not. He's ours and the British don't dare move against him on the one percent chance that they are wrong. They were not willing to give Kennedy anything to hit them over the head with. Not that that matters any longer."

"I see," Dulles said slowly. "How did you come by this information, Jonathan, and are you convinced it is accurate?"

"I am, sir. As to how I got it, I think it's best you not know, in case there's a need for a future disclaimer of responsibility."

Dulles looked at him reflectively.

"All right then, give me the names."

When Cabot did so he noticed a tremor to the older man's fingers as he reached for his beer.

"Just those three of them?"

Cabot nodded. "The British have their favorite." He spoke a single name.

"Jesus Christ Almighty! They—you—can't be serious!"

"They are and I think they're right."

"But this person—"

"Is probably the deepest traitor anywhere in the United States government," Cabot finished for him. "And I'll finish this for you. But to do that I need something from you, sir."

Dulles looked at him suspiciously.

"The truth as to what my real mission is over here," Cabot said quietly.

"You're pushing, Jonathan," Dulles warned him. "That's awfully close to calling the President—never mind me—a liar."

"Not at all, sir," Cabot said. "Two weeks ago in Washington I was told what I needed to know. I accepted it then and until I nailed Frye. But you didn't send me over here *just* for that. Getting to Frye was the first step. Even you are surprised there would be something between that and the next stage, namely the real traitor. But there is a next stage, sir. Getting rid of Frye was a matter of clearing the way for it."

Cabot lit a cigarette and drew deeply on the smoke.

"The plant won't surface unless I offer honest bait. That's why I need the truth."

"Listen to yourself," Dulles whispered. "How can you even conceive of using such intelligence to flush someone who might, just might, take it to Berlin? If you were to know what it is, what is involved—"

"I don't plan to use the truth, sir, at least not the way I hear it from you," Cabot said. "But if I can take one element of what you say and build a tight, plausible story around it—something airtight—then I think that will be good enough. But nothing less. If this operation you're planning is so important, then I can tell you it won't be worth a damn as long as the deep agent is in place."

For the next several minutes Allen Dulles smoked and sipped his beer in silence.

"There is a second operation, *the* operation," Dulles said at last. "You were to be carrying it from the beginning. I had my bags packed a week after you left, ready to fly over the minute I received word that the embassy was clean. Furthermore, the President has authorized me to bring you up to date—fully—at this point. I will do so soon, not here but in the car. Once I have told you what is at stake, you will tell me if there is still the chance of building this Trojan Horse you hope will work. But know now, Jonathan, if I feel there is the slightest jeopardy to the overall mission, I'll veto your proposal—and every one you come up with after that until I'm satisfied."

Dulles drained his beer and shifted around the corner of the table.

"You may think I'm an old curmudgeon, but after you hear what I have to say you'll know what it's like to carry the war on *your* shoulders!"

15

On the evening of June 1, the dining table at Ten Downing Street had been set for five. In addition to Winston Churchill and his unexpected guest, Allen Dulles, were Jonathan Cabot, Mackenzie McConnell and Edward Pearce. After the service had been cleared away and the staff withdrew, the Prime Minister rose at the head of the table.

"I should like," he said ponderously, "to offer a toast to my good friend from America, Allen Dulles. But before I do so there is some news I must impart."

Churchill glanced up and down the table.

"As you have heard, the Luftwaffe has stepped up its attacks against Dunkirk. On this day alone four destroyers have been sunk, five large ships sent to the bottom and a host of smaller craft, including several Channel ferries.

"The cost," Churchill rumbled, "has been enormous . . . But in spite of it the evacuation has been and continues to be more successful than we ever dreamed possible. On this day alone 64,429 men were taken off the beaches . . . With God's help we shall have another twenty-four hours, perhaps forty-eight, in which to save even more lives. My commanders tell me we will now be able to save some three hundred and forty thousand men, two-thirds of these English, the rest French.

"What this means, ladies and gentlemen, is that Britain has the wherewithal to fight once more!" Churchill declared. "We have the men who will be leading the fight to liberate not only France but all of Europe from the yoke of German oppression. And tonight I am proud to announce to you that very soon we shall have the means to provide armed support for these men."

Churchill raised his glass. "To the United States of America, the arsenal of democracy!"

As the champagne was sipped all eyes turned on Allen Dulles.

"Thank you, Prime Minister," the envoy said. "And in turn let me salute you and the people of this brave nation for achievements which will shine in the annals of history."

Dulles fixed his attention on Cabot, Pearce and Mackenzie McConnell.

"But the fight is far from over. The Dunkirk evacuation has provided a core of fighting men around which future armies will be formed. However, the cost in matériel has been enormous. Thousands upon thousands of guns, tanks, vehicles and pieces of support equipment have been left behind in France.

"It is true, as the Prime Minister has said, that by default the United States has become the arsenal of democracy. As you know, we have been shipping to Britain a certain amount of war matériel over the last year. However, the volume, in terms of need, has been negligible. That situation must and will be rectified."

"Excuse me, sir, but does that mean we will declare war on Germany?" Pearce asked.

"No, Mr. Pearce. Unfortunately the situation is far more complicated than that. The isolationist mood in Congress—indeed in the entire country—is still strong. No, sir, what the President has elected to do is something altogether different."

Dulles drew on his cigar, blowing the smoke up toward the chandelier suspended over the table.

"I must remind you that everything said here tonight must remain utterly secret," Dulles said somberly. "Even the slightest breach in security can be fatal."

A pause emphasized Dulles's words.

"The President is well aware of the huge arms losses sustained by Britain," he continued. "He also realizes that the Cash and Carry scheme which has been in effect for some time now is woefully inadequate to meet current demands and conditions. Yet to supply Britain directly, on the scale that is necessary, could be construed by the Germans as active U.S. participation in this war. It is conceivable that Hitler would use this as an excuse to declare war upon America. I need not go into the immense repercussions which would follow. Suffice to say that the President would lose a great deal of his political persuasion—and probably the next election. If that is the case the next occupant of the White House might well shut down any and *all* schemes to service Britain militarily.

"In view of this the President has declared that he will sell all Britain needs to Canada, which can then ship the arms anywhere it chooses without any constraints. Even now plans are being finalized to ready the sea-lanes and rail links between the United States and Canada so that the shipments can proceed without undue delay. Once the equipment has crossed the border, what is done with it is no longer an American concern. Naturally all matériel will then be shipped from Canadian ports on board Canadian or British vessels."

The enormity of what Dulles had said stunned Mackenzie McConnell. She looked at Cabot, sitting on her right, but his face was impassive, the eyes locked on the cigarette he was rolling between his fingers.

He already knew, she thought.

But that was not the case with Edward Pearce, who was slowly shaking his head.

"One hell of an undertaking," Pearce murmured. "If the

Germans learned of this arrangement and went public . . . hell, Congress could still force the President to shut it down. Hitler's propaganda could touch off an isolationist backlash before the first case of rifles crossed the border. The operation would be stillborn.

"And then," Churchill finished, "the situation would be very grim indeed."

"Unfortunately, as the Prime Minister is aware, there is a further complication," Dulles said. "We had already discussed organizing the three of you into an operational team, headquartering you in the Downing Street annex. That was before we were apprised of this, um, outstanding matter. Jonathan, would you elaborate?"

"Excuse me, gentlemen," Edward Pearce spoke up. "But in view of recent . . . developments at the embassy I suggest that my participation in this be reconsidered before anything more is said."

"Jonathan's report absolves you of any wrongdoing or negligence, Mr. Pearce," Dulles said. "That's good enough for both the Prime Minister and myself."

"Besides, Edward," Cabot murmured, "before this thing gets off the ground there is a loose end to tie up. And I need *both* your help."

Pearce and Mackenzie McConnell looked at him askance.

"There's another agent in the embassy."

"What?" Mackenzie cried. "That's impossible!"

"I wish so too, but it's not," Cabot told her. "Frye didn't die instantaneously. He managed to hang on long enough for me to get over to him. I know the code name of his control. I know this person is embassy personnel."

"Who is it?" Pearce asked softly.

"One of three possibles. We'll go over the names later."

"But you *will* have this person inoperative by the end of three days," Dulles said. It was a statement not a question.

"No question of that," Cabot said.

"You have proven yourself a resourceful man, Mr. Cabot," Churchill said. "Given your recent actions, I have no reason to question your confidence. But, Mr. Cabot, I beg of you to understand that you cannot possibly begin your new task until the situation at your embassy is absolutely secure. And every day you use up is a day lost to us."

"Mr. Prime Minister, I promise you: no more than three days. After that we go into high gear."

The man's crazy!

That single thought kept revolving in Pearce's mind as he sat in his living room, swathed in darkness, a snifter of brandy in one hand.

After they had left Ten Downing Street, Pearce drove Cabot and McConnell back to her apartment. On the way Cabot had dropped his bombshell: he had given them the three names of the people he suspected. But he offered no other details. Those would be discussed at an early morning meeting tomorrow at the embassy.

Kennedy's personal secretary, the chargé d'affaires, the naval attaché . . . Three people whose loyalty Pearce would have vouched for without hesitation. The naval attaché was a drinking buddy, from his part of the country, Texas. The chargé was a Caspar Milquetoast, a fussy little man who preferred to remain in the background. As for Kennedy's personal secretary, Sue Ann Dunn, she had been with the Ambassador back in the States!

But Cabot said he was certain. And he didn't think it would take twenty-four hours, much less seventy-two, to unearth the traitor. He had a plan . . .

Pearce drained his cognac, hurling silent epithets at the deceased Leonard Frye. He should have died as soon as the bullet hit his throat. Pearce had seen the wound. He wouldn't have given Frye one chance in a thousand of surviving more than thirty seconds. But the miserable son of a bitch had lived; long enough to say something that had convinced Cabot the game wasn't finished yet.

Now Cabot was moving again—in the wrong direction, but moving. He'd make life a living hell for each of the three people involved before he realized he was wrong. Kennedy wouldn't dare interfere because of Frye. There was no one to stop Cabot now.

That was what concerned Pearce, made him realize that for all the mistakes Cabot was committing he would, sooner or later, home in on Pearce himself. Cabot's investigations would clear the three suspects. Which would tell Cabot that the deep plant was someone else. Given Cabot's tenacity, even the blind spot he had for Pearce because of their friendship wouldn't last forever. All of which meant that Pearce's time in London was limited now. It was no longer a matter of weeks but days.

Except one factor had changed the circumstances: Pearce was no longer responsible only for himself. Somewhere in England was the agent Berlin had sent over. Where he was, if in fact he had even landed yet, Pearce did not know.

Perhaps it's better this way, Pearce thought to himself. He had been prepared to punish Berlin for forcing him into the unknown. But now there was no question that Pearce had to save himself. He would set the agent up with whatever he could. He would stay and cooperate, according to orders, until the last possible moment. But when Cabot came too close he would abandon Berlin's man and activate his contingency routes to the Continent. Yes, Berlin would be ready to put his head on a platter for what it would consider desertion of his post. But Pearce would silence this fury quickly enough. After all, he would be bringing Hitler everything he knew of Roosevelt's secret plan to arm Britain via Canada, the one weapon the Führer needed to destroy the Anglo-American alliance.

That, Pearce reflected, would surely be worth the life of one man, no matter how important his mission.

II

MASQUERADE

16

"**C**orporal Henry Schiffer?"

There were two of them, standing on the left of the bed. The one who had asked the question was tall, reed-thin, with a toothbrush ginger mustache, aquiline nose and very cold green eyes. He wore the uniform of an Army colonel.

The other was British Navy, shorter, heavyset, with a florid face, thick red lips and bulbous nose. From his uniform Guderian identified him as a commander.

"You *are* Henry Schiffer?" the Colonel repeated.

"Yes, sir," Guderian rasped and coughed to clear his throat.

Fear swelled up in his stomach as he pushed himself up against the pillows, burning through the cobwebs and fuzziness in his mind.

My God, how long have I lain here? What's been done to me . . . And how much did I say—what did I tell them—that I can't remember?

Guderian grimaced as his shoulder pressed against the headboard. The Navy Commander solicitously adjusted the pillow for him.

"My name is Blake," the Colonel said, the stiletto smile robbing his words of any warmth. "This is Commander Rawlins, who represents Admiral Ramsay of the Dover Fleet."

"How d'you do?" Guderian muttered and coughed, his hand across his mouth.

His attention was on the room now. It wasn't like any hospital he had ever been in but resembled more of a private bedroom. The wallpaper was patterned in cheerful yellow and white stripes, the dresser, night tables and rocking chair obvious antiques. The bed itself smelled fresh, with no trace of harsh hospital lye, and was covered with a dark blue quilt.

"Where am I?" Guderian asked in a breaking voice.

"London, Corporal," Commander Rawlins said gruffly. "You've taken a nasty blow to the head and the surgeons took some shrapnel out of your shoulder. But all that is on the mend. You should be fit as a fiddle in a day or two."

"I don't know . . ." Guderian said slowly. "I can't remember anything . . ."

But at once he did and the officers recognized the glazed expression in his eyes.

"That's right, Corporal," Rawlins said. "You were evacuated from Dunkirk. Do you remember the S18?"

"Yes." Guderian nodded. "The bastard was shooting up anything that moved in the water. Then he started coming towards us . . ."

"The skipper of our CMB said he's never seen such shooting as when you took over on the gun," Rawlins said. "He figured everyone on board the CMB was about to become fish bait. If that S18 had finished you off, not only the wounded on board but hundreds of others would have perished. The Jerry could have shot up every boat around him until he ran out of fuel and ammunition."

Rawlins paused, appearing embarrassed and sincere at the same time.

"I don't know how many men owe you their lives, Corporal, but it's a good number. I am proud to have met you."

"As the representative of the British Army I wish to add our congratulations for the services you've performed," Colonel Blake said. "And I have here"—he pulled out a long brown envelope from his tunic pocket—"a letter from the Prime Minister himself with his congratulations, as well as a note from General Dill stating that you be recommended for the Distinguished Service Order."

Guderian looked from one officer to the other, incredulous.

"I . . . I don't know what to say," he murmured. "I just did what I could . . ."

"Corporal, you're much too modest," Blake said. "Although I think I understand how at a loss you must feel at this moment. Disorientation, you know. You will stay here until the doctors feel you're fit to return to active duty. At that time you will report directly to me at the War Ministry at Whitehall. I look forward to receiving you, Corporal Schiffer."

Blake handed him the sealed brown envelope, then both men

stepped back and saluted. Guderian managed to raise his right arm in a shaky facsimile.

When the door closed behind the two officers, Guderian tore open the envelope and read both letters. Suddenly he began to laugh, his chest heaving as tears streamed from his eyes. Tears of relief, not mirth. Instead of being taken out and shot he had received a personal commendation from Winston Churchill himself and was about to become a British war hero! How Gerd Jaunich would have loved this moment . . .

"It's dreadfully unfair of you not to share the joke."

Guderian never heard her come in. Dressed in a nurse's starched whites, she was no more than twenty. The red hair fell in thick soft waves to her shoulders, framing a pretty face with large blue eyes, a pert nose and fine, laughing mouth. As she approached the bed Guderian saw she was taller than the average woman, perhaps five feet ten, with a full, Rubensesque figure.

"Now tell me what is so funny," she demanded.

Guderian waved the letters in his hand.

"I don't understand what this is all about."

The nurse took the letters, read them through quickly and handed them back.

"Well, Corporal Schiffer, I do believe you are my first bona fide hero."

Guderian grimaced. "Not that at all. And who might you be?"

"Christine Harloch."

Her hand was cool to the touch, and without being aware of it Guderian held on to it longer than convention dictated.

"Christine . . . That's a lovely name. I take it you work here, at this clinic . . .?"

She blushed. "This is my home."

Guderian was bewildered. "I'm sorry, I don't understand."

Her fingers were against his forehead.

"You've a bit of a temperature but otherwise you're fine. I have a few moments now, would you like to hear what happened to you?"

"Very much so," Guderian said softly.

"I was at Dover when your boat came in," Christine Harloch began. "You were unconscious, still hanging on to that damn gun. The CMB commander literally had to pry your fingers off it . . . At any rate, they brought you off the docks into one of my tents. You have to realize just what a mess Dover was—still is, undoubtedly. Wounded have been arriving for days on end. The hospitals for miles around were full. We were putting the sick wherever we could.

"After the doctor examined you and decided you could travel you were transferred to a hospital train. Six or seven of the men on your boat were with you. The whole lot of you came here."

"But you say you live here," Guderian protested.

"This is the largest house on Berkeley Square." Christine smiled. "There are dozens of empty rooms. I convinced the authorities that in cases such as yours there was no need to take up hospital beds. It's a common thing nowadays, people giving up what room they have for those coming in from Dunkirk. I have three other girls here and a doctor who comes round once a day to check up on the patients."

"Incredible," Guderian murmured. "I've been so lucky . . ."

"More than you know," Christine Harloch said gently. "I saw the boat when it came into the docks. How it made the Channel is a wonder in itself."

"How long will I be here?"

"I should say a week at least. Your upper chest and shoulder will be quite tender for a while and we have to make certain there's no danger of infection."

Her voice dropped a little and she hesitated.

"After that you're welcome to stay here for as long as you like . . . unless of course you have somewhere else to go to."

Guderian smiled into her azure eyes.

"No, I have nowhere to go," he said.

For more reasons than he dared tell her . . .

"Right then!" Christine said brightly. "Now that that's out of the way, how is your appetite? Lunch will be ready in about an hour. Nothing terribly fancy to start with, I'm afraid, but nourishing nevertheless."

She turned to leave when Guderian called her back.

"Miss Harloch, before I left . . . for Dunkirk, I mean, I had some friends living in the West End. I'd like to telephone them later, see if there's any word as to what happened . . ."

"Of course," she said sympathetically. "This is the ground

floor. My flat is right in the back. The door is always open. The telephone is in the hall."

"Thank you . . . Thanks very much."

"But I want you to rest," Christine said, her voice trying to affect a no-nonsense attitude. It had no chance against her smile. "That way you'll be up and about in no time."

Sooner than that, Guderian thought, his eyes holding hers. Much sooner.

As soon as Christine Harloch had gone, Guderian sat up against the pillows and, using his left arm, slowly drew back the quilt. The shoulder and chest muscles rippled, but as he applied more pressure pain streaked through the tissues. After what seemed like an eternity, with his face bathed in sweat and the left hand trembling violently, the quilt and top sheet had been laid back.

Guderian slumped back against the pillows. The shrapnel wounds had to have been deep to cause such pain. A week, he estimated, perhaps ten days, for the muscle fiber to heal. The stiffness would linger on because nerves healed much more slowly. Another two weeks to regain the loss of strength. Twenty-one to twenty-four days. He didn't have half of that in his timetable. Still, he had made it to England. He was alive. The cover was working better than he could have hoped for. As for his shoulder, he would simply have to ignore it.

Guderian forced himself up by his abdominal muscles and swung his legs over the side of the bed. As soon as his bare feet touched the cold, pine-scented floorboards he had to grab hold of his pajama trousers. The pajamas were most definitely not standard hospital issue. Woven out of fine soft Egyptian cotton, they were dyed a rich Burgundy with white trim. But the top hung loosely even at Guderian's shoulders while the rest billowed out like a Scout's pup tent. He tied the trouser strings twice around his waist and shuffled over to the closet, where he found a silk robe of equally gargantuan proportions as well as some slippers.

As he moved past the bed Guderian glanced at the clock on the night table. Fifteen minutes before eleven. The contact time between himself and Darius was between ten and eleven o'clock in the morning, six to seven at night. There were six numbers he could call, three in each time frame.

As his fingers gripped the large cut-glass knob, the pain that had settled into a dull throbbing suddenly coursed through his neck, setting off rockets behind his eyes. His knees almost buckled but he refused to surrender.

Tonight! Call tonight! His mind screamed at him.

But his fingers turned the knob and the door opened.

The sight that greeted him was one Guderian could never have expected. He stood facing the center hall of the house, the grand twin circular staircase winding up to his left. As he moved around it he passed the front parlor doors behind whose frosted glass panes he saw a double line of cots and men supine upon them; some sleeping, others staring starkly at nothing, enveloped in pain and the horror of memories. He crossed the hall, stepping across a maroon runner carpet and pulled open the door of what had once been the music room. The Bechstein grand had been relegated to one corner, its broad expanse covered by a sheet. The instrument now did double duty as a medicine cabinet.

All the plants had been removed, the watermarks from their pots still visible on the outcropping beneath the leaded bay window. In the center of the room, standing on dull floorboards, was an operating table, the linens smelling of disinfectant and alcohol. Around the table were cabinets filled with medicines, drugs, surgical instruments. At the far end of the room, beneath the rolled-up carpet, were a half dozen basins lined up like shiny helmets and a hot plate with a large pot of water on it.

Guderian closed the door behind him and moved toward the righthand side of the staircase. The house was very quiet. If he strained his ears he could hear the soft voices somewhere high above him. In the back, where he figured the kitchens were, someone was pouring water into a galvanized sink. He listened to the clatter of plates and the snatches of song he couldn't identify.

Guderian retraced his steps around the staircase and knocked softly on the door at the end. Upon receiving no answer, he opened it.

"Miss Harloch?"

The room belonged to her, undeniably. The scent he remembered on her skin was the same that hung in the still air.

Guderian called her name once more, but was moving down the corridor even as he did so, past the hastily constructed bookcases, smelling of raw conifers, the titles—poetry, mythology, picture books on art, history and tattered travel diaries—past the foot tables with bric-a-brac set on Irish lace doilies and into the large bed-sitting room that, with its private bath, resembled a suite at the Ritz. Beyond the French windows Guderian saw a bricked patio with yellow wicker furniture and a three-sided wall which effectively cut this garden off from the rest of the grounds. This was where Christine Harloch dwelt.

For a moment Guderian stood very still, his senses drinking in everything around him. When he heard the faint ticking of the wall clock he moved back into the hall and, making sure the door was closed, lifted the telephone receiver. The other party answered on the second ring.

"Grosvenor oh-two, three-eight."

"I wish to speak to Darius," Guderian said, adopting a French accent.

The pause on the other end of the line was no more than a heartbeat, but enough to confirm he had made contact.

"One if by land, two if by sea," was the reply.

"Two if by sea," Guderian replied.

"Welcome," the voice said softly.

"We must meet."

"My time here is at an end," the voice continued on, disregarding Guderian's statement. "There is a message for you. Use the third option." A pause. "The third option."

The connection was broken. Guderian watched the sweatmarks on the receiver evaporate into two damp spots.

My time is at an end.

Guderian shuddered. What had gone wrong? What could possibly have happened to Edward Pearce in the last four days since the transmission from Berlin alerting him to Guderian's impending arrival? Surely if the Americans had by some incredible stroke of luck ferreted him out, Guderian would never have been able to speak to him. But he had, and Pearce hadn't used the few words which would have told Guderian the American was blown. And he could have spoken these words as easily as any others . . .

Use the third option.

Not only was Darius still able to communicate, but he also had freedom of movement. There would be written details, an explanation, at the third option, and—

"Corporal Schiffer!"

He whirled around to see Christine Harloch standing in the door frame, both hands on her hips, frowning. Then at once her expression softened and she was by his side, one arm around his waist, the other on his good arm.

"You called?" she asked softly.

"They didn't make it," Guderian said, looking straight ahead. "Not one of them."

Without another word he allowed her to lead him back to his room. There was nothing he could do at the moment . . . nothing save keep his frustration in check.

With the help of sedatives Erik Guderian slept right through lunch and well into the afternoon. He awoke briefly at five o'clock, rolled over and glanced at the clock on the nightstand, then closed his eyes again. When Christine Harloch looked in on him an hour later she didn't have the heart to wake him for his dinner.

Guderian's mental alarm went off at half past eight. Without bothering with the light he got out of bed and opened the door a crack. Across the hall, in the music room, he saw Christine and another girl folding towels and sheets.

Guderian moved silently into Christine's room and made another telephone call. He returned to his room without incident, helped himself to an extra dose of painkillers, whose side effect would put him to sleep, and slipped in between the sheets. For the next nine hours he slept without memory, like of the dead.

"You're mad!" Christine was laughing. "I can't possibly leave here right now. And neither can *you!*"

At half past seven on the morning of June 1, an hour after Guderian awoke, Christine Harloch had appeared to change his dressing. His shoulder was stiff and the arm tender down to the elbow, but he thought he could actually feel the healing process and he willed for it to continue. After she was done Guderian washed himself thoroughly with a rough sponge, brushed his teeth and carefully combed his hair. He threw the sweat-sodden pajamas into the laundry hamper and, with only a towel wrapped around his waist, padded across the room to the closet.

The only clothes he had in the world consisted of his uniform. Guderian held it at arm's length, noting that someone had gone to the trouble of giving it a thorough cleaning and carefully mending the tears in the shoulder and trouser legs. In the dresser he found his socks, underwear and shirt as well as Schiffer's personal effects: an inexpensive but serviceable watch, two handkerchiefs, a black comb, twelve pounds and some coins. Underneath the coins was his military identification. Guderian put on everything except the shirt, which he couldn't manage alone. He had just finished tying his boots when Christine Harloch returned from her rounds.

"You're crazy," she repeated. "Breakfast at the Grosvenor!"

"Miss Harloch, I'm starved," Guderian protested. "And the Grosvenor serves real American food."

"What's wrong with British fare?" she demanded archly. "And please, no more 'Miss Harloch.' My name is Christine."

"Look," Guderian said, stepping closer to her, so close he could feel her breath on his chest. "You've done so much for me. You've got me on the mend, all my clothes are clean and stitched up. I've been sleeping for the last two days. Now it's June—look outside! The day's beautiful. Surely you can take off an hour . . ."

Her fingers were on his skin, the nails moving lightly across the bandage.

"Your wound . . ." she murmured.

"If you help me with my shirt we can put the arm in a sling."

"You're impossible," she said, stepping back.

"I wouldn't ask for something like this if you were alone here, or there was a new batch of wounded coming in," Guderian said soberly. "But that isn't the case. So please, let me take you to the Grosvenor. Let's walk together in the spring air and forget about hospitals and the war for a little while. That's not asking for too much, is it?"

She pursed her lips and the frown cut two deep furrows between her eyes.

"Please," he said softly. "Besides, there's something else I should do."

She didn't say a word but reached for his shirt and helped him into it and buttoned it.

"Drink your tea, Corporal," she said severely. "I have other people to feed, rounds to make, a replacement to find and a sling to make for you. If you like you can wait for me in the garden."

Guderian took her advice and had his tea in the garden. The stone walls were still blotted with dark patches where the water had worked its way in. Tufts of grass were sprouting between the bricks, and the two apple trees in the corner were coming into blossom. From somewhere on the second or third story Guderian heard the strains of a Schumann symphony wafting through the open windows, but when he looked up he felt as though the music were descending directly from the peerless blue sky above him.

Erik Guderian did not move from his chair for almost an hour. Using the background music as counterpoint, he methodically reviewed what had to be done, examining each detail in the plan he had formulated. When he was satisfied that he had covered the major contingencies, he thought ahead to the days from now when he would be acting in concert with men he knew only as ciphers, whose loyalties and abilities he would have to take on faith. In Berlin he had had every confidence in these unknown people. Their past work and the results engendered spoke eloquently for them. But Darius had poisoned that trust.

My time here is at an end.

So Guderian searched for the fallback positions, alternatives, avenues of escape—the factors which would ensure that he would never find himself without resources, forced into a cul-de-sac. Step by step he reviewed the plan as it had been formulated in Germany, modified and refined in France. Yet no matter which way he approached the details, he found himself coming back to the one man who should have been his strongest card yet who had metamorphosed into the joker— Darius. The conclusion was inescapable: until he knew exactly what it was that had prompted Darius to run—what he could be carrying *with* him—Guderian could not move to the next stage of the plan.

"I'd give you much more than a penny, but I'm not sure if I want to know those thoughts."

Guderian started, the chair legs scraping against the stone. Gone was the uniform which was the only clothing he had seen her in. In its place was a colorful spring skirt that fell to midcalf. The blouse was the color of peaches and the sweater a dark cashmere which was set off by a blue silk scarf tied loosely at her throat. Her hair had been carefully brushed and begged for fingers to run through it. There was a hint of rouge at the cheeks and some mascara to accent the eyes.

"Even a penny is too much," Guderian said. "What happened over there—the futility and stupidity of it all . . ." He looked away from her. "It will take a little while to learn to live with it . . ."

Guderian rose and took her by the elbow.

"But not even that is going to spoil breakfast," he declared. "And since we're walking we had better get started."

"Let's go out the back way," Christine said quickly.

When Guderian looked at her askance, she blushed.

"Too late." He laughed and pointed to the second-floor windows where a half dozen giggling females were waving to them. Christine grabbed his good arm and they made for the gate.

There was no war in London that day. As they turned the corner on Mount Street, Guderian and Christine Harloch gazed at the people hurrying along in the street, at the traffic which flowed with a smoothness particular to the city. In the soft spring wind they talked to each other as though there were nothing around to distract them.

It was Guderian who monopolized the dialogue. He answered her questions easily—about what Henry Schiffer had been doing in London before signing up, who his friends were, where they had lived, what he had studied and how was it that he had chosen to come to London in the first place. He told the story almost verbatim as he had heard it from the real man and found his voice rising and dipping at particular points just as Schiffer's had done. And he knew Christine believed every word, because he had Schiffer's young, frightened face, the hollow, beaten eyes in his mind's eye as he spoke.

As they passed the gates of St. Crispin's church, Guderian stepped over to an old woman seated on a bench. Flowers, their stems wrapped in newspaper, were arranged in tin cups of water, forming a semicircle. Guderian chose white carnations.

"I'll only be a moment," he said, guiding Christine into the churchyard. Around the back of the church was a small gravesite, most of the headstones worn and blackened over time. She squeezed his hand and offered an understanding smile.

There was no one else in the graveyard. Guderian walked on

alone, slowly, eyes roving, skimming past trees, the sexton's hut, the rear door of the small church. Nothing.

Although he knew exactly where to go, Guderian paused at the foot of the path leading into the plots. He looked around as one would to get one's bearings, then proceeded up the center path, turned left at the next set of plots and counted off five stones.

RIDLEY MAJOR
1919–1939
BELOVED BROTHER OF JONATHAN
RIP

The grave was one of the few fresh ones, the limestone tablet still bone white. Standing at the foot, Guderian crossed himself, then proceeded to the marker where he knelt and placed the flowers. In that same motion his fingers scooped away the dirt at the foot of the gravestone. The sun caught the metal of an aluminum capsule, and for an instant there was a spark of light before Guderian palmed the cylinder.

"Was he a friend?" Christine asked as he met her at the gate.

"I didn't know him at all," Guderian said. "But I promised a buddy of mine I would visit the grave . . . if he couldn't get here himself."

"I'm sorry," Christine said.

"So am I," Guderian murmured.

But the third option had been carried out. The message had been received. It was now a matter of translation.

At the corner of Rex Place he drew her into a bookstore, where he purchased stationery, envelopes, a street guide to the city and a novel.

"Oh, you're one for the French, are you?" Christine teased him, weighing the hefty copy of Stendhal's *Red and Black* in her palm.

"It's much better than a sedative," Guderian told her, handing the clerk the money.

He asked for and paid a few pence more for a bag.

"I could have carried that for you in my purse," Christine protested when they were on the street.

"Nonsense. Stendhal is a weighty matter."

She giggled. "You sound just like Andrew."

"An older brother?" Guderian ventured.

"No, just a friend. Andrew is a Navy commander, attached, at least for the time being, to the Admiralty. We were very close . . . once."

"I'm sorry if I was prying," he apologized.

"You really *don't* know who I am, do you?" she asked at once.

"Who you *really* are, as far as I'm concerned, is a beautiful nurse who took a wreck of a man off some godforsaken boat, absconded with him to London where you nursed him back to health in the best tradition of Florence Nightingale. What more could a man need to know?"

Her eyes remained downcast, as though she were watching the cracks in the sidewalk, careful lest she step on one and, as in the children's game, die.

"It's just that sometimes people aren't comfortable with me once they learn who my family are," she said in a small voice.

"They're villains all, are they!" he laughed.

"No, just depressingly, incredibly rich . . . And not well liked by some people."

"Should that make a difference?"

"It does at times," she said with a hint of desperation, as though he were failing to read between the lines she was giving him. "Look, I know you're a Canadian, but doesn't the name Harloch mean *anything* to you?"

It did and he should have made the connection well before now.

"The newspaper people?"

She nodded. "The same."

"And that's supposed to be some sort of black mark, a warning?" he asked her, his tone light, teasing.

He waited a moment but she would neither answer nor look at him.

"You've done a tremendous amount for me," Guderian said, picking up the slack. "I shall always be in your debt, for the kindness, the caring . . . For heaven's sake, you took a complete stranger, battered and alone, into your own home!"

"I don't want you to think that what I do is charity," she blurted out. "I worked damn hard to become a nurse and I'm a good one. But I don't want you to turn away from me because . . ."

Gently he gripped her by the shoulders, stopping her, forcing her to look at him. "Why should I ever do that?" he asked softly.

"Because sooner or later who I am, my family, always becomes a part of it," she whispered. "They can frighten people . . ."

"I think I can manage if it comes to that," Guderian said gently.

For the first time she looked directly at him, her eyes measuring, weighing.

"Perhaps you can. You seem much older than you really are . . . experienced."

He took her elbow and they started walking again.

"Sometimes it helps to talk to a stranger," he said. "There's not much to lose that way."

She hesitated at first, then the words came out haltingly as though she was afraid they were somehow inadequate. But he encouraged her; with his eyes, with small gestures, using his hands and fingers, coaxing her to trust him, anticipating her hesitations and leading her over them, softly encouraging her to give herself up to him.

Her story was a fairy tale and he believed her because he knew she was of the rich, whose lives easily lent themselves to the magical and wondrous.

She was born two years after the Great War, the second of two children, born a girl when every family was praying for sons. The money was on her father's side, its source being the great Harloch textile and shoe factories stretching from London in the south into the towns and cities of Lancashire in the north.

Christine's first dozen years were spent in a Wonderland isolation. She did not attend school but received tutors at her home. She was vaguely aware of a thing called poverty, but grew up believing it was something you saw inadvertently from the window of the Rolls when the driver took a back street. There were instructors in dance and etiquette in the London house; riding captains of dubious East European gentility at Harloch House in East Anglia. There was also the memory of a mother, a beautiful singer-entertainer whom Bartholomew Harloch had married in his days as a young rake and who died shortly after Christine was born.

In 1939, at the age of nineteen, Christine and two maiden aunts were on the Grand Tour of the Continent, the final piece of the mosaic in her education. For a reason that was never quite clear to begin with, the three women found themselves in Madrid on precisely the day Franco launched his final assault upon the city. The aunts immediately found shelter for themselves and their charge in the British embassy, but they were quite powerless to stop what happened next.

When Christine spoke of this moment she called it one which, at the time, seemed predestined to arrive. It was as though everything she had been doing up to now had led up to it. Elements within her which until then were confused, erratic or inscrutable suddenly fell into place, their meaning perfectly clear. It was as though the world had finally succeeded in breaking open her chrysalis, leaving her no choice but to confront it. The fairy tale had come to an end.

"Early next morning I broke into the dispensary in the physician's office," Christine said. "I took as much morphine, sulfa, bandages and ointments as I could, got past the embassy security cordon and made for the Loyalist lines. Looking back on it I still wonder how I wasn't killed, what with all the German planes bombing us night and day . . ."

"How long did you stay in Spain?" Guderian asked.

"Almost six months. They needed doctors and nurses so badly. I had had some training in first aid, not much more than the Girl Scout variety, but the sight of blood didn't bother me. Even if it had, there wasn't time to worry about it, not with everything else that was going on. Almost everything I know now is a result of Madrid."

And then Guderian saw her in a completely different light. He had never experienced Madrid or Guernica firsthand but knew, from the accounts of others, the depth of human misery those names had created. They formed a crucible of suffering which broke the souls of men, yet here was this girl, seemingly sheltered and fragile, who had emerged tempered, whole.

"You are a remarkable woman," Guderian said. "I don't think I've met anyone quite like yourself before."

Christine blushed but did not look away.

"Nor I you," she replied quickly and then swept past the doorkeeper of the Grosvenor, who touched his cap.

The captain greeted them at the entry to the breakfast room, murmured a word of sympathy about Guderian's wound and stepped past Christine, menus tucked under his arm. As he skirted a round table with an enormous vase of art flowers as the centerpiece, Guderian saw that part of the room which had been previously blocked off. Half a dozen tables were occupied, all but one with solitary diners. The seventh had three people around it: a tall, stunningly attractive woman with golden hair, one man on her right, powerfully built and obviously the woman's companion . . . and Darius. Guderian was no more than fifteen feet away when the man, in reaching for his cigarettes, presented himself in profile to him. Guderian did not break stride. The smile he had for Christine, who was seating herself on the banquette, remained frozen on his lips. He allowed the maître d' to pull the chair back for him and murmured his thanks. Yet that part of him which was the eternal observer, like a disembodied twin who watched over even his own progress, was still seized by disbelief. He knew that man! He had memorized his photograph and the details found in the Abwehr file. Jonathan Baylor Cabot. The man who could not be defined, categorized as working for any particular department or agency of the American government. The man who had Dulles's ear. Who had laid and sprung the trap in which Beth Davis had been slain. Who had followed the twisted skein to London and taken the man Darius had used as a shield. Who was now breaking bread with Darius himself . . .

God in heaven, did Darius really believe he could run from *this* man!

My time is at an end . . .

As though it had been before his eyes all the time, like a mirage floating before his vision but just beyond his physical grasp, Guderian's alter ego seized the answer. Of course it wasn't Darius who controlled the situation any longer! It was Cabot, without question. Yet obviously Darius was not afraid of Cabot. He would not have been sitting with him at breakfast, chatting Cabot up like the old friend he was. No, Darius didn't suspect any danger from Cabot, at least not the immediate kind. He was getting ready to move for another reason altogether. Because Cabot had tempted him with a forbidden fruit until the temptation to pluck it and bite into it had proven irresistible . . .

This bait—was it genuine as Darius obviously believed? Or was it, like the Apple of Paradise, tainted? The answer lay only inches away, in the capsule in his breast pocket.

"Henry—are you all right?"

Guderian glanced up at Christine Harloch.

"You've been staring at the menu as though it's written in Arabic. Are you sure you're all right?"

"Perfectly," Guderian said and pushed back his chair. "I have to use the facilities. All those liquids you've been feeding me. Order for the both of us, would you? The full American breakfast—and lots of coffee."

He was gone before Christine could utter a word in reply.

The elderly attendant in the washroom greeted Guderian with a deferential nod and pushed open a cubicle door. The German locked the door behind him and played out the charade, dropping his trousers. Quickly he reached into his pocket, pulled out the aluminum capsule and tapped out the rolled-up paper. There were seven columns of numbers across, seven down, inscribed on the paper in precise handwriting. Guderian pulled out the text of *Red and Black* and set to work. The message was, as he had suspected, succinct and brief, yet Guderian decoded it twice because he could not believe what he was reading.

Darius's words spelled out not only what he wanted to say, but also his own condemnation. Guderian could almost picture the excitement of the man as he penned the message, the feverish joy which overtakes an agent when he is on the receiving end of what he believes is an intelligence coup. Even the best can be infected, refuse to see the real from the fabricated, the lie veiled as the truth.

It was Edward Pearce—Darius—who had sent the message, yes. But the words, the text, those belonged to the tall, heavily built man who walked so quietly and smoothly at his side. Jonathan Baylor Cabot, the man who had put a ring through Pearce's nose without Pearce's ever knowing it.

Guderian tore the paper into fragments and flushed the toilet. Christine was waiting. If he stayed away too long, her concern might cause someone to come looking for him. Guderian tightened his belt and stepped out of the cubicle. The attendant turned the faucet on for him and stood by, a towel in his hands. Guderian washed his hands, then splashed water on his face, catching his reflection in the mirror.

Too damn close! Guderian cursed silently. If Pearce hadn't said those few words, *My time here is at an end*, Guderian would never have thought to intercept him at Grosvenor. He gave silent thanks to the details in Darius's file, which had provided a clear picture of Pearce's daily habits.

And if I hadn't come today, Guderian thought to himself, accepting the towel, not seen Cabot here, before reading the message, I would never have made the connection between the two.

Guderian dropped a few pence on the plate and left the washroom. Pearce was valueless to him now. Worse, he was dangerous. But there was more he had to know before deciding on a course of action.

As he reentered the breakfast room Guderian saw the concern with which Christine was looking at him. He smiled back, hoping to reassure her. Intuitively he felt he would need her now, be able to use her. How and when was unclear. But he recognized that she could serve as his mantle—the perfect cloak behind which he could hide until the issue of Darius was settled. It was only a matter of days . . .

17

E dward Pearce awoke to the shrill rattle of the alarm clock. He rolled over and slammed his palm down on the timepiece. The temptation to go back to sleep was overwhelming. What little rest he had managed to get had been fraught with rushing nightmares. He couldn't remember a single sequence, but the ache behind his eyes and throbbing pain in his legs were lingering evidence of what he must have suffered through. Sleep was never kind to him on the eve of a journey, but this was the worst he could remember. Pearce felt as though he had been physically beaten.

After he showered under the trickle of water that could be coaxed from the pipes, Pearce walked slowly through the apartment, coffee cup in hand. There was no question of taking anything with him. Even if he had something to take. The apartment, with its three square rooms painted a neutral cream color, the petulant gas radiator, the makeshift kitchen with hot plates and breadbox-size icebox, was devoid of any character or reflection of the man who lived in them. Even the few concessions to decoration weren't his own: the prints and two watercolors had come from the embassy storerooms—pieces no one else wanted; the two dozen books on the shelves belonged to the embassy library. The bric-a-brac on the living room mantelpiece—two glass minstrel figurines, a cigarette box, a vase with dried flowers—had all been bestowed upon Pearce by women who had come and long since departed.

As he dressed, Pearce inventoried his wardrobe, carefully selecting the clothes he would wear today—nothing too tight, no material that chafed. He didn't know how long he would be in them. Warmth and comfort were the determining factors.

From a wire hanger he removed a wide leather belt, flipped it over and unzipped the back. He laid the belt lengthwise across the bed. From the shoebox at the bottom of the closet he took a hammer and from the shelf above his bed, a large seashell that doubled as a bookend. He took both into the kitchen and, placing the shell into the sink, methodically smashed its leaves until he had reached the innermost coil. From within the recess he pulled out three gold-certificate deposits, a thousand dollars in hundred-dollar denominations and a meticulously forged identity card which made him out to be a representative of the American Red Cross. A corresponding passport, bearing the same name, was already tucked away in a false padding of his jacket's shoulder.

Pearce carefully gathered up the fragments of the seashell and deposited them in a paper bag. On his way out he would drop the bag into the trashcan outside the gate, thirty minutes before the scheduled pickup.

Everything must appear normal, nothing out of place . . . Pearce's final mocking salute to those who would come after him. And he knew they would, with Cabot in the lead. But by then they would be chasing shadows.

Pearce took one last walk through the apartment. This would be the last time he would ever find himself in such ugly, anonymous surroundings. In Switzerland was freedom, bought by the gold certificates. In Lisbon, his second stop, even more bounty when he delivered his information to the Germans. Wealth which equaled freedom . . .

The pink underbelly of dawn was showing against the blue-black remnants of the night sky. Pearce locked the door behind him and skipped down the half dozen steps to the street. He tossed the paper bag into the bin and replaced the lid. Somewhere down the street but still out of sight he could hear the rattle of milk bottles in the metal racks of the milk wagon.

As he began to walk Pearce could not repress a smile. Berlin had commanded Pearce to put himself at the disposal of the incoming agent. The head of security at Grosvenor Square pondered the man's possible reactions when he had deciphered Pearce's message. Outrage? Disbelief? Perhaps both. Pearce knew he would shortly have the opportunity to find out for himself. He had made a counterdemand: the agent must contact him by three o'clock this afternoon and arrange a meeting for a time no more than five hours later. Pearce would give him everything: agents' names, safe houses, dead-drops, money supplies, a list of specialists in everything from armaments to chemicals. He would hand it all over on a platter—except for himself. Because Edward Pearce believed he carried in his head the information which would enable Berlin to put a quick, brutal end to the war. No other agent, no other mission, no matter how highly rated, could even begin to compare.

"Where is Nurse Harloch?"

The question was too abrupt and Guderian knew it as soon as he heard his own words.

The girl standing beside the bed was younger than Christine, eighteen perhaps, petite, with curly red hair and freckled complexion.

"She said she had some errands to run, sir. She will look in on you as soon as she returns."

The nurse paused. "This is Doctor Bacal. He's come to examine you and change the dressing."

He was, without a doubt, the gentlest man Guderian had ever seen, in appearance so much like Albert Einstein that Guderian was stunned by the resemblance. His expression gave him away.

"I see you recognize me, Corporal Schiffer," Bacal said, a Viennese lilt still evident beneath the harder English accent. The blue eyes sparkled in amusement.

"But you're not—" Guderian started to say.

"Doctor Einstein?" Bacal cocked his head of frizzy hair to one side. "No, sir, most assuredly not. I regret that I am in no way related to that illustrious gentleman. The only thing we have in common, aside from this striking resemblance in appearance, is our Hebraic persuasion."

Even as he spoke Bacal was in the process of removing the dressing on Guderian's shoulder, his fingers moving so lightly that Guderian scarcely felt them.

"You're Canadian, are you?" the physician murmured, discarding the bandage into a metal tray. He looked closely at the wound, fingertips brushing the red, raw flesh.

"Yes. From Kitchener."

"German descent?"

Something in the tone made Guderian recoil.

"My father was German," Guderian said.

"A fine people," Bacal commented softly. "Decent, generous, industrious . . ."

The words trailed off, lackluster, as though they represented qualities no longer applicable to the character. Hidden behind them Guderian sensed a profound regret.

"You are in excellent physical condition, Corporal," Bacal said, applying ointment. "Are you a sportsman?"

"A teacher," Guderian said.

"But you are very active nonetheless, yes?"

"I used to do a fair bit of mountain climbing."

"Of course!" Bacal exclaimed softly. "That would explain the strength of your upper torso."

A fresh pack was applied over the ointment and Bacal set it in place with white surgical tape. He stood back, hands folded across a slight paunch, surveying his handiwork.

"I wish all my ministrations could be done so simply, with such excellent results." He sighed. "You will rest for a few more days, Corporal Schiffer, but after that I see no reason why you can't be discharged. Naturally I expect you not to undertake any strenuous activities for a few weeks. I will prescribe certain therapy to prevent loss of muscle strength, but basically it is a matter of time."

Bacal paused. "You have been fortunate, Corporal. I only wish you had lived *not* to fight another day. But I'm afraid you shall."

Guderian looked up at him and said, "Thank you, doctor."

Although he spoke these words with heartfelt sincerity, Guderian felt somehow unclean, as though he had physically stolen something from this man. Deceit was strange that way.

After the examination came breakfast. Guderian took his

time over the soft-boiled eggs, dry toast and tea, letting his mind work through the next steps of what had to be done. When he had eaten he set the tray aside and went into the bathroom to wash up. As he examined himself critically in the mirror he realized Bacal was right: he had lost weight, too much of it. But it wouldn't be therapy that would restore the fine pitch to his body.

Guderian slipped into the oversized maroon robe and left his room. In the hall he almost ran into the pretty redheaded nurse who had assisted Bacal.

"Corporal," she said, "you shouldn't be running about like this."

"If I'm being discharged in a couple days I'd best see if my old landlady will have me back," Guderian said cheerfully.

"I shouldn't be worrying about that if I were you," the nurse laughed as she proceeded up the stairs.

"What do you mean?" Guderian called after her.

But she never answered him and for a moment he stood there looking up at the second-floor gallery, listening to the echoes of the soft laughter.

As usual the door to Christine Harloch's suite was unlocked. Guderian's first call, to Darius, was answered promptly. Guderian identified himself and without pause outlined his suggestion as to how and when the meeting should take place. There was a silence when he finished. Guderian could almost sense the objections which were being formed into words on the other end of the line. He was wrong.

"Agreed."

That was all Darius said before breaking the connection.

Guderian dialed a second number and prayed that the party would answer. The call was coming in fifteen minutes after the appointed time frame for contact. The phone was ringing . . . twice, three times, four. An answer. Guderian identified himself by a fictitious name and added the password sentence. It was reciprocated at once. Within fifteen seconds a time and place for a meeting had been agreed upon. Guderian hung up and returned to his room to dress.

As he carefully worked the shirt around his injured shoulder, questions streamed through his mind double-time. Could this man arrange what was necessary on such short notice? Would it be possible for him to get away without raising suspicion? Was the location the best one possible?

Guderian slipped on his jacket and felt the inside pocket. The scalpel which he had stolen from the dispensary was there, hard and smooth against his fingertips. His eye caught sight of the navy blue cloth which was made up as the sling. He considered asking a nurse to wrap his arm in it but rejected the idea. Uniforms were the common dress in London streets today. His would go unnoticed.

Guderian had to walk up to Carlos Place before he was able to find a taxi, and even then it was a matter of luck. As soon as the driver discharged his passenger he raised the off-duty flag. Guderian shouted at him then started to run, keeping his left arm stiff against his body. The result was the exaggerated movement of a cripple, but it had the intended effect: the driver waved him inside. As it turned out the driver was headed home to the East End. The slight detour which took him to the National Gallery in Trafalgar Square was more than compensated for by the tip Guderian left him.

England at war, he thought, puzzled, amused and respectful all at the same time. Below him, in the Square itself, the pillar of Nelson rose toward the blue cloudless sky as though challenging anyone who would dare strike it. At the base were the swarms of people, sitting along the edges of the fountains, walking around the cinder paths between tracts of grass still wet from yesterday's rain, or milling about the various stands and kiosks where peddlers hawked everything from newspapers to ices dipped in syrup.

Is Berlin still like this? he asked himself. Do children still play in the Zoo and ride the carousels in the parks along the Unter den Linden? Berlin seemed incredibly far away.

Guderian shivered and shook his shoulders as though ridding himself of some miasma. All at once he felt utterly severed from his country. It wasn't only a matter of physical distance. Berlin, Germany, what was happening there, was all another universe, quite apart from the rest of humanity.

We are going to lose, he thought to himself suddenly. If the war continues much longer we will lose and our children will suffer the victors' fury and condemn us for all time.

The realization was so pure that he could not believe it was not real. It stunned him at first, but as he stood there watching the children chase the hundreds of pigeons which lifted off in great clouds to escape, he realized that what he had glimpsed at was the truth. He had heard and read about such things coming upon other men. He had tried to understand it then, what a man felt when the veil of history was dropped for a microsecond and he was permitted a glimpse of the future. Guderian was seized by it now: stark, unrelenting terror, brought on by atrocities which a single man was impotent to prevent from coming to pass.

Or was he?

It can't happen, Guderian thought savagely. I won't *permit* it to happen!

Brusquely he turned and began his ascent up the tiered steps toward the Gallery, moving quickly, driven by an insane hollow laughter from a figure he didn't dare turn around and face.

The man Guderian had come to meet was sitting exactly where he said he would be: in a shell-like alcove which housed the Statue of Pegasus, a mediocre example from the Roman period. Around the base of the shell were half-moon benches carved out of marble. As he approached the recess Guderian saw the black, brilliantly shined shoes first, then the battered oxblood leather briefcase with the initials J.D. burned into the clasp, finally the immaculately dressed figure of medium build who had one leg crossed over the other. Guderian could almost touch the raw strength emanating from the man, like that of a coiled snake. As he sat down Guderian noticed that a trick of light had cast the face in the shadows. Accident or intention? He looked at the man carefully, his eyes recording the outlines of the face, probing behind the darkness to complete the image. If the stranger took offense at such scrutiny it did not show in his voice.

"Doctor Livingstone, I presume?"

The voice was soft, like a child's, but spoken with obvious effort. Guderian filed the point away: a throat injury. Also the dry, mocking tone.

"Indeed," Guderian answered.

For a moment neither man said a word. They were far enough apart so that they could see almost around the corner from where the other was sitting and into the main hall. The floors were terrazzo. Even though there were very few people here today, the echoes of their footsteps would provide a comfortable cover to their conversation. Footsteps on stone would also serve to warn them if anyone came too close.

"You come from Darius," the man stated.

"I come from Berlin," Guderian corrected him.

"Darius made no mention of you."

"But I knew who you are and how to reach you without using him."

The man considered the rebuttal, then said:

"Very well. I know Darius is secure. If you knew me without going through him you must be all right."

"This is where you're mistaken," Guderian said. "Darius is no longer secure."

"That's impossible," the man said tonelessly. "I wouldn't have come without ascertaining that Darius is still operational."

"You called him?"

"There is no need. I have access to his movements."

"He doesn't know he's been taken," Guderian said. "He's been fed some tainted bait. He swallowed it. The minute he tries to run, and he intends to do so tonight, they will take him."

Again silence, then: "Who else is compromised?"

"I believe no one. They are waiting to see where he will take them. If they can get a few more for the price of one, they'll do so. . . . Then wring the rest of the names out later."

"What is it you want me to do?"

"We are the only hope Darius has. We have to help him— tonight. I have arranged to meet with him."

"But if he's tainted then he's being followed," the man countered.

"This is what I propose," Guderian continued on as though there hadn't been any interruption.

In deft strokes he outlined the plan he had in mind.

"Do you think it's feasible?" he asked the man.

"Feasible, certainly. But we need more details."

A few minutes later the initial idea had the necessary hues and shades.

"So you see, it is possible although there are certain factors which are beyond our control. We cannot predict the number of men who will form the umbrella around Darius. Nor can we be absolutely certain that they will respond to anything happening to Cabot rather than going after their primary target. There is also the matter of escape, for both of us. Berlin did not send me here on a suicide mission. We'd best leave that to the Japanese, who have experience in such affairs."

It was Guderian's turn to fall silent.

"Comments?" he asked at last.

"Some," the man said softly.

When the man had finished, Guderian smiled inwardly. Sometimes it was much better to allow people to draw for themselves the conclusion you had in mind all along. Guderian had given the man the variables and also had hoped he had arranged them in the only possible way. Guderian's way.

"You're sure you haven't overlooked any points that concern you directly?" Guderian asked.

"None," the man whispered.

"Very well. Until tonight then."

"Good day, Doctor Livingstone."

The clock struck midnight and June 2 passed into oblivion. Forty-eight of Cabot's seventy-two hours had elapsed, empty hours, inconclusive, which brought him no closer to his goal.

Jonathan Cabot continued to wait. He was alone in Pearce's office at the embassy, sitting in the comfortable leather swivel chair, his body hunched forward across the desk. The gooseneck lamp spilled its light across the charts and pages carefully laid out on the green blotter. On either side of him were telephones: a permanently open line to Queen Anne's Gate and Mackenzie McConnell, a clear outside line to Pearce, the Downing Street line, and finally three circuits routed through the Security Service boards giving Cabot direct access to Mackenzie's men in the field.

Not a few men either, but a force of thirty, the best MI5 had to offer. Cabot had examined the service records of each one before confirming their participation. They were tough, resilient men who walked the streets like panthers and could remain at a surveillance post for hours on end, invisible chameleons.

Ten men for each suspect. That was what Cabot had ordered and no one questioned him. Churchill himself had made it perfectly clear to all concerned that he wanted this man, no matter the time and resources it took to bring him to ground. And Cabot was his instrument.

Yet the instrument was ineffectual without a target. The bait, suitably disguised, had been presented to each of the three suspects at the end of the working day, June 1. From that moment on there wasn't a single minute in which the targets were out of Cabot's sight. The instant they stepped off the embassy grounds the tag teams picked them up, covering their movements across the city. If one took the subway, an agent planted at the entrance followed him, with a support team within fifty feet. Two had private cars which, while they were parked in the embassy compound, had had magnetic radio-direction beepers installed underneath the rocker panels. A list of shops, restaurants, homes of friends, favorite pubs, hair-dressers and barbers had been compiled, their locations marked across a wall-sized map of London. Appointment calendars had been appropriated during the noon hour, the pages photo-graphed, the details studied. As a result reservations were made in certain restaurants, seats bought for performances in theaters along the Haymarket and four agents sent out, with appropriate female escorts, in black-tie attire.

Nor was surveillance limited to the streets. Each suspect's apartment had been invaded by groups of MI5 Technical Branch specialists. Telephone receivers had been gutted, their interiors intricately realigned so that both speakers' voices would be amplified. The cords had been carefully unwound, the wire covers stripped and new wires added. These were connected to the switch boxes in the basement of the buildings, where a team of two monitored all incoming-outgoing calls, taping every word.

All three apartments had radios, two in the living room, one in the dining room. The guts of these were intricately rear-ranged so that the units functioned as receivers not only of incoming programs of the BBC but also as recorders of conver-sations taking place within the room. The text of all sound within a radius of thirty feet was recorded on an ultra-slow tape secreted into the radio's cabinet.

As a final backup measure Cabot had had MI5 specialists look over the buildings adjacent to the suspects' apartments. If there was a flat whose windows looked across into the sur-veillance territory, the people who occupied it were quietly informed that His Majesty's government required their prem-ises for a short time. Four such people found themselves con-fronted by a quiet-spoken man who shepherded them out of the building into black saloon cars and quickly deposited them in security-controlled suites in the Camden Hotel on Bayswater. In their place arrived the best speech therapists and lip-readers the Security Service could find. Technical Branch provided the high-powered binoculars and the silent, ever-present babysitters.

A telephone whirred softly on his left. Cabot listened for a moment, murmured a few words and broke the connection. He penciled in another mark on his map: the Ambassador's secretary, who had been to Covent Garden with the British Commercial Liaison, had just arrived home from a late supper at the Ritz. Her escort, a man in his fifties, widower, with an impeccable service record, had seen her to the door, where he had said goodnight. The secretary had brushed him a kiss on the cheek and gone inside. A separate team picked up the Liaison and followed him to his own home five blocks away. According to the lip-readers watching from across the way, the secretary hadn't even gone into the living room, where they could have "read" any conversation that took place. The bedroom light had come on briefly and a moment later was extinguished.

Cabot sat back in the chair, the tip of the pencil tapping lightly on the edge of the desk. All present and accounted for, all safely in their beds. Cabot was not discouraged. Whichever of the three was his ultimate target would move soon enough. He or she would work on a private timetable according to laws and conditions Cabot could only guess at. But the movement would come. That much he was certain of. In the meantime he would wait, watch the hours move past him like a stream running silently through forest darkness. He would wait and listen for that almost inaudible sound of something breaking the waters . . .

At noon, after five hours' sleep, Jonathan Cabot arrived at Queen Anne's Gate.

"Go home and get yourself some sleep," he advised Mackenzie McConnell.

"You look as though *you* could do with more."

Cabot winced.

"It's not quite *that* bad, Jonathan," she laughed, touching his cheek.

"I left Pearce at the embassy. I'll cover for you here."

"There's no time to go home," she said stubbornly.

"Mackenzie—"

"I'll break out a cot upstairs. I'll be fine, Jonathan, really." She paused. "You'll call me as soon as the run starts?"

"I will. But that won't be until five o'clock, when the embassy begins to empty."

But by midafternoon events were overtaking him.

"I just got the word—she's leaving early."

Cabot recognized the urgency beneath Pearce's laconic tone.

"Hold on."

Cabot picked up a phone that linked him to the mobile surveillance units stationed near Grosvenor Square.

"Dunn, Kennedy's secretary, is moving now. Make sure you have all exits covered to pick her up. Two units stay on her, the rest hold back. Call me as soon as you have a visual."

Cabot was back on the other line.

"How did you find out?"

"I was having coffee with the steno girl," Pearce told him. "It was she who mentioned that Dunn would be cutting out early. She overheard something about a fitting at some dress shop."

"Is she still in the building?"

"Probably. I called as soon as I got word. Two minutes—no more."

"They will pick her up," Cabot said tightly.

"Would you like some help with that?" Pearce asked.

"I need you where you are," Cabot told him. "She may be the number one suspect now, but we have two others, and as far as I know both are still at the embassy."

There was a silence on the line, then Cabot let out a deep sigh.

"I'm sorry, Edward. There was no reason for me to run off at the mouth like that."

"It's the endgame, Johnny," Pearce said, not unkindly. "You're the man in the hot seat. I know how you feel. I've been there."

"I'll keep the line open," Cabot said. "Thanks."

Edward Pearce replaced the receiver in the cradle, staring thoughtfully at it.

"You'll have to wait a long time for me to answer it, Johnny," he said softly. "A very long time!"

The chief of security for the American embassy plucked his coat off the rack and closed the door to his office but left it unlocked. He took the elevator to the basement, where he checked in on the cipher rooms. There had been no traffic since lunch. Pity, Pearce thought. It would have been nice to take along an extra nugget. He said goodnight to his operators and went back to the first floor, making for the Blackbourne Mews exit. As he expected, the surveillance vans were nowhere in sight. Cabot had run out of time. Whatever evidence he had on the Ambassador's secretary, evidence he didn't share with Pearce, would turn to ashes in his hands. Cabot, so convinced that it had to be one of the three, had let the clock run down until the last moment. In a little over an hour the two other suspects would be leaving the grounds and would require surveillance. The chase would be on and it would continue until Cabot realized how false the quarry was. Naturally he would try to contact him, Pearce, and upon receiving no answer would assume that one of the three had taken him out of the play. Which would only redouble Cabot's determination to convict one of the three suspects.

He'll try, Pearce thought, moving swiftly down Bolton Street, God knows what he'll do to those people before he can accept the truth, that I've taken him . . . that I've taken them all.

The Cafe Imperial, situated on the northwest side of Regent Street, was built in the first year of the Great War. A five-story structure, its unique feature was the so-called window-wall, an appropriate nomenclature since the side of the building facing the street was done almost entirely of glass—all five tiers.

The first two levels were designated Salon and Mezzanine, where lunch and high tea could be enjoyed to the strains of Vivaldi in an atmosphere not unlike the Hanging Gardens of Babylon. It was said that the lush tropical vegetation that had been imported for these rooms could have passed for a small jungle.

The third floor was known simply as the Bar, from which the female sex was excluded. In very short order the Bar became the private preserve of a hundred or so gentlemen who earned the sobriquet of the Century. While the Bar was technically open to the public, strangers were invariably made to feel out of place. By 1940, however, with the influx of foreign soldiers, who had little or no understanding of such unspoken rules, and whose money was more than welcome at the till, the Bar lost its clubby atmosphere and became just another military watering hole.

The last two floors, the Ballroom and Aerie, had not been used in sixteen months. In fact the last true gala that was held there was in 1938 when the guest of honor was Neville Chamberlain, an appropriate choice since the theme was "Peace in Our Time." Now Chamberlain was just another embarrassing skeleton rattling around in the political closet, and the illusion of peace had been shattered by the hollow-eyed men returning from Dunkirk.

From the National Gallery the man known to Guderian as Mr. Stanley went directly to the Cafe Imperial. He took a light lunch at the Salon, sitting by the windows at street level. When he had finished he asked the waiter to serve him coffee in the Mezzanine since the noise outside was distracting him from his reading. Mr. Stanley spent a half hour over a single espresso before settling his bill and moving up to the almost deserted Bar. There too he took a seat by the window, which gave him a vantage view in three directions: north to Glasshouse Street, west toward the offices of the Empire Life Assurance Company, and south, across Regent Street, to the vast arcade known as Man in Moon Pass. He studied the buildings very carefully, taking note of the windows on the upper floors, which he could see from where he was sitting. He looked across the lounge area and followed the progress of the sun's light as it passed across the blue-gray carpet. He tapped lightly on the glass, an eccentric gesture to anyone who might have been watching, and judged how badly bullets of various calibers would be deflected by its density.

Mr. Stanley folded his newspaper, left a decent but not extravagant tip and departed while the bartender had disappeared into the stockroom. Luck was with him and he managed to step into a taxi that had just discharged a passenger at the Cafe before the porter could slam the door shut. At half past two Mr. Stanley arrived at his home in Gower Mews across from the British Museum. Upon entering he was pleased to see that his cleaning lady had come and gone. It would have complicated matters to have her there.

The case he was looking for was hidden under the floorboards in a cupboard under the sink. Mr. Stanley made sure the curtains were drawn, then removed the box and set it down on the circular breakfast table. He flipped the latches and began his assembly.

The De Lisle carbine was one of two sniper rifles the British

Army had developed, the other being a modification of the Lee Enfield called Rifle No. 4, Mark I(T). Mr. Stanley had been one of the first people to test-fire the De Lisle and had sworn by it since then—as he well should have since he had three successful kills to date. Based on the SMLE .303 rifle, the De Lisle had been rechambered for a .45-ACP round. In addition to telescopic sights, the weapon was equipped with a highly effective silencer which, while muffling the shot, did not detract from its accuracy to the degree other silencers did. It was, in Mr. Stanley's opinion, the weapon of choice for the task at hand.

By three o'clock the rifle had been broken down, its component parts cleaned, the pieces returned to their felt indentations in the carrying case. Mr. Stanley checked his watch, calculated the amount of time he would have to arrive at the Empire Life Assurance building and decided he might as well leave now. Although he had a car, there was no question of using it. Taxis were haphazard at best, although one had a better chance at the cab station by the Museum than on the street. If he left now he could count on arriving in Glasshouse Street within the half hour. The executive offices of the Empire Life Assurance Company would begin emptying fifteen minutes thereafter, with the secretarial and clerical staff following punctually at four o'clock.

As he left his house Mr. Stanley permitted himself a small smile. The Berlin agent, Dr. Livingstone, must have known that the Empire Life Assurance Company had instituted a policy of getting its workers into the offices earlier in the morning and sending them home earlier in the afternoon so that during the shorter winter days they could do some shopping before the blackout. The policy was to have ended a few days ago but had been extended indefinitely by government order. It was always a pleasure, he reflected, to do business with a professional.

The tempo of traffic around Piccadilly Circus had picked up since the early afternoon. Cavalcades of buses and trucks roared around the sandbagged, boarded-up statue of Eros, their exhausts drowning out the sound of the fountains, the tiers empty of the usual crowds that sat on them to watch London revolve. Mr. Stanley left the cab on Shaftesbury Avenue, stepped into the crowd flow and allowed himself to be carried by it across Piccadilly, around the back of the Cafe Imperial and onto Glasshouse Street. A moment later he was standing in the foyer of Empire Life, beneath a cerulean dome that had the constellations studded in miniature lights across its expanse.

Keeping close to the marble wall, Mr. Stanley started to move against the onslaught of human traffic that thundered at him. When he reached the banks of elevators he chose one of three which the company had had automated before the war. Alone in the car, he rode up to the seventh floor where the senior executive officers were. As he expected, the corridors were empty, the offices behind the frosted glass doors devoid of lamplight. Following the map etched out in his mind, he proceeded to the easternmost part of the building, which narrowed into a curved point at the height of the triangular building. Mr. Stanley didn't bother knocking on the door of one Robert Moss, Executive Vice-President, but picked the lock, using an ingenious tool that resembled a hatpin. Moving swiftly through the barristers' gate, he passed through the secretaries' offices and into the well-appointed suite whose high windows glowed in the afternoon light. So much the better. The sunlight would offer a protective glaze. Even if anyone looked up all they would see would be heat reflection.

The windowsill had two spider plants and an African violet on it. Mr. Stanley removed these to the executive's desk, threw down two pillows from the sofa onto the floor directly under the window and dropped to his knees. A moment later the De Lisle rifle was assembled, one round in the breech, three extra in the chamber. He set the rifle on the sill, undid the bottom latch and pushed the right window open a fraction. The rifle barrel was laid flush with the frame, invisible. Mr. Stanley leaned into the gun, adjusting his knees so that they provided the leverage and pressed his eye against the hard rubber of the scope.

Sixty-two yards away, at an angle of thirty degrees, he spotted Dr. Livingstone sitting at a window table in the Bar. The scope power was so fine Mr. Stanley could almost read the label on the matches in the ashtray on the table. He made a fractional adjustment on the scope, watching as Livingstone consulted his watch, then rose and walked away from the table, his drink unfinished.

Mr. Stanley angled the rifle barrel to the Mezzanine. Almost directly below where the Berlin man had been sitting was Darius, also occupying a window table, with a cigarette burning in the ashtray, the chair opposite him empty. The barrel moved to the left, the crosshairs on the center of the back of the chintz-covered chair.

Where was the other man?

The same question was running through the mind of Edward Pearce. The time was thirty-two minutes past four o'clock. The German should have been here at exactly half past the hour, the time he himself had specified. Pearce looked through the glass into the pandemonium below. The scene in the street resembled a gigantic mime, with thousands of players rushing soundlessly to and fro across a stage that was central London. He shook his head slightly as though amused by the senselessness of it all and adjusted his vision so that he could focus on the reflection of what was happening behind him.

The tables were being taken up quickly, primarily by groups of middle-aged women. Consequently the noise level in the Mezzanine had risen appreciably. There were no more than two dozen men in the room, most of them older, dressed in business suits or sporting blazers and slacks. The useless and the idle, Pearce judged. But his eyes continued to roam, trying to catch a glimpse of the telltale surveillance before contact.

Pearce shifted in his seat to get a better view of the reception area. He craned his head around a matron's Easter bonnet but saw only more of the same surrounding the Mezzanine entry. It was nothing he saw or heard, only instinct, that made him turn around.

"Hello, Edward."

The surprise was so total that Pearce knew he could not deny it. He had no idea how Cabot had managed to get across the room without being seen by him. But that was the least of his worries at the moment.

How had Cabot found him? How had he known Pearce would be here?

"Remember the monitors we put on Frye's line, Edward?" Cabot asked gently. He was reading Pearce's thoughts as though they were his own. "No, that's the one thing you did forget. I guess when you had Frye killed you thought your troubles were over with. But the equipment was still there. I made a few adjustments, transplanted the clips to your line."

"Johnny . . ." Pearce said, trying to smile.

Cabot let one hand drop across his coat, neatly folded on his lap, to his side. From the way the coat lay Pearce knew the submachine gun was hidden in the folds. Cabot's right hand was in his jacket pocket, the dummy pocket, and his fingers on the butt of the gun.

"The shooters in the park were yours, weren't they, Edward?" Cabot continued on in that same soft conversational tone. "They were the same bastards who hit us in Leatherhead. Tell me, were they really gunning for me or did you just want to scare me, throw me off balance? I think it was the latter. You thought I might fumble the investigation if I had to keep looking over my shoulder. But in case I didn't you were prepared to throw me Frye. Not that I would ever get to him while he was alive. If Frye was dead he couldn't tell me that he had nothing to do with Leatherhead. . . ."

Cabot paused, staring deeply into Pearce's expressionless eyes.

"That was when you decided on a two-for-one, didn't you? You set Frye up for me, then sent your gunners to take us both down. That way there would be only your version of what happened: Frye had brought the gunners with him. You and Mackenzie managed to get them *and* him—but not before I was dead. That was how the official report would have read, wasn't it?"

Cabot fished out a cigarette with one hand and lit it.

"Still no comment, Edward," he said, the smoke curling from his mouth. "No, I suppose not. Not after so much killing . . . Did you know your driver, the young kid, Robertson, was an MI5 plant? Ah, you didn't. Well, he was. You see, Edward, the British had been suspicious of you for some time now. They were well into their surveillance on you by the time I arrived but had nothing to show. Why? Because you were working out of a place they couldn't get into: the embassy. Outside you were as pure as new-driven snow."

"Johnny," Pearce said at last. "You're making a big mistake. The secretary—"

"Kennedy's secretary was working with us for the last few days," Cabot cut him off harshly. "Her file was doctored; I choreographed her every movement for the last forty-eight hours. The surveillance teams on her and the others were the big show, Edward, all done up just like Broadway for an audience of one—you."

Pearce lounged back in his chair, a grin spreading across his lips.

"Fantasy, Johnny," he said. "Sheer fantasy. Show me proof that I was involved with the shooters in the park and Leatherhead, proof that I passed information across to Beth Davis, that somehow I am, in fact, a traitor. The point is, you can't. Because it's all too unreal."

"Is it, Edward?" Cabot said. "I knew you were supposed to meet someone here. He hasn't shown. Perhaps he saw me or my people. On the other hand maybe he never intended to show. . . . Because he knew, from the moment he was talking to you, that you were tainted. You were to meet him to pass along the information I fed you, about the arms-through-Canada deal Roosevelt wanted to move around Congress. You thought the information was worth stepping out for. This was the big one you had been waiting for. Even the Germans would have forgiven you had you brought it to them. Forgiven you until they realized it was all a smokescreen.

"I think your man realized this first. I think he arranged a backup for this meeting. I think, Edward," Cabot said sadly, "that somewhere in this room, or in the street, is a gun just for you. And I'm the only chance you have of getting out of here alive."

Cabot hesitated, his eyes filled with pain. "And I want to know why you did it, Edward. For Christ's sake, you owe me at least that much!"

Pearce was grinning now, that lopsided toothy smile that was as much his signature as the Stetson or the Texas drawl. Even the milky blue eyes refused to give him away. But Cabot knew that somewhere within that hard, sun-baked shell a vulnerable nerve had been touched: doubt.

The man from Berlin isn't going to show, Pearce thought, looking at a point somewhere over Cabot's shoulder. He could have followed me in and I never would have known it because he *is* Berlin and that good. While I was watching out for him he was checking for people on me. And he saw them . . . must have because otherwise . . . otherwise.

They'll find the forged papers and the gold certificates. Cabot will put me on the hot seat and try to sweat me. When I don't crack he'll give me to the British. But sooner or later they'll have to bring me out into the open, into a court. But if I can hold out on them they will deal. They'll have to. They can't afford to put me in front of a judge.

Pearce placed both hands on the armrests of his chair.

"You're making a terrible mistake, Johnny," he said quietly. "You've reached all sorts of conclusions by jumping around like a frog from lilypad to lilypad. But if you're here to take me then do it and let's go."

"Spare me the down-home bullshit," Cabot said tonelessly. "Stand up slowly and put your hands on the table. Someone will come over to us."

Edward Pearce was halfway out of his chair when the bullet hit him. It passed cleanly through the thick plateglass but was deflected nonetheless. Had there been nothing in its path it would have struck Pearce in the temple. As it was, the .45-caliber projectile tore away the carotid artery, exploded just behind the brain stem and ripped through most of the delicate bone structure that supports the head.

The instant Cabot saw the blood he tipped his chair backward, flinging himself over the side. The second bullet tore up the carpet inches from his left knee. Cabot jammed the sub-machine gun against his shoulder and took aim at the Empire Life Assurance building. More glass was shattered as twenty-five bullets streamed across the expanse of Regent Street, gouging at the limestone frescoes that adorned the roof ramparts. Cabot had not dared aim any lower. There were half a dozen windows where the shot might have come from, and behind some, innocent people. But he wanted the killer to know that his target could shoot back.

A few seconds passed but there were no more shots. Cabot's fusillade had silenced the crowd in the Mezzanine. The silence was being broken by soft whimpering and moans as people opened their eyes and fearfully began to look around. The woman who had been sitting at the table behind Pearce and who was now sprawled across the carpet turned over. As she tried to prop herself up, her hand slipped in the pool of blood next to Pearce's head. Her scream broke the shocked paralysis and the stampede began.

Cabot barely glanced at Pearce as he waded into the crowd, holding the gun over his head. Using his height and strength he pushed and plowed his way across the room. But halfway to the door further movement became impossible. The crowd had choked the exit. Behind him Cabot felt bodies leaning into him, threatening to topple him. Twenty feet away Cabot saw one of Mackenzie McConnell's men squirming his way through.

"The street!" Cabot roared. "Tell them to cover that insurance building and the street!"

The agent's eyes met his briefly and he shook his head. The signal was clear: the men in the room could not get out in time to warn those in the lobby of what had happened. The surveillance units in the street would be more concerned with what was going on inside the Cafe Imperial than where the shots had come from. If they had heard any shots.

Suddenly Cabot reversed his direction and plowed back to the tables by the window, crockery and glass grinding under his heel. He thrust his head out the shattered windowpane and looked down upon the crowds which had run off the sidewalk when the glass shattered and were now in Regent Street, groups of bodies jammed between immobile vehicles. The din from the stalled traffic was deafening.

Cabot scanned a dozen of the faces that were staring up at him. He ignored their cries and his gaze shifted to the Empire Life Assurance building, the top floors. From where he stood he couldn't tell if one of the windows was ajar. The sun's glare covered the glass with a blinding patina.

Cabot turned away and looked down at Pearce.

You were Berlin's best agent, he thought. Yet Berlin sacrificed you. What could have been so important that you had to die . . . at the precise moment you were running for shelter? What was it you knew that Berlin could not afford to have *us* know?

Cabot knelt beside him and gently rolled him over.

"Christ, Edward, why?" he whispered, feeling the sting of tears.

He reached out and passed his fingers over Pearce's face, closing his friend's eyes forever.

"What's all the commotion downstairs?" Guderian asked the bartender as another whiskey and soda was placed before him.

Everyone in the Bar had heard the sound of breaking glass and a muffled cry that might have been a scream. The patrons looked at one another; most shrugged and resumed their conversations. One or two wandered over to the windows.

"Don't rightly know, sir," the bartender said. "Some minor accident, I should think. Nothing to worry about."

"No," Guderian murmured, looking at his cold, pitiless reflection in the mirror behind the bottles. "I'm sure there isn't."

18

"We shall go on to the end . . . We shall fight on the beaches, we shall fight on the landing grounds, we shall fight in the fields and in the streets, we shall fight in the hills; we shall never surrender . . ."

It was the afternoon of June 4. Winston Churchill had just returned to Ten Downing Street from the House of Commons where he had delivered what would become his most famous address. But sitting alone in his study, with Nelson's mounted uniform facing him, he was not the same man whose words would rally an empire. That tattered historic uniform seemed to speak for all his doubts: Would the New World, with its power and might, step forth to the rescue and liberation of the Old? Would it rescue you from the lies you have foisted upon your own people?

That same morning, 26,175 men were evacuated during the final stages of Operation Dynamo, swelling the official total rescued to an astounding 338,226, of which 112,000 were French troops. Englishmen rejoiced because in their eyes Dunkirk was a victory, moral if not physical, of spirit over armor. That was how Churchill had portrayed it, what he wanted them to believe. Yet he knew better. Almost all the BEF's heavy equipment—tanks, trucks, artillery pieces—had been left behind. Most of the returning men had thrown away not only their rifles but the basic kits. The Admiralty reported no less than 80 percent of the merchant fleet lost along with countless smaller, private vessels. Nine destroyers had been sent to the bottom by the Luftwaffe, followed by a score of CMBs. RAF Fighter Command tallied up eighty pilots dead, one hundred and five aircraft destroyed, with twice that number now grounded for essential repairs . . .

But the English people rejoiced because they did not know this and Churchill fostered their ignorance. For if they knew otherwise the entire country would face a demise of the soul. And that was what Churchill feared most. He knew he had to give his people hope, no matter how ephemeral it might be. They could endure, he knew as much, but only if they believed that someone was standing with them, that they had not been abandoned.

But the mendacity had not stopped there. He hadn't told his people that their freedom, if they were destined to be free at all, would be dearly paid for by stinking yellow metal. The time had come when an Englishman's birthright—liberty— had a price upon it, like so much chattel.

Do not condemn me too quickly, Churchill asked of Nelson's ghost. Like yourself, I too am an old fox in these woods . . .

His reverie was broken by the punctual arrival of his visitors. Churchill greeted Allen Dulles, Mackenzie McConnell and Cabot in turn, dismissed the manservant and poured drinks himself.

"An excellent speech, Winston," Allen Dulles commented. "Perhaps your best."

"Thank you, Allen," Churchill replied gruffly. "May we *never* find ourselves fighting on the beaches."

"Amen to that," Dulles echoed.

"From what Allen told me, Mr. Cabot, you and Miss Mc-Connell appear to have had a rather trying day," Churchill commented, drawing a cigar from his leather case. "Pray, enlighten me."

Cabot replaced his drink on the stand and leaned forward, elbows on his knees. In a voice which betrayed the residue of fatigue, he sketched out the sequence of events that began with Frye's murder. He spoke rapidly but omitted nothing. Only when he reached the part about Edward Pearce, the suspicions MI5 had had concerning him, did he falter and fall silent. Mackenzie McConnell picked up the narrative smoothly and outlined the trap that had been laid for Pearce, how successful it had been—up to a point—and the bloody conclusion which had taken place during the carnage at the Cafe Imperial.

"Allen, how does that affect matters at the embassy?" Churchill murmured, rolling a length of ash into the tray.

"We're playing the death of Pearce as an out-and-out killing. We circulated the story of some kind of Nazi reprisal—"

He held up his hand to ward off Churchill's protest.

"We had to go this route," Dulles said. "You can't hide something like a shooting at the Cafe Imperial. By bringing Nazis into it we cover the matter with a security blanket— which means the details are off-limits to the press. We can't bury the incident completely, but we sure as hell can throw cold water on any Fleet Street investigation."

"I take it Mr. Kennedy had no objections to such procedure?" Churchill queried dryly, not entirely successful in keeping the malice from his tone.

"I've told Joe the truth," Dulles said. "To say that he's in a state of shock is putting it mildly. I can guarantee you that this incident has tamed Joe's somewhat freewheeling style. It's safe to say that you can expect every cooperation from Grosvenor Square."

"Then the Ambassador will be staying on." It was a statement, not a question.

"The President has assured him that the post is his indefinitely," Dulles said. "I think you can see, Mr. Prime Minister, where it would be to everyone's advantage to keep Kennedy here, where we can see him."

"Yes, of course," Churchill murmured. In Roosevelt's position he would have done exactly the same thing: a potentially dangerous adversary had been severely compromised by his own people. As a result much political strength had been lost. It was time for the victor, Roosevelt, to show compassion and understanding, express sympathy for, and confidence in, the vanquished. Crocodile tears to be sure, but every reference to the debacle, no matter how kind or sympathetic, would be a sharp tug on Joe Kennedy's leash.

"And the embassy security?" Churchill ventured.

"I will be remaining in England indefinitely until a suitable successor is appointed and arrives."

"I'm glad to hear that, Allen," the Prime Minister said quietly. "Very, very glad."

He sipped his cognac, then looked at Cabot and Mackenzie McConnell.

"So I suppose the time has come to tell these young people exactly what it is they have—unknowingly—been involved in," he said.

"It's time," Dulles agreed and fixed himself another drink.

Mackenzie McConnell glanced over at Cabot, her cat's eyes sending a stream of questions. She remembered what he had said: that in a few days she would know everything. But his reply was a shrug punctuated by raised eyebrows as though he didn't care. The anger floating off Cabot was unmistakable. She could almost smell the rank, bitter odor.

He can't tear himself away from the betrayal, she thought. Pearce had been too close to him, the treachery he had perpetrated had cut too deeply. And the worst of it is that Jonathan will never know why. Pearce never had a chance for confession, if there was going to be one at all.

But that didn't matter to Cabot. A man possessed to make sense out of the puzzle of treason, he tore apart Pearce's life in London. The result was silent mockery. Pearce's rooms were as neutral as those of a boardinghouse; the women he was involved with vacuous, with all the depth of a puddle after a summer shower.

Nor had the shooter been tagged. Jonathan believed that the voice on the tapes which made the arrangements for the Cafe Imperial belonged to him. But it remained only that, a voice. When the Security Service had burst into the office that had been used as the vantage point, the agents found no blood, no rifles, only two shell casings and shattered glass which testified to the almost inhuman accuracy of Cabot's aim.

There was nothing to give away the man behind the trigger, the ghost Berlin must have had at Pearce's side since the day they started to run him. In all likelihood Pearce probably never knew of his existence. But the assassin had been there all the time, Berlin's insurance that if Pearce faltered, was about to be taken, he would not live to incriminate a soul.

That's what Jonathan blames himself for most of all, Mackenzie reflected. He might have waited a little longer before taking Pearce. He knew contact had to be made. The taps on Pearce's line were proof enough. He waited and still no one showed, so he made his move, made it because he knew that if he didn't I would have . . . because by then I had broken security, told him we had suspected Pearce all along . . .

"Miss McConnell, are you with us?" Dulles asked, rather too loudly, she thought.

"I'm sorry, sir. Yes, of course."

"What is past is past," he said, not unkindly. "And there is a great deal more that will be required of you." Dulles paused.

"The reason the President sent Jonathan over here was to take care of the leak at Grosvenor Square which was feeding an agent in Washington. The President and I thought there would be only one deep-penetration agent involved. As it turned out we got more than we bargained for . . . much more."

Dulles nodded in Cabot's direction.

"When it came to taking Pearce or the second agent, Jonathan needed some bait, very high-quality information which would be accepted without question as genuine and which would be valuable enough to spook our man into running. It was agreed between Mr. Churchill and myself that a fictitious arrangement to ship arms from the States to England via Canada would serve adequately."

"Except it wasn't fiction, was it?" Cabot interrupted, lifting his head up and looking coldly at Dulles. "You didn't sent me over here *just* to take care of Frye . . . and Pearce!"

As he spoke, Dulles tapped down the pungent tobacco in his pipe.

"You're anticipating me, Jonathan," he said softly, the rebuke unmistakable. "As both you and Miss McConnell are aware, the U.S. has been shipping arms to England since the winter of thirty-nine. What you may not know are the terms of the agreement under which this matériel is paid for.

"Winston, perhaps you would take over at this point."

Churchill grunted and moved his chair slightly so that the late-afternoon sun burning through the French doors didn't fall on his face.

"Several months before the Polish invasion," he opened slowly, "the President and I concluded a gentlemen's agreement whereby America would provide Britain with armament. The sobriquet applied to this matter was rather quaint: Cash and Carry, a term used, I believe, by American department stores. Nonetheless it illustrates the point precisely. The American Congress is not enamored with the idea of involving its country in another European conflict. However, its representatives understand that their constituent workers will be kept happy and productive so long as the factories operate at capacity. I refer specifically to the arms manufacturers and of course their attendant industries: steel, mining, chemicals, shipbuilding, automotive assembly, textiles. But Congress demanded that any such exports be paid for upon receipt, or in some cases even prior to delivery. Since America has become, per force, the arsenal of democracy, we had little choice but to comply with these terms.

"What this meant, Mr. Cabot, Miss McConnell, was that Britain has been paying the U.S. Treasury for these purchases out of gold that has been on deposit in the city of New York prior to the outbreak of hostilities. Thus far we have managed quite well. However, in the last month two things have happened which have upset our arrangement:

"First, because of the debacle at Dunkirk and the complete collapse of the French armies, Britain stands alone. She will need—nay, needs *now*—more than everything: foodstuffs, armament, naval vessels, ammunition, clothing, fuel. Without these we cannot fight.

"Second, our resources at the Federal Reserve have been exhausted. At last count, I am informed, we can barely cover our purchases made thirty days ago. That was before Dunkirk . . ."

Churchill paused to roll off more ash. As he removed the cigar from his mouth, Cabot saw how chewed up the tip was. He remembered Dulles telling him that Churchill never, never chewed his cigars.

"President Roosevelt and I discussed this state of affairs some weeks ago," the Prime Minister continued. "He assured me that America would continue to supply us as long as Congress was satisfied that payments were being made on schedule. This of course I could not, under present circumstances, guarantee. Yet neither could the lifeline be ruptured. So an agreement was struck, a plan which revolved around your success, Mr. Cabot, at Grosvenor Square. Since you have not disappointed us, we may proceed."

Churchill took a deep breath.

"The operation bears the code name Prometheus. The Greek god of the same name was, you may recall, the one who brought fire, gold fire, to the mortals. *It involves transferring the entire fiscal wealth of this nation—every last bar of bullion and piece of negotiable paper—to the United States.*"

The silence lasted only a few seconds but it was deafening.

"Mr. Prime Minister, are you suggesting—" Mackenzie McConnell started to say.

"I am not suggesting anything!" Churchill snapped. "I am stating what is given. On my own authority, without asking the permission of either the Chancellor of the Exchequer or the combined Houses of Parliament, I have concluded such an agreement with the President of the United States."

"Forgive me, Prime Minister, but I very much doubt you had any such authority," Mackenzie McConnell held her ground. "You are talking about the common wealth of the nation, the coin of the realm. There are hundreds of thousands of investors, corporate and private banking individuals, who entrusted their funds to British banks. You can't simply remove it like that . . . in one fell swoop. It's nothing short of robbery!"

Mackenzie McConnell wasn't even aware of it, but she was standing up, almost shouting at the Prime Minister, who was letting her carry on.

"Your point has been taken," Churchill said tonelessly.

Mackenzie took a couple of tentative steps back toward her chair and sat down. Her face was flushed, hot, and she was furious with herself for having been drawn into an untenable position. She glanced over to Cabot for support but he hadn't taken his eyes off Churchill.

"There are, as you say, Miss McConnell, a great number of questions, practical as well as ethical, with which we must concern ourselves," Churchill said. "Pray, confine yourself to the former and the qualities of the latter will become evident soon enough."

"How much money are we talking about?" Cabot asked softly.

"In round figures, sir, some two hundred and fifty million pounds sterling."

"Mr. Prime Minister, I'm not a financial expert, but if I'm not mistaken that would be about as much as the Bank of England holds—in gold and negotiable securities."

"Exactly, Mr. Cabot. When I said the entire wealth of this nation would be moved, I meant it—literally!"

"Then there has to be another reason," Cabot said. "That figure will buy you a large percentage of everything Du Pont, General Motors, Standard of New Jersey and Liberty Shipyards can produce in the next five years. I don't think you expect the war to go on for that long, Mr. Prime Minister. A hundred million would cover whatever arrangement you have with the President. That much again, and more. . . ."

"It's Dunkirk, Jonathan," Mackenzie McConnell said slowly. "Don't you see? No one expected the French to hold out. As soon as the Germans got around that bloody Maginot Line the writing was on the wall. Now the Germans will roll up France. That means they get the submarine pens at Saint-Nazaire, which in turn moves the U-boat wolf packs that much closer to the Atlantic sea-lanes."

She turned to Churchill. "That is how you intend to move

the bullion, isn't it, Prime Minister? By capital ship or submarine?"

"That matter is under advisement. But you are tending in the right direction, Miss McConnell. The fall of France has placed this nation in the greatest jeopardy it has had to face since the Spanish Armada. As of now Hitler has his jumping-off point: Calais is no more than thirty-five miles from the cliffs of Dover. I believe you can appreciate exactly the magnitude of the calamity which would befall us if an invasion were to *succeed* . . . and this gold hadn't been moved!"

"Britain would be bankrupt," Cabot said coldly. "She wouldn't be able to feed her people much less finance any kind of war effort. On top of that you'd end up giving the Nazis over two hundred and fifty million pounds to use as they please."

"Berlin wouldn't have to go that far, Jonathan," Dulles interjected. "If Hitler got word that Prometheus was even being considered, never mind it being a full-fledged operation, he would sacrifice as much money, as many agents as necessary, in order to pinpoint the bullion carrier. Then the German Navy could string out U-boats, raiders, even throw in the damn *Lützow*, across the Atlantic. Chances are better than even that with their equipment the Germans could send our boat to the bottom—along with the gold. And once the bullion is gone, what is Britain left to pay with? She would *have* to sue for peace."

"On Hitler's terms," Mackenzie McConnell whispered. "Your President would let it come to that?"

"Miss McConnell," Dulles said, "never forget that the biggest supporter your country has resides in the White House. But the President answers to Congress, where a fair number of members espouse the isolationist principle. Bottom line? Yes, I think there is every chance that Roosevelt could *not* get you the necessary credits if the gold ends up at the bottom of the Atlantic!"

"But—"

Churchill cut her off. "It is a hypothetical bridge which, with God's grace, we shall never have to cross. But the question of Prometheus does not go away. You, Miss McConnell and Mr. Cabot, have been chosen to construct a plan for the greatest transfer of wealth in the history of the world. I do not indulge in hyperboles or flights of fancy when I say the fate of this nation and indeed, civilization as we know it, rests on the perfection of such a scheme, not only in conception but in execution."

"Mr. Prime Minister, exactly how many other people are aware of Prometheus?" Cabot asked quietly.

"We have consulted no one as yet. Allen and myself have drawn up a list of those whose participation we consider indispensable. After you and Miss McConnell have studied it you might want to add some names."

"The time factor?" Mackenzie McConnell spoke up.

"You yourself mentioned the constraints you'll be working under," Churchill said. "The increased German naval activity is one. The absolute necessity for secrecy is another. The third has to do with our abysmal balance of funds at the Federal Reserve in New York. I suggest to you that the operation must be put into effect no more than two weeks from today."

"Forgive me, Prime Minister, but have you considered how much work—the planning, the organization and coordination of various departments, finally the physical transfer of the bullion—is involved?" she asked, incredulous.

"Yes, I have," Churchill said soberly. "But I shall make provisions for you and Mr. Cabot to have the full authority of this office for the duration of Prometheus. Whatever individuals or offices you feel you need to assist you will be contacted by me personally. In short there will be nothing you won't have access to. For the next ten to fourteen days Prometheus has priority over all business in the country."

"You've failed to mention the most obvious 'constraint,'" Cabot said quietly. "A factor which, unfortunately, doesn't give a damn about your office or its authority, Mr. Prime Minister. But one which is far more lethal than anything the German Navy has."

"Pray, what is that, Mr. Cabot?"

"Our third man. The agent from Berlin who, if he didn't pull the trigger on Pearce himself, was certainly behind the trap. Someone your Double-cross people don't have a line on, who doesn't have a face or a name or a past. Yet Pearce was readily sacrificed to preserve this man's anonymity. That makes him very important . . . extremely dangerous."

Cabot paused. "And I don't like that sort of coincidence. I don't like the sudden appearance of Berlin in London at precisely the point when something as big as Prometheus is about to start running."

"What are you suggesting, Jonathan?" Dulles asked him.

Cabot could not believe that he had heard the question correctly. Dulles knew exactly what he was suggesting! Beth Davis *had* passed on the transcript with its reference to Prometheus! And someone very clever in Berlin might have divined its meaning . . .

The realization of what was happening stunned him. *No one had told the British that Berlin could have heard the term Prometheus, much less have any inkling as to what it stood for!* Roosevelt had never shared this information with Churchill. Because if he had, Churchill might have had very serious second thoughts about committing the coin of the realm to America.

"Jonathan, you had something to tell us?" Dulles asked softly.

"It goes back to everything that's happened," Cabot said, choosing his words carefully. "Is it possible that Berlin has somehow found out about Prometheus?"

"Impossible!" Churchill snorted. "Prometheus has been mentioned only once in all my discussions with the President, and even then the reference was deliberately vague. Certainly there is nothing in writing. And as I told you, no one outside this room has been apprised of even the *possibility* of such an operation."

And once was more than enough, Cabot thought, sickened by the deception.

"But if it *suspects*?" Cabot said, embracing the falsehood. "What if some clever people in the Reichschancellery sat down and came to exactly the same conclusion as you have, Mr. Prime Minister: *that Britain would have to move its gold to the States for the very reason you talked about?*"

"Are you suggesting that this agent, if he exists, was sent to determine whether or not an operation such as Prometheus is being considered, or is under way?" Churchill demanded.

"It's possible," Cabot replied. "Especially if Berlin chose the right man."

"And have you any thoughts as to who this right man would be?" Churchill's tone had a sarcastic edge to it.

Cabot's eyes clouded and his voice was as cold as a fresh grave.

"A specialist in international finance," he said softly. "Someone who, prior to the war, would have been an expert on

European banking systems. A man who would have traveled to London frequently, knew the City, perhaps even broken bread with the Governor at the Bank of England . . . A very special man."

"And if he did the shooting, he would also be an expert rifleman," Mackenzie added. "We found two shell casings on the floor of one of the offices of the Empire Life Assurance Building. The gun used was a De Lisle sniper rifle."

"British manufacture?" Churchill asked sharply.

"Yes, Prime Minister. But in itself that isn't much help. De Lisle exported over five thousand such rifles prior to 1939. Special units in half a dozen armies used them."

"Miss McConnell, you said *if* this man did the shooting," Dulles said. "What did you mean by that?"

"It's possible that because of his seniority, this particular agent would have a cloak, someone who moves alongside or behind him, covering his blind spots, protecting him from any surprises. This would give our man a lot of mobility and allow him to concentrate exclusively on his mission."

"And who would be such a cloak?" Churchill queried.

"Anybody, Prime Minister, whom Berlin trusts absolutely."

"We have to find whoever it is Berlin has sent, Mr. Prime Minister," Cabot said suddenly. "And we have to do it concurrently with the organization of Prometheus. If the killing of Pearce is handled by MI5, then Mackenzie can mobilize whatever resources she wants and lead the investigation along the lines which hopefully would bring us to the killer—without anyone else in counterintelligence being any the wiser as to the real reason we want this man. I will handle the arrangements for Prometheus, at least in the preliminary stages. If Miss McConnell discovers that Pearce's death had nothing to do with Prometheus, then we can leave the investigation with the Security Service."

"Miss McConnell?" Dulles asked.

"I agree with Cabot, sir," she said. "It's best if pinpointing the identity of this third man, and that of the assassin—if they are two different people—be left with me."

"I confess I am distressed by this development," Churchill said. "It divides your efforts, costs us precious time, which I assure you is of the essence at this stage."

Churchill rose and, pulling out a tiny key, unlocked the top drawer of his desk. He handed an unmarked buff file to Cabot.

"Allen and I have sketched out what we believe to be an effective cover. According to rumors which we will foster, a joint Anglo-American intelligence force is to come into being, information-sharing that will cut across service lines, hence your mandate to draw upon any sources whatever—Army, Navy, Air Force. Both your names will be given to the heads of the above services with unequivocal instructions that whatever you need whenever you need it is to be rendered by their subordinates—without question. It will be made perfectly clear that when you act you do so at the behest of this office.

"I suggest both of you avail yourselves of the adjoining conference room and study the possibilities. When you are through you will return the file, along with any notations, to me. No papers regarding Prometheus are to leave Downing Street. A separate office, next door with a secure line, will be at your disposal. Kindly use the Whitehall entry to avoid being seen in the street. The staff has been told to expect your coming and going and of course you will have immediate access to me at any time."

Churchill looked from Cabot to Mackenzie McConnell.

"There is really nothing else for me to add at this moment. If there are no questions I suggest you study these notes. It would be comforting if we might have an initial report by the end of the day."

At half past one she knew he still wasn't asleep. Mackenzie McConnell rolled over and shifted her long body against Cabot's, her breasts pressing against his forearm. One hand snaked out from under the covers and passed slowly through his dark, curly hair.

"Old Churchill was disappointed," Cabot said, his voice disembodied in the darkness. "I guess he actually expected some kind of report to read with his dinner."

Mackenzie McConnell continued to touch him, gently massaging the left temple, her other arm coming around to hold him. Cabot would have stayed in that damn office all night if she had let him, poring over the dossiers and papers messengers had been ferrying in from various Whitehall departments all night. No one, she thought, had actually realized the enormity of what they were asking him to do. The coordination required for such a project was unheard of, the logistics defying anyone to make sense out of them. And over everything lay the final complication: the necessity for secrecy, to limit the number of people who would be involved to the absolute essential minimum. And to vet even these . . .

As she lay beside him feeling the pulse of his body beat against her own, Mackenzie could almost see the permutations and combinations, the possibilities and probabilities being turned over in his mind, like the multicolored chips of glass in a child's kaleidoscope.

"Sleep, my love," she breathed, kissing the edge of his lips.

Cabot moved over on his side and his head slipped down to her throat, coming to rest in the warmth of her breasts.

"Sleep . . ." she whispered and curled up against him, stroking him even as she herself fell asleep.

Six hours later Mackenzie awoke to find Cabot gone. She sat up abruptly, infuriated. Normally she was a light sleeper who stirred if the delivery truck at Harrods rumbled by too loudly. But with *this* man her sleep was dark and fathomless, the mental alarm she depended upon useless. And she did not like to wake up alone, without her lover.

But this morning there was no time for recrimination. At eleven o'clock she had a meeting with Army Registration at Whitehall. Before that . . . Mackenzie McConnell shuddered as the cold, still air enveloped her nakedness. Before that there was Kim Philby.

Mackenzie McConnell arrived at Queen Anne's Gate at half past eight. She went directly to the third-floor conference room and found Kim Philby delicately stirring a cup of tea, cigarette jammed into one corner of his mouth.

"Good morning, Mackenzie," Philby said brightly. "You look much too fine for me to believe there's a flap on."

Mackenzie took the seat opposite him. "I'm sorry I'm late. I know you shifted your schedule to accommodate me."

Philby held up his hand. "No problem. What can I do you for?"

"Kim, you're head of SIS Iberian sector. Have there been any Abwehr special operations originating out of Lisbon or Madrid in the last fortnight? Any unusual activities such as launching a hastily assembled force to England?"

Although Philby was liaison between MI6 and the Security Service, MI5, he also ran the Iberian sector for the Secret Intelligence Service. He had been given the post not only because of his pre-war experience in Madrid and Lisbon but because a great many Abwehr operations were in the last months originating from Spain and Portugal. Whatever he gleaned from the Iberian peninsula Philby passed on to MI5.

"Actually it's been rather quiet," he said, the calm gray eyes riveted on Mackenzie McConnell. "Most of the action has of course been in France. I have the odd feeling that as soon as the Germans reach Paris we'll see more and more emphasis on that sector."

He paused. "Anything in particular you would be looking for, Mackenzie?"

"We believe that the Abwehr has slipped us a new agent, someone who came in around the Double-cross System."

Philby raised his eyebrows.

"This shared supposition wouldn't have had anything to do with the shooting of the security head of the American embassy, would it?"

You fox! Mackenzie thought and said: "I'm afraid, Kim, that I'm not at liberty to say."

"Yes, of course," Philby murmured. "If the Americans are involved . . . But then again perhaps you just answered, yes?"

"Regardless of where this suspicion has originated," Mackenzie continued on, ignoring the gambit, "the point is that the Prime Minister has chosen to accept it at face value. I have been asked to investigate the possibility of such penetration via the troops returning from Dunkirk."

"Mackenzie, I don't know who your sources are," Philby said thoughtfully, "but have they—and you—considered the fact that not even the Army knows exactly who did and didn't make it off those beaches? The casualties have been staggering, as has been the confusion. I think you're asking for the moon if you expect Whitehall to give anything resembling an accurate list. Besides, it's possible that this agent would be masquerading as a *French* soldier. God knows we took enough of them from Dunkirk."

"Kim, I don't think the latter is a likely possibility," Mackenzie replied. "A Frenchman would be packed off to the special camps the Army has readied in Kent. He wouldn't have the mobility he needs. As for the Army records, the figures they have for the dead *are* accurate. But that's not what I'm interested in. I want the missing in action, the list of MIAs. These are the identities the Nazis could have collected ever since the breakthrough along the Maginot Line, doctored and passed on to their own people. A British soldier, unaccounted for, wouldn't be the object of any great search, at least not right now."

Sterling silver rattled against porcelain as Philby pushed his cup away.

"I suppose it has occurred to you that if such a man exists, and if he is so important to Berlin, then he could have retained the services of the Abwehr's best forgers? There wouldn't be any need for him to go the circuitous route of trifling with one of our chaps' identification."

"Not necessarily," Mackenzie shot back. "As good as our forgers are, I happen to know that SIS prefers stolen or recovered original documents for agents being sent into Europe. Berlin too prefers bona fide paper to a copy, especially if the agent intends to move around quite a bit in enemy territory."

"But if you presume this is the case, as you obviously do, then what you are suggesting is that the Double-cross System has been penetrated," Philby said, leaning forward on the table, fingertips drumming to some silent rhythm only he could hear.

"Not at all, Kim. What I *am* saying is that we mustn't allow ourselves to believe that these are the *only* agents the Germans intended to use against us."

"And you suspect that the Iberian sector was this unknown's jumping-off point," Philby concluded.

"Yes."

Philby clapped his hands. "Very well. I'll pull all the information we have accumulated over the last two months and go through it. If there's nothing there, we'll go back further."

"I truly appreciate this, Kim," Mackenzie said.

"A word of caution," Philby suggested. "I'm not asking you to reveal what you can't. But if this operation is a joint effort with our Yank cousins, you might want to keep the lines of communication open to SIS. Americans are rich and blustery and all that, but when it comes to our line of work they're babes in the woods. If things become sticky, do call on me."

"Thanks, Kim. You know I will."

They left Queen Anne's Gate together. Mackenzie offered Philby a lift but he begged off, saying he was headed in the opposite direction. The last person he wanted to be seen with was a representative of the Security Service—not when he was on his way to meet with Ernst, his NKVD, Soviet Security, control in London. Philby thought the Kremlin would very much like to know that something exceedingly sensitive, involving the Americans, had just been born in the British capital.

19

Less than two minutes from Queen Anne's Gate, in Berkeley Square, Dr. Harold Bacal was completing the discharge examination of the patient he knew as Corporal Henry Schiffer.

"The healing has been nothing short of remarkable," the physician said, putting away his stethoscope.

Guderian drew his shirtsleeve over the bandage. The pain was still there, throbbing lightly, persistently, like a metronome. But by now it had become a familiar condition, something he had incorporated into his movements and so was all but unaware of it.

"I was lucky," Guderian said. "And I'm more than happy to give the bed to someone who really needs it."

"Unfortunately there are plenty of those," Bacal sighed.

Both men knew this was true enough. The evacuees in the last shiploads had been among the worst off. They had been fighting the German air attacks and tank bombardments for well over a week. The number of casualties was more than 75 percent for many units. Guderian had been watching the wounded arrive at Berkeley Square for the last forty-eight hours. When bed space had run out, cots and mattresses were laid out in the center hall and along the corridors on the two upper levels. From God knows where Christine Harloch had managed to procure more sheets, blankets, dressings and morphine. Guderian suspected a contact somewhere in the black market but didn't raise the issue. He had hoped to be able to stay on at Berkeley Square for at least a few more days, but given his improved physical condition, it was impossible to keep a room all to himself. He now was, as he had to remind himself, a hero of the British Empire. Magnanimity demanded that he make the correct gesture.

"I suppose you will be returning to active service shortly," Bacal said, fixing the clasp on his worn leather bag.

"As soon as the Army decides where it is it wants me."

"Give yourself some time, son," Bacal said, placing a feathery hand on Guderian's shoulder. "Look around you. What is left of the Army will take a long time to organize, to heal. Hitler has all of Europe now. The more he consolidates his gains the stronger he'll become. To send these men—*boys*—back to the shores of Normandy without support would be folly. So don't be too anxious. Believe me, your time will come soon enough."

Even as Bacal was speaking a nurse entered and began stripping the bed.

"You have a place to stay, do you?" the physician asked.

"Yes, thanks. I'll be all right."

"I expect you to come by in ten days so we can have a look at that shoulder." Bacal's eyes twinkled. "If you don't show up I shall have to send Christine after you."

Guderian saw her standing by the door.

"Remember, my dear, ten days, no more," Bacal said to her.

"He'll be here, doctor, I guarantee it."

They watched as the elderly physician made his way down the narrow aisle between two rows of cots.

Guderian stepped back as two tradesmen maneuvered past him carrying boxes and a lamp he recognized. He looked underneath the staircase and saw the door to Christine's room was open, the bookshelves stripped. Two more men were pushing a large mattress across the threshold.

"Don't tell me—" he started to say.

"I'm afraid so," Christine answered. "There is an awful lot of space in that suite. Right now we can set up ten cots, perhaps more, and still have room for all the extra linen and supplies."

"But what about yourself?" Guderian protested.

She grinned. "Come along, Corporal, and I'll show you."

As soon as they were outside she led him to a grass path that curved around the house and into the trees that formed a miniature park.

"And you, Henry?" Christine asked. Although her voice was light he felt some hesitation. "You don't have a place, do you?"

He looked at her sharply. "Now why would you say a thing like that?"

"I know you were out the day before yesterday," she told him. "I stopped by your room and . . . you were gone. So was your uniform."

When he didn't reply she stopped, her hand on his arm.

"I didn't mean to pry, Henry, really I didn't. I . . . was worried, that's all." .

He cupped her cheek with his palm and brushed away a stray wisp of hair that had fallen across her forehead.

"I know," he said softly. "And I appreciate the thought."

They walked on in silence, the leafy canopy broken by shafts of light with dust motes dancing, suspended in the warm, clean air. The roar of the city seemed to have receded, and at that moment London could have been very far away.

"But you're right," Guderian said at last. "The room is gone. The landlady was good enough to store my trunk and a few personal items in the basement, but I'll have to move them out soon."

"You don't have anywhere in particular in mind, do you?"

"Not at the moment, no."

"Do you think this would do?" she asked quietly.

The carriage house was a storybook structure set in the corner of the lot where the two walls that bounded the property converged. The swinging double doors that once admitted carriages and horses had been removed, replaced by a fresh stucco wall into which was set a long, rectangular window. The rest of the building was original, constructed out of hewn stone. On the top level was a half-moon window behind which, Guderian guessed, was the sleeping loft.

Christine opened the door and ushered him into the small central living room.

"One bedroom over here on the right," she said. "Across the way, the kitchen and breakfast room. Upstairs is the original bedroom and lavatory."

Holding his hand she whirled around and asked breathlessly, "So, what do you think?"

"It's r–really very nice," Guderian stammered. "But, Christine . . ."

"I'll give you your choice," she said with mock *politesse*. "Upstairs or downstairs."

He gripped her by the shoulders and made her face him.

"And where are *you* going to live now that you've given up your room in the main house?"

"Why, here, of course." She looked at him coyly. "Come now, Henry, don't tell me you're still shy about such things."

"Christine—"

She placed a finger to his lips. "Hush, now. I'm not about to let you go wandering around London looking for some miserable garret. Besides, Bacal may have discharged you, but you're still my patient."

"But I don't have that much money," Guderian protested. "There's so much I have to do . . ."

"And you shall do it," she said firmly. "All in good time."

His arms dropped slowly down her back, then tightened around her.

"Christine—"

"Shh, don't say a word," she whispered. "Men can be so blind and foolish sometimes."

Her lips were against his, pressing hard, her arms around his wide shoulders, drawing his body tightly against hers.

"People will talk, you know," Guderian murmured, the words sliding across her cheek.

"And they'll be so jealous!" Christine whispered back, her hand sliding inside his shirt, the fingers passing through the hair on his chest. "So jealous . . ."

It took Mackenzie McConnell only a few minutes to drive to Horse Guards Avenue, located between Whitehall and the Victoria Embankment. She swept by the War Ministry building facing the Admiralty and drew the Jaguar into a parking space at the side of a squat four-story structure whose first two levels had no windows. Her pass was examined by guards posted before two massive steel doors with angular Art Deco designs carved into them. She was admitted and found herself in a large, circular reception area dominated by a single desk.

"Miss McConnell?"

The woman who materialized by her side was tall, in her late fifties or early sixties, with pinned-back gray hair and an elongated, horsey face. Her gray skirt and blazer, ruffled silk blouse and cameo at the throat was the costume of a country squire's wife ready to greet weekend guests. But the handshake was firm and the manner that of a lady accustomed to command.

"I am Millicent Balfour, head archivist."

"Yes, of course. We spoke over the telephone."

"If you would come this way, please, I shall introduce you to my staff."

Millicent Balfour took the lead, the thick heels of her commonsense brogues hitting the marble with Guards' precision. She guided Mackenzie into a stairwell, talking as she descended.

"I suppose I should tell you that Mr. Churchill called me yesterday telling me to expect you. He asked that you be given every cooperation from me and my staff—and that is precisely what you shall have."

"Thank you," Mackenzie murmured.

"However, the Prime Minister did not disclose the exact nature of what it is you are looking for. I trust you shall elucidate."

"I shall indeed."

"My boys and girls are the very best archivists and researchers to be found anywhere," Millicent Balfour continued on, keeping up the brisk pace down a long, narrow corridor. "I trained every one of them. They are not with the Army, which in my opinion couldn't locate a tank on an empty field. Most have had experience at both the British Museum as well as at the University of London. Two are directly from Oxbridge. So long as you give us the essentials, rest assured we shall ferret out what you want."

The corridor ended in a cavernous room that was lit as bright as day by high-intensity bulbs. A long counter, worn down to a natural sheen, ran almost the length, behind which were the stacks: if the six-foot-high metal cases were placed end to end Mackenzie was certain they would stretch for a mile if not more. Each of the six levels on every stack was crammed with files.

"Those are my boys and girls," Millicent Balfour said, her pride obvious.

Mackenzie swore that the six men and three women came to attention before the counter. The women were of indeterminate middle age, their plain, expressionless faces reminding Mackenzie of librarians during her schoolgirl days. The men were generally younger, two so fresh-faced that she had difficulty in believing they had ever finished grammar school much less university. The grandfather of the lot hid behind thick round spectacles and when Mackenzie held out her hand the old man's shot out, missing hers completely. Not blind, surely!

"Perhaps you would care to explain to us exactly what it is you need, Miss McConnell," the head of the troops said, taking her place before the rank.

"Yes, well. . . ." Mackenzie stumbled, suddenly at a loss for words.

"We are looking for one particular man," she started again. "At the moment we have no name, no face, no rank, no unit number. It is believed however that the identity of this man has been espoused by a German intelligence agent of considerable importance. This underlies the urgency of our mission.

"There are two possible ways in which the Germans could have procured this identity: from the body of a soldier killed in action or from one missing in action. For various reasons we believe that the Germans chose the latter.

"We also believe that the agent using this identity slipped into England during the Dunkirk evacuations, more precisely during the earlier days, sometime between May 26 and May 30.

"Assuming that the man survived the Channel crossing and arrived here safely, what sort of identity would he have favored? We feel that the Germans would have taken the papers of a British soldier who was part of a unit engaged in the heaviest fighting at the time: in this case Boulogne or Calais. It is in this sector then that I suggest you begin your search, which might take a twofold approach."

"A dual assault," Millicent Balfour interjected. "Yes, indeed, a splendid suggestion." She pivoted toward her assistants.

"First we must check the records of all those missing in action who belonged to units fighting at Boulogne or Calais," she said briskly. "Second, we correlate whatever the Army has in its files on the circumstances of such a disappearance with the accounts of survivors in the unit. Did anyone see a man who, although dressed in a British uniform, was not familiar to them? Were there stragglers who attached themselves to a retreating unit? Did someone from another company suddenly materialize in a place where he shouldn't have been? In short we are looking for anomalies, discrepancies, anything which doesn't fit the pattern. Naturally this involves substantial field-work—each MIA account which hasn't been corroborated to our satisfaction must be presented to the unit survivors. In this way we can reduce the number of possibilities dramatically.

"I should warn you, my dears," Millicent Balfour forged ahead. "There isn't very much time in which this man must be found. As Miss McConnell has already explained, this project is particular to Ten Downing Street."

She turned to Mackenzie. "In fact there is only one outstanding question: What is it *you* will be doing, Miss McConnell?"

"I thought I might be of some assistance to you here," Mackenzie McConnell said timidly.

"Have you had archival experience?"

"No, but—"

"Then I suggest you help carry out the fieldwork," Miss Balfour said with crisp finality. "If we all stay within our area of expertise the work will be done that much more quickly. Don't you agree?"

"Whatever you think is best," Mackenzie said helplessly.

Millicent Balfour knitted her brows at her watch.

"If we begin now, then you should have the first files within a few hours. My dears, let's go find Mr. Churchill his man!"

Across the English Channel and fourteen hundred kilometers into what was now Occupied Europe, the object of Millicent Balfour's singular attention, Corporal Henry Schiffer, was still sleeping in a dreamless peace.

Henry Schiffer's lot hadn't been a harsh one. He still didn't understand why a commando force (as he thought of Action Group) should have singled him out for special attention. Because of fatigue, induced as much by drink as by the interrogation, he slept during the flight to Germany. When he arrived at the training barracks in the Black Forest he was assigned an entire hut to himself, which had its own outhouse and a primitive but functional shower stall. He was given a substantial meal every day and was permitted two hours of exercise in the afternoons, always in the company of several of the men who had brought him here. But the rest of the day he was required to stay inside, although through the barrack windows he saw the arrival and departure of various Wehrmacht trucks which brought everything from lumber to gargantuan iron boxes he surmised were vaults. Since he heard explosions every day he also assumed this was some sort of training ground for demolition teams. All in all Schiffer considered himself quite fortunate.

Karl Horst, who had soundlessly opened the door to Schiffer's hut and was now standing over the sleeping man, also thought that Schiffer was a lucky man. His last memory would be that of peace, and that was much more than so many had when they died.

Only an hour ago the giant *Feldwebel* had received the message from Berlin he had been waiting for, which his friend and superior, Major Kleemann, had told him to expect if all went according to plan. Horst remembered well how the Major's voice had broken when, after Schiffer's interrogation, he had told Horst what had to be done.

"For every step I take, Karl," the Major had said, "I shall leave a bloody imprint. I can live with this because I must. What savages me is the fact that this one time it will not be my hands that do the killing."

"Tell me what it is you want, *Herr Major*," Horst had told him.

And when he had, Horst understood his Major's agony.

The *Feldwebel* drew out his commando knife. You will never know, he said silently to the sleeping man, what this has cost. In one fell motion he buried the dagger into Schiffer's heart. The body jerked under the impact but the Canadian soldier never opened his eyes. A soft sigh expired as Horst withdrew the bloodied steel.

"Now there is no one who can say you are not Schiffer," Horst whispered. "He was the final witness!"

Quickly Karl Horst wrapped the body in the bedding and carried it outside, past the kitchens and into the woods where he had dug the grave. The *Feldwebel* did not realize how wrong he was: there were witnesses who had seen Schiffer, briefly talked to him, prepared his meals for him. And they were watching from the kitchen window as Horst shouldered his burden into the trees.

At four o'clock in the afternoon Christine Harloch left the coach house for her shift at the clinic. Erik Guderian was relieved to see her disappear among the trees. He needed time alone to think about and to evaluate what had to be done. Yet another part was ashamed of this. This feeling sullied the generosity she showered him with, the love she had thrust upon him the previous night when, even after they lay spent and exhausted, he continued to cling to her out of some inexplicable fear. It was more than desire, for Guderian could recognize blind passion when it coursed through his body. It was the need to simply hold another human being and, in the midst of the depravity the world was thrown into, push back mortality and the omnipresence of death.

Guderian stepped away from the window and went back into the bedroom, throwing open the doors of the massive antique armoire. Three soft wool suits from Josephson's of Savile Row hung side by side. Beside them were two sportscoats, with matching trousers from Burberry. A half-dozen shirts and assorted neckties had come from Jermyn Street while the boots and shoes, while not made to order, were the best Frye's of St. James's had on hand.

What Guderian had agreed to—the purchase of essential clothing until he had straightened out his financial status with the Army (so he had told Christine)—had run away into a buying spree, leaving him embarrassed. Yet Christine was oblivious to his protests. Obviously her name was known in the shops, for she dealt with the staff with an easy informality and received hushed exacting service in return. No money changed hands, everything was signed for. She would have shopped for his underwear and socks had Guderian not insisted that this he would do on his own. It wasn't a matter of prudery but precaution. At Blackwells, a small inexpensive department store, he bought shorts but also light black trousers, running shoes, two navy blue sweatshirts and a dark windbreaker. At the moment he needed these far more than he did Savile Row tailoring.

He finished dressing in the dark clothing, slipped the scalpel, set in an improvised leather sheath once used for a nailfile, into the pocket of the windbreaker, and left the carriage house. He did not go toward the main house but went out through a little-used gate cut into the wall near the carriage house. Moving swiftly across Berkeley Square, he entered Bruton Street, heading for a small mews on the lefthand side. There, halfway down, was a garage with the numeral 14 branded into the soft, green-painted wood.

The key which opened the lock was one of three on the ring. The others were for the carriage and main houses. Christine overlooked nothing. Guderian drew back the doors and stepped around the first of two Rolls-Royces housed therein. Lord Harloch's favorite, a 1937 P-3, was covered with a soft body cloth. Guderian stepped around the car's flank, lifted the cloth and drew it back over the rear end of the vehicle, exposing the twelve-foot-square trunk.

Christine had told him that because of her work at the hospital she had extra petrol rations. During the first days of the evacuation, when the number of casualties had overwhelmed the capacity of the ambulances, as many private vehicles as possible had been pressed into service. The P-3 had made half a dozen trips to Dover and back, ferrying servicemen who did not require stretchers. As a result the Army, according to Christine, had provided her not only with the coupons but a siphon kit as well. Guderian unbuckled the leather clasps on the trunk, popped the lid open and found exactly what he needed: a hollow rubber tube which fitted into a small air pump, a large flashlight, several liter bottles and a metal siphon: all the components necessary to transfer gasoline from a drum into a gas tank without the help of a conventional pump. Guderian examined every piece carefully to make certain it would function properly, then set everything back in its place and locked up the trunk. A few minutes later he was descending into the subway station, whose line would take him up to Euston Square station.

According to the effects Guderian had found on his person, Corporal Henry Schiffer had been living in a boardinghouse on Taviton Street directly behind University College of the University of London. Located halfway down the block, it was one of eight which lined the street. Guderian recognized the sort from his own university days, although he had never had to lodge in one: a narrow five-story structure with the cheapest rooms in the attic, the concierge's flat on the ground floor, rickety railing staircase that slipped past lime-green walls with dusty naked bulbs dangling overhead. The rooms would be of the bed-sitting variety, with an alcove that had an ancient icebox, hot plate and a table that would double as a desk. There would be a common bathroom at the end of each corridor.

The rent would be cheap, five pounds a week perhaps, the rules of the house, in most cases, inapplicable to the needs and character of university students but enforced nonetheless by a matron with beefy forearms, florid complexion and metal hair-curlers nesting beneath an oily kerchief.

Guderian grimaced at his evaluation and crossed the street, carefully mounting the chipped stone steps. He pressed the button that had BUILDING SUPERVISOR stenciled beside it.

"What you want, then?"

The querulous voice came from his left, through an open window on whose ledge rested two bony elbows. A turkey's neck appeared next, followed by a wizened, toothless face with a pair of dark vulture's eyes.

"I'm looking for the building supervisor," Guderian said to the old man.

"Ain't here."

"Do you know—"

"Want a room, do ye? Don't know what she has. Lots of strangers comin' by lately!"

"Where can I find Mrs. . . ."

"Glendower, Annie Glendower," the apparition cackled. "Be down at the White Horse by now I should think."

"Do you have storage, for extra trunks and suitcases?"

"Basement's full of them. All belong to lads who went off to France." The ghostly voice was troubled. "Was very bad, I hear. Very bad. Only one who's lived here has come back since. But we keep everything they left behind, not to worry."

"And Mrs. Glendower is at the White Horse?"

"Right as rain, old son. At the end of the street."

Guderian waved his thanks and headed off toward Endsleigh Place.

The White Horse, if one believed the rusting metal crest over the door, had been founded in 1742. A dark, dusty place with a tiresome floral wallpaper that English pubs for some reason favored, it served students as well as locals. The older citizens had carved out a territory along the bar proper and in the front parlor. The second room, where someone was grimly playing a guitar against a tide of male and female laughter, had been surrendered to the "others."

Guderian ordered a beer and carefully scrutinized the early evening clientele. He had to wait only a few minutes before a large woman, whose pink housecoat did not entirely hide her pendulous breasts, waddled over to the bar, a cigarette clamped in her mouth, her breathing coming in wheezing asthmatic gasps.

"If ye don't stop with the fags, Annie, you'll be dead before your time," the bartender said cheerfully, drawing her another Guinness.

"*This* is stuff that keeps me alive, mate!" Annie Glendower shouted back. She raised her glass and to the applause of her neighbors, drank the entire glass down.

During the next hour Henry Schiffer's landlady repeated her performance three times. Between the applause she also sipped a smokey Scotch whiskey, savoring it as though it were sacramental wine. In that time she smoked ten cigarettes, whose butts were deposited into a Players tin. Guderian made careful note of this and of Annie Glendower's rolling carriage when she finally departed.

Erik Guderian waited five minutes, finished his beer and left the White Horse. At a grocery on Gower Place he purchased a bottle of the same brand of whiskey Annie Glendower had been drinking as well as two tins of Players Navy Cut cigarettes. He gave a pimply-faced boy a few pence to deliver both to Taviton Street and enclosed a short note, written with his left hand, informing the landlady that one of her old lodgers had returned from France and wanted to show his appreciation for her having held on to his things. He signed the note with the initials A.P. Guderian didn't know if a lodger with such initials existed, but he doubted Annie Glendower would dwell on the matter. She wasn't the kind to pass up a gift horse.

Guderian walked up to Euston Station. In the company of anonymous travelers who had disembarked from trains coming in from Glasgow, Cardiff and Birmingham, he ate an unremarkable dinner of fried whitefish and chips and washed it down with a glass of thin white wine. Leaving the station, he retraced his steps to the garage in the mews, where he spent twenty minutes siphoning out a quart of gasoline from the tank of the P-3 Rolls-Royce. He deposited the jar along with other materials into a cheap canvas carrying case purchased at Euston Station. Guderian locked up the garage and at nine o'clock, with the blackout in effect, was on his way once more to the boardinghouse.

Even though the night was studded with stars, there were only shadows along Taviton Street. Guderian moved swiftly, more on account of a possible police patrol than being seen by someone who might be peeking out from behind the blackout curtains. When he reached the front door of the boardinghouse he grasped the knob in his right hand and twisted it. Annie Glendower might have been well into her cups, but she had remembered to lock the door after coming home. Guderian turned the knob to the right as far as he could and slipped a thin nailfile against the lock. Metal ground upon metal as the lock gave. Guderian stepped into the alcove and froze.

The black-and-white-checkered linoleum was filthy. A single yellow light bulb did little more than illuminate patches of water-stained plaster on the ceiling. Through the door directly before him Guderian heard the faint sounds of a BBC transmission, the announcer's voice broken by sporadic, heavy snoring. The whiskey had done its work. There only remained the question of whether Annie Glendower was alone in that room or whether the old man who had spoken to Guderian was still with her. Not that this really mattered . . .

Guderian stepped lightly to the back of the hall. He found a small door cut into the wall that concealed the staircase and opened it. The flashlight he had taken from the Rolls-Royce emergency kit illuminated narrow stairs descending steeply into a basement whose earthen walls were reinforced by set stone. Guderian began to move down slowly, testing each of the slippery wooden steps before he put his full weight on it.

The old man hadn't been lying. Stacked across the back part of the basement and up against one wall were a dozen large steamer trunks, an assortment of suitcases, large and small, and cardboard boxes bound with twine. Each one was tagged with an identical card although the handwriting on most was different. Annie Glendower made certain her lodgers had clearly identified their pieces prior to storage.

Guderian found one trunk and a suitcase belonging to Henry Schiffer. For an instant he closed his eyes and silently murmured a few lines of prayer. By now Henry Schiffer had been returned to the earth.

The powerful flashlight beam picked up another set of stairs at the very end of the basement. Guderian noted the angle at which they ascended and matched the point at which they reached the first floor with the possible layout of Annie Glendower's apartment directly above. When he tested the door at the top of the landing he discovered it was unlocked . . . and opened upon Annie's matchbox-size kitchen.

From where he stood he could see her in profile, sprawled in a rocking chair, her head lolling to one side. The radio was playing a ballroom melody. The smell of cigarettes and whiskey hung over the stale odor of boiled potatoes.

Where was the old man?

Guderian moved forward, almost sliding his steps across the bleached linoleum. He was five feet from Annie Glendower when a snore erupted from her lips, waking her up.

The shudder that passed through her body made the chair swing back. The countermomentum then pulled the rocker forward. Using this as leverage, Annie gripped both armrests to help raise herself. As she was beginning to stand, her head turned, an instant before Guderian's right hand clamped on her throat.

His fingers plunged into the folds of fat under the chin, the thumb seeking the carotid artery. Her eyes were staring up at him, rolling in terror, as a soft gurgling emerged from her throat. Guderian sidestepped the weak flailing of her arms and brought his left hand around the side of her head. He gave one final squeeze at the throat, knowing that this would incapacitate the windpipe for at least a few seconds, and gripped the hair on the right side of her head. Annie Glendower kicked out, her heavy legs bruising Guderian's shinbone. The German spread his legs in a fighting stance, as much to avoid another kick as to plant himself firmly for maximum leverage. His hands shot out in opposite directions, one pulling Annie's head toward him, the other pushing it away. The crack of brittle bone resounded like a gunshot. Annie Glendower's arm shot up in an involuntary reaction, but she was dead before it came down again, limp at her side.

Guderian loosened his grip on the head, slipped an arm under Annie's shoulder and guided the body back into the chair. Aside from the creaking of the rocker the apartment was still. Guderian moved around a small table covered with remnants of fabric and an open sewing kit and stepped into the darkened bedroom. It was empty. As was the bathroom. Either the old man had gone or else he lived somewhere else.

Guderian returned to the body and bending over, cantilevered Annie Glendower's dead weight onto his right shoulder. The muscles in his chest turned to fire as he stood up, his left arm, thrown across the back of the landlady's legs becoming numb. Ignoring the pain, he carried the corpse into the kitchen and stood it up against the opening to the basement. He faced Annie Glendower toward the staircase . . . then pushed.

The sickening sound of snapping bones echoed in his ears as he returned swiftly to the parlor, picked up Annie's cigarettes as well as the half-full tumbler of whiskey she hadn't been able to finish. He brought these down into the basement, smashing the glass not far from one outstretched hand, scattering the cigarettes across the floor.

Guderian knelt down by the canvas bag he had brought with him and took out the jar of gasoline. Covering the opening with cheesecloth, he sprinkled the fuel over all the trucks and cartons, leaving enough to soak Annie Glendower's housecoat. He packed the bag carefully, making certain every item he had brought had been replaced.

Guderian moved over to the foot of the stairs, standing in the pale shaft of light that flowed down from the kitchen. Without pause he lit the first match, let the flame consume half of the wooden splinter and tossed it onto a suitcase. The gasoline erupted, spreading furiously across the floor, flames licking at the trunks. Guderian retreated up the stairs and lit another match. He let this one burn down as well, then dropped it into the half-filled box. The box was still in midair when it erupted. Then like a torch it dropped on Annie Glendower's back. The wall of flame rose from the body, driving Guderian farther up the stairs. When he finally stepped onto the kitchen landing there wasn't anything—or anyone—he could see in the basement.

20

Located in the financial district of London known as the City, the Bank of England occupies a rectangular area bounded by Threadneedle Street on the south, Princes Street on the west, Lothbury Street at the north end and Bartholomew Lane to the east.

The outer screen wall facing Threadneedle Street was designed by Sir John Soane and built between 1794 and 1827. Set into this stone wall, broken by Doric-style columns, is the front entrance of the Bank, presided over by the Senior Gatekeeper, resplendent in scarlet robe with gold tassels and a bicorn hat. On the morning of June 6, fifteen minutes before the start of the business day, ten o'clock, the Gatekeeper had been advised to admit a single visitor whose name he did not know. What made this order even more extraordinary was the fact that the Governor himself, Reginald Saint John Reading, had accompanied the Gatekeeper to the doors, waited the two minutes until the appointed hour, then signaled him to draw back one of the two bronze portals. The man waiting stepped through like a shadow, and the Gatekeeper was still securing the locks when the two men disappeared up the staircase. If asked to describe the man who had entered, the Gatekeeper would have been at a complete loss to do so, which was precisely the intention.

"Welcome to the Bank of England, M–Mr. C–Cabot," Reading said, a slight stutter playing on the front syllables of his last words.

Cabot had been told what to expect: a tall, slender man, impeccably dressed in chalk-stripe suit with a wine-red tie. The face was craggy, with a long, heavy nose that dominated the slightly hollow cheekbones with deep perpendicular ridges running to both ends of a wide, fleshy mouth. The hair was wavy and carefully tossed to one side, gold and silver mixing in equal proportions. The eyes, a deceptive soft brown, reflected absolutely nothing.

"I suppose we both wish it was under different circumstances," Cabot replied.

He was watching carefully for Reading's reaction. Churchill had met with Cabot late last evening shortly after informing Reading of the intention to move the gold.

"A sphinx!" Churchill had declared. "The man has either gold dust or nothing at all in his veins. He listened without a word as I explained the decision that had been reached, that you were in charge of the operation and exactly what was required of the Bank. Naturally I did not mention *how* the bullion was to be shipped or when. Frankly, Mr. Cabot, I expected outrage. Yet Reading did not utter a single contrary word!"

"Mr. Cabot, I am very pleased that it *is* under these particular circumstances," Reading said. The smile was sad yet somehow resolute. "We find ourselves in an extraordinary predicament, for which we must find equally innovative solutions. I assured the Prime Minister unequivocally that I realize what has to be done and why. You have only to ask for any cooperation to receive it—without question."

Cabot breathed a sigh of relief and fell into step with Reading as he proceeded to the second level.

The Court Room is the most opulent room of the Bank. Running seventy feet along the southeast wing, it is, appropriately enough, done in pale lemon yellow. Double-column arches run directly behind the doors and open up on two magnificent fireplaces hewn from henna marble. Over one is a Lafarge clock, over the second, a Turner landscape. The thirty-foot ceiling is inlaid with ornate frescoes, while the area between the tops of the columns and the ceiling is studded with large cameos, salmon pink, of British monarchs. The room is dominated by a brilliantly polished conference table that accommodates ten chairs lengthwise and two at either end, one for each of the Directors. This morning none of these chairs was occupied.

"Please, Mr. Cabot, do sit down," the Governor said, indicating the last chair in one of the long rows. He himself took his usual place at the head of the table.

Reading made a steeple of his bony, nicotine-stained fingers and sighed at his reflection in the high-gloss veneer.

"I can honestly say, Mr. Cabot, that I never believed I would live to witness such a day," he said, his voice betraying an infinite sadness. "For centuries the Bank has been the repository and custodian for the wealth of *other* nations, whose trust in it was unquestioned. Now . . ."

Reading drew out a single cigarette along with a kitchen match which he ignited with his thumbnail, a gesture totally out of keeping with the character of the man. He carefully broke the match in two before depositing it in the ashtray.

"But do not misunderstand me," Reading continued. "The Prime Minister is absolutely correct: it would be an unmitigated disaster for the gold and negotiable securities to fall into Nazi hands. A calamity of only slightly lesser proportions would ensue if the gold were to be lost en route to its haven. Therefore rest assured I am in complete agreement with the Prime Minister as far as this project is concerned and am prepared to be of service in any way I can."

"Your help will be invaluable," Cabot said.

"Then perhaps you would begin your queries?"

"From the information given me by the Prime Minister I have a rough figure for the amount of gold and securities to be moved," Cabot said. "What I need now are the precise figures."

"Currently the Bank has one hundred and twenty-four tons of bullion in its vaults." Reading looked up with a quizzical smile. "That figure doesn't intimidate you?"

"It's close enough to what I had before," Cabot said. "But frankly, I can't *imagine* that much gold. There's no reference point."

"Believe me, I understand," Reading said lightly. "But to continue. This weight is distributed into eight thousand, nine hundred sixteen bricks, each one weighing twenty-eight pounds, measuring thirteen and a half by nine by seven inches. When gold is shipped, whether overland or by sea, it is sent in specially reinforced wooden cases. In total then we are speaking of just under one hundred thirty-nine million dollars in gold that must be transferred."

"That figure doesn't tally with ones I've been given," Cabot said at once, recalling the figure of two hundred and fifty million pounds sterling that Churchill had quoted.

Reading held up his hand.

"I was referring only to the *physical* gold, Mr. Cabot. There is also some one hundred and ten million in sterling in gold certificates on the Bank's South African holdings."

Reading slid a single sheet of paper across the lacquered surface.

"You will appreciate that the paper is far less bulky than the gold itself, a factor which may assist you in the actual transfer."

Cabot scanned the sheet. He doubted that Reading was fishing, but the Governor had no need to know how the transfer would be effected and so Cabot said nothing.

"Finally, there is also the matter of a hundred million pounds in negotiable securities," Reading continued. He pushed another sheet across the table. "The packing details. However, I should tell you that that figure is at best arbitrary."

Cabot glanced up quickly.

"No, not because of inaccuracy," Reading assured him. "It is a matter of market conditions. The figure on each share is the *nominal value, not the market value as listed*. It's quite likely, for example, that on any given day a hundred-pound bond could be sold at triple or quadruple its face value. Therefore I tend to think this paper is worth at least double the figure of one hundred fifty million pounds."

"So the bottom line is *four hundred and fifty million pounds*," Cabot said softly.

"And possibly half as much again," Reading confirmed. "Pushing the total to two billion, seven hundred million of your dollars."

The Governor sat back in his chair and regarded the dispassionate man on his right. From somewhere inside his withered soul a wretched cry issued forth, because for the first time since speaking to Churchill Reading truly understood that this man would take everything. The money . . . that was only a part of it. The tradition of which Reading was a part, that hurt more. Reading had given his life to the Bank. Nothing beyond its walls was of any import to him. Yet this cold, hard man had walked in and with a few words brought shame upon him, as the Governor who would be remembered as having presided over the emptying of the coffers. Coffers which, despite Churchill's pledges, would never be replenished. Reading shuddered, realizing that he was witnessing the death of the only thing he had ever come to love.

"Are you all right?"

The Governor glanced at Cabot. "A touch of the flu, I suspect. Forgive me, but you were asking . . . ?"

"How long would it take to assemble the bullion and securities from the Bank's branch offices and the head offices of the other institutions holding them?"

"Why, everything has already been collected," Reading answered.

"I'm sorry but I don't follow," Cabot said tonelessly.

"Nothing mysterious about it," Reading said petulantly. "I should have thought the Prime Minister would have explained: as soon as war was declared in September 1939, the branch offices of the Bank and head offices of other institutions deposited all their bullion and securities with us. They were required to do so by law."

"I see," Cabot murmured. "So it is ready for shipment."

"Only the packing remains to be done."

"And who handles that?" Cabot asked.

"We have twenty porters engaged full-time," Reading told him. "Of course a great deal of work is mechanical, although the actual packing is still done by hand. To anticipate your next question, to pack all the bullion would take this team some eleven hours, since each man can crate about ten boxes per hour. The securities, of course, could be handled much more quickly."

"Your central loading depot opens up on Bartholomew Lane?"

"Yes. As with most other essentials the Bank has its own fleet of armored trucks which we lease between our own shipments. Not a novel idea, really, since most of our deliveries are scheduled at regular intervals."

"The same thing applied to the drivers and escorts, as far as being vetted?"

Reading gave him a wintry smile. "We have a double-A rating with Lloyd's, Mr. Cabot. They are rather parsimonious with such a standard."

"What is the maximum weight your vehicles can carry?"

"Two tons, although we much prefer to ration out any load, even if it means two trucks carry only a few hundred pounds each."

Cabot sat back in his chair, studying the gauzy reflection of the chandelier in the brilliantine mahogany.

"Governor," he said slowly, "at what time do your trucks leave the building? That is, when do those gates on Bartholomew Lane open?"

"All deliveries are made very early in the morning," Reading told him. "Depending on the volume of the shipment, the counting and packing generally begins between midnight and two o'clock in the morning. The trucks leave a few minutes before dawn."

"But you also deliver on Sundays."

Reading inclined his head. "Yes, in fact we prefer Sunday if the delivery is to be made within the City or London proper. There's far less congestion in the streets that day."

"I'll need several things," Cabot said. "The records for all drivers, escorts and packagers; all records for the trucks from the date of purchase; the name of your liaison at the police; and a portfolio of your security personnel."

"If you tell me where, I can send that information around this afternoon."

"The Prime Minister's residence," Cabot said. "This is a number I can be reached at."

He handed Reading a blank card with a telephone number handwritten across the face.

"Every time I give the number out, that person's name goes on a master list," Cabot cautioned him. "If there is any unauthorized caller the number will be changed immediately and we'll all be knee-deep in a full security investigation."

"I think I understand, Mr. Cabot," Reading said dryly, glancing at his watch. "If we are through perhaps I can offer you tea—or coffee—in my office?"

"No, thank you," Cabot said. "There's one item we haven't covered."

"And what is that?" Reading asked, surprised.

"I'd like to know more about the King William tunnels," Cabot said.

The stunned expression on Reading's face confirmed for Cabot what Churchill had told him. As far as the venerable Bank of England was concerned, these tunnels did not exist.

Erik Guderian read all about it in the morning edition of the *Daily Telegraph*. The fire in Taviton Street had completely destroyed one boardinghouse and badly damaged two others on adjacent sides. While there were a number of minor casualties, there was, miraculously enough, only one fatality: Annie Glendower, the landlady of Number 42. The fire marshal was quoted as saying that the cause of the blaze was carelessness. An empty bottle of whiskey had been found in Annie Glendower's parlor. By the body were fragments of a glass as well as a charred cigarette tin. The landlady had been seen at the White Horse pub earlier on, drinking liberally. A grocery boy remembered delivering a fresh bottle to her apartment shortly after she had left the pub. The circumstantial evidence was damning: Annie Glendower had tied one on, stumbled on the stairs leading to the basement. The resulting fall had broken her neck, the burning cigarette she carried ignited the dry cartons stacked around her . . . The rest was chain reaction.

Guderian read through the piece carefully while Christine Harloch slept on in the bedroom. Satisfied that the fire marshal had no cause to suspect foul play, he folded the paper to the editorial section and left it on the breakfast table. Before leaving he washed out his teacup and put away the orange preserve he had had with his muffins. Christine didn't stir as he locked the door after himself.

The day was brisk, with a strong wind creating racing clouds across a blue canvas. Guderian stepped out onto Berkeley Square and decided to walk the distance to Whitehall. The killing of Annie Glendower had eliminated the first of two traces Henry Schiffer had left behind him. Even if by some stroke of the imagination someone came looking for Schiffer, all they would find would be a heap of ashes. But there existed a second source, one that could not be burned, or otherwise destroyed. Not because such a thing was impossible, rather it did not fit Guderian's overall scheme.

Erik Guderian had planned to slip into England under the cover of the chaos that existed both at Dunkirk and the Channel ports. It would be impossible for British Army authorities to look after each and every man coming off the boats. There would be hundreds, if not thousands, of stragglers—men who were shell-shocked, had lost their units or had simply wandered away. It would take weeks to track them all down.

Although fate had given him safe passage, it had also provided its own cruel twist: Henry Schiffer had returned from Dunkirk alive but also a hero. From the moment he had seen the Army officer and Navy commander standing by his bed, Guderian realized that he had to deal with Schiffer's file, which would undoubtedly have a photograph of him, as quickly as possible. But his convalescence had cost him four precious days, his sudden affair with Christine and the move into the coach house another two. And Annie Glendower . . .

Because of Schiffer's heroism and the attention it drew to the man, Guderian had been robbed of the chance to get at the Canadian soldier's file as soon as circumstances warranted. By the same token the file should have already made its way to the desk of the Army colonel who had become so interested in Schiffer! Yet for an unknown reason this had not happened . . . not unless he was, even now, walking into a trap . . .

Guderian shivered in the harsh cold sunlight. He drew his coat around him and quickened his stride.

At the desk in the center lobby of the Ministry of War, Guderian gave his identification and the name of the officer he wanted to see to the sergeant on duty. Less than a minute later a young woman in mufti came up to Guderian, introduced herself as Colonel Blake's secretary and escorted him to the elevator, which took them to the fourth floor. The Colonel's office was in the center of the seemingly endless corridor, which was filled with men and women, most of them in uniform, moving briskly with papers in hand.

"Come in, old chap, come in!"

The voice boomed at him from the larger inner office. As he thanked the secretary Guderian glimpsed a uniform rising from a chair behind the desk. The next instant Blake was shaking his hand and clapping him on the back as he led him inside.

"You're looking particularly fit, Schiffer," Blake said, staring up and down at Guderian. "Treated you well at Berkeley Square, have they?"

"Very well, sir."

"Sit down, sit down." Blake waved at him. "Actually I was going to call you later on in the day—see how you were getting along."

Guderian smiled, glancing across the papers on Blake's desk. The man was a model of neatness. There was nothing but a letter on the blotter, no files in either of the metal trays on the lefthand side.

Guderian smiled. "Must be telepathy, sir."

"Well, whatever, Corporal, I have finally had some time to devote to your case," Blake said. "What with all the men coming in from France, I tell you the last several days have been sheer hell. Not only a matter of our lads, you understand. We took off about twenty thousand Frenchies in the last day and a half. Got to feed them, clothe them and resettle them, you know."

"An enormous logistical problem, sir," Guderian agreed.

"But not that I've forgotten about you." Blake wagged his finger at Guderian. "Not at all. I was going to call the hospital to see if you were fit enough to take part in the awards ceremony. I see that obviously you are."

"Sir, I'm not sure I understand," Guderian said, with what he thought was an appropriate amount of puzzlement.

"Surely you didn't think that what the Commander and I told you at the hospital was so much nonsense!" Blake cried. "I can tell you, Corporal, that in the midst of this crisis I still had a chance to review the testimonials given on your behalf by the CMB commander as well as by some of the wounded who saw what you did. *And* . . . it is my considered opinion that nothing short of the Distinguished Service Order is what you merit for your bravery!"

"Sir—"

"Furthermore, I have suggested to General Avery, and he has agreed, that the awards ceremony take place as soon as possible," Blake continued on relentlessly. "I must be frank with you, Schiffer. At a time like this, when the country is still reeling from what happened to us at Dunkirk, we need to show the people exactly what our mettle is made of. We are *not* a defeated army!"

"Sir, I'm flattered, really, that you feel I can contribute to this . . . this effort," Guderian said. "Naturally I would be happy to follow whatever orders you have in mind."

Blake slapped the desk with both palms.

"Excellent!" he said. "I shall inform the General that the awards ceremony can be scheduled for sometime next week. I haven't had a chance as yet to review your file, what with all the mess we're in at the moment—"

"Sir," Guderian interrupted. "If I may, the reason I came here today was to request permission to go into the Royal Artillery archives. You see, I know that at least two of my friends were killed in Calais. I haven't been able to locate the others. But I knew those two well. I thought of sending a letter to their parents, telling them exactly how their sons fell. I think it would make all the difference in the world."

Blake raised his eyebrows and nodded slowly.

"Yes, I think that would be an excellent idea," he said thoughtfully. "In fact, we might mention their names at the ceremony . . . Yes, I have no objection to that. In fact I can have the files sent over by courier."

"If it's all the same to you, sir, I'd rather look them up myself," Guderian said. "It's just that I'm not doing anything at the moment and I've been thinking about them quite a lot . . ."

"Of course, I understand completely," Blake said sympathetically. "Awfully difficult to forget. I'll get Miss Pritchett to draft authorization for you. At the same time, if you could bring your own file by this might save me time and bother. The couriers are very busy these days . . ."

"Of course, sir," Guderian said, rising. "It would be my pleasure."

Fifteen minutes later, when Blake's secretary handed him the necessary authorization, Guderian understood why the Colonel had mentioned the need for couriers.

"You wouldn't be expected to know," the secretary said. "We have a completely different set of records for Commonwealth soldiers. *British* files are kept here, of course. But someone such as yourself, from Canada, or Australia, wherever, who enlisted in the Army, would have his papers out at the Earls Court center."

She looked up at him curiously. "Your friends whose files you need—they were Canadian, weren't they?"

"Yes," Guderian said quickly.

"Otherwise, you see, there wouldn't be any need for you to go all the way out there. It's just that we had no other storage facilities, and now when you want something the dispatch office stirs up such a fuss . . ."

Her voice trailed off as though talking about the difficulties were tiring enough.

"I appreciate your consideration," Guderian said sympathetically. "Still, I imagine it'll all be straightened out in due course."

"I suppose," the secretary replied, unconvinced.

Her phone was ringing and Guderian saw the opening to leave. He hurried out of the office and managed to squeeze into the elevator just as the grille was closing. Outside on the front steps he flagged down a taxi just as it was pulling away. Guderian gave the driver the Earls Court address and sat back, breathing hard.

All because there wasn't enough space, he thought. On such infinitesimal twists of fate did major operations succeed or fail. The negligible detail, the obvious that went unseen, the decision which, when made, did not reveal the minute ramifications that would inexorably flow from it. Not he, not Berlin itself, could have foreseen that the British Army, out of regimented stupidity, would not keep all personnel records in one place. Trust the British to divide even paperwork into that belonging to "us" as opposed to "them" . . . as if "they" weren't shedding blood as rich as that of any British soldier.

Then too Guderian realized why Colonel Blake had been so anxious about the awards ceremony. The Army didn't give a damn about "Corporal Schiffer's" act of bravery. What it had was a propaganda coup: award a major citation to a soldier of the Commonwealth and show the whole Empire just how steadfast support for Britian was. Plaster Schiffer's face in every recruiting station from Toronto, Canada, to Sydney, Australia, and show those innocents what kind of glory could be theirs for the asking.

Guderian smiled. He would love to have indulged in that charade. Gerd Jaunich would think it splendid. But he knew better than to tempt the Fates . . .

The Army depot was a ramshackle building that had been requisitioned from the Earls Court Exhibition Foundation. Formerly a storage house for the Exhibition, it was relegated to the southern end of the acreage between Eardley Crescent and Kempsford Gardens, standing alone like a poor but tolerated relation.

Colonel Blake's signature was not unfamiliar to the duty officer who called one of the clerks to take Guderian to the "Tombs" as the archives were cheerfully referred to. While they waited for the clerk to appear, the duty officer, an overweight youngster of twenty or so, plied Guderian with questions about what was going on at "headquarters." It was evident he considered the Earls Court assignment as something slightly worse than Purgatory. Mercifully, the clerk appeared quickly enough.

The second level of the building was a vast open area, with black, rusting girders overhead and a floor of raw plywood boards that threatened to splinter under one's weight.

"You have the names you want, then?" the clerk asked over his shoulder as he sauntered between metal skeleton shelves that were twice his height.

"Yes, I do," Guderian told him.

"Let's have 'em, mate. I can handle this lot quicker than you."

"Look, I'm sure that's true," Guderian began and launched into another version of the story he had given Blake. The clerk seemed unimpressed but shrugged.

"If you want to dig for them yourself, that's fine with me. But at least give me the last names anyway. Otherwise you'll be here all night."

"Sanderson and Thompson," Guderian said.

"Right . . . S and T . . . The Ss are over here in rank seven. And the Ts in rank ten. There's a desk at the other end. No ink or paper, though."

"I brought my own," Guderian assured him.

It took Guderian no more than five minutes to find Henry Schiffer's file. He brought it over to what passed for a desk—a sheet of plywood mounted across two sawhorses, and opened to the first page.

The photograph jolted him. It was a standard Army photo, two inches by an inch and half, closely cropped, printed on cheap thin paper. But it wasn't the quality of the picture that bothered him. It was Schiffer, grinning into the camera, teeth wide and straight, only his eyes betraying the desperation behind the humor with which he tried to glaze his uncertainty. That must have been the exact moment he truly realized what it was he had gotten himself into. And even at that moment he had been deceived. No one had talked to him about dying.

Even as he read the particulars of the file, all facts he already knew save one or two obscure references the military had taken note of, Guderian was easing the scalpel from its sheath. His hand dropped by his right leg, the razor's edge moving swiftly across the stitching along the top of the boot.

From the beginning Guderian had known that the documentation which would convert him to Henry Schiffer would have to be carried to England on his person.

Although the list of "sleepers" Jaunich had provided him with included the names of three forgers, Guderian had argued that as soon as the papermen linked a face to the name of Henry Schiffer they would have to be eliminated—a further complication.

Carrying the papers had also presented a unique problem. Since Guderian was to travel by sea, there was no way in which the documentation could be sewn into his uniform. This generally favored method was complicated not only by the fact that the clothing would in all likelihood become wet, but also that it would be taken away from Guderian once he had arrived in England. At some point he would be given a fresh dry uniform . . .

But not so the boots. Next to his rifle, boots were a soldier's most prized possession, not only because they were in scarce supply but also because they had been broken in. By its very nature an army moved, and the soldier could travel only as quickly and comfortably as his boots would permit.

Guderian palmed the scalpel into his pocket. Reaching down, he pried his finger in between the two layers of leather whose stitching he had cut. Plucking the threads away, he dug in until his fingers touched the thin, waterproof envelope. He withdrew it, slit it open and plucked out the photograph of himself.

At the other end of the building someone was arguing about misplaced files. The anger resounded off the girders, traveling around and around until it lost momentum and fell away. Guderian slipped his hand into his pocket and brought out a matchbox. Using the scalpel, he quickly pried the photo of Henry Schiffer off the sheet, slipping it into the breast pocket of his tunic. Taking his own picture, he licked the back, making sure it was moistened well, then sprinkled the powder from the matchbox across the top. The powder began to dissolve instantly, creating a sticky paste. Guderian picked up the photograph with the tips of his fingers and very carefully turned it over. Gingerly he lowered the photograph until it was exactly where Schiffer's had been. Then, slowly, he pressed it into place, running his finger along the edges a dozen times to make certain there wasn't a seam. Guderian closely examined the photograph and found it impossible to distinguish it from the original. Now the other details, which would have compounded suspicion, receded to nothingness:

Schiffer was six feet, Guderian, a few inches taller.

Schiffer's weight was listed at one hundred seventy pounds. Guderian had been ten pounds heavier but had probably lost as much during his convalescence.

Schiffer's hair was listed as light brown. The ambiguity made Guderian's flaxen acceptable.

Fortuitously, both men had gray eyes.

Guderian rose and, tucking the file under his arm, started the long walk down the center aisle. The final piece in the deception was in place. He *was* Corporal Henry Schiffer. Now he could begin what he had come to England to do.

21

The wind was cold along the river; the oily, gray waters rolling along in frothy waves, monotonously wearing away the wooden piles, as thick as a man's torso, that supported the great docks along the river Thames. Standing on the bow of the Royal Navy launch, Cabot watched as the bridges of London—Waterloo, Blackfriars, Southwark, London—slipped over and past him.

The previous evening couriers had arrived at Cabot's Downing Street annex with cartons of files, designs, blueprints and data sheets relating to every category of fighting vessel, surface and submerged, that was to be found in the Royal Navy's arsenal. He had discarded what was obviously of no value to him and concentrated on those vessels whose specifications matched the requirements he needed: carrying capacity, armament, and above all speed, the factor Cabot regarded as most crucial. To his dismay several of the ships were unavailable to him. They were either in dry dock for major repairs or at dockside being outfitted with new equipment or replacement parts. Other vessels were woefully undermanned, lying idle in the vast yards off the Clyde, or, having been fatally wounded during the Dunkirk retreat, had been stripped of all usable parts and their shorn hulks towed out to sea and sunk. Still others were scattered around the oceans of the world, from the frigid North Atlantic to the sweltering doldrums of the Indian Ocean.

Nonetheless Cabot had found two ships, either of which would serve the plan he had in mind. At seven o'clock on the morning of June 7, Winston Churchill telephoned the Admiralty and ordered that the cruisers *Jade* and *Victorious* stand by to receive an officer from Ten Downing Street. Any orders that the First Sea Lord had issued for either vessel were as of that moment suspended. The captains of both were to make themselves and their crew available to the man who would be speaking for Winston Churchill.

The Royal Docks came into view, then their estuaries, cranes and piers slid by. Garbage scows, three or four to a link, were being towed downriver. Pleasure boats passed on the right, women's laughter being caught on the wind like kites. As the launch made yet another adjustment to follow its serpentine course, the yellow-brown of the land gave way to green. Greenwich was only a few minutes away.

The Royal Observatory pierced the horizon. The launch veered out to the center of the channel and Cabot saw them: *Jade, Victorious*, riding high a hundred yards off in the swell that lapped against Greenwich Pier.

They were Dido class cruisers, the first of their kind, built by Cammell Laird of Birkenhead. With funding provided in the 1935 Estimates, their keels had been laid down in October of the following year. Both *Jade* and *Victorious* were launched in the summer of 1939, the final work on them completed five months later after sea trials in the North Atlantic.

The launch slowed as it drew into the shadows of *Victorious*, moving along the massive gray flank. The proportions were staggering: six thousand seven hundred tons when fully loaded, spread along five hundred and six feet in length, fifty in width. According to specifications provided by the Admiralty, *Victorious* had a maximum range of 4400 miles at twelve knots. But she could do much much better, as the sea trials records verified: 3480 miles at twenty knots, and an amazing twenty-five knots if that distance were reduced by a thousand miles.

A sailor brushed by Cabot, and, standing on the prow, caught the line thrown from the platform. The launch was secured and Cabot stepped off it, moving up the rickety metal staircase that ran along the ship's flank at a forty-five-degree angle.

"The Admiral's compliments, sir!"

The officer who addressed him was wearing dress whites with lieutenant's epaulets. He was over six feet, with reddish-brown sideburns, and emerald-green eyes, a sharp contrast with the pale, almost milky complexion of his face. His grip was firm and in it Cabot felt the strength of a man who in spite of sea or office duty kept himself very fit.

"Lieutenant Andrew Simmons, at your service, sir," the officer said, stepping back. "If you would follow me, Admiral Runnymeade is expecting you in the sea cabin."

"Thank you, Lieutenant," Cabot said, falling in stride beside him.

Cabot would have preferred to meet with Runnymeade

alone, but when the Admiralty had contacted him Runnymeade made it very clear that his Lieutenant, Simmons, would participate in any discussions that had to do with *Victorious*. The Admiralty had passed the message along to Cabot, who had promptly called up Simmons's Navy file. After a quick perusal he understood why Runnymeade had taken such a position.

Besides being a graduate of the Dartmouth Navy Academy, Runnymeade's alma mater, Simmons was also a naval engineer with a degree from the University of Edinburgh. His qualifications assured him an officer's rank and he was assigned to oversee the drafting and design work of the Dido class cruisers. Simmons did more. He stayed on during the actual constructions, initiating improvements and innovative designs along the way. In the whole of the Royal Navy there wasn't another man who knew more about the actual workings and capabilities of this vessel than Simmons. But Runnymeade's loyalty to his junior lay equally in the fact that Simmons had proven himself as adept at running a ship at sea as he was at building one. Runnymeade, at fifty-five a legend in the Fleet, was grooming Simmons for his own command.

The Captain's day cabin was behind the wheelhouse and remote-control office. The quarters were spartan: a narrow couch that doubled as a bed set against one wall, a metal desk pushed up under a porthole, steel shelves riveted into the metal panels, stacked with books and maps, and a narrow head crammed against a dollhouse-size locker.

The dimensions of the cabin made the man appear bigger than he was. Nathanial Runnymeade was the archetypal image of the seaman: no more than five foot eight, he was standing facing the door, short thick legs spread apart, a barrel chest thrust out, heavy drayman's forearms ending in powerful hands. The hair was completely white, the face etched in wrinkles placed there by the natural elements—from the blazing heat of the Indian Ocean, which had been his most recent posting, to the cold fury of the Cape of Good Hope where, in the twenties, Runnymeade's ships served as escorts for merchantmen plying the South African sea-lanes. Runnymeade was also one of the most decorated officers of the Royal Navy, one of two who held the highest honor of the realm: the Victoria Cross.

"Mr. Cabot, isn't it?" Runnymeade said, stepping forward and offering his hand.

"It's an honor, Admiral," Cabot replied.

"Oh, I think the honor is ours," Runnymeade said, the flame-blue eyes lighting up for an instant. "After all, it's not every day that we receive an emissary from Mr Churchill."

"Will there be anything else, sir?" Simmons asked deferentially.

"Yes, Andrew. Lock up, will you, and make yourself comfortable." Runnymeade turned to Cabot. "I trust the Prime Minister has authorized Simmons to sit in."

"Lieutenant Simmons has been vetted by my office," Cabot confirmed. "I feel he would make a valuable contribution to this project."

"Just what is your office, sir?" Runnymeade asked softly.

"A room at Ten Downing Street, Admiral," Cabot told him. "This is a one-time operation, to be executed within seven days if all goes well. It has nothing to do with any branch of Whitehall or the Armed Forces. I have the authority to choose whatever people I feel are best suited for the operation, tap any resources that are needed."

"I suppose we should be flattered, Andrew," Runnymeade said dryly, "to be included in such august company. But you mentioned that no British offices, other than that of the Prime Minister, are involved. Are we to assume that since you are an American this is somehow tied in with your people?"

"The only American who is aware of the project is the President of the United States," Cabot said.

"I see," Runnymeade said thoughtfully. "This puts us in select company indeed and, I might add, is quite intriguing. Mr. Cabot, would you care for a bracer before you begin?"

"No, thank you," Cabot said. "I'd like to ask you and the Lieutenant a few questions concerning Victorious."

"By all means."

"First of all, I have to know whether she passed all her sea trials to your satisfaction," Cabot said. "Was there anything on the machinery or performance you are dissatisfied with?"

Runnymeade cocked his head. "Andrew?"

"Mr. Cabot," the younger man said, "Victorious, and her sister ship, Jade, cleared sea trials with near perfect records. I say near perfect because I'm something of a stickler for details. We've had some difficulty with the A turrets on both vessels. The swivel mechanism wasn't as smooth in rough weather as it should be. This problem has, I feel, been solved, but we can't be absolutely certain until we run actual test firings."

"That's it?"

"That's all, Mr. Cabot."

"How much fuel do you carry when fully loaded?"

"Eleven hundred tons."

"Ammunition?"

"Eight two-pound and eight five-inch antiaircraft guns, six twenty-one-inch torpedo tubes, and of course the ten 5.25-inch main batteries. All told about four hundred and six tons of ammunition to feed our weaponry."

"What about the protective armor?"

"A main belt of three-inch plate over all machinery spaces closed in by one-inch traverse bulkheads and a one-inch deck. There is a central armored platform two inches thick over the forward and after magazines which thins out to half that in the space between the magazine and forward boiler room. The waterline has three-quarter-inch plating while the turrets themselves are protected by one to one-and-a-half inches of plate. The same is true of the steering gear."

"And the generators?" asked Cabot.

"Each one is in a separate watertight compartment," Simmons explained. "The ring main extends fore and aft behind the armor and below the waterline. The steam lines are arranged so that any generator could be supplied from either the forward or aft boiler rooms."

"Is there any possibility of some dead weight being stripped from the ship without critical effect?"

Simmons glanced uneasily at Runnymeade, who nodded.

"The whole concept behind the Dido class cruiser was to create a very fast yet heavily armed vessel," Simmons said. "To do this certain modifications had to be implemented in both the design and construction stages. For example, copper piping was used for pump flooding, draining systems and domestic lines. A common fitting shot was built instead of one for each trade. The handling room between the magazine and turret was eliminated because during the mock-up stage we learned there was no possibility of flash penetrating the magazine.

"Weight was also saved in the armament area. We carry no spare barrels for the 5.25 guns. As well the turrets are armed with the four-ton Mark IV instead of the five-and-three-quarter-ton Mark V weapons that quite rightly belong on the King George V class battleships.

"I doubt, Mr. Cabot, that very much more could be trimmed without jeopardizing some operation on the vessel."

"You carry a complement of five hundred and eight men," Cabot said. "How many of them are *absolutely essential* to the running of the ship?"

"Mr. Cabot," Runnymeade interrupted, "each man has an integral role to fulfill on this ship. It would be unthinkable to try to reduce the numbers."

"I'm afraid it will be necessary, Admiral," Cabot said. "Not only from the point of view of security but also from dead weight. Hypothetically, if you were ordered to sail from where we are now to a point on the Eastern Seaboard of the United States, and if your orders read that you were to avoid any and all contact with the enemy, that in effect you were running, how many men would you need to control the ship?"

Simmons shot a quizzical look at his superior, but Runnymeade ignored it.

"If we reduce the number of Royal Marines," he said slowly, "and possibly some seamen, then we shouldn't need as many mess hands or cooks . . . A hundred and fifty, Andrew? Could we take away that many and still remain effective, as Mr. Cabot says?"

"If we run, sir, literally run across the Atlantic, we might be able to do it with that number," Simmons said. "But three hundred and fifty is the bare minimum. There are two considerations Mr. Cabot hasn't taken into account: the weather out at sea at this time of year and the *possibility* of enemy engagement. If we were noticed by the U-boats, chances are we'd have to fight. As far as the German capital ships are concerned, we could probably outrun them providing we received early enough warning."

"There you have it, Mr. Cabot," Runnymeade said. "Would such a staff reduction be acceptable? And before you answer be advised that I would not countenance jeopardizing my ship or crew for *any* mission by sailing undermanned or underarmed. I have as much responsibility to them as to your orders."

"I appreciate that, Admiral," Cabot said. "But I'm afraid that won't be enough. On this mission *Victorious* will be handling very special cargo, a one-shot mission across the Atlantic. One hundred and fifty men less translates into roughly fourteen tons. What I need to bring on board is *one hundred twenty-four tons.* Which means reducing *Victorious*'s armament capability."

Cabot paused.

"Before I outline the details, I'll take you up on that offer of a drink."

"I believe we could *all* use one, sir!" Runnymeade said softly.

It was clear from his expression that he considered the American quite mad.

It was five o'clock in the afternoon when the Navy launch nudged the dock at Westminster Pier and Cabot jumped off. The driver of the Humber staff car took Cabot's briefcase and escorted his passenger to the vehicle. A moment later the Humber was threading its way through the evening traffic along the Victoria Embankment, its destination the Royal Marines compound in Waltham Forest, north of London.

Settled in the back seat, Cabot reviewed the results of his six-hour discussion—cut through with tooth-and-nail arguments—on board *Victorious.* To their credit both Runnymeade and Simmons had heard Cabot out on his proposal to trim weight by cutting back on the amount of munitions the vessel would take on. Runnymeade was the more vociferous of the two in his objections. But after he learned what *Victorious* would carry, even the bantam Admiral conceded that possibly some accommodation could be made.

At this point Simmons proved himself invaluable. Although he would no more countenance sending *Victorious* on a suicide mission than would Runnymeade, the Lieutenant proposed that *Victorious* reduce her usual torpedo load from twenty-four fish to none, and her shell loads to a meager three rounds per gun. He reasoned that given the secrecy of the mission, speed not weaponry was the critical factor. After some heated debate Runnymeade concurred, but only on the condition that on the return voyage *Victorious* carry full armament. Cabot quickly gave his assurances.

The second obstacle was the loading. Cabot insisted that if at all possible *Victorious* take on her cargo while lying off Greenwich. Tidal charts were brought out. Water levels during the proposed loading hours were examined, a margin for error and minute miscalculations built in. After prolonged debate Runnymeade and Simmons concurred: it could be done.

From the myriad of terms and limitations, Cabot's plan necessitated only one that caused outright resentment: crew members who would not be part of the ship's complement had to be effectively quarantined. Runnymeade bridled at the thought of his men being confined to their barracks by shore patrol for as long as eight days. Along with Simmons he offered a number of alternatives, but each one failed the ultimate test: given the importance of the mission and the safety of those who would be taking part in it, could Runnymeade guarantee, absolutely, that the men left behind would not, in any way, jeopardize the mission?

In the end both Runnymeade and Simmons concluded that quarantine was the only answer, no matter how distasteful.

The task of selecting the three hundred and fifty-eight men who would man the ship proved to be backbreaking. Cabot insisted that first to be chosen should be those who could do more than one job, so that there was no duplication of assignments. Runnymeade argued for the most experienced hands, who could be counted on to improvise if something went wrong. From the ship's hold strongboxes of dossiers were brought into the Captain's sea cabin and the already parsimonious quarters became even more cramped. Because of time constraints Cabot left the final selection up to Runnymeade and Simmons. He would approve the final roster but doubted he would have any quarrel with their choices. It was agreed that the crew would be confined to quarters during the loading of the ship.

Equally important was the matter of cargo storage. The one hundred twenty-four tons Cabot proposed to bring on board had to be distributed in such a way as to maximize the efficiency of the ship's operations. But the crates also had to be placed where, in the worst of all possible circumstances, the majority of them, if not all, could be jettisoned. Blueprints of *Victorious*'s interior were rolled out, the holds and storage compartments carefully examined.

Cabot would have stayed on had that been possible, but he had no reservations about leaving the remaining details to Runnymeade and Simmons. Both men were now part of Prometheus, and Cabot knew he couldn't have asked for two better officers.

The Royal Marine compound was in fact a temporary transportation pool built beside the Banbury Reservoir. An electrified barbwire fence defined the perimeter. The buildings themselves were a jumble of Quonset huts, which served as living quarters for the mechanics, and domes of corrugated steel, not unlike aircraft hangers, where Marine vehicles were stored and worked on. But the officer who was coming out of the guardhouse by the camp's gate was much more than a mechanic. Although his uniform identified him as a Marine major, the small inconspicuous flashes on either shoulder indicated he belonged to the elite: the Advance Strike Force.

"Mr. Cabot?" the officer asked as Cabot rolled down his window.

Cabot nodded and the Major, without comment, got into the car.

"That garage on the left, Sergeant," he said to the driver and turned to Cabot. "The name's Nesbitt, sir, Major Charles Nesbitt."

There was a soft Scottish burr to his words, as quiet and self-contained as the man himself appeared to be. Nesbitt was a big man, rawboned, with the muscular arms of a farmer. Although five years younger than Cabot, his face was deeply etched, the lines creasing skin that seemed perpetually tanned. According to his dossier, Nesbitt's last assignment had been in Palestine.

They drove straight into the depot, the doors rattling to a close behind them. There were over a hundred trucks inside, lined up in five rows, all ten-ton canvas-back diesel vehicles manufactured by Leyland and called, appropriately enough, Hippos.

"Major, you're in command of the First Royal Commando platoon, currently stationed at Hemmingford, outside London," Cabot said, following Nesbitt out of the car.

"I have that honor, sir, yes," Nesbitt replied tonelessly.

The locations of the commandos' training facilities and barracks were on the Restricted List, circulation limited to only the Chiefs of Staff, the Secret Intelligence Service and the Prime Minister's office. Cabot understood Nesbitt's reservations about an outsider being privy to such knowledge, no matter that it had been Churchill himself who had called upon the Major's cooperation.

"How many of your men can drive these vehicles?" Cabot asked him, indicating the Hippos.

"All of them, sir. They can also swim two miles with thirty pounds on their backs and hike through rough terrain for the better part of sixteen hours."

"They won't be called upon to do that," Cabot told him. "How long would it take a hundred of these same men to load one hundred twenty-four tons of crates onto those trucks?"

Cabot gave Nesbitt the dimensions of the boxes, adding: "There will be an overhead crane at their disposal, as well as pneumatic dollies."

"No more than eight hours, working at a steady pace," the officer replied.

"The work has to be done in six," Cabot said.

Nesbitt considered. "Yes, it's possible."

"And then if the same quantity had to be unloaded, within the space of, say, three hours, would they be able to handle that?"

"I've put them through worse paces," Nesbitt confirmed.

"I've drawn up another set of exercises for your men, Major," Cabot said, handing him a sheaf of papers. "You'll find a requisition order for twenty Hippos. You will drive these out tonight to Hemmingford. Within two days a dummy set of boxes will be delivered to you. As of then you will begin to put your men through the exercises outlined in these notes. Six hours is the cutoff point, Major. Every minute you can shave off that time will be of enormous value to this operation."

"Is the drill to be run indoors or out?" Nesbitt asked.

"Indoors. And one other point: once the trucks are in your possession, no one except your men is to go near them. Check them over after you take them out. Make certain every engine, drivetrain and suspension is checked."

"What about security, sir?" Nesbitt asked, placing the papers on one of the Hippos' massive front fenders.

"You'll need twenty-five men for that," Cabot said. "You might consider the possibility of rotating security teams, giving twenty-five at a time a rest while they handle security. But there must be a full complement of arms. I want every man to have his weapon ready during the transfer. Further details, such as the exact date, time, and location, will be given you in a few days. If you have any questions you can reach me at this number."

Cabot passed him a card with six digits and brought out his lighter. Even before the flame was up Nesbitt handed him back the card.

"I've only one question," Nesbitt said softly. "What is it we are really going to move, sir?"

"A king's ransom," Cabot said enigmatically, and watched as the flame began to eat into the paper.

Erik Guderian moved with the press of the crowd up the narrow subway stairwell and emerged at the point where Threadneedle Street intersects with Cornhill. On his right was the Royal Exchange; dead ahead, the Bank of England. Guderian did not notice the change in the traffic light, but instinctively followed the momentum of the other pedestrians, stepping off the curb and falling into the swift, measured pace that characterized the City walk. His eyes remained fixed on the door to the Bank, closed now, as solid as the stone slabs which sealed the tombs of the pharaohs. He remembered them from another time, almost another age, when, during his tenure with Krupp, he had walked through them and into the massive financial heart which circulated the patrimony of centuries of Empire. From five continents resources too vast to be imagined had poured into this edifice, been cleansed, converted and then sent out again so that even more might be brought back. It was, Guderian had thought then, a fitting monument to this nation of shopkeepers, who through the ages had patiently applied a glossy veneer of respectability over piracy, rapaciousness, theft and greed.

He walked along Threadneedle Street, brushing the limestone blocks of the façade, and turned down Bartholomew Lane, catching a glimpse of a stolid face behind the grille cut into the steel garage doors. Five years had elapsed since he had last spoken with either the Governor, Reginald Saint John Reading, or any one of the fourteen Directors, yet he saw their faces as clearly as though it had been only yesterday. Changes were few and far between where the Bank was concerned. Therein lay its strength, but also a weakness Guderian knew he could exploit. He had been on intimate terms with these men, broken bread with them and listened as liquor got the better of their tongues. But because they had all been gentlemen, belonged to the same clubs, were peers in the same profession, they had trusted him without reservation. It was a piece of stupidity that would cost them dearly.

He rounded the corner off Lothbury Street and was moving up Princes Street, taking care to stay by the side of the building. Even though the financial day was done, with the streets clogged with girls moving smartly along the sidewalks, their heels tapping out a staccato rhythm that reflected their haste. There were almost no young men—the brokers, traders, junior executives who would normally have been the traffic. They were gone now—or dead. In their place uniformed porters, rheumy-eyed and limping, hurried as best they could from office to office, sagging canvas bags bending already weak spines.

Reading, Guderian thought. He is the key to it all.

Guderian knew as much about the Bank's security as any man alive: the electronic devices in the vaults, the almost funereal ritual of transfer by armored truck, the presence of invisible but omnipresent young men who prowled the Bank corridors, alert for that one tiny clue which signaled chaos but which a mortal could not discern.

No, the Bank was impervious to a frontal assault and Guderian had not wasted a moment's consideration upon it. It was the man who had ultimate responsibility for what was stored therein, without whose cooperation and expertise Prometheus could not come to fruition, who was vulnerable: Reginald Saint John Reading.

More than a year ago, when he had sketched out the initial tentative outline for his assault on the Bank, Guderian had concluded that Reading had to be one of the key pivots upon which any transfer would turn. Logic dictated this: Reading alone was privy to *all* the information—how much bullion was on hand, how long it would take to gather together the negotiable securities from other City banks, the transport required, the option of routes, and finally, the arrangements that had to be concluded with Morganthau of the Federal Reserve for an orderly disbursement of the funds. To get to Reading meant penetrating the transfer in one fluid motion. And Guderian was certain he could do just that.

By the time he had tabled his proposal before Hitler, Guderian knew more about Reading than any other person alive. Abwehr, SS and independent sources in England and

Switzerland provided him with minutiae which, when pieced together, provided a composite of an assault plan upon the man. Not that Guderian had any intention of harming Reading, his wife of thirty-one years or his daughter, who had recently failed her midterm examinations at an exclusive boarding school. The whole object was to get close enough to Reading, by taking advantage of his habits, to unearth the exact moment when the Governor would have to have the transfer details in his possession. To strike at that precise instant without Reading's ever realizing that he had been victimized . . .

Knowing the Governor so intimately, Guderian understood this was possible. And had he been a man of lesser talents, blinded by the sheen of his own plan, Guderian might easily have missed the sudden opportunity that was thrust at him . . .

It was the car which first attracted his attention. Thinking back, Guderian realized it could scarcely have done otherwise. The fact that the vehicle was a Rolls-Royce was in itself exceptional, given the severe rationing imposed on gasoline used in private vehicles. But it was a vintage automobile, a 1932 Silver Ghost. Less than a hundred had been built, and there was probably only one with such an extravagant color scheme: the long hood was done completely in wasp yellow, the shade made all that more startling by the gleaming black lacquer that coated the massive fenders. The body panels were also done in yellow, with a black running board to highlight the gleaming chrome bordering a yellow trunk.

Guderian was back on Threadneedle Street. Without breaking stride he stepped closer to the curb, falling in behind a pair of secretaries hurrying along arm in arm. He had a direct line of view between their shoulders. The driver of the car had come around and was holding the door open for a short, silver-haired gentleman in uniform. The cuffs had one wide and three medium gold-lace rings with a curl on the uppermost. The shoulder straps were done in gold lace with a silver-embroidered crown, three eight-pointed stars ensigned by crossed baton and sword. The peak of the cap was embroidered in an oval of oak leaves. It was the uniform of a full admiral of the British Fleet.

Guderian dropped farther behind the two women. The officer glanced briskly at the traffic along the sidewalk, and, spying an opening, shot across toward the Bank steps. Guderian's gaze flitted toward the doors and he saw him: a man had slipped out and was standing on the threshold of the bronze portals, a tall, heavyset man who had moved into position like a shadow. The Admiral said something to him but the man did not reply. Instead, he stepped aside to let the officer pass, then glanced out onto Threadneedle Street, his gaze drifting across the pedestrians walking by. At that instant Guderian began moving as well. The man was watching for anyone stationary—surveillance which might have followed the officer and positioned itself near the Bank. Guderian swore he felt the eyes run by him, like a sudden cold current that flows under a swimmer's belly. When it passed, Guderian looked up and Jonathan Cabot had disappeared, the great bronze doors shimmering in the afternoon sunlight as though glazed with molten gold.

Erik Guderian caught up to the secretaries, who were waiting for the light to change, and crossed the street with them, moving into the shadow of the Royal Exchange. He buckled his coat tightly against a wind that suddenly had become cold and breathed deeply to still the fierce pounding of his heart against his chest.

Jonathan Baylor Cabot—American intelligence but related to no known division. The man who had caught Darius, Edward Pearce, and the agent Pearce had controlled, Leonard Frye . . . who had been Beth Davis's source. Cabot, who had unraveled the whole twisted skein.

I should have had you killed, Guderian thought furiously, wiping away the sheen of sweat from his forehead. I should have ordered Mr. Stanley to put the first bullet into you and to take Pearce with the second shot . . .

But at that time I believed you were a danger to me only through Pearce. Pearce had decided to break with the orders from Berlin. He had become renegade, unpredictable. So I took the most prudent course: I had had the threat to myself and my mission eliminated. I had believed the bullet would stop you as effectively as it had Pearce. With your chief of security dead, you had nothing more to investigate. The string was broken.

Then why was Cabot still here?

Did you come for something else? Were Frye and Pearce only *part* of your objective?

That has to be, because there is no other reason for a counterintelligence agent to remain in position after an operation . . .

The enormity of the realization sweeping over him was staggering.

Of course Cabot was still here! He, Guderian, had made the mistake of defining Cabot as counterintelligence because of his actions against Pearce. Once Cabot had been denied Pearce, Guderian thought the American would leave. But he hadn't. *Because Cabot had been on an offensive intelligence mission during the whole of that time*! Getting to and neutralizing Pearce had been only the first step, the mandatory groundwork, before the mission could begin.

A mission that had to do with, at least in part, an admiral of the British Fleet.

And the Bank of England.

Five city blocks away, the bells of St. Paul's sounded the hour. The door to the Bank of England remained locked. Erik Guderian had no idea how long Cabot and his visitor would remain sequestered inside. Within the hour the City offices would empty themselves of staff. The streets would become silent, a lone man sorely conspicuous. It was also possible that the two men would leave separately, using any one of a dozen exits.

Guderian started to walk along the square in front of the Exchange. All his discipline was required to keep his head down, avoid looking at the Bank. There were too many windows, too many unseen eyes that might be watching.

I cannot come after you! Guderian thought fiercely. As much as I yearn to do so, because you are the worst threat. I cannot follow where you now walk. The temptation itself is madness!

But the yellow Rolls-Royce . . . and the Admiral to whom it undoubtedly belonged, that was another matter.

As soon as he turned down King William Street, Guderian lifted his face to the wind. The blood ran furiously in his veins, and fear had been replaced by the cloying scent of a new path, barely discernible as yet but there nonetheless. Yes, there was much that remained unknown and time was working against him. But he firmly believed that Cabot had inadvertently handed him the key to victory. Guderian knew exactly what it was he would be looking for.

22

June 8 marked the fifth day of Private David Renny's stay at the Sacred Heart clinic. It was also the day of his discharge and he couldn't wait to get out.

David Renny remembered nothing of how he came to be at Sacred Heart. His last recollection was of a tent somewhere on the Dunkirk beach. His old sarge, Mackelhose, was leaning over him, shouting something, but Renny couldn't hear, not over all the screaming and gunfire around him, the flapping of the tent and sand that was blowing around him. A shell exploded, awfully close by the sounds of it. The earth heaved beneath him and he felt himself falling, screaming and falling into blackness . . .

Only to wake up in London. With his right arm and shoulder set in a cast that still smelled of fresh plaster and ointment. Renny had craned his head around, looking at the rows of beds opposite him, each with a wounded man in it, then up at the high ceiling with its ornate frescoes and large dusty chandeliers. He started to laugh softly, then began to sob as tears spilled from his eyes. By the time the sister arrived at his side he was asleep again.

Renny wished he had been able to sleep through his entire stay. The following day he was asked to vacate his bed. The evacuees from Dunkirk were still pouring in. His wound wasn't serious enough to warrant a bed and he was moved to the day lounge, where he spent the better part of the day sitting by the window looking down at the grime and soot of Waterloo Station across the road.

By the end of the third day David Renny had managed to badger the doctor into giving him an early discharge. He had called his mother, who lived in Notting Hill and wasn't even aware that her son had returned from France, and got her to come to Sacred Heart to sign the necessary papers. The tearful reunion was the sole highlight of Renny's convalescence. He had read every book in the sparse library collection. He tried to play cards with some of the other patients but found that one hand was simply not enough for poker. The constant noise of the hospital, the clatter of gurneys, the moaning and cries of patients, the ceaseless traffic of doctors and sisters in the halls, all conspired to rob him of sleep at night and peace of mind during the day. The worst of it was that his mum hadn't been able to get hold of Mackelhose. Renny was certain that if the old sarge could see what his unit member was going through he'd have him out of this pit in a flash.

At twelve noon Renny was in his usual seat at the window in the day room. The sisters were doling out a watery brown broth that was to pass for stew, clucking at the patients to eat up. The first couple of meals had come with biscuits which could be dipped into the soup, give a man something to chew on. Renny hadn't had bread since then, and the only meat was the faint taste from the soup bones.

A sister slid a bowl in front of him and dropped a mimeographed list of names, forty pages thick, beside it.

"Eat up, now." She smiled cheerfully and bustled over to the next poor victim.

Renny caught the odor steaming from the bowl and reached for the list instead. Across the top of the front page was written, in uneven type:

MISSING IN ACTION
IF YOU SAW ANY OF THESE MEN FALL OR BE RESCUED
PLEASE CALL THE NUMBER PROVIDED IMMEDIATELY.

David Renny had been reading the list carefully ever since it had appeared three days ago. He did so out of boredom and a twinge of conscience. If it hadn't been for the sarge and the other lads, his name and Lennon's could have ended up on that paper. So Renny began to move his finger down the first column of names, listed alphabetically, the soldier's unit placed alongside. He was through the Es before the sister came by and scolded him for not eating. Renny gulped down the broth, trying to taste as little of it as possible. As soon as he was done he went back to his reading.

The sun coming through the window made him sleepy but Renny persevered. He saw the name and heard the voice at the same time.

"Davey, you old sod, still lounging about, are you!"

Mackelhose swaggered his way through the room. His ham-fisted hand came down hard on Renny's good shoulder.

"Jesus, Sarge, you got to be careful!" Renny cried. "I can feel that on the other side too!"

"Aw, they're babying you, son!" Mackelhose boomed. "You're ready to get back to your old sarge, ain't ye?"

"My mum—"

"Sent me to take you home, lad. The old dear, bless her heart, managed to find me in spite of all that Army runaround. When I heard where you were and that you'd be getting out, I told her I'd look out for you. Just like in Dunkirk, eh, son?"

"Sarge, this name," Renny said, excited. "Yeah, this one here. Isn't that the fellow who shot up the Nazi car, the one we rode into Dunkirk?"

Mackelhose leaned over his shoulder and Renny smelled the rank odor of beer.

"Schiffer, Henry . . . Yeah, that was his name, all right."

"And he was Royal Artillery, right, Sarge?"

"Yeah," Mackelhose said, straightening up. "I remember the flashes. A piece of luck that we ran into him when we did. Saved us a hell of a walk, that boyo did."

"Did he come off with us?" Renny asked.

"No, he helped get you and Lennon into the shelters, then made a run for it. I remember seeing him heading for the water. There was a CMB not too far off, taking on whoever swam close enough."

"That means he made it!" Renny exclaimed. "He ain't MIA!"

"Whoa, son," Mackelhose said. "I didn't say I saw him reach the boat. Last I knew he was swimming for it. Matter of fact I thought him a bit of a bastard, running off like that. Figured he should have stayed with us, seeing as how we came all that way together."

"I don't know if I can blame him, Sarge," Renny said. "Like you say, he helped us out a lot. Lennon probably wouldn't have made it without the ride. And me . . . Sarge, do me a favor, would you? Call the number. Tell whoever it is that . . . Schiffer, yeah, that he's alive."

"Sure, Davey, I'll do just that—as soon as I get you to your mum," Mackelhose grinned.

But Renny knew his sergeant better than that. Mackelhose

was the most unselfish man alive as far as he was concerned. There wasn't anything he wouldn't do for his men. But strangers were another matter.

"Sarge," Renny said quietly, "my mum didn't know I was alive until I called her from this place. Not the doctors or the fucking Army gave any thought to the poor woman. Maybe somewhere Schiffer's mum is waiting to hear. Maybe they've already told her he's MIA. But if he is alive think of what it would mean to her . . ."

Mackelhose looked down at his private, at the pleading eyes, and saw how much this meant to the boy.

"All right, I promise I'll call as soon as we get you home," he said.

"My mum doesn't have a phone," Renny told him. "She has to use the landlady's. Please, Sarge, it will only take a minute."

"Sweet Jesus!" Mackelhose sighed. "We'll do it for the mums of the world. You get to your room or wherever it is they've stored your stuff. I want to see you ready to move out when I'm through."

"Thanks, Sarge," Renny said.

"I'm a prince, lad," Mackelhose laughed as he walked away. "This'll only take a minute."

But Sergeant Mackelhose was wrong. He dialed the number and spoke to a woman he imagined to be some luscious young thing at some central registry. Millicent Balfour, who had the voice of a nightingale, took Mackelhose's name, Army number, the person he was calling about and where the call was originating from.

"You will remain exactly where you are, Sergeant," she said crisply.

"Now listen here, woman," Mackelhose started in on her. "I've a mate who I have to take home."

"Was he present with you when this soldier, Schiffer, was last seen?"

"Yes, but—"

"Fine, then bring him along."

"You don't understand!" Mackelhose shouted.

"No, Sergeant, it is *you* who are laboring under misconceptions," Millicent Balfour said icily. "This is a Security Service matter. Two representatives and transportation will be at the Sacred Heart in a matter of a few minutes. They will expect to find you waiting at the front door. Should you *not* be there I personally will have your balls for bullocks. Do I make myself clear, Sergeant?"

Mackelhose was so mortified by the language that all he could do was stare wonderingly at the receiver in his hand.

Mackenzie McConnell had been ready to call it a day when the redoubtable Miss Balfour told her that the Security Service would be bringing in a Sergeant Mackelhose. Mackenzie groaned inwardly but thanked the librarian and wearily reached for the latest MIA figures delivered by Whitehall courier only a few minutes earlier.

Since she had started her search for the man who did not yet exist, the distinction between day and night had blurred. Mackenzie found herself going home at two or three in the morning, only to wake up from a restless sleep four hours later. After a cold shower she would head back to that Whitehall basement and start in on the latest MIA sheets. Or else Millicent Balfour would spot her and hand her a list of soldiers who had called in with a report but who couldn't leave their beds. In the last four days Mackenzie had been to every London hospital she had ever heard of—and some of the new temporary clinics. Each visit ended with another soldier being identified as dead.

Of those dozen or so who were alive, none had been placed on the suspect list. The man Mackenzie McConnell was seeking would have to be highly mobile. The men she visited were either bedridden by their injuries or had broken arms or legs. Nevertheless each injury was checked out and the file not closed until the physician of record had attested to it.

So it went on, the running, the interviewing, the wading through the horror which Dunkirk had washed upon the city. Moments were snatched to have something to eat, to sleep a few hours, before the conscience nagged one back to reality one never really escaped from . . .

"They've arrived, Mackenzie. Security is bringing them down now."

Mackenzie McConnell looked up and smiled. She couldn't have done without Robert Ogilvy either.

He had come back on active duty three days ago although his convalescence had been deemed indefinite. At first, Mackenzie admitted she had been shocked at the sight of him. The surgeons had done the best they could during the first operation.

The glass and metal splinters were removed, the cuts cleaned and sutured and bandages applied. But as the swelling went down and the dressing was removed, the scars began to show—deep, red, inverted welts across both cheeks, a grotesque parody of Heidelberg dueling scars. Across the forehead ran a ridge of sutures that pinched the skin, turning it into a deathly white color.

Ogilvy had had himself discharged at the first possible opportunity. He met with Mackenzie, convinced her he was ready to get back to work and refused to leave until she acquiesced. Mackenzie had been reluctant, but she understood that a man like Robert would only waste away doing nothing. In a way she owed him the chance. She discussed the research operation with him, using the half-truth of a German agent who had slipped into England during the Dunkirk evacuation, and found Ogilvy eager to help. But it was the fact that not once did he refer to the ugly words spoken between them at the hospital that convinced her. Perhaps he had accepted the inevitable. If so, he was too valuable an agent not to use.

"Have you heard from Cabot?" Ogilvy asked, sliding onto the edge of her desk.

"No, I haven't."

Curious, she had just been thinking about Jonathan herself. She had called Downing Street a few times, but the operator who rang the number said no one was answering. Mackenzie knew she had only to identify herself and Cabot would be found wherever he was. But not for matters of the heart . . . God, how she missed him!

She was wondering if the conversation was going to take a bitter twist when there was a knock on the door.

"Here they come now," Ogilvy said.

They were an odd couple—the young, slim man with a grotesque cast on the left shoulder and the beefy, older sergeant whose stomping echoed throughout the Archives. The security escorts handed Mackenzie a slip of paper and withdrew.

"Sergeant Mackelhose?" she called out.

"That's me," he growled.

"And you're Private Renny?"

"Yes, ma'am."

"Perhaps you'd care to sit down, Private," Mackenzie said. "You'll be more comfortable that way."

"He'd be more comfortable at home, in a bed," Mackelhose retorted, "where he belongs."

The welts on Ogilvy's cheeks reddened as his eyes bored into Mackelhose's.

"We have no quarrel with that, Sergeant," he said icily. "And the faster we get through here the quicker he'll go home."

Mackelhose dropped into a chair and tugged out a tin of cigarettes.

"It's about Schiffer, right?" he said.

"Since Private Renny recognized the name, perhaps he should be the one to tell us about Schiffer," Mackenzie suggested.

"Eh, ma'am," Renny stuttered, "If–if it's all the s—same, I'd rather the sergeant tell you. You see, I just recognized the name. But it was Sergeant Mackelhose who first saw him."

"Is that true, Sergeant?"

"Yes, it is, ma'am." Mackelhose nodded. "But before we go any further, I think the boy and I got a right to know what this is all about."

"This is all about ascertaining exactly who should or should not be listed as an MIA," Mackenzie replied crisply.

"I'll bet," Mackelhose breathed.

"Do you think we can get on with it now, Sergeant?"

"All right. Not that I know all that much, you understand."

As it turned out, Mackelhose had a fine eye for detail and a memory to support it. He talked for the better part of a half hour, stopping only to light a cigarette. His narrative began with the incident at the Nazi scout car where he first saw Schiffer and ended with the Dunkirk sequence where he watched the corporal swimming toward the CMB.

"Do you agree with everything the sergeant has told us?" Mackenzie asked Renny.

"Yes, ma'am!" the blond private said enthusiastically, "except that I didn't see Schiffer in the water, seein' as how I was already in the tent."

"All right," Mackenzie said, looking back at Mackelhose. "You said Schiffer was a Canadian, right?"

"That I did," Mackelhose said sagely.

Mackenzie gestured toward Ogilvy and whispered, "See what's holding up Miss Balfour on Schiffer's file."

"Can you describe him to me, Sergeant?"

"He was a good-looking man, I suppose," Mackelhose mused. "Older than anyone I ever met with that rank. Said he was a schoolteacher so I guess that made sense . . . being drafted at the last minute as it were. Strong fellow, tall, dirty-blond hair, narrow nose, tight mouth. Gray eyes, if I recall rightly. Yeah, gray."

"Any identifying marks?"

"No, I don't think so . . ."

Ogilvy returned and sat on the desk with his back to the two soldiers.

"She doesn't have the records here," he said softly. "All the Commonwealth soldiers' files are up at the Earls Court depot. Balfour is ringing them now."

"Get a team over there now," Mackenzie told him. "I want that file down here as quickly as possible."

"Something?"

"I don't know," Mackenzie said slowly. "Something's not right and I can't put my finger on it."

"Stay with it," Ogilvy advised her. "I've seen that famous intuition of yours at work before."

"Either that or I'm bone-tired and imagining things," Mackenzie muttered.

She turned back to Mackelhose. "Sergeant, you're sure of the date, May 28."

"It's not one you'd forget, would you—when you managed to get your arse out of Dunkirk?"

"And you're equally certain it was a CMB he was swimming for?"

"I've seen enough of those in my time, ma'am."

"All right, Sergeant," Mackenzie said wearily, too tired to fight the rudeness any longer. "We have your unit's location and Private Renny's address. If we need anything more we'll call on you."

"Still don't trust us to say what it's all about then?" Mackelhose said bitterly.

"MIAs, Sergeant. All we're trying to do is take a little of the uncertainty out of some people's lives. *That's all.*"

When the two soldiers had gone Ogilvy returned with Millicent Balfour.

"It's a *most* curious development," the archivist said. "The records at Earls Court have been checked and the one pertaining to a Corporal Henry Schiffer has been removed."

"By whom?" Mackenzie asked instantly.

"Well, that's the odd thing about it," Miss Balfour said. "It seems that the corporal appeared with authorization to check the records of two members of his unit who were killed at Dunkirk. He wanted to write a personal note to the boys' parents. At the same time he removed his own file."

"But how could he do that?" Mackenzie cried.

"Now, miss, I trained the boys and girls at Earls Court myself," Millicent Balfour admonished her. "They wouldn't let anyone into the archives without proper authorization."

"Whose was it?" Ogilvy asked quietly.

"A Colonel Blake here at Whitehall," Miss Balfour said triumphantly. "I took the liberty of calling him myself. He indeed gave the corporal authorization to remove his dossier and bring it to the Colonel's office."

"Did the Colonel say why?" Mackenzie demanded.

"Apparently Corporal Schiffer is to be decorated for exceptional bravery while under fire," Miss Balfour announced as though she were making the presentation then and there. "He saved an entire boatload of wounded off Dunkirk."

"Good morning," Guderian said amiably. "Can I help you?"

His smile didn't falter even though every instinct in him screamed out warning.

The man standing in the doorway of the gatehouse wore the uniform of a Navy lieutenant. He was in his mid-twenties, quite thin, with reddish-brown hair, a ginger mustache and green eyes that were wide in surprise. A slow blush was spreading over both cheeks—a combination of embarrassment and fear, Guderian guessed.

"I'm here to see Lady Christine," Andrew Simmons said stiffly, not bothering to introduce himself.

Guderian stepped to one side, reaching for his coat and swinging it over his shoulders.

"She'll be out in a minute—" he started to say.

"Henry, have you gone yet?" Her voice carried clearly from the kitchen.

"There's someone at the door for you," Guderian called out.

Christine Harloch came out, wiping her hands on a dish towel. She hesitated for a fraction of a second, her lips forming a silent O, then marched straight up to the visitor and embraced him lightly, offering him her cheek.

"Andrew, what a pleasant surprise!" she exclaimed. "It's been ages!"

She turned, almost pirouetted, on one foot, placing herself between the two men.

"You've met Corporal Henry Schiffer," she said brightly. "Henry, this is Lieutenant Simmons, an old and dear friend of mine."

"Pleased to meet you," Simmons muttered.

"Likewise," Guderian said easily and stepped over the threshold. "Well, I must be off. I'll see you later, Christine . . . ?"

There was the hint of a question in his words.

"Yes, Henry, do . . ." she replied, flustered.

Before she could say anything more, Guderian was gone. The door closed behind him.

"I do hope I wasn't intruding," Andrew Simmons said.

His tone was sharper than he had intended.

Christine regarded him silently, then said calmly, "I was just making tea. Please sit down. I'll be back in a minute."

"May I use the facilities?"

"Of course," she called back from the kitchen. "You know where they are."

Damn him! Christine thought, on the verge of tears, as she rattled the cups and saucers. Why did he have to come *now*?

In truth she had forgotten all about Andrew since meeting Henry and suddenly felt quite ashamed. She had known Andrew since they had been children. They belonged to the same set, shared identical backgrounds, amused the same people when seen together . . . people who took it for granted that one day, as surely as there is an England, Andrew Simmons and Christine Harloch would become husband and wife.

And if the war hadn't come along, Christine thought, carrying a laden tray into the dining room, that's exactly what would have happened by now. It never could now.

Not that Andrew was an ogre. Far from it. He was a considerate, gentle man who had never shown her anything other than kindness. But never love, for perhaps he was still too young to allow that to come forth. Or else it had been bred out of him like other raw, primeval emotions the upper classes had no use for. There had been a time when she would have accepted his offering, play her role as a complement to his own, because she too had been weaned on the same thin millet. But not now.

Not since the crucible of Spain. Not since she discovered the delectable, flagrant, yes, even obscene, passion in the arms of Henry Schiffer.

"Is he staying here with you?"

The question was spoken so quietly, in such a dead monotone, that it startled her. Andrew walked across the pegged boards and sat opposite her, his back ramrod stiff, eyes on the condiments.

"Henry has the spare bedroom," she replied. "He was wounded at Dunkirk, Andrew. He saved a boatload of soldiers and sank a German ship in the process. They're going to give him a medal . . ."

She smiled faintly. "He's Canadian and he doesn't have anyone here . . ."

Andrew Simmons sat back in his chair, regarding the woman he loved and knew he was losing. He had seen a man's kit in the bathroom, but that wasn't what gave it away. There was a rank odor in this house, a smell particular to two people, an odor of intimacy, all-knowing, consuming. He knew he could press her with questions and she would tell him what he wanted to know. Christine had changed that way. She had learned to speak her mind, defend her thoughts and actions, question the need for apologies or shame. In the end, he didn't want to know.

"I came by to remind you about the party," Andrew Simmons said. His voice seemed very faint to him. He could scarcely hear it over the pounding of blood at his temples. He heard her reply that she remembered.

"Yes, that's right," he heard himself say. "I'll fetch you at two o'clock."

He was on his feet, his back to her, walking toward the door. His hand was on the cut-glass knob when he turned around, fully expecting her to have materialized by his side, her arm on his, coaxing him to come back. But Christine hadn't moved. She remained seated at the table, smiling at him, her eyes bright, glistening. Whatever she was saying, Andrew Simmons heard not a word. He raised his arm in a feeble salute and fled out the door.

The yellow Rolls-Royce was exactly where Erik Guderian had thought it would be: in a reserved parking space next to the wide steps that led into the Admiralty headquarters. The presence of the car determined what happened next.

At half past nine Guderian was invited into Commander Rawlins's office. The Navy officer who had been present when Guderian first regained consciousness after Dunkirk was sorting out the morning's paperwork, but insisted Guderian take a cup of tea with him. Guderian listened patiently as Rawlins carried on about the arrangements being drawn up for the awards ceremony, searching for that one lapse in the monologue to get a word in edgewise. It came when Rawlins stoked his pipe. Quickly Guderian asked the Commander whether he might have a copy of the official commendation letter. He had already written to his parents in Canada saying he was all right, but if he could post a copy of the letter . . . well, they would be thrilled, probably send it to the local newspaper.

Rawlins grasped the implication immediately and thought it a splendid idea. Twenty minutes later Guderian left the Commander's bureau with not only an official copy but a short note to Schiffer's parents from Rawlins himself. He destroyed the latter in the men's washroom before leaving the building.

The Rolls-Royce was still there. Guderian paused on the steps to adjust his splint, which he had carefully affixed after leaving the gatehouse, then proceeded past the Royal Marine sentries and out the gates onto Whitehall. He waited for a break in traffic, walked swiftly across the wide boulevard to a vendor's cart situated not too far from the Horse Guards. He bought a cup of tea he had no intention of drinking and sat down on the small ledge that jutted out from the foundation of the Treasury Office. From this vantage point he saw the front half of the yellow Rolls-Royce.

There had been several options open to him. He could have mentioned noticing the car to Rawlins who, given his loquacity, might have been forthcoming about its owner. But in spite of his cheerful dullness, Rawlins was not a stupid man. If asked later on he might remember who it was who had expressed an interest in the car.

The same was true of the Marine sentries, to whom the car was undoubtedly a familiar sight. Guderian wore his arm splint like a badge, and it would earn him a degree of sympathy. But again, someone might remember a casual inquiry later on . . . at precisely the wrong moment.

So for thirty minutes he waited on the opposite side of

Whitehall, thinking about the unexpected complication that had arisen this morning.

Andrew Simmons was not Christine's lover, he was certain of that. The boy was too keen, too raw. But he was a suitor, an anxious one, of long standing, who had come across another male on territory he considered his exclusive preserve. Nor was the man a fool. If Christine didn't tell him Guderian was staying with her, Simmons would deduce that for himself. Which meant that Corporal Henry Schiffer had made an enemy for himself, someone who might take it upon himself, whether for his own purposes or on behalf of a lady's virtue, to make inquiries about a stranger, an interloper. Christine would have to tell him all about Andrew Simmons . . .

The vendor had moved farther down Whitehall, toward Westminster, and Guderian returned to his post by the Treasury Office. Given the traffic that swirled around him, he was not concerned about someone spotting a lone, wounded soldier sitting alone. There were too many wounded men to make a difference.

When Big Ben sounded twelve, Guderian moved.

He recognized the driver first, an older man of medium height with a distinct limp to his left leg. By the time Guderian was halfway across Whitehall, the driver had disappeared around the car. Caught with oncoming traffic to his right, Guderian waited, catching glimpses of the great car being maneuvered to the foot of the steps.

The driver got out, came around the grillwork and stood by the passenger door. As Guderian ran across the cobblestones of Whitehall he saw an officer—not the Admiral who had ridden in the car yesterday—come down the steps and speak to the driver. The officer handed him a small package. The driver shrugged and limped back around the car.

Guderian was well back along the sidewalk as the gates were drawn back. He saw a flash of yellow as the car rolled toward the slight bump between the sidewalk and the lot. The driver glanced right, hands turning the wheel, a look of impatience on his features at the three women who slipped across his right of way. Thinking that only a blind man or fool would fail to notice the gleaming carriage, the driver depressed the accelerator, feeding enough momentum to the wheels to climb the slight ridge.

At that instant Guderian stepped forward, awkwardly, as

though he had been pushed from behind. The massive curved fender smashed squarely into his hip, spinning him around. He heard cries as he struggled to regain his balance. His good arm shot out, flailing widely, but the momentum was too great and he fell heavily to the concrete. The ugly black tires of the Rolls-Royce squealed to a halt only inches before his face.

"Good Christ, didn't ye see where you were going!"

He felt hands clamped on his good arm, pulling him away. The driver was beside him, kneeling, throwing an arm under his good shoulder.

"Can ye stand up, son?" he was saying, the bearded face flushed, gray eyes half-angry, half-fearful.

"I'm—I'm all right," Guderian stammered. "It was all my fault, wasn't watching where I was going!"

Two Marine sentries had run out of the lot and were pushing back the gawkers. Another shouldered his way through the crowd toward the driver.

"You hurt, son?" he bawled.

Guderian slipped his hand off the driver's shoulder, putting his full weight on his left leg. He took a couple of experimental steps and winced.

"Nothing broken." He grinned. "There'll be one hell of a bruise, though."

"You didn't see him, sir?" the Marine sergeant asked the driver.

Guderian noticed the crossed foul anchors ensigned by a crown on the driver's upper sleeve. The uniform of a petty officer.

"Came out of nowhere, sor." The driver shook his head. "Mercy that I wasn't travelin' at speed."

He passed the sergeant his identity papers.

"Admiral Runnymeade's vehicle," the sergeant stated.

"Exactly, sor."

The Marine looked over at Guderian.

"I'll be needing some identification from you as well."

Guderian dug into his breast pocket, careful to hand over both his Army pass and the commendation letter. As he hoped, the Marine read both.

"You almost ran down a bleedin' 'ero," he said to the driver, handing him the letter.

"The good Lord have mercy, sor," the driver intoned. "If the Admiral was to have seen this . . ."

"Look, there's no harm done," Guderian said, taking back his papers.

"But your shoulder, Corporal!" the driver exclaimed.

"It's fine," Guderian assured him. "Officer . . ."

"Hinkley, sor," the driver said promptly. "Albert Hinkley, Royal Navy retired, at your service."

"If there's nothing more, then I suggest you move your vehicle off the sidewalk," the Marine sergeant said.

He called out to his men to return to their posts, the incident already fading from his mind.

"Sor, it's against regulations, but I do have liberties with the vehicle," Hinkley was saying. "May I offer to drive you wherever it is you may be going? If you don't mind riding in the front seat, that is—"

Suddenly the retired Petty Officer groaned.

"Lord love a duck! The damn bottles!"

Guderian looked inside and saw two shattered bottles of claret lying in the footwell. Gingerly Hinkley picked up a large piece of glass and checked the label.

"Ah, it's all right!" he said, obviously relieved. "There's more where this came from."

"I'm awfully sorry," Guderian murmured. "Is it expensive wine?"

"The very best, sor," Hinkley said proudly. "The Admiral hosts a ship's supper before sailing date. Mercifully, that is four days away. Don't you worry, these can be replaced. Are you sure I can't run you somewhere?"

"You're very kind." Guderian smiled. "But my appointment is just up the street. And I do apologize about the wine . . ."

"Not to worry, sor," the Petty Officer said, relieved nonetheless.

As he moved off, his arm raised in a half-salute, Guderian considered how much more he might have learned about Admiral Runnymeade had he taken Hinkley up on his offer. And he would have, had the Petty Officer's destination been any other than Threadneedle Street. The Bank of England was where he had glimpsed the man whose path he dared not cross. Besides, Guderian considered, there was a great deal to be done now and time seemed to be spinning out faster and faster.

He had not set foot in the Reading Room of the British Museum since his days at Cambridge, almost twenty years ago. Yet the instant Erik Guderian walked through the double doors it was as though he had been there only yesterday.

The scent was the most familiar thing: a cloying mixture of aging leather, dehydrating paper and decades of yellow wax that had worked its way into the wormy floorboards. He had chanced to smell such an odor only once before, when he had examined a piece of papyrus from the Morgan Collection. Here it emanated from walls that held over five and a half million volumes. The reading desks were as he remembered them: slanting boards with a short bookcase at the top, inkwell on the right, a narrow hard bench with barely room enough for one to shift one's buttocks and not bump the neighbor. He walked along the outermost of a hundred concentric rings of desks, fingertips brushing the ancient wood, feeling the scars that millions of students, scholars and passers-through had left as their testimonial. The only difference was the supreme quiet, different from the silence of the past when a thousand bodies were packed in beneath the dome. Today he counted barely a hundred, most of them old men or girls, researchers from one or the other Ministry.

Guderian draped his coat over a bench, looked around a final time and set to work.

From the central desk he received the old-fashioned nib pen familiar to every European schoolboy and two sheets of gray, squared paper. He crossed over to the reference section and pulled the latest volume of Who's Who. Returning to his desk, he quickly found the half-page devoted to Admiral Runnymeade, scanned the biographical details and carefully penned two facts which seemed to be the most promising starting points. He returned the Who's Who to its proper place and searched out the *Navy Club Journal*.

The car is the key!

As Guderian suspected, Runnymeade was very much a private man. During his thirty-year association with the Navy Club he had never held an elected office. His contributions to charities and worthwhile causes had been generous but not overly so given his rank at the time. He remained a studious bachelor and had, as one writer editorialized, "a single, all-consuming passion: The devilish automobile!" Guderian placed the *Navy Club Journal*s to one side and went in search of the Rolls-Royce Owners Association yearbooks.

Two hours later both sides of the grainy papers were filled in

Guderian's small, careful script. The information in the year-books exceeded what he had hoped to find. Admiral Runnymeade was more than an aficionado of the motor car. His collection included over a dozen specimens of the marque. Some, like the first Rolls ever assembled, were on loan to museums. Others remained in storage at his country estate in East Anglia, where, as the writer of the article took pains to point out, "the drive material consists not of gravel or other stone but of crushed meteorite to eliminate the raising of dust and other debris as the cars are driven over it."

From this source Guderian also learned how Runnymeade could have afforded such a hobby, given the Navy's parsimonious wages. The answer lay in a series of photographs of Runnymeade's sister and her husband, who was a director of the Westminster Bank. The Admiral's inheritance, excluding the East Anglia and London properties, had been a half-million pounds, and he had been quite content to allow his brother-in-law to handle his finances while he was in the service of the Crown. Given the returns, the hobby of car collecting was not in the least extravagant.

At half past five the porter stopped by Guderian's bench to inform him the Room would be closing in thirty minutes. Dutifully Guderian went about replacing all the journals, but suddenly stopped when he had one of the yearbooks in his hand. Quickly he flipped through the pages to a photograph that had caught his attention: Runnymeade on the front lawn of his estate with two cars behind him and a complement of ship officers on either side. Guderian placed the yearbook aside and checked the latest social register in which Runnymeade's sister was featured. The picture was almost identical in composition. There were the two cars and some thirty officers in Navy uniform. But the automotive yearbook had no caption to its photograph. The one in the register did.

The words leaped off the page, slamming into his consciousness. If these connections were truly valid and not some spoor he had mistaken for a true path, then he had come far closer to Prometheus than he dared believe possible.

"Sir . . . time, I'm afraid."

Guderian nodded and quickly filed the remaining references. He had taken a half day to come this far. Still, it wasn't enough. He would have to return and go through the National Historical Register, the Bible of England's grand homes.

But when? Guderian thought as he bade the porter good night. There was another vital factor to be looked after, and he didn't know how long that would take.

The wind nipped at the seams of his coat as he stepped into the leaden afternoon, the noise from the traffic raucous after the peace within the reading room. The margin for error had narrowed to almost nothing. Because somewhere across the city Jonathan Baylor Cabot had set a clock in motion whose time Guderian had to abide by. . . . If in fact he had correctly deciphered Cabot's countdown.

Yet, as he walked across Russell Square, another figure huddling in the crowds, he felt the surge of victory, the unerring belief that he had already targeted the quarry.

23

B y the time Robert Ogilvy returned with the third pot of tea the afternoon light had fled from the office at Queen Anne's Gate. He set the tray on the corner of the desk, leaned across and switched on the light.

Mackenzie McConnell sat back, startled.

"You're going to ruin yourself if you keep going like that," Ogilvy said.

Mackenzie rubbed her eyes with her fingertips.

"I've been through this damn file the better part of a dozen times," she said, stifling a yawn. "And I'm no closer to what I want to find than I was before."

Ogilvy handed her a cup. "Perhaps because there's nothing to find," he suggested. "Over and above what's in there . . . the obvious."

"Christ, Robert, I just don't know anymore," Mackenzie muttered, pushing away an overflowing ashtray.

"You know what I mentioned about your intuition," Ogilvy said, sitting down in a chair opposite her desk. "I've seen it work miracles. But I also recall times when it was wrong. Then you had the good sense to admit as much and not beat your head against the wall."

Mackenzie sipped her tea and stared into the wisps of steam as though trying to divine their meaning.

"I've tried to let it go, Robert," she said quietly. "I've picked up half a dozen other MIA cases—we've solved every one. But this one keeps coming back like a ghost from an unquiet grave."

"But it's *not* an MIA case!" Ogilvy objected. "For God's sakes, Henry Schiffer is alive and quite well in London, thank you very much!"

She knew his exasperation was justified. In the last thirty-six hours Ogilvy had been her eyes, mouth and legs, moving from one point of London to another gathering every scrap of information that was available on Corporal Henry Schiffer. But the question remained unanswered: of all the units that had returned from Dunkirk, why was there no information *at all* on the fate of the other men in Schiffer's unit?

Other units had been decimated, but from each there were at least several survivors whose accounts tallied to form a clear picture of what had taken place. But this was not the case with the Royal Artillery soldiers manning the searchlights at the Citadel in Calais.

Ogilvy had begun his inquiry at the source: Whitehall, and the office of Colonel Blake, who had had Schiffer's file brought over from the Archives office at Earls Court. At first the Colonel had been more than willing to discuss the matter of Corporal Schiffer. He had waxed long and eloquent on the upcoming ceremony at which the Canadian soldier would be honored, expounding on the details of the propaganda campaign that was quickly taking shape. Ogilvy listened politely, then asked for Schiffer's file. The Colonel's jovial attitude dissolved quickly when Ogilvy refused to tell him why the Security Service was interested in Schiffer. It became glacial when Ogilvy invoked the Service's authority to requisition the file whether or not the Colonel wished to part with it.

Having delivered the file to Queen Anne's Gate, Ogilvy searched out supplementary material. From the University of London records he brought back Schiffer's academic records and letters of reference from Canada. At St. Simon's hospital he met with Dr. Bacal, received written authorization to pull

Schiffer's medical records and procure the same from the clinic at Berkeley Square. It was at Berkeley Square that Ogilvy also learned, from some chitchat with the head matron, about Schiffer's affair with Christine Harloch.

"He certainly didn't waste any time, did he?" Mackenzie McConnell commented.

"The man's a hero." Ogilvy shrugged and dropped yet another report on her desk. "From the commander of the CMB which had taken Schiffer off Dunkirk. Read all about it."

She did—several times over, especially the official transcripts of Schiffer's account of his last hours at Calais.

But it was, Mackenzie reflected, only one-sided. There was still no corroborating testimony as to what had happened at Calais. Mackenzie had raised the idea of bringing Schiffer in but had met with resistance.

"I'll do it, if you like," Ogilvy had told her. "It's not as though we don't know where he is. But our inquiries have already ruffled a few feathers."

"You don't think he'd be able to give us anything new?"

"Not a damn thing." Ogilvy shook his head. Then he added: "I feel you're beginning to look upon Schiffer as a suspect. Why I haven't any idea. But that could be the wrong tangent to go off on. If you want to find out what happened at Calais there's only one person who can tell you that: the unit commander, Lieutenant Clarke. The only problem there is that Clarke is in a mental hospital . . ."

That was where the conversation had ended then. Mackenzie returned to her notes and files and spent the whole day going through them. She even went out to Berkeley Square on her lunch break, but there hadn't been anyone at the coach house.

Mackenzie rose and drew the curtains, leaning against the windowsill, her arms folded across her breasts. She wished to God she could talk this out with Cabot, but he was still sequestered at the Bank of England.

"All right," she said at last. "Let me play out the final hand and if nothing comes of it, I'll gracefully retire."

"Which means?"

"That I'm going to see Clarke at the mental hospital, as you so elegantly phrase it."

"Oh, Lord!" Ogilvy exclaimed. "You've seen the reports, Mackenzie. The man's insane! He hasn't said a reasonable word since he was brought in there."

"Maybe that's so because no one has asked him the right questions," Mackenzie said slowly."

St. Joseph's Hospital for the Emotionally Disabled was a red-brick Victorian pile built at the turn of the century, when the Shoreditch area of London was still considered country. Standing at the end of Worship Street, its five acres of grounds had been whittled away to less than one. The hospital was in fact a charity ward, administered by Franciscans. Since it was not a wealthy order, the Franciscans depended as much on the archdiocese of London for financial support as on individual contributors. In recent years both sources proved scarcely adequate. With the outbreak of war and especially since the evacuation at Dunkirk the facilities of St. Joseph's had become severely strained.

"You see, Miss McConnell, no one anticipated how terrible the effect of a first battle would be on our young men," Brother Terence was saying as he led her along a corridor whose tiles might once have been white but were now gray and over which lay an odor of disinfectant so strong it burned her nostrils.

Brother Terence, a monk of forty who had both nurse's training and three years of psychoanalytic study to his credit, was responsible for those he called "the silent ones."

"People forgot very quickly about the thousands of cases of shell-shock that were brought home during and after the Great War," the monk continued. "We've been caring for some of these poor souls for over twenty years. And this time, if Dunkirk is any harbinger of what we can expect, matters will be far worse."

"Why is that?" Mackenzie McConnell asked him.

"Because no one in the Armed Forces tells the young men the truth," Brother Terence answered sadly. "All the posters show brilliant young men in heroic postures. The Army drill instills a sense of awe and exultation in the young. Day after day after day history is cannibalized for its glories and presented as though this were all there is to war. No one speaks of the terror, Miss McConnell, that awesome fear which erupts when a soldier watches the man next to him fall or feels the bullet in himself and realizes, so much to his surprise, that he is mortal.

"And that is only the beginning. Young men, Miss McConnell, were forced to make decisions which other young men died because of. That's when their courage deserted them—not because they saw themselves as cowards but because their actions caused death. It was not their fault, yet others, their superiors, made it so.

"So where were these to run if one survived while others perished? Only madness. That is their final refuge."

"How many men, 'silent ones,' do you have here?" Mackenzie asked him.

"Over five hundred," the monk said sadly.

Brother Terence stopped before an iron door and selected a key from his ring.

"We took in only as many as we could decently care for. Here each man has his own cell, small to be sure, but clean and quiet. He isn't forced to mingle with others. Every day I can look in on him, spend a half hour, perhaps forty minutes, trying to coax a phrase or sentence, even a single word, out of him. Sometimes I succeed, most often I do not."

Brother Terence was about to pull back the door when Mackenzie laid a hand on his arm.

"Lieutenant Clarke . . . ?"

"I thank God that at last his screaming has stopped," the monk said. "Because it wasn't really screaming but howling, like that of some demented soul struggling to climb out of Lucifer's well. When Lieutenant Clarke was brought here he was raving about the massacre of his men. I learned from the authorities that he was the only survivor. There is so much guilt within that poor man . . ."

"Is Clarke quiet now?" Mackenzie asked.

"I treated him with drugs almost constantly," Brother Terence said. "Otherwise he would have injured himself. Now it's exactly the opposite: He's retreated into himself. He doesn't talk to me during my visits, but I know he understands what I'm saying. With time, patience . . . love, he may become whole again."

"Brother Terence, I have to talk to him about Calais," Mackenzie said urgently. "There are details I must have, questions I need answered."

The monk regarded her steadily. "You realize what you could do to him if you tear open that scar."

"Believe me, I have no choice," Mackenzie told him.

"I know I cannot go against your authority," Brother

Terence said. "I'm only asking if you have settled this matter with your own conscience."

"I doubt if I'll ever be able to do that," Mackenzie said softly. "But I have something to offer him: Lieutenant Clarke wasn't the only survivor in his unit. That much is true. If he believes me then perhaps he will forgive me for what I have to do."

Brother Terence nodded and opened the door. At the same instant he switched on the light, flooding the cell with a soft yellow glow, and quickly began to speak.

"Richard, it's Brother Terence . . . there's nothing to be afraid of."

The cell was small, no more than six feet by eight, spotlessly clean, the walls scrubbed, the tile floor glistening under the light. There was a window high in the corner and a crucifix beneath it. A small cot was pushed up against one wall. On a small table was a plastic basin, water pitcher and soap.

Lieutenant Richard Clarke, formerly with the Royal Artillery Regiment, was half lying, half sitting on the cot, his back propped up by a pillow against the wall. Mackenzie McConnell recoiled at the sight of him. Clarke could not have been more than twenty, but he appeared far younger. His soft blond hair had grown long, almost covering his ears, and the face, highlighted by cornflower-blue eyes, was angelic, the effect heightened by the soft golden down of a beard. He smiled at Brother Terence but uttered nothing.

"Richard, I've brought someone to see you," the monk said.

Clarke's gaze passed from him to Mackenzie. The smile faltered briefly but then reappeared. Mackenzie walked over to the cot and sat down on the edge.

"Hello, Richard," she said gently.

There was no response.

"Richard," she began carefully, "do you remember a man called Henry Schiffer? He was a corporal in your unit, at Calais."

Abruptly Clarke swung his head away, staring at the wall. His feet curled up toward his body and the knuckles bunched into fists.

"He is alive, Richard."

Clarke shook his head violently.

"Yes, he is," Mackenzie said, gently but firmly. "He's here in London. He returned from Dunkirk."

Clarke curled up his body more tightly, jerking himself into the corner of the walls. Suddenly Mackenzie reached out and gripped his face with both hands, forcing him to look at her.

"He *is* alive!" she said fiercely.

Clarke moaned, his eyes blazing out at her like those of a frightened animal.

"Richard, will you try to remember?" she coaxed him. "Please, it's so very important . . ."

She held on to him, stroking his face, whispering softly until the smile broke over his lips. Gingerly she removed her hands and reached for the dossier she had brought with her.

Clarke stared vacantly at the photograph of Henry Schiffer. He ran his fingertips over the grainy surface and turned away. Mackenzie looked over her shoulder at Brother Terence, who nodded encouragingly. Mackenzie waited until she was certain the man had calmed down.

"Richard, if you like I can bring Henry to see you," she said. "I know he would—"

"They were all murdered, you know," Clarke said suddenly, sitting up, pulling his knees up against his chest and wrapping his arms around them.

"What did you say?" Mackenzie whispered.

"My men were all murdered," Clarke said calmly, speaking to the wall.

His fingers began moving restlessly, intertwining, then coming apart . . .

"You see, I really thought we had made it," he said in a madman's conversational tone. "I mean we survived the worst Jerry could throw at us. I was so proud of the lads. They hadn't faltered for a moment . . .

"But around midnight the planes came back. There must have been a hundred of them, perhaps more. The bombs kept falling around the Citadel, never on us but all around. The men were screaming, firing blindly because the generators were already burned out. That's when the killing began . . .

"I was at the other end of the Citadel, near the supply depot. We needed shells. I couldn't have been gone for more than twenty minutes. When I returned . . ."

"What did you see when you returned?" Mackenzie prodded him gently.

"They were all dead," Clarke said in a puzzled tone, as though even now he couldn't grasp the fact. "Every one of them . . . I walked around to each one of them. They had been murdered, throats cut or stabbed in the back. And we were going to Dunkirk in a few hours. We survived *everything* and we were going home. But they were murdered and I wasn't there to help them . . ."

Clarke began shivering and drew his arms tightly around himself.

"They weren't all murdered," Mackenzie said.

"Yes!" he screamed. "Yes, they were killed like cattle and it was my fault . . . all my fault."

"No, it wasn't!" Mackenzie shot back. "Some of your men *were* murdered. But not all of them! Not this one!"

She thrust an enlarged photograph of Erik Guderian at Clarke.

"Henry Schiffer—he survived!"

Clarke stared at the picture, then suddenly started to giggle.

"That's not Henry," he gasped. "I knew Henry and that's not him!"

Clarke threw back his head and laughed. "I couldn't find Henry. I knew he was dead like the rest of them—"

"It is Schiffer!" Mackenzie cried.

"That's not Henry!" Clarke screamed. He grabbed the photograph from her fingers and began tearing it apart. "Henry didn't look anything like that. You're lying to me. I killed him, just like I killed the others. I should have stayed with them—"

Suddenly Clarke flung himself off the bed, arms working like windmills, his right hand striking Mackenzie across the cheek. If it hadn't been for Brother Terence he would have made it out of the cell.

The monk grabbed Clarke and twisted one arm behind his back, pinning him against the wall.

"Hold him!" he roared.

Mackenzie leaped up and pressed herself against Clarke. Out of the corner of her eye she saw the spittle dribbling from the soldier's lips.

The monk brought out a syringe from the folds of his robes. Uncapping it, he slid the needle into Clarke's arm.

"Don't let go," he warned Mackenzie. "The morphine needs a few seconds to take effect."

Mackenzie tightened her grip on Clarke.

"That's not Henry!"

The words echoed in her mind, shattering the truth as she had known it only moments ago.

Then who is the man in the photograph? Who is Henry Schiffer?

24

Davey Jones's Locker was called an alehouse, not a pub, by the seamen who frequented it. Located south of the Eastern Docks on Wapping High Street above the Wapping Dock Stairs, it had stood on the same barren piece of ground for over four hundred years. The erosion of the riverbank was held back by timbers, twelve inches square, driven into the loamy soil. Below the waterline was a fine wire mesh anchored into the riverbed to prevent rats from gnawing at the beams.

On the right side of the alehouse was the Seamen's Church where sailors, a particularly superstitious lot, offered up pennies to the poorbox as soon as their ships docked. The next step was to Davey Jones's Locker, the last to the Great Cumberland Hotel, on the left, where beds with stained, erupting mattresses were rented out at two shillings a night, three if the sailor brought along company.

And there was plenty of that, Guderian observed, stepping out of the bright sunlight into a large room whose shutters were nailed to the windowframes. There was no natural light, no clocks in Davey Jones's Locker. Time ceased to exist as soon as one stepped past the soot-laden glass doors. On the right, along a drinking rail illuminated by red and blue bulbs, stood the girls, all in a row like ducks in a shooting gallery. Some of them were old—or at least they appeared that way, their pasted-on smiles revealing blackened teeth, the skin along the face and hands pitted or broken by ugly red sores. Some, the ones who wore the most *maquillage*, had colored and treated their hair so that it frizzed out from their scalps like a Brillo pad. The painted nails and scarlet slashes of lipstick across the mouth completed the grotesque picture.

"You alone then, love?"

Guderian recoiled at the touch of her fingers on his hand. The girl was no more than sixteen, her skin alabaster white broken by a strawberry birthmark on the right side of her neck. She was grinning at him, her breath foul with cheap gin.

"I'm looking for a man," Guderian said.

The girl tittered. "Ooh, you've come to the wrong place!"

"The assistant harbormaster," Guderian said and held up a pound note. "Know where I can find him?"

"You mean Billy, don't you?"

Her eyes were those of a vampire, fixed on the bill between his fingers.

"That's right."

The girl looked around nervously, standing on tiptoes, straining to see over or around the Royal Navy uniforms at the bar.

"Don't see him just now," she said. "But if you like I'll go fetch him. He's probably still at the Great Cumberland."

Her hand was very quick but Guderian was faster; her fingers grasped only at air. Slowly Guderian tore the note in half.

"You get half now—if you get him here in fifteen minutes," he said coldly, "When he sits down at my table I'll give you the other half."

She was mesmerized by the torn bill.

"Would you be wanting anything else?" she asked. "For a little extra—"

"Just bring me Billy," Guderian told her. "Tell him his Canadian cousin arrived from Dunkirk."

"Canadian, are you? Thought you was a Yank."

"Fifteen minutes."

Guderian left her and pushed his way to the bar, taking note of men around him. The old mariners, in grimy, stained overalls, boots and woolen shirts, were Merchant Marine. The younger ones were, to a man, wearing the uniform of the Royal Navy, and were holding on to girls who cadged drinks as fast as they could put them down. The merchant seamen watched, old vultures who knew that the goslings wouldn't last very long. When gin and rum had done its work, the pride of the

Empire's Navy would be pickpocketed or waylaid outside, whatever money was left stolen, the watches and anything else of value stripped off, the drunken body left in the alley. It was almost a ritual.

Guderian paid for his warm gin and brought it over to an empty booth. At the table beside him four sailors were playing cards. Guderian pushed his drink aside, his right hand on his coat pocket, fingers resting lightly on the warm handle of the scalpel. He heard laughter and glanced up to see a cursing Billy Booth being led, an ox in tow, by the girl. She half dragged, half marched him up to where Guderian was sitting.

"Here he is, mate!" she announced, eyes cold.

"Sit down, Billy," Guderian said.

"I don't know you!" Captain William T. Booth roared. He wasn't a tall man but thick, with a barrel chest and arms like oak boughs. His salt and pepper beard was matted with bits of dead skin and crumbs clinging to the strands, eyes shot through with broken red veins. He wiped his runny nose with the back of his shirtsleeve.

"Don't know you!" Billy Booth repeated and swung around to the girl. "Is this what you woke me for, whore—"

He raised his arm, about to bring it down on the girl, when Guderian moved. His right hand shot out, thumb and forefinger spread wide apart, slamming under the double chins of the assistant harbormaster's throat. The grip tightened at once, and as the artery was squeezed his eyes began to bulge.

"Here's your money," Guderian said, handing the girl the other half of the pound note. "Leave us now."

He turned back to the assistant harbormaster. "Doctor Livingstone, Billy. You remember the name, don't you?"

Suddenly Guderian released his grip and Booth began coughing, spewing phlegm over the floor. A few of the men began jeering him. Guderian pushed the assistant harbormaster into the booth and nodded at the gin.

"Drink up before you choke."

Billy Booth looked at him murderously, but his trembling fingers reached for the glass. Dr. Livingstone . . . He had almost forgotten what the words meant.

Guderian brought out a tin of cigarettes, laid it on the table and indicated that Booth should help himself.

"This isn't the place to talk, you know," Booth muttered, drawing one out.

Guderian looked around at the din and smiled. "Oh, I rather like the atmosphere, don't you?"

"What the bleedin' hell do you want?"

Guderian rose, went over to the bar and came back with two glasses of gin.

"How are things with you, Billy?" he asked casually. "Everything all right? No funny little men coming round asking questions?"

Booth snorted. "The fuck they want with me? With bleedin' Dunkirk I've been working my arse off. I ain't ever seen so many ships in my life!"

"I'm interested only in the Royal Navy, Billy."

Booth laughed, a sharp barking sound like that of a seal.

"Dream on, chum! You couldn't get within a hundred yards of any of the ships in the pools. The Marines have standing orders to shoot anyone without the right papers."

"Not the ships, Billy," Guderian said patiently. "Only the quartermaster stores in Greenwich. You could manage that."

Booth ran a thick, dirty hand along his beard, stroking the tuft under his chin. He drank from the second glass of gin and took another cigarette.

"Can't be done," he said at last. "Whatever material we've got left is like fucking gold. Because we don't know when the next Yank ship will get through. Oil, food stores, maintenance equipment—you name it—it's all under lock and key."

"I have to see the Quartermaster's records," Guderian said softly. "Not to steal anything, just look around."

"You ain't been listening!" Billy snarled. "I told you the stuff is like the fucking Crown Jewels. Why only yesterday a new detachment of Marines came in—as though the hundred or so they had there already wasn't enough."

"But you go into the compound regularly," Guderian said. "That's where you get the gas for your Morris-Commercial—along with a few extra gallons you sell off to friends. You do your maintenance on the vehicles in the compound—where you replace perfectly good parts with new ones—and sell the old ones in the market. You help yourself to the clothing stores though God knows why you don't keep any for yourself. You take out food from ships' rations so while some poor bastard goes without in the middle of the Atlantic you're waxing fat. I'm right, aren't I, Billy?"

The assistant harbormaster said nothing and stared out into

the melée of Davey Jones's Locker. If it weren't for what he'd been able to steal during these last three years he'd be like the rest of these poor bastards in here, living hand to mouth with the hand not reaching the mouth half the time. And God knows he had come close.

Billy Booth had taken to the sea at the age of fourteen and in ten years had learned all there was to know about ships. He had come back to London with a stake, married, applied to the Harbour Commission and studied hard for his pilot's license. He passed his examinations and became a harbormaster's assistant. The men, from captains down to mates, respected him because Billy Booth could guide a tanker through fog and settle her in the right berth as gently as you please . . . At one time he had had it all.

Three years ago, a few days after he had been promoted to assistant harbormaster, his wife, a working-class girl from the docks, suddenly and inexplicably deserted him. In time Booth discovered her lover's identity and where they had fled to. But he could never understand—or accept—why she had done what she did. And Buenos Aires was too far to go in search of an answer.

It was then that the drinking started, days to be lost in stupor, nights to violence. The charity and pity felt for him throughout the Eastern Docks evaporated quickly as did the savings which Booth gambled away in less than three weeks, leaving himself prey for the lenders, who flocked to him, pecking away at what was left. In two months' time he was in debt for over a thousand pounds. The Harbour Commission was talking quietly of letting him go. Too many errors had been made while he had been guiding ships.

Many a time Booth wondered whether it wouldn't have been better for his life to have ended then and there. But somewhere in his besotted soul he continually found that last shred of will to live. And that was why he had grabbed at the hands reaching out for him.

They belonged to two quiet gentlemen, one English, the other obviously German by the accent in his voice. Their proposition was simple: All of Booth's outstanding debts would be paid off immediately. He would be given a stipend of one hundred pounds deposited in cash into a safety deposit box at the end of each month. He would, in short, be able to start all over again with a clean slate. In return the men expected only two things: that Booth would clean himself up so that there was no chance of his losing his job, and that he would furnish a written report at the end of every week on the activity along the Thames—not only what he did or was involved in but the dock gossip as well. This report would not carry his signature. Rather it would bear his thumbprint.

When Booth asked who was all so interested in what was happening along the Thames's docks he was told it was none of his business. All he had to do was watch and file his reports.

"And if I don't?" he had demanded belligerently.

"Then the man who comes for your report will also come to kill you."

Whether out of greed or a sad, terrible frustration, or a kind of twisted revenge on the docks that had destroyed his life, William T. Booth accepted. He filed his first report the following week and when a young man had come for it he saw the thumbprint at the bottom of the page but took another one.

"To be absolutely certain, you understand."

Booth understood. He had become a traitor, no matter that the accent was English. Yet it was all so painless, to the point where he even stopped checking the safety deposit box. He had gone to the bank five consecutive weeks, each time finding ten new ten-pound notes. But Booth understood even then that he wasn't being paid for what he wrote each week, at least that wasn't the whole of it. As he lived and breathed, one day a man would arrive and introduce himself as Doctor Livingstone. Then and only then would he truly begin to earn his money.

"You go back on duty tonight, don't you?" Guderian asked him.

Booth nodded. "Nine o'clock."

"Drive by the Wapping Station," Guderian said. "I'll be there at half past eight. And this is what I want you to bring . . ."

The quartermaster stores was a series of five hundred hastily constructed Quonset huts set in the open field between Trafalgar Road and the river Thames. The area was bordered by a ten-foot-high chain-link fence with strands of barbed wire across the top. Because the stores included such strategic reserves as oil, diesel fuel, and ammunition there were Navy foot patrols on the inside and dogs on the outside perimeter.

"Evening, Billy. What brings you around at this time of night?"

The sentry at the front gate didn't bother shining the flashlight at the assistant harbormaster. The weak light filtering onto the dirt road from the guardhouse illuminated the figure behind the wheel of the Morris canvas-top truck.

"I got me a run coming to Southampton," Billy Booth said, grinning at the young Marine. "Came in to sign out a new tire." He jerked his thumb at the deflated tire in the rear.

"Jesus, Billy, I don't have nothin' in the day book about your coming," the Marine objected.

"Well that's no great problem, is it now?" Booth said, giving him a wink. "Come here before unannounced. Just help myself, sign so that everything's on the up and up."

"Yeah, well, they've changed the regulations, Billy. I ain't supposed to let nobody in till morning."

"Sure, and I ain't suppose to have these, much less be showing them to you, are I now?"

Booth thrust a handful of pornographic magazines at the Marine.

"Billy!"

"Come off it, lad," Booth scoffed. "You think I haven't seen the other stuff I bring you making the rounds in the compound? You're a man after my own heart—you don't give it away."

The soldier grinned nervously, pretending not to look at the magazines.

"And for you—and a lady friend—two passes to the Palladium. Open tickets. You could hawk them for a king's ransom, but if I were you I'd hang on to them. If you got a special girl who's been shy this will bring her round."

The Marine licked his lips nervously.

"I'm all alone," he said. "Freddie's nipped out for some coffee at the Tavern. Barmaid gives it to him out back . . ."

"So where's the problem?" Booth shrugged. "The stuff I need is right by the Quartermaster's office. You know I have the passkey. Take all of two minutes to load up and I'll be on my way."

"The other two—"

"Ring them up. Tell 'em it's a bleedin' emergency, which it is. I have something for them as well."

"I don't know, Billy . . ." the young Marine said.

"Look, son, make up your mind!" Booth snapped. "I've

treated you like family. If you don't care to remember that. . . ."

"All right, all right!"

The soldier stepped back into the guardhouse and reached for the telephone. Billy Booth came around the Morris and pushed back the gate. He got back into the vehicle and gunned the engine. The Marine didn't look back as he drove off.

Booth covered fifty yards, then slowed the vehicle as he turned around the corner of one of the huts. Reaching back with one hand, he pushed aside the tire and flung back the black canvas covering. Moonlight glinted off the scalpel in Erik Guderian's hand.

"Put it away and get ready to jump!" Booth whispered at him. "Remember what I told you: two huts down, one across. You'll be able to see the car from there. I'll leave the running lights on."

Guderian eased the scalpel back into its sheath, tucking it away. Bracing himself on the frame, he pushed his body up and squatted by the tailgate.

"Now!"

Pressing down hard, Guderian vaulted over the tailgate. He hit the ground hard, feetfirst, tucking his body in and rolling with the vehicle's momentum. He saw Booth look back, waved and began running for the side of the Quonset hut.

Guderian pressed himself against the cold metal and waited until he caught his breath. He was clad entirely in black, his face stained with burnt cork, his running shoes snug on his feet. Somewhere up ahead he heard the engine die.

He covered the remaining forty yards in only a few seconds, running hard but softly, staying on the grass that bordered each hut. He saw Booth getting out of the Morris-Commercial, gesturing at the two Marines, who were already moving in his direction. Booth slapped one of them on the shoulder, held out something in his other hand.

Guderian was moving again, racing for the side of the Quartermaster's office. He slipped around the length of the hut and crouched low. The door was four feet away. The two Marines, backs turned to him, less than thirty.

Booth was walking toward another hut, rolling the tire he had slashed earlier on. The two Marines ambled behind him, laughing softly. Guderian slithered to the door, the key sweaty in his palm. For all his seeming carelessness Billy Booth was a man who covered his bets. When the compound had been built he had been given a master key. He had had two duplicates made because, as he said, one could never tell . . .

The crash of the tire against corrugated steel startled Guderian as much as it did the two soldiers. Booth started cursing about the damn thing getting away from him. The Marines were shouting at him to keep quiet. Guderian slipped the key into the lock, turned the knob and was inside, the door closed behind him.

The Quartermaster's office was a waist-high wood frame rectangle with glass panels set between four by four studs. Guderian tried the door and found it wasn't locked. Once inside he turned on the flashlight, swinging it along the forty feet of olive-green filing cabinets. It took him almost a full minute to examine tags taped to the cabinet doors before he found the reference he wanted. Another fifteen seconds elapsed as he pulled out two files only to discover that what he was looking for had been cross-referenced in another section. Guderian glanced down at the luminous face on his watch, the second hand making its relentless sweep past the numbers . . .

The drawer he wanted was down at the far end. Unlike the others it was locked. Guderian swore softly and drew out a chamois cloth with four sheaths sewn into it. He had asked Booth for a set of instruments with which he could pick locks, and although the assistant harbormaster had assured him that once inside the hut he wouldn't find anything locked, Guderian had insisted. Booth hadn't been told what it was Guderian was after.

The two minutes elapsed just as the lock turned and the file rolled out toward him. Guderian clamped the butt end of the flashlight between his teeth. His fingers started rifling through the top stubs of the files, moving as quickly as his eye could read the titles. He was thirty seconds over the allotted time when he plucked out the file. He read the first page, flipped the second over, when the door to the hut rattled. Guderian slipped the file back into place, doused the light and rolled the cabinet back into its recess, locking it with a soft click.

He was moving again, part of his mind committing to memory the words he had read while at the same time trying to grapple with the enormity of their meaning. The other part was focused on his survival. As Guderian stepped across the door and around a stack of crates he heard Booth's querulous voice.

"Come on, lads, you don't have to drink it all at once, you know . . ."

The lock rattled and the door swung open. Boots thudded across the rubber mats which covered an earthen floor. The two Marines passed by so close that Guderian could smell the leather of their field kits, the sweat soaked into the uniforms.

"Get in here, Billy!" one of them whispered. He was the one with the bottle Booth had brought along.

Booth entered, looking from side to side, then followed the two Marines into the glassed-in office.

"Just get us some cups . . ." one of the soldiers muttered. "A little drinkee after that hard work . . . Why'd you leave the door open, Billy?"

Because Booth hadn't given up, Guderian thought. He knew that if Guderian didn't get out now, while the guards were having a swig, he wouldn't come out at all.

A faint light snapped on and Guderian saw that all three men were in the office, one bending over a small counter, the other twisting the cap off the bottle. The assistant harbormaster had stepped to one side, but even so if the soldiers turned around they would be able to see the door—and at the wrong moment, someone going through it.

Guderian moved around the crates. Four steps brought him to the door.

"Pour out a bit more, Charlie! No time to be cheap. . . ."

"Should have closed that door. . . ."

"Aw, leave it alone—we'll be out of here in a minute."

Guderian's fingers slipped around the scalpel handle. He had no doubt that he could kill the two soldiers. But even if the bodies weren't found until late morning, the assistant harbormaster's usefulness would be finished. And Guderian still needed him.

Guderian watched the three men raise their glasses, then throw back their heads to down the liquor. At that precise instant he hurtled out the door, running the way he had come. By the time he reached the place where he had jumped off, he heard the Morris-Commercial being fired up. Two thin slats of light pierced the darkness and Booth shifted into gear. Guderian watched as the vehicle moved slowly between the row of huts. When it came abreast he leaped into the back, scrambling to throw back the tarpaulin.

"Thank Christ!" Booth muttered and increased speed.

Guderian slipped under the tarpaulin and dragged the new tire over his body. He felt the Morris slow, heard Booth say something to the young Marine at the gate and laugh. The flaps of the tarpaulin began to snap in the wind as the Morris started down the main road.

25

"It is now . . ." Churchill looked up at the grandfather clock beneath the portrait of Nelson, "one o'clock, the tenth of June. You say, Mr. Cabot, that you could have Prometheus under way within forty-eight hours?"

The Prime Minister was seated behind his desk, elbows on the leather blotter, his head bowed but propped up by both hands. Before him was the report Cabot had drafted only three hours earlier.

"Possibly less, Prime Minister," Cabot replied. "The transfer of bullion from the Bank of England to the ship was coordinated this afternoon. The logistics are in place. The Royal Marines are on standby. All we need now is the final word."

Churchill closed the dossier, removed his glasses and rubbed his eyes.

"Are we ready to give the word, Allen?" he asked looking up.

"Everything seems to be in place," Dulles commented.

"Not quite everything, gentlemen."

Mackenzie McConnell stepped past the Scotland Yard detective. She smiled briefly at Cabot, but he could see from her strained expression that something was wrong.

"There remains the issue of our unknown agent," Mackenzie McConnell said, depositing a dossier before the Prime Minister and handing copies to both Dulles and Cabot. "I feel I'm close, but I need, among other things, a little more time."

"Time is one thing we've not a lot of, Miss McConnell," Dulles said frostily.

"I appreciate that, sir," Mackenzie replied. "But if you hear me out I think you will understand the importance of what I've found."

"Let us listen to what the lass has to tell us, Allen," Churchill murmured.

Mackenzie reached out for one of Cabot's cigarettes and lit it. She outlined the process of elimination she had set up with the Archives staff, how the parameters of the search had first been defined and then narrowed. She spoke of her meeting with Sergeant Mackelhose and Private Renny, recounting how they met a survivor from a unit whose members were all supposed to have been killed . . . which brought her to Lieutenant Clarke, the commander who believed himself to be the only survivor of the Royal Artillery group. Mackenzie took extra time here, repeating almost verbatim what Clarke had told her about the way in which his men had been murdered and how he had found all of them except one, Corporal Henry Schiffer. Except that Lieutenant Clarke did not recognize the photo of Schiffer, taken from the Army files, when she had shown it to him.

"And a last curious development," Mackenzie said. "At almost exactly the time Schiffer was discharged from the Berkeley Square clinic, the boardinghouse where he had lived prior to his departure for Dunkirk burned to the ground. The fire marshal's report lists this as an accident. The landlady had been drinking that night and managed to torch the whole place. But interestingly enough, the fire started in the basement, where tenants kept their lockers, suitcases and packages. Everything that Schiffer had stored there was destroyed . . . along with anything that might have been of interest to us."

"Mackenzie, what are you really saying?" Cabot asked her.

"It's possible that the man the Army knows as Henry Schiffer, whom it intends to honor for bravery under fire, isn't the same Schiffer who arrived on the beaches of France last month," she answered quietly.

"There's not enough in this report to warrant such a conclusion," Dulles objected. "It seems to me that you have far more information on Schiffer being *exactly* who he is rather than someone else."

"Except that Clarke couldn't identify him as the man attached to his unit," Mackenzie reminded him.

"You say that Clarke is in a mental institution, suffering

from battle fatigue," Churchill commented. "Are you suggesting that his condition is *not* as severe as the hospital report indicates?"

"I'm saying, Prime Minister, that for a few moments Clarke was lucid," Mackenzie replied evenly. "He described in accurate detail exactly what happened at Calais. Only when I showed him Schiffer's picture and insisted that this was the man who had also survived did Clarke begin to fall apart. But if you're asking me whether I believe him when he couldn't identify Schiffer, the answer is yes."

"Dicey thing to do, take the word of such a man," Dulles said dubiously.

Mackenzie was about to retort but Cabot broke in.

"What have you done about Schiffer?"

"Robert Ogilvy has been watching him for the last six hours," Mackenzie said. "No unusual activity. So far."

"You could clear this whole thing up in a few hours," Dulles pointed out. "Pick him up for interrogation."

"I'm afraid it's not that simple," Mackenzie told him.

She mentioned how the investigation had already come to the attention of the Army officer who had recommended Schiffer for the medal.

"Apparently he was not amused," Mackenzie said, "and referred the matter to his superiors. Since an inquiry from the Admiralty has already reached my desk, I don't think it prudent to move along official channels.

"Furthermore, if we pluck him now we run the risk of moving too soon. We only *assume* that Schiffer is working alone and that his target is Prometheus. But there are at least six other projects—none of them as vital as Prometheus at the moment—which he might be attempting to infiltrate. If he's as good an agent as I believe, we will never know for certain what his target is or how much he has already passed on. I would say that we watch him carefully but do not intercede."

"On the face of it I'd say there's not much for us to do at this point," Dulles offered, tapping out his pipe. "Jonathan has his operation ready to go. I say we run with it. Keep this Schiffer character under surveillance, to be sure, but let's not stop because of a possibility."

"Somehow I don't think Mackenzie is quite finished—are you?" Cabot raised his eyebrows.

"Not at all," she answered, returning his look. "In fact,

given what I've heard tonight, what I'll be asking for is tantamount to apostasy." She looked directly at the Prime Minister. "I suggest, sir, that you postpone Prometheus for forty-eight hours."

Allen Dulles's pipe clattered in the tray.

"I would really like to believe I hadn't heard you correctly, Miss McConnell," he said sharply.

Cabot, who knew the signs of Dulles's anger, shook his head minutely, trying to warn Mackenzie.

"You did, sir," she said.

"Really, Winston—" Dulles started to say.

"Prime Minister, Mr. Dulles," Mackenzie said quickly. "I understand as well as any of you the importance of Prometheus. There can be no dry run. Everything will go the first time and, as you yourself said, Prime Minister, the fate of this nation goes with that ship and its cargo. I cannot guarantee at this moment that Schiffer is our man, but *any* risk must be investigated, and if ascertained, then neutralized.

"Personally I do not believe that we can do this in England. The answer lies elsewhere, specifically Geneva."

Cabot raised his eyes at the mention of that city. He looked at Mackenzie and wondered if she would follow through with the gambit he thought she was working on.

"There are two aspects to my proposal," Mackenzie continued. "The first concerns a joint MI5–SIS operation that's been running in Geneva for over a year now. We have managed to secure excellent contacts with German nationals who travel to Switzerland on a regular basis. These are people, some in key areas, others in professions which require travel, who move not only around Germany but are privy to sources in the Nazi Party, the Wehrmacht and Abwehr, which we could never infiltrate. This afternoon I received a message from Geneva stating that one of the couriers we run will be in Switzerland tomorrow. Apparently this man has information regarding British prisoners taken during the offensives on Calais, Boulogne and Dunkirk.

"The second part of my plan concerns *your* resources, Mr. Dulles. It is well known, even within our secretive communities, that you maintain extremely close and sensitive lines of communications with certain Germans via Geneva. Some would say that your pipeline extends even into the Reichschancellery itself. I fervently hope this is all true because what I am about to suggest is based on it. We know that the man sent over to England must have been of senior rank. If he is in fact masquerading as Schiffer then we even have a photograph with which to work. I am asking you, Mr. Dulles, to send Mr. Cabot to Geneva to talk with your sources. They alone can tell us exactly which senior intelligence officers were absent from Berlin at the time Schiffer was either killed or disappeared. If we know that, then we can eliminate certain considerations. If we are truly lucky, perhaps one of your people will recognize the man in the photograph. With a bona fide identification we'll know exactly what branch of German intelligence this man works for. Given that, we can determine, accurately, whether Prometheus was his target. If not, we will at least have eliminated the one outstanding threat to the operation. If Prometheus *is* on his list then we know what we have to do to neutralize it."

Mackenzie paused. "And by sending Cabot, no one's sources are compromised," she concluded diplomatically.

After a few seconds of silence Dulles asked, "Is that *all* you want, Miss McConnell?"

"Under the circumstances, sir, I feel my proposal is reasonable enough."

"I'm inclined to agree, Allen," Churchill said. "It would give us all peace of mind if we knew that Prometheus was a hundred percent secure. But I take it you have specific objections."

"Time," Dulles said flatly. "The sooner we make the shipment the less time there is for *anything* to go wrong. Even if this Schiffer is a Nazi agent, what could he have passed on to Berlin in so short a time? As far as I'm aware, there haven't been any reports of attempted penetration, much less documented security leaks."

He looked at Cabot. "Isn't that the case, Jonathan?"

"The operation is, if you'll pardon the expression, watertight," Cabot said. "But there is something I'd like to remind you of, sir. Whoever this man is, whether he's Schiffer or someone else, he is responsible for a hell of a lot of blood. Beginning with the shooting in Leatherhead. Then Leonard Frye. Finally Pearce."

Cabot paused.

"It's Pearce who's been bothering me all along. He was the best agent Berlin had in England, yet they subordinated him to

someone coming over, someone who needed Pearce's resources, his contacts, his unquestioned safety, which could be
used as a shield. But something went wrong. Pearce became
renegade, refused to cooperate with this man and must have
communicated as much. What he didn't know was that the man
from Berlin was not traveling alone. He had his own protection.

"So what was so damn important that it made Pearce ex-
pendable?" Cabot asked rhetorically. "Only Prometheus. But
could the Germans have divined its meaning? To answer that I
went back into the intelligence that London managed to get out
of the Low Countries, Belgium, Czechoslovakia and Poland.
*What I discovered is evidence of systematic looting of the
central banks and allegedly secret vaults in those countries.*"

"Systematic, Mr. Cabot?" Churchill queried skeptically.
"Pray, how have you deduced this?"

"Prime Minister, if you were to study the German advance
into any one of those countries you would see that at certain
points regular Army units were deliberately split away from the
main thrust . . . toward the central banks or vaults. In addition,
there is evidence of a special commando force—on which we
have no hard intelligence—*that was already in place* when this
support arrived.

"I can only conclude that someone within German intelligence mapped out and executed a campaign designed to sever
the economic lifeline of the target countries. If the Germans
had gone this far they could have taken the next logical step."

"Projected what we, the British, would do," Churchill said,
almost inaudibly. "Prometheus . . ."

"It seems very likely," Cabot replied. "Now this agent is on
his own—at least to a great extent. And he's probably a man
we've never heard of, but we do know his expertise—finance,
on a massive scale. This gives us a starting point."

He turned to Mackenzie.

"With all due respect to the Double-cross System I don't
think an agent of this caliber would be relying on the network
in place. Even if Berlin is convinced that its agents are functioning normally, this man wouldn't risk using them. He would
want people who haven't been raised yet, the sleepers he himself could activate, use and discard if necessary."

"What's the bottom line, Jonathan?" Dulles asked softly, as
though he didn't want to hear the reply.

"If it were just a matter of setting up this son of a bitch because of what he tried to do through Pearce, I'd say let it go," Cabot said coldly. "But I feel he's a lot more dangerous than that. I think he's figured out what we want to do and he'll try to stop us any way he can. I can hold the operation for forty-eight hours. Assuming I have clear access in Geneva, I can be back well before then.

"It's worth a try, sir," Cabot concluded. "All the way around."

"Maybe," Dulles said slowly. "But even if I concur, we'll still need to inform the President. I suggest we consider it overnight and make a final decision tomorrow morning."

Kurt and Anna Moelders were both fifty-six years old. They had lived in Munich all their lives and had until the early twenties operated a very successful restaurant in the Schwabing district of the city. After the postwar Depression, they moved to Regensburg and bought a small, bankrupt inn which was just starting to show a profit when Erik Guderian and *Die Piraten* arrived to set up their base of operations. As compensation for virtually putting them out of business, Guderian arranged for the Moelderses to cook for and look after his men as well as those of the SS support unit. Over a period of two years Guderian came to trust them without reservation and had vouched for their loyalty to the Reich when the Gestapo had run the usual background investigation on anyone being employed in a "sensitive" area. The inquiry turned out to be nothing more than a formality and the Moelderses were duly accredited to the compound. What neither Guderian nor the Gestapo ever suspected was that both husband and wife were avowed anti-Fascists. Recruited by men and women now long dead, the Moelderses had worked for the British Secret Service since 1919 as independent agents reporting to a single man.

On Thursday of each week the Moelderses left the Regensburg compound in the early morning to shop for themselves and their charges in Munich. For this occasion they were given the use of a car and the necessary gasoline coupons. Each time, because they assumed someone might be watching, the Moelderses adhered to an exact routine: the butcher first, followed by the vegetable store, baker and dry goods store. Whatever they could not carry back themselves would be delivered.

And, as usual, for lunch Kurt escorted Anna to the elegant Hohenzollern Cafe, where they were shown to their table on the terrace, overlooking the river. It was there, exactly on schedule, as they were drinking their Viennese coffees, that contact was made.

"Kurt . . . Kurt Moelders!"

The man who had been sitting at the other end of the terrace and was threading his way toward them was short and slim, dressed in a dark three-piece suit, his silver, swept-back mane and the deep creases adding a craggy appearance to his features. When he came up to the Moelderses' table his smile widened and he kissed Anna on both cheeks.

"My goodness!" Gustav Herder exclaimed, gripping Kurt's hand. "Who would have thought that of all people I would run into you today."

"Gustav, it is so good to see you!" Anna beamed. "Have you been in Munich long?"

"I arrived yesterday," Herder told her, signaling the waiter for coffee. "An old patient isn't faring so well, I'm afraid."

While Anna clucked sympathetically, Herder glanced at the tables around them. He had seen the Moelderses the minute they had entered the Hohenzollern. Deliberately he had eaten his own lunch slowly, watching as the noontime diners who had come in with them finished their own meals and for the most part departed, leaving only a handful of people remaining on the terrace, none within earshot of their table.

"It's been too long, my friends," Herder said, gazing fondly at both of them. "How have you been faring?"

In fact it had only been six weeks since the last contact. At that time Herder had come down from Berlin, where he had an exclusive practice consisting of senior administrative officials who worked in every department from the Finanzministerium through to Speer's Ministry of Armaments. Almost exactly a year ago Herder had come within an ace of being included as a consultant on Hitler's personal medical staff. The Führer's physician, Morell, had spoken highly of him to Hitler, but in the last minute the Führer had deemed Herder's practice too extensive and valuable to remove him from it.

"We have been well enough, Gustav," Moelders said amiably. "But quite a bit has been happening, as you'll soon hear . . ."

If an observer had been watching the three people he would

have concluded that a perfectly harmless conversation was taking place. All three participated. There was laughter and several times Anna Moelders had blushed. Except that every gesture was part of an elaborate charade. The words were incongruous with the smiles and hand movements, which were meant to disguise the horror of what was being said.

Kurt Moelders described the latest prisoners to arrive at Dachau, only a few kilometers from Regensburg. From information passed to him by a cousin, he detailed the plans for new medical installations and the use of special vans which were to take prisoners to the killing grounds, vans designed to somehow kill their passengers en route so that the SS wouldn't have to waste bullets. Apparently a study had been done by someone called Eichmann, who found that shooting was not a cost-effective way to deal with the problem.

To this Anna added what she had overheard from the talk between the SS and Regensburg guards; her singsong voice gave details of beatings, forced labor and brutal living conditions as though they were quite ordinary, everyday affairs. Herder watched her closely but not once did her pleasant expression falter or her voice break.

"There is one more thing, Gustav," Kurt Moelders said, reaching for the check. "Something quite extraordinary which I can't really make sense of, but could be quite important—as far as the British are concerned . . ."

As he counted out the money Moelders told his control about the mysterious appearance at Regensburg of a young British soldier by the name of Henry Schiffer.

"He wasn't actually British," Anna corrected him. "He spoke more like an American. Ah, yes, he was Canadian."

"Thank you, my dear." Her husband nodded. "That's quite right. As you know, Gustav, Regensburg, being a commando base, has never yielded any hard intelligence. The men involved are simply too tight-lipped. That is why we have been concentrating our efforts on Dachau. But suddenly a British— or Canadian—prisoner of war arrives. Why? Regensburg isn't a detention center. In any case this soldier is very well treated. He has his own hut, we make his meals for him, he exercises with the soldiers."

Kurt Moelders's voice dropped. "Then one day we see a big *Feldwebel* carrying a body wrapped in bloodstained sheets into the woods. After that the soldier is never seen again. Two nights later I go into the woods and find a shallow grave. It is the same soldier."

"The SS is killing British prisoners of war!" Herder whispered.

Silence descended over the table as the waiter picked up the money.

"We do not understand it," Moelders said quietly. "It is unthinkable but—"

"Have you a name?" Herder demanded.

"The men called him Schiffer," Anna said. "When talking about him they used the rank of corporal."

The three of them rose and embraced one another as old friends would.

"I shall report this to London as quickly as possible," Herder said. "You are certain of the name and rank?"

"Absolutely."

"He may have been something much more than a corporal if they were holding him at Regensburg," Herder murmured. "Holding him until they killed him—for whatever reason."

"But what else could he have been?" Anna asked anxiously.

Herder shrugged. "Who knows. Let us not forget that Hitler was once a corporal as well."

He shook Kurt Moelders's hand once more.

"One last thing: what is the name of the *Feldwebel*'s supervisor? He alone could have given the execution order."

"Kleemann. It had to have been Major Helmut Kleemann . . ."

26

The journey between Greenwich and East End London was accomplished without incident—something Guderian considered no small miracle given the maniacal way in which the assistant harbormaster had driven. When he shook off the tarpaulin the German felt bruised and battered, as though he had been systematically beaten.

"It was reckless to drive so quickly," Guderian said, stepping away from the weak pool of light that illuminated what had once been the loading dock of the Great Cumberland Hotel.

"Got us here in one piece, didn't I?" Booth retorted.

Something skittered in the darkness, knocking over an empty bottle. Without warning Billy Booth's left foot shot out, the heavy boot slicing cleanly through a rotting crate.

"What the hell do you think you're doing!" Guderian said savagely, seizing Booth by his coat and driving him up against the tailgate of the Morris-Commercial.

Booth's eyes glazed over, his breath coming out in short, fierce grunts.

"Get the hell away from me!" he whispered, and twisted away from Guderian's grip. "You got what you came for, didn't you? Now get away and leave me well enough alone!"

Guderian stepped back, moving carefully around the refuse, his ears tuned to the scraping of footsteps, the opening of a window. But if someone had heard the commotion, they knew enough to mind their own business. It was the law of the docks.

Yes, he had gotten what he came for—the papers in the Greenwich files. The sheer gall of the plan! Its incredible simplicity and velvet cunning! It was almost too perfect!

Yet for all his ingenuity Runnymeade—and behind him Jonathan Baylor Cabot—had allowed a single, vital factor to slip between the cracks.

Napoleon said that an army travels on its stomach, Guderian thought. It is made up of men, and men must eat and drink . . .

"Why y're looking at me like that?" Booth challenged him. "We're done, ain't we?"

"Yes, we're done," Guderian said quietly. But he knew this to be a lie.

Booth drew himself away from the utility truck, his expression wary.

"Then you'll not be needin' me no more," he said cautiously.

"No, I don't think so. In any event I know where to find you if I must."

Booth was about to say something but thought better of it.

"I'll look after the truck," he muttered, moving away. "You'll find your own way out."

"Don't worry about me."

He watched the assistant harbormaster stumble away as though drunk. Twice Booth glanced back but the second time Guderian knew he hadn't seen him. The German had disappeared into the shadows.

As Guderian had expected, Booth did not go into the Great Cumberland Hotel but made directly for Davey Jones's Locker. The ring of drunken laughter tinkled out onto the street when Booth pulled open the door. Guderian stole to a vantage point farther along the street and settled into a doorway to wait.

The assistant harbormaster almost took him by surprise, exiting from the alehouse less than thirty minutes later. He walked in long strides, like a man who had had nothing to drink. Guderian knew the opposite was true: certain men needed their ration of liquor to function in what appeared to be a normal manner. Billy Booth could have absorbed a full quart of whiskey and the adrenaline that was churning within him would have absorbed it like a sponge.

Skipping behind him, her hand clutching a tattered shawl, was a young whore. At the door of the Great Cumberland Hotel Booth handed her what must have been a key but did not follow her in. Booth made for the Wapping Dock Stairs and the riverbank.

Guderian did not set foot on the mossy concrete until he heard the sound of creaking timber. A few seconds later a weak shaft of light floated across the oily waters. Guderian scrambled down the steps, careful to stay on the earthen bank beside the dock, and made for the launch moored at the pier. The permeated sand sucked at his boots, each footstep bringing up a soft gurgle. He waded into the water to his chest, holding his arms straight out, until the fingers touched the gunwale. Slowly he shifted himself around and lifted himself out of the water just enough for his head to clear the transom.

There was no one in the cockpit. As Guderian's pupils dilated he could discern coils of rope, diesel fuel canisters, several crates, life jackets, life preservers and a salvage pole. In one motion he lifted himself out of the water, gritting his teeth against the shaft of pain digging into his shoulder, and rolled gently across the rough, wet deck. He was on his feet in seconds, scrambling crabwise toward the deckhouse, eyes trained on the sliver of lamplight escaping from the crack in the trapdoor.

Suddenly the light burst upon him as though from an exploding star. The trapdoor had been slammed back and the hulking figure of the assistant harbormaster loomed not three feet away. Not a word passed between the two men. Guderian threw himself to one side as Booth launched his entire body forward. Booth's left fist drove into his shoulder, causing Guderian's head to spin. In spite of the drink Booth was moving quickly, scrambling after Guderian, catching him by the belt and hauling him back. Guderian lashed out with a free leg, feeling the boot connect with flesh, hearing the gasp of pain as Booth's fingers loosened their hold. He twisted away, catching Booth with another kick, shattering ribs, then dived forward, the knuckles of his right hand forming a deadly spear. The breastbone shattered under the impact. Guderian ducked a last desperate roundhouse punch, delivered a vicious elbow thrust into Booth's already broken chest, then jerked his knee hard against the assistant harbormaster's jaw as Booth doubled over.

Guderian staggered back, glaring at the fallen man. He dropped to his knees, leaned forward and touched Booth's jaw. The assistant harbormaster's head rolled to one side like that of a hanged man. Sickened, Guderian shifted away and crawled down into the cockpit.

For a moment he remained sprawled under the weak lamplight, the pounding in his temples threatening to catapult him into unconsciousness. Guderian stared down at his slick hands. Too much blood . . . There was always too much blood. Henry Schiffer, the men in Calais, then Annie Glendower, now Booth. And who in God's name knew how many corpses were still waiting for him before this was all finished? All because they had seen his face or had been connected with the man who had been the first domino to fall: Henry Schiffer.

Slowly Guderian wiped the blood on his sodden trousers. He reached out and dragged over a can of gasoline, unscrewed the cap and tipped the five- gallon container on its side, watching mutely as the liquid sloshed across the hold. He found another and doused the assistant harbormaster's body. Nothing could be left to chance now. Booth's death had to appear an accident, otherwise the ensuing investigation would be relentless. Greenwich would come under suspicion. Cabot, Runnymeade, would raise their noses to the wind. A fire, set by a known drunkard, whose whore was still waiting for him, would purge everything.

Guderian stepped off the harbor cruiser and reached inside his breast pocket for matches in a waterproof case. The flint sparkled and the flame winked in the night. He was scarcely aware of the gasp of air behind him as the gasoline ignited. For him the ashes of the evening were already cold.

Erik Guderian's eyes snapped open but he lay completely still, staring at the tiny wavering spider-web between the whitewashed ceiling and a dark-brown timber beam. Slowly he turned his head and saw what had awakened him: Christine was lying beside him, propped up on one elbow, looking at him silently.

"Christine . . ." he started to say hoarsely, remembering.

She placed a finger on his lips. Her eyes . . . he couldn't bear them. They were a predator's eyes, like those of Delilah when she had gazed upon Samson. A harlot's eyes, ravenous, all-consuming.

Christine drew back the sheet that covered them both and he saw the angry marks on her shoulders and breasts. As her tongue slid over his chest and her legs parted he glimpsed patches of red along her inner thigh . . . where his beard had scraped . . . She cupped his balls and the fingers curled around his cock, her tongue like that of a hummingbird.

The images flooded his memory so painfully that he gasped aloud, squeezing his eyes shut against the tears. Of his throwing open the door in the early hours of the morning, staggering in, clothes dripping . . . Christine running from the bedroom, seizing him, stripping him, demanding to know what had happened.

But there was nothing he could say to her, and instead he seized her without a word, setting upon her body, greedily exploring every curve and orifice, forcing her to submit, then join him in every act he demanded. He was aware of her cries, part hurt, part passion, but did not hear them. And in the end, when he had spent himself, he had fallen away like Lucifer from heaven, falling forever . . . into screaming darkness.

Guderian's back arched as her lips moved frantically over his shaft. Her mouth consumed him with the greed of a supplicant, her hair tossing from side to side as she drained him.

When he saw the tantalizing smile he knew she was done . . . And gone, without a word, leaving him lying there, heart heaving against his chest.

The next time he saw her she was dressed, standing beside the bed.

"I have to know if you'll be here when I return," she said in a matter-of-fact tone.

"I'll be here," he whispered.

She smiled and laid a cool hand on his shoulder.

"There's a party I promised Andrew I would attend with him," she said. "It will be the last time I'll be with him. You won't ever see him here again." She paused. "Just the two of us . . . and I will do whatever you want."

He started to say something but she shook her head and quickly fled from the room.

My God, she thinks it's Simmons! That I didn't come home out of jealousy because he was here . . .

It was the final deception, created by herself, without a single word or suggestion from himself. Guderian started to laugh, not out of malice or disgust with her but because that was what the caprice of the gods demanded. Tears were rolling down his face when the telephone sounded. He staggered toward it, naked, and lifted the receiver. As soon as he recognized the voice on the other end his possession passed.

Guderian took a quick sponge bath, shaved and donned his uniform. He left by the back gate, crossed Berkeley Square and headed for the garage in the mews on Bruton Street. As he inserted the key into the lock he examined it for any sign of forced entry. There was none. He swung back the garage door just enough to slip in, turned on the lights and closed the door behind him. In the corner was the BSA motorcycle he had used the previous day. Nothing was out of place. There was no sound.

"Doctor Livingstone."

Robert Ogilvy, the man known to Guderian as Mr. Stanley, his lethal cloak who interceded when the German needed him, materialized from the side of the great car.

"One day you must tell me about the way you get through locked doors."

"One day," Ogilvy said. "But not now. We have very little time. I'm afraid the Security Service has become far too interested in you. In Henry Schiffer, that is."

Guderian took two steps toward him, his eyes burning. "There's been no cause—"

"There *should* have been no cause," Ogilvy corrected. "But MI5, at least one operative in MI5, has latched on to the idea that a German agent infiltrated England during the Dunkirk evacuation."

"There has to be some mistake," Guderian said.

"I'm afraid not." Ogilvy shook his head. "Mackenzie McConnell is convinced that Henry Schiffer deserves intense scrutiny. And whatever her suspicions are based upon, it's enough to have Cabot's support."

Guderian sucked in his breath at the mention of the American.

"In fact the enquiry is being run independently of *both* the Security Service and MI6, channeled directly through Ten Downing Street. Not even I, who was appointed to cover you, am aware as to why Cabot and McConnell should be so concerned about this agent. But I can tell you the search has narrowed down to one Henry Schiffer."

"If they suspect, why haven't I been taken?" Guderian demanded.

"Because what evidence there is, is either circumstantial or flimsy. It seems that Schiffer's entire unit was murdered at the Citadel . . . I don't suppose you'd know anything about that, would you? Not that it matters—except for one factor: whoever was responsible for the massacre overlooked one thing: the unit commander was never taken. He returned to find his men slaughtered and has, as far as I know, been driven insane. Yet it turns out that his condition is not as advanced as I had thought. Otherwise of course I would have killed him. Apparently our Lieutenant Clarke has periods of lucidity. McConnell went over to interview him, and after telling him that Schiffer was still alive and showing him your photograph, managed to get through to Clarke. Clarke told her that the man in the photograph was not the one *he* knew as Schiffer."

"And MI5 is now taking the word of madmen?" Guderian asked, the disbelief soft, lethal.

"That Clarke is almost certifiable is part of your saving grace," Ogilvy told him flatly. "The other factor is that *you* are still looked upon as a hero. There have already been rumblings from the Admiralty about McConnell's investigation. Since officially no such investigation is under way, she has to tread carefully."

"But she suspects," Guderian said softly. "And she has enough authority to order surveillance on me."

"Fortunately Mackenzie and I worked very closely in the past," Ogilvy commented. "Even though she could not tell me the whole of what is going on, she trusts me enough to carry out discreet but effective surveillance."

Guderian walked around to the monstrous BSA and ran his hand along the shining chrome handlebars.

"What is her next move?" he asked without turning around.

"Interestingly enough, it will be Cabot who makes it. A decision was reached this morning to send him to Geneva. I don't know why, except that Geneva is a clearinghouse for our sources within Germany."

"Dulles also has his own listening posts there," Guderian murmured. He turned back to Ogilvy. "Cabot is going to try to match up the information he has on Schiffer with whatever he can get from British and American sources in Germany."

Ogilvy nodded. "That's very likely the case. And I can't protect you there, I'm afraid."

Guderian began to pace around the motorcycle, fist slapping into open palm.

"No, that's all right," he said softly. "As long as MI5 won't move on me until he returns, everything is all right."

"I don't see how Mackenzie can do anything else," Ogilvy agreed. "Cabot is running a very special operation. For him to leave now means that she convinced him that you're important enough to merit such attention. It *also* means she has no other resources."

"How long will Cabot be gone for?" Guderian demanded.

"No more than forty-eight hours."

That means I have less than half that, Guderian thought to himself. But Cabot was the primary consideration now.

"You won't be able to watch me twenty-four hours a day," he said. "Do you know your relief man?"

"Not yet, but he's coming at noon—unless I call in and say you're on the move."

"I need three hours," Guderian said urgently. "Then it doesn't matter who is watching."

"I can give you that," Ogilvy replied. "Is there anything you'd like done about Cabot?"

"No . . ." Guderian said grimly. "It wouldn't do for anything to happen to him here."

He turned to the British agent. "I have to call on someone. I'll give you a few minutes to get your car. Make absolutely certain no one is following you. I can't compromise this contact."

"Don't worry," Ogilvy told him. "They've given you all to myself."

The big BSA swooped into the traffic moving swiftly up St. James's Street, Guderian sitting low, his body thrust forward over the gasoline tank. He swung around a lumbering bus and turned off into Ryder Street, slowing the machine almost to a crawl, riding hard over the cobblestones. He waited for the oncoming milk wagon to pull out of the lane and guided the motorcycle in behind the blackened granite blocks that made up the rear of Bentley's, a private club whose exclusivity rivaled White's. Guderian eased the machine onto its kickstand, tugged out a brown manila envelope from inside his jacket and went up the steps to the shiny black door.

"What can I do fer ye?"

The boy was no more than fourteen, shirtsleeves rolled up to puny biceps, face spotted with acne. His fingers were grimy, the nails almost completely black. In his left hand he was holding a half-peeled potato.

"Special delivery for a Mr. Alfred Morell," Guderian said, adding: "Official Army business."

The kitchen boy held out his hand. "I'll take it to him."

"I'm afraid Mr. Morell has to sign for it," Guderian said pleasantly. "There may also be a reply."

The boy gave an exasperated sigh, then looked around.

"You got a fag?"

Guderian handed him a half-full tin. "Rations tomorrow. I can spare them."

Someone with a thick French accent shouted from the kitchen. The boy grinned at Guderian, slipping the tin into his trousers pocket.

"Good on ye! I'll fetch Mr. Morell."

He ran off, oblivious to the curses streaming after him. Guderian stepped inside and quietly closed the door.

"May I be of assistance to you, sir?"

Alfred Morell materialized behind Guderian so silently that

the German never guessed he was there. Despite his years—
Guderian guessed late sixties—he remained a tall man. His
silver hair fell sharply on either side of a widow's peak, making his face appear narrower than it already was. The high
forehead gave way to a smooth, aquiline nose, defined by deep
creases on either side which fell around the mouth and tapered
off toward the narrow jaw. The eyes were those of an old
man's: brown-blue flecked with white cataracts. But the voice
was clear, the enunciation perfect upper-class English.

Alfred Morell moved his hands across a shiny brown leather
apron that covered the front part of his starched shirt and the
black trousers to the knees. Guderian smelled the odor of
graphite and from the blackened cloth tucked away in the
apron's pouch deduced that Alfred Morell, chief steward of
Bentley's for over a decade, had been polishing the silver.

"Army pension office, sir," Guderian said, loud enough for
anyone around the corner to hear. "Regarding the matter of
Charles Evans."

Alfred Morell's features displayed no emotion at the mention of this name, but Guderian saw the flash of pain register in
the eyes, the imperceptible squint of the crow's-feet that told
him Morell remembered the name—much to his grief.

"Yes, of course, sir," the steward said calmly. "I was told to
expect you. If you would care to follow me." Morell indicated
the steep, narrow staircase.

The steps ascended to what was ground level. Morell led the
way to a cramped birdcage elevator which took them to the
sixth and uppermost floor.

"The servants' quarters," he commented, walking smoothly
along the frayed carpet. "Four of us live here, including myself. There was a time when members would use those rooms
to sleep over, but since the Depression . . . well, you understand."

Guderian said nothing. Every sense was alert, listening and
watching for, trying to intuit, any sign of danger. The corridor
was silent. No sounds came from behind any of the doors they
passed.

"You needn't concern yourself about anyone else," Morell
said, pulling out a gold keychain from his pocket. He looked
directly at Guderian.

"I know who you are and where you have come from. I've
been expecting you for a long, long time," he added softly.

The room was a reflection of the man: neat, uncluttered, the few furnishings old but obviously of excellent quality. On the mantlepiece above the tiny fireplace was a large silver frame holding a rectangular photograph of a family.

Guderian stepped over to have a better look at the individual members. The photograph was the original of one he had seen in Morell's file in Berlin.

"My wife's name was Katherine," Morell said, his voice hollow like the noise in a seashell. "But I suppose you already knew that . . . We were born and raised in the same town in Germany, Emmaus. When I came to London to study architecture she stayed behind. After I received my degree I became a British citizen and sent for her.

"We had two children: a boy, Rolfe, and a little girl whom we also named Katherine . . . In 1914, when the world ended for us, Rolfe was only five, Katherine three.

"The British came for my wife on the second day of hostilities. She had German papers, you see. They took her from our home and drove her to a concentration camp somewhere in Kent. A week later they returned for me. Even though I was a British subject and had pledged my allegiance to the monarchy, they took me as well. Not as a prisoner, really. At least that's how they explained it to me. They put me in charge of serving food at a men's camp. That's where I learned my future trade. An architect doling out gruel . . .

"Our children were placed with a British family by the name of Evans. Katherine was the first to die. I was told it was dysentery but when I saw her body I knew it was malnutrition. She couldn't have weighed more than twenty-five pounds . . .

"Our boy was murdered. The police said it was an accident, that he had been playing with matches. But where had the matches come from? I knew the other boys had set him on fire . . .

"My wife never recovered from this. I was permitted to visit her once a month, and each time I saw her I knew she was slipping further and further into madness. One day they found her hanging from a barrack beam . . ."

Alfred Morell moved over to the dormer window and drew aside the gaily colored curtains.

"I am telling you this so that you understand that you have nothing to fear from me," he said, looking out through the glass. "The British destroyed my life with such cruelty that even now I have moments when I cannot believe that it all actually happened. After the war one of the officers in the camp took pity upon me and used his influence to find me work here. But I have never forgotten. From the day I walked through the gates of that camp, into a world where I had nothing anymore, I became a German again. The only meaning I have derived from my life since then is the service I have performed for my country."

Morell turned around. "I have been waiting a long time to hear the words you spoke. I place myself at your service."

Guderian had listened to the old man's narrative, drawn in by the soft cadence his words rode on. For the first time since his arrival in England did he feel truly safe.

"I need to send a message to Germany immediately," Guderian said. "I was told you were the best communications man in the country."

"Quite possibly," Alfred Morell said. If the destination of the message surprised him at all, he didn't show it.

He stepped over to the Victor radio which stood in the corner of the room next to the fireplace. The unit was ten years old at least, four feet high, its wood frame nicked and scarred. The half-moon glass covering the dial was a pale yellow and there were four knobs lined up underneath it. Morell knelt down in front of the radio and ran his fingers along the base, a board five inches high, eighteen across.

"It has been some time since I had occasion to do this," he said.

Suddenly with a sharp squeal of wood moving against wood the baseboard popped out. Carefully Morell placed it aside and reached inside the cavity, pulling out a wooden box four inches high, fourteen inches square. Gripping it by the handle, he carried it over to the small table underneath the slanted dormer windows.

"Do you recognize it?" he asked, throwing the catches and flipping back the top.

"An ENIGMA," Guderian said softly.

"This is one of the first," Alfred Morell said proudly. "It was shipped to me in four different pieces. This was possible because Berlin remembered I had been an architect, with special training in electronics. It wasn't difficult to hook up and align the components."

The machine resembled a typewriter both in dimensions and

physical appearance. ENIGMA could encipher and decipher messages by illuminating substitute letters behind the keyboard. When the operator depressed a key, an electronic impulse was activated, traveling along one of billions of possible paths through jack connections in the plyboard at the front of tho machine and rotor contacts at the back. When the operator moved a key he also shifted one or more of the rotors so that ENIGMA's internal settings varied from letter to letter. Guderian knew all this because ENIGMA had been developed specifically on his instructions, by the best man in the electronic-cipher field. Professor Aaron Steinfeldt . . .

"Do you have a set contact time?"

"Yes," Morell replied. "But there is also an emergency procedure at my disposal. Instead of the message going directly to Regensburg, which takes far longer, I type in a series of code words which activates a sister machine in the nearest U-boat. I assume you would want the emergency routing."

"You can make contact with a U-boat a hundred miles away?" Guderian asked incredulously.

"I have added certain modifications to this machine." Morell smiled. "Instead of an antenna I have constructed a booster-battery pack which triples the ENIGMA's sending and receiving range. The pack also allows me to send longer messages if I must."

"What about radio-location trucks?" Guderian queried. "British counterintelligence monitors the airwaves twenty-four hours a day. Their initial concern isn't so much the text, which is virtually indecipherable, as the location where it originated."

"Does your message require a lengthy reply?"

"Only an acknowledgment."

"Very well," Morell said. "We will proceed thusly: Contact is made with the U-boat. That will take less than twenty seconds. Assuming the ENIGMA operator on board is alert, a reply should be forthcoming in half a minute. Next, if your message is ready, we send it immediately. If not, I kill the machine until you are ready. Finally, at the end of the message we request a confirmation of receipt. As soon as we have that, the machine is switched off. All told, the British would have less than two minutes, depending on the length of your text, to try to implement their tracking procedure. That is nowhere near enough time to confirm coordinates of a city sector, much less pinpoint a given street or building."

"But the British have the new mobile vans," Guderian objected. "The last word Berlin had on these was that they move around London constantly, covering sectors at random. If one of them should be in the vicinity . . ."

"I have heard about these special trucks," Morell said calmly. "In fact I've seen them in the streets. I can't disagree with you that they are a threat, but under the circumstances the risks are acceptable."

Guderian sat down at the desk and drafted his message. He read it through and shortened it as much as he dared. It had to be clear enough so that there was no possibility of misinterpretation on Regensburg's part. But it was still too long. He went through the text two more times, deleting a word here, reducing a phrase there.

"That's the best I can do," he said, handing the paper to Morell.

The elderly steward frowned as he read the thirty sentences.

"This will take three minutes, perhaps longer, to send," he said at last.

"I can't shorten it any more than that."

Alfred Morell sighed, then smiled faintly. "I can see now why you were concerned with the directional trucks."

He pulled another chair over to the table and sat down, fingers poised over the keys.

"I suggest you leave as soon as we are done," he said quietly. "There's not much use in both of us tempting fate."

Alfred Morell took a deep breath, threw the switch and ENIGMA came to life.

27

"You look after yourself in Geneva," Mackenzie McConnell whispered.

The wind caught Mackenzie's hair, splashing it across her

face. Cabot reached out and brushed it away and as he did she held his fingers to her lips. Thirty yards away from the Jaguar sports car, the engines of the Pan American Atlantic flight to Lisbon burst into life. Cabot encircled her in his arms.

"Just come back to me," Mackenzie said, her words scarcely audible over the roar. "Come back so we can finish this and then . . ."

"You don't have to say anything more," he murmured and brought his lips down upon hers, feeling her long fingers digging into his back as she clung to him. A moment later they were walking to the plane together.

Mackenzie watched him climb the ramp and returned the final salute he gave her. She turned on her heel and walked quickly to her car, getting in and watching as the aircraft lumbered out onto the runway. She was still looking after it when the plane was taxiing . . .. and someone was rapping on the car window. Mackenzie recognized the agent from MI5 and rolled down the car window.

"The directional truck we have at Berkeley Square is picking up a transmission," the agent said without preamble.

"From the clinic?" Mackenzie asked eagerly.

"No, but within the same quadrant. At last report the sender was staying on for a good long while. The unit commander believes we have a good chance for a fix."

"Let's see if we do," Mackenzie said. "I'll follow your lead."

Dr. Gustav Herder had driven the Mercedes 120 sedan flat-out along the new autobahn, constructed only four years ago, between Munich and St. Rémy-le-Pauvre on the Swiss border.

As a student Herder had had secret fantasies about becoming a racing driver; as a doctor he remained a devotee of the sport and had, prior to the war, volunteered his services as a track physician to the Porsche team at the annual Mille Miglia in Milan. At night, when there were almost no other cars to contend with and darkness enveloped the vehicle like a cocoon, the Mercedes was transformed into a living, breathing entity, giving Herder a serenity he hungered for. And always those hours dissolved far too quickly. As he wove his way along the twisting roads down from the Alps foothills, Herder could already discern the lights of St. Rémy-le-Pauvre flickering in the valley below.

The road flattened out only in the last two kilometers.
Herder did not slow down as he leaned the car into the stretch,
and he was unprepared for what happened next. Suddenly his
headlights became useless. The fresh blacktop glittered like a
sequined ribbon as the klieg lights—high-intensity lamps from
which antiaircraft searchlights had evolved—snapped on.
Herder dared not look up, for he knew he would be blinded. He
saw the pines rushing past him, then the blockhouse on the left
side of the road, the thick red-and-white candystripe barrier,
seemingly suspended in the air four feet above the ground . . .
the tank traps beyond it with the twisted bunches of barbed
wire, the spikes glistening like snow under the lights.

At the last possible moment he downshifted. The Mercedes
spat and roared, its momentum decreasing. The physician applied the brakes, managing to stop the vehicle only inches from
the barrier.

"*Halt*! Turn off the engine!"

The officer standing by the driver's window was not the one
Herder had expected. The commander of the border detail
should have been an overweight, pale boy whose family, as
Herder had learned, dealt in agricultural machinery and had
virtually bought him this safe commission. The officer staring
down at him was older, a major sporting the black uniform and
high-peaked cap with the silver death's-head of the SS.

Herder stepped out of the car, briefcase in hand. Without a
word he opened it and handed the thin, sallow-faced officer his
traveling papers.

"You are Doctor Herder," the officer said even before he
opened the passport.

"Yes, I am," the physician said calmly. He looked and saw
that all the uniforms belonged to the SS. He placed his hands
on the small of his back and slowly thrust his body forward,
arching his back like a man who has been sitting in one position for too long. How he wished he could have seen the night
sky, brilliant with stars, but the SS lights had stolen even
those.

"Why are you going to Geneva?" the Major asked. Herder
noticed that he spoke with an infinitesimal impediment.

"My papers state the reason quite clearly," Herder said. "I
travel to Geneva frequently to purchase medical supplies."

"Which you bring back with you in that little car?" the

officer queried. When he raised his eyebrows the skin on his forehead crinkled like that of an old man.

"I am only the broker, not the shipper," Herder explained patiently. "I am authorized to examine the goods, pay for them out of a Swiss account and arrange for shipment, which generally follows a week later. I do not bring anything back myself."

"Open the trunk."

The officer didn't bother with Herder's bag. He flipped back the blanket lying on the trunk floor and pulled forward a wooden crate. The top slats were not nailed down.

"And what is this?" he asked, holding up a slim green bottle of Moselle wine.

"A small gift for Lieutenant Kreutzer, the officer I generally see here."

Herder saw no reason to lie. Obviously something was about to happen or had happened to Kreutzer, in which case the SS knew everything they needed to.

"I see," the SS said. "And what does Lieutenant Kreutzer do to deserve this small gift?"

"Nothing at all, Major," Herder replied coldly. "There is nothing I require him to do. He simply enjoys the wine of the district where he was born. It isn't too much of a favor to do for a soldier of the Fatherland."

"Lieutenant Kreutzer will not be returning to his post," the officer said, eyes darting around the trunk, following the quick movements of his hands and fingers as they tapped and padded around the outline.

If he finds the papers I am a dead man, Herder thought.

Herder's tongue slipped around the tooth, probing in the silver lining cavity.

"You will have to bite down hard," the dentist had warned him. "The silver will harden over time. There may also be food particles. Bite down and gnash your teeth. You can do this without anyone noticing—at least they won't if they don't know what to look for. The seal will break and release the cyanide . . ."

For over seven hundred days he had lived with death in his mouth. Had the moment come when he would have to release it? The physician had no illusions about his courage under the torture the SS practiced. He could not permit them to take him alive.

"What do you wish to do with the wine?" the SS asked abruptly.

"I beg your pardon?"

"You are going over the Swiss frontier. Do you wish to declare it or leave it here and take it back with you tomorrow?"

"I . . . I suppose I might as well leave it here," Herder said.

The SS snapped his fingers. One of the corporals ran up and hoisted the crate from the car.

"Your wine will be safe with us—untouched," the officer smirked.

The SS swung his arm and the barrier was raised. Men dragged back the barbed wire enough for the car to get through.

"Have a good journey, *Herr Doktor*," he said softly.

Herder's actions were automatic. He wasn't conscious of tossing his papers onto the passenger seat, nor of stubbing the starter button with his forefinger, nor of shifting gears. He was almost surprised when the car shot forward through the opening, the wire flashing by. He wanted to shout, to scream out his relief, so that his muscles would stop trembling. God rode with you this night! he kept repeating to himself. If He believes in what you have, so must the British!

It was raining when the airliner touched down at Lisbon. The June heat trapped the moisture in the air, and by the time Cabot and the other passengers walked from the aircraft into the terminal building their clothing was drenched with sweat. After the immigration formalities Cabot presented his papers at the Lufthansa office. A sturdy, dour-faced blond girl checked his name against those on the passenger manifest, snatched his passport away and handed him a boarding pass. The passport, she informed him, would be returned to him on the plane.

Cabot washed up as best as he could in the men's lavatory, had a mug of black, bitter coffee in the canteen and then strolled to the Lufthansa office again. He asked the same girl some pointless questions about the length of the flight and what kind of weather he could expect in Geneva. She answered with the customary brusqueness but Cabot hardly heard a word. He was watching the two men behind the glass partition as they matched passports against the transit visas. Nothing seemed out of place. He couldn't sense anything going against him.

Cabot thanked the girl in grammar school German and entered the transit lounge. The Portuguese customs officer stamped his boarding pass and encouraged him to purchase some duty-free sherry. Cabot thanked him but declined. Out of the corner of his eye he had seen one of the Germans walk over to the embarkation gate. Punctually at six o'clock the announcement was made over the loudspeaker: Lufthansa Flight 01 was ready to take on its passengers. Cabot smiled graciously at the glacial blonde as he filed through the last checkpoint. He was less than four hours away from Geneva.

The previous evening Willi Trapp, communications specialist for *Die Piraten*, committed an act of extraordinary valor when he interrupted Karl Horst's dinner. The giant *Feldwebel* was concentrating fiercely on the dismemberment of a whole roast chicken when Trapp came in and shepherded him out of the mess hall. After Horst read the decoded text the chicken might never have existed. There could be no mistaking the sender: not only was the code word correct but the phraseology matched the way Kleemann spoke. The message itself left him numb.

Ordering Trapp to say nothing about the transmission, Karl Horst sequestered himself in his Major's office. From the recesses of the safe he withdrew a sealed envelope that bore his name as well as the file on Jonathan Baylor Cabot. He broke the seal on the envelope and pulled out the letter.

My Dear Comrade,

Because you are reading this, one of two things has come to pass: either you have received word of my death, in which case there is little for me to say except farewell, or else I am still alive, proceeding with my mission, and now need your help.

Assuming it is the latter, I ask you and the others to forgive me for the deception I perpetrated upon you in Calais. As soon as we had found our man I knew I would not be returning with you. But at the time I could not say as much. Subsequent details are inconsequential. Suffice to say I have espoused Schiffer's identity and am using it in a solo operation in London. That I am reaching out to you means something untoward has occurred which I myself cannot correct.

It is critical that you follow exactly whatever instructions you receive. Jaunich is privy to this operation and will assist you in any way. But the action part lies, as it always has, in the hands of *Die Piraten*. I understand I have already placed a heavy burden upon you in my last order, the execution of Corporal Henry Schiffer. Perhaps one day I will be able to absolve you of the consequences, which should have been mine. But now I must have your trust and skills once again. If we succeed, then the war will soon be over for all of us. The ultimate mission of *Die Piraten* will have been accomplished.

Take my message to Jaunich, prepare yourselves and soon we will meet again.

Alles Gute,
MAJOR HELMUT KLEEMANN

Karl Horst sighed deeply and pocketed the letter. Yes, he had been surprised—and hurt—when the Major had told him he would be staying behind . . . without explanation. But his loyalty to the man remained stalwart: the *Feldwebel* hadn't flinched when the Major had told him that one day, soon after the unit's return to Germany, Jaunich would call and activate his order for Schiffer's execution. A killing Horst would carry out on his Major's behalf . . .

The *Feldwebel* opened the dossier on Jonathan Baylor Cabot and read the details. Aside from the obvious, that Cabot was an officer in an obscure branch of American counterintelligence, the contents yielded no clues as to why the Major had demanded this man's execution when Cabot arrived in Geneva . . . tomorrow. But all the same he would have it, Horst vowed. Of that there was no question.

"Trapp!"

The communications specialist had been waiting, unbidden, in the outer office.

"Get Jaunich in Berlin—priority!"

"*Zu Befehl*!" Trapp turned away, then at once looked back at Horst. "From Major Kleemann?" he asked softly.

Horst nodded. "Action."

Trapp could not restrain the grin. He positioned himself before the switchboard and put the call through, conscious of the adrenaline coursing through his blood. Yet the euphoria died as quickly as it had been born.

"We're out of luck," Trapp said, coming back into Guderian's office. "Jaunich left Berlin an hour ago. If anyone at the Reichschancellery knows where he went they're not saying."

"*Scheiss!*" Horst swore. "Didn't they at least tell you when he'd be back?"

"I received the distinct impression that queries were strictly *verboten*," Trapp said mildly. He paused. "I suggest, *Feldwebel*, that we may have to handle this ourselves."

"Get the men together," Horst told him.

Ten minutes later *Die Piraten* had assembled in Horst's quarters. They listened as the *Feldwebel* read the message and explained the circumstances.

"Technically we are not permitted to use our initiative without Berlin's approval," Horst rumbled. "Yet neither can we let down Major Kleemann, who is expecting us to act. I remember that when we first came together the Major explained the chain of command like this: we answer to him, he to Jaunich, Jaunich to the Führer. Well, Jaunich isn't to be found, and if we go to Hitler God only knows what will happen. In the meantime the Major waits, counting on us. Since I am the next in command I will go to Geneva. Klaus, the text specifically asks for you. But I am keeping this on a strictly volunteer basis. You have every right to refuse the request."

Klaus Langer, the weapons specialist, slowly coiled his thin, sprawled frame and rose to his full height of six feet five inches. He removed his spectacles and carefully wiped them with a linen handkerchief. Langer's fastidiousness was the butt of gentle humor among the men, but there was no better expert with any kind of firearm or explosive than this soft-spoken, angelic-looking Silesian.

"Since when have we listened to *anyone* who told us not to use our initiative?" he said softly.

Within the hour Horst and Langer had become civilians. Their suits, cut in Berlin, gave them the appearance of the industrial engineers their papers made them out to be. From Regensburg they drove along the foothills of the Bavarian Alps, following the contours of the range, until they crossed the border at Lörrach and entered Basel. Although Swiss customs examined the vehicle carefully, they never came close to discovering the weaponry secreted in the chassis. On the outskirts of Basel the two men drove off onto a deserted side-road, brought out the weapons and placed these in small suitcases whose contents were then buried. They made it into the city proper and found the railway station twenty minutes before the overnight Geneva express was to depart. Klaus Langer convinced the frugal Horst that their hard driving merited the comfort of first-class accommodations.

The two members of *Die Piraten* arrived in Geneva at half past two in the afternoon. From the train station Horst and Langer, fully armed now, took a taxi directly to the airport. The message from London speculated that the target, Cabot, would be arriving in Switzerland via Portugal. There was only one flight a day between Lisbon and Geneva and it wasn't due for another two hours. Since there were no arrivals scheduled in the interim Karl Horst adjourned for lunch, leaving Langer to procure a car. At four forty-five both were back in the main concourse watching the disembarking passengers from Lufthansa Flight 01.

"And there he is," Karl Horst breathed.

Jonathan Cabot, carrying a Gladstone bag, cleared customs without formality and made his way to a taxi stand.

"I imagine we want to do this neatly," Langer murmured, opening the driver's door of the Citroën sedan.

Horst hadn't taken his eyes off the quarry.

"Very," he said grimly. "Have no fear, my young friend. Before the day is out we shall take him. A man, especially one who has traveled for as long as he has, will want to sleep."

As soon as the words were out of his mouth the *Feldwebel* remembered the young Canadian soldier. Because he had read Cabot's file he tried to tell himself this time was different. Yet he didn't know how . . .

The highest point in Geneva's Old Town rises 1326 feet above the lake. Situated on that vantage point is one of Europe's oldest churches, the Cathedral of St. Pierre, built on the ruins of Roman temples and early Christian churches that hark back to the fifth and sixth centuries. As he passed through the lush gardens which surround the cathedral, Cabot saw the two black, weathered stone towers, dating back to the twelfth century, that had never been completed. To those who didn't know, the effect was that of a ruin rather than unfinished work.

At half past five on a workday there were few people around the cathedral. Two gardeners were tending to the shrubbery; a group of ministers, whispering in Schweizerdeutsch, swept by him, disappearing through an archway into the central courtyard. Cabot walked around the cathedral, pausing now and then to look out toward the Rade de Genève or, in the opposite direction, toward the Gothic structures that made up the Hôtel de Ville. Nothing was out of place. He heard nothing except the twittering of birds in the pear and cherry trees. Cabot entered the cathedral through the original western doorway.

The interior of St. Pierre is over two hundred feet long, the walls soaring toward three vaulted domes. The effect is at once humbling yet simple, precisely the combination intended in Calvinist churches. The nave, divided by four aisles each with rows of chiseled pews, has a gallery, blind arcading and triforium. Light filters in through seven stained-glass windows on either wall as well as from the chandeliers suspended from the center of the domes. The white-yellow effect is broken by the ruby-red shadows from glass candleholders on either side of the altar.

Cabot paused to allow his eyes to adjust to the light. Against the left wall, by the gravestones of long-dead ecclesiastics, a group of pilgrims was gathered before the "Chaise de Calvin," a triangular chair said to have been used by the Reformer. Across the way the chapels were silent, iron bars across half-moon doors. There were no more than half a dozen people in the pews. Cabot counted five women, kerchiefs over their hair, scattered randomly across the first six pews before the altar. There was also one man, well in the back, on the second-to-last pew, sitting right at the edge.

Cabot slipped his hand into his jacket pocket and moved down the aisle toward the last pew. He slipped onto the hard, polished wood and knelt down on the padded rail. The gun came up, the barrel pointed directly at the pew before him.

"Yesterday Big Ben struck seven times at six o'clock," he said softly.

The man's head stiffened. He slipped the red and yellow scarf, the identification mark, from his neck and rose. Throwing the coat back on his shoulders, he swung the scarf around his neck and stepped out into the aisle, shrugging his coat back on. Cabot moved directly behind the man, following him out. As they stepped outside, Dr. Gustav Herder suddenly turned to his left, onto a narrow footpath that followed the cathedral's south flank. Cabot stayed with him, his eyes moving ceaselessly across the expanse of lawn on the left. The nearest cover was ten meters away in a hedgerow that marked the perimeter of the garden.

As they rounded the corner Cabot stepped quickly to Herder's side so that the physician would be the one exposed as they made the turn. Herder looked up at him with a faint ironic smile but did not break his pace. He led the way to a small opening around a dormant fountain.

Gustav Herder sat down and examined the man still standing before him.

"You are wrong," he said. "Big Ben chimed six times at seven o'clock."

"Doctor Gustav Herder," Cabot said.

"And you are not English," Herder replied.

"Mackenzie McConnell sends her regards—and this."

In his left hand Cabot produced a velvet jeweler's box and handed it to the physician. When Herder opened it he saw the cameo pin with the image of Diana the Huntress. It was the pin he had given Mackenzie McConnell a year ago. Herder closed the box and held it out to Cabot.

"She won't be coming anymore." It was more of a sigh than a statement.

"Nothing's happened to her," Cabot told him. "She'll be here the next time."

Herder scrutinized him carefully. "We all pray there will be a next time, Herr . . . ?"

"Doctor Herder, Mackenzie sent me because you have something of special interest for her," Cabot said, ignoring the physician's attempt to elicit a name. "That was the message London received."

Herder crossed one leg over the other and folded his hands around one knee.

"Does the name Dachau mean anything to you?"

Herder caught the sharp intake of breath, air whistling through the teeth as though he had touched the man beside him with a scarlet branding iron.

"Dachau means a great deal to me, Doctor."

Oh, God, Orit!

Herder's words had, in one savage motion, peeled back the balm that lay over the wound, had almost become part of it, so that only in his most private moments did Cabot recognize it as not being part of his own flesh.

"What of Dachau?" he demanded, his words a fierce whisper.

"I have brought photographs," Herder said quickly, realizing that this man had to be much more than just a messenger. "The camp is being enlarged. There was also a meeting held there three weeks ago. Among those present was a man called Eichmann. I understand that there are preparations under way to create more camps, bigger camps, quite possibly in Poland."

Cabot glanced down at the elegant satchel at Herder's feet. It was his now, along with all the horrors Herder and God knows how many others had risked their lives to obtain and transmit. They did this because they believed that a handful of men in London and Washington would look upon this evidence and bring the wrath of God upon the perpetrators. Herder and those like him dreamed of a fiery vengeance because what they lived in the midst of demanded no less. Yet those whose compassion they sought were not so pure. Giants were governed by laws and considerations that ordinary men could never comprehend.

"You know about Dachau," Herder observed.

"Yes, I know," Cabot said. "And that in spite of the hell that is born there you never before used the emergency routing to contact London. There is more, isn't there."

He saw Herder flinch before the callousness of the words.

"In Regensburg, fifty kilometers outside Dachau, is a commando camp," the physician said in a dead voice. "The British know of its existence and the fact that it is guarded by the SS. Nothing more because the men who train there are among the best. Even my sources, as close as they are, have not been able to determine exactly what goes on. But a few days ago something unusual happened there. That was the reason for the emergency routing . . ."

Speaking in a monotone Gustav Herder outlined the details Kurt and Anna Moelders had provided.

"And the curious thing is that this soldier was later killed— in cold blood. You see, we believe that he was someone quite other than who he appeared, possibly a British agent who had been posing as a corporal. It seemed he was kept alive for a purpose, for a specific time, until—"

Cabot had scooped up a handful of pebbles and was about to toss them into the fountain. His hand froze in midair.

"A corporal!"

"Yes—"

"Does he have a name?"

Herder flinched at the brutality behind the question.

"Schiffer. His name was Henry Schiffer."

Cabot's fist opened and the pebbles dropped away. Herder saw blood where the stones had dug into the American's flesh.

She was right! Mackenzie had been right all along!

"You're certain he was British," Cabot said, testing. "Schiffer is a German name. He may have been an Abwehr or SD double."

"I only said he had been with the British Army," Herder corrected him. "The man himself was a Canadian."

Cabot straightened up and looked at Herder for what the physician thought was a very long time. But it may have been that the intensity behind the American's gaze never caused him to blink.

"I want you to tell me everything you can about Schiffer," he said quietly.

"There isn't anything else to add," Herder protested.

"Do you have a photograph?"

"No—"

"A description!"

He would beg for anything, a scrap to take back to London, to prove to Dulles and Churchill that Mackenzie had been right!

"Then repeat what you do know," Cabot said at last, spent. "And for the love of God don't leave anything out!"

The physician hesitated, then began his recital again. Cabot remained immobile, a blind statue, looking straight ahead but seeing nothing . . .

Even if he had he would never have questioned the presence of two men who were strolling away toward the twin unfinished towers of St. Pierre. He might have noticed that one man had a firm grip on the other's elbow.

It took all of Klaus Langer's strength to guide Horst away from the proximity of the two men. He did not release his grip until they had turned the corner of the tower.

"You can let go of me now, Klaus," Horst said.

He pulled his arm away as easily as though it had been held by a child.

"Can you believe it?" he whispered. "Gustav Herder, eminent physician, lifetime friend of the Moelderses . . . a thieving traitor!"

"So what does that make the Moelderses?" Langer asked quietly. He had placed himself in such a position that he never lost sight of either the American or Herder.

Karl Horst shuddered. He knew that every person in the Regensburg compound was, to whatever degree, under random surveillance by the Gestapo. *Die Piraten* found this a joke and sometimes played little games with Himmler's "trenchcoats." But on others, especially the civilians who had dealings with Regensburg, the scrutiny was constant—and the results shared with the officers of the compound. Because he was Kleemann's second in command, Horst had seen photographs taken of the Moelderses when they were in Munich . . . shopping, having lunch, by chance meeting an old friend. Gustav Herder. The couple whom *Die Piraten* considered aunt and uncle were traitors, killers as deadly as any they had ever encouraged. The cruelty of the betrayal broke the giant's heart.

"Are they still there?"

"They're getting up," Langer told him. "If they separate do you want to take Herder now?"

"No," the *Feldwebel* said softly. "He's ours any time. We stay with the American—and see what other little surprises he has for us!"

Dusk had fallen by the time Cabot arrived at the Beau Rivage, Geneva's grand address on the lakefront. He registered under the name on his American Red Cross passport, had his one bag sent up to his suite, and followed the manager into the vaults where he deposited Gustav Herder's briefcase for safekeeping. All the while his mind was churning.

Schiffer . . . the one man in the company whose body Clarke hadn't been able to find. Because Schiffer wasn't dead then. He had been taken alive, needed alive. His would be the identity of a man coming to England, under the cover of Dunkirk evacuation. That agent would need every scrap of information about Schiffer, so what better source than the man himself, a tired, hungry, desperate soldier who never thought twice about talking about himself . . .

But who was the man, connected to Regensburg, who had conceived, and so brilliantly executed, the operation? Who was Schiffer now?

Cabot knew that upon leaving Herder he should have gone directly to the U.S. mission. From there a coded text could have been sent to London. Mackenzie had to be notified and Schiffer picked up at once! The Regensburg connection made him lethal!

But he had run out of time. Even now, as he walked into the suite, Cabot realized he was late. Dulles's contact, the fount of priceless information known as Source Mainstream, would not wait. A delay meant something had gone wrong. Source Mainstream would disappear before Cabot ever got to him.

And he had to make contact! *Because for the first time in over a year Source Mainstream had contacted Dulles first.* Only hours before Dulles was to have sent his own signal, Source Mainstream had demanded a meeting, immediately— something he had never done before. Dulles had looked up at Cabot and quietly asked: "Now what in hell could be so important for him to lose control?"

Neither man had an answer at that moment, but the same unspoken question was in both their minds: *had Berlin anticipated them?*

Cabot adjusted his shoulder-holster strap and moved over to the connecting door between his suite and the adjacent one. It opened soundlessly, revealing a space a foot wide, then another door. Cabot brought the gun out and his hand pushed down the handle.

Klaus Langer and Karl Horst had no difficulty in determining which suite belonged to Cabot. Langer merely followed the porter bearing Cabot's bag while Horst maintained surveillance on the American in the lobby. He watched as Cabot was escorted to the vaults by the manager and patiently waited for him to return. In the interim the weapons specialist returned.

"He travels in style," was Langer's only comment.

Both men watched as Cabot entered the elevator, following the swing of the needle to the seventh floor.

"I think he's settled in for the night," Langer said matter-of-factly. "I know what you want, Karl. But Herder was an accident, a fortunate one but an accident nonetheless. Our primary objective is Cabot. We should take him now, cleanly, quietly."

Karl Horst said nothing.

"We have the Major's orders," Langer persisted. "We also have Herder. The briefcase is no longer important. If Cabot doesn't claim it the hotel will simply give it to the next of kin. And we know in Cabot's case that is a moot point."

The *Feldwebel* hesitated, then finally spat out the words: "All right, we take him now!"

But Karl Horst didn't take a single step. Both men froze as a figure they instantly recognized came through the swinging doors of the lounge and entered an elevator. They watched in silent disbelief as the needle told them to which floor the only passenger in the car ascended. It was the seventh. And the man in question was Gerd Jaunich . . .

"You would be well advised to put your weapon away."

The voice was as steady as the hand holding the Beretta whose barrel was trained on his heart. Slowly but without hesitation Cabot slipped his revolver into its holster.

Now at last he could believe it.

"Gerd Jaunich," he said softly, as though the words would somehow add reality to the man.

One of Germany's faceless leaders. The man who saved Hitler's life during the First War, who had instant access to him, night or day. The confidant and evaluator of every important project brought before the Führer. Source Mainstream. Cabot had not believed it when Dulles had first uttered the name behind the code.

"Who are you to Potomac?" Jaunich asked, using Dulles's cipher.

"Clipper."

With an elegant gesture the German deposited the weapon on the end table.

"You are late. Was there a problem?"

"No."

Of course not, Gerd Jaunich considered silently. Not for a man like yourself, handpicked by Potomac, my alter ego for so many years now, without anyone being the wiser—not even Churchill, who thought I spoke only to him. Untrue . . . Dulles was my first and most secret correspondent, my window on the Potomac just as I am his on Berlin.

But I could tell from your expression, Clipper, that you were privy to none of this. Yet I know as much as there is to know about you, the kind of man you are, what you have done and where. Your presence was not unexpected and it has absolved me of what I am about to do.

"You have something for Potomac," Cabot said, never taking his eyes off the other man. Behind Jaunich's iron-will control he sensed hesitation, the misgiving of a secret man who must suddenly expose his heart.

"Tell me," Jaunich said. "Why did Potomac send you?"

"I was available."

"That means you were already in London. Why?"

"I am looking for a man."

The words were spoken with such ruthless indifference that Jaunich shuddered.

I must tell him now! he thought. I can betray Erik in this moment while I still have the will and tell Clipper about the operation running against Prometheus . . . If I do this perhaps he will put aside his hatred. Erik can be taken alive, returned to Germany under the guise of a trade . . . Yet there is no guarantee that Erik will *permit* himself to be taken alive. He is succeeding against all odds. I know it because Dulles has pitted Clipper against him . . .

Yet I was the one who helped plan the operation. I induced Erik to undergo tremendous pain on its account. God help me, I never would have done it had I known about Sea Lion . . .

Gerd Jaunich reached across the sofa and handed Cabot an accordion-style paper case.

"Before you open it, Clipper, I wish to ask you a question: Are you cognizant of an Allied operation code-named Prometheus?"

"I'm afraid not," Cabot said.

"Don't be flippant!" Jaunich barked. "You are a hard man and one day that will work against you. But at this moment you might remember we are not adversaries."

Cabot would not take his eyes off the German. Any movement now would betray the terrible exultation he felt. Berlin *had* been moving against Prometheus—from the day Cabot had allowed that last message from Beth Davis to reach Berlin. It had all begun then, and now the circle had come full turn: he had been responsible for Berlin's learning about Prometheus. He would also be the one who would stop its attempt to destroy it.

"You *do* know!" Jaunich said softly. "Go ahead, open the case."

Cabot did so and pulled out two manila envelopes, both numbered.

"Open the first one."

To think it all began with Sea Lion only forty-eight hours

ago, Jaunich thought to himself. Hitler summons me to the Reichschancellery. The General Staff is present, as is the rest of the court: Himmler, Goebbels, Goering, Ribbentrop. Hitler picks up a pointer and walks over to the map of Europe hanging on the wall. He taps the blue of the English Channel and begins his recital. He has been reading all accounts of attempts to invade England. He recalls the success of William the Conqueror, the disaster of the Spanish Armada, Napoleon's engineering dream of boring a tunnel between the Continent and Dover. He concludes by stating that there is only one possible way to humble England . . .

At this moment I am afraid. Hitler is about to reveal the operation against Prometheus, violate every promise he made to myself and Erik! But what he says is far more horrible . . .

Hitler speaks of a new operation. Jodl, ever the sycophant, chimes in with the code name: Sea Lion. The invasion of England . . .

I cannot believe what I am hearing, yet I force myself to listen. A vast armada is being prepared. Millions of men readied, paratroopers, naval assault teams, a fifth column. Casualties of up to 80 percent on the initial beachhead assault are deemed acceptable—even necessary! To show the English what we are willing to sacrifice . . .

The recital ends and everyone applauds. I feel my hands clapping together mechanically and I am ashamed. All this time Hitler has been watching me. When the meeting is over he asks me to stay behind.

Everyone has gone. Hitler states that I disapprove of Sea Lion. I seize the opportunity and ask him why, after the endless discussions we have had, he has not only returned to the subject—*but committed the resources of Germany to it!*

Hitler is conciliatory. He tells me he understands why I am angry, because I was the one who had convinced him that an invasion was impossible and he believed me—then. His voice becomes more animated. He is, he says, overwhelmed by the irony: yes, he believed me—yet couldn't I see that I was also the one who unlocked the riddle? Invasion was impossible because Britain could still fight. *But the operation against Prometheus, when it succeeded, would provide the very springboard the assault needed!*

At that moment I confess I lost control of myself, shouting that the entire object of Prometheus was to *save* German lives.

We had conceived the most daring operation of the war in order to humble the English in one fell swoop, force them to sue for surrender. It was insanity to believe any force could subjugate them!

Even then Hitler did not lose his composure. He told me to reconsider it, making certain I understood that nothing I could say would change his mind . . . And I have. I have thought about nothing else until I accepted what it was I had to do. Sea Lion had to be crippled, and there was only one way to do that: Erik's mission against Prometheus had to be stopped. If the British succeeded in sending the coin of the realm to America, Roosevelt would continue to ship back arms. Instead of invading a husk, Hitler's generals would be faced with a fortress! And, even if sanity did not prevail and Sea Lion were not dismissed, it would have to be postponed . . . long enough for even the most myopic to accept its folly.

That is why I have betrayed you, Erik, on the eve of what could have been your greatest triumph. God willing, we will meet soon and I shall explain to you that in this betrayal I tried to keep alive the reasons why you undertook so much: to save life. Now I must save yours. If I can do that it will bring me peace enough . . .

Gerd Jaunich tightened his lips and gazed up at Cabot. The American had not opened either of the two envelopes.

"You mustn't be polite on account of an old man's reveries," Jaunich told him. "Go ahead, open them."

"Perhaps you have something to tell me before I do," Cabot said.

"The contents will speak for themselves, Clipper."

Cabot tore open the flap on the first and drew out a three-by-five glossy print.

"Schiffer!" he whispered.

"Your quarry, is he not?" Jaunich said.

"But why—"

"The betrayal?" Jaunich broke in. "An honest question, Clipper, but one which I will not answer at this moment. You are one who would understand how men choose to turn away from what is painful. Besides, there is no need for you to know."

Jaunich paused. "He is the one you are seeking. I have given him to you and I pray that you find him. He is very good, Clipper, as good if not better than you. But now the advantage is yours. You have a face—and overwhelming resources to throw against him."

"Yes, I have him now," Cabot whispered.

"I want you to promise me one thing," Jaunich said sharply.

"If I can."

"I want you to bring him to me alive. It is not a condition I can enforce, and perhaps he himself will make it impossible for you to do so. But, Clipper, you must promise me to try!"

"Who is he to you?" Cabot asked warily.

Jaunich gestured at the second envelope. "Let us say that I am responsible for controlling his destiny. I am giving what I can to correct the mistakes I forced upon him."

The second photograph was in Cabot's hand.

"It can't be!" he whispered. "They can't be one and the same man."

"They are," Jaunich said. "They are both Erik Guderian."

The photograph slipped through Cabot's fingers. He realized Jaunich was staring at him and that his face had been bled white. Slowly he shook his head, trying to comprehend the incomprehensible. A picture of Orit smashed into his consciousness and he groaned. The irony was complete: Jaunich had betrayed Guderian in order to save him. Yet he had done so to the one man who could never permit him to live . . .

Cabot reached down to retrieve the photo. He rose, not daring to look at it again, and found a gun in Gerd Jaunich's steady hand. A second later the door behind him was smashed open.

"It *was* him . . ." Karl Horst whispered. Yet a question mark pervaded his words.

"It was Jaunich," Langer said quietly. "No mistake."

"And he went to the same floor as Cabot, as though he had been waiting, watching for him to come . . ." the *Feldwebel* murmured. "Klaus, it can't be what I'm thinking!"

"You yourself said Cabot might lead us to other quarry," the young weapons specialist said. "Jaunich is a senior official of the Reichschancellery—Hitler's confidant. He is *not* an operative or even control. So what business does he have with the man Major Kleemann sent us to eliminate?"

"Enough!" Horst said viciously.

But the implications of Langer's question still paralyzed them. Was it conceivable that a man of Jaunich's background and stature was liaisoning with a known American agent? Could Jaunich, the guiding hand behind *Die Piraten*, also be a traitor—working with the very man they had come to kill? *Was that why Major Kleemann had sent the Regensburg message, because he had known that Jaunich would not be in Berlin but in Geneva . . . meeting Cabot*?

"Find out which suite Jaunich has taken," the *Feldwebel* said tersely. "I will meet you on the seventh floor. If they're together . . ."

Five minutes later Karl Horst had his answer.

"Their suites are side by side," Klaus Langer said coldly, meeting Horst in the corridor.

"God help us all," the *Feldwebel* breathed. "All right. We take Cabot first—alive if possible. But Jaunich *must* be returned to Regensburg. I want him to answer to the Major."

Horst withdrew a fifteen-shot Mauser and screwed in the bulbous silencer. Langer was already kneeling by the door, picking the lock. The door swung open and Horst stepped smoothly into the room, the barrel weaving. Langer slipped by him, checking the bedroom and bathroom. Nothing. The weapons expert pointed to the door set in the middle of the wall. Horst nodded, turned the handle and drew it back. Voices were heard, one of them unmistakably Jaunich's.

The *Feldwebel* nodded to Langer, who pressed himself up against the wall. Karl Horst stepped back, raised one leg, then slammed his heel against the wood. The door burst open and *Die Piraten* spilled into the room, crouching as they did, their weapons trained on the one man standing, the other holding a gun on him.

Gerd Jaunich had heard the turn of the handle. Someone was in the partition between the two rooms. Whoever they were they did not belong to Clipper, which left only two alternatives: someone had followed either him or Clipper to Geneva. At that moment Jaunich picked up the gun and raised it at the same time as Cabot straightened up. The door burst open.

Jaunich was not certain of what registered first: Cabot's whirling about at the crash or his own recognition of the two men who were suddenly in the room. But Jaunich knew exactly what he had to do, what it had all been leading up to. His last conscious thought was to ask Erik to forgive him—for everything.

The first bullet from the Beretta sang by Cabot's temple and buried itself in Karl Horst's forehead. The big man's head snapped back and he fell forward, the last of his momentum sending him crashing against a lamp. But Langer responded automatically. The silenced Mauser spat out bullets into Gerd Jaunich's body, the firestream swinging toward Cabot. Cabot was faster. The Hanyatti was in his hand, finger swinging back the trigger even as the arm was still moving. The single shot ripped through Klaus Langer's chest, exploding on impact, tearing away the heart and everything else in its path. It was all over in less than five seconds.

Cabot stepped over the two men and kicked their weapons beyond their reach. He lifted Gerd Jaunich up against the cushions, feeling the blood pulse out of the shattered body.

"You must . . ." Jaunich started to say, then suddenly gagged. Cabot swung Jaunich's head back, listening to the unearthly gasps. Jaunich's fingers clamped on his hand.

"Save him . . ." he whispered, not having the strength to even open his eyes. "Save him . . . for all of us!"

In the next instant Potomac's window on Berlin closed forever.

28

The second week of June brought with it the promise of an extraordinary summer. It was difficult to believe, in those peerless days of azure skies and brilliant sunshine, that the war existed at all. The illusion was heightened as the Dunkirk evacuees were absorbed into the mainstream of city life. All but the most serious cases had been discharged, permitted to return to kith and kin. At hospitals and clinics those who had worked ceaselessly for days on end were given a much deserved furlough. As the Army slowly reorganized itself, the number of khaki uniforms seen around the city dwindled: New orders were received; companies, battalions and whole divisions were being re-formed at camps set up in the south of England. But even as the wounds began to heal and the shock was absorbed, men looked ahead to the next conflict, knowing with a fatalistic certainty that it would come as surely as the sun rose and set.

At half past eight on the morning of June 14 Erik Guderian was standing by the side of the bed in the room he shared with Christine Harloch. He did up the top button on his jacket, watching the gentle rise and fall of her breast as she slept, and silently asked her to forgive him. She had given herself to him without hesitation or reserve, and in her love he had carved out a refuge for himself. Now he was abandoning her, leaving her defenseless against the hunters who would turn her life into a living hell . . . the same hunters who would, if his mission failed and he was on the run, deny him this refuge because they would already have made Christine their bait.

Guderian leaned over and brushed his lips against her warm skin, inhaled deeply of her scent and listened as she murmured in her dreams.

"Forgive me, my love," he whispered. An instant later he was gone.

The motorcycle waited in the garage, its tank full, the major engine parts carefully examined for any defects. Beside the machine was the knapsack he had packed last night with what he thought he might need: a change of clothing, gloves, towel, the essentials of a first-aid kit, a flashlight, a length of strong, corded rope and a large piece of charcoal wrapped in tissue. Guderian completed the inventory, drew open the garage doors and walked the BSA out. After locking up he proceeded halfway down the mews before climbing aboard and jumping on the kick starter.

Traffic was light and he arrived at Russell Square in less than fifteen minutes. The next two hours were spent in the Reading Room of the British Museum, where he examined issues of the National Historical Register dating back to the turn of the century. When he had gleaned what he could from that source Guderian ferreted out a half dozen historical works dealing with a little-known aspect of sixteenth-century English history: the story of a group of men called the *Poursuivants* . . .

At twelve o'clock, his research completed, Guderian left the

Reading Room. He kicked the motorcycle to life and carefully threaded his way across London to Old Kent Road, a major artery heading south. At Lewisham he chose a less traveled route that took him through Downe and along the bypass curving around Sevenoaks.

The day was crisp, with a cloudless sky and only a hint of a breeze. Guderian made Tonbridge in less than forty minutes, crossed Robertsbridge at one o'clock and entered Battle a few minutes later. He drove off the road onto a farmer's dirt path to relieve himself, then slowed as he entered Hastings proper. He drove through the site of that ancient battle without stopping, staying on the secondary road that paralleled the cliffs, then swung due north. Two miles beyond the limits of Hastings he arrived at his destination.

The village of Ipswich-Colby had been founded in the fourteenth century. From what Guderian had read its population had never exceeded more than a few hundred souls. The main street, cobbled, with narrow sidewalks, was still lit by gas lamps. There was one of everything: a pub, bakery, dry goods store, grocery store, dairy outlet (for the regionally famous Colby cheese), post office, barbershop (for both sexes if the sign were to be believed), constabulary and a smith's shop. Guderian drove slowly over the cobblestones, taking note of the idle but not uncurious glances given him by the villagefolk. They were people of the land, tenant farmers who had tilled the acreage of their forefathers for as long as memory served. An insular, almost inbred people, they regarded strangers with a benign suspicion. To learn what he needed to know would take patience and not a little subterfuge.

Guderian leaned the BSA on its kickstand, swung his arms out side to side and stretched his legs. He unstrapped his knapsack, and swinging it over his good shoulder pushed through the swinging doors of the Mermaid alehouse.

The pub was a study in Victoriana, consisting of one large room with a hexagonal bar in the center. The seats and benches were covered in ancient needlepoint, the fabric fastened to furniture frame by brass tacks. The floor was generously strewn with sawdust (to absorb both the dirt and the odor of field earth that dropped from farmers' boots), and the island behind the bar was ringed with a brass loop from which hung brilliantly polished pewter mugs. The odor of tobacco impregnated wood whose dull sheen testified to its centenarian age.

There were half a dozen men present, four at the bar, two sitting at a table near the green-veined marble fireplace. Guderian held the inquisitive glances for a few seconds, a faint smile on his lips. He placed his knapsack by the footrail and shifted his weight against the bar.

"A pint of bitter, please."

The barmaid was a raven-haired beauty with locks streaming down to her waist. She gave Guderian a saucy smile, violet eyes laughing.

"My pleasure, sir."

The accent was broad, thick like fresh cold butter. But no one else spoke while she drew Guderian's bitter and with a coquette's shake of her hip palmed his money.

"I didn't think I'd be seeing ye agin, sor. Specially not in these parts."

A rush of fear contracted Guderian's fingers, and for an instant he thought he would squeeze the glass hard enough to shatter the pint. He glanced down the bar, past the three men who separated him from Albert Hinkley, Royal Navy retired, Admiral Runnymeade's driver.

"Good Lord, you gave me a start!" Guderian exclaimed, smiling broadly. "Albert Hinkley, isn't it?"

The driver nodded. "The same, sor, the same."

He picked up his beer and came around to where Guderian stood.

"This is the fine gentleman I was telling ye about," Hinkley announced to the pub, "Made it off Dunkirk almost to meet his Maker on Whitehall!"

There were smiles, but no one joined Hinkley's quiet laughter. The watery hazel eyes regarded Guderian steadily, the questions behind them all too obvious.

"I'm sure it wasn't all that close," Guderian said, raising his glass.

"And many thanks for that, sor," Hinkley said, his blue-veined, liver-spotted hand lifting his own drink. But his lips didn't touch the bitter.

"And what would be bringing you down here on this fine day, sor?" Hinkley inquired softly.

It was a pivotal question, laced with suspicion. Yet Guderian realized that with luck he might be able to turn it to his advantage.

"I have to report in the day after tomorrow," he said.

"Reassignment. But I've always wanted to see something of England other than London. Actually, bumping into you, as it were, gave me the idea of coming down here."

"Did it now, sor?"

"It's an easy drive from London." Guderian shrugged. "I'm an engineer by training. There's not another part of the country so close to London where I can literally walk through centuries of English architecture."

"True enough," Hinkley said without inflection.

"But perhaps I've come at the wrong time," Guderian said, pushing away the empty glass. "I feel I'm intruding, so . . ."

A horny, calloused hand slapped down upon his shoulder.

"Bring Corporal Schiffer another pint, Mary," Hinkley ordered. "He'll not go away thinking any the poorer of us!"

The beer was scarcely in his hand when Guderian was turned around. Hinkley had accepted what he had been told and that was all the invitation needed. One by one Guderian shook hands with the others at the bar. They were tall, beefy men, with red, weathered faces, grizzled beards and hands the size and texture of picnic hams. Their rough camaraderie matched their voices and clothing, and in the space of a minute they had formed a semicircle around him, pressing him with questions about the war and Dunkirk in particular. Each had at least one boy in the service, and while they knew that the chances of Corporal Henry Schiffer's knowing anything about any one of the lads were slim, the questions, pent up for so long, tumbled out. It was, Guderian thought, as though he were a talisman, someone who had passed through the inferno and survived. Perhaps they believed that if they touched him his magic would be transmitted through a desperate love to offspring as yet unheard from.

"Not such a bad lot, are we then?" Hinkley said quietly when the others had gone, chores waiting.

"I wish I could have told them something definite," Guderian said sincerely. "The pain of not knowing . . ."

"Aye, it's evil, lad, that it is," Hinkley mused sadly.

He gestured to Mary to replenish their glasses but Guderian placed a palm over his.

"There's still a lot I want to see before nightfall," he said. "It won't do to have me careening about the countryside drunk as a lord. On a borrowed motorcycle yet!"

Hinkley laughed heartily, wiping his nicotine-stained mustache with a curiously dainty gesture.

"Right you are, Henry," he said. "And if it were any other night I'd offer you the hospitality of the manor. But tonight's the Ship's Supper and we won't be havin' any visitors about."

"Ship's Supper?" Guderian asked, feigning ignorance. Obviously Runnymeade's driver had forgotten his unintentional reference to the supper after the accident at the Admiralty Gates. The supper that should have been held two nights ago had Cabot not suddenly altered the schedule.

Hinkley leaned back on the bar, his eyes twinkling like those of an elf.

"It's a tradition, lad," he said, the words rolling off his tongue lovingly. "Before his ship sails the Admiral holds a dinner for his officers and their ladies. God knows it will be too long before any of them have another chance to spend some easy time, to say nothing of the table that awaits them."

"A very generous thing to do," Guderian murmured.

A hundred questions streamed into his mind but he held back. The Petty Officer was far from drunk and the trust he had shown would disappear the moment Guderian asked something which an Army corporal could not possibly have been interested in.

"The Admiral's that kind of man," Hinkley agreed, removing a dull gold hunter from the pocket of his chamois vest. "And I should be getting along. There's still enough to do."

"I can imagine," Guderian commented. "You must be expecting close to a hundred people."

"That's true," Hinkley nodded. "The women here have been cooking for the past two days. But there's still the beer to deliver, the workmen to be rounded up."

"Decorations?" Guderian queried.

"No, lad, the manor itself," Hinkley corrected him. "If ye're interested in the houses of these parts ye'd have heard of Topcliffe Hall."

Guderian expressed the appropriate surprise.

"That's Admiral Runnymeade's residence?"

"Ye have heard of it," Hinkley laughed, obviously pleased.

"Well, of course!" Guderian exclaimed. "It's one of the most famous houses in the district."

"Then ye understand why it grieves me not to be able to extend ye an invitation," Hinkley said sadly. "Any other time but today or tomorrow. There'll be no chance of your coming by this way again, will there?"

Guderian shook his head. "I have to report in. Who knows where they'll send me next."

"Ah well, ye never know what will happen," Hinkley said, slapping him on the back.

Guderian reached down and retrieved his knapsack.

"I think you'll be wanting these, sir."

Mary flipped her gleaming mane back with one hand and pushed two thick sandwiches bound in wax paper toward Guderian. He could smell the pungent aroma of the cheese through the wrapping.

"You didn't have to," he said, digging into his pocket for some coins.

"And I won't be taking your money neither," Mary laughed, "if you promise to stop by later."

"I'll try," Guderian promised.

As they stepped outside, Albert Hinkley winked at him.

"I think ye've made yerself a friend," he chortled. "She's a good girl, Mary. Maybe ye'll think twice about coming to see Topcliffe Hall!"

Guderian swung one leg over the BSA saddle. "I wouldn't want to poach," he said, smiling.

"No worry with Mary," Hinkley assured him. "She's a high-spirited girl but doesn't belong to any of the local lads. No one will hold it against you."

"Tell me," Guderian said. "Do you think I might drive by Topcliffe Hall, just to see it at a distance, I mean?"

"Surely. There's a dirt path that winds over the hillocks to the east. Not good for a car but your machine will climb it nicely. Ye'll have a grand view from there."

"It would be a pity not to see it," Guderian said. "Just in case."

"I know what ye means, lad," Hinkley said quietly. "We live in uncertain times. Best to see and do what we can today."

He paused. "It was good seeing ye, Henry Schiffer, and I'm proud to have made your acquaintance. If there's anything I can be of service for ye, ye know where to find me."

Guderian gripped his hand. "I'm grateful for your hospitality."

The motorcycle roared to life and Guderian started down the cobblestone street. He was no longer worried about his ma-

chine attracting the attention of the local population. The men
at the bar would have seen the BSA and by now word would
have spread that a friend of Albert Hinkley's had visited. Nor
would Runnymeade hear of his presence. It was obvious that
Hinkley hadn't mentioned the near-accident to his employer,
only to his friends, who he knew would keep it among themselves.

Guderian had asked direction to Topcliffe Hall only for
form; he had memorized the directions off a local map before
leaving London. Half a mile from Ipswich-Colby he turned off
the main road and started up the dirt path. The BSA climbed
the hill easily enough and in a few minutes Guderian was
standing at the top of the rise, overlooking the shallow, saucer-
like terrain which constituted the manor's acreage. He removed the field glasses from his knapsack and began a slow
scan.

The entrance to Topcliffe Hall was a narrow but well-graded
road threading between two rows of cypresses. Better than half
of the hundred acres was woodland; another third had been
cleared and was used as pasture. The remaining portion, undoubtedly with the richest soil, remained farmland, bordered
on the south by a large pool of water that was fed by a fast-
rushing stream. Below the pool were falls. The house itself
was situated on the west side of the water, at the very edge of
the pond.

Guderian swung his glasses back to the entrance and his
breath quickened. He hadn't been expecting to see them and so
his eye had passed them by: Royal Marines, two of them . . .
three, walking along the edge of the cypress rows, submachine
guns slung over their shoulders.

Marines for the Ship's Supper?

Guderian wiped the sweat from his brow and crouched to the
earth. He trained the glasses on the forest perimeter, moving
them with painstaking slowness across the treeline. He spotted
another complement of men and two vehicles, both with
mounted machine guns and spotlights. There were a half dozen
more on the actual grounds of the house. Guderian quickly
calculated the number he had seen and figured there was at
least a full company.

For security . . . there was no other explanation. But what
kind of trouble could Admiral Runnymeade be expecting that
would justify forty armed and waiting men?

Guderian replaced the field glasses in the case, eased the motorcycle off its stand and walked it down the hill, making sure no one from the house could see him, before he started it up.

There could be a dozen reasons why Runnymeade would want security, he thought as the BSA roared toward the main road. A last-minute guest, so important that his—or her—presence justified the show of force. A royal guest perhaps. Even Churchill himself.

But no! Guderian told himself fiercely, unable to restrain his jubilation any longer. I *am* right!

The security was the last piece of evidence to confirm that what he thought would take place was actually going to happen.

He drove down the main road until he figured he was was within two hundred yards of Topcliffe Hall drive, then veered left and cut across the edge of a fallow field. The precaution was small, but in Guderian's mind justifiable. Given the security, the Marines would make mental note of a young soldier on a motorcycle. Questions might be asked of the villagers who came to work or served at the manor.

When he came back onto the main road he headed east, calculating the distance to the pond by keeping track of the stone fences that partitioned the fields. He passed a farmer on the road, who lifted his hand in greeting. Guderian waved as he flashed by, recalling the man from the Mermaid. His assumption had been correct: Albert Hinkley's word was all the locals needed to accept a stranger in their midst. He turned off about a half mile from the manor drive, endured a jolting ride along a badly pitted path and killed the engine as soon as he glimpsed the lake. Removing his knapsack, Guderian pushed the motorcycle behind a clump of bushes and walked the rest of the way.

The setting was exactly as he had envisioned it. The land rose slightly from the lake, the beeches and evergreens providing more than adequate cover. There were a few yards of tall grass between the treeline and water's edge where blackened rocks poked out of the water. Directly across the lake was the house. Guderian unpacked one of the two sandwiches Mary had made for him, settled his back against a young oak and began to eat slowly. He never took his eyes off the manor.

Less than a third of Topcliffe Hall faced the lake. There was a vast, slate terrace that dominated the foreground and beyond it a tall hedgerow that hid the lower part of the windows that belonged to the billiard room. The roof of the far wing, the servants' quarters, angled sharply and was broken by an exceptionally wide chimney. The second visible part, adjacent to the terrace, had a much smaller roof. Here the windows were tall and narrow, covered with gaily colored curtains. That was the kitchen. Guderian adjusted the field glasses and framed a field of vision along the base of the wing. The concrete foundation ran straight into the water, exactly as the detailed drawings in the National Historical Register had indicated. The width was seventeen feet before the kitchen met the terrace. He lifted the glasses and fixed the location on the brass weathervane, then calculated the angle to the edge of the foundation. He figured his margin of error to be some three or four feet. But given that he would be working in darkness, even so little space to search would cost him valuable time.

Guderian folded the wax paper and replaced it in the knapsack. It was half past four but the sun was still high in the sky. He crawled farther into the trees and found himself a reasonably dry and level patch of ground. Using the pack as a pillow he stretched himself out and closed his eyes. He had at least three hours to wait and would use these to rest. There would be no sleep for him this coming night.

It had been the most splendid Ship's Supper Runnymeade could remember. He was standing on the gallery that ran three-quarters of the way around the walnut-paneled dining room below, looking down upon his officers, forty-two of them resplendent in dress whites, their wives or girls decked out in dazzling finery of magenta, emerald and sunburst. The local ladies, hired as they were for every such occasion, moved around them bearing trays of coffee and tea. The table, cleared away, now held a dozen bottles of exotic brandies and liqueurs.

And what a magnificent table it had been. The village women had truly outdone themselves, preparing a feast that would have done the Scottish lairds proud. They had started with fish chowder and thick-cut salmon steak followed by roasted pheasant with cornbread and apple stuffing, smoked quail and a whole smoked lamb surrounded by grilled lamb chops. There had been a mixed grill and platter of smoked short ribs complemented by colcannon, sautéed carrots and green beans. There followed scones, oatcakes and monk's bread baked in the kitchen hearth, whiskey nutcake, raspberry shortcake and bread pudding. Pears and grapes were served to clear the palate before the entry of a cheeseboard the size of large bellows.

Before dinner the Admiral himself had gone around replenishing the quaiches from a stag's head decanter while throughout the repast Albert Hinkley, decked out in a Montrose doublet, jabot and sporran, served the finest reserves of Topcliffe Hall's cellars.

It was, Runnymeade considered, drawing gently on his cigar, an evening all would remember. He took a last, almost wistful look at the party below, the chatter and laughter cascading to the rafters, and returned to his study. He longed for it not to end and by rights it shouldn't have. Another time the terrace would have been strung with Japanese lanterns and a small orchestra would have played until dawn. Runnymeade regretted not having the chance to dance with his hostess of the evening, Mackenzie McConnell.

But at least I have kept with tradition, he thought, rolling his chair up against the ancient desk. I gave them the proper send-off, and God knows it will be months before they see a table like that again. Some never will . . .

As he rolled the ash off his cigar Runnymeade wondered just how curious his officers were. They wouldn't have missed the presence of the Marines; nor had Mackenzie McConnell, a representative of the Security Service, gone unnoticed.

Yet the men hadn't raised so much as a whisper of speculation. Well, their patience would be rewarded in a few minutes. Runnymeade leaned across and tugged a golden sash. One of the panels along the wall opened and Hinkley appeared as silently as a wraith.

"Sor?"

"I want the men assembled here in exactly two minutes, Mr. Hinkley."

"Sor!"—the Petty Officer inclined—"and the womenfolk?"

Runnymeade smiled at the sailor's anachronism.

"There are amusements in the card room. Perhaps you'll see to it that no one is left wanting."

"Very good, sor."

As Hinkley withdrew, the Garrard timepiece sounded nine o'clock. Runnymeade rose, lifted out a silver keychain and came over to a curio cabinet. He unlocked the glass doors, removed two figurines from the middle shelf, removed the shelf itself and tapped lightly along the top of the backboard. The wood slid down neatly and he removed three rolled-up nautical charts. He replaced the panel, shelf and figurines, carried and rolled out the charts, placing lead weights on all corners.

I have the war in the very palm of my hand, he thought silently. God help me if anything should go awry now.

He was still standing like that, hands folded on the small of his back, head bowed, white teeth tugging at the lower lip, when Hinkley knocked at the door, then opened it. After the officers filed in, the door was locked from the outside. Hinkley pocketed the key and went in search of the ladies, ready with a repertory of sea tales.

The security details pertaining to Topcliffe Hall on the evening of June 14 had been finalized by both Admiral Runnymeade and Mackenzie McConnell. Both had agreed that a company of Royal Marines was more than an adequate force to patrol the perimeters. Equally, every man and woman entering the property, whether an officer and his lady, a tradesman or cleaning woman, had been vetted. But what Runnymeade and McConnell had overlooked was the fact that Topcliffe Hall itself was a potential enemy.

The original manor had been constructed by Charles LaBray in 1491. In the next seventy-five years a number of wings were added on, expanding the house to better than twice its original size. And along with the usual construction came modifications which LaBray made entirely by himself, in the greatest secrecy. Because LaBray was a "hidden" Catholic.

Sixteenth-century England was a cruel land to professed Roman Catholics. Known as Recusants because of their refusal to adopt the Protestant faith, they practiced their rituals in secret, all too aware of the informers around them who would, for a single gold piece, betray them to the *Poursuivants*, vigilantes who hunted down priests.

Charles LaBray was outwardly a staunch supporter of English law. Yet by night he opened his doors to Jesuits fleeing the *Poursuivants*. Time and time again armed men hammered on the doors of the manor at midnight and searched it from top to bottom in an effort to find the "priest holes" and other sanctuaries. But LaBray was too imaginative, too efficient for them.

If one were able to physically slice Topcliffe Hall down the center, providing a cutaway view of the interior, one would see a manor riddled with boltholes, secret passages, dummy walls and false floors. In fact Topcliffe Hall contained some of the most ingenious hiding places of all the Catholic stately manors in England. When the Runnymeade family purchased the property in the early 1820s, a complete history of Topcliffe Hall was compiled. Every false panel and tunnel referred to in Catholic writings was unearthed, examined and if necessary, meticulously restored. The work was chronicled in the architectural digests of the period, which were eventually reprinted in the definitive work on English country homes, the National Historical Register. Which was where Erik Guderian found the drawings, drafting plans, details of reconstruction and restoration of the hiding places.

It was this source that revealed to him the existence of an old sewer network that ran beneath the present basement of Topcliffe Hall, where it emptied into the lake, and the restoration that had been carried out on the tunnel not fifty years ago. Had it not been for the National Historical Register or the fact that the Runnymeade family felt it an obligation to meticulously maintain the heritage of the manor's past, Erik Guderian might never have gained entry to Topcliffe Hall at all.

When Guderian awoke, the first thing he saw was the luminous dots around the circumference of his watch. The time was 9:07. He pulled himself up and massaged the stiffness out of his shoulder.

As he had expected, there were no Marine patrols on this side of the pond. If it had been his command he would have left the water alone as well. No one would anticipate an assault across the pond, in the darkness. Even a full commando force rising out of the bank would be decimated before it hit hard earth. Except that he had no intention of making for either the terrace or the lawn.

Guderian stripped to his shorts, gooseflesh breaking out over his skin. The wind was light but cold enough. He bundled the clothing together and jammed it into a hollow at the base of a tree. He emptied the knapsack, placing light running shoes, trousers, dark sweater, small towel and flashlight into the wa-

terproof canvas, securing it tightly. He strapped the scalpel to
his right calf with adhesive, careful not to cut off the circulation.

He slithered down the riverbank, wincing as his feet touched
the icy water, and checked his coordinates. Topcliffe Hall was
blazing with light, the reflection rippling off the water, casting
light shadows across the roof. The brass weathervane was
clearly visible. Guderian waded into the pond, trying to ignore
the frigidity of the water, and pushed off the pebbled bottom,
keeping his left arm in the air, the waterproof bag gripped
between whitened fingers. Using a slow, steady, one-armed
crawl, he covered the fifty yards in less than two minutes.

There was a small ledge jutting out from the foundation
some two feet above the waterline. Guderian trod water and
carefully placed his waterproof bag on the cement outcropping.
To his right the pool glittered in the reflection cast by the
manor lights. Looking around, he tried to catch a glimpse of
the armed patrols but saw nothing. On his left was darkness,
the single advantage he had. So long as he worked quietly there
was no reason for anyone to see him.

Guderian took four deep breaths, then slowly allowed himself to sink, his fingertips exploring the crusted cement beneath
the waves.

It was one of the most horrible sensations he had ever had,
dropping slowly in total darkness, all his senses except for
touch shut out. He didn't know how deep the pond was at this
point . . . nor could he dispel that irrational human fear of
something waiting for him at the bottom, its jaws open, golden
eyes glittering . . .

His feet, almost numb now, touched something round, hard
but soft at the same time. With one thrust Guderian propelled
himself toward the surface, breaking the water cleanly, his
arms desperately searching for the ledge so that he wouldn't
fall back into the water. His fingers clamped onto the rough
concrete and for a few seconds he hung like that, his back
muscles rippling as much from fear as from the cold. Slowly he
lowered himself back into the water and started deep-breathing
again. The entry was there! It had to be! An instant later he had
disappeared and the pond was calm once more.

It took Erik Guderian twenty minutes of painstaking searching by touch before his fingers curled around the wire mesh
grille that covered the ancient sewer. Three times he had to

dive, work his way down the wall, get a grip on the mesh, and, with his feet braced against the slippery foundation, try to curl back enough of the mesh so that he could pass through. It wasn't until later that he saw the blood on his hands where the wire had bitten through the skin.

When he was certain there was enough room for him to pass, Guderian returned to the surface for the last time. He hung onto the ledge for as long as he could, giving his body a moment's respite, then grabbed the waterproof kit and disappeared beneath the water. He reached the sewer entrance almost immediately, and, twisting his body sideways, swam into the brick-lined tunnel.

Guderian stayed along the edge of the tunnel, one hand scrabbling to catch the edges of bricks to help propel himself along. His legs worked furiously, the pumping momentum generated by a primeval fear of never emerging from this conduit. Images of a watery grave rushed through his mind, of himself floating for all eternity in this sewer while his body became a feeding ground for things that waited somewhere in the darkness.

The air in his lungs was almost gone. He felt a gentle squeeze as though a fist were slowly tightening around his chest. Guderian flipped over on his back and with one hand above him began to pull himself along the roof of the tunnel. He felt himself becoming dizzy and inadvertently opened his mouth a crack. The water tasted sour, pouring down his throat. He took one final lunge, then tried to break the surface. His head slammed into the brick, causing him to spin away.

And this is how it ends, Guderian thought as he drifted along the side of the sewer. His knees scraped the bottom and bumped into something hard. He laid his arms out in front of him like a supplicant before some idol. He thought he could smell the spring resin of a forest and knew he was dying.

But something was carrying him forward. He felt himself rising but idly dismissed this. He was falling . . . Without Guderian's being aware of it, his hands were continually pulling him forward. The will to survive had replaced reason. His body was working to save him in spite of himself.

One chance, he thought weakly. He summoned whatever energy was left in his legs and pushed himself forward. His knees scraped stone, then his belly. He arched his body . . . and his head came out of the water.

It was Norway rats, brown, sleek, with fiery red eyes gazing unblinkingly upon him that forced Guderian to move. He didn't know how long he had lain on the cold stone steps edging out of the sewer. The crystal on his watch had shattered.

Guderian fumbled inside the waterproof kit and took out the flashlight. The rats retreated before the beam, skittering over the narrow ledge. He played the light over the massive timber beams that formed the basement floor and found the trapdoor. It was exactly where the plans had indicated.

He toweled as best he could, then pulled on the trousers and thick sweater. He jammed his feet into the sneakers and adjusted the woolen cap over his wet hair. His knees buckled under the first crouching step, but he managed to crawl toward the trapdoor and, squatting beneath it, pushed it up.

Dust and dirt filtered onto his face. He turned his head aside and buried a racking cough into the crook of his arm. When the spasm passed he pushed the trapdoor aside completely and shined the light into the gaping darkness.

The shaft was at least thirty feet high, four feet square. Along the side of the false wall were wooden brackets driven in by brass nails. A loop of rope hung down and was connected to a pulley which in turn was affixed to a crossbeam at the top of the shaft. Guderian pulled on the rope tentatively and found it held. Slowly he added more downward pressure. The pulley creaked faintly but the rope, although old, appeared sound. Nevertheless he drew out its entire length, examining every foot under the beam to make certain it wasn't frayed.

When he was satisfied the rope would hold, Guderian clamped the flashlight between his teeth, placed both hands on the rope and cantilevered himself up so that both feet caught the first bracket. Somewhere high above him the pulley groaned, but the rope held. He drew himself up, chest and shoulder muscles straining, until he was flush against the wall. Below he heard the squeal of rats.

Move! he thought furiously. For God's sake move!

It took Guderian a full twenty minutes to climb the shaft. With the beam playing on the brick wall only inches from his face, he climbed, one bracket at a time, until, two-thirds of the way up he bumped against the ledge jutting out into the shaft. He swung to one side and pushed against the door cut into the brick. The panel swung in, revealing a cubbyhole no more than five feet square. Guderian squirmed his way inside the cavity.

The chamber rested beneath the floor of the room above it. The flashlight found the outline of another trapdoor which, if nothing had been changed, would open up into the southwest corner of the Admiral's bedroom. Guderian waited until his breathing became normal once more, then rose, his shoulders pushing against the weight of the trapdoor.

The room was swathed in darkness, the scent of a man's cologne pervading the air. Guderian pulled himself out of the chamber and quickly lowered the trap. He didn't hesitate but scrambled over to the fireplace. He stepped carefully over the brass log-cradles and into the chimney proper, fingers seeking the panel he knew had to be there.

It was. The fireplace in Runnymeade's bedroom was false. The chimney was in fact part of an old ventilation shaft hidden on the righthand side, concealed by a false brick wall and mortar blackened to resemble a flue. Guderian pulled the panel away and stepped into the aperture, drawing the wall shut behind him. He felt his way in the darkness, taking only three steps before coming up against another wall. Erik Guderian was now in the study, standing behind a panel adjacent to the fireplace in that room. Less than a centimeter of wood separated him from those present. He heard every word.

"That's it then," Mackenzie McConnell was saying after the officers had left the room. "They know exactly what has to be done and when."

"But not why," Runnymeade replied.

Both he and Mackenzie McConnell were standing beside the refectory pine table, the charts still spread out along its length. Runnymeade was lighting another cigar.

"You know, Admiral, that we can't reveal that," Mackenzie said gently. She understood how much Runnymeade despised not telling his men everything. It was obscene to send them into battle without their knowing why they might die.

"Yes, I know," Runnymeade said, the smoke stinging his eyes. "But that doesn't make it right."

"Is there anything else we need go over?" Mackenzie asked him. She wanted to go downstairs and telephone London. Contact from Jonathan was overdue.

"I think we're done here," Runnymeade said. He reached for the sash and Hinkley appeared at the silent summons.

"Lock up after us, will you, please," Runnymeade said, escorting Mackenzie to the door.

"Very good, sor," Hinkley said sonorously.

He waited until the Admiral and his lady were in the hall, then closed the door firmly and from his trousers pocket pulled out a thin chain with a single golden key. Hinkley was about to insert the key when a sudden crash above startled him.

"It's all right, sor!" he called to Runnymeade who, with Mackenzie, had stopped at the staircase landing. "One of the Petty Officers was up a moment ago. Looked a little weathered, I'd say, so I told him to go upstairs for a spell."

"Perhaps he is *in extremis*," Runnymeade said and made to turn around.

"Don't you be worrin' about it, sor," Hinkley assured him, already making for the third floor. "I'll see to it no harm comes to him."

Then the corridor was silent. A heartbeat later Erik Guderian was in the study.

For a few seconds he could not believe where he was. The journey that had begun in Berlin an eternity ago had at last come to an end. Yet he felt no elation nor any relief. He was thinking of Gerd Jaunich, who had conceived the operation; of Hitler, who had personally demanded Guderian bring him England . . .

The paralysis broke. Guderian crossed the thick Chinese rug and stood over the pine table. His eyes focused on the charts before him, greedily absorbing the routes, latitude and longitudes traced across the pale green paper. So intent was he in committing these to memory that he never heard the door open and whirled around only when Christine Harloch called out his name in a soft, tentative voice.

"Henry . . . ?"

Guderian had never seen her look more beautiful, flaming hair swept across one shoulder, the red colliding with the soft white silk of her gown. Her eyes were impossibly huge, those of a doe startled by the hunter, vulnerable, frightened yet at the same time trusting. He took a step toward her and she backed away.

"Christine . . ."

"What are you doing here, Henry?"

The question came out as a strangled whisper. He could almost sense the horror of the truth shattering the illusion. Guderian uncoiled himself, springing at her. His right hand shot out, flashing by eyes that welled with terror, and slammed into the side of her head. Beyond the impact he heard the crackle of bone. Christine fell before he could catch her. Swiftly Guderian reached behind him, closed the door to the study, then turned over her inert form. Blood was gathering in her ear.

In one motion he scooped her up and carried her into Runnymeade's bedroom, again careful to close the door behind him. He laid her on the satin quilt and instantly began backing away, his eyes never leaving her.

I should kill her, he thought to himself. She has seen my face, knows who I am, just like the others! But the body refused the mind. Guderian lifted his hand only to find he was already at the panel by the fireplace. Escape or murder, the choice was his . . . Guderian stooped down and disappeared into the stone.

The trapdoor was sprung and he jumped into the chamber. A second later his hands found the rope. Guderian swung himself into the darkness and began sliding down the side of the shaft. He dropped the last few feet to the basement, lifted the second trapdoor and disappeared into the medieval sewers. The rats skittered away as he flung off his clothing and waded into the waters. Taking three deep breaths, he dived in, his fingertips guiding him along the top of the sewer. When he was into the pond he ignored his screaming lungs and rose slowly, making certain only his face broke the surface. But even so he heard the frantic shouting and the pounding boots along the terrace. Guderian kicked off and sank beneath the waters, swimming steadily for the opposite shore.

He staggered out among the rocks and crawled up the embankment on his belly, not daring to cast even the palest shadows. His clothing was exactly where he had left it, and in a minute he was dressed, moving swiftly along the path toward the hedges where he had hidden the motorcycle. The only reason he saw the Royal Marine was because of the moonlight glinting off the gun barrel.

The soldier was only a few yards from the motorcycle, holding the submachine gun in one hand, a radio in the other. Guderian moved close enough to the man to hear the faint crackle of static. He drove the scalpel into the Marine's side, cutting him off in midsentence. The soldier, a tall brutish man, still managed to swing around, his expression one of utter astonishment. Guderian twisted the scalpel out, hearing the man groan as he dropped to his knees. He brought his foot down viciously on the radio and thrashed through the tall grass toward his machine. The final run had begun.

III
DOUBLE-CROSS

29

A light, almost invisible drizzle was falling over London as Jonathan Cabot descended the ramp wheeled up against the Pan American flight from Lisbon. He turned his collar against the needlelike rain and walked quickly to the customs office. Through the water-streaked window he saw Allen Dulles, sitting alone behind a government-issue desk.

"Schiffer's our man," Cabot said, slamming the door behind him. "Otherwise known as Erik Guderian. And he's after Prometheus. There's no mistake."

"Guderian!"

Dulles was stunned, but he was already dialing.

"Why in God's name didn't you relay this from Geneva?"

"We don't have time for that now!"

And then Dulles realized something terrible had happened in Geneva. The man before him was not the same one he had sent to Source Mainstream.

"I just hope we can pick him up in time," Dulles said. He passed Cabot the receiver. "Mackenzie's down at Runnymeade's estate in Sussex for the final briefing of the ships' officers."

"Who's watching Schiffer?"

"She put Robert Ogilvy onto him. He wants that bastard as badly as you do."

But as Cabot began to speak to Albert Hinkley at Topcliffe Hall, neither he nor Dulles was aware that at that moment a Tonbridge county constable on his way home from his patrol had just come across a black Jaguar sedan whose front end had plowed into a ditch. The constable took ten precious minutes to examine the accident and twice failed to hear the sound of a wounded man. The third time Robert Ogilvy cried he lost consciousness. It took the constable another few minutes to find Ogilvy's identification before realizing what he had come upon. Matters might have turned out completely different at that point. But the constable was almost four miles from Tonbridge. The nearest farm which he knew had a phone was two miles down the road. And because of gasoline rationing, all he had was a bicycle . . .

Lieutenant Andrew Simmons had watched Christine walk, or rather stumble, her way up the staircase. It hadn't been until halfway through the meal that Simmons had realized Christine was drunk. Up to that point the evening had been a pleasure. Being the kind of man he was, he had dismissed the memory of that Army corporal from his mind, easily enough done after he had managed to convince himself there was really no one between him and the woman he loved. Christine helped foster the illusion, chatting happily as they drove from London to Ipswich-Colby, staying on his arm as he paraded her through the party. Yet somehow, perhaps because his own happiness had blinded him, Andrew Simmons missed the slow inebriation that had come over her, a condition that was bordering on the frightful by the time he had returned from the briefing.

He closed his eyes lightly as he watched her careen past the Admiral, who was coming along the gallery with Mackenzie McConnell. Andrew Simmons turned away, angered by the way her behavior was making a fool of him.

"Is Christine not feeling well?"

Runnymeade materialized at his Lieutenant's side, his voice expressing a genuine concern.

"A bit under the weather, sir," Simmons mumbled.

He felt a hand on his arm.

"I think you should go look for her," Mackenzie McConnell said gently. "If she's not feeling well, call me."

"Perhaps you're right, ma'am," Simmons said, suddenly ashamed of himself.

"And tell me if she needs anything," Mackenzie called after him.

But Simmons was already trotting up the stairs, crossing the gallery in his long strides, certain he would find her in the upstairs bathroom. Andrew knocked and the door eased open. The bathroom was empty. Frowning, he went to the guest bedroom overlooking the front terrace, but there was no one inside. His pace quickened as he retraced his steps, checking the second guest room at the opposite side of the gallery. Nothing.

Christine Harloch would have remained undiscovered for at least another few minutes had Lieutenant Simmons not noticed that the door to the Admiral's bedroom was ajar. Could she really have been that drunk as to have stumbled into this sanctum? Simmons gave the door a tentative push.

"Christine . . ."

He saw her lying on the bed and went up to her, his hands around her shoulders shaking her. It was then that he saw the pool of blood spreading across the satin . . .

Mackenzie McConnell was entering the music room when the screams erupted. Even as Simmons's cries were echoing in the hall she was running toward the staircase, her hand jammed in her purse, fingers seeking the small .32-caliber pistol she carried. Mackenzie found the Lieutenant kneeling by the body of Christine Harloch, her head in his lap, the blood staining his dress whites. Simmons stared at her with the eyes of the dead.

"Get the ship's doctor!" Mackenzie cried to a Royal Marine who had pounded up behind her. "Contact all units. I want a full security alert in effect at once!"

"She's not dead," Simmons was muttering as though he were trying to convince himself. "She *can't* be."

Mackenzie pulled him away and knelt beside the injured girl, placing a hand on her throat.

"She's alive, thank God! Give me a handkerchief, anything to put on the bleeding!"

Dr. Adrian Silander, physician assigned to *Victorious*, elbowed his way through the throng at the door, Runnymeade close behind. Swiftly he examined the wound and ordered a cot or stretcher be found. The bleeding had to have been severe but was clotting now, a positive sign. There were no apparent injuries to the neck nor any broken bones. But Silander couldn't judge just how bad the concussion was.

"Admiral, I've asked for a complete security alert," Mackenzie said. "If you—"

"I will look after it personally," Runnymeade assured her. He lowered his voice. "It couldn't have been him . . ."

The doubt in his tone mitigated the need for a reply. Mackenzie McConnell was certain that somehow a lone man had penetrated Topcliffe Hall. Which meant that in all probability

Robert Ogilvy, assigned to watch over the man known as Henry Schiffer, was dead.

"I want this room cleared—right now!" Mackenzie called out, elbowing her way through the crowd.

She made her way along the banister to Runnymeade's study, the Admiral at her heels. Runnymeade stooped over the lock, a thin golden key in his fingers.

"Doesn't appear jimmied," he said, trying the handle.

He slipped the key in and the double bolts shot back.

"He didn't get in here," Runnymeade said with evident relief. "The charts are exactly as we left them. Nothing has been touched, I'd stake my life on it!"

Mackenzie had no reason to doubt him. Runnymeade knew his study so well he could account for every speck of dust—if there was any. And everything *was* in place, she thought, counting the Admiralty charts just to be certain. Nothing was out of place.

She calculated the time between her and Runnymeade's leaving the room and the moment Simmons had discovered Christine Harloch. Schiffer must have been hiding somewhere, waiting for the conference to finish. When it had and when he thought the hall was clear he made his move. Only to run into a tipsy Christine Harloch. Schiffer struck her down the instant he realized Christine not only recognized him but would also demand an explanation. At that point panic got the better of him and he ran.

That's the only way it *could* have happened, Mackenzie told herself. Because the lock was intact. The double bolts would have frustrated even an expert. And the bolts themselves had no scratches on them . . . But something still nagged at her— an uneasiness she couldn't shake off. It was as though she were looking at something but not seeing what it was. Only Christine Harloch had seen anything.

"I'll attend to my men," Runnymeade said, following her out. "I hope you have an imaginative explanation prepared."

Mackenzie grimaced and quickly returned to the Admiral's bedroom. The ship's doctor was buckling up his medical bag.

"How soon can I talk with her, doctor?"

"I'm afraid that's not in my power to predict," Silander replied somberly. "If she's lucky she'll come out of it in a few hours. But if not then we're dealing with a very nasty concussion indeed. I can't give you any predictions in that case. But I do know I have to move her to London immediately."

"Isn't there something you can give her, just so I can talk to her for a moment?"

"Miss McConnell, I'm aware of how your department functions and some of the methods you subscribe to," Silander replied icily. "But I do not propose to endanger my patient so that you can chat with her!"

"Doctor, you don't know what's at stake!"

"A human life!" Silander retorted. "If I were to give Miss Harloch the kind of medication that would induce her to speak—if such a move would be successful, which I doubt—I would be placing her life in grave jeopardy."

She couldn't reconcile the emotions within her. Christine Harloch was the only person who had actually seen Schiffer, could tell her exactly what, if anything, had transpired in that hall. Yet Silander was right: to induce Christine to speak could mean killing her.

"I want her transferred to MI5 facilities in London," Mackenzie said abruptly. "If she shows any sign of regaining consciousness *please* call me immediately."

A Marine sergeant materialized by her side.

"Begging your pardon, ma'am," he said, anger making him sound breathless. "A patrol found one of my men in the field across the pond. He's badly off, a knife wound in the back."

"Christ, Sergeant, I'm—"

"He's alive, ma'am. He's managed to tell us that the man who tried to kill him had driven off on a motorcycle."

"Call up whatever reserves you need, Sergeant," Mackenzie said instantly. "Start your men off on every road heading to London. We'll crowd him out, flush him and take him—alive, if we can!"

"Very good, ma'am," the Marine said grimly. "And, ma'am, I almost forgot myself: there's a telephone call for you. A Mr. Cabot from London."

"He was there all along. He managed to get through the security, into that damn house and out again!"

Jonathan Baylor Cabot stared at the black plastic receiver, shaking his head.

"Did he get anything?" Dulles asked softly.

"No. Both Mackenzie *and* Runnymeade swear to that. His girl, Christine Harloch, walked in on him. Guderian hit her and ran, taking out a Marine who found his motorcycle."

"Vicious bastard, isn't he," Dulles murmured. "And now he's on the run. What are the chances of picking him up before he reaches London?"

Cabot pointed at the mantelpiece clock. "Next to nonexistent. He's had too much of a head start. Even though we know what Guderian is driving, he's already gone past most of the points where roadblocks have been thrown up. Our only hope is the unexpected—trouble with the bike, an accident because he was moving too fast."

"You don't put too much stock in that."

Cabot shook his head. "We're going to have to take him in London."

"And Prometheus?" Dulles asked. "How much has Guderian learned? How much is already in Berlin?"

Cabot stared out the window. Outside, in the blue light cast by the moon, he saw the shadows of the plane that had brought him to his man.

"I don't know, but we have to keep Prometheus on schedule," Cabot said.

Allen Dulles looked away, removed his bifocals and rubbed his eyes.

"Churchill will ask me how far Guderian penetrated the operation," he said. "He'll want every guarantee of safe passage we can give him. How can we do that without knowing how much—if anything—Guderian has learned?"

"That line of thinking will freeze the operation," Cabot said flatly. "Regardless of how many men I throw into the search, there is no guarantee we'll find Guderian before Prometheus has to start," Cabot continued. "Look at the way the son of a bitch has been operating. Obviously he has support facilities. But *who* are they and *where*? We don't have a handle on him. If we try to get one we'll be committing a major error: we'll be playing by *his* timetable. That gives him hours or days to dig in even further. But if we go with the operation as planned, Guderian is thrown off balance. Whatever bits and pieces he's managed to feed Berlin will be worthless. Berlin won't be able to mount a counteroffensive in time."

"Let me play out the devil's advocate here," Dulles said. "Guderian had the Navy angle figured out before he even left

Dunkirk. He could have calculated exactly what the British reserves were. That figure would give him the only viable means of transportation: submarine or surface ship. Given the abysmal state of England's undersea fleet, he gambled on the latter. And was right. Assuming he *has* passed his suspicions to Berlin, isn't it likely the German Navy will be stringing out a battle fleet to intercept the cruiser? Or send in the wolf packs?"

"That's exactly why I want to move now," Cabot said. "Even if Berlin agrees to send out its capital ships, they are so slow they wouldn't reach the cutoff points in the Atlantic for at least two days. The problem would be with the subs. But there too Berlin would have to string out its forces across a thousand miles. The submarine commanders would not know what type of vessel they were looking for, much less where to find it. We might send it out alone, we could surround it with a convoy, we could place it on the fringe of a convoy. They would have to cover too many possibilities."

"How soon do you want to move?" Dulles asked him.

"Less than thirty hours from now," Cabot said. "The *Victorious* should weigh anchor at three o'clock on the morning of June 16."

"Can you have everything done by then?" Dulles asked, the doubt rising in his voice.

"If I start now."

"Then start. I'll talk to Churchill as soon as he returns from the House of Commons. I will also go to bat for you before Roosevelt if it comes to that."

"If I have to stop the operation in midstream we'll be worse off than before," Cabot warned him. "Secrecy depends on my being able to get this done in one fast shot."

"Do it," Dulles ordered bluntly.

Even before Dulles was out the door Jonathan Cabot was back on the telephone. His first three calls went to the commander of the Royal Marine base in the north of London, the second to Reading's home, where the Governor of the Bank of England was reading Thackeray to his wife, the last to Admiral Runnymeade at Topcliffe Hall in Ipswich-Colby. He spoke only a few minutes to each man, activating their particular part in Prometheus. There were no questions from any of the principals. The details had been hammered out, committed to memory, long before.

When he was through, Cabot called the home number of the head of Scotland Yard's Criminal Investigation Division. A meeting was arranged for within the hour. The Inspector would contact the head of the London Metropolitan Police Force, who would meet him and Cabot at Scotland Yard.

He's coming into the city, Cabot thought. He's running now, heading for a nest. He will have to rest, at least for a little while. Then in the morning he will have to come out.

Dawn . . . Cabot had to have his snares in place by then.

He pushed the motorcycle hard, almost recklessly, his driving a reflection of the decision he had made when he had reached the junction of the main highway stretching toward London.

Erik Guderian had a choice: to use the secondary roads that meandered through Sussex toward London or else take his chances on the main thoroughfare, MI. Guderian had no illusions about his chances if he came up against a roadblock. His only hope was to literally outrun the barriers—pass the points where they *would be* erected. Guderian lost no more than a few seconds at the junction before wheeling the bike onto the highway. If he chose the slower route he was giving Cabot time to set up that many more traps at the access routes into London proper. A fatal mistake.

Driving flat-out, the headlight blazing a path of yellow ahead of him, Guderian reached East Grinstead in less than twenty minutes. He followed the MI as it curled around the sleepy town, his eyes never off the road, oblivious of the roadhouse cafes and beyond them the sterile row housing that was silhouetted against the full moon. Every few minutes he glanced at the fuel gauge. The motorcycle's tanks had been half full when he had left, which meant he should have enough gas to reach at least the outer limits of the city.

He cleared Sevenoaks a half hour later, reaching Greater London at Caterham and Warlingham. He flew past Croydon a few minutes later, slowing down as he approached Merton. Guderian killed his own headlight as soon as he spotted the flickering lamps a mile away. He geared down the bike and proceeded cautiously, using only moonlight to guide him along the glittering blacktop. Three hundred yards later he saw the revolving blue strobe of a police vehicle. Then two more.

Guderian cursed softly and brought the motorcycle to a stop.

Eight miles to Lambeth, ten to Southwark. He could cover that distance quickly enough on foot, but he would be all the more vulnerable, a lone man walking the fringe of the highway at night. If he encountered any sort of patrol, motorized or pedestrian, he wouldn't stand a chance. They would run him to the ground or at the very least radio a position before he had a chance to kill them all.

Watching the lights blink in the darkness, Guderian found himself mesmerized by them and realized how close he was to total exhaustion. The muscles in his arms, legs and neck were strung out, hard and taut. His left shoulder had begun to throb once more. So close, only a dozen miles between himself and his goal . . . He made his decision and depressed the clutch.

Guderian swung off the MI at the last exit, entered Merton and began weaving his way around the city, seeking the alternate route that would take him out of Merton, past the checkpoint and up toward London on a secondary route. Precious time was lost as he moved along unfamiliar streets, detoured and twice went around in a circle. But at last he found the artery he was looking for.

At half past one on the morning of June 15 Guderian passed less than two hundred yards from the checkpoint on the MI. The secondary route, which had swung away from the main highway, inexplicably veered parallel to it, with only pasture separating the two thoroughfares. Guderian had no way of knowing whether the police, having heard an engine growling in the darkness, would automatically signal an alert. Nevertheless he didn't switch on the headlight until he was well beyond the blue strobe lights. As soon as these disappeared he gave the motorcycle its head.

Seven miles later, in the winding streets of Lambeth, his luck ran out.

Guderian almost didn't hear the spotter plane on account of the BSA's engine. But he saw the light coming directly at him, the floodlights attached to the undercarriage creating a stream of light he couldn't avoid. The plane roared overhead, then swung around for another pass. Guderian swung hard left, sending the bike into a skid, the rear end crashing against a lamppost. The reflex action saved his life. On the second pass the machine-gunners opened up, the bullets stitching a wavy path along the cobblestones he had been driving on.

Guderian killed the engine and was running before the spotter craft had time to make another overflight. Looking around, he discovered he had driven straight into one of London's main food terminals: the boarded-up stall fronts all bore the names of fruit and vegetable merchants. Which meant that he had to be close to the river. Guderian rolled beneath a stall as the plane came around again, then scrambled to his feet and started running again. He disappeared into a narrow lane and found that it led downhill. The river was close. He could smell it.

As he ran Guderian could almost hear the frantic radio communications between the plane and home base. In the dispatcher's office men would be checking a central board to pinpoint coordinates, speaking urgently into microphones linking them to mobile units. It would all depend how quickly central control could flood armed men into the area, how many search teams were on hand, how much area they could initially cover.

Guderian ran on, past darkened warehouses, low-slung factory buildings and shuttered pubs. He had almost reached the breakwater when the darkness disappeared and a blinding light struck him. He couldn't make out the monstrous shape behind, but heard the sickening whine of metal upon metal as the gears ground down. He threw himself away just as the London Transit Authority bus brushed by him, close enough for one fender to tear at his trouser leg.

"What the bloody hell d'you think you're doing!"

The driver had pulled back his window and was staring down at the man lying in the street.

Guderian rose slowly, placing both hands on the bumper and straining to get back on his feet. He staggered around to the door and pounded on it until the driver opened up.

"Good Christ, man, you're bleeding like a stuck pig! Here, let me help you—"

As soon as the driver was within reach, Guderian clamped both hands on his shoulder and heaved him out the door. He dropped beside the fallen man and gripping his head, smashed it against the pavement. Guderian staggered back, staring at the dead driver. He uttered an oath and climbed back into the bus. The motor had been left running and he managed to shift into the proper gear. Seconds later a lumbering London Transit Authority bus was headed across Lambeth Bridge into central London.

Guderian was not conscious of how he ever drove as far as the foot of St. James's Street. He clung to the massive wheel as though it were his last lifeline, steering through now familiar streets, eyes darting toward the rearview mirror for any sign of pursuit.

At St. James's he deliberately flooded the engine and applied the emergency brake. If a patrol spotted the bus it might assume that it had broken down and the driver had gone to the nearest phone booth. Which was exactly where Guderian was headed. He half-ran, half-staggered into the warren of streets behind St. James's and found a phone booth next to a haberdasher's. Guderian dialed the number, then jammed in the necessary coins. He slumped against the glass, the receiver pressed against his ear, eyes always on the street.

"Yes?"

The voice was soft, modulated, giving no hint that Alfred Morell had been asleep.

"I need to have something delivered," Guderian said, his voice breaking over a cough.

"Come round to the back. And be very careful."

He was moving again, staying in the shadows of the smart shops, checking each street intersection for traffic before running across. When Guderian reached the alley behind Bentley's, he saw the service door was ajar, a shaft of pale light streaming over the garbage bins.

"Quickly!"

Morell reached for his arm and pulled him inside. Without a word he propped Guderian up and led him up the back staircase to his room, taking care to keep the German's bloodied hands away from the wall. As soon as they were inside, Morell laid Guderian out on the bed and locked the door.

"A message . . ." Guderian gasped. "I have to get a message through to Berlin!"

"They are looking for you," Morell said, coming out of the bathroom with a washcloth in his hand. "It was on the BBC not twenty minutes ago. The police, Army, the Security Service—all searching for a Corporal Henry Schiffer."

Morell paused, then added calmly: "I presumed that was yourself."

"What else?" Guderian demanded hoarsely, propping himself up on one elbow.

"They say you attacked and gravely injured a Security Service agent . . . and that you hurt a woman. They're not sure if she will live."

Guderian closed his eyes. "She'll live. That's just an excuse to bring the police in on the hunt. She'll live . . ."

Alfred wiped away the filth and blood from Guderian's face and helped him to sit up.

"They will be listening for transmission," he said quietly. "They will be expecting one."

"No choice," Guderian said and looked at Alfred.

"I will send whatever you want," the old man assured him.

"Then let's not give them any more time!" Guderian said fiercely.

As Alfred began to assemble his equipment, he said over his shoulder: "You can't go anywhere tonight, not with the hunt up and you like that. You'll have to rest here. In the morning I can move you . . ."

Erik Guderian nodded and with the last vestige of his strength drew himself up, his head cradled in his hands. Somewhere very far away he heard Alfred Morell call out to him. Then the old man's hands were around his shoulders, shaking him.

". . . message. I need the message!"

Guderian opened his eyes only to see the room pulsating before him. In a hollow voice that could not possibly have belonged to him he uttered the half dozen sentences that had been imprinted on his mind since Topcliffe Hall. Then he felt himself falling over, tumbling back. No sooner than Morell laid his head on the pillow did the terror and fatigue of the last day explode over Guderian and he fled from it into eternal darkness.

30

At two-twenty on the morning of June 15 the communications link between Cabot at Ten Downing Street and field operations sounded. Sixty seconds later Cabot had spoken to both the commander at the Southwark roadblock and the pilot of the spotter plane. When Cabot broke the connection his hand was trembling as much from exhaustion as from anticipation. Erik Guderian, otherwise known as Corporal Henry Schiffer, had abandoned the motorcycle. He was on foot, possibly injured if the plane's surveillance officer's description of his flight was accurate. On foot and alone. Vulnerable. But more important, Guderian was on ground that could become a controlled perimeter.

In the next two minutes Cabot contacted the night watch commander of the London Metropolitan Police Force, the Duty Superintendent at Scotland Yard and the Duty Officer at the Army's Wellington Barracks along Birdcage Walk. He waited until each man had been patched into his single line, then gave them the essential details. Before he was through a second phone rang: a police patrol vehicle, guided by the spotter plane, had discovered a body on Stamford Street. Cabot ordered the other callers to hold.

The constable on Stamford Street reported in: the deceased was a bus driver. He had been beaten to death. There was no sign of the vehicle.

Cabot swore and returned to his three waiting callers. From the London police he ordered a dozen mobile teams organized and ready to move in fifteen minutes. In the meantime every available officer in the Southwark area was to be contacted and told to be on the lookout for a London Transit Authority bus. The vehicle was to be disabled if possible, but above all its location filed at once with police central control.

Similar directives were issued to Scotland Yard, except that Cabot wanted its flying squads out *now* covering the north approaches to Blackfriars, Waterloo and Westminster bridges.

The commando units were also to roll immediately. They would be responsible for the area between the Victoria Embankment and St. James's Park all the way up to the Mall and Strand. The standing orders remained as before: apprehend if possible but shoot to kill if Guderian ran.

Cabot got back to the constable on Stamford Street. He and whatever other men were in the area were to work the district south of Stamford Street as far as Borough Road. Any contact was to be reported immediately. The officer requested that the plane stay in their area. Aerial surveillance would be invaluable in this street-congested district. Cabot overruled him. He had other plans for the aircraft.

Swiveling in his chair, Cabot studied the grids on the wall

map of London. Seconds later he was speaking to the pilot, ordering him to overfly the following route: Stamford Street to York Road, which cuts into Westminster Bridge; across the river and along the perimeter of St. James's Park to the Mall; then east again over Waterloo Bridge. By the time the pilot completed this tour a second, possibly a third, plane would be in the air.

As he waited for the connection to be put through to RAF Barrows Field outside Gatwick, Cabot again studied the map, then checked the time. Seventeen minutes had elapsed since the time the bus driver had been found. Add another five to ten since the killing and theft had taken place. Given the maximum speed a London bus was capable of, the inexperience of Guderian in handling such a machine, and the disorientation of driving in the dark, he assessed that the perimeters given to the pilot represented the maximum distance Guderian could have traveled in that time. The liability lay in the fact that for a reason he himself did not understand, Cabot was gambling on Guderian's heading either north or west, not south and east. The sooner more planes got off the ground the faster he would be able to blanket the other areas.

RAF Barrows responded immediately. Cabot ordered all available spotter planes into the air on a scramble basis. Luck was with him: Barrows Field had three in readiness. But even as the pilots were roused out of their sleep by the wail of sirens, the situation was overtaking them. The original spotter plane, with its twin high-density beams, had cleared Westminster Bridge. It was now approaching the darkness of St. James's Park and was less than a minute away from where Erik Guderian had abandoned the stolen bus.

Cabot kept one line open to the spotter plane, listening in as the pilot established individual radio channels for each of the three ground forces.

"Starling to Army One . . ."

The military reply crackled back an acknowledgment.

"Visual sighting of a stationary vehicle at St. James's Street at the Royal Opera Arcade. Am turning about for a better look."

Cabot stared into the microphone, oblivious to the faint snapping of static.

"This is Starling," the pilot said. "Vehicle identified as London Transport Authority bus. No driver in sight."

"Starling, this is Annex. Head for the park! Repeat: Head for the park! Instruct Starling Two from Barrows to line up with you."

Cabot snatched up another receiver. Orders streamed across the wires to the Wellington Barracks where Ford light-reconnaissance vehicles, engines running, four-man crews in place, began to roar down Birdcage Walk.

"We estimate arrival time in two minutes, sir," the duty officer informed Cabot.

"Keep this line open to the lead vehicle," Cabot said. A moment later he was speaking to Barrows Field, telling the controller exactly what patterns he wanted Starlings Three and Four, the remaining spotter planes, to fly.

Two minutes . . . Cabot thought. How far can he run in that time? And if he's hurt . . .

Only ninety seconds had elapsed before Wellington Barracks re-established contact.

"Our patrol has reached the bus, sir," the dispatcher informed him. "The vehicle is empty. There are bloodstains on the wheel and the floorboards."

Now you're mine! Cabot thought fiercely.

"Listen very carefully," Cabot said, looking at the map. "St. James's Park is to be sealed off from the Queen Victoria Memorial to Horse Guards Road. Additional units are to cordon off the following perimeter: Piccadilly, Regent Street, The Mall, Green Park. Advise all men that the London police and Scotland Yard will be establishing safe quadrants *adjacent* to these areas. They will remain there until you can move in troops."

"And what are the other areas, sir?" the duty officer queried.

"Whitehall to Victoria Embankment to Northumberland Avenue on the east. To the north, the area from the Admiralty Arch up to New Coventry Street along St. Martins Street."

"I understand, sir. The directive regarding the suspect is still in effect?"

"It damn well is!"

"What about vehicular and pedestrian traffic?"

"Nothing moves into the fire zones. Anything or anyone coming out is to be stopped, scrutinized, all transport searched. And I mean thoroughly!"

Cabot detected a hesitation in the duty officer's voice.

"Sir, it's now twenty to three. Traffic won't be a problem for a few hours, but as soon as the Underground starts up at dawn. . . ."

"No trains will stop at any of the stations in the zone," Cabot said.

"But the morning rush hour—"

"That's precisely why the Army will relieve the London police as soon as possible," Cabot cut him off. "Until the suspect is found no one gets out of the zones. I'll call you back with instructions for the search teams."

Cabot hung up before the duty officer had a chance to raise another objection. He spoke to the police units stationed in Southwark and told them to get across the river to predetermined coordinates. The same message went to the London Metropolitan Police headquarters and Scotland Yard. The forces against Guderian were now fully mobilized. Cabot jammed a package of cigarettes into his pocket and took his coat off the rack. The submachine gun bumped against his ribs.

The night air cleared his head almost at once and Cabot breathed deeply, thankful to be outside. He hadn't realized how stifling his command post had become.

"Sir?"

One of the eight paratroopers assigned to the Annex came up and saluted smartly.

"We have a fix on the son of a bitch," Cabot said. "It's a large area but I think we can run him to ground."

The sergeant, who, as Cabot's escort, was privy to the ongoing hunt, flashed a grin.

"Where to, sir?"

"Berkeley Square," Cabot said softly. "I think Guderian headed north after ditching the bus. I think he was going to the one place where he would have cached fresh identification, clothing, weapons. He's at the Harloch house . . . and that's where we'll take him!"

But that wasn't the case at all.

As a false dawn spilled over London, the city's core remained an armed fortress. All security points previously manned by London police were now patrolled by the military. The quarantine was holding. Only essential personnel—doctors, nurses, hospital-supply vehicles and emergency ambulance cases—had been allowed through. Armed commandos also patrolled the subway stations, above ground and below, where they took up positions at both ends of each ramp. The London Transit Authority had reluctantly agreed that no trains would stop at any of these stations. The underground patrols were to make sure that each trainman knew exactly what was waiting for him if the cars even slowed down on their way through.

Above, the situation was becoming increasingly more difficult. First light brought with it the early morning traffic. The BBC had been broadcasting continually, advising that no entry would be permitted into the cordons. The London police had set up patrols to guide commercial traffic around the area as well as keep pedestrian traffic from spilling over into the restricted zones. Cabot was monitoring the situation from a mobile command post at the foot of St. James's Street. At six o'clock he ordered fresh police reinforcements into the sectors where the pressure on the cordon was greatest. Cabot realized that if one barrier came down, even for a few minutes, the flood of traffic, onlookers and curiosity seekers would break into the neutral zone between the police and soldiers. Bloodshed would be inevitable. The commandos had standing orders to fire at will and would, Cabot knew, do just that. Whatever questions they might have had about their mission dissolved when Winston Churchill had personally inspected the various perimeters an hour earlier.

But it was the situation inside the zone that gnawed away at Cabot. Teams of Scotland Yard detectives had fanned out in a circular search pattern using the bus as a hub. While Army units, with the help of the spotter planes, beat the bushes in both St. James's and Green parks, the plainclothes squad began picking the locks of whatever buildings didn't have a night watchman. The process was excruciatingly slow, in spite of the fact that the Yard called out every available officer. Later in the morning, Cabot knew he would be able to send troops in to help.

For Cabot personally there was the bitter taste of defeat because his hunch had proved wrong; Erik Guderian hadn't been at the coach house in Berkeley Square. There was no evidence that he had gone near it or the clinic in the main house.

"Which means," Cabot said to Mackenzie as she passed him tea from the field kitchen brought in to take some of the edge off the troops' tempers, "that he's either bleeding to death in some cellar or else he's found his niche."

Mackenzie took a look at the lightening sky, gray streaked through with pink and yellow.

"How long do you think the cordons will hold?" she asked him.

"As long as they have to," he answered grimly.

"Jonathan, you have an entire city pressing around you. The merchants are up in arms because they can't get in to open their stores. Businesses are screaming because employees can't get to work. Families have been ordered to remain inside. You're going to start running into a food shortage sooner or later. Tempers will flare."

"I know," Cabot said quietly. "That's why I *have* to find him. Time is the only thing Guderian has going for him. He's in the area, aware of what's going on. He's going to try and wait it out. I can't allow him to do that. As long as he hears or sees what's happening he won't be able to rest. Tired, careless, maybe he'll make a mistake."

"And try to run?"

"In the best of all possible worlds," Cabot said softly.

"I'm sorry for all this ruckus, sir," the young Scotland Yard detective said, palming away his identification. "I'm afraid we have a bit of a flap on our hands."

Alfred Morell glanced over the detective's shoulder at the six other men clustered on the front steps of Bentley's.

"Obviously," he said dryly. "Well, you had better come in."

The detectives gathered around the statue of Diana in the antechamber and looked about themselves self-consciously.

"Now, gentlemen, how may I be of service to you?" Morell asked the detective.

"We have orders to search the entire premises, sir," the detective told him. "If you—"

"What is it you're looking for, Sergeant?" Morell demanded.

"A man, sir," the detective said, thrusting the police sketch of Erik Guderian at the chief steward.

"I see," Morell said noncommittally. "Am I to assume this man has committed some sort of crime?"

"You might say that, sir," the detective replied grimly.

"And *when* was this to have taken place?"

"We cornered him in this area about four hours ago, sir."

Morell raised his eyebrows. "There has been a great deal of commotion here far earlier than that, Sergeant. It is now ten o'clock. You mean to say that you think he is still in the area?"

"Absolutely, sir. The perimeters have been effectively sealed. He couldn't have slipped away."

"I also listen to the BBC, Sergeant," Morell informed the detective. "Very well. I know you have martial law authority. I suppose the best thing would be to have the staff guide your men through. Be faster that way, don't you think?"

"We appreciate the cooperation, sir!" the detective answered smartly.

What Scotland Yard had no way of knowing was that Morell had already prepared his staff for their arrival. As soon as he had heard the BBC news broadcast, the head steward had assembled the two cooks, three stewards and a dish boy who had worked last night's late shift and so hadn't been allowed out of the cordon. To each he explained exactly what was to be done. An hour later when the chairman of the club board called, Morell received his consent for absolute cooperation with the authorities—even if they wouldn't tell him exactly what was going on.

"I'll take you up to the top floor—the living quarters—myself," Alfred told the detective. "The other men can follow the staff into the basements, wine cellar, storage areas."

"I don't suppose anyone heard something unusual last night?" the detective queried.

"I'm afraid not. You see, after the staff was sent back by your men, they all spent the night in the members' quarters. That's why I'm afraid the rooms are somewhat unkempt. It's conceivable, I suppose, for an intruder to have broken in through one of the basement windows. In such a large house . . ."

Morell left the obvious unsaid. He guided the detective along the corridor.

"Three stewards slept here," he said, indicating the unmade beds. "The cooks were in the next room, where a cot had been set up for the kitchen boy. There's a common bathroom at the other end of the hall."

As the detective brushed by him, Morell felt the hardness of the knife hidden by the jacket. He waited patiently as the man from Scotland Yard checked both rooms thoroughly, looking under the beds, opening the closets.

"This one is yours, is it, sir?"

"That's correct, Sergeant."

By contrast Morell's room was neat as a pin. Except that all the detective had to do was turn back the sheets and he would find them bloodied. There hadn't been the opportunity to either change or dispose of them.

The police officer walked over to the ancient RCA radio.

"My mum and dad had one just like this," he said, smiling wanly, squatting down in front of the set.

The detective's feet were almost touching the false-front panel. If he nudged it—

As he rose, the detective's left shoe bumped against the panel, which immediately fell forward.

"Now look what I've done—"

"Don't worry," Morell said, stepping over quickly and picking up the piece of wood. "It came unglued ages ago. I simply haven't gotten round to having it fixed."

Because the detective was so close to the set he couldn't see more than half an inch into the recess. A few centimeters more and he would have noticed the amplifier immediately.

"If you would step aside for a moment," Morell said.

"Sorry."

At the same instant as the detective took a step back, Alfred slid the panel back into place.

"What's that, then?" the detective asked.

The chief steward looked up carefully. At the same time, his hand dropped into his pocket as he rose to his feet, the thumb-nail seeking the notch in the blade.

"What's what, Sergeant?"

"Up on the ceiling. Have you been having a water problem?"

The Scotland Yard officer was pointing to one of the panels that made up the ceiling of the room. There was a dark-brown jagged stain along the one directly above him.

"Nothing like that," Morell assured him. "We used to keep paint and things like that up there once. At some point a workman must have spilled something. I had forgotten all about it, actually."

The detective was a tall man. When he raised himself on his

toes and extended his arm and hand, his fingers were able to push the panel up a half inch. Silvery dust filtered into the air.

"It's empty space up there, is it?" the detective said slowly.

"I believe so, yes."

The steward was watching the man intently. The blade had come free . . .

"Perhaps I had better have a look," the officer said.

"Really, Sergeant," Morell said. "I was asleep in this room all night. Someone could scarcely have tiptoed in, pulled up the chair, moved the panel and climbed up without my being aware of it."

He paused. "Nevertheless, you do have your duty," he said, the irony obvious, and began to pull up a chair.

"Never mind," the detective said, slapping his hands together. "That's stretching it a bit far, I think . . ."

Lying prone on the floor of the triangular attic, Erik Guderian heard the door close and lock. Only then did he relax his grip on the revolver handle.

Carefully he rolled himself over in the darkness, away from the puddle of brown-stained turpentine he had inadvertently knocked over. His fingers gripped the edge of the panel and raised it a few centimeters. Immediately Guderian brought his nose directly into the opening and breathed deeply. In the confined quarters, with nowhere for the evil stench to dissipate, he was slowly choking to death.

"Where in devil's name can he be?"

Winston Churchill stripped a sodden shirt off his back and flung it to the floor. He brought the undershirt over his head, crumpled that up, glowered at Jonathan Cabot and stomped off into the bathroom.

"Speak up, Mr. Cabot!" Churchill shouted over the stream of running water. "I can't hear you in here!"

From where he stood Cabot saw Churchill's reflection in the medicine cabinet mirror. The Prime Minister was vigorously scrubbing his face. Cabot didn't say a word.

Churchill strode back into the bedroom, a towel hung around his neck. He opened the doors of an enormous armoire and began rifling through fresh shirts.

"Guderian is still somewhere in the cordon, Mr. Prime Minister," Cabot said.

"But you have searched the entire area!"

"Almost," Cabot admitted. "I think we missed him. He's in there but we missed him."

"It is now four o'clock," Churchill informed him, fumbling with the buttons of his shirt. "You are running out of time, sir!"

Churchill finished knotting his tie and turned on his heel.

"Well, sir?"

"Before I came here, Mr. Prime Minister, I checked in with Allen Dulles at the embassy," Cabot said. "The President has been kept informed of the situation. In spite of the fact that we haven't been able to run down Guderian, he is of the opinion that Prometheus should begin on schedule."

Cabot paused. "Naturally the final decision is in your hands, Prime Minister. The President reiterated that he will defer to you in these circumstances."

"Damn you, Cabot, for not finding him!" Churchill said viciously.

Almost immediately his expression of anger became one of astonishment.

"Good Lord—forgive me for saying such a thing," Churchill murmured. "I don't know what came over me. It's just that . . ."

"No offense taken," Cabot assured him. "I don't envy you your position, Prime Minister."

"You realize I can't keep central London closed off like this indefinitely," Churchill said. "The people are howling for a decent explanation, not the tripe we have been doling out. Parliament is demanding a full account of what is going on. The Army tells me that at certain points the barricades have been challenged by people trying to get out for food . . ."

"I realize that," Cabot said. "It's a credit to your security that the cordon is holding as tightly as it is."

Cabot watched as Churchill buttoned up his waistcoat.

"I need eleven hours, Prime Minister. Less if everything works as it should and I can eliminate the contingency time I set aside. After that it won't matter where the hell Guderian is. He won't be able to stop Prometheus."

"What then? We lift the cordon without any assurances to the public that the emergency has been satisfactorily dealt with?"

"The entire city has been inundated with posters of Guderian's picture," Cabot said. "Even if we open up the cordon, chances of his getting out are marginal. He's playing for time because it's his last weapon. When we deny him that, he'll have to run."

"I have your assurance that when that happens *and we fail to catch him* Guderian still has no chance to interfere with Prometheus?"

"After three o'clock tomorrow morning, none," Cabot said.

Churchill opened his hunter.

"I'm due in the House in twenty minutes," he muttered, speaking more to himself than to Cabot.

Suddenly he swung around to the American.

"Do it, Mr. Cabot! Do it and godspeed to you!"

He handed Cabot the letter.

When Jonathan Cabot left Downing Street he did not go directly to the Bank of England. Instead he instructed his driver to take him to the north end of London Bridge, in the area between Lower Thames Street and the river. Once there, Cabot walked out onto the bridge and looked downriver, past Billingsgate fish market, alive with activity now, past the rows of small fishing vessels that were disgorging their loads and the garbage scows lined up waiting for their loads. Somewhere beyond the bends of the river the cruiser *Victorious* waited.

Cabot returned to the car and told the driver to head for Threadneedle Street. When he arrived the bank porters were already outside, an indication that the Bank was in the process of closing. Cabot waited in his vehicle as the last of the City men came out, then ran up the steps and slipped inside. Reading, the Governor, was waiting for him in the domed antechamber, alone.

"Mr. Cabot, what is our situation?" Reading demanded. Clearly he was not amused about having had to wait until the last minute.

"We go."

"So you managed to apprehend the infiltrator!" Reading said, his relief evident.

"No," Cabot told him. "He's still somewhere in cordon."

"But that means—"

"That the quarantine will remain in effect until we've finished our job," Cabot interrupted him. "He won't have a chance to get near us."

"I don't know if we can proceed on that basis," Reading was saying. "I must have certain assurances . . ."

Cabot handed him Churchill's letter.

"The Prime Minister has accepted full responsibility."

Reading glanced down at the paper, his expression one of wonder and fear.

"I wish I could say this absolves me of my responsibility," he said softly. "But it doesn't . . ."

He looked up at Cabot. "I suppose we had better get on with it then."

Behind them the great doors closed, the echoes of bolts slamming into place chasing the two men as they proceeded quickly down the staircase, which stopped before a single elevator door. Reading inserted a key into the magnetic lock and ushered Cabot into the car. The one-hundred-foot descent into the vaults lasted precisely thirty seconds. As the doors parted, the Governor and Cabot walked the final link between the vaults and the outside world. Once he and Reading passed into the central chamber, there was no way out except through the shipment section, which had its own individual security.

Reading lifted the receiver of the telephone set in the wall and spoke softly into the mouthpiece. Automatically Cabot looked up. High on the wall to his right a Judas hole popped open, an unblinking eye scrutinized the two men. An instant later the fifteen-hundred-pound door rumbled aside. Cabot and Reading stepped across the threshold into a large rectangular room, one wall of which was one complete sheet of specially reinforced glass. Along the other side were three desks, a battery of telephones, twelve feet of filing cabinets that ran straight up to the ten-foot ceiling, and one man.

"Mr. Cabot, may I introduce you to Mr. Geoffry Draper, chief clerk of the Bullion Office," Reading said.

Draper rose from behind his desk and extended his hand to Cabot. He was a short, heavyset man with wavy blond hair that still managed to hide a balding scalp. His black, thick-frame glasses accentuated the calm eyes and a ready smile.

"We are ready to proceed any time you are, sir," Draper said quietly and gazed reverently through the glass.

There it is, Cabot thought. Everything that has been responsible for the duplicity and killing . . .

In the chamber, which measured sixty feet by eighty-five, with a twenty-four-foot ceiling, was the gold, stacked up in a crisscross pattern on wooden pallets that had been arranged in neat rows along the length of the room. Up against one wall were the boxes in which the bars would be packed, all eight thousand nine hundred and sixteen of them. In the center of the room was a conveyor belt that broke off into an L-shape which disappeared through a small square cut into the walls. Beyond that was the loading depot.

"Are all the telephones functional?" Cabot asked Draper.

"The Army Signal Corps men were here earlier, sir," Draper confirmed. "Everything is working as it should."

"Then let's do it," Cabot said softly.

Cabot slid into Draper's chair and reached for one of the telephones. The first call went out to the mobile command post at St. James's Street. The Colonel in charge of the search operation reported no status change. Next he spoke with Allen Dulles at Grosvenor Square. Since Churchill was in Parliament Dulles would act as both operations control and liaison until the Prime Minister returned to Downing Street.

Cabot checked his watch and dialed a third number. The commander of the Royal Marine force at the north London depot informed him that his men were ready. Cabot told him to start them rolling at exactly five o'clock, fifteen minutes from now.

"Do you have the figures?" Cabot asked Draper.

The chief clerk handed him the master list, which had the serial numbers of each and every bar that was to be shipped. A second set of figures pertained to the numbers the boxes had been stamped with.

"Mr. Draper, open up the doors and get your squad in there!"

Geoffry Draper spoke softly into an internal-line phone. Even before he and Cabot had entered the vault a side door had opened and forty men, identically dressed in blue Farmer John overalls, work boots and heavy gloves trooped in, forming a line between the first row of gold and the conveyor belt.

Cabot passed by them quickly. Even though every man in the room had been with the Bank for at least ten years and was bonded by Lloyd's, an MI5 security check had been carried out. For the duration of the operation the men would be guarded by a contingent of the Bank security force which was now making its way in from the holding rooms. The packers would not be allowed to leave the Bank premises until Cabot had personally called the security commander.

As the men spread themselves along the belt, standing five feet apart from one another, Cabot ducked into the loading bay on the other side of the vault. It was a massive rectangular room, with overhead winches and pulleys, three forklifts lined up against one wall, and a ceiling half of which was the bottom platform of a freight elevator that could handle forty-ton vehicles.

Cabot reached for the wall phone.

"Bring them down," he said.

He walked beneath the second half of the ceiling which wasn't there—yet—and craned his head to look up into the dark shaft. The elevator machinery started up, chains rattling somewhere high above him. At the same time he felt the rush of cold air on his cheek as the giant fans began recirculating the air in the chamber.

It took six minutes for the three-ton Austin K5s to appear on the descending ramp. Even before the ramp was flush with the floor, members of a Royal Marines demolition squad were jumping out of the bed. A ruddy, ginger-haired officer trotted over to Cabot.

"Lieutenant Matthews reporting, *sir!*"

"Your men have all been briefed?" Cabot asked.

"To the last detail, *sir!*"

"You have ten minutes, Lieutenant, to blow the wall and clear the debris."

"Understood, *sir!*"

Cabot stood back watching as the men hoisted their equipment on their backs and made for the far wall. The demolition team had been waiting in the Bank of England's street-level depot for thirty minutes, having been sent earlier on than the units which by now, Cabot figured, were no more than ten minutes away from Threadneedle Street.

"Send that truck back up!" Cabot shouted into the telephone receiver.

The demolition team began to align charges at precise spots along the far wall. Sticks of dynamite, specially manufactured for interior work, were taped to the plaster, the detonator wires fixed into the triggers, then strung out along the floor to the detonator box itself. Wiring the wall took three minutes.

Cabot was back on the line talking to a Marine sergeant who

was working the elevator. All the time he was watching the demolition team members make the final checks on the explosives and begin to tie all the wires into a central lead that would be connected to the box.

"Warn the people on the other side," Cabot said softly as the Lieutenant gave him the thumbs-up signal.

Cabot listened to the reply, hung up and at the same instant heard the final locks snap in on the elevator gears.

"Any time you're ready, Lieutenant," he called out.

The demolition experts huddled in two of the far corners, pulling protective padding over themselves.

"Fire in the hole!" the Lieutenant roared, then dropped out of sight.

Although the explosion was a small one, the noise was deafening in the confined area. As charges placed along the base and ceiling of the far wall impacted, the entire sheet of plaster, wood and mortar crumpled.

Even as the fans began drawing the smoke into the exhaust ducts, the demolition team was moving. Quickly the debris was shoveled aside, exposing a sheet metal wall that was the wall's final reinforcement. Two of the men crouched beside the wall, running their gloved fingers along its edge.

"Torches!" someone shouted.

Cabot saw that the top portion of the wall was already hanging away from its frame. But closer to the base the explosions hadn't made severance complete.

For the next two minutes the room filled with acrid smoke as acetylene torches cut through the last shards of metal holding the wall up. Sledgehammer teams were brought in for the final ear-splitting knockdown. With a screech of bolts being torn from their housings, the wall fell back into the tunnel that should not have existed behind it.

Cabot jumped onto the metal sheet, staying close to the wall for support. One by one he picked out the lamps set on the ground on either side of the tunnel, giving the impression of a short, irregular runway. A soldier materialized out of the gloom, paratroop beret and flashes identifying him as an Advance Strike Force commando. It was the tough, weathered Major from Hemmingford.

"Are your men in position?" Cabot demanded.

"They are, sir!" Nesbitt replied.

"Communications with the river?"

Nesbitt motioned for his radioman to step forward, the portable set wedged tightly against his back.

"We shall open up the other side as soon as you give the word, sir," he said.

Cabot heard the elevator start up in the underground depot.

"Tell them to stand by," he said.

As he made his way back, the demolition unit began placing thick boards across the fallen metal wall. Cabot approached the team's Lieutenant.

"Time?"

"Two minutes ahead of schedule, *sir!*"

Cabot nodded, watching the ramp descend with the first of the ten-ton Hippo trucks.

No one, not even Erik Guderian, could have imagined that there was a way other than surface transport by which to move the gold from the vaults beneath Threadneedle Street to the waiting cruiser. Yet there was, and Jonathan Cabot had found it in architectural plans that dated back to 1911.

In that year the Bank of England had undertaken a complete overhaul of its vault system, enlarging the capacity, facilitating egress and ingress. At the same time the street-level depot had been fitted with an elevator strong enough to handle projected loads of twenty tons each. It was during the reconstruction that Charles Cullington, chief designer, had discovered the King William Tunnel.

Part of London's earliest sewer system, fourteen feet high, its sides set in glazed brick, the King William Tunnel ran from the edge of Threadneedle straight down King William Street and emptied into the Thames beneath London Bridge. It had been closed off since 1888 when a new system had been installed.

Cullington immediately recognized that the Tunnel was the solution to a major problem which had continually troubled him: there was no way, other than by the freight elevator, to move the gold. In a national emergency or natural disaster this could prove catastrophic. Having completed an engineering survey, he presented the Bank's Board of Governors with a daring and unique plan. Since the Tunnel floor was solid bedrock, an underground rail line, the kind used in mines, could be installed. In the event of a crisis in which the street-level access had been severed or could not be used, a series of small, flatbed carriages could ferry the bullion safely to the foot of the river. The cars would be powered by independent electric generators which need not rely on the Bank's link to the city's electrical sources.

The Board unanimously approved Cullington's plan. A rail system was laid along the bedrock, four generators installed along the quarter-mile route, and upon completion, the river entrance was sealed with a thick concrete plug while the Bank entrance was closed off by a metal wall. The project was carried out by a special team from the Army Engineer Corps and took four months to complete. All engineering plans and drafting plans were subsequently destroyed. The men who had worked on the Tunnel, from the Army architect through to the lowliest private, signed the Official Secrets affidavit. As it happened a great many of these same men perished in the trenches of France three years later, thereby further ensuring the security of the entire project.

If Jonathan Cabot hadn't had access to the Black Book, a blueprint for government organization and contingency plans in the event of rebellion or invasion, he too would never have known about the "King William option." As it was, the Tunnel satisfied every one of Cabot's security requirements for the transfer, including the duration—which had to be kept as brief as possible.

At three o'clock this morning the same team of demolition experts that was in the vault now, supported by a commando unit, had blown the concrete plug at the river entrance. In the next four hours the tunnel had been thoroughly examined for any sign of erosion or decay. The team didn't bother with the condition of either the generators or the tracks. These were superfluous to Cabot's intentions. When the inspection was completed, the opening was temporarily camouflaged and guarded by the commando unit operating from a berthed river-patrol vessel.

At the same time as Cabot arrived at the Bank, two hours ago, the river entrance had been uncovered to admit a force of sixty armed soldiers who took up positions along the length of the tunnel. They had been told exactly what would be taking place on the other side of the metal wall and so were not caught off-guard by the explosions. The passageway was secure and ready.

At precisely 6:05 the elevator carrying the first of the three Hippo-class Army trucks ground to a halt. The canvas was

thrown back and a dozen commandos jumped out. They
stacked their weapons and lined up in single file next to the
opening through which the conveyor belt passed into the loading bay. Two commandos remained on the truck itself.

Cabot moved back into the vault, his eyes sweeping over the
row of packers who stood beside the still motionless conveyor
belt. The expressions on their faces revealed neither surprise
nor curiosity. Reading had assured Cabot that while their job of
preparing gold for transfer may have appeared mundane, the
variety of circumstances under which they had worked had
made even the extraordinary commonplace. No two shipments
out of the vault were ever the same.

Cabot headed toward Draper, the chief clerk, who was at the
head of the line.

"Ready when you are," he said.

Draper raised his copy of the master list and from his overalls withdrew a stopwatch.

"Your attention, gentlemen!" he called out. "Loading will
begin in precisely ten seconds."

He dropped his hand on the control lever of the belt and
counted off.

"Go!" And hit the button on the watch.

As soon as the first man on the line touched a brick, he
called out the serial number imprinted on the face. Draper
immediately checked it off on the master list. The movement
of the conveyor belt was synchronized so that as the gold bars
were slapped down each made its way to its designated man at
the exact moment the previous packer had counted his off. The
result was an uninterrupted staccato roll call that lasted fifty-
seven minutes.

As the full crates disappeared through the opening into the
depot, they were snatched by commandos who slammed on the
lid and, using pneumatic hammers, drove six nails into each
crate. The crates were swung onto the bed of the waiting Hippo
and stacked onto waiting pallets.

At seven o'clock work ceased as the first truck's consignment was filled. The driver fired up the Hippo and cautiously maneuvered his vehicle onto the wooden beams spread
between the floor and the jagged edges of the metal wall. By
the time the vehicle was driven one hundred feet into the tunnel
and engine killed, the elevator was on its way up to street level,
where the second truck was waiting.

By half past nine these initial stages of Prometheus repeated themselves two more times. Even though Cabot had allowed for an hour of spillover time—the elevator's moving back and forth, the few minutes lost for the trucks to be driven into the tunnels—he was still twenty-eight minutes ahead of schedule.

"The next truck that comes down will have everything you need to seal up this hold," he told the demolition team leader. "I want you to start pulling sheet back in place as soon as we're out of here. Don't worry about cosmetics, just make sure the exit is secure."

He went back inside the vault and into the overhead glassed-in office where Reading was waiting.

"Nothing?" Cabot asked, gesturing at the phones.

"Quiet as the grave," the Governor of the Bank replied.

He looked out at the line of packers sitting on the conveyor belt, some of them working out kinks in their muscles. Behind them an entire row of pallets stood empty.

"They did a splendid job," Reading murmured.

The door opened and Draper ran in. He gave his master list to the Governor.

"Every brick accounted for, sir," he said, breathing hard.

Reading glanced through the lists perfunctorily, uncapped his pen and scribbled his signature above the authorization line.

"Thank you, Draper," he said absently and turned to Cabot.

"You are ready to proceed." It was a statement, not a question.

Cabot was about to reply when one of the telephones sounded. Reading snatched up the receiver, listened silently, then said:

"Very well. Send her down."

"It seems that Miss McConnell has arrived," he informed Cabot. "Will you wait for her?"

Cabot was tempted. A sudden urge to hold her, to let her warmth and touch shield him from what he had to do, rose up in him. Another minute wouldn't make any difference. He wanted to say something more, to leave a few personal words so she would know that even now he was still thinking of her.

"She knows what to do," he answered instead.

"Good luck, Mr. Cabot," Reading called out.

Cabot paused at the door to the depot and looked back.

"Thank you, sir."

The demolition squad was unloading its tools from the vehicle standing on the elevator ramp. Cabot ran past them and into the King William Tunnel, moving swiftly toward the lead truck. The driver was behind the wheel, the leader of the commando force beside him. Cabot jumped onto the running board, fingers curling around the rods that held the rearview mirror in place.

"Go!" he shouted.

The lights of the lead truck snapped on, illuminating the Tunnel cavity. Up ahead Cabot saw soldiers moving alongside the truck, picking up the lanterns as they headed for the river entrance. The sound of gnashing gears filled the confine, and the lead truck lurched forward, the separate axles climbing over the railway ties in a rocking motion.

Cabot leaned out and glanced back. The other two trucks had fired up their engines and were beginning to follow at a distance of forty feet. As they passed, the commandos in the Tunnel jumped onto the running boards.

The quarter-mile journey took twenty minutes. As the headlights of the lead vehicle were seen by the unit waiting at the river, the order was given to the tugboat captain to bring the first barge alongside the makeshift dock. When Cabot saw the pale moonlight illuminating the exit, he shouted to the driver to douse his lights. The truck clattered over the last dozen ties and hit the sandy bar between the Tunnel and the plank pier. The mammoth tires bit into the loose earth, clawing for traction. With sand above the wheel rim, the truck almost drove itself into the bank before the front tires caught the planks and with a splintering of wood heaved the vehicle onto the boards. The driver gunned the engine and slowly maneuvered the truck into the center of the waiting barge.

Cabot jumped off and sprinted to the bank, hurdling the recesses the truck had gouged out of the sand. Desperately he waved the second vehicle, emerging from the Tunnel, to a halt.

"Get some wood up here!"

Within minutes a makeshift timber platform was in place. Walking backwards, Cabot motioned for the second Hippo to inch forward. The planks sank into the sand but the vehicle made it onto the next barge in the towline.

"Get number three on!" Cabot shouted over the roar of the tugboat engine as it churned fifteen yards forward.

He ran up the pier and leaped onto the second barge.

"Move on the camouflage!"

The stink of garbage was hideous but that was exactly what Cabot wanted.

A major problem in the Prometheus transfer had been the matter of getting the bullion downriver to where *Victorious* waited. Even though the shipment would be made under the cover of night, Cabot would not countenance moving the load overland. Aside from the ideal targets the lumbering Army vehicles provided, there was the problem of the dock activity involved in the unloading and loading of the vessel. At either point the vulnerability of the shipment was unacceptable.

Cabot had spent hours along the river Thames seeking a solution. When he at last came upon it he cursed because it had been before his very eyes all the time.

Two tugboats with their three, four or five garbage scows in tow . . . plying the river every hour of the day, so common a waterfront sight that no one paid any attention to it. The obvious had become the invisible.

Cabot had quickly established that each of the scows could carry far more than the tonnage he required of them. From that point on it had been a simple enough matter to work out the logistics with Admiral Runnymeade. When Runnymeade approved the plan, his aide, Lieutenant Simmons, had gone down to the Port Authority Office and requisitioned a tug and three barges. He politely refused the Authority's offer to man the vessel. The Navy team which would guide the barges to *Victorious* had already been selected.

The final detail had been the garbage itself. For the Army to have approached the London Sanitation Department was out of the question. Too many tongues would waggle if officers came around asking for several tons of refuse. The problem was solved by using an existing Army base in north London. At the same time as the bullion was being loaded beneath Threadneedle Street, a convoy of Army vehicles arrived at the pier below London Bridge. Within hours refuse was piled high along the sides of the scows. But the center of each scow was empty. That was where the trucks now stood, half hidden by refuse.

As Cabot watched, the commandos drew an enormous net strewn with bits of newspaper and shredded cloth over the trucks. From a distance the vehicles would appear to be only a mountain of refuse. Even if a spotlight were shone on the

scows little or nothing would be seen. All windows and lights
on the vehicles were being hastily coated with flat black paint.

Cabot made his way to the stern of the tugboat and, stepping
back, leaped over the four-foot expanse of water between it
and the scow. A young officer in battle fatigues materialized at
his side.

"The men are just about through, sir," he said. "We shall be
able to push off in five minutes."

Cabot accepted a light from the officer and looked out over
the lapping, black waters.

"How long to our destination?"

"Thirty minutes, sir!"

And another forty-five to unload, Cabot thought. I need
seventy-five minutes, Guderian, just seventy-five. After that
you can rot in whatever hole you managed to crawl into . . .

The air crews, culled from the Luftwaffe's finest pilots and
navigators, had left their air base in Alsace-Lorraine ninety
minutes earlier. At two-thirty A.M. their aircraft, Dornier 17Z
bombers, were approaching the French coast at maximum air-
speed of 255 miles per hour. The squadron leader ordered his
command to reduce altitude and speed immediately. The first
had to do with evasion techniques designed to penetrate the
British radar barrier. The second was related directly to the
mission: the bombers were not to be over their target area until
exactly thirty minutes from now.

The squadron leader of the six ships throttled back his aircraft to one hundred and seventy miles per hour and sent the
machine even closer to the moonlit Channel waters. The
urgency of carrying out his orders to the letter had been im-
pressed upon him twice over by his commanding officer. Not
that this had been necessary. The squadron leader had had his
late dinner interrupted by an urgent telephone call. The final
briefing, if it could be called that, had been given by Adolf
Hitler himself, who spent a full thirty minutes quizzing the
leader on every facet of the operation. Although the Führer did
not state this in so many words, the squadron leader understood
that this mission could have only one of two endings: either he
and his men would succeed, in which case all who survived
were guaranteed an Iron Cross First Class to be presented by
Hitler personally, or else they must die in the attempt to hit the
target. There was no middle ground.

There was also no protection, the squadron leader reflected with a trace of bitterness. He had raised the question of fighter support but Hitler had turned it down quickly and with finality. The whole object of the attack was to move in fast, devastate the target and get out. Fighter cover meant that much more metal for English radar to pick up, a hazard to the primary and only objective.

The commander had one further objection but he wisely eschewed mentioning it. His planes were overloaded. The maximum bomb weight the Dorniers had been designed to carry was two thousand pounds. Each now bore six four-hundred-pound fused devices. If British radar did pick them up and got to them before the planes were over target, the three machine guns at the nose, ventral and dorsal positions would be utterly ineffectual against the Spitfires and Hurricanes.

The commander chewed hard on his cigarillo, tasting the bitter juice under his tongue. He eased his machine to less than one hundred meters above the waves. When he checked his watch he realized that he was already halfway across the Channel. Thirty minutes to the Thames estuary . . .

The radar station at Knob Hill Farms on the English coast picked up six blips at two-forty. Thirty seconds later, after confirmation came in that the RAF had no planes in the sky and the flight must be considered hostile, the fighter field at Lichfield Downs went on scramble.

Within ten minutes six RAF Spitfires were roaring down the runway. Their estimated interception time was fourteen minutes.

At this point the Dornier bombers were less than eight minutes away from target.

Cabot shielded his eyes from the glare emanating from the four giant spotlights rigged on the superstructure of the *Victorious*. He watched as the eighth of nine pallets was swung across the air, hung suspended for a moment, then was slowly lowered on deck. Even before the pallet touched down a group of sailors swarmed around it, untying and flinging off the thin steel wires that were hooked up to the crane's central cable. Steel clattered against steel as the wires were pulled from under the pallet. The crane operator threw a lever and the cable was reeled in at the same time as he swung the boom across the stern of *Victorious*.

Cabot watched as the cable descended toward the bed of the truck on the third barge. The camouflage netting had been dragged off the vehicle and the canvas top rolled back. The white-hot glare of the lights penetrated the slits in the wooden crates, the gold bars glittering fiercely as though they had just been minted and still retained the heat of the forge.

Ten minutes ahead of schedule. The most critical part of Prometheus, the point at which work *had* to be carried out with light, was almost over with. Even though *Victorious* was lying dead center in the Thames, Cabot knew that such activity would not go unnoticed. His only strength lay in the speed with which the transfer could be accomplished. As the shout came to raise the pallet, Cabot stepped onto the last layer of gold bricks. Holding on to the wires, he waved his arm and the crane began its swing.

"Get the barges out of here!" he roared. The captain of the tug anticipated the order. As Cabot and the gold were being lowered onto the *Victorious*'s deck the engines caught and the tug pulled away from the cruiser's flank, heading into the shallows.

Cabot jumped onto the deck and surveyed the pallets lined up in an uneven row. Beneath the armor plating he felt the vibrations of the mighty engines, idling. In a few moments *Victorious* would be under way. By the time she reached the mouth of the Thames, half the boxes would be stored below decks.

"Sir, a message from RAF, Knob Hill Farms," the radio operator said stepping up to him. He lowered his voice and added: "Bombers on the way . . ."

"Christ no!" Cabot whispered. "Not now!"

But already he could hear them, the persistent unearthly drone that pulsed out of the moonlit sky.

"Two o'clock, sir!" the radio operator shouted.

They came out from behind the clouds, flying low over the city, in single file, their trajectory such that for the last half mile they would be following the river . . . straight to *Victorious*.

"Abandon ship!" Cabot shouted. He grabbed the radio telephone and repeated the order to the bridge. Seconds later the sirens began blaring. Men froze, stared up at the sky, then literally dropped whatever they were carrying and began backing away toward the guardrails.

"Get the hell off this vessel!" Cabot screamed.

The paralysis broke. As the bombers thundered from the dead of night, their target brilliantly illuminated for them, men flung themselves into the murky water and swam frantically for the riverbank. Cabot waited until the lead plane was almost over him before he too dived for the safety of the depths.

The lead Dornier was flying at just above stalling speed. Hunched over his viewfinder, the bombardier threw the first set of toggles and a four-hundred-pound charge dropped away. The bomb spun away toward *Victorious*, impacting exactly on the tip of the bow. The explosion sheared away the paint storeroom and the working space above the torpedo gunners' room. Its concussive effect blew away four watertight compartments, buckling the waterline plates.

The second and third bombs fell on either side of the forward funnel. The entire area below the nine-meter rangefinder was destroyed—the transmitting office, remote control office, wheelhouse, and lobby. In the Petty Officers' pantry the ceiling caved in. The third charge was the most devastating, falling directly onto the torpedo workshop, splintering the interior funnel lines and causing B boiler room to explode. The *Victorious* was blazing.

Jonathan Cabot watched transfixed as the first Dornier completed its run and peeled away, clawing for altitude. Out of the corner of his eye he saw pinpricks of light appear. The Dornier shuddered as Spitfire machine guns racked the exposed underbelly. But the explosion of the dying airship was nothing compared to the horror that was taking place on the *Victorious*.

The second Dornier had dropped two bombs simultaneously, destroying both stern turrets as well as completely obliterating whatever was on deck. The pallets laden with crates disintegrated before Cabot's eyes. The third ship, when it followed through, completed the job. Its three bombs plunged straight through the naval storeroom and exploded above the X and Y magazines. The ensuing explosion was so great that not only did the entire stern of the *Victorious* heave itself out of the water, but the fourth bomber, coming in far too low, was literally torn apart in midair by the concussions.

Swimming on his back, Cabot continued to kick for the shore. His body was almost numb from the frigid waters, and he could feel shock setting in. Desperately he kept on moving, his eyes on the sky. The Spitfires had pounced on the last two Dorniers and were gunning them in a vicious crossfire. One of the German ships plunged into the Thames not fifty feet from Blackfriars Bridge. Another burned out over the docks, driving its nose low into a warehouse. As its explosives ignited, the warehouse collapsed onto the Dornier.

Cabot struggled out of the water, his hands and knees sinking into the mud and sludge of the bank. Even at this distance the light from the fury in the river illuminated the seawall behind him, and beyond that, the steps that led to the first row of granaries. He staggered to his feet, leaning against the porous blackened seawall.

Goddamn you, you managed to do it! he thought viciously. Somehow you knew exactly what I would do and you worked your operation around it . . . But in the end you lost. *You don't know it yet but you lost*!

Cabot clambered up the steps of the seawall, listening to the wail of emergency vehicles. Guderian had accomplished what he had come to England to do, but Cabot's real work was just about to start.

31

Erik Guderian was smiling. Standing by the window of Morell's room, the blackout curtains pulled back an inch from the frame, he saw the leaping brilliant flames as they lighted up the sky above the river Thames. The explosions had been thunderous and with each shudder that rumbled through the night Guderian had rejoiced. Not even the fiery loss of the Dorniers that had carried out the destruction tempered the exaltation of victory. They were necessary sacrifices placed upon the altar of British and American defeat. Thirty-six men . . . in comparison to what had been gained, a small enough price to render up.

Behind him the door opened and closed softly. Guderian did not turn around. He had seen Morell's reflection in the window.

"They are dismantling the cordon," Morell said, breathing hard, having just run up the staircase from the ground floor.

"You're certain?" Guderian demanded.

"There's too much activity for them *not* to be moving out," the chief steward said. "Let me turn the radio on. There's bound to be some word from the BBC."

Guderian drew the blackout curtains together and carefully examined himself in the full-length mirror on the closet door. He was dressed in a heavy flannel workshirt, corduroy trousers, thick woolen socks and Army boots. Morell handed him a military-style greatcoat and a black beret.

"Up close you won't stand a chance," he said. "But at night, at a distance, you will pass for a soldier."

There were other changes as well. Guderian's hair had been cut *en brosse* and dyed black. A six-day growth of beard had been scraped away, but the budding mustache retained. There wasn't much else that could be done with what Morell had had to work with. Darkness would be the best protection.

Guderian tucked his revolver into the coat pocket.

"Did you manage?" he asked Morell.

The old man's head bobbed frantically. He dug into his pocket and produced a packet the size of a thick bundle of pound notes. As Guderian took it he felt the paper crackle beneath the cheesecloth.

"I took all the pharmacist had on hand," Morell breathed. "Mixed it exactly as you told me."

"No one saw you?"

"On my word, no. The Bond brothers have been supplying us for years. I've gone there often enough to have members' prescriptions filled. Know exactly where everything is . . ."

"But when you had to break in—"

"No one saw me!" Morell repeated vehemently. "There's a back door with a lock on it older than I . . ."

Guderian slipped the packet into his greatcoat and turned away.

"There seems to be a great deal of activity along King Street," Morell was saying. "That might be your best way out."

Guderian said nothing. He had already decided how he

would break out of the already disintegrating quarantine. He
had to get out of London quickly, with a vehicle, because his
job, like Cabot's, wasn't over yet.

"It is now almost three-fifteen," Guderian said. "I want you
to send the final message at exactly six o'clock, later this
morning."

He paused, gripping Morell by the shoulder.

"You saved my life many times over," he whispered
fiercely. "When this is all over and we have succeeded I will
come back for you. You deserve the Führer's recognition for
what you've done!"

The chief steward blinked rapidly, trying to hold back his
tears.

"Succeed in what you set out to do!" he said vehemently.
"Not for me or yourself but for the Fatherland. God willing we
shall meet again. But if not, at least I can die knowing that I
too served!"

Morell stepped out the door first, making sure that the corridor was empty. He led the way down the back staircase,
through the darkened kitchen, and opened the door to the service entrance.

"Godspeed!" he whispered. "The message will be sent . . ."

Guderian did not look back. He stepped into the alley and
immediately pressed himself against the brick wall as an armored personnel carrier roared through the sidestreet. He
needed transportation—but not that kind.

For the next twenty minutes Guderian remained in the alley,
allowing four trucks and another carrier to pass by. He was
about to move when he heard the unmistakable sound of a
Morris-Commercial coming toward him. Guderian leaped into
the sidestreet and started flagging down the vehicle. Because of
the blinding headlights he couldn't determine if the driver was
alone.

"Over here!" Guderian shouted.

The paratroop corporal, who was on his way to the command post at the foot of St. James's Street, geared the Morris
down and stared at the figure running toward him. His eye
caught the greatcoat and beret and so the mind registered the
soldier as friendly.

"There's a body in there," Guderian gasped, gesturing at the
alley. "It might be him. I heard some groaning . . ."

As the corporal turned in the direction Guderian had indicated, the German brought out the gun from his pocket. The blow hit the paratrooper on the side of the face, stunning him. As he fell over, Guderian jumped on him, hitting him viciously across the exposed neck.

Without wasting a movement Guderian dragged the body into the small space behind the seats and laid the driver out on his back. If anyone stopped him now, he could say he was rushing an accident victim to one of the hospitals. The blood on the paratrooper's face would be more than convincing.

Guderian jumped behind the wheel and threw the Army truck into gear. Swinging it onto St. James's, he drove as fast as he could toward Piccadilly, lights blazing, waving and yelling at the other military traffic to get out of his way. The checkpoint at Piccadilly was in the process of being dismantled. The Army trucks that had been stationed across the street in single file were backing away toward groups of waiting troops. Guderian slowed to a halt and leaped out of the truck.

"Get that vehicle out of the way!" he shouted at a driver. "I have a wounded man here!"

Startled, the driver threw his machine into reverse. As he swung behind the wheel Guderian heard pounding feet coming at him.

"What's going on here?"

The paratroop sergeant had his weapon leveled at Guderian.

"He got hit by one of our own trucks!" Guderian shouted back. "I've got to get him to the clinic at Berkeley Square!"

The sergeant looked over at the soldier thrashing feebly in the rear of the vehicle. He turned to say something to Guderian when two personnel carriers roared up behind him. The commander of the armored unit was screaming for everyone to get out of his way.

"Get going!" the paratrooper roared.

Guderian stomped on the accelerator and the Morris-Commercial shot forward. Since Piccadilly was still closed off, he made what would have been an illegal left and headed toward Dover Street. Less than a minute later he saw the outline of the house where he himself had been taken and cared for after his arrival from Dunkirk. Everything that had happened then seemed so long ago . . . almost unreal.

Guderian swung off Dover Street into Hay Hill. The truck lurched as he drove it onto the sidewalk close to the wrought-iron fence that framed the park. He doused the lights and got out.

The young soldier had almost regained consciousness. His eyelids were fluttering and he was moaning softly. The corporal opened his eyes to see a gloved hand descending toward his mouth. In a futile gesture he tried to ward it off with one arm, but Guderian knocked it away easily. He clamped one hand over the soldier's mouth and brought the other around the back of his head. Guderian fed power into his arms and shoulders and with a vicious twist broke the young soldier's neck.

Night birds fluttered at the sound of cracking bone. Guderian pulled the soldier's body out, squatting down so the dead weight lay across his shoulder. He moved over to the side of the fence and dropped on his haunches, rose swiftly, at the same time heaving the corpse over the spikes and into the bushes.

Guderian staggered backward. Suddenly he leaned on the fender and vomited out the tension and horror that had welled up inside him.

Just a little bit more, he thought desperately. A little more strength. I've almost made it. It's so very close now.

Somewhere in the distance a dog barked, the sound followed by a low whistle. Guderian got back into the truck and started up the engine. Slowly he pulled the vehicle off the curb and using only parking lights sped out of Berkeley Square, heading south. He breathed deeply of the clean night air, trying to clear his mouth of the sour bile. But even as he drove he could not forget the image of that soldier, the terror-stricken eyes burning into his own.

"You're certain you are quite all right, Mr. Cabot?"

Winston Churchill, tie askew, spectacles drooping far down on his bulbous nose, regarded the American with uncertainty. Across the room Allen Dulles's concern was unspoken but evident. Cabot's lips were still a pale blue from the exposure in the icy waters. But the scalding bath and fresh warm clothing controlled the shivering that had overtaken Cabot when he had arrived at Downing Street. A few shots of premium whiskey hadn't hurt either.

"I'm fine, Prime Minister, thank you," Cabot said and refilled his glass.

"I think I shall join you," Churchill said wearily. "In fact I am sorely tempted to dispose of the entire contents of this decanter. Later in the day, Parliament will be howling for my head. I don't suppose they would care what condition it is in."

Churchill held up the decanter. "Allen?"

Dulles shook his head. He had been monitoring the bullion transfer from the embassy. As soon as he heard the air raid sirens go off he was over at Ten Downing. At that point Dulles had no way of knowing whether Jonathan Cabot was still alive.

"Guderian got to us, didn't he?" Dulles said, looking at Cabot, who was lighting a cigarette.

"What's the latest casualty?" asked Cabot, ignoring the gambit.

Dulles read from a sheet of paper on his lap.

"The barge crew managed to get away in time. No damage there. As for the men on board *Victorious,* eighteen of the twenty are accounted for. The other two haven't been found yet."

"They should have gotten off in time," Cabot murmured. "Goddamn it, there was enough time."

He hesitated. "What about *Victorious*?"

"The only thing that can be seen of her are the funnels," Dulles said. "Her battle days are over."

"Still, I suppose it wasn't a total loss," Churchill commented sarcastically. "The RAF shot down all six Dorniers without sustaining any losses. Two hundred and fifty million pounds sterling in gold and negotiable securities—a small price to pay for a half dozen German warplanes, wouldn't you say?"

They really don't know, Cabot thought to himself, glancing from Dulles to Churchill. Throughout this entire affair they never suspected a damn thing!

Cabot rose and stepped back so he could look at both men.

"The gold and securities are completely safe," he said.

Churchill and Dulles stared at him.

"Really, Mr. Cabot," the Prime Minister started to say. "Such a joke is in very bad taste at this point in—"

"It's true," Cabot repeated. "The shipment is intact. It was never on board the barges, much less the *Victorious.* But Guderian believed that. The bombing raid proved as much. And you gentlemen also believed it—the final proof that Prometheus is still secure."

"I'm afraid I still don't understand," Churchill said in a faltering voice. "Everything was planned to the last detail.

There were no last-minute changes in schedule or transport . . ."

"None that you *knew* of," Cabot corrected him. "But yes—there were changes. I simply didn't inform you of them."

"I beg your pardon?" Churchill demanded in a strangled whisper. "You didn't tell us—"

"Exactly what *did* you do with the gold, Jonathan?" Dulles interrupted quietly.

"As long as Guderian was out there I had to work on the assumption that Berlin knew not only when the shipment was going but how," Cabot explained. "This was an unacceptable risk. The only way to ensure that the transfer would be secure was to lead everyone, except the people who were an integral part of the ruse, in the direction I wanted them to go."

"And we were not considered integral?" the Prime Minister asked, his voice bristling with irony.

"No, sir. Neither of you were," Cabot said flatly.

"Besides," he added, "I had no way of knowing that you would approve the plan—if it meant the almost certain loss of *Victorious*."

"You're damn right we might have had second thoughts!" Churchill thundered. "*Victorious* is irreplaceable!"

"Given the circumstances, Prime Minister, it was either the ship or the gold," Cabot replied evenly. "I couldn't give you both. I'm sorry. Not with Guderian loose."

"What was the actual plan, Jonathan?" Dulles asked, trying to keep the account on track.

"Governor Reading informed me that among other safeguards the Bank of England maintains a set of phony gold bars," Cabot said. "These bricks are lead, with a very fine layer of gold over them. In weight, shape, size, even serial numbers, they are identical to the genuine article. Those were the bricks that were being loaded last night when I was in the vault. Everything that took place last night did so under an illusion. Yet there was no other way. The demolition team, the Marines, the commandos on the barges, the Royal Navy personnel on *Victorious*, *everyone* had to believe that what they were handling was the actual bullion. Only the absence of the negotiable securities would have raised suspicion. But no one picked up on that."

"A decoy," Churchill muttered. "A bloody incredible decoy . . ."

"Exactly." Cabot nodded. "As soon as I left the vault Mackenzie McConnell arrived. Waiting in the Bank's courtyard were ten Hippo vehicles. It was she who supervised the packing of the real gold—along with the securities—and getting it onto the trucks."

"You *trucked* the bullion out of the Bank?" Dulles cried.

"Using a variation of the shell game," Cabot confirmed. "Not all the Hippos were loaded. Moreover, it was the safest way to go. Ironically, Guderian did us a favor by running for London. We were able to pin him in the city and use the Army to enforce a quarantine. Not only did we deny him freedom of movement at a critical time, but we also had a ready-made excuse for the Army's presence. Given all the troop movements and military vehicles, the Hippo convoy didn't cause any suspicion whatsoever. It simply blended into the existing situation."

"That was why you were so insistent on the cordons!" Churchill exclaimed. "You wanted to get the shipment out as much to keep Guderian in!"

"That was the intention," Cabot told him. "Or both of them, if you will. I think you understand now why I reacted so quickly to Guderian's being at Topcliffe Hall."

"How could Guderian have learned that *Victorious* was to carry the bullion?" Churchill asked, shaking his head. "Even though it was a decoy, you nonetheless had absolute security around the transfer."

"Guderian didn't guess, Prime Minister," Cabot said, his voice hard. "His penetration into England was based on the almost certain knowledge that you would move the gold. The banker in him deduced as much early on in the game. As for how he focused on *Victorious*, I can only tell you that Guderian had to have had help over here. In spite of the successes of the Double-cross System there are obviously agents active and operating in critical areas."

Cabot paused. "Because not only did Guderian home in on *Victorious*, he also had to have had help getting his message to Berlin so that the Dorniers could fly."

At the final words Churchill paled. Their implication was deadly.

"Where did the trucks take the gold, Mr. Cabot?" he asked softly.

"By now, Mr. Prime Minister, the trucks will have reached

their destination," Cabot said. "Southampton . . . where Prometheus will be loaded onto the cruiser *Jade*."

"*Jade!*" Churchill whispered. "*Victorious*'s sister ship!"

"On my instructions Captain Runnymeade pulled *Jade* out of the Thames early yesterday evening. As much as I hated it, I had to leave *Victorious* as a possible target ship. If Berlin was sending bombers, I wanted Goering to know that they had found their target. Of equal importance was Guderian's either witnessing or learning of the ship's destruction. Because he had access to a radio. The deception had to be played out to the final card in order for it to work. But I can assure you now that as far as Berlin is concerned the shipment has been completely obliterated. It will be interesting, Prime Minister, to see what kind of propaganda Berlin spews out about their . . . *victory*."

"And there is no chance of Guderian's *not* having been taken in by your rather spectacular play?" Churchill demanded.

"None, Prime Minister."

"Allen, I for one want to leave for Southampton immediately," Churchill said. He turned back to Cabot. "It's not that I do not trust what you've told us, you understand. But I won't be able to sleep tonight in any event and I think it would do something for my own morale to see *Jade* depart."

"I thought you might have something like that in mind, Prime Minister," Cabot said. "There is a military transport waiting for us at Waterloo Station."

But unknown to these three men, a fourth had already reached Southampton. His target too was the *Jade*, but his purpose was quite different from a congratulatory farewell.

The Southampton Cartage Company (SCC) was the city's oldest transport firm, having gone into business in 1889 with three teams of dray horses and as many wagons. By 1940 SCC had a fleet of forty long-distance trucks and a staff of over one hundred. The foundation of the company's success lay with long-standing Royal Navy contracts for hauling away garbage and bringing in ships' supplies.

At three o'clock in the morning on June 16, Freddie Tompkins, a twenty-four-year-old driver who had been with SCC for five years, released the air brakes and slowly maneuvered his Leyland Blue Star rig out of the garage. Tompkins was exempt from war service because of an asthmatic condition. Given what he had heard and seen about Southampton after the Dunkirk retreat, he was grateful for the infirmity. Nevertheless Freddie believed that those who remained at home also served. Whenever he ran up against soldiers in the Windsor Arms pub he made a point of mentioning his work for the Royal Navy.

Tompkins guided the Blue Star with its attendant eight-wheel tanker through the silent, empty streets of the city. He briefly wondered what was happening at the naval yards that necessitated this sudden shipment. Usually all vessels were victualled, supplied, and their freshwater tanks filled the evening prior to sailing. But the call from the Southampton's Quartermaster's Office hadn't come in until after midnight. The SCC dispatcher had been none too pleased about having to get out of his warm bed to head for the office and arrange the paperwork.

But Tompkins didn't mind the loss of sleep in the least. He was between girls and the overtime would make a handsome addition to his Post Office savings account. Besides, if the truth were known, Freddie Tompkins had a fascination for the big ships. He had become a familiar face among the civilian workers at the yards and Navy shore-duty personnel.

Twenty minutes after leaving the garage, Tompkins pulled up his transport under the immense water tower which dominated the landscape of the suburban row houses. Four sixty-foot-high steel pillars provided the cradle on which the tank, an oval laid on its side, rested. There was a series of control boxes and pipes which released, monitored and carried the flow of fresh water from the hundred-thousand-gallon-capacity reservoir. Tompkins drove the tanker between the mammoth circular piles and eased it to a halt so that the tanker's top ports were directly beneath the pipe hookups. He applied the air brakes and shut off the engine.

The District Waterworks Supervisor had also had his sleep broken by a call from the Navy dispatcher. When Tompkins entered his shed the supervisor had the paperwork ready. Tompkins filled out the necessary details—his driver's number, time of loading, estimated time of departure, load (a tanker's capacity, five thousand gallons)—and fixed his signature at the bottom.

"Who we doin' this for, then?" he asked the supervisor. "Ain't seen any ships in port that had a five-thousand-gallon water tank."

"Neither did I," the supervisor replied sourly. "They wouldn't tell me what's going on. Just to get the water down to Pier Three by five o'clock."

"Damn strange—but that's the Navy for you!" Tompkins said cheerfully and clambered up the rail to the top of the tanker.

He scampered along the eight-inch-wide panel that ran the length of the tanker, flipping open the port covers. Working his way back, he fed in the thick rubber hoses that hung, like cows' nipples, from the overhead pipeline, which in turn was connected to the pipes that stretched straight up into the giant reservoir. When he had double-checked each hose, Tompkins clambered down and ran over to the control boxes the supervisor had unlocked.

"Ready?"

Tompkins nodded. The supervisor began to turn the wheel that opened the pipes up top. Tompkins waited a moment for gravity to do its work, then went over to the side of the tanker. At eye level was a cap tightly fitted into its grooves. This covered the relief pressure mechanism. In the event of an emergency, when there was too much water pressure in the tanker, the cap would blow, allowing the excess to shoot out. Tompkins didn't have to cock his ear next to the feed-in pipe. He heard the water rushing into the tanker as soon as the cap was off.

"Moving nicely!" he shouted to the supervisor, who waved back in reply.

Tompkins screwed the cap back into position. The loading would take the better part of an hour. But there was no need to hang about listening to the slosh of water. The supervisor had a hot plate in the shack and the better half of a bottle of rum Tompkins had brought him earlier in the week. Tea and a dram and a couple cigarettes . . . a civilized way in which to pass the time.

Guderian had left the Morris-Commercial around the back of an all-night roadhouse, parking it well away from the main building and the fuel pumps that serviced the interdistrict trucks. He walked the stiffness from his legs and disappeared behind a copse of trees to urinate. When he finished he dipped into his coat pocket and threw the vehicle's keys farther into the woods. It was 3:40 in the morning of June 16.

Guderian paused a moment to collect himself. From where he stood he could see the glow of lights, a half mile off, from the reservoir. Even though the blackout was in effect, the supervisor had to have received special dispensation. It was impossible to load five thousand gallons of water in darkness.

And Guderian knew that that was the exact capacity of the tanker standing beneath the reservoir. Just as he knew the name of the company to which it belonged, the time it had to arrive at the depot, and when it was expected at the docks. This information had been in the files of the Quartermaster's office at the Central Naval Depot at Greenwich . . . which Guderian had broken into and rifled. That was why he had had to leave London when he did . . . and murder an innocent soldier for his vehicle, which would get him to Southampton. That was why there was another corpse fifty miles away, that of a gasoline station owner whom Guderian had woken up, then killed as soon as he had the keys to the pumps.

The bloody trail had led him to within a few miles of his target. The last leg of the journey was only several hundred yards away.

Erik Guderian slipped off the greatcoat. He laid it out on the ground, removed his revolver and the package Alfred Morell had prepared for him, from his pockets. He checked the gun thoroughly, then stuffed the firearm into the waistband of his trousers and covered the butt with the heavy workman's shirt.

He brought the package into the moonlight and turned it over in his hand. Its contents weighed less than half a pound, but Morell had assured him that was more than enough for Guderian's purpose. He examined the packet carefully, made certain there were no tears and slipped it into the lefthand breast pocket of his shirt. He threw the commando beret onto the coat, rolled up the coat into a tight ball, knotting it with the sleeves, and threw it as far as he could into the woods. He was ready.

Guderian crossed the highway fifty yards from the roadhouse, disappearing into the ditch between the unpaved shoulder and the plank fences that defined the backyards of the row houses. The ditch was damp and after a crouching run of twenty yards he elected to move to higher ground. The mud sucking at his boots gave too much away in the otherwise silent dawn.

The row houses ended at a small soccer field. Diagonally

across it was Southampton's main steam plant. Beyond that, partially blocked out by the brick stacks, loomed the gigantic shadow of the overhead reservoir. Guderian calculated that the safer route lay around the perimeter of the soccer field, along the darkened streets. But going straight across would save him valuable minutes. The tradeoff was that the lights of the steam plant already bathed the playing field in a milky white light.

Guderian started running, the grass slippery beneath the thick rubber soles of the boots. But he made good time and reached the chainlink fence that bounded the steam plant without incident. Minutes later he had skirted the plant's maintenance yard and was headed in the direction of the water tower.

The tanker rested in the glow of a dozen lamps, the light so powerful that it sparkled off the quartz chips imbedded in the gravel. Twenty yards to the left was a shack, also lit up. Even from where he stood Guderian could hear the rumble of water in the pipes. He was so close to the target, yet the distance between himself and the tanker represented the maximum threat to his mission. For a given period of time he would be completely at the mercy of the floodlights. The area beneath the tower was barren. Only the vehicle itself presented any sort of cover.

Guderian started his run, legs pumping furiously, the crunch of crushed stone bedlam to his ears. The driver and supervisor must be inside the hut. It was unlikely they would hear anything unless he fell. But a casual glance out the windows would be enough. Guderian didn't know how much time he had, when the filling had begun, and whether or not anyone would come out to check the valves. He tried to dismiss the questions from his mind, but they continued to hammer at him. He was only a few feet away from the Blue Star cab when the shed door opened.

Guderian clutched at the bar welded into the side of the cab frame and curled both hands around it. He held on, arms stiffening, the rest of his body still flying because of his forward momentum, then suddenly being jerked to a halt as the grip held. He felt as though his arms were being wrenched from their sockets, but he stifled the scream and clung to the bar, feet now on the running board.

Footsteps crunched over gravel. A palm slapped the tanker twice, the echo resounding in the night.

"Halfway there," a voice called out. "Right on schedule."

The footsteps retreated, the door to the shack was slammed shut.

Guderian dropped to the ground and hobbled along the tanker's flank, arms numb, hanging uselessly at his sides. He found the pressure-release cap immediately and forced his arm up. The pain was so great that for an instant he thought he would black out. With a final effort he clamped his fingers around the cap and twisted it open.

Water sloshed out, spilling onto his shirt. Guderian slipped the cap back on to prevent any more telltale water from staining the gravel and dug into his pocket for the cheesecloth packet. Holding that in his left hand, he brought out the scalpel he still carried with him, sheathed and taped to the inside of his shirt, and cut through the cloth and the heavy paper beneath it. When he was certain the incision was large enough, he pulled off the cap, let the spillover created by the sloshing water come out, then pressed the packet against the open funnel. Within seconds the white powder was streaming into the hold of the tanker and was being mixed into the entire supply by the currents fed from the pipes.

When he was certain the package was empty, Guderian screwed the cap on firmly, wiped away any residue and stuffed the empty packet into his shirt. He took a last look at the ground around him to make sure nothing had fallen out, then ran toward the cab of the Blue Star. Jumping onto the running board, he opened the door just enough to squeeze into the passenger seat.

The Blue Star had been built for long-distance hauling. As a result it had a compartment behind the front seats in which the driver could stretch out for some rest. Guderian slid back the curtains and dropped into the narrow confine. There was a pillow, a frayed blanket and a kit bag filled with a change of clothing. Guderian disturbed nothing. He curled his body so that his legs were drawn against the wall of the cab. This way he occupied only slightly more than half the allotted space. There was the chance that if the driver drew back the curtain he would not bother to look round, but only reach back for what he wanted. Guderian was grateful that he had found no food in the compartment.

He brought out the scalpel and laid it on the blanket. If he had to kill the driver he would do so only as a last resort, to save himself. If he were discovered after the tanker had entered the naval compound, even that would be a futile gesture. There was no middle ground anymore. Cabot had seen to that, had hunted him with a ferocity Guderian thought was almost inhuman. And Cabot was still out there, not too far away, waiting. Guderian knew he had a single advantage: Cabot would be thinking that he, Guderian, had believed the gold transfer destroyed by the Dorniers' bombing run. Even though he hadn't cornered Guderian in London, he wouldn't be expecting him here. Because Guderian wasn't supposed to know what Cabot knew.

A piece of dirty brown canvas separating the driver from his hidden passenger . . . The measure between success and failure was less than one centimeter. As long as the driver didn't notice a slightly different smell, or his suspicions weren't kindled by intuition . . . As long as he just wanted to get his job over with . . . There was nothing to do but wait.

At 4:57 on the morning of June 16 the loading of the *Jade* was completed. The giant cranes, which had lifted pallets stacked with boxes of gold, swung their booms away from the ship. The Army Hippos had been moved to the far end of the wharf, leaving the approach to the bow clear for the water tanker that had pulled into the compound. After the last crate had disappeared into the hold, Mackenzie McConnell did her final walk-through. She began at the soda fountain and lobby located beneath the Admiral's quarters, then clambered down the ladder to the lower lobby, which opened up on the Petty Officers' pantry. Even though she had checked the serial number of each and every crate as it came off the pallets, she nonetheless now repeated the process, placing another series of ticks on the master list. The bullion and securities, stacked up from floor to ceiling along the four compartment walls, rested almost dead center in the ship, where the weight distribution was even. As Mackenzie closed the watertight entries behind her she affixed a canvas tape seal across the doors. From this moment on, the lobbies were off bounds to all crew members. When *Jade* docked in Halifax to refuel, a contingent of Royal Canadian Mounted Police would come on board to inspect the integrity of the seals. No one would be permitted to disembark until the police had made their inspection.

Tucking her clipboard with its master list under her arm,

Mackenzie scrambled up the steep metal stairs to the upper lobby and out the door by the Number 3 forward turret.

"Jonathan!"

He was standing behind the guns, Dulles and Churchill flanking him.

"Prime Minister, Mr. Dulles, an unexpected pleasure."

"We thought it would be appropriate to come by and wish the *Jade* bon voyage," Churchill said laconically. "I assume everything proceeded without incident?"

Mackenzie did not miss the irony beneath his words. For the past three hours she had been expecting some sort of communication from Downing Street. Cabot had told her that at the last minute he would inform Churchill and Dulles about the switch in ships. He would run interference for her as long as possible, freeing her to complete supervision of the loading. But Mackenzie understood that sooner or later she would be summoned by the Prime Minister. An explanation would be demanded as to why she participated in Cabot's phenomenal ruse, why she hadn't alerted Ten Downing Street. She had had her arguments ready, yet they crumbled in her mouth before the presence of the man.

Mackenzie took a deep breath and handed Churchill the master sheet.

"Every brick accounted for, Prime Minister. The compartments have been sealed. The Royal Marines have standing orders to admit no one into them."

Churchill glanced through the pages and handed them to Dulles.

"There you have it, Allen," he said, his voice catching. "The financial patrimony of the Empire. I trust Franklin will be able to put it to good use."

"The very best, Prime Minister," Dulles replied quietly. "As soon as we return to London I'll call Washington and inform the President that the check has cleared, as it were. The first shipments will be ready to leave Norfolk, Brooklyn and Boston as soon as *Jade* docks."

Churchill nodded absently and turned away, raising his hand to greet Admiral Runnymeade, who was coming up on deck, accompanied by Andrew Simmons.

Cabot took the opportunity to draw Mackenzie aside.

"Is the Bank sealed up?" he asked her.

"I left Reading wandering around in an empty vault, lost to the world," she said. "It staggers the imagination . . . what we've done, I mean. It wasn't until I actually saw all those securities, and the bars . . ."

"We're *almost* done," he corrected her. "There's still three thousand miles of ocean to contend with."

"But nothing's come up—"

"Everything is fine," Cabot assured her. "Even the long-range weather forecast looks good. Thank God for small mercies. I don't know if I could have handled eight days of rolling seas."

"So you are going along, are you?"

She tried to keep the emotion out of her voice but failed—badly. Mackenzie had known from the outset that Cabot would be sailing with the bullion. But just as with the gold, nothing seemed real until it was actually upon her.

"The turnaround time will be short," he said softly. "As soon as the shipment reaches the Federal Reserve in New York and I hand in my final report to the President, I'll be on the way back. Three weeks, no longer."

As the first shimmering rays of dawn glanced off the smoky waters and the sky opened in the promise of a new day, Cabot reached out and cupped Mackenzie's face with both hands.

"Oh, to hell with them!" Mackenzie said fiercely and flung her arms around his neck.

Their lips sealed upon each other, tongues probing deeply, straining to convey a passion, a need that could no longer be withheld. As his hands slid to her waist, Mackenzie buried her lips in his neck.

"Not an inch further, my darling. Otherwise I won't be responsible for my actions. Just promise me you won't do anything foolish. I don't want to see a single scratch on you when you return!"

"It's all past us," Cabot murmured, running his fingers through her golden mane. "There's nothing that can touch us now!"

Less than fifty yards away Freddie Tompkins was being given the final go-ahead to move his tanker into position.

As expected Tompkins had had no difficulty bringing his load into the compound. He and the on-duty Marine were on a first-name basis, and while the soldier had checked the bills of lading, a steady stream of gossip passed between the two men.

"Sure you're not carrying anything in the sleeper, son?" the Marine joked.

"Just some medicine I'll be glad to share when you get off duty," Tompkins laughed.

"Not today, old son," the Marine answered regretfully. "Double shift for everyone."

Tompkins nodded but knew better than to pursue the matter. The activity around the base was obvious, as were the extra guards he drove by on his way to the dock. Something was up all right, but it wasn't any business of an SCC driver.

Tompkins maneuvered his vehicle toward the bow of the vessel, lying silent and forbidding beneath the gantry lights. He never failed to feel awed by the immensity of such craft, the latent power in the triple turrets and bristling antiaircraft batteries. But he kept his eyes steady on the road ahead. The trickiest part of the haul was coming up.

The *Jade*'s freshwater tank, like that of all Dido class cruisers, was buried deep in the bow, between the diesel stowage compartment and the sonar room, below the waterline. A single shaft, ten inches in diameter, ran straight to the bow and was capped by a steel plate only a few feet from the end of Number 1 turret. In order to fill the tank a hose had been set between this funnel and the tanker's egress points at the back of the oval tank. Once in place the pumping could be controlled from the truck's cab. The trick was to get the vehicle close enough to the freshwater funnel.

Since it was impossible for so heavy a truck to drive onto the cruiser, a special ramp had been built. Because its incline was gradual, the ramp's lowest angle was thirty yards from the vessel. Supported by timber pillars, it rose at an angle of twenty degrees until it reached the level platform, set fifteen feet above the ground, that formed the bridge between the dock and the edge of the pier. The platform itself was constructed of reinforced metal sheets with a tubular steel railing. Freddie Tompkins knew from experience that the railing was little more than matchwood and wouldn't help stop his vehicle if its wheels strayed off the center of the platform.

And sometimes they did, because the truck had to be backed up the ramp, pushing rather than pulling its load. One miscalculation on the accelerator or gearshift and the entire load would be out of control.

Tompkins jumped out of the Blue Star, passed his papers to the Marine and began to carefully inspect every foot of the ramp. He checked the platform, then climbed down to ground level and walked beneath it, examining the piles. Only when he was satisfied that there were no obvious structural defects did he return to his truck and tell the Marine he was ready.

Back in the cab Tompkins made a minuscule adjustment to the outside rearview mirror and hastily crossed himself. At the same instant as his hand fell on the stickshift his feet began working the clutch and accelerator. With a roar of diesel exhaust the truck began backing up.

Tompkins never had any problem with the ramp. The grade was gentle enough so that he could maneuver his vehicle without difficulty. The critical moment came at the point where ramp and platform met. He had to give just enough gas so that the rear wheels would pass onto the metal sheet without slipping. At the same time he had to control the acceleration to prevent a possible fishtailing effect.

As soon as he heard the telltale groan of metal Tompkins fed power into his wheels. The tanker slid a foot to the left, then as Tompkins compensated with a turn of the wheel, straightened out. As soon as he had the front wheels flush with the platform, Tompkins slumped forward on the wheel and let out a long, slow whistle of relief. He saw the Marines on the dock signaling clear, waved in return and backed the tanker all the way along the platform. A moment later, with the engine still running but all brakes on, Tompkins jumped from the cab and threaded his way between the railing and the vehicle to the end of the platform. Below he saw two sailors readying the connecting hoses.

In the rear compartment of the Blue Star cab Erik Guderian moved as soon as Tompkins's footsteps faded away. Slowly he stretched himself out and began to massage his thighs and calves, fingers digging into the muscles to restore circulation, prevent the cramps which would seize him as soon as he had to move. Guderian figured on about two minutes for the hookup to be completed. In that time he reviewed every single detail about the loading that Booth, the assistant harbormaster, had provided him with. He closed his eyes and drew a mental image of the funnel that disappeared into the bowels of the ship

. . . and the iron-rung ladder which ran parallel to it, a ladder that could be used by only one man, going down or coming up. He had to be that one man.

Guderian heard Tompkins climb back into the cab. Switches were thrown, and as the diesel roared, the pumps attached to the belly of the tanker started up. The door opened again and the driver was gone.

Again Guderian waited. If Booth had been correct then Tompkins shouldn't be returning to the cab until the off-loading was almost finished.

"No point for a driver to hang about in the cab with all that rattling going on," Booth had told him. "He'll be on the outside, checking the hose and funnel, but once the water's running and the valves are tight he has nothing to do. Forty, forty-five minutes is a long time to sit around on deck, especially if it's cold. He'll be close by, but you might have the chance . . ."

He *had* to have the chance.

The cab of the Blue Star was pointed in the direction of the dock. Because of the windshield and side windows Guderian knew that anyone looking in the direction of the cab would see the movement from the rear compartment into the front seat. His only advantage was the fifteen-foot difference in height. That and the irregular shadows which covered the pier might be enough to hide his forward motion.

Guderian took a deep breath, pulled the curtain back and uncoiled his body, using his flexed knees to push off the back wall of the compartment. He dropped headfirst into the seat, slithered to the floor, then scrambled across the patched leather to the driver's door.

The driver's window faced the eastern exposure of the pier. There was no movement among the alleys that ran between the long, low warehouses. The front end of the ramp was empty. Guderian opened the door and slipped onto the metal sheeting, one foot at a time. Immediately he stepped behind the wheel so that his boots wouldn't be seen by anyone on the other side.

Guderian started toward the end of the tanker, his hands swinging lightly by his sides. To run would be to create too much noise on the metal sheets. And a Marine would be more likely to catch and fire on a moving target as opposed to a man who walked with the authority of someone who belonged there.

Guderian reached the end of the tanker and was now four feet from the end of the platform, standing next to the slick black hose that dropped over the edge ten feet onto the deck of *Jade*. A makeshift ladder had been set up against the platform. It was steep and because of the angle Guderian couldn't count the number of rungs. The ladder or a ten-foot jump . . .

The driver was standing fifteen feet away from the funnel, talking to a sailor who was lighting a cigarette. Because the wind was out of the east, Guderian couldn't catch their words. The sailor gestured at an unknown point on the ship and the driver agreed with whatever he said. The two men turned and took half a dozen steps away from the funnel. Guderian moved.

He had reached the ladder and was squatting above the uppermost rung when the driver suddenly turned back.

There was no way in which the driver couldn't see him!

Freddie Tompkins was all for going behind the shelter of Number 1 turret where, as the sailor told him, he could wait for a cup of hot tea the galley was making up. The wind had stiffened and drove right through the heavy sweater he was wearing. There was no shelter on the open deck and he didn't fancy hopping about from one leg to another for three-quarters of an hour. Still he was conscientious enough to make a final check on the hose to make certain the seals were holding.

When Tompkins turned around the sun hit him squarely in the eyes. He cursed and immediately lowered his eyes, keeping them on the deck, and blinked rapidly to dispel the dancing golden dots before his vision. He stooped down to check the hose and the clips that fixed it firmly to the funnel, rubbed his fingers together for any sign of moisture, then carefully pivoted on the balls of his feet, standing only when his back was to the sun.

Guderian was half walking, half sliding down the short ladder as soon as Tompkins was on his way toward the turret. He made for the open hatch in a crouching run, always keeping his eyes on the driver's retreating back. The driver was the only one who mattered now. Any one of a hundred different pairs of eyes might see him, but Guderian refused to consider them. He was six feet from the hatch.

As Tompkins reached the top of the gun mounted on the turret he thought he heard the sound of metal striking metal. He turned around, palm over his eyes, and squinted across the deck. There was no one there. The sound of the pump was steady.

If Freddie Tompkins had been three feet closer to the hatch he would have made out a pair of knuckles, the skin stretched white, curled around the first rung of the ladder that descended at a ninety-degree angle into the hold of *Jade*. If he had stepped even closer he would have found himself looking into the cold fierce eyes of Erik Guderian . . . and the living death of Prometheus. But Tompkins knew nothing of either Guderian or Prometheus, as he would repeatedly explain to his interrogators later on. He was simply a young man who was tired of the cold and wanted some shelter and hot drink.

As he heard the echoes of boots against metal fade, Erik Guderian began his descent, not daring to look up again. The mental image in his mind changed and he conjured up the detailed blueprint of the area around the water tank. He accounted for each watertight door he passed but kept on going until he had reached the end of the ladder and was standing on the roof of the tank itself. Guderian stepped around the funnel and spun the wheel on the oval iron door. An instant later he was in the sonar compartment, facing a stepladder that would take him to the cable locker. Beyond that was the narrow corridor which connected the entire forward part of the ship.

Erik Guderian had found his way into the very heart of Prometheus.

32

Although Erik Guderian had no way of knowing, two completely unrelated factors were combining to influence the destiny of Prometheus in a way he couldn't have anticipated. The first was a sudden shift in London weather; the second, a particular dietary consideration.

The clear night sky which had helped the Dornier bombers find their target so easily had, at half past four in the morning, disappeared behind a rolling fog. The rains started to pelt down thirty minutes later and would last until noon. Nevertheless the sudden arrival of inclement weather did not prevent the chief steward of Bentley's from braving the elements.

As the cordon around central London was broken down, mercantile traffic began to trickle into the quarantined areas. Because there was no question of getting any sleep after his anonymous guest left, Alfred Morell passed the hours sitting in a high rocker by the windows that overlooked the street. At times the rocker's movements lulled him into a doze, but like many older people he slept fitfully and never more than a few hours at a time. At half past five he heard the telltale sound of the milk wagon being drawn in the lane next to the club.

Morell doused his face with cold water, carefully brushed his hair back and reached inside the cupboard for his old black mackintosh. A moment later he was hurrying through the empty kitchens and was out the back door. The steady drizzle created beads on the wax of his wingtips, but Morell stepped into the lane and started off at a half trot after the milk wagon, which had stopped forty yards farther on, before a still shuttered grocery store.

The milkman had been on this route for the last five years. He greeted Morell warmly and gave him two pints of buttermilk for the price of one.

"For coming out in this bleedin' rain!"

Morell tucked the bottles under one arm and started to walk back. The bottoms of his trousers were thoroughly wet by now and he felt the trickle of water down his neck. But for the last day his stomach had been churning. The digestive system, accustomed to delicate treatment, began to feed off the acids which had accumulated in the stomach. Usually these were dissolved by the buttermilk Morell drank each day. But the kitchen had run short and he hadn't had the opportunity to buy his own. As he stepped under the long, low awnings of the dress shops Morell could already sense his relief. He wanted nothing to distract him from the task the man from Berlin had entrusted him with.

The Army troop carrier had no business being in the lane at all. It was eight tons of vintage Leyland, with an extended, canvas-top bed, high cab, and fenders that flared far out over the wheels. The driver was a nineteen-year-old private from the depot in Battersea, who had been ordered to pick up a consignment of men on the Haymarket and who had lost his way. For the last ten minutes he had been frantically going up and down the warren around St. James's, trying to find the right one-way street. The fog made his task all that more difficult. The fact that the cab rode so high, obscuring the side views, made the accident inevitable.

Alfred Morell heard the rumble of the truck soon enough. Prudently he moved even closer to the shop windows. Had he actually stepped into a doorway the vehicle would never have touched him.

As he roared down the lane the driver caught the sudden shift of fog, which revealed a lamppost on the lefthand side. Instinctively he swung the wheel, veering the carrier to the right. The front wheels jumped the curb. The fender, dented and mud-spattered, with a jagged piece that had gone unrepaired from an earlier mishap, sheared across Alfred Morell's chest, spinning him around and dropping him like a stone.

The driver never heard the crash of milk bottles on the pavement. He never felt the encounter. The truck plunged on into the fog. Somewhere in the distance a curse was flung at the driver as the milkman's horse tried to bolt.

Alfred Morell groaned and rolled over on his side. Immediately he felt the fire in his chest. With trembling fingers he patted the front of his coat. The cloth was frayed. As he pushed his hand into his clothing he felt something warm . . . then hard. The chief steward inclined his head and saw that half his chest had been ripped away. Blood was trickling through his fingers, mixing with the rain, which had also washed the exposed breastbone clean.

God, it hurt so much!

Alfred Morell staggered to his feet, clutching the slippery façade of a haberdashery wall. His mind began to fade in and out of consciousness, like a flickering lamp. He thrust his face into the rain and screamed:

"Berlin!"

It was a ferocity only those who know they are dying could have unleashed. Alfred Morell lurched across the street toward the back door of Bentley's. If anyone had challenged him they would have seen a murderous gaze in his eyes. Morell understood that no one could be permitted to stop him, help him. He was beyond that.

He staggered up the four steps, opened the back door, mercifully left unlocked, and stepped into the light. When he saw how slick his hands were he groaned softly. But the biggest obstacle was still to come: the staircase to his room.

It took the chief steward a full twenty minutes to climb to the uppermost floor. Twice his grasp on the wooden rail slipped and he almost plummeted backwards. But somehow his legs responded to the mind's command. Even as the sustenance of his life dribbled onto the drab, worn carpet, he moved on, driven by the thought of Berlin.

Alfred Morell made it into his room and locked the door only seconds before one of the cooks emerged from his own, shuffling toward the bathroom, scratching his neck. The water was running before Alfred collapsed in front of the Victor radio. For a few minutes he lay there, a brutalized animal, then slowly one hand reached out and pushed against the bottom panel, which popped out.

Staying on his knees, the chief steward pulled out the secret radio assembly. He wet his fingers with his tongue to get some of the sticky blood off and painstakingly attached the appropriate wires. He reached out and switched on the control button to allow the set to warm up, then dragged the wire antenna across the floor. Moving sideways like a crab, Morell leaned on the windowsill and hoisted himself up. After opening the window he threaded the wires through the tiny finishing nails driven into the exterior frame.

The chief steward slid to the floor, the runner carpet bunching up at his feet. He slumped back against the wainscotting, his chest rising and falling rapidly. The trickle of blood had become a steady stream.

Without getting up, the chief steward pushed himself across the floor toward the set. He managed to pull the headset over his ears and threw the switch that opened his frequencies. With faltering fingers he began to tap out his message.

Alfred Morell had no idea of how long he continued to send the same six coded sentences. He lost count after four. As he sat there stabbing at the keys a red haze descended over his vision. His head lolled and he felt his entire body swaying. But he persevered, punching the sticky keys from memory. He never felt the last spasm of pain as it tore apart what remained of his chest. He didn't feel himself falling over, almost in slow motion.

When Alfred Morell's head crashed onto the floorboards he lost consciousness forever. He wasn't dead yet but his life's blood was now streaming out of the chest cavity. And the transmitter remained alive, sending its pulses into the ether, a homing beacon for anyone who happened to be listening . . .

At 7:04 on the morning of June 16 the cruiser *Jade* slipped her moorings and began to steam out the tidal basin that separated the city from the sea. Five miles out she cleared the coastal town of Calshot and headed into The Solent between the mainland and the Isle of Wight. Two hours out of Southampton, moving at top speed of thirty knots, *Jade* cleared Lymington and arrived at latitude 50°, forty-five miles beyond Mitford-on-Sea.

"From here we swing directly west," Admiral Runnymeade said, binoculars pressed against his eyes, scanning the windswept horizon of the Atlantic. "The weather will hold until we reach Land's End, then Meteorology tells me a warm front has moved in off the Irish coast. Seas will stay calm until we're well out, but the fog is expected to be thick."

"That much more cover for us," Cabot said softly. "If we can get into the open sea without anyone seeing us we'll be able to reduce some speed."

"And still hope that the oilers and destroyer escorts that are supposed to meet us off the Canadian waters actually appear," Andrew Simmons added. "The Atlantic is unpredictable this time of year. We might have relative calm straight across or else something will come up on us on the blind side and we'll still burn up extra fuel just maintaining medium speed."

Cabot looked over at Simmons, who flanked the Admiral's seat in the wheelhouse. Simmons was a natural leader who maintained an easy familiarity with his men. They responded to his orders instantly, and he knew each of them well enough never to repeat a command. Although he held authority firmly he also delegated command, making each sailor aware of just how important his duties were to the whole effort.

And an effort it would be. When Cabot, Runnymeade and Simmons had drawn up the initial plans, one of the primary considerations had been the final weight of the ship. Because of the gold and securities, weight had to be taken off in another area. The cut also had to take into consideration the extra fuel *Jade* would carry. Her run across the Atlantic had to be made at the best possible speed. But at thirty knots, her radius was fifteen hundred miles. This improved substantially if she were to travel at twenty- to twenty-five knots, which would give her between 3480 and 2440 miles. Yet the figures related to optimum conditions, not taking into account evasive maneuvers or unforeseen situations. It was therefore decided that in order to carry the contingency fuel the ammunition holds would have to be emptied. As a result *Jade* was carrying a meager three rounds per gun in each of the five turrets. Only her antiaircraft systems were fully loaded. A fighting vessel, she had been ignominiously stripped of that which gave her her marque.

Cabot tapped Simmons on the shoulder and drew him toward an empty corner of the wheelhouse.

"I'm sorry, but there was no word on improvement in Christine's condition," he said. "She's still unconscious . . ."

Simmons shook his head as though dispelling the words. He had scrupulously avoided speaking to Cabot when the American had boarded his vessel, busying himself with the last-minute details before cast-off. Even in the wheelhouse he had addressed only Runnymeade, oblivious to the presence of the other man.

Simmons's eyes glittered with tears.

"She'll come out of it," he whispered. "I know she will!"

Before Cabot could answer, Simmons turned on his heel and left the wheelhouse.

"Can't really blame him, can you?" Runnymeade said, stepping over softly.

"No, not in the least," Cabot murmured.

Runnymeade glanced at his watch.

"We won't pass Land's End for nearly eight hours yet. I suggest you take advantage of the easy seas and get yourself some rest. There mightn't be the opportunity later on."

Runnymeade turned his back on him and walked toward the wheel, stopping to check the instrument consoles along the way. Cabot buttoned up his heavy woolen vest and stepped out into the cold sea spray. The thought of sleep was too inviting, too necessary, to pass up.

Twenty feet below the forward decks, in a room that had no light and where the air was warm and motionless, Erik Guderian had just stretched himself out on the cold metal-plate floor. He was in the lower righthand quarter of what was usually the seamen's mess. Except that on this voyage the chairs and tables had been unbolted from the floor. There were no ration cases and the cupboards had been emptied of their condiments. In their place were crates upon crates of England's wealth, each one stamped with the insignia of the Old Lady of Threadneedle and manifest numbers which were meaningless to Guderian.

The numbers didn't matter. In fact, nothing did anymore. Guderian had reached the inner sanctum, and as tired as he was, that single thought kept his pulse racing.

He had left the sonar room well before the antisubmarine-equipment operators had. The escape ladder between sonar and the seamen's mess was the only entry in or out. Once the ship was under way, the hatch to the freshwater tank would be sealed, as would the door to the A shell room (now carrying fuel) on the opposite side. The operators, who had entered through the mess in the company of a Royal Marine, would remain at their posts for the next twelve hours until relief. Once they were inside, the Marine left the mess, locking the latch from the inside. Those few seconds it took the soldier to cross the mess represented the only time Guderian might have been discovered. But the Marine acted on his training: his duty was to stand guard outside. What was piled up in the mess was none of his concern. Therefore he never noticed that a half dozen of the crates had been moved to what would have appeared to an experienced seaman's eye an unacceptable, even dangerous, position.

Each row of crates was tied by thick oily rope to hooks welded into the plates. Guderian had managed to loosen the ropes around a stack piled up against the wall. With his back against the cold bulkhead, he used his legs as a press to push the crates out just enough to create enough space for him to slide into. Guderian knew this could be an unnecessary precaution. There was no reason why anyone should enter the mess once *Jade* had turned out to sea. But to cover that last percentile, to give himself at least a few seconds' time in which to react, he had carved out this niche.

Guderian smiled in the darkness, shifting his weight so that the small of his back rested on the end of his sweater, not on the deathly cold plates. Even if Cabot were to stumble upon him now, it was too late. He would be able to hold him for a few hours, six at the most. Somewhere in that time Cabot would drink water, whether in tea or coffee or straight from a glass. That was all the advantage Guderian would need . . .

Guderian ran his fingertips along the crate beside him. Beyond the half inch of wood lay the gold. Victory, he exulted, was literally within his grasp.

Captain Klaus Brennecke looked over the shoulder of his navigator, who had been plotting the intercept course.

"What is our position?" he asked quietly.

The navigator, a fresh-faced boy of twenty-two whose youth belied four years of hard experience, tapped the tip of the pencil compass against his teeth.

"One hundred miles southeast off Mizen Head on the Irish coast. At this speed we should reach our rendezvous point off Land's End in about seven and a half hours."

He looked up at his captain.

"*Can* we hold at twenty knots?"

Brennecke stepped over to the console and checked the fuel gauge. It read better than half full. Under normal circumstances he would have had no doubts that *Atlantis* could go into one more engagement and still have sufficient diesel to reach her refueling ship, which was now heading toward prearranged coordinates in the Atlantic. Yet these were anything but normal circumstances.

Less than thirty minutes earlier, at 6:35, Berlin had broken radio silence, something only an emergency dictated. Brennecke was to break off his roving attacks and proceed to certain coordinates dangerously close to the English coast. He was to do this at the best possible speed since it was imperative he reach the designated coordinates not only on a given day but at a certain hour. As any commander would have, Brennecke challenged the transmission. The sea around Ireland was fertile hunting ground for English warships which shepherded the convoys through the last part of their journey. Brennecke requested elaboration and to his amazement received a radio message originating within the Reichschancellery itself. The signature at the end was that of Adolf Hitler. The Führer demanded that Brennecke follow his orders without question. His target was the British cruiser *Jade*, which would be making out to open sea but which would become incapacitated at certain coordinates off Land's End. *Atlantis*'s task was to intercept *Jade* and pirate her cargo. There was a man on board who would somehow cripple the cruiser; show them exactly what was to be taken. This agent, code-named Thor, was to be regarded as the Führer's personal representative. His orders were final. After the cargo was safely on board, *Atlantis* was to break for Germany with all possible speed. Any, repeat *any* sacrifice was to be made in order to get this cargo to Bremen. *Atlantis* was to stop for nothing, keep away from all engagement with the enemy. U-boats had been already dispatched to escort her home.

What in the name of God is on board that vessel? Brennecke asked himself for the hundredth time. How could the Führer possibly believe that a single man might sabotage the pride of the British Fleet? And the ultimate question: if this Thor failed, how was *Atlantis* to be any match for a Dido class cruiser?

Yet Brennecke knew he would have to devise a way. Not only was he the captain of *Atlantis*, he was also, by designation of Hitler himself, the guiding force behind the raider program. This, coupled with his miraculous record, had made both him and his vessel legendary.

Built in 1937, *Atlantis*, then known as the freighter *Goldenfels*, had hardly any nautical wear and tear on her before Brennecke's shipwrights began gutting her. Fuel capacity was increased from 1368 to 3000. Water tanks swelled to 1200 tons, while coal bunkers which powered the condensers came in at 1000 tons. The area between decks was razed and space made to house prisoners, sand ballast, mines, crew's quarters and a small barnyard. (Pigs and chickens held up remarkably well at sea; rabbits did not.)

After the ventilation was in place, Brennecke started on the armament. Although only 7862 tons, 61 feet wide and 488 feet in length, *Atlantis* literally bristled with hidden weaponry. She carried six 5.9-inch guns, one 755mm cannon, one twin 37mm and four 20mm. There were four 21-inch torpedo tubes, 92 mines and one Heinkel 114 reconnaissance aircraft. The decks had been stiffened to hold the extra weight. Hatches with specially raised coamings held 30 percent of the armament, while the rest was hidden inside folding deckhouses, false bulwarks or belowdecks. To ensure that the weapons would be instantly available for use, the heavy steel flaps, precisely balanced, were operated by independent hydraulic levers.

By January 1940 *Atlantis* alone was responsible for over 100,000 tons of Allied shipping sunk. Flying half a dozen different flags, she had enough false panels and mountings to turn herself into four different merchantmen. As much as her armament, disguise and the ability to confuse her victims were her most powerful weapons. She preyed on merchantmen of every nationality, her attacks concentrated in the sea-lanes these vessels had to sail without naval escort. On those rare occasions when Brennecke encountered a destroyer or frigate he managed to overwhelm the opposition by his advantage of surprise.

Brennecke removed the scarred pipestem from his mouth and stepped out onto the bridge. The weather was holding, seas rolling slightly, his vessel making excellent time. The captain of *Atlantis* looked up at the slowly catapulting head clouds and stared across the waters.

Where was Jade *now*? *Did she know she was sailing into a trap*? *And what was she carrying*?

Brennecke shook his head and crossed himself, his lips moving soundlessly in the prayer all seamen utter when they feel death riding on the waves.

33

One of the reasons the British Security Service had opted for the Double-cross System as a means of neutralizing German spies was its pointed lack of success in pinpointing unauthorized radio transmissions. The Service's Transmission Intercept Unit was, in 1940, still in its infancy, the technology largely experimental and oftentimes unreliable. Nevertheless the Unit persevered, adding to its equipment and experience daily. Such persistence was rewarded when, at half past six on the morning of June 16, an operator in the East London station came upon and managed to hold an active channel coming from somewhere in the city's west-central area.

Mobile units were dispatched at once in an effort to triangulate the exact location. By seven-twenty the search was narrowed to an area bounded by Green Park, Piccadilly, Haymarket and The Mall. But the effort was impeded by the

inordinate amount of traffic that was pouring through this previously restricted area. Thousands of shopkeepers, busi-
nessmen, deliverymen and clerks choked the streets in an effort
to get to work after a twenty-four-hour absence. The difficulties were compounded not only by the slow-moving traffic
but also by the breakdown of one of the three operating units.
As a result the first quiet gentlemen from MI5, led by Robert
Ogilvy, did not arrive at Bentley's until well after nine o'clock.

Ogilvy, still aching from the injuries of the car accident and
stung by Mackenzie McConnell's reprimand over his carelessness, brushed by the steward who answered the door, ordering his men to fan out through the building. He silenced the
servant's outrage by producing his revolver and told the man that
if he uttered so much as a squeak he would come to appreciate
the term justifiable homicide. Leaving two men to take care of
the staff, Ogilvy and a team of three headed for the top floor.
Assured by the operators in the mobile unit that the signal was
still alive, they knew that the antenna would be the giveaway.

The roof yielded nothing. Back inside, the team began a
systematic search of the rooms used by the staff. When they
came to the chief steward's door and found it locked, Ogilvy
stepped back and calmly shot away the lock. The time was ten-
fifteen. Alfred Morell had been dead for over two hours. The
transmitter was scalding to the touch. Ogilvy swore softly and
ran downstairs. He was the first person to notice the sticky
substance on the staircase handrail which later proved to be
blood. Yelling for his men to seal off the building and call up
reinforcements, Ogilvy put a call through to Queen Anne's
Gate. Mackenzie McConnell answered on the first ring.

She had arrived back in London not sixty minutes earlier. En
route, traveling in the same train compartment as the Prime
Minister and Allen Dulles, Mackenzie had tried to keep up
with the conversation. But she found her thoughts straying
back to Cabot and the ship, which by now had reached the
open waters. The primary objective of Prometheus had been
accomplished: the bullion and negotiable securities were safely
under way to America. So even though she knew the hunt for
Erik Guderian had to continue unabated, Mackenzie could
scarcely summon up the energy to focus her attention on what
was waiting to be done in London. The clickety-clack of
wheels upon rails, the swaying of the carriage and drone of

conversation between Churchill and Dulles all conspired against her. Exhausted from over forty hours without sleep, she closed her eyes for an instant and was gone. The next thing she remembered was Dulles gently shaking her shoulder, telling her they were pulling into Waterloo Station.

Mackenzie declined Churchill's invitation to drive her to Queen Anne's Gate and instead took a taxi home. Within the hour she appeared in her office, refreshed by a hot shower and change of clothing, and began to work her way through the field reports concerning the search for Erik Guderian. She had read only two when the phone rang and she was on the fly once again.

"How long has the radio been live?" Mackenzie asked Ogilvy.

They were standing in Morell's room, watching as the coroner completed his initial examination of the body.

"The first signals were picked up four hours ago."

Mackenzie closed her eyes and shook her head. Four hours . . . The entire text of a day's Parliamentary proceedings could have been sent in that time.

"But he's been dead for over two," Ogilvy volunteered.

"What killed him?" Mackenzie asked harshly.

The coroner, a young man who worked exclusively for MI5, stood up.

"Something tore his chest open," he said, lighting a cigarette. "A jagged metal instrument. There is also evidence of contusions, as though he were hit by a moving vehicle."

"That would make sense given the amount of blood we've found on the back staircase and the delivery entrance," Ogilvy murmured. "The rain's washed away whatever evidence we might have found in the lane."

"Something cut him open like that and he still managed to crawl up here and send off a signal," Mackenzie said in disbelief.

"He must have been a very determined man," the coroner said quietly. "He had to have known he was dying as soon as he was hit. That he crawled all the way up here, bleeding like that, and still had the presence of mind to send out a signal . . ."

"God knows whatever hit him should have broken his treasonous neck!" Mackenzie whispered savagely.

She remembered the drone of the Dornier bombers, the inferno that had engulfed *Victorious* and the explosions that had rocked the Thames. Cabot had been on the *Victorious*, along with dozens of other men . . . two of whom had died. And the man lying at her feet was responsible for the carnage.

"Get him the hell out of here," Mackenzie said tonelessly.

She turned to Ogilvy. "Get a team to take the walls off this room. I mean that literally. I want to know what else the bastard was hiding from us. Has the manager arrived yet?"

"The chairman of the board is on his way in," Ogilvy replied.

As she walked down the back staircase and through the kitchens, Mackenzie asked herself what message had been so important to Alfred Morell that he had fought back death in order to send it to Berlin. Success of the raid, that was the obvious answer. That Guderian was still loose, running toward the rendezvous point where he would be picked up? That too, possibly. But could there be something else, something that had to do with Prometheus?

There is nothing else! she told herself fiercely. Guderian got his message to Berlin, Berlin sent in the Dorniers. Jonathan's ruse worked. I saw the gold being loaded in the vaults. I was at Southampton when *Jade* took on her cargo and set sail. It's finished! Guderian failed . . .

But there was something worrying her mind, a slender thread that drifted on the winds of doubt, something she could sense but not reach out and grasp.

"This is the club steward who let us in," Ogilvy was saying.

Mackenzie stepped before the cowed little man and said, "I need the membership and employee records—now!"

The steward winced as though she'd physically struck him.

"Th—they're in the chairman's office," he stammered. "B—but it's locked."

"Do you have the key for it?"

"No, I—"

"Shoot the lock," Mackenzie said, turning to Ogilvy. "Get some people from Queen Anne's Gate to pick up all the staff and bring them down there."

"What about the members?"

"I'll go through the list quickly," Mackenzie told him. "If I see anything out of place I'll let you know. It's the staff I want questioned first. They're the ones who would be most familiar with Morell's habits and movements."

Two hours later Mackenzie realized how wrong she was.

Neither the other stewards, the kitchen staff, nor the club chairman, when he arrived, could offer any tangible information on the dead man. The picture that emerged from their remembrances did not add anything to the detailed personnel file Mackenzie and Ogilvy had gone through twice. Alfred Morell had had no friends outside the club; his family, which he never spoke of, had died a long time ago. Among his personal effects Mackenzie found mementos of trips to France, Italy and Malta, all brought back during the two weeks' vacation Morell took each year, but his passport showed no entry or exit stamps for Germany.

"The man was too good to be true," was Mackenzie's bitter summation. "He made this place a virtual fiefdom and ran it so that no one could ever question anything he did."

"What do we do now?" Ogilvy asked her. "Start in on the members?"

"I'm beginning to wonder if that's necessary," Mackenzie said. "There's no question Morell was working for the Germans. They turned him after his wife and daughter passed away and trained him as a deep sleeper. Given his position, he was so valuable to Berlin—in terms of the gossip he could pick up from this place—that it didn't dare integrate him into its other networks. Which is why we never picked up his scent. God knows how much he's passed to a human control. But the radio wasn't to be used until something very big came along, worth the risk of exposure."

"Like Guderian," Ogilvy suggested.

"Like him."

"So you don't think there's a link between Morell and any one of the members?"

"No, but we still have to run that gauntlet," Mackenzie said. "Churchill will demand it. The old adage about leaving no stone unturned—"

"Excuse me, Miss McConnell, there's a call for you from Harmsworth Hospital," an agent interrupted. "The officer in charge of looking after Miss Harloch. He says it's urgent."

"Christine!" Mackenzie murmured.

The conversation was brief and one-sided, with Mackenzie uttering no more than half a dozen words. She looked at Ogilvy and ran one hand through her hair.

"Christine Harloch has regained consciousness," she said, eyes flashing. "It's a beginning."

The Security Service babysitter at Harmsworth Hospital was Charlie Watson, who had been specially chosen by Mackenzie. Watson was an older man, with the lumbering carriage of a circus bear and the soul of an Irish poet. He was always the "soft" man of an interrogation team, the one who sided with the accused, played every role from father confessor to sad but forgiving parent. He was the kind of man whom Mackenzie wanted by Christine Harloch's bedside if the girl regained consciousness.

"Hello, luv."

Watson intercepted her outside the hospital room door.

"What's happened, Charlie?" Mackenzie asked point-blank.

"The lass came to about forty minutes ago," Watson said. "I called for the doctor, who examined her. From what he says it's not unusual for the effects of a concussion to fade away like a bad dream. The lass was disorientated, wanted to know what happened to her—"

Did she say anything?

"She started to cry," Watson said softly. "She called for someone named Henry. Bones wanted to give her a shot, but I persuaded him not to. I thought you would want to speak with her right away."

"That I do!"

Watson held on to Mackenzie's arm as she was about to open the door.

"Go gently with her, luv," he advised. "She's very skittish."

The instant Mackenzie saw her she realized Christine Harloch had lost more than weight. Her face was pinched an unnatural white, the cheekbones gaunt. The eyes, which must have been beautiful once, were empty, soulless reflections of pain.

"Hello, Christine," Mackenzie said softly and spoke her name.

"Miss McConnell . . ."

"I'm very glad you're all right," Mackenzie said, pulling up a chair. "The doctor says that all you need is rest."

Christine Harloch cast her eyes down, her fingers twisting a lace handkerchief, tearing it at the edges.

"Christine, do you know who I work for?"

"The police," the girl said, barely mouthing the words.

"For the Security Service. And I have to ask you some

questions. It's very, *very* important that you answer as best you can. Will you try?"

Christine Harloch nodded mutely. Mackenzie hesitated but knew she had no choice. The girl was very weak and the time she had, limited. She had only cruelty to use on her.

"Christine, why did Henry do this to you? What was it you saw?"

"Henry wouldn't hurt me!" the girl moaned. "He loved me. Why would he hurt me?"

"Henry is not his real name," Mackenzie told her. "The man you fell in love with is Erik Guderian. He's a German spy."

Christine's eyes widened, whether in fear or surprise, Mackenzie wasn't certain. Her heart went out to the young girl because, Mackenzie knew, she had no idea of the duplicity Guderian had woven around her.

"I can't believe that," Christine said weakly. "Henry wasn't like that. You didn't know him—"

"We know him very well," Mackenzie said grimly. In quick broad strokes she outlined a bloodied sketch of Guderian's actions in England.

"He fooled us all, Christine," she finished. "You, me, the Army, anyone he came in contact with. He lied to everyone . . . and we didn't just believe him, we rewarded him."

"But he never wanted anything from me," Christine protested. "He never asked me for anything!"

"He didn't have to," Mackenzie said. "You were so generous to him that it wasn't necessary for him to ask for what he needed. But he used you, Christine, as surely as he did others. You were invaluable to him precisely because of who you were. He hid behind your name, traded on the influence that surrounds it. He took advantage of the shelter you gave him, the transportation he could use . . . the trust you offered him."

Mackenzie paused. "If he loved you so much why did he hit you?"

That question shattered the fragile illusion Christine Harloch had clung to. It destroyed every rationalization she had built around the horror she had suffered. Its light penetrated the darkness of her ignorance as to why Henry had hurt her like that. The shame followed quickly, sweeping over her relentlessly, forcing her to confront her gullibility, the stupidity she had allowed to blind her.

Mackenzie let the tears wash out as much of the sickness as

they could. All the while she held on to the girl, stroking her hair, whispering softly to her. When the worst had passed she started again.

"We have to know a great many things about Guderian," she said. "You're the only one who can tell us what he did during the time he stayed with you. You're the one he was closest to. You had a chance to listen to what he said. Perhaps he mentioned some names or places that really didn't mean anything to you then. Now these could be very important. We need your help, Christine, desperately."

"What are you going to do to him?" the girl whispered fearfully.

"He'll be put on trial for espionage," Mackenzie said. "It's possible that if we get to him soon enough, the courts will take into consideration the fact that he could have killed you but chose not to."

"Henry is a hero, you know," Christine murmured. "He's going to receive a medal . . ."

"That too will be taken into account," Mackenzie agreed. "We will let you talk to him if you like. Perhaps if he cooperates with us the Justices will see fit to offer leniency."

Mackenzie despised herself for what she was doing to the girl. There wasn't a chance in hell Guderian wouldn't hang in the courtyard within the Wormwood Scrubs prison. But until Christine had told her everything, Mackenzie knew this final deception had to be perfect.

"You haven't found him?" she asked in a small voice.

"No, not yet."

"Is he still in London?"

"We believe so, yes."

"I still want you to tell me when Henry's . . . when he's found."

"You have my word I will," Mackenzie said.

"I was drunk," Christine said. "I went to the Ship's Supper with Andrew only because he had asked me long ago. I didn't love him—not the way he thought—but I went because of a promise. All the time I was thinking of Henry, where he was and what he might be doing. I wanted so badly to be with him. That's why I was drinking . . ."

Christine gazed up at Mackenzie, a faint smile on her lips. But her voice was puzzled.

"I was thinking of him and suddenly there he was . . ."

"Where, Christine?"

"I was on the second-floor balcony, looking for the bathroom. I thought I was going to be sick. I opened a door but it was the Admiral's study. That's when I saw Henry. He was standing over a long table. There were papers on it, charts and drawings . . . He was looking at them."

"Christine, that door was locked!" Mackenzie said desperately.

"No, it wasn't," the girl replied solemnly. "Otherwise I could never had opened it, could I? And seen Henry . . ."

"No . . ." Mackenzie whispered.

Her mind churned furiously, replaying those few seconds after she and Runnymeade had left the study. A crash from the floor above . . . Runnymeade stepping onto the landing . . . . Hinkley bent over the door, key in hand, then straightening up and looking up . . . The exchange between the two men, something about an officer taken ill . . . Hinkley going upstairs.

He never locked the door! Mackenzie thought wildly. *Hinkley was in the process of turning the key, but the crash . . . And after he came back down he never stopped to check!*

"Miss McConnell, are you all right?" Christine asked faintly.

"Yes . . . of course," Mackenzie said, her throat dry, the words echoing as the blood pounded at her temples. "And you said Henry saw you?"

"He was very surprised, just as I was. I think I asked him what he wanted. Then he came *towards* me, his arm raised . . ."

Christine Harloch began to cry softly.

It can't be! Mackenzie thought furiously. The door to the study *had* been locked—Runnymeade had had to open it with his gold key. She had seen him do it . . .

Unless Guderian had been in the study all along! Which meant he had found a way into the house.

At that instant Mackenzie remembered the injured Marine found on the other side of the pond . . .

Yes, Guderian had gotten in and heard everything. But even after everyone had gone downstairs he had remained, to look at the charts . . .

The horrific implication swept over Mackenzie. Guderian

had invaded Runnymeade's house not because he wanted the names of the ships, as she and Cabot believed. And thought they were proved right when the bombers had singled out *Victorious*. The attack had convinced Cabot that Guderian had managed to send the *wrong* information to Berlin . . . and so the danger was over if both the agent and his control believed the gold destroyed.

But Guderian already knew that Jade *was the bullion carrier.* He had played Cabot's game, but then twisted the end. It wasn't the carrier's name he had needed, but the course *Jade* would follow . . .

And Jonathan was on board Jade.

"You don't remember anything after he hit you?" Mackenzie asked, her throat dry.

Christine shook her head. "Nothing."

It doesn't matter, Mackenzie thought savagely, because it had been Guderian who had locked the study door after himself, before carrying you into Runnymeade's bedroom. He couldn't bring himself to kill you, but he left you, hoping you would die. When we found you, the locked study door made us think you intercepted him *before* he had gotten into the study, not after . . . when he was making his run.

"I'll be back," Mackenzie said suddenly.

She flew into the corridor, colliding with Charlie Watson.

Mackenzie ran the length of the room, wrenched open the door and was halfway down the corridor before Watson caught up to her.

"No one gets in to see her," Mackenzie cried over her shoulder. "Absolutely no one! Call Queen Anne's Gate and get some support personnel!"

"But—"

"She knows something that doesn't exist! I don't want her talking to anyone!"

Before Watson could reply she was hurtling down the staircase, making for the front doors. The Jaguar pulled away from the curb with a squeal of tires and Mackenzie flung the car into traffic. She drove like one possessed, running lights and cutting off traffic, driven by the one thought that was burning in her mind.

Jonathan is on board Jade!

She didn't slow until she had reached the entrance to Downing Street. Even then she paused only long enough for the Military Police to glimpse her identification.

Detective Inspector Thompson, Churchill's bodyguard, drew back when he opened the door on this obviously mad woman.

"Where is he?" Mackenzie demanded.

"Taking lunch with some Cabinet—"

"Get him out here!" Mackenzie whispered, leaning against the wall, fighting back tears. "For the love of God, get him out!"

At that instant Churchill appeared.

"Mackenzie—"

"Prime Minister, it is imperative I speak with you at once—privately."

Without a word Churchill took her aside.

"What's happened?" he asked softly.

Mackenzie stared at him, not knowing how to say what could no longer be left unsaid.

"Guderian knows about *Jade* . . . about the last-minute transfer, sailing time, course, everything."

"That's not possible!"

"Please, Prime Minister. Hear me out."

As quickly as she could Mackenzie recounted Christine's story as well as what had transpired at Bentley's on St. James's Street.

"Now we know what it is Alfred Morell sent on to Berlin. That's why he crawled up into his room even though by all rights he should have died in that street! *He had Guderian's last message for Berlin—telling them about* Jade's *course!*"

The Prime Minister closed his eyes.

"You're certain of all this?" he whispered.

"We have no choice but to assume that Berlin has made plans to intercept *Jade*," Mackenzie said vehemently. "Prime Minister, we must warn her!"

Churchill walked over to his desk and picked up the receiver.

"Get me the Admiralty communications room—at once!"

The connection was made in a few seconds.

"This is Churchill. To whom am I speaking . . . Very well, Commander. I want you to send the following message to *Jade* immediately . . . I beg your pardon . . . *When did this happen*? Twenty minutes ago! And no one thought to inform me! Commander, you may expect me there posthaste!"

The Prime Minister slammed the receiver down on its hook and leaned on it heavily.

"They can't raise the ship . . ." He looked around at Mackenzie. "They lost contact with *Jade*. She never made her scheduled call!"

34

The first cases of sickness were isolated: three from the kitchen itself, twice that number from the boiler rooms and a few among the Marines. When presented with the symptoms, the ship's doctor was not unduly alarmed. A number of frail sealegs were to be expected. Moreover, he had no idea when or what the afflicted had last eaten. The rule of thumb was that an unwelcome parasite within the digestive tract would be expelled within twelve hours. Until then the men would live on bromides . . . which they took with water.

All this happened before the first mess call at noon, where each man consumed at least one glass of fresh water along with tea, soup and meat sauces. Forty minutes later, the second sitting began. Seamen and officers who could not leave their posts had trays brought to them . . .

The contaminant Erik Guderian had poured into the tanker at the Southampton depot was a derivative of curare. The drug was lethal even when mixed with as little as thirty parts per million of water. A lesser amount was nonetheless devastating. When ingested with water the compound passed swiftly through the digestive tract and entered the bloodstream. From there it preyed on the nervous system. The first symptoms consisted of cold shivers and uncontrolled trembling followed by excruciating stomach pains and vomiting. Even after the stomach had been voided, the cramps persisted, causing shortness of breath and finally paralysis. If only an infinitesimal amount of poison had been digested, and the victim was generally healthy, the symptoms would pass in seven or eight hours. Those with respiratory ailments or heart conditions were not expected to live.

By half past one, no more than sixty minutes after they had eaten, men on the first lunch shift began clutching their bellies. They dropped to their knees wherever they stood, doubling up in agony and vomiting, then pitching forward and curling up in the fetal position as paralysis seized them. It was a credit to those who ate second that they managed to haul as many of the afflicted as they did to the infirmary and later to the bunks before they themselves succumbed. In the torpedo workshop, Number 1 low-power room, compressor room, stokers' mess, Number 1 transmitter room, men were crying and screaming in agony. Within two hours of the first mess sitting, *Jade* had become a rogue ship, plowing through the waves without anyone to guide her.

Erik Guderian was standing by the hatch of the seamen's mess. Beyond the bulkhead he heard the groans followed by sickening thuds of bodies hitting cold iron. He checked his watch and at 2:45 spun the wheel to open the hatch. Cautiously he pulled it back. The quaking features of the Royal Marine stared up at him as the guard's head fell back across the steel frame. For an instant Guderian was frozen by the sight of the stricken man, covered in his own filth, his mouth opening and closing like that of a landed fish. The only sound the guard could make was a soft gurgling at the back of his throat.

Guderian knelt down and picked up the submachine gun. He was turning away when he saw the handcuffs and pocketed these as well. He stepped over the guard's legs and moved swiftly down the corridor. Although Alfred Morell had assured him that even one cup of the contaminated water would be enough to render a man impotent, Guderian could not presume that everyone on board had drunk. He wheeled back the hatch into the second mess and stepped through.

The odor was foul enough to make him gag. Across the room, curled up at the foot of the tables and benches, were over fifty seamen. Some clawed at his feet as he ran over and by them but Guderian kicked off their feeble grips. In swift succession he made it through the other two mess halls and began his descent into Number 1 transmitter room. If anyone were still functioning on board *Jade* he would try to get to the radios. The first thought would be to warn London.

But no one in this room would be doing that. Both operators had already lost consciousness. The food on the trays on the makeshift table was almost all consumed. Guderian swung the gun across the instruments and was about to squeeze the trigger when he heard something clatter to the floor.

The latch between transmitter rooms 1 and 2 was open a fraction. Guderian pushed at it with his foot, gun held level. He saw himself looking into the pain-twisted face of Andrew Simmons.

"You!"

The single word was no more than a croak. Simmons, who had half raised himself off the floor, was clutching at the edge of the wide metal ledge that the transmitting units were bolted to. A few inches from his fingers, beside the microphone, was a Navy-issue revolver.

"Get away from there," Guderian said softly.

"Killer," Simmons gasped.

With a final heave he managed to slide onto the chair, fingers stretching out toward the gun.

"Move away, Simmons," Guderian repeated. "I don't have to kill you."

Simmons grinned like a madman. "You didn't have to kill her either, did you?" he whispered in a tortured voice. "We belong together—"

Guderian had misjudged the depth of Simmons's rage. With the last of his strength Simmons swept his hand toward the gun. Guderian reacted instantly, the submachine gun barked and four bullets tore open Simmons's neck. Without pausing, Guderian pointed the barrel at the instrument panel and fired off the rest of the clip.

Stepping over the bodies in transmitter room 1, Guderian slammed in a fresh load and in an almost lazy, sweeping gesture shredded the primary radios. As he made certain that the transmitters were beyond salvage, he suddenly stopped and looked down at his feet. There were no vibrations coming off the floor plates. The engines must have stopped. *Jade* was dead in the water.

Jonathan Cabot had slept far longer than he had intended.

Given a berth in a small storage room next to the Admiral's quarters, he had asked to be awakened in four hours. Even though no one came for him he still might have awakened had his mental alarm gone off. But the roll of the ship and the bone-numbing fatigue conspired against him . . .

Cabot awoke a few minutes before three o'clock. The sight that greeted him when he stepped out into the passageway might have been from a charnel house: along the length of the corridor were bodies, grotesquely displayed, contorted in unimaginable positions. Cabot drew back inside the cabin and quietly reached for the Hanyatti.

It took him fifteen minutes to traverse the ship and reach the wheelhouse. He gave up stopping to examine the afflicted men after he had examined three. The symptoms appeared to be the same, yet he had no idea what could have caused them. Only one thought pounded through his mind: *Erik Guderian had managed to find out about* Jade.

Which also meant that the German could be on board. How Guderian had gotten on was irrelevant. What he was after was clear enough. The remaining question was how did he intend to get at it. The ship's complement was helpless. The engines had been stopped. Cabot shuddered as he slipped onto the bridge and saw the prostrate form of Admiral Runnymeade. The older man was not breathing. Beside him the young wheelman and navigator were curled up, unconscious. Cabot saw streaks of blood along the metal sheeting where desperation had driven men to mutilate their fingers in an attempt to stand up.

Cabot stepped over to the reinforced plate glass that looked out over the bow turrets. Not five hundred yards away he saw a freighter streaming at *Jade*. He snatched up a pair of binoculars and focused them on the flag hoisted high above the bridge. She was Dutch! An Allied merchantman! There was still a chance . . .

"I'm afraid you're mistaken," a voice behind him called out softly. "She is my ship, not yours. And please, slide your weapon onto the Captain's chair. There's no point in dying, not now."

Cabot did as he was bade, then slowly turned around. He knew exactly who it was he would face and so there was no surprise in his expression.

"Guderian . . ."

"Step away from your weapon," Guderian said.

Cabot moved to the right, his eyes never leaving Guderian's. The man who was ultimately responsible for Orit's death and whom he had sworn to kill. A murderer whom a dying man had begged Cabot to save. The circle had come round.

"What's killing them?" he demanded harshly.

"They won't die," Guderian answered. "It's a poison—"

"That's another mistake you made," Cabot cut him off. "Runnymeade is dead!"

The gambit didn't work. Guderian did not even glance at the body.

"Sometimes it happens that way," he said softly. "But most of the men will be all right in a few hours."

"It was the water supply," Cabot said rhetorically. "No gas would have worked as effectively."

"Please turn around and place your hands on the small of your back," Guderian ordered.

"But your biggest mistake was to stop the ship here," Cabot continued.

He had to keep Guderian talking, *force* him to reply. When a man talked he couldn't focus his entire attention on what he was doing. One infinitesimal error was all Cabot needed.

He felt the gun barrel press against his spine, then the icy hook of the first lock of the handcuffs. The barrel dug deeper into him as the second bracelet was locked into place.

"It can't work," Cabot said. "You won't have time for a transfer. If we miss one radio contact—"

"What will happen, Mr. Cabot?" Guderian asked him and immediately answered. "Nothing at all. We are eight hours out of Southampton. The nearest British Navy vessels are at least that far away. I know that *Jade*'s course was set to run in *exactly the opposite direction* of other naval activity. A spoor, if you will. RAF aircraft may be dispatched, but even if they do find us the raider is more than capable of repulsing them. So you see there is really nothing out there to stop us."

Cabot looked out at the approaching merchantman and cursed silently, the muscles in his forearms bulging as anger pumped through his blood. He had anticipated a leak, the destruction of *Victorious*, a possible submarine attack, but not piracy. Never raiders!

"You have to stop, Erik," Cabot said quietly.

The use of his Christian name made Guderian hesitate.

"How did you uncover my identity?" Guderian asked him.

There was a hint of fear in his voice because he realized that when Cabot had first seen him he had called him by his true name.

"I found Schiffer," Cabot said. "But I could never have found the man behind the mask. Not unless I had help . . . from the one person who knew who he really was."

"You're not making sense," Guderian said.

"But I am," Cabot answered. "I've been hunting you long before Prometheus was conceived. I want to ask you: do you remember a man named Aaron Steinfeldt?"

"Steinfeldt!" Guderian said in a daze. "What has he to do with this?"

"He was in charge of developing new communications systems for you at Regensburg. You had him brought there because you demanded the best. And he was it. Steinfeldt died in Regensburg because he was worked to death."

"That was not my fault!" Guderian shouted. "It's true I needed Steinfeldt for a certain project. But it was Berlin which made the actual arrangements. The SS running the compound were fools, totally irresponsible. When I heard what had happened I had their heads for it! Steinfeldt was too valuable—"

"He died nonetheless," Cabot said tonelessly. "But before that his daughter was also arrested. Himmler said she died while committing defenestration. I was coming back for Orit that same day. We were going to get her father out and when we did she was going to become my wife."

Guderian's entire body sagged as though he had been struck from behind by a terrible force.

"That is why you have hunted me," he said sadly. "Because without knowing it I robbed you of your future . . . Yours and hers together."

"I wanted to kill you," Cabot said as though he hadn't heard Guderian's words. "I hunted you but you had disappeared. No one knew anything about you, nothing at all. It wasn't until I saw the photograph of the way you look now that I understood."

"There are no photographs," Guderian whispered.

"Yes, there is one. A man showed it to me in Geneva. He had been Dulles's 'window on Berlin' as he called himself, a loyal German, an intimate of Hitler, yet one who understood that special lines of communications had to be maintained between special men on both sides. He contacted Dulles and told him he had extraordinary information. I was dispatched to see what it was."

Cabot paused. "It was you, Erik. This man showed me your photograph after surgery. He was a central figure behind the attempt against Prometheus, yet he must have learned something that convinced him of exactly the opposite: Prometheus had to succeed! For everyone's sake."

"You're insane," Guderian said hoarsely.

"No, it was he who was trying to save sanity. He knew he was betraying you, yet in that same betrayal he was trying to help you. Before he died he begged *me* to save *you*, to bring you home alive . . ."

"Gerd is dead?"

"He was killed saving my life," Cabot said. "We were in his suite in Geneva when two men, undoubtedly commandos judging by their armament, broke in. There was no reason for them to have come after Jaunich. Someone had sent them for me. Someone who knew I was going to be in Geneva that day—"

"No!" Guderian screamed. "No, no, no!"

The message he had sent to Berlin after meeting with Ogilvy burned in his mind. Karl Horst had received the order, acted upon it, met up with Cabot in Geneva. *Except that neither Karl nor his partner could have ever guessed whom Cabot was going to meet*! They chose precisely the wrong moment, when the two men were together . . .

Guderian uttered a moan that tore at the very fabric of his heart.

His men had come upon Cabot and Jaunich. But what happened next could not have come to pass as Cabot wanted him to believe.

"You have been lying to me," Guderian said dully. "You promised yourself vengeance and now you are extracting what you can."

"Erik—"

"No, listen! The very fact that you are alive means that my men are dead! You bested them in Geneva, something I would not have thought possible. But this fantasy about Jaunich's being dead is your last ruse. Yes, I ordered your execution in Geneva! Even after taking Pearce you weren't satisfied. You persisted in digging beneath him . . . and so you were coming too close to me.

"But you didn't speak with Jaunich in Geneva or anywhere

else. You couldn't have because I sent two other messages to Berlin, the first to send in the bombers to destroy *Victorious* so that you would think I took your tainted bait, the second to bring the raider to its intercept point. Both orders have been obeyed! And only one man could have seen to that!"

"You're wrong, Erik!" Cabot shouted. "And you still haven't answered the biggest question of all: *how did I know who you really were*? For Christ's sake, you still have a chance to learn the truth: send a text to Berlin via the raider! Demand that Jaunich answer! He must have a code prefix to guarantee authenticity of the reply. *I swear to you it won't be on the message*!"

For an instant Erik Guderian was tempted to yield to his doubt. But he remembered where he had lain in the ship, waiting for the poison to take effect . . . the crates of gold surrounding him. Cabot had come so close to convincing him, the honeyed words almost lulling him into belief. But beneath his feet lay the end of the war. That was all he needed to remember.

Without a word Guderian stepped over to Cabot and prodded him over to the Captain's chair, brushing Cabot's gun to the deck. With the muzzle of the gun pressed into Cabot's spine, Guderian undid one clasp of the cuffs and in the same motion snapped that through the frame of the chair.

"Guderian!" Cabot roared.

The German paused at the hatch.

"I'm sorry for your loss," he called back. "I wish . . ."

And then he was gone.

"Sir, a signal from the British ship!"

Captain Klaus Brennecke of the raider *Atlantis* followed the Ensign's thrust-out arm. On the deck of *Jade* he saw a lone figure, a signal lamp in hand, the white light flashing in Morse.

"Thor," Brennecke whispered. "Our man!"

"Sir, there's more!" the Ensign shouted and slowly read off the message:

VESSEL CREW NEUTRALIZED. PREPARE BOARDING PARTY. TWENTY MEN AND CRANE.

The Ensign turned to Brennecke. "Sir?"

But Brennecke had already gripped the megaphone.

"Prepare to swing overhead crane!" Brennecke's voice

boomed over the raider's decks. He turned around to his helmsman.

"Bring us in as close as you can," he said, gritting his teeth. "Thank Christ the sea is almost dead!"

Brennecke took the wheel himself, shouting at the engine room to give him more power. *Atlantis* was less than ten yards away from the floundering cruiser when the crane, its webbing holding a dozen men, began its swing across the water, arcing across the cruiser's bow turrets.

"Lower the net!" he shouted over the megaphone.

The webbing plunged onto the deck of *Jade*. Brennecke saw the man he knew only as Thor scramble to help the sailors out.

"Shoot the lines across!" Brennecke roared.

He watched as the heavy ropes were propelled across the ten yards of sea separating the two ships. Immediately his men on board the cruiser began tying up the two ships. Brennecke could not help but envy Thor: the man had the gods beside him. Such a maneuver would have been unthinkable in anything other than a calm sea.

Brennecke watched as the second complement of men was swung over and off-loaded. Thor was wasting no time. He already had the first detachment working on the deck before the forward turret. Brennecke's first thought was that Thor had blundered: a British cruiser had no hatches on the forward deck. But the skipper of *Atlantis* was not privy, as Guderian was, to the last-minute modifications effected on the cruiser.

It would have been possible to load the gold crates onto the ship by using fifty sailors to form a chain along which the cargo was passed piece by piece into the holds. But Runnymeade had suggested that since the bullion was to be stored in the seamen's mess in the forward part of the ship, a patch of deck be cut open, hinged, then drawn back to allow access for a crane. After the loading was completed, a watertight seal would be fitted around the trap. It was this plan which Guderian was now reversing.

As soon as the hatch was open sailors from *Atlantis* dropped into the hold. The crane operator on board the raider followed the Morse signals precisely and dropped his rigging into the opening. It took the Germans less than two minutes to secure the ropes beneath and around the first pallet, which was then lifted clear of the hold and swung over to *Atlantis*.

Brennecke had quit the bridge and joined his men on the

lower deck, wading into their midst to help with the off-loading. He labored like a man possessed, realizing what it was he was handling as soon as he saw the burned-in seals on the crates. He was also aware that at any moment his signals officer might cry out a warning, that another ship was on the horizon, or worse, aircraft.

"Get the other crane into the job!" he cried.

It took the men of *Atlantis* less than an hour to empty the cargo contained in the seamen's mess on board *Jade*. As the crane descended for the last time, Brennecke leaped across to help Thor out of the webbing.

"May I suggest you get us the hell away from here as fast as possible, *Herr Kapitän*," Guderian said, his face a sheen of sweat.

"Don't bother with the ropes!" Brennecke shouted. "Cut them. Give me maximum speed!"

"I need to send a message to Berlin," Guderian said.

"Follow me, my friend." Brennecke grinned. "I'm sure Berlin will be wanting to hear from you as well."

The radio room was adjacent to the wheelhouse. Guderian pushed aside the operator, twisted the dials to the correct frequency and began to transmit.

THOR TO ZEUS. THE FIRE HAS BEEN BROUGHT TO EARTH.

He repeated the message twice and pushed himself away from the set, stepping out onto the bridge.

"Call me the instant the reply comes in," he told the radio operator.

Guderian stared through the glass at the dwindling image of *Jade* and spotted the figure standing by the Captain's chair. He drew his hand up in an informal salute.

"Goodbye," he whispered. "And forgive me!"

"Is it true?" Brennecke asked, stepping beside Guderian. "We have English gold?"

"Yes, it's true, *Herr Kapitän*," Guderian said softly.

Brennecke shook his head in disbelief. "It makes all of us very rich men." He laughed. "If Berlin would only let us keep our booty!"

But Erik Guderian was not thinking of the gold any longer. He was staring down at his watch, counting off the seconds. Doubt like a wisp of smoke from a fire now quite dead curled up within him. Why was Zeus not acknowledging his transmission?

Jonathan Baylor Cabot watched the raider steam away, becoming smaller and smaller as it moved at top speed. His mind was numb, empty of thoughts and emotions. He had even forgotten about the pressure on his wrist because of the handcuffs. Guderian had robbed him, utterly and completely. He had sailed with Britain's gold and Cabot's vengeance toward a destiny he himself knew nothing of . . . because Gerd Jaunich had never told Cabot why the betrayal had been necessary. If Cabot had known that, then perhaps . . .

Now there remained only one thing for Cabot to do. It would be a small victory, meaningless in what had come before, but he hungered for it, out of revenge and to keep the enormity of his defeat at bay. Cabot was still thinking about it when the flash on the horizon blinded him and the force of the explosions ripped across the silent sea, creating a golden aura across the sky.

35

The first vessel to reach *Jade* was the British T-class submarine *Orion*. Diverted by Admiralty order from a patrol off the south coast of England, it reached the stricken cruiser at 6:04 P.M. on June 16. Twenty minutes later, after an armed boarding party had at last made its way onto the bridge, Jonathan Cabot had had the handcuffs sawn off from his swollen right wrist. By that time the lights on the onrushing destroyer, *Proteus*, could be seen on the horizon.

At that point Cabot did not question the inexplicable arrival of *Orion*. Only later would he realize the role it had ultimately played in a drama in which he had unwittingly participated.

At 7:30 the PBY Catalina flying boat Dulles had dispatched

from Southampton arrived. A launch took Cabot from *Jade* to the waiting aircraft, which took off immediately. Ninety minutes later the Catalina was easing into its berth on the east side of the Southampton docks. Cabot thrust open the door, seeing Dulles walking down the jetty. He turned back to the pilot and said:

"Remember what I told you."

The pilot, a young Britisher who had been privy to the transmissions Cabot had had with London on the way in, nodded grimly.

"Just say the word, guv," he said softly. "I'll fly you through hell if I must!"

"Thank God you're still in one piece!" Dulles said, gripping Cabot by the shoulders. "What in hell was going on out there?"

It took Cabot less than two minutes to explain to Dulles exactly how Guderian had penetrated, incapacitated and finally pirated the ship.

"What I don't understand is the explosion," he finished. "You should get vessels out there immediately, see if you can pick up any survivors."

"Guderian?" Dulles asked.

Cabot looked over his shoulder at the woman standing alone on the docks. He could feel Christine Harloch's eyes upon him.

"Yes, for her as well."

He turned to Dulles and asked urgently:

"Where is Mackenzie?"

"I called her at Queen Anne's Gate before leaving London. She wasn't there nor did anyone seem to know where she was."

A slow pounding started up at Cabot's temple.

"Was Ogilvy there?"

"No, both of them were gone . . . Jonathan, what's wrong?"

Cabot wheeled around and began running back to the plane.

"Jonathan, where are you going?" Dulles shouted after him. "For Christ's sake there's a lot you don't know . . ."

Cabot didn't hear the rest. He jumped in beside the pilot and slammed the hatch.

"London's been calling," the pilot said as he opened up the engines.

Cabot nodded mutely. For an instant he felt totally paralyzed by the sensation of loss, as though what he was about to do was utterly futile. Then the image of Mackenzie swam before his eyes.

"She's still alive!" he whispered savagely. "God help me but she's still alive!"

He grabbed the microphone and twisted the radio knobs to find the correct wavelength. A moment later, over the drone of the Catalina's engines, he was shouting instructions to Kim Philby in London.

Three hours before the Catalina lifted off from Southampton, Mackenzie McConnell, sequestered in the Admiralty Crisis Room, learned that not only had *Jade* been located but that Jonathan Cabot was unharmed. She immediately petitioned for and received the Prime Minister's permission to go to Southampton to meet him. Mackenzie and Robert Ogilvy, who had been with her throughout the nerve-racking wait, left the Admiralty together. She had agreed to drop him off at Queen Anne's Gate before meeting Allen Dulles. They were inside her Jaguar, clearing the Admiralty gates, when he took her.

"Make a left at the next intersection, Mackenzie."

For an instant she thought he was joking, but the coldness in his voice made her look around. And she saw the gun, only inches from her ribs.

"Robert . . ."

The rest of her words were choked off by the realization rising in her gorge. All the tiny discrepancies, the minute factors that had been out of place, the inconsistencies she had not been able to explain, all coalesced into a single coherent mosaic: betrayal.

"*Left*, Mackenzie, please!"

The barrel was hard against her flesh. Mackenzie signaled and turned.

"Give it up, Robert," she said quietly. "Killing me won't do you any good—"

"I have no intention of killing you," Ogilvy said in the same dead tone. "You're no use to me that way. Take the next right and head into Mayfair, Bloom Street."

"Why, Robert?" she asked softly, eyes directly ahead. But her peripheral vision kept flitting to him, searching for that one opportunity.

"The most easily understood motive of all," Ogilvy said. "Revenge. The boy from a redbrick university playing servant to his betters from Oxbridge . . . being used by them, sent out on missions for whose success they later claimed credit . . ."

His voice broke. "Betrayed by the woman he loved. Revenge, Mackenzie—it's really so easy to understand if you just stop and think about it."

She cast a glance at him, saw how red the terrible welts on his face had become, pulsating as though they had suddenly taken on a life of their own.

"How long, Robert?" Mackenzie asked.

"Years, my love."

"When we were together?"

"No. We were the only thing keeping me back. I could have started then, but you see, I still believed . . ."

"And when you stopped believing you became a traitor," she said savagely.

The barrel dug into her ribs and she uttered a weak cry. Involuntarily her foot punched down on the accelerator and the supercharged car shot through a red light.

"Gently, my love, very gently," Ogilvy said through his teeth. "We wouldn't want an accident now, would we?"

"You don't know what you've done," Mackenzie whispered through her pain. "What you've *failed* to do!"

"You mean about *Jade* and the gold?" Ogilvy mocked her.

She stared at him in horror, tears stinging her eyes as he laughed at her.

"I knew all about Guderian!" Ogilvy cried out. "Who do you think was his long gun in London, who took out Pearce? I was the shadow of Berlin!"

"And I assigned you to follow Guderian!" Mackenzie cried weakly. "My God—"

"Which I did, my love, very carefully."

"And Jonathan—" The realization of how she had jeopardized his safety sickened Mackenzie.

"Yes, I'm surprised he's still alive," Ogilvy said. "Guderian didn't complete his work after all."

"Which is why you're running," she said dully. "That's why you insisted on coming with me to the Admiralty, because you had to know if Jonathan had survived. If not then you were safe. He was the only man who could put the pieces together." She paused, her voice dropping. "And like a fool I let you come with me because I thought you knew nothing about *Jade*. To you it would just be part of the operation against Guderian, having nothing to do with any gold . . ."

"Unfortunately the truth will not make you free," Ogilvy

said. "By the time Cabot learns of it, it will be too late. Pity, I should have liked to repay him in full for this."

Ogilvy lightly ran his fingers over his twisted face.

"Pull into that mews!" he said suddenly.

Mackenzie did so, stopping behind a black Austin taxicab flanked by two men. The door to the Jaguar was wrenched open and she was dragged out. A hood was pulled over her head, the cords tightened around her neck. She heard Ogilvy telling one of the men to leave her car where it was. The Spaniard answered that it was dangerous to do so but Ogilvy cut him off.

They led her to the car and forced her to the floor, one of them keeping a firm grip on the noose about her neck. As the taxi jolted over the cobblestones Mackenzie bowed her head and silently begged Jonathan to forgive her. In that instant she knew, with utter certainty, that she would never see him again.

"They shall crucify you for this," Kim Philby said as he ushered Cabot into a van that waited under Tower Bridge. Only moments before, he had helped Cabot disembark from the Catalina, which had made a heart-stopping landing on the river Thames, at this hour nothing more than an inky, ill-defined ribbon. Now the pilot was turning his craft around before the harbor police arrived.

"Dulles has been screaming from Southampton—" Philby started to say.

"What about Mackenzie?" Cabot demanded, slamming the doors behind him.

"We found her car near the Spanish embassy just as you suspected," Philby told him. "We have an inside source. He's reported Mackenzie and Ogilvy are in there."

Philby hesitated. "How could you have possibly known? No one suspected Ogilvy . . . He was too close to Mackenzie."

Cabot remembered Guderian telling him how he had known Cabot would be in Geneva. Mackenzie, Dulles and Churchill were the only ones aware of his mission. But Guderian had known too . . . and his only possible source had been a mistake on the part of one of the three people. By process of elimination it had to be Mackenzie . . . and from her to Ogilvy. But there was no need to tell Philby this.

"Guderian had too much help, knew too much in advance," Cabot said instead. "Ogilvy was his shadow, tipping him off, even assigned to cover him, for God's sake! It was that 'accident' outside Tonbridge that finally made me think twice about him."

"And as soon as the flap about *Jade* was on, Ogilvy knew there was a chance you were still alive," Philby murmured. "After the first Admiralty reports came in he realized you'd be after him as soon as you touched dry land. That's when he decided to run . . . taking Mackenzie with him . . . as a shield."

Philby looked up at Cabot. "You knew that too, didn't you?"

Cabot didn't answer and began sorting out the equipment lying on the bed of the truck.

"Are you certain we can get her out this way?" Philby asked quietly. "I still think we should have brought the Service in on this—"

"If we go in en masse she's as good as dead," Cabot flung back at him. "I can't allow that to happen! And if your information is accurate—and it better be—then we know exactly the route Ogilvy will take. It will be our first and last chance."

Cabot threw off his jacket and quickly stripped to his shorts. Philby handed him the woolen underwear.

"You don't have to stay after I go in," Cabot said, pulling on the thick-weave garment. "If you leave the truck I can get her out myself."

Philby passed him the bottom half of the diving suit.

"Nonsense, old boy. In for the penny, in for the pound."

Philby handed him the rubber jacket and helped draw it over Cabot's arm.

"You'll have to forgive the flippancy," he added suddenly. "I'm afraid we've made quite a mess about Ogilvy. Serves us all right. I just hope you can bring Mackenzie out."

Cabot braced himself on the panels as the vehicle took a sharp turn.

"I'll bring her out."

Cabot adjusted twenty pounds of lead, strung out in a belt, around his waist. The truck was slowing, the road becoming bumpy as the tires hit across the bricks. Cabot knew they had arrived at the waterfront.

The dank smell of the river curled his nostrils as Cabot jumped off the truck bed. The brisk wind sang low under Blackfriars Bridge, whose lights were the only reference points, and stroked the waters. Beyond the edge of the Hermitage Stairs Cabot heard the waves lapping against the moss-covered concrete embankment.

"She's a hundred yards downriver," Philby said.

Cabot threw the Mae West over his neck and fed the straps under his groin and around his waist. He strained to see anything in the darkness but was able to make out only a single blue lamp.

"The current's with you," Philby said. "They'll have men posted on watch, but I reckon you can drift down seventy-five yards before going under."

Cabot squatted and fed his arms through the webbing that was hitched to a sixty-cubic-foot iron cylinder. He rose and buckled that securely to his waist. Philby flipped the regulator over Cabot's right shoulder.

"The remote control will be in the truck, along with anything else you need," he said. "No more than twenty yards from Wapping Old Stairs."

He handed Cabot a mesh sack that weighed some thirty pounds.

"For God's sake don't bump against anything!" he whispered.

Hunched forward, Cabot walked to the edge of the stairs and carefully descended to the water's edge. He put on the flippers, spat into his mask and wiped the plate.

"I don't want to see you when I come up," he said to Philby. "Cover yourself. You've done more than enough."

"Just bring her out!" was the hushed response from the darkness.

Slowly Cabot slid into the frigid river, the water streaming into his suit. Within a few minutes his own body temperature would warm it, but until then he had to ignore the numbing cold. There was a soft hiss of air as the Mae West filled to the size of a man's forearm. Cabot gripped the mesh sack and slowly kicked away from the stairs, heading into the river to catch the outgoing current.

Although his head was above water Cabot continued to breathe through the regulator. He had at least forty minutes of air in the iron tank, more than enough. He put his back to the open water and kicked out in smooth, rhythmic strokes, feeling the current catch him and bear him downstream. He estimated the distance as best he could by keeping the blue light in view.

Thirty yards from the Spanish freighter *Barcelona* he let the air out of his Mae West and sank beneath the waters.

The river Thames was so silt-ridden that even with the help of the lamp, Cabot saw no more than five feet ahead. He was up against the vessel even before he knew it and had to push himself off the barnacle-laden hull lest his tank bump against it. Under water, sound, not light, was the enemy. Using his knife to scrape away the residue, Cabot reached into the sack and drew out a mine. Carefully he set the charge, then placed its magnetic back against the hull of the *Barcelona*. He moved ten yards, allowed himself to sink a few feet and set another charge. The procedure was repeated three more times, by which time Cabot had worked his way to the bow of the vessel.

Wapping Old Stairs was no more than sixty yards to the west. Cabot released the buckle on his weight belt and let the lead sink to the bottom. When he broke the surface he undid the tank clasps and pushed the iron lung away. The Mae West was the last piece to be discarded. Unencumbered, Cabot swam out of the current, making for the steps that descended to the water's edge. He heaved himself out of the river, ripped off the flippers and hood and scrambled toward the van Philby had parked by the side of the terminal warehouse.

If he hadn't been moving so quickly the lights from a car turning the corner would have pinpointed him. Cabot dived for the side of the truck, crouching, watching as the sedan pulled by him.

Ogilvy had arrived.

Even as he opened the door he continued to watch the car. The remote-control detonator was on the seat. Cabot checked it and clipped it to the webbing around his waist. He reached behind the seat and tore the Hanyatti submachine gun from its carrier.

The vehicle had stopped near the ramp that led onto the *Barcelona*. As though on cue the freighter's high-intensity spotlights came on, bathing the dock in a cold white glare. Two men got out of the car and looked around. Then a third, from the rear seat. The last man spoke to the other two, who made their way toward the gangplank. Cabot chose his moment.

"Ogilvy!"

The call was so low that for an instant Ogilvy wasn't sure he had heard it. Instinctively he turned in the direction of the voice, and through the gloom made out the figure standing there. A sharp command was barked out in Spanish. The two men on the gangplank froze, then turned back and ran toward the car.

"Jonathan Cabot," Ogilvy said conversationally, slowly walking toward him.

Cabot stepped into the light, the gun held level in one hand. Behind Ogilvy the two men took up flanking positions, a crossfire. The double agent came within three feet of Cabot and stopped, his eyes evaluating the condition and circumstance of the man before him.

"You don't need her," Cabot said. "And I don't want you. It's over with. You've won. You walk on that ship and I can't touch you. But you don't need to take her with you."

"It's so comforting to hear you beg, Cabot," Ogilvy laughed.

He regarded Cabot for what seemed a very long time.

"You want me to think, by your appearance, that the ship is mined," he said at last. "You want me to give her up because that is the only way I can escape."

Ogilvy smiled faintly. "I choose to believe you are bluffing, Cabot."

Cabot watched him turn on his heel and walk toward the car. As the two men moved in closer Ogilvy opened the rear door. He reached inside, then drew back, hauling Mackenzie McConnell by the arms. Once out, Mackenzie stumbled as Ogilvy began pushing her toward the gangplank.

"No!" Cabot whispered. The sight of Mackenzie, with a hood drawn over her head, revolted him. "No! Not again!"

His left hand fell to his side, the palm scarcely brushing the detonator trigger. It was enough.

The mines along the hull of the *Barcelona* detonated simultaneously. The vessel heaved itself out of the water, the metal sheets along the waterline ripping and tearing themselves along the concrete pier. Then the horrible screeching of metal against stone tore the night air as the vessel ripped itself against the dock. Within seconds the *Barcelona* began to list as a reflection of orange flame seared across the black Thames.

Cabot was moving even as the charges went off. The blast hurtled into him with the force of a hurricane, but because he knew it was coming he threw his body into it. Keeping low to the ground, he ran toward the car, watching as Ogilvy's security took the full force of the explosion. One was hurtled back into the windshield, the other's body struck the grillwork on the front. Even in the holocaust Cabot was close enough to hear the dry snapping of bone.

Cabot dived at Ogilvy who, with Mackenzie, had been protected from the worst of the blast by the position of the car. He brought his knee into Ogilvy's belly and drove a clenched fist into the side of his jaw. Ogilvy collapsed as the secondary explosions began to tear the guts out of the *Barcelona*. Cabot drew back and shot him cleanly through the temple.

Cabot threw away his weapon and scooped up Mackenzie McConnell in his arms. She flung her arms around his neck and buried her face in his neck, sobbing, repeating his name over and over again. Cabot tightened his grip on her, aching to feel his skin against hers. He was running now, staggering toward the direction of the warehouse. Within seconds the fuel on the vessel would blow.

He saw the lights of vehicles before the roar of the engine reached him. Cabot staggered against the side of the warehouse, trying to look beyond the yellow glare bearing down on him. Mackenzie looked around, and seeing the car bear down on them, uttered a low scream. A backup, Cabot thought. The son of a bitch had a backup!

He cradled Mackenzie's face and brushed his lips on hers. To have come all this way . . . but not to lose her, not this time.

"Get in!"

At the last instant the Jaguar swerved, the rear doors flying open. Philby!

"For God's sake, man—"

But Cabot was in motion, sliding Mackenzie into the back seat of the still-rocking chassis. He had barely enough time to follow her in before the last explosion hurtled at them. The car fishtailed down the alley between the warehouses, outrunning the blast and flames. Cabot raised his head and looked out the rear window at the disintegration. He felt a hand on his cheek and lips kissing his own. Somewhere far away he felt the warm embrace of love . . .

EPILOGUE
1965

"In the end we got what we wanted, and some of the supplies, like the Sherman tanks, were worth their weight in gold. But in the long run we paid a high price for saving the world from Nazi tyranny. Our dollars came to an end and we ceased, for the time being, to be an exporting country. We sacrificed our future to protect the future of civilization."

Jonathan Cabot finished reading the installment of Prime Minister Macmillan's memoirs from *The Times*, folded the paper and placed it by his drink. The oblique reference to gold by the man who in 1942 had been the country's foremost expert on wartime supplies was as close as anyone, including Churchill in his writings, had come to alluding to Prometheus. One of the reasons Jonathan had traveled to England was to ensure that Whitehall extended its quarter century of secrecy on that operation indefinitely. The British people were never to know just how terrible their final price for victory had been.

"A penny for your thoughts?"

He felt a cool hand cover his own and looked up. She still had the power to take his breath away! The golden hair was streaked with regal silver now. There were smooth straight lines across her forehead and ridges that accented the cheeks. But those turquoise eyes were as alive and filled with love as ever, the lips still generous in what they gave to him. In the midst of the busy luncheon crowd at Overton's of St. James's Cabot raised her hand to his lips.

"I was thinking of you," he said. "We have been husband and wife for twenty-five years, yet I love you now as I did that first day. I know you so well, yet I never tire of discovering you . . ."

She squeezed his hand, then glanced at the article she had already read.

"If they only knew," she murmured.

Mackenzie seldom thought back to those final days of Prometheus. There was, even after a quarter century, too much pain. She preferred to remember other, softer memories: her marriage to this man in whom she found the meaning of love, his being with her when, on the eve of Germany's surrender the twins had been born, the beginning of their life in America after the war.

Out of the corner of her eye Mackenzie saw the two quiet men who always traveled in Jonathan's shadow when he was abroad. Unlike her, who had left the secret world forever to write historical nonfiction, he had remained within it. But he had also kept his promise to her: after the war there had been no more active operations. Nevertheless, as the President's Special Advisor on Security Affairs, Jonathan merited the human cloak.

"If anyone could write the truth, it would be you," Jonathan said quietly. "But it can't be done, not now, probably not ever. The upheaval would be staggering."

Mackenzie pursed her lips and smiled ruefully. "I know." But her eyes were clouded over, and she was remembering that last day as though it was yesterday . . .

The early morning was bathed in warm silence. There were four people sitting around the wrought-iron bistro table beneath the oak that bloomed in the garden behind Ten Downing. The steward poured tea and coffee, left a large basket of fresh bread and pastries and quietly departed.

"You could have told me about Ogilvy," Dulles said, sweetening his coffee.

Cabot reached across and took Mackenzie's hand. She smiled at him, returning his grip, sharing the need to touch.

"What will happen now?" Cabot asked. "The gold is either in Germany or at the bottom of the sea."

He still hadn't been told exactly what the explosion he had witnessed was all about.

"You're quite right," Churchill said. "The German raider that pirated you was sunk."

The Prime Minister drained his teacup. He reached inside his breast pocket and tugged out a yellow paper, handing it to Cabot.

"This may be of interest to you," he said noncommittally.

The date was today's, the origin, Halifax, Canada. The message was succinct: PROMETHEUS UNBOUND.

Cabot let the paper flutter into his lap.

"It's wrong!" he said softly, as Mackenzie picked it up. "It has to be."

Churchill chuckled at Mackenzie McConnell's gasp of astonishment.

"No, Mr. Cabot, it's quite true. The bullion has arrived safely in Canada. At this very moment it is being transferred by rail from Halifax to Montreal. From there it will be shipped directly to the Federal Reserve in New York."

"I don't understand, Prime Minister," Mackenzie said weakly.

"Ah, you were such a clever pair!" Churchill rejoined. "You thoroughly outwitted me with that ruse concerning *Victorious*. *But what you didn't know, were never meant to know, was that there was never any real bullion in the Bank—ever!* You were aware of one fraudulent set, but there were actually *two*. The real gold and securities had been shipped from the Bank a fortnight earlier, using the transfer of the Royal Art Treasures as a cover. The entire consignment was driven to Wales. The treasures were transferred to a mine shaft at a place called Blaenau-Ffestiniog. The gold was loaded on board another cruiser waiting in Portmadoc in Cardigan Bay."

"B–but why . . ." Mackenzie stammered.

"I *wanted* the Germans to succeed," Churchill said gravely. "Or at least *think* that they succeeded. If Berlin believed its man had the booty, then Hitler would be convinced we could no longer fight. As a result a major policy shift would ensue. And thanks to Allen, we have learned that it has."

"Hitler had a plan on the boards called Sea Lion," Dulles explained. "The invasion of England. But when Berlin received word that the raiders had the gold, the schedule for Sea Lion was rolled back. It wasn't brought forward even after the raiders were sunk. Hitler believed he had achieved his objective either way. So he has turned his attention to another invasion, that of Russia: Operation Barbarossa."

"And that's why Jaunich blew Guderian's cover to me!" Cabot said softly. "Because he had sent Guderian to England without knowing Sea Lion existed. When he discovered it he could not allow Guderian to sacrifice himself . . . for nothing."

He paused. "Then there was the incident at the Bank, when

Reading mentioned that *the bullion and securities had already been gathered from the branch and head offices*! Damn it, but I should have seen what was happening. Reading's explanation was so flimsy . . ."

Cabot looked at Churchill. "And finally the submarine. *Orion*. It was shadowing *Jade* all along. As soon as the piracy had been carried out, she took off after the raider."

"The Captain had strict orders to wait until Guderian communicated his victory to Berlin before sending them to the bottom," Churchill said.

"There's no trace of Guderian?" asked Cabot.

"The search vessels have reported only debris," Dulles told him. "His chances of still being alive . . ."

It was unnecessary to finish the sentence. Mackenzie Mc-Connell thought of the girl waiting for a man who would never return.

"Did you know about this?" Cabot said, turning to Dulles. "Was this the way the operation was to run from the very beginning?"

The American glanced at Churchill.

"Permit me, Mr. Cabot, to answer a question with a question," the bulldog said shyly. "Do you *really* believe I would entrust the patrimony of the Empire into the hands of Americans . . ."

"He fooled us all, didn't he—that swinish man!" Mackenzie said suddenly, her laughter ringing throughout the restaurant.

And Cabot was laughing as well, his arm thrown across her shoulders, hugging her. He turned his head, felt her hair brush his face and he inhaled the scent of her, oblivious to the mystified glances from other diners.

"Good grief!" Baylor Cabot said. "They're at it again!"

Beside him his twin sister, Cynthia, a stunning twenty-year-old image of Mackenzie, rolled her eyes. Both Jonathan and Mackenzie looked up at their children in frank admiration.

"You're late," Cabot said gruffly. "As usual."

"The *train* from Cambridge was *late*," Cynthia said, sitting opposite her father.

"Cyn, don't fib," her brother admonished her. "The truth of the matter is there was this incredibly interesting fellow in our compartment. We'd seen him around the university but never figured out what he did there—"

"*Très sophistiqué!*" Cynthia exclaimed.

"And the curious thing is that once we told him our names he seemed to know all about you two," Baylor finished.

Mackenzie looked up from her perusal of the menu.

"What do you mean, he seemed to know all about us?" she asked quietly.

"Oh, what you did in the war," Cynthia answered. "Especially about something called Prometheus—which *I* had never heard of."

Cynthia's teasing smile faded as she saw her mother's stunned expression.

"Jonathan . . ." Mackenzie's voice shook. "It isn't possible, is it? I mean, he didn't *survive*!"

"What was the name of the man on the train?" Cabot demanded, the fury in his voice startling the twins. "What did he say about Prometheus?"

Cynthia fished in her canvas tote bag and pulled out a set of publisher's bound galleys. "He gave us this."

Mackenzie pressed herself against her husband, reading over his shoulder.

THE PROMETHEUS LEGEND

"Oh, dear God!" Mackenzie sucked in her breath. "It *is* possible."

Cabot gripped her hand.

"No, it's all right," he said softly. "Nothing will really change."

He traced his finger to the bottom of the jacket where in small print Mackenzie read:

A NOVEL BY ERIC GUDERIAN